METRO 2033

DMITRY GLUKHOVSKY

GOLLANCZ

LONDON

Typeset at The Spartan Press Ltd,
Lymington, Hants

Printed in Great Britain by Clays Ltd,
St Ives plc

www.nibbe-wiedling.de
www.orionbooks.co.uk

Dear Muscovites and guests to our capital!

*The Moscow metro is a form of transportation
which involves a heightened level of danger.*

– A notice in the metro

CHAPTER 1

The End of the Earth

'Who's there? Artyom – go have a look!'

Artyom rose reluctantly from his seat by the fire and, shifting the machine gun from his back to his chest, headed towards the darkness. He stood right at the edge of the lighted area and then, as loudly and threateningly as he could, he clicked the slide on his gun and shouted gruffly, 'Stop! Password!'

He could hear quick, staccato footsteps in the darkness where moments ago he'd heard a strange rustle and hollow-sounding murmurings. Someone was retreating into the depths of the tunnel, frightened away by Artyom's gruff voice and the rattling of his weapon. Artyom hurriedly returned to the fire and flung an answer at Pyotr Andreevich:

'Nope, no one came forward. No response, they just ran off.'

'You idiot! You were clearly told. If they don't respond, then shoot immediately! How do you know who that was? Maybe the dark ones are getting closer!'

'No . . . I don't think they were people . . . The sounds were really strange . . . And the footsteps weren't human either. What? You think I don't know what human footsteps sound like? And anyway, when have the dark ones ever run off like that? You know it yourself, Pyotr Andreevich. Lately they've been lunging forward without hesitation. They attacked a patrol with nothing but their bare hands, marching straight into machine-gun fire. But this thing, it ran off straight away . . . Like some kind of scared animal.'

'All right, Artyom! You're too smart for your own good. But you've got instructions – so follow them, don't think about it. Maybe it was a scout. And now it knows how few of us are here, and how much ammunition they'd need . . . They might just wipe us out here and now for fun. Put a knife to our throat, and butcher the

1

entire station, just like at *Polezhaevskaya* – and all just because you didn't get rid of that rat . . . Watch it! Next time I'll make you run after them into the tunnel!'

It made Artyom shudder to imagine the tunnel beyond the seven-hundredth metre. It was horrifying just to think about it. No one had the guts to go beyond the seven-hundredth metre to the north. Patrols had made it to the five-hundredth, and having illuminated the boundary post with the spotlight on the trolley and convinced themselves that no scum had crossed it, they hastily returned. Even the scouts – big guys, former marines – would stop at the six hundred and eightieth metre. They'd turn their burning cigarettes into their cupped palms and stand stock-still, clinging to their night-vision instruments. And then, they'd slowly, quietly head back, without taking their eyes off the tunnel, and never turning their backs to it.

They were now on patrol at the four hundred and fiftieth metre, fifty metres from the boundary post. The boundary was checked once a day and today's inspection had been completed several hours ago. Now their post was the outermost and, since the last check, the beasts that the last patrol might have scared off would have certainly begun to crawl closer once again. They were drawn to the flame, to people . . .

Artyom settled back down into his seat and asked, 'So what actually happened at *Polezhaevskaya*?'

Although he already knew this blood-curdling story (from the traders at the station), he had an urge to hear it again, like a child who feels an irrepressible urge to hear scary stories about headless mutants and dark ones who kidnap young children.

'At *Polezhaevskaya*? What, you didn't hear about it? It was a strange story. Strange and frightening. First their scouts began disappearing. Went off into the tunnels and didn't come back. Granted, their scouts are completely green, nothing like ours, but then again, their station's smaller, a lot less people live there . . . well, used to live there. So anyway, their scouts start disappearing. One detachment leaves – and vanishes. At first they thought something was holding them up – up there the tunnel twists and turns just like it does here . . .' Artyom felt ill at ease when he heard these words. 'And neither the patrols, nor those at the station could see anything, no matter how much light they threw at it. No one appeared – for half an hour, then for an hour, then two. They wondered where the scouts could have gone – they were only going one kilometre in.

They weren't allowed to go any further and anyway, they aren't total idiots . . . Long story short, they couldn't wait to find out. They sent reinforcements who searched and searched, and shouted and shouted – but it was all in vain. The patrol was gone. The scouts had vanished. And it wasn't just that no one had seen what had happened to them. The worst part was that they hadn't heard a sound . . . not a sound. There was no trace of them whatsoever.'

Artyom was already beginning to regret that he had asked Pyotr Andreevich to recount the story of *Polezhaevskaya*. Pyotr Andreevich was either better informed, or was embellishing the story somewhat; but in any case, he was telling details of the sort that the traders couldn't have dreamed, despite being masters and true enthusiasts of story-telling. The story's details sent a chill over Artyom's skin, and he became uncomfortable even sitting next to the fire. Any rustlings from the tunnel, even the most innocent, were now exciting his imagination.

'So, there you have it. They hadn't heard any gunfire so they decided that the scouts had simply left them – maybe they were dissatisfied with something, and had decided to run. So, to hell with them. If it's an easy life they want, if they want to run around with all kinds of riff-raff, then let them run around to their hearts' content. It was simpler to see it that way. Easier. But a week later, yet another scout team disappeared. And they weren't supposed to go any further than half a kilometre from the station. And again, the same old story. Not a sound, not a trace. Like they'd vanished into thin air. So then they started getting worried back at the station. Now they had a real mess on their hands – two squadrons had disappeared within a week. They'd have to do something about it. Meaning, they'd have to take measures. Well, they set up a cordon at the three-hundredth metre. They dragged sandbags to the cordon, set up machine guns and a spotlight – according to the rules of fortification. They sent a runner to *Begovaya* – they'd established a confederation with *Begovaya* and *1905 Street*. Initially, *October Field* had also been included, but then something had happened, no one knows exactly what – some kind of accident. Conditions there had become unliveable, and everyone had fled.

'Anyway, then they sent a runner to *Begovaya*, to warn them that, as they said, trouble was afoot, and to ask for help, should anything happen. The first runner had only just made it to *Begovaya* – and the people there were still considering their answer – when a second runner arrived at *Begovaya*, lathered in sweat, and said that their reinforced cordon had perished to a man, without firing a single shot. Every last one of them had been slaughtered. And it was as if they'd been butchered in their sleep – that's what was scary! But they wouldn't have fallen asleep, not after the scare they'd had, not to mention the orders and instructions. At this point, the people at *Begovaya* understood that if they did nothing, the same story would begin in their neck of the woods as well. They equipped a strike force of veterans, about a hundred men, machine guns, and grenade launchers. Of course, that all took a bit of time, about a day and a half, but all the same, they dispatched the group to go and help. And when the group entered *Polezhaevskaya*, there wasn't a living soul to be seen. There weren't even bodies – just blood everywhere. There you go. And who knows who the hell did it. I, for one, don't believe that humans are capable of such a thing.'

'And what happened to *Begovaya*?' Artyom's voice sounded unusual, unlike him.

'Nothing happened to them. They saw what the deal was, and exploded the tunnel that led to *Polezhaevskaya*. I hear forty metres' worth of tunnel is collapsed; there's no digging through it without special machinery, and even with machinery, I bet you wouldn't get very far . . . And where are you going to find that kind of machinery, anyway? Our machinery rotted away fifteen years ago already . . .'

Pyotr Andreevich fell silent, gazing into the fire. Artyom gave a loud cough and said,

'Yeah . . . I should've shot the thing, of course . . . I was an idiot.'

A shout came from the south, from the direction of the station:

'Hey there, at the four-hundredth metre! Everything OK there?'

Pyotr Andreevich folded his hands into the shape of a megaphone and shouted in reply:

'Come closer! We've got a situation here!'

Three figures approached in the tunnel, from the station, their flashlights shining – probably patrol members from the three-hundredth metre. Stepping into the light of the fire, they put out their flashlights and sat down.

'Hi there, Pyotr! So it's you here. And I'm thinking to myself – who'd they send off to the edge of the earth today?' said the senior patrolman, smiling and shaking a cigarette from his pack.

'Listen, Andryukha! One of my guys saw someone up here. But he didn't get to shoot . . . It hid in the tunnel. He says it didn't look human.'

4

'Didn't look human? What did it look like, then?' Andrey turned to Artyom.

'I didn't even see it . . . I just asked for the password, and it ran right off, heading north. But the footsteps weren't human – they were light, and very quick, as if it had four legs instead of two . . .'

'Or three!' winked Andrey, making a scary face.

Artyom choked, remembering the stories about the three-legged people from the *Filevskaya* line where some of the stations went up to the surface, and the tunnel didn't run very deep at all, so they had almost no protection from the radiation. There were three-legged things, two-headed things and all kinds of weird shit crawling all over the metro from those parts.

Andrey took a drag of his cigarette and said to his men, 'All right, guys, since we're already here why don't we sit down for a while? If any three-legged things crawl up on these guys again, we'll lend a hand. Hey, Artyom! Got a kettle?'

Pyotr Andreevich got up and poured some water from a canister into a beat-up, soot-covered kettle, and hung it over the flame. In a few minutes, the kettle began to whistle as it came to a boil. The sound, so domestic and comforting, made Artyom feel warmer and calmer. He looked around at the men who were sitting at the fire: all of them strong dependable people, hardened by the challenging life they led here. You could trust men like these; you could count on them. Their station always had the reputation for being the most successful along the entire line – and that was all thanks to the men gathered here, and to others like them. They were all connected to each other with warm, almost brotherly bonds.

Artyom was just over twenty years old and had come into the world when life was still up there, on the surface. He wasn't as thin and pale as the others who'd been born in the metro, who wouldn't dare go up to the surface for fear of radiation and the searing rays of the sun, which are so ruinous for underground dwellers. True, even Artyom, as far as he could remember, had been on the surface only once, and then it was only for a moment – the background radiation there had been so bad that anyone who got a bit too curious would be completely fried within a couple of hours, before he'd even managed to enjoy a good stroll, and see his fill of the bizarre world that lay on the surface.

He didn't remember his father at all. His mother had been with him until he was five years old. They lived at *Timiryazevskaya*. Things had been good, and life had gone smoothly and peacefully, until *Timiryazevskaya* fell victim to a rat infestation.

One day, huge, grey, wet rats poured from one of the tunnels on the dark side of the station without any warning. It was a tunnel that plunged off to the side, a disregarded branch of the primary northern leg, which descended to great depths, only to become lost in the complex network of hundreds of corridors – freezing, stinking labyrinths of horror. The tunnel stretched into the kingdom of rats, where even the most hopeless adventurer wouldn't dare to go. Even a wanderer who was lost and couldn't find his way using underground maps and paths, would stop at this threshold, sensing instinctively the black and sinister danger emerging from it, and would have rushed away from the gaping crevasse of that entrance as though from the gates of a plague-infested city.

No one bothered the rats. No one descended into their dominions. No one dared to violate their borders.

They came to the people.

Many people perished that day, when a living torrent of gigantic rats – bigger than had ever been seen at either the stations or in the tunnels – had flooded through the cordons and the station, burying all of its defenders and its population, muffling their dying screams with the mass of its bodies. Consuming everything in their path – the living, the dead, and their own fallen comrades – the rats tore ahead, further and further, blindly, inexorably, propelled by a force beyond human comprehension.

Only a few men remained alive. No women, no old men or children – none of the people who would normally have been saved first, but rather five healthy men who had managed to keep ahead of the death-wreaking torrent. And the only reason they'd outrun it was because they'd happened to be standing near a trolley, on watch in the southern tunnel. Hearing the shouts from the station, one of them sprinted to see what had happened. *Timiryazevskaya* was already perishing when he caught sight of it as he entered the station. At the station's entrance, he understood what had happened from the first rivulets of rats seeping onto the platform and he was about to turn back, knowing that he couldn't possibly help those who were defending the station, when suddenly his hand was seized from behind. He turned around and a woman, her face contorted with horror, pulling insistently at his sleeve, shouted, in an effort to overcome the many-voiced choir of despair, 'Save him, soldier! Have mercy!'

He saw that she was handing him a child's hand, a small, chubby hand, and he grabbed the hand without even thinking that he was saving someone's life. And, pulling the child behind him and then picking him up and tucking him under his arm, he raced off with the frontrunner rats in a race with death – forward through the tunnel, where the trolley was waiting with his fellow patrolmen. He started to shout at them from afar, from a distance of fifty metres or so, telling them to start up the trolley. Their trolley was motorized, the only one of its kind in the surrounding ten stations, and it was only because of it that they were able to outrun the rats. The patrolmen raced forward, and flew through the abandoned station of *Dmitrovskaya* at full speed, where a few hermits had sought shelter, just managing to shout to them: 'Run! Rats!' (Without realizing that there was no chance of the hermits saving themselves.) As they approached the cordons of *Savyolovskaya* (with whom, thank God, they had peaceful arrangements), they slowed down so they wouldn't be fired at. They would have been taken for raiders at such high speed. And they shouted at the top of their lungs to the guards, 'Rats! The rats are coming!' They were prepared to keep running right through *Savyolovskaya*, and further along the line, prepared to beg to be let through, as long as there was somewhere further to go, as long as the grey lava hadn't inundated the entire metro.

But luckily, there was something at *Savyolovskaya* that would save them, the station and perhaps the entire *Serpukhovsko-Timiryazevskaya* branch. They were nearly at the station, soaked in sweat, shouting at the *Savyolovskaya* guards about their narrow escape from death. Meanwhile, the guards at the post were quickly pulling the cover off of some kind of impressive-looking piece of kit.

It was a flame-thrower, assembled by the local craftsmen from spare parts – homemade, but incredibly powerful. When the first ranks of rats became visible, gathering force, and you could hear the rustling and the scratching of a thousand rats' paws from the darkness, the guards fired up the flame-thrower. And they didn't turn it off until the fuel was spent. A howling orange flame filled the tunnel for tens of metres and burned the rats, burned them all, without stopping, for ten, fifteen, twenty minutes. The tunnel was filled with the repulsive stench of burnt flesh and the wild screeching of rats. And behind the guards of *Savyolovskaya*, who had become heroes and had earned fame along the entire metro line, the trolley came to a stop, cooling down. On it were the five men who had fled from *Timiryazevskaya* station, and there was one more – the child they had saved. A boy. Artyom.

The rats retreated. Their blind will had been broken by one of the last inventions of human military genius. Humans had always been better at killing than any other living thing.

The rats flowed backwards and returned to their enormous kingdom, whose true dimensions were known to no one. All of these labyrinths, lying at incredible depth, were so mysterious and, it seemed, completely useless for the functioning of the metro. It was hard to believe, despite the assurances of various persons of authority on the matter, that all of this was built by ordinary metro-builders.

One such person of authority had once worked as a conductor's assistant on an electric train in the old days. There were hardly any of his kind left and they were greatly valued, because at first they had proven to be the only ones who could find their way around. And they didn't give in to fear the moment they found themselves outside the comfortable and safe capsules of the train, in the dark tunnels of the Moscow metro, in these stone bowels of the great metropolis. Everyone at the station treated the conductor's assistant with respect, and taught their children to do the same; it was for that reason, probably, that Artyom had remembered him, remembered him all his life: a thin, haggard man, emaciated by the long years of work underground who wore a threadbare and faded metro employee uniform that had long ago lost its chic but that he donned with the same pride a retired admiral would feel when putting on his parade uniform. Even Artyom, still just a kid at that time, had seen a certain dignity and power in the sickly figure of the conductor's assistant . . .

Of course he did. For all those who survived, the employees of the metro were like local guides to scientific expeditions in the jungles. They were religiously believed, they were depended upon completely, and the survival of everyone else depended on their knowledge and skill. Many of them became the heads of stations when the united system of government disintegrated, and the metro was transformed from a complex object of civil defence, a huge fallout shelter, into a multitude of stations unconnected by a single power, and was plunged into chaos and anarchy. The stations became independent and self-sufficient, distinctive dwarf states, with their own ideologies and regimes, their own leaders and armies. They warred against each other, they joined to form federations and confederations. They became metropolitan centres of rising empire one day, only to be subjugated and colonized the next, by their erstwhile friends or slaves. They formed short-term unions against a common threat,

8

only to fall at each other's throats again with renewed energy the moment that threat had passed. They scrapped over everything with total abandon: over living spaces, over food – over the plantings of albuminous yeast, the crops of mushrooms that didn't require any sunlight, the chicken coops and pig-farms, where pale subterranean pigs and emaciated chicks were raised on colourless underground mushrooms. They fought, of course, over water – that is, over filters. Barbarians, who didn't know how to repair filtration systems that had fallen into disuse, and were dying from water that was poisoned by radiation, threw themselves with animal rage upon the bastions of civilized life, at the stations where the dynamo-machines and small home-made hydroelectric stations functioned correctly, where filters were repaired and cleaned regularly, where, tended by the caring female hands, the damp ground was punctuated with the little white caps of champignons, and well-fed pigs grunted in their pens.

They were driven forward, in their endless and desperate on-slaught, by an instinct for self-preservation, and by that eternal revolutionary principle: conquer and divide. The defenders of successful stations, organized into battle-ready divisions by former military professionals, stood up to the assaults of vandals, to the very last drop of their blood. They went on to launch counter-attacks and won back every metre of the inter-station tunnels with a fight. The stations amassed their military power in order to answer any incursions with punitive expeditions; in order to push their civilized neighbours from territory that was important for sustaining life, if they hadn't managed to attain these agreements by peaceful means; and in order to offer resistance to the crap that was climbing out of every hole and tunnel. These were strange, freakish, and dangerous creatures, the likes of which might well have brought Darwin himself to despair with their obvious lack of conformity to the laws of evolutionary development. As much as these beasts might differ from the animals humans were used to, and whether they had been reborn under the invisible and ruinous rays of sunlight, turned from inoffensive representatives of urban fauna into the spawn of hell, or whether they had always dwelled in the depths, only now to be disturbed by man – still, they were an evident part of life on earth. Disfigured, perverted – but a part of life here all the same. And they remained subject to that very same driving impulse known to every organic thing on this planet.

Survive. Survive at any cost.

Artyom accepted a white, enamelled cup, in which some of their homemade station tea was splashing around. Of course, it wasn't really tea at all, but an infusion of dried mushrooms and other additives. Real tea was a rarity. They rationed it and drank it only at major holidays, and it fetched a price dozens of times higher than the price of the mushroom infusion. Nevertheless, they liked their own station brew and were even proud enough of it to call it 'tea.' It's true that strangers would spit it out at first, since they weren't used to its taste; but soon they got used to it. And the fame of their tea spread beyond the bounds of their station – even the traders came to get it, one by one, risking life and limb, and soon after their tea made it down the whole metro line – even the Hanseatic League had started to become interested in it and great caravans of the magical infusion rolled towards *VDNKh*. Cash started to flow. And wherever there was money, there were weapons, there was firewood and there were vitamins. And there was life. Ever since they started making the very same tea at *VDNKh*, the station had begun to grow strong; people from the nearby stations moved to the station and stretches of track were laid to the station; prosperity had come. They were also very proud of their pigs at *VDNKh*, and legend had it that it was precisely from this station that the pigs had entered the metro: back at the very beginning of things when certain daredevils had made their way to the 'pig-breeding pavilion' at the Exhibition and managed to herd the animals back down to the station.

'Listen, Artyom – how are things going with Sukhoi?' asked Andrey, drinking his tea with small, cautious sips and blowing on it carefully.

'With Uncle Sasha? Everything's fine. He came back a little while ago from a hike down the line with some of our people. An expedition. As you probably know.'

Andrey was about fifteen years older than Artyom. Generally speaking, he was a scout, and rarely stood at a watch nearer than the four hundred and fiftieth metre, and then only as a cordon commander. And here they'd posted him at the three-hundredth metre, with good cover, but all the same, he felt the urge to head deeper, and made use of any pretext, any false alarm, to get closer to the darkness, closer to the secret. He loved the tunnel and knew its branches very well but, at the station, he felt uncomfortable among the farmers, the workers, the businessmen and the administration – he felt unneeded, perhaps. He couldn't bring himself to hoe the earth for mushrooms, or, even worse, stuff the fat pigs at the station's farms with mushrooms, standing up to his knees in manure. And he couldn't be a trader either – he'd been unable to stand traders from the day he was born. He had always been a soldier, a warrior, and he believed with all his soul that this was the only occupation worthy of a man. He was proud that he had done nothing his entire life but defend the stinking farmers, the fussy traders, the administrators who were business-like to a fault, and the women and children. Women were attracted to his arrogant strength, to his total confidence in himself, to his sense of calm in relation to himself and those around him (because he was always capable of defending them). Women promised him love, they promised him comfort, but he could only feel comfortable beyond the fiftieth metre, beyond the turning point, where the station lights were hidden. And the women didn't follow him. Why not?

Now he'd warmed up nicely as a result of the tea, and he removed his old black beret and wiped his moustache, damp from the steam, with his sleeve. Then he began to question Artyom eagerly for news and rumours from the south, brought by the last expedition, by Artyom's stepfather – by the very man who, nineteen years ago had torn Artyom from the rats at *Timiryazevskaya*, unable to abandon a child, and had raised him.

'I myself might know a thing or two, but I'll listen with pleasure, even for a second time. What – do you mind?' insisted Andrey.

He didn't have to spend any time persuading him: Artyom himself enjoyed recalling and retelling his stepfather's stories – after all, everyone would listen to them, their mouths agape.

'Well, you probably know where they went . . .' began Artyom.

'I know they went south. They're so top-secret, those "hikers" of yours,' laughed Andrey. 'They are special missions of the administration, you know!' he winked at one of his people.

'Come on, there wasn't anything secret about it,' Artyom waved his hand dismissively. 'The expedition was for reconnaissance, the collection of information . . . Reliable information. Because you can't believe strangers, the traders who wag their tongues at us at the station – they could be traders or they could be provocateurs, spreading misinformation.'

'You can never trust traders,' grumbled Andrey. 'They're out for their own good. How are you supposed to know whether to trust one – one day he'll sell your tea to the Hansa, and the next he'll sell you and your entrails to someone else. They may well be collecting information here, among us. To be honest, I don't particularly trust ours either.'

'Well, you're wrong to go after our own, Andrey Arkadych. Our guys are all OK. I know almost all of them myself. They're people, just like people anywhere. They love money, too. They want to live better than others do, they're striving towards something,' said Artyom, attempting to defend the local traders.

'There it is. That's exactly what I'm talking about. They love money. They want to live better than everyone else does. And who knows what they do when they go off into the tunnel? Can you tell me with certainty that at the very next station they aren't recruited by agents? Can you – or not?'

'Which agents? Whose agents did our traders submit to?'

'Here's what I'll say, Artyom. You're still young, and there's a lot you don't know. You should listen to your elders – pay attention, and you'll stick around a bit longer.'

'Someone has to do their work! If it weren't for the traders, we'd be sitting here without military supplies, with *Berdan* rifles, and we'd be tossing salt at the dark ones and drinking our tea,' said Artyom, not backing down.

'All right, all right, we've got an economist in our midst . . . Simmer down now. You'd do better to tell us what Sukhoi saw there. What's going on there with the neighbours? At *Alekseevskaya*? At *Rizhskaya*?'

'At *Alekseevskaya*? Nothing new. They're growing mushrooms. And what is *Alekseevskaya* anyway? A farmyard, that's all . . . So they say.' Then Artyom lowered his voice in light of the secrecy of the information he was about to give: 'They want to join us. And *Rizhskaya* isn't against it either. They're facing growing pressure over there from the south. There's a sombre mood – everyone's whispering about some sort of threat, everyone's afraid of something, but of what, nobody knows. It's either that there's some sort of new empire at the far end of the line, or that they're afraid of the Hansa, thinking they might want to expand, or it's something else altogether. And all of these barnyards are starting to cuddle up to us. *Rizhskaya* and *Alekseevskaya* both.'

'But what do they want, in concrete terms? What are they offering?' asked Andrey.

'They want to create a federation with us that has a common defence system, to strengthen the borders on both ends, to establish constant illumination inside the inter-station tunnels, to organize a police force, to plug up the side tunnels and corridors, to launch transport trolleys, to lay a telephone cable, to designate any available space for mushroom-growing . . . They want a common economy – to work, and to help each other, should it prove necessary.'

'And where were they when we needed them? Where were they when there was vermin crawling at us from the Botanical Gardens, from *Medvedkov*? When the dark ones were attacking us, where were they?' growled Andrey.

'Don't jinx us, Andrey, be careful!' interceded Pyotr Andreevich. 'There aren't any dark ones here for the time being, and all's well. It wasn't us who defeated them. Something happened that was of their own doing, it was something among themselves, and now they've quietened down. They might be saving up their strength for now. So a union won't hurt us. All the more so, if we unify with our neighbours. It'll be to their benefit, and for our good as well.'

'And we'll have freedom, and equality, and brotherhood!' said Andrey ironically, counting on his fingers.

'What, you don't want to listen?' asked Artyom, offended.

'No, go ahead, Artyom, continue,' said Andrey. 'We'll have it out with Pyotr later. This is a long-standing argument between us.'

'All right then. And, they say that their chief supposedly agrees. Doesn't have any fundamental objections. It's just necessary to consider the details. Soon there'll be an assembly. And then, a referendum.'

'What do you mean, a referendum? If the people say yes, then it's a yes. If they say no, then the people didn't think hard enough. Let the people think again,' quipped Andrey.

'Well, Artyom, and what's going on beyond *Rizhskaya*?' asked Pyotr Andreevich, not paying attention to Andrey.

'What's next? *Prospect Mir* station. Well, and it makes sense that it's *Prospect Mir*. That's the boundary of the Hanseatic League. My stepfather says that everything's still the same between the Hansa and the Reds – they've kept the peace. No one there gives a thought to the war anymore,' said Artyom.

'The Hanseatic League' was the name of the 'Concord of Ring Line Stations.' These stations were located at the intersection of all the other lines, and, therefore of all the trade routes. The lines were linked to one another by tunnels, which became a meeting place for businessmen from all over the metro. These businessmen grew rich with fantastic speed, and soon, knowing that their wealth was arousing the envy of too many, they decided to join forces. The official name was too unwieldy though, and among the people, the Concord was nicknamed the 'Hansa' (someone had once accurately compared

13

them to the union of trade cities in Medieval Germany). The short word was catchy, and it stuck. At the beginning, the Hansa consisted of only a few stations; the Concord only came together gradually. The part of the Ring from *Kievskaya* to *Prospect Mir*, what's called the Northern Arc, and that included *Kurskaya*, *Taganskaya* and *Oktyabrskaya*. Then *Paveletskaya* and *Dobrynskaya* joined in and formed another Arc, the Southern Arc. But the biggest problem and the biggest hindrance to uniting the Northern and Southern Arcs was the Sokol Line.

The thing was, Artyom's stepfather told him, the Sokol line was always sort of special. When you glance at the map, your attention is immediately drawn to it. First of all, it's a straight line, straight as an arrow. Secondly, it was marked in bright red on metro maps. And its station names contributed too: *Krasnoselskaya*, *Krasne Vorota*, *Komsomolskaya*, *Biblioteka imena Lenina* and *Leninskie Gori*. And whether it was because of these names or because of something else, the line would draw to itself everyone who was nostalgic for the glorious Soviet past. The idea of a resurrection of the Soviet state took easily there. At first, just one station returned to communist ideals and a socialist form of rule, and then the one next to it, and then people from the tunnel on the other side caught wind of this optimistic revolution and chucked out their administration and so on and so on. The veterans who were still alive, former Komsomol men and Party officials, permanent members of the proletariat – they all came together at the revolutionary stations. They founded a committee, responsible for the dissemination of this new revolution and its communist idea throughout the metro system, under the almost Lenin-era name of 'Interstational.' It prepared divisions of professional revolutionaries and propagandists and sent them to enemy stations. In general, little blood was spilt since the starving inhabitants of the Sokol line were thirsting for the restoration of justice, for which, as far as they understood, apart from unjustified egalitarianism, there was no other option. So the whole branch, having flared up at one end, was soon engulfed by the crimson flames of revolution. The stations returned to their old, Soviet names: *Chistye Prudy* became *Kirovskaya* again; *Lubyanka* became *Dzerzhinskaya*; *Okhotnyi Ryad* became *Prospect Marx*. The stations with neutral names were renamed with something more ideologically clear: *Sportivnaya* became *Kommunisticheskaya*; *Sokolniki* became *Stalinskaya*; *Preobrazhenskaya Ploshchhad* where it all began, became *Znamya Revolutsya*. And the line itself, once Sokol, was now called by most the

'Red Line' – it was usual in the old days for Muscovites to call their metro lines by their colours on the map anyway, but now the line was officially called the 'Red Line.'

But it didn't go any further.

When the Red Line had formed itself and had ideas about spreading itself through the metro, patience quickly wore thin at other stations. Too many people remembered the Soviet era. Too many people saw the agitators that were sent by the Interstational throughout the metro as a tumour that was metastasising, threatening to kill the whole organism. And as much as the agitators and propagandists promised electricity for the whole metro, that by joining with the Soviet powers they would experience real communism (it was unlikely that this had come from any actual slogan of Lenin's – it was so exploitative), people beyond their boundaries weren't tempted. The Interstational sloganeers were caught and thrown back to their Soviet territory. Then the Red leadership decided that it was time to act more resolutely: if the rest of the metro wouldn't take up the merry revolution flame then they needed to be lit from underneath. Neighbouring stations, worried about the strengthening communist propaganda, also came to the same conclusion. Historical experience demonstrates well that there isn't a better way of injecting communist bacilli into an area than with a bayonet.

And the thunder rumbled.

The coalition of anti-communist stations, directed by the Hansa, broke the Red Line and wanting to close the Ring circle took up the call. The Reds, of course, didn't expect the organized resistance and overestimated their own strength. The easy victory they had anticipated couldn't even be seen in their distant future. The war turned out to be long and bloody, wearing on and on – meanwhile, the population of the metro wasn't all that large . . . It went on for almost a year and a half and mostly consisted of battles for position involving guerrilla excursions and diversions, the barricading of tunnels, the execution of prisoners, and several other atrocities committed by either side. All sorts of things happened: Army operations, encirclement, the breaking of encirclement, various feats, there were commanders, heroes and traitors. But the main feature of this war was that neither of belligerent parties could shift the front line any considerable distance.

Sometimes, it seemed that one side was gaining an edge, would take over an adjacent station, but their opponent resisted, mobilized additional forces – and the scales were tipped to the other side.

But the war exhausted resources. The war eliminated the best people. The war was generally exhausting. And those that survived grew tired of it. The revolutionary government had subtly replaced their initial problems with more modest ones. In the beginning, they strove for the distribution of socialist power and communistic ideas throughout the underground but now the Reds only wanted to have control over what they saw as the inner sanctum: the station called Revolution Square. Firstly, because of its name and secondly because it was closer than the any other station in the metro to the Red Square and to the Kremlin, the towers of which were still adorned with ruby stars if you believed the brave men who were so ideologically strong that they broke the surface just to look at them. But, of course, there at the surface, near the Kremlin, right in the centre of the Red Square was the Mausoleum. Whether Lenin's body was still there or not, no one knew, but that didn't really matter. For the many years of the Soviet era, the mausoleum had ceased to be a tomb and had become its own shrine, a sacred symbol of the continuity of power.

Great leaders of the past started their parades there. Current leaders aspired to it. Also, they say that from the offices of the Revolution Square station there are secret passages to the covert laboratories of the mausoleum, which lead directly to the coffin itself.

The Reds still had *Prospect Marx*, formerly *Okhotnyi Ryad*, which was fortified and had become a base from which attacks on Revolution Square were launched. More than one crusade was blessed by the revolutionary leadership and sent to liberate this station and its tomb. But its defenders also understood what meaning it held for the Reds and they stood to the last. Revolution Square had turned into an unapproachable fortress. The most severe and bloody fights took place at the approach to the station. The biggest number of people was killed there. There were plenty of heroics, those that faced bullets with their chests, and brave men who tied grenades to themselves to blow themselves up together with an enemy artillery point, and those that used forbidden flame-throwers against people . . . Everything was in vain. They recaptured the station for a day but didn't manage to fortify it, and they were defeated, retreating the next day when the coalition came back with a counterattack.

Exactly the same thing was happening at Lenin Library. That was the Reds' fort and the coalition forces repeatedly tried to seize it from them. The station had huge strategic value because they could split the Red Line in two parts there, and then they would have a direct passage to the three other lines with which the Red Line doesn't intersect anywhere else. It was the only place. It was like a lymph gland, infected with the Red plague, which would then be spread across the whole organism. And, to prevent this, they had to take the Lenin Library, had to take it at any cost.

But as unsuccessful as the Reds' attempts were to take Revolution Square, the efforts of the coalition to squeeze them out of Lenin Library were equally fruitless. Meanwhile, people were tiring of the fight. Desertion was already rife, and there were incidents of fraternization when soldiers from both sides laid down their arms upon confrontation . . . But, unlike the First World War, the Reds didn't gain an advantage. Their revolutionary fuse fizzled out quietly. The coalition didn't fare much better: dissatisfied with the fact that they had to constantly tremble for their lives, people picked themselves up and went off in whole family groups from the central stations to the outer stations. The Hansa emptied and weakened. The war had badly affected trade; traders found other ways around the system, and the important trading routes because empty and quiet . . .

The politicians, who were supported by fewer and fewer soldiers, had to urgently find a way to end the war, before the guns turned against them. So, under the strictest of secret conditions and at a necessarily neutral station, the leaders from enemy sides met: the Hansa president, Loginov, and the head of the Arbat Confederation, Kolpakov.

They quickly signed a peace agreement. The parties exchanged stations. The Red Line received the dilapidated Revolution Square but conceded the Lenin Library to the Arbat Confederation. It wasn't an easy step for either to make. The confederation lost one of its parts along with its influence over the north-west. The Red Line became punctuated since there was now a station in the middle of it that didn't belong to it and cut it in half. Despite the fact that both parties guaranteed each other the right to free transit through their former territories, that sort of situation couldn't help but upset the Reds . . . But what the coalition was proposing was too tempting. And the Red Line didn't resist. The Hansa gained more of an advantage from the agreement, of course, because they could now close the Ring, removing the final obstacles to their prosperity.

They agreed to observe the status quo, and an interdiction about conducting propaganda and subversive activities in the territory of their former opponent. Everyone was satisfied. And now, when the cannons and the politicians had gone silent, it was the turn of the propagandists to explain to the masses that their own side had managed an outstanding diplomatic feat and, in essence, had won the war.

Years have passed since that memorable day when the peace agreement was signed. It was observed by both parties too – the Hansa found in the Red Line a favourable economic partner and the latter left behind its aggressive intentions: comrade Moskvin, the secretary general of Communist party of the Moscow Underground in the name of V.I.Lenin, dialectically proved the possibility of constructing communism in one separate metro line. The old enmity was forgotten.

Artyom remembered this lesson in recent history well, just as he strived to remember everything his stepfather told him.

'It's good that the slaughter came to an end,' Pyotr Andreevich said. 'It was impossible to go anywhere near the Ring for a year and a half: there were cordons everywhere, and they would check your documents a hundred times. I had dealings there at the time and there was no way to get through apart from past the Hansa. And they stopped me right at *Prospect Mir*. They almost put me up against a wall.'

'And? You've never told us about this, Pyotr . . . How did it work out?' Andrey was interested.

Artyom slouched slightly, seeing that the story-teller's flashlight had been passed from his hands. But this promised to be interested so he didn't bother to butt in.

'Well . . . It was very simple. They took me for a Red spy. So, I'm coming out of the tunnel at *Prospect Mir*, on our line. And *Prospect* is also under the Hansa. It's an annexe, so to speak. Well, things aren't so strict there yet – they've got a market there, a trading zone. As you know, it's the same everywhere with the Hansa: the stations on the Ring itself form something like their home territory. And the transfer passages from the Ring stations are like radials – and they've put customs and passport controls there . . .'

'Come on, we all know that, what are you lecturing us for . . . Tell us instead what happened to you there!' Andrey interrupted him.

'Passport controls,' repeated Pyotr Andreevich, sternly drawing his eyebrows together, determined to make a point. 'At the radial stations, they have markets, bazaars . . . Foreigners are allowed there. But you can't cross the border – no way. I got out at *Prospect Mir*, I had half a kilo of tea with me . . . I needed some ammunition for my rifle. I thought I'd make a trade. Well, turns out they're under martial law. They won't let go of any military supplies. I ask one person, then another – they all make excuses, and sidle away from me. Only one whispered to me: "What ammunition, you moron . . . Get the hell out of here, and quick – they've probably already informed on you." I thanked him and headed quietly back into the tunnel. And right at the exit, a patrol stops me, and whistles ring out from the station, and still another detachment is running towards us. They ask for my documents. I give them my passport, with our station's stamp. They look at it carefully and ask, "And where's your pass?" I answer, surprised, "What pass?" It turns out that to get to the station, you're obliged to get a pass: near the tunnel exit there's a little table, and they have an office there. They check identification and issue a pass when necessary. They're up to their ears in bureaucracy, the rats . . .

'How I made it past that table, I don't know . . . Why didn't the blockheads stop me? And now I'm the one who has to explain myself to the patrol. So this muscle-head stands there with his shaved skull and his camouflage and says, "He slipped past! He snuck past! He crept past!" He flips further through my passport, and sees the Sokol stamp there. I lived there earlier, at Sokol . . . He sees this stamp, and his eyes all but filled with blood. Like a bull seeing red. He jerked his gun from his shoulder and roars, "Hands above your head, you scum!" His level of training was immediately apparent. He grabs me by the scruff of my neck and drags me across the entire station, to the pass point in the transfer passage, to his superior. And he says, threateningly, "Just you wait, all I need is to get permission from command – and you'll be against the wall, spy." I was about to be sick. So I try to justify myself, I say, "What kind of a spy am I? I'm a businessman! I brought some tea from *VDNKh*." And he replies that he'll stuff my mouth full of tea and ram it in with the barrel of his gun. I can see that I'm not very convincing, and that, if his brass gives their approval, he'll lead me off to the two-hundredth metre, put my face to the pipes, and shoot me full of holes, in accordance with the laws of war. Things weren't turning out too well, I thought . . . We approached the pass point, and this muscle-head of mine went to discuss the best place to shoot me. I looked at his boss, and it was as if a burden fell from my shoulders: it was Pashka Fedotov, my former classmate – we'd remained friends even after school, and then we'd lost track of each other . . .'

'Well fuck! You scared the hell out of me! And I already thought you were done for, that they'd killed you,' inserted Andrey venomously, and all of the men who were gathered tightly around the campfire at the four hundred and fiftieth metre burst into friendly laughter.

Even Pyotr Andreevich himself, first glancing angrily at Andrey, couldn't restrain himself and smiled. Laughter sounded along the tunnel, giving birth, somewhere in its depths, to a distorted echo, a sinister screech that sounded unlike anything . . . And everyone gradually fell silent upon hearing it.

From the depths of the tunnel, form the north, the suspicious sounds were rather distinct now: there were rustlings and light rhythmic steps.

Andrey, of course, was the first to hear them. He went silent instantly and waved a hand to signal the others to be quiet too, and he picked up his machine gun from the ground and jumped up from where he was sitting.

Slowly undoing his safety catch and loading a cartridge, his back to the wall, he silently moved from the fireside into the tunnel. Artyom got up too – he was curious to see who he had missed the last time but Andrey turned back and frowned at him angrily. He stopped at the border of the darkness, put his gun to his shoulder and lay down flat shouting, 'Give me some light!'

One of his guys, holding a powerful accumulator flashlight, which had been assembled from old car headlights, turned it on, and the bright beam ripped through the darkness. Snatched from the darkness, a fuzzy silhouette appeared on the floor for a second. It was something small, something not really scary looking, something which rushed back to the north.

Artyom couldn't restrain himself and he cried out:

'Shoot! It's getting away!'

But for some reason Andrey did not shoot. Pyotr Andreevich got up too, keeping his machine gun at the ready, and shouted:

'Andryukha! You still alive?'

The guys sitting at the fire whispered in agitation, hearing the lock of Andrey's gun slide back. Finally Andrey appeared in the light of the flashlight, dusting off his jacket.

'Yes, I'm alive, I'm alive!' he said, laughing.

'Why you snorting?' Pyotr Andreevich asked him suspiciously.

'It had three feet! And two heads. Mutants! The dark ones are here! They'll cut our throats! Shoot, or they'll get away! Must have been a lot of them! Must have!' Andrey continued to laugh.

'Why didn't you shoot? Fine, my young man might not have but he's young, didn't get it. But why did you mess it up? You're not new to this, after all. You know what happened at *Polezhaevskaya*?' asked Pyotr Andreevich angrily when Andrey had returned to the fire.

'Yes I've heard about *Polezhaevskaya* a dozen times!' Andrey waved him away. – 'It was a dog! A puppy, not even a dog . . . It's already the second time it's tried to get close to the fire, towards the heat and the light. And you almost took him out and now you're asking me why I'm being too considerate. Knackers!'

'How was I supposed to know it was a dog?' Artyom had taken offence. 'It gave out such sounds . . . And then, a week ago they were talking about seeing a rat the size of a pig.'

'You believe in fairy tales! Wait a second and I'll bring you your rat!' Andrey said, throwing his machine gun over his shoulder and walking off into the darkness.

A minute later, they heard a fine whistle from the darkness. And then a voice called out, affectionately, coaxingly:

'Come here, come here little one, don't be afraid!'

He spent a long time convincing it, about ten minutes, calling it and whistling to it and then finally his figure appeared again in the twilight.

He returned to the fire and smiled triumphantly as he opened his jacket. A puppy fell out onto the ground, shivering, piteous, wet and intolerably dirty, with matted fur of an indistinct colour, and black eyes full of horror, and flattened ears.

Once on the ground, he immediately tried to get away but Andrey's firm hand grabbed it and held it in place. Petting it on its head, he removed his jacket and covered the little dog.

'The puppy needs to be warmed up,' he explained.

'Come on, Andrey, it's a fleabag!' Pyotr Andreevich tried to bring Andrey to his senses. 'And he might even have worms. And generally you might pick up an infection and spread it through the station . . .'

'OK, Pyotr, that's enough, stop whining. Just look at it!' And he pulled back the flaps of his jacket showing Pyotr the muzzle of the puppy that was still shivering either out of fear or cold. 'Look at its eyes – those eyes could never lie!'

Pyotr Andreevich looked at the puppy sceptically. They were frightened eyes but they were undoubtedly honest. Pyotr Andreevich thawed a bit.

'All right . . . You nature-lover . . . Wait, I'll find something for him to chew on,' he muttered and started to look in his rucksack.

'Have a look, have a look. You never know, maybe something useful will grow from it – a German Shepherd for example,' Andrey said and moved the jacket containing the puppy closer to the fire.

'But where could a puppy come from to get here? There aren't any people in that direction. Only dark ones. Do the dark ones keep dogs?' one of Andrey's men, a thin man with tousled hair who hadn't said anything until now asked as he looked suspiciously at the puppy who had dozed off in the heat.

'You're right, of course, Kirill,' Andrey answered seriously. 'The dark ones don't keep pets as far as I know.'

'Well how do they live then? What do they eat, anyway?' asked another man, scratching his unshaven jaw with a light, electric crackling sound.

He was tall and obviously battle-hardened, broad-shouldered and thickset, with a completely shaven head. He was dressed in a long and well-sewn leather cloak, which, in this day and age, was a rarity.

'What do they eat? They say they eat all kinds of junk. They eat carrion. They eat rats. They eat humans. They're not picky, you know,' answered Andrey, contorting his face in disgust.

'Cannibals?' asked the man with the shaved head, without a shadow of surprise – and it sounded as though he'd come across cannibals before.

'Cannibals . . . They're not even human. They're undead. Who knows what the hell they are! It's good they don't have weapons, so we're able to fend them off. For the time being. Pyotr! Remember, six months ago we managed to take one of them captive?'

'I remember,' spoke up Pyotr Andreevich. 'He sat in our lock-up for two weeks, wouldn't drink our water, didn't touch our food, and then croaked.'

'You didn't interrogate him?' asked the man.

'He didn't understand a word we said, in our language. They'd speak plain Russian to him, and he'd keep quiet. He kept quiet the entire time. Like his mouth was full of water. They'd beat him too, and he said nothing. And they'd give him something to eat, and he'd say nothing. He'd just growl every once in a while. And he howled so loudly just before he died that the whole station woke up . . .'

'So how'd the dog get here anyway?' Kirill reminded them.

'Who the hell knows how it got here . . . Maybe it ran away from them. Maybe they wanted to eat it. It's about two kilometres to here.

Couldn't a dog have run here from there? Maybe it belongs to someone. Maybe someone was coming from the north and fell on the dark ones. And the little dog managed to get away. Doesn't matter anyway how she got here. Look at her yourself. Does she look like a monster? Like a mutant? No, she's a little puppy dog, nothing special. And she's drawn to people – that means she's used to us. Otherwise why would she have tried three times to get close to the fire?'

Kirill went silent, thinking through the argument. Pyotr Andreevich filled up the kettle with water from the canister, and asked: 'Anyone want more tea? Let's have a final cup, soon it'll be time for us to be relieved.'

'Tea – now you're talking! Let's have some,' Andrey said. The others became animated at the idea as well.

The kettle came to a boil. Pyotr Andreevich poured another cup for those who wanted it, and made a request:

'You guys . . . There's no point in talking about the dark ones. The last time we were sitting like this and talking about them, they crawled up. Other guys have told me that the very same thing happened to them. Maybe it's just a coincidence, I'm not super-stitious – but what if it's not? What if they can sense it? Our shift's almost over already, what do we need these shenanigans for at the last minute?'

'Yeah, actually . . . It's probably not worth it,' seconded Artyom.

'OK, that's enough, man, don't chicken out on us! We'll get there in the end!' said Andrey, trying to cheer up Artyom but not really succeeding in convincing him.

The mere thought of the dark ones sent an unpleasant shiver through everyone, including Andrey, although he tried to hide it. He didn't fear humans of any kind: not bandits, not cutthroat anar-chists, not soldiers of the Red Army. But the undead disgusted him, and it wasn't that he was afraid of them, but that he couldn't stay calm when he thought about them or indeed any other danger.

Everyone fell quiet. A heavy, oppressive silence came over the men grouped around the fire. The knobbly logs in the fire were crackling, and to the north, a muted, deep-chested croaking sound in the tunnel could be heard from time to time in the distance, as if the Moscow metro were the giant intestine of some unknown monster. And these sounds were really terrifying.

CHAPTER 2

The Hunter

Once again, all sorts of nonsense started filling Artyom's head. The dark ones . . . He'd come across those damn non-humans only once during his watch, and he'd been scared silly – but how could he not have been . . .

So, you're sitting there on watch. You're warming yourself by the fire. And suddenly you hear it: from the tunnel, from somewhere in the depths, a regular, dull knocking rings out – first, in the distance, quietly, and then, ever closer, and ever louder . . . And suddenly your ears are struck by a horrible, graveyard howl, and it's coming closer . . . And then complete mayhem! Everyone jumps up; they heap the sandbags and crates on which they'd been sitting into a barrier – quickly so that there'd be something to hide behind. And the most senior among them shouts with all his might, at the top of his lungs, 'Alert!'

Reserves rush in from the station to give support; at the three-hundredth metre where the main blow will have to be absorbed, they pull the cover from the machine gun, and people throw themselves to the ground, behind the sandbags, directing their guns at the mouth of the tunnel, taking aim . . . Finally, having waited for the dark ones to draw closer, they turn on the spotlight, and strange, delirious silhouettes become visible in its beam. They're naked, covered in black, glossy skin, with huge eyes and mouths like gashes . . . They're striding rhythmically ahead, towards the fortifications, towards death, with reckless abandon, without wavering, closer and closer . . . There are three . . . Five . . . Eight beasts . . . And the first among them suddenly throws back its head and emits a howl like a requiem.

You feel a shiver along your skin; you resist the urge to jump up and run, to toss your gun aside, to abandon your comrades, to throw everything to the devil and run . . . The spotlight is aimed straight into the muzzles of these nightmarish creatures to strike their pupils with its bright light, but it's obvious that they're not even squinting, they're not throwing up their hands, but they are looking into the spotlight with eyes wide open, and continuing to move steadily onward, onward . . . Do they even have pupils?

And now, finally, the guys run up from the three-hundredth metre with more machine guns; they lie down alongside, commands fly overhead . . . Everything's ready . . . The long-awaited 'Fire!' thunders. At once, several guns begin to rattle, and the big machine gun rumbles. But the dark ones don't stop, they don't crouch; they stride ahead fully erect, without slowing their pace, just as steadily and calmly as before. In the light of the spotlight, you can see how the bullets tear at their glossy bodies, how they're being pushed backwards, how they fall; but they get right back up again, rise to their full height, and march on. And again, hoarsely now, because its throat has already been pierced, a sinister howl rings out. Several minutes more will pass as the steel tempest finally breaks this inhuman, unthinking obstinacy. And then, when all of these ghouls have tumbled, breathless and motionless, the guys will finish them off with shots to the head from five metres, just to be sure. And even when everything's over, when the corpses have been tossed into the shaft, that same sinister image will continue to hover before your eyes, for a long time to come – bullets plunging into those black bodies, the spotlight scalding those wide-open eyes – but they kept on marching, as steadily as ever, onwards . . .

Artyom convulsed at the thought. Yes, of course, it'd be better not to chat about them, he thought. Just in case.

'Hey, Andreich! Get ready! We're on our way!' they shouted from the south, from the darkness. 'Your shift's over!'

The men at the fire began to move about, throwing off their stupor, rising to their feet, stretching, putting on their backpacks and weapons and Andrey picked up the little puppy. Pyotr Andreevich and Artyom were returning to the station while Andrey and his men were returning to the three hundredth metre since their shift there hadn't quite ended.

Their replacements walked up and exchanged handshakes, ascertained whether or not anything strange or peculiar had happened, wished each other the relaxation they deserved, and sat down a bit closer to the fire, continuing a conversation they'd begun earlier.

When everyone was already headed south along the tunnel,

towards the station, Pyotr Andreevich began speaking heatedly with Andrey about something, apparently returning to one of their eternal disputes; and the husky guy with the shaved head, who had questioned them concerning the dark ones' eating habits, fell away from them, drawing even with Artyom, and beginning to walk in step with him.

'So then, you know Sukhoi?' he asked Artyom in a low, muffled voice, without looking him in the eye.

'Uncle Sasha! Well, yes! He's my stepfather. I live with him,' answered Artyom honestly.

'You don't say . . . Your stepfather? I've never heard of such . . .' muttered the man.

'And what's your name?' Artyom decided to ask, having reasoned that if someone questions you about your own relative, then that gives you the right to ask a question in return.

'My name?' asked the man, surprised. 'Why do you need to know?'

'Well, I'll tell Uncle Sasha, Sukhoi, that you were asking after him.'

'Tell him that Hunter was asking. Hunter. Tell him I said hello.'

'Hunter? That's an odd name. What is it, your last name? Your nickname?' Artyom asked.

'Last name? Hmm . . .' Hunter smirked. 'What of it? It's totally . . . No, son, it's not a last name. It's . . . how should I put it . . . A profession. And what's your name?'

'Artyom.'

'Fine then. Nice to meet you. I'm sure we'll see each other again. And fairly soon at that. Cheers!'

Giving Artyom a wink before parting, he remained behind at the three-hundredth metre, along with Andrey.

There wasn't much further to go; from a distance, the lively noise of the station could already be heard. Pyotr Andreevich, walking alongside Artyom, asked him worriedly:

'Listen, Artyom, who was that, anyway? What was he saying to you back there?'

'He was a strange sort of guy . . . He was asking about Uncle Sasha. An acquaintance of his, I guess? Do you know him?'

'Don't seem to . . . He's just come to our station for a couple of days, on some sort of business, it seems. Looks like Andrey has already met him; he was the one who insisted on being on the same watch with him. Who the hell knows why he found that so necessary! His face is somehow familiar . . .'

'Yeah. It's probably hard to forget an appearance like that,' said Artyom.

'Exactly. Where was it that I saw him? What's his name – do you know?' inquired Pyotr Andreevich.

'Hunter. That's what he said – Hunter. Just try and figure out what that's supposed to be.'

'Hunter? Not a Russian name . . .' frowned Pyotr Andreevich.

In the distance, a red glow had already appeared. *VDNKh* like the majority of stations, didn't have normal lighting and, for thirty years now, people had lived under scarlet emergency lights. Only occasionally were there normal electric light bulbs in their 'apartments' – their tents and rooms. And only a few of the wealthiest metro stations were illuminated by the light of genuine mercury lamps. Legends had formed around them, and provincial types, from distant, god-forsaken substations, would nourish the dream for years on end of making it there and beholding this miracle.

At the tunnel exit, they handed over their weapons to the other guards, and signed their names in the ledger. Pyotr Andreevich shook Artyom's hand before parting and said:

'It's about time we hit the sack! I can barely stand on my feet, and you're probably ready to sleep standing up yourself. Give Sukhoi my warmest regards. He should pay me a visit.'

Artyom said goodbye and feeling the sudden onset of fatigue, took himself off to his 'apartment.'

Two hundred people lived at *VDNKh*. Some in the service quarters, but the majority in tents on the platform. The tents were army-issue, now old, tattered, but still intact. They didn't have to contend with wind or rain underground, and they were well maintained so it was easily possible to live in them. They didn't lose heat or light, and they even kept out the noise. What more could one ask of one's housing? . . .

The tents were tucked up against the wall on either side – both along the tracks, and in the central hall. The platform had been turned into something resembling a street: there was a fairly wide passage along its middle. Some of the tents were large, housing the more numerous families and they occupied the space beneath the archways. But several arches remained free for passage – at each end of the hall, and at its centre. There were other accommodations below the platforms as well, but the ceiling there wasn't very high, and they weren't very suitable for habitation. They used them at *VDNKh* for the storage of provisions.

The two northern tunnels were joined by a side tunnel, several tens of metres beyond the station, which, once upon a time, allowed trains to turn around and head back in the other direction. Now one of these two tunnels was plugged up; the other led to the north, towards the Botanical Garden, and almost to *Mytischi*. They'd left it as a retreat route in the case of extreme circumstance, and it was there that Artyom had been on watch. The remaining segment of the second tunnel, and the unified stretch between the two tunnels, was designated for mushroom plantations. The rails there had been dismantled and the ground had been tilled and fertilized – they hauled waste products there from the cesspit. Tidy rows of mushroom caps shone white along the tunnel. One of the two southern tunnels had been collapsed as well, at the three-hundredth metre, and they used that area for chicken coops and pigpens.

Artyom's home stood on the main thoroughfare – he lived there in one of the smaller tents together with his stepfather. His stepfather was an important man associated with the administration. He maintained contact with other stations so the powers that be reserved the tent for him – it was granted to him as his own personal tent, and it was a first-rate one at that. His stepfather would frequently disappear for two or three weeks at a time, and never took Artyom with him, excusing himself by saying that he was occupied with matters too dangerous, and didn't want to subject Artyom to any risk. He'd return from his trips thinner, his hair unkempt, sometimes wounded. But the first evening of his return he would always sit with Artyom, telling him things that were hard to believe even for a resident of this grotesque little world, and one who was used to unbelievable stories.

Artyom felt the urge to travel himself, but to wander around in the metro for no good reason was too dangerous. The patrol guards at independent stations were very suspicious, and wouldn't let a person pass with a weapon – and heading off into the tunnels without a weapon meant certain death. And so, ever since he and his grandfather had come from *Savyolovskaya*, Artyom hadn't had the chance to take part in any decent excursions. He'd sometimes be sent to *Alekseevskaya* on business but he didn't go alone, of course. They went in group, sometimes as far as *Rizhskaya*. But on top of that, he had one more trip under his belt, about which he couldn't tell anyone, although he desperately wanted to . . .

It happened a long, long time ago, when there wasn't even the slightest hint of the dark ones at the Botanical Garden, when it was

28

simply an abandoned and dark station, and patrols from *VDNKh* were stationed much further to the north. At the time Artyom himself was still just a kid. Back then, he and his buddies decided to take a risk: during a shift change, they stole past the outer cordon with flashlights and a double-barrelled rifle stolen from someone's parents, and crawled for a long time around the Botanical Garden station. It was eerie, but it was interesting. In the light of the flashlights, you could see the remnants of human habitation everywhere: ash, singed books, broken toys, torn clothing . . . Rats darted about, and from time to time, strange rumbling sounds would ring out from the northern tunnel. One of Artyom's friends – he didn't even remember who it was anymore but it was probably Zhenya, the most lively and most curious of the three – said, 'What if we try to take down the barrier and go up to the surface, up the escalator . . . just to see what it's like there? To see what's there?'

Artyom had said right away that he was against it. The recent tales his stepfather told him about people who had spent time on the surface were fresh in his mind, about how afterwards they had long been sick, and about the sorts of horrors sometimes seen up there. But they immediately began to argue that this was a rare opportunity. When else would they manage to make it, with no adults, to an abandoned station, as they had now? And now they had the chance to go up to the surface too, and see, see with their own eyes, what it's like to have nothing above your head. And, resigning all hope of convincing him nicely, they declared that if he was such a coward, then he could sit down below and wait for them to come back. The thought of staying alone in an abandoned station, and, on top of that, besmirching his reputation in the eyes of his two best friends, was completely unbearable to Artyom. So, summoning his courage, he consented.

To everyone's surprise, the mechanism that brought the barrier dividing the platform from the escalator into motion actually worked. And it was Artyom himself who managed to start it up after half an hour of desperate attempts. The rusty iron wall moved aside with a nasty grating sound and before their eyes stood the short row of steps of the escalator, leading upwards. Some of the steps had collapsed and, through the yawning gaps, in the light of the flashlights, one could see colossal gears that had stopped years ago, corroded with rust, grown over with something brownish that was moving, just barely noticeably . . . It wasn't easy for them to force themselves to go up there. Several times, the steps they stepped on

29

gave way with a screech, and dropped below, and they climbed across the chasm, clinging to the old hulls of the metro lamps. The path to the surface wasn't long, but their initial determination was evaporating after that first collapsed step; and in order to raise their spirits, they imagined themselves to be real stalkers.

Stalkers . . .

The word, strange and foreign to the Russian language, had caught on very well nonetheless. Earlier, this was the name given to people whose poverty compelled them to make their way to abandoned military firing ranges, take apart unexploded missiles and bombs and redeem brass casings with those who bought non-ferrous metals. It was also given to those strange people who, in times of peace, climbed around in the sewers. But all of these meanings had something in common: it was always an extremely dangerous profession, always a confrontation with the unknown, the mysterious, the ominous . . . Who knows what happened at those abandoned ranges, where the radioactive earth, disfigured by thousands of explosions, ploughed with trenches and pitted with catacombs, put forth monstrous sprouts? And one could only guess what might dwell in the sewers of a teeming metropolis once the builders had closed the hatches behind them, leaving those gloomy, narrow, reeking corridors forever.

In the metro, the rare daredevils who had the guts to venture to the surface were called stalkers. In protective suits and gas masks with tinted glass, they were heavily armed as they ascended to the surface in search of items that were necessities for everyone: military supplies, equipment, replacement parts, fuel . . . There were hundreds of men who dared to do this. Those who were able to make it back alive could be counted on one's fingers – and these men were worth their weight in gold. They were valued even more highly than former metro employees. All kinds of dangers awaited those who dared to go up above – from the radiation to the ghoulish creatures it had created. There was life there too, on the surface, but it was no longer life according to the customary human conception of it.

Every stalker became a living legend, a demigod, whom everyone, young and old, regarded with rapt amazement. In a world in which there was nowhere left to sail or fly, and the words 'pilot' and 'sailor' were becoming dull and losing their meaning, children dreamed of becoming stalkers. To strike out, clothed in shining armour, accompanied by hundreds of gazes of adoration and gratitude, climbing to the surface, to the realm of the gods, to do battle with

30

monsters and, returning underground, to bring the people fuel, military supplies, light and fire. To bring life.

Artyom, his friend Zhenya, and Vitalik the Splinter, all wanted to become stalkers. And, compelling themselves to climb upwards along the horrifying, screeching escalator with its collapsing steps, they imagined themselves in protective suits, with radiation damage monitors, with hulking machine guns at the ready, just as one would expect of real stalkers. But they had neither radiation monitors, nor protection, and instead of imposing army-issue machine guns, they had only the ancient double-barrelled rifle, which, perhaps, didn't even shoot at all . . .

Before long, their ascent was complete, and they found themselves almost on the surface. Fortunately, it was night; otherwise, they would have been blinded. Eyes accustomed to darkness and to the crimson light of bonfires and emergency lamps in their many years of life underground wouldn't have withstood the glare. Blinded and helpless, they would have been unlikely to make it back home again.

The vestibule of the Botanical Garden station was almost destroyed; half of the roof had collapsed, and through it one could see the radioactive dust of the dark-blue summer sky, already cleansed of clouds, and strewn with myriad stars. But what was a starry sky for a child who wasn't even capable of imagining that a ceiling might not be above his head? When you lift your gaze, and it doesn't run up against concrete coverings and rotten networks of wires and pipes, but is lost instead in a dark-blue abyss, gaping suddenly above your head – what an impression! And the stars! Could anyone who had never seen stars possibly imagine what infinity is, when, most likely, the very concept of infinity first appeared among humans inspired, once upon a time, by the nocturnal vault of the heavens? Millions of shining lights, silver nails driven into a dome of dark blue velvet . . .

The boys stood for three, five, then ten minutes, unable to utter a word. They wouldn't even have moved, and by morning would certainly have been cooked alive, if they hadn't heard a blood-curdling howl ring out nearby. Coming to their senses, they rushed headlong back to the escalator, and raced down it as fast as their legs could carry them, having thrown all caution to the wind, and several times nearly plunging downwards, into the teeth of the gears. Supporting each other, and pulling each other out, they made the journey back in a matter of seconds.

Spinning down the final ten steps like a top, having lost the double-barrelled rifle along the way, they immediately lunged for the control panel of the barrier. But, damn it, the rusted old iron had become wedged, and it didn't want to return to its place. Scared half to death that the monsters would pursue them from the surface, they raced off homewards, to the northern cordon.

But, remembering that they'd probably done something very bad, having left the hermetic gates open, and had possibly left the path downward, into the metro, and to people, open for the mutants, they found the time to agree to keep their lips sealed, and not to tell any of the adults where they'd been. At the cordon, they said that they'd gone to a side tunnel to hunt for rats, but had lost their gun, become frightened, and returned.

Artyom, of course, caught hell from his stepfather. His rear end smarted for a long time from that officer's belt, but Artyom held up like a captive partisan, and didn't blurt out his military secret. And his comrades kept silent as well.

Everyone believed them.

But now, when he thought of their escapade, Artyom fell, more and more often, into reflection. Was this journey, and, more importantly, the barrier they'd opened, connected somehow to the scum that had been assaulting their cordons for the last several years?

Greeting passers-by, stopping now and then to hear some news, to shake hands with a friend, to land a kiss on the cheek of a familiar girl, to tell the older generations about his stepfather's dealings, Artyom finally reached his home. Nobody was there, and he decided not to wait for his stepfather but to go to bed: an eight-hour watch was enough to take anyone off their feet. He threw off his boots, took off his jacket and planted his face in the pillow. Sleep didn't make him wait.

The flaps of the tent were lifted and a massive figure slipped quietly inside, whose face couldn't be seen. The only thing visible was the ominous gleam of a smooth skull reflecting the red emergency lights. A muffled voice was heard: 'We meet again. Your stepfather, I see, is not here. Doesn't matter. We'll find him. Sooner or later. He won't get away. For now, you'll come with me. We have something to talk about. For example, the barrier at the Botanical Gardens.'

Artyom, frozen, recognized the guy he had met at the cordon earlier, the man who had introduced himself as Hunter.

The man came closer, slowly, silently, and his face was still not visible. For some reason the light was falling in a strange way. Artyom wanted to call for help, but a powerful hand, as cold as death, clamped onto his mouth. At last he managed to grab hold of a lantern, turn it on and light up the person's face. What he saw, rendered him powerless for a moment and filled him with horror: what loomed in front of him was not a human face, but a terrible black muzzle with two huge, vacant and white-less eyes and a gaping maw.

Artyom darted and threw himself out of the tent. The light suddenly went out and the station became totally dark. There was only some weak reflected light from a small fire somewhere in the distance. Without pausing for thought, Artyom rushed in that direction, toward the light. The ghoul jumped towards him from behind, growling, 'Stop! You have nowhere to run!' He roared with terrifying laughter, which slowly became a familiar graveyard howl. Artyom ran off, without turning to look, hearing the footfalls of heavy boots behind him, unhurried, even, as if his pursuer knew that there was nowhere to run, that Artyom would be caught sooner or later.

Artyom ran up to the fire and saw a figure sitting there with its back to him. He was going to tap the sitting person on the shoulder and ask for help, but the person suddenly fell backwards and it was clear that he had been dead a long time and his face was covered with hoarfrost for some reason. And in the face of this frozen person, Artyom recognized Uncle Sasha, his stepfather.

'Hey, Artyom! That was a good sleep! Now get up! You've been snoozing for seven hours in a row already . . . get up sleepyhead! We have guests coming!' Sukhoi's voice rang out.

Artyom sat up in bed and stared at him, stunned. 'Oh, Uncle Sash . . . You . . . Is everything OK with you?' he asked at last, after a minute of blinking. It was hard for him to overcome the urge to ask him if he was alive or not, and that was only because the fact of it was standing in front of him.

'Yes, as you can see! Come on, come on, get up, no point lying about. I want to introduce you to my friend,' said Sukhoi. There was a familiar but muffled voice nearby, and Artyom was covered in perspiration, remembering his recent nightmare.

'So, you've met already?' Sukhoi was surprised. 'Well, Artyom, you're sharp!'

Finally, the visitor squeezed into the tent. Artyom shuddered and pressed against the tent wall – it was Hunter. The nightmare came alive again: dark, vacant eyes; the roar of heavy boots behind him; the stiff corpse sitting at the fire . . .

'Yes. We've met.' Artyom managed to squeeze out his reply and

33

reluctantly extended a hand to the visitor. Hunter's hand was hot and dry, and Artyom slowly started to convince himself that it was just a dream, that there was nothing sinister about this person, that it was just his imagination, ignited with fear after eight hours at the cordon, playing out in his dreams.

'Listen, Artyom! Do us a favour! Boil some water for tea! Have you tried our tea?' Sukhoi winked at the visitor. 'A poisonous potion!'

'I know it,' Hunter responded, nodding. 'Good tea. They make it at *Pechatniki* too. Pig's swill. But here, it's a different matter.'

Artyom went to get the water, then to the communal fire to boil the kettle. It was strictly forbidden to make fires inside tents: a couple of stations had burnt down due to tent fires before now.

On the way he thought about *Pechatniki* – it was at the other end of the metro system, and who knows how long it would take to get there, how many transfers, crossings, through how many stations you'd have to go – lying sometimes, fighting sometimes, other times getting through thanks to connections . . . And this guy says casually, 'They make it at *Pechatniki* too . . .' Yes, he's an interesting character, even if a little scary. His grip squeezes like a vice, and Artyom wasn't a weakling – he was always eager to compare strength with a good handshake.

Having boiled the kettle, he returned to the tent. Hunter had already thrown off his raincoat under which you could see a black polo-neck jumper, tightly filled with a powerful neck and a bulging, strong body, and military trousers drawn tight with an officer's belt. On top of the polo-neck, he was wearing a vest with lots of pockets, and a holster hung under his arm containing a burnished pistol of monstrous size. Upon closer inspection, Artyom could see that it was a 'Stechkin' with a long silencer, and it had something attached to it, which by the looks of it was a laser sight. A monster like that would cost you all you had. The weapon, Artyom noted immediately, was not a simple one – not for self-defence, that was for sure. And then he remembered that when Hunter introduced himself he added, 'as in someone who hunts.'

'So, Artyom, pour the visitor some tea! Yes, and you Hunter, take a seat! Tell us how you are!' Sukhoi was excited. 'Devil knows how long it's been since I last saw you!'

'I'll tell you about myself later. There's not much to say. But strange things are going on with you, I hear. Goblins are crawling around. Coming from the north. Today I was listening to fairy stories while standing with the patrol. What's up?' Hunter spoke in brief, choppy phrases.

'It's death, Hunter,' Sukhoi's mood suddenly darkened. 'It's our death stealing up from the future. Our fate is creeping in. That's what it is.'

'Why death? I heard that you crushed them very successfully. That they're disarmed. Well? Where are they from and who are they? I've never heard anything like this at any of the other stations. Never. And that means that it isn't happening anywhere else. I want to know what's up. I'm sensing a great danger. I want to know the level of danger, I want to understand its nature. That's why I'm here.'

'Danger should be liquidated, right Hunter? You're still a cowboy, Hunter. But can danger be liquidated – that's the question.' Sukhoi grinned sadly. 'That's the hitch. Everything here is more complicated than it seems to you. A lot more complicated. This is not just zombies and corpses walking across cinema screens. That's too simple: you load a revolver with silver bullets,' Sukhoi demonstrated by putting his palms together and pretending to point a pistol as he continued, 'pow-pow! And the forces of evil are slain. But this is something different. Something frightening . . . And as you well know, it's hard to scare me.'

'You're panicking?' Hunter asked, surprised.

'Their main weapon is horror. The people are barely maintaining their positions. People are sleeping with machine guns, with uzis – and they're coming at us unarmed. And everybody knows that there's a higher quality and quantity of them still to come, they are almost running away, going crazy from the horror of it – some have already gone crazy, between you and me. And this isn't just fear, Hunter!' Sukhoi lowered his voice. 'This . . . I don't even know how to explain it to you plainly . . . It gets stronger every time. They are getting into our heads somehow . . . And it seems to me that they're doing it on purpose. You can sense them from afar, and the feeling gets stronger and stronger, and the agitation is so vile that your knees start to shake. And you can't hear anything yet, and you can't see anything, but you already know that they're coming nearer . . . nearer . . . And then there's a howl – and you just want to run . . . But they're coming closer – and you're starting to shake. And a while later you can see them walking with open eyes into the searchlights . . .'

Artyom shuddered. It seemed that he wasn't the only one tormented by nightmares. He used to try not to talk about it to anyone before. He was afraid that they would take him for a coward or for a lunatic.

'They're crippling our minds, the reptiles!' Sukhoi continued. 'And you know, it's like they adjust themselves to your wavelength, and the next time they come, you feel them even more strongly, and you're even more afraid. And this isn't just fear, I can tell you.'

He went silent. Hunter was sitting there without moving, studying him, and apparently thinking over what he'd heard. Then he took a mouthful of hot brew and spoke, slowly and quietly: 'This is a threat to everybody, Sukhoi. To the whole filthy metro, not just to your station.'

Sukhoi was silent, as though he didn't want to reply, but suddenly he burst out: 'The whole metro you think? No. Not just the metro. This is a threat to the progress of mankind, which got itself into trouble with its progress already. It's time to pay! It's a battle of species, Hunter! A battle of species. And these dark ones are not evil spirits, and they aren't some kind of ghoul. This is Homo novus – the next stage in evolution, better adapted to the environment than us. The future is behind them, Hunter! Maybe, Homo sapiens will rot for another couple of decades, or for another fifty in these demonic holes that we've dug for ourselves, back when there was plenty and not everyone could fit above ground so the poorer folk were driven underground in the daytime. We will become as pale and sick as Wells' Morlocks. Remember them? From *The Time Machine* where beasts of the future lived underground? They too were once Homo sapiens. Yes, we are optimistic – we don't want to die! We will cultivate mushrooms with our own dung, and the pig will become man's best friend, as they say, and our partner in survival. And we will guzzle multivitamins with an appetizing crunch that were prepared by our careful ancestors in the tonnes. We will shyly crawl up to the surface to quickly steal another canister of petrol, a few more rags, and if you're really lucky, a handful of cartridges – only to quickly run back down into the stuffy vaults, looking shiftily around like thieves to see if anyone noticed. Because we aren't at home there on the surface anymore. The world doesn't belong to us anymore, Hunter . . . The world doesn't belong to us anymore.'

Sukhoi fell silent, looking at the steam slowly rising from his cup of tea and condensing in the twilight of the tent. Hunter said nothing, and Artyom suddenly realized that he had never heard anything like it from his stepfather. There was nothing left of his former confidence in the fact that everything would necessarily be fine; nothing left of his 'don't panic, we'll get through it!'; and nothing left of his encouraging winks . . . Or was that just all for show?

'You don't have anything to say, Hunter? Nothing? Go on, contradict me! Where are your arguments? Where is that optimism of yours? Last time when I spoke to you, you were certain that the levels of radiation would lower, and people could return to the surface again. Eh, Hunter . . . "The sun will rise over the woods, but just not for me . . ."' Sukhoi sang in a teasing voice. 'We'll seize life with our teeth, we will hold onto it with all our strength – but what would the philosophers have said and the sectarians confirmed, if there was suddenly nothing to grab? You don't want to believe it, can't believe it, but somewhere in the depths of your soul you know that that's how it is . . . But we like this whole business, Hunter, don't we? Me and you, we really love living! We will crawl through the stinking underground, sleep in an embrace with pigs, eat rats, but we will survive! Right? Wake up, Hunter! No one will write a book about you called *The story of a real person*, no one will sing about your will to live, your hypertrophic instinct for self-preservation . . . How long will you last on mushrooms, multivitamins and pork? Surrender, Homo sapiens! You are no longer the king of nature! You've been dethroned! No, you don't have to die instantly, nobody will insist on that. Crawl on a little more in agony, choking on your own excrement . . . But know this, Homo sapiens: you are obsolete! Evolution, the laws of which you understood, has already created its new branch, and you are no longer the latest stage, the crown of creation. You are a dinosaur. Now you must step aside for a new, more perfect species. No need to be egotistical. Game over, it's time you let others play. Your time is up. You're extinct. And let future generations wrack their brains over the question of what made Homo sapiens extinct. Though, I doubt anyone will be interested . . .'

Hunter who was studying his fingernails through this monologue, raised his eyes to Sukhoi and said gravely, 'You have really given up on everything since I last saw you. I remember that you were telling me that if we preserve culture, if we don't turn sour, if we don't stop using proper Russian, if our children learn to read and write, then we'll be fine and we'll last here underground . . . Didn't you say all that – or wasn't it you? And now, look at you – surrender, Homo sapiens . . . What the hell is that?'

'Yeah, well, I just figured out a thing or two, Hunter. I have felt something which you have yet to get, and maybe you'll never get it: we are dinosaurs, and we are living the last days of our life . . . It might take ten or even a hundred years, but all the same . . .'

'Resistance is futile, right?' Hunter offered, in a mean voice. 'What are you driving at?'

Sukhoi was silent, his eyes downcast. Clearly this had cost him a lot – having never admitted his weaknesses to anybody, or said such a thing to an old friend. Even worse that it was in front of Artyom. It was painful to him to hold up a white flag.

'But no! You won't wait!' Hunter slowly said, standing up to full height. 'And they won't wait! New species you say? Evolution? Inevitable extinction? Dung? Pigs? Vitamins? I'm not there yet. I'm not afraid of it either. Got it? I am not putting my hand up to volunteer. The instinct of self-preservation? You call it that. Yes, I will sink my teeth into life. Fuck your evolution. Let other species wait their turn. I'm not a lamb being led to slaughter. Capitulate and go off with your more perfect and more adapted beings – give them your place in history! If you feel that you've fought all you can fight, then go ahead and desert, I won't judge you. But don't try to scare me. And don't try to drag me along with you into the slaughter-house. Why are you giving me a sermon? If you don't do it alone, if you need to do it collectively, you won't be so ashamed? Or has the enemy promised you a bowl of hot porridge for each person that you bring to them in captivity? My fight is hopeless? You say that we're at the edge of the abyss? I spit on your abyss. If you think that your place is at the bottom of the abyss then take a deep breath and forward march. But I'm not coming for the ride. If rational man, refined and civilised Homo sapiens chooses to capitulate – then I refuse to be called one and would rather become a beast. And I will, like a beast, sink my teeth into life and gnaw on the throats of others in order to survive. And I will survive. Got it?! I will survive!'

He sat down and quietly asked Artyom for another splash of tea. Sukhoi stood up himself and went to fill and heat the kettle, gloomily and silently. Artyom stayed in the tent alone with Hunter. His last words were ringing with contempt; his malicious confidence that he would survive lit a fire in Artyom. For a long time he was trying to decide whether to say something. And then Hunter turned to him and said: 'And what do you think my friend? Tell me, don't be shy . . . You want to turn into vegetation too? Like a dinosaur? To sit on your things and wait until someone comes for you? Do you know the parable about the frog in the cream? Two frogs landed in a pail of cream. One, thinking rationally, understood straight away that there was no point in resistance and that you can't deceive destiny. But then what if there's an afterlife – why bother jumping around, entertaining false hopes in vain? He crossed his legs and sank to the bottom. The second, the fool, was probably an atheist. And she started to flop around. It would seem that she had no reason to flail about if everything was predestined. But she flopped around and flopped around anyway . . . Meanwhile, the cream turned to butter. And she crawled out. We honour the memory of this second frog's friend, eternally damned for the sake of progress and rational thought.'

'Who are you?' Artyom ventured at last.

'Who am I? You already know who I am. The one who hunts.'

'But what does that mean – the one who hunts? What do you do? Hunt?'

'How can I explain it to you? You know how the human body is built? It's made up of millions of tiny cells – some emit electrical signals, others store information, others still soak up nutrients, transfer oxygen. But all of them – even the most important among them – would be dead in less than a day, and the whole organism would die, if it wasn't for cells responsible for immunity. They're called macrophages. They work methodically and regularly like a clock, a metronome. When an infection gets into an organism, they find it, track it down, wherever it's hiding, and sooner or later, they get to it and . . .' He made a gesture as though he was wringing someone's neck and let out an unpleasant crunching sound. 'Liquidate it.'

'But what relevance does that have to your job?' Artyom insisted.

'Imagine that the whole metro was a human organism. A complex organism, made up of about forty thousand cells. I am the macrophage. The hunter. This is my job. Any danger that is sufficiently serious as to threaten the whole organism must be liquidated. That's what I do.'

Sukhoi finally came back with the kettle and poured the boiling brew into the mugs. He had obviously gathered his thoughts in the meantime, and he said to Hunter, 'So you're going to take on the liquidation of the source of danger, cowboy? You're going to go hunting and shoot down all the dark ones? It's hardly possible that anything will come of it. There's nothing to be done, Hunter. Nothing.'

'There is always one last option – the last resort. To blow your northern tunnel to pieces. Collapse it completely. To cut off that new species of yours. Let them procreate from above and leave us moles alone. The underground is now our natural habitat.'

'I'll tell you something interesting. Only a few people know about this at the station. They've already blown up one tunnel. But above us, above the northern tunnel, there is a stream of ground water. And, when they blew up the second northern tunnel, we were almost flooded. If the explosion had been just a bit stronger – goodbye my dear *VDNKh*. So, if we now blow up the remaining northern tunnel, then we'll be flooded. We'll be covered in radioactive swill. Then that will be the end, not only for us. Therein lies the real danger to the metro. If you start an inter-species battle now and in this way, then our species will lose. As they say in chess: check.'

'What about the hermetic gate? Surely we can simply close the hermetic gate in that tunnel?' Hunter said.

'The hermetic gate was already dismantled along with the rest of the lines gates fifteen years ago by some smart guys – and they sent the material to fortify one of the stations. No one remembers which one anymore. Surely you knew about this? There you go, check again.'

'Tell me . . . Have they increased their pressure recently?' Hunter, it seems, was conceding and shifting the conversation to another tack.

'Increasing? And how! It's hard to believe that it was only a little while ago that we didn't know they existed. And now, here they are – a major threat. And believe me, the day is near when they will sweep us away, with all of our fortifications, searchlights and machine-guns. It's impossible to raise the whole metro to defend one good-for-nothing station . . . Yes, we make pretty good tea, but it's unlikely that anyone will risk their life even for such excellent tea as ours. In the end, there's always competition with *Pechatniki*. . . . check again!' Sukhoi grinned sadly. 'No one needs us. We ourselves will soon not be in any condition to handle the onslaught. We can't blow up the tunnel and cut them off. We also don't have the means to go to the surface and burn them down, for obvious reasons . . . Checkmate. Checkmate to you, Hunter! And checkmate to me. Checkmate to all of us in the near future, if you see what I mean.' Sukhoi grinned sourly.

'We'll see,' Hunter snapped back. 'We'll see.'

They sat there a little longer, discussing all kinds of things. Many of the names mentioned weren't familiar to Artyom. There were references to bits and pieces of stories. Every once in a while an old argument would spark up, of which Artyom understood little, but their discussions had clearly been going on for years, abating if the men hadn't seen each other in a while and flaring up again when they met.

Finally, Hunter stood up and said it was time he went to bed because he, unlike Artyom, hadn't slept since his patrol. He said goodbye to Sukhoi. But before leaving he suddenly turned to Artyom and whispered to him: 'Come out for a minute.'

Artyom jumped up straightaway and followed him, not paying attention to the surprised look on his stepfather's face. Hunter waited for him outside, silently buttoning up his raincoat and lifting the latch on the gate.

'Shall we go through?' he suggested and he quickly stepped forward onto the platform towards the guest tent where he was staying. Artyom hesitantly moved to follow him, trying to guess what this man wanted to discuss with him, a mere boy really, who had done nothing significant or even useful for anyone so far.

'What do you think about the job that I do?' Hunter asked.

'It's cool . . . I mean if it wasn't for you . . . Well, and the others like you – if there are such people . . . Then we would have long ago . . .' Artyom mumbled uncomfortably.

His tongue was twisted and he felt hot suddenly. As soon as someone like Hunter paid him attention and wanted to tell him something, even just asking him to come outside for a minute, to be alone, without his stepfather, he blushed like a virgin and started agonizing, bleating like a lamb . . .

'You think highly of it? Well, then, if people think highly of it,' Hunter grinned, 'that means there's no point in listening to the defeatists among us. Your stepfather is being a coward, that's all. But he's really a brave man. In any case, he was once. Something horrific is happening here Artyom. Something that can't be allowed to continue. Your stepfather's right: these aren't just the goblins we've seen at dozens of other stations, these aren't vandals, they're not just degenerates. This is something new. Something meaner. There's a chill in the air. There's death in the air. I've only been here two days and I am already being penetrated by the fear here. And the more you know about them, the more you study them, the more you see them, the stronger the fear, as far as I understand. You, for example, have you seen them often?'

'Only once so far. I've only just started on the northern patrol, though,' Artyom confessed. 'But if I'm honest, once was enough. I've been tortured by nightmares ever since. Like today for example. And it was a while ago that I saw them!'

'Nightmares you say? You too?' Hunter frowned. 'Yes, it doesn't look like a coincidence. . . . And if I live here a bit longer, another couple of months, and go on patrols regularly, then it's not out of the question that I'll turn sour too . . . No, my lad. Your stepfather is mistaken. It isn't him speaking. It's not his thinking. It's them thinking for him, and it's them speaking for him. Give up, they say, resistance is futile. And he's their mouthpiece. And he probably doesn't even know it himself . . . And it's right, I guess, that they tune in and impress themselves on the psyche. Fiends! Tell me, Artyom,' Hunter turned to him straight on, and the boy understood: he was about to tell him something really important. 'Do you have a secret? Something that you wouldn't tell anyone on the station, but that you could tell a passer-by perhaps?'

'Well . . .' Artyom hesitated and for a perceptive person that would have been enough in order to understand that such a secret existed.

'And I have a secret too. Why don't we swap. I need to share this secret with someone but I want to be sure that they won't blab. That's why you give me yours – and don't let it be any crap about a girl, but something serious, something that no one else should ever hear. And I'll tell you something. This is important to me. Very important – you understand?'

Artyom wavered. Curiosity, of course, had got him, but he was frightened of telling his secret to a man who was not only interesting to talk to and who had seen many adventures but, by the looks of things, was also a cold-blooded murderer, who wouldn't hesitate in the slightest to remove any obstacle in his path. And what if Artyom happened to have been an accessory to the incursion of the dark ones . . .

Hunter looked into his eyes reassuringly. 'You have nothing to be afraid of in me. I guarantee inviolability!' And he winked fraternally.

They had walked up to the guest tent that had been given to Hunter for the night but they remained outside. Artyom thought again for the last time and decided what to do. He took in some more air and then hurriedly, in one breath, laid out the whole story of the expedition to the Botanical Gardens. When he was finished, Hunter was silent for a time, digesting what he'd heard. Then, in a hoarse voice, he said, 'Well, generally speaking, you and your friends should be killed for doing that, from a disciplinary point of view. However, I already guaranteed you inviolability. But that doesn't extend to your friends . . .'

Artyom's heart jumped, he felt his body freeze in fear and his legs falter. He wasn't able to speak and so he waited in silence for the verdict.

'But in light of your age and the general brainlessness of that event, and also the fact that it happened a while ago, you are pardoned. Go on.' And so that Artyom could be brought out of his prostration sooner, Hunter winked again at him, this time even more reassuringly. 'But know that you'd be shown no mercy by your fellow inhabitants at this station. So you have voluntarily given over to me a powerful weapon against you yourself. And now listen to my secret . . .'

And while Artyom was regretting his big mouth, Hunter continued:

'I haven't come across the whole metro system to this station for no reason. I'm not giving up on my own task. Danger should be eliminated, as you have probably heard many times today. Should and will be eliminated. I do that. Your stepfather is afraid of it. He is slowly turning into their instrument, as far as I can see. He is resisting them more and more reluctantly and he's trying to get me to join him. If the ground water thing is true then the option of exploding the tunnel is, of course, obsolete. But your story has clarified something for me. If the dark ones first made their way here after your expedition, then they're coming from the Botanical Gardens. Something has been growing there that isn't right, in that Botanical Garden, if that's where they were born . . . And that means that you can block them there, closer to the surface. Without the threat of unleashing the ground waters. But the devil knows what's happening at the seven-hundredth metre of the northern tunnel. That's where your powers end. That's where the powers of darkness begin – the most widespread form of government in the whole Moscow metro system. I'm going there. No one should know this. Tell Sukhoi that I asked you lots of questions about conditions at the station, and that will be the truth. You don't have to explain anything, right – if everything goes smoothly, I'll explain everything to whoever needs to know. But it might be that . . .' He stopped short for a second, and looked at Artyom more closely. 'That I don't come back. Whether there's an explosion or not, if I don't come back before the following morning, someone should say what's happened to me, and tell my colleagues about the fiends that are making trouble in your northern tunnels. I have seen all my former acquaint-ances here at this station today, including your stepfather. And I feel, I almost see, that there's a little worm of doubt and horror crawl-ing through the brains of everyone who has been exposed to their influence. I can't rely on people with worm-eaten brains. I need a healthy person, whose ability to reason has not yet been stormed by these ghouls. I need you.'

'Me? But how can I help you?' Artyom was surprised.

'Listen to me. If I don't come back, then you have to, at any cost – at any cost you hear! – you have to go to *Polis*. To *Gorod* . . . And look there for a man with the nickname Melnik. Tell him the whole story. And one other thing. I will give you something, which you will give to him as proof that I sent you. Come inside for a minute.'

Hunter took the lock off the entrance, lifted the flap of the tent and ushered Artyom inside.

There wasn't much room in the tent due to the huge camouflage rucksack and the impressively large trunk which were standing on the floor. By the light of the lantern, Artyom saw a dark shimmering gun-barrel in the depths of the bag, which, by the looks of it, was a reassembled army hand machine gun. Before Hunter could manage to close the bag so he wouldn't see, Artyom caught a glimpse of a matte black metal box containing machine-gun magazines, laid in a dense row next to the weapon, and small green anti-personnel grenades on the other side of it.

Without any commentary on this arsenal, Hunter opened the side-pocket of his rucksack and withdrew a small metal capsule from it, made of a machine-gun cartridge case. The side where there should have been a bullet was screwed up into a little twist.

'Here, take this. Don't wait for me if I've been gone two days. And don't be afraid. You will meet people everywhere who will help you. You have to do this! You know that everything depends on you. I don't have to explain that to you – right? That's it. Wish me success and get out of here. I need to catch up on some sleep.'

Artyom managed to utter a word of goodbye, shook Hunter's hand and started wandering over to his tent, stooping under the weight of the mission on his shoulders.

CHAPTER 3

If I Don't Come Back

Artyom was sure he would be cross-examined as soon as he got home. His stepfather would shake him down, trying to find out what he spoke about with Hunter. But, contrary to his expectations, his stepfather wasn't awaiting him with a rack and Spanish boots but was snoring peacefully – he hadn't had a chance to sleep in the last twenty-four hours.

Since he'd been on night patrol and slept that day, Artyom was again going to have to work the night shift – this time at the tea-factory.

Decades of life underground, in the darkness interspersed with patches of dull-red light, makes you lose a true sense of day and night. At night, the station's lighting was a little weaker (as it was on the trains of long ago so that people could sleep) but the lights never went out completely except in the case of an accident. Though it had become aggravated by years of living in darkness, human vision was nonetheless comparable with the eyesight of the other creatures that lived in the tunnels and abandoned passages.

The division of 'day' and 'night' had probably come about by force of habit, rather than by necessity. 'Night' made sense because the majority of inhabitants at the station were more comfortable with the idea of everyone sleeping at the same time, letting the cattle rest, turning down the lights and imposing restrictions on noise. The inhabitants of the station could find out the time by the two station clocks, placed over the entrance to the tunnels on either side. These clocks were considered to be as important as strategic objects like the arms store, the water filters and the electric generator. They were always looked after, and the smallest problems with them were immediately dealt with, and any delinquents attempting to take them down were dealt with very strictly, sometimes sent into exile from the station.

Here there was a criminal code, by which the *VDNKh* judged criminals in swift trials, and it was always being applied to extra-ordinary situations which were resolved and then new rules were established. Any actions against strategic objects brought about the most severe punishments. For smoking and the setting of fires on platforms, as well as the careless handling of weapons and explosives, you would be immediately expelled from the station and your property confiscated.

These draconian measures can be explained by the fact that several stations had already been burnt to nothing. Fire spread instantly through the small tent cities, devouring everything, and the wild screams of awful pain would echo in the ears of the neighbouring stations for months afterwards. Charred bodies stuck to the melted plastic and canvas, and sets of teeth, cracked from the inconceivable heat of the flames, gnashed in the light of the lanterns held by frightened traders who had accidentally come upon this traveller's hell.

In order to avoid the repetition of such a grim fate in the rest of the stations, the careless setting of fires became a serious criminal offence. Theft, sabotage and the deliberate avoidance of labour were also punished with exile. But, considering that almost everyone was always visible to each other and that there were only two hundred or so people at the station, these kinds of crimes were rare and usually perpetrated by strangers.

Labour was compulsory, and everyone, young and old, had to fulfil a daily quota. The pig farm, the mushroom plantation, the tea-factory, the meat-packing plant, the fire and engineer services, the weapon shop – every inhabitant worked in one or two of these places. Men were also required to go on military duty in one of the tunnels once every forty-eight hours. And when some kind of conflict arose, or some new danger appeared from the depths of the metro, the patrols were strengthened and they put a reserve force on the pathways, at the ready.

Life was so meticulously arranged here, and *VDNKh* had estab-lished such a reputation for it that there were many wishing to live there. But it was very rare for outsiders to be taken into the settlement.

There was a few more hours until his night shift at the tea-factory and Artyom, not knowing what to do with himself, trudged over to see his friend Zhenya, the same one with whom he undertook the headspinning adventure to the surface. Zhenya was his age, but unlike Artyom, he lived with his own real family: his father, mother, and younger sister. There were only a handful of incidents where a whole family had been saved, and Artyom secretly envied his friend. Of course, he loved his stepfather very much and respected him even now that the man's nerves had got the better of him. But nonetheless, he knew that Sukhoi wasn't his father, and wasn't his kin altogether – and he never called him 'Dad'.'

At the beginning Sukhoi asked Artyom to call him 'Uncle Sasha' but later regretted it. Years had gone by and the old tunnel wolf hadn't managed to start a family of his own, he didn't even have a woman who would wait for him to return from expeditions. His heart would beat harder when he saw a mother and child, and he dreamed about the possibility that one day he wouldn't have to go out into the darkness, disappearing from the life of the station for days and weeks, and maybe forever. And then, he hoped that he would find a woman who would be prepared to be his wife, and to bear him children, which, when they learnt to speak would not call him 'Uncle Sasha' but 'Father.'

Old age and feebleness were getting ever closer, and there was less and less time remaining, and he needed to hurry, but all the same it would be hard to pull off. Task followed task and he couldn't find anyone to take over his work, no one to trust with his connections and his professional secrets, in order to finally start doing some non-manual work at the station. He had already long considered doing work that was a bit more peaceful, and he even knew that he could fall back on a supervisory role at the station thanks to his authority, his stellar record and his friendly relations with the administration. But for now, there was no one capable of replacing him, not even on the horizon, so he entertained himself with thoughts of a happy future and he lived for today, postponing his final return and continuing to spend his sweat and blood for the sake of the granite of other stations and the concrete of far-off tunnels.

Artyom knew that his stepfather, despite showing fatherly love towards him, didn't think of him as his successor in professional matters and mostly thought of Artyom as a nitwit, and completely undeserving of such responsibility. He didn't take Artyom on long expeditions, ignoring the fact that Artyom had grown up and could no longer be persuaded that he was still too young and that zombies would drag him off or rats would eat him. He didn't understand expressing a lack of confidence in Artyom had pushed the boy into desperate escapades for which Sukhoi had to punish him afterwards. He had probably wanted not to subject Artyom to the senseless mortal danger of wandering the metro but allow the boy to live the way Sukhoi wanted to live himself: in peace and safety, working and raising children, not wasting his youth unnecessarily. But in wanting such a life for Artyom, he was forgetting to strive for such a life himself, and had passed through fire and water, had succeeded in surviving hundreds of adventures and was satisfied with them. And the wisdom acquired with years wasn't speaking to him anymore, all that spoke to him were the years themselves and the fatigue they brought. Artyom had energy boiling inside him. He had only just started living, and the prospect of drudging through the vegetative existence of crumbling and drying mushrooms, and changing diapers, and never going beyond the five-hundredth metre seemed absolutely inconceivable. The desire to get away from the station grew in him every day, as he understood more and more clearly what life his stepfather was moulding for him. A career as a tea-factory worker and the role of a father with many children was less appealing than anything on earth.

He was drawn to adventure, wanted to be carried along like tumbleweed in the tunnel draughts, and to follow these draughts into uncertainty, to meet his fate – and that's what Hunter probably saw in him, asking him to take part in a venture of such enormous risk. This Hunter fellow had a subtle sense of smell when it came to people, and after an hour of conversation he understood that he could propose the plan to Artyom. Even if Artyom didn't ever get to the designated place, at least there was the prospect of leaving the station, in accordance with his orders in the event that something should happen to Hunter at the Botanical Gardens.

And the hunter wasn't mistaken in his choice.

Luckily, Zhenya was at home and now Artyom could pass the evening discussing the latest gossip and having conversations about the future over strong tea.

'Great!' his friend exclaimed in response to Artyom's greeting. 'You're also on night duty at the factory today? They put me there too. I'm so sick of it that I wanted to ask the boss to switch me. But if they put you with me then that's fine, I can handle it. You were on patrol today, right? Well, tell me! I heard that you had a state of emergency there. What happened?'

Artyom cast a sidelong look at Zhenya's younger sister with great emphasis as she had become so interested in the conversation that she had stopped stuffing mushroom waste into the ragdoll that her mother had sewn for her, and was watching them with bated breath and round eyes from the corner of the tent.

'Listen, little one!' Zhenya said strictly, having understood what Artyom meant. 'You, now, go on, get out of here with your little thing and go and play at the neighbours'. I think Katya invited you over. We have to be nice to the neighbours. So, go on, and take your dollies with you.'

The little girl squeaked indignantly and started to gather her things with a gloomy look on her face, meanwhile making suggestions to her doll, who was blankly looking up at the ceiling with her semi-erased eyes. 'You think you're so important! I know everything anyway! You're going to talk about your mushrooms!' she said contemptuously as she left.

'You, Lenka, are still too small to discuss mushrooms. The milk on your lips hasn't even dried yet!' Artyom put her in her place.

'What's milk?' the girl asked, puzzled, touching her lips.

But neither of them bothered to explain and the question hung in the air.

When she left, Zhenya fastened the flaps of the tent and asked, 'Well, what happened? Go on, spill it! I've heard quite a lot about it already. One guy says that a huge rat crawled out of the tunnel. Another guy says that you scared off a spy for the dark ones and that you even wounded him. Who should I believe?'

'Don't believe anyone!' Artyom advised. 'They're all lying. It was a dog. A little puppy. Andrei the marine picked it up. He said that it was a German Shepherd.' Artyom smiled.

'Yeah but I heard from Andrei that it was a rat!' Zhenya said, perplexed. 'Did he lie on purpose or what?'

'You don't know? That's his favourite catchphrase – the one about the rats the size of pigs. He's a comedian, you see,' Artyom responded. 'So what's new with you? What have you heard from the boys?'

Zhenya's friends were traders, delivering teas and pork to the market at *Prospect Mir*. They brought back multivitamins, cloth, all sorts of junk, sometimes they even got hold of oil; sometimes they'd bring dirt-stained books, often with pages missing, which had mysteriously ended up at *Prospect Mir*, having travelled through half the metro system, passing from one trunk to the next, from one pocket to the next, from one merchant to another, before finally finding their rightful owners.

At *VDNKh*, they were proud of the fact that, despite their distance from the centre and the main trade routes, the settlers there were able not just to survive conditions that worsened every day, but to maintain, at least within the station, human culture, which was quickly dying out underground.

The administration of the station had strived to give this issue as much attention as possible. It was mandatory to teach children to read, and the station even had its own small library, to which all the books that they managed to acquire at markets were added. The problem was that the traders didn't really choose the books, they just brought what they were given and they collected it as though it was scrap paper.

But the attitude of the people at the station towards books was such that they wouldn't rip even one page out of the silliest pulp fiction. People revered books as though they were relics, as a final reminder of the wonderful world that had sunk into oblivion. Adults, who held sacred every second of a memoir they read, transferred this love of books to their children, who had nothing to remember of the other world and only knew the endlessly intersecting and gloomy tunnels, corridors and passages.

In the metro there were just a few places where the written word was idolized like this, and the inhabitants of *VDNKh* considered themselves to be one of the last strongholds of culture, the northern-most post of civilization on the *Kaluzhsko-Rizhskoi* line. Artyom also read books and Zhenya did too. Zhenya awaited the return of his friends from the market and when they arrived he would rush up to them to ask if they'd brought anything new. And so, books almost always got into Zhenya's hands first, and then they went to the library.

Artyom's stepfather brought him books from his expeditions and they had almost a whole bookshelf of books in their tent. The books lay on the shelf, yellowing and sometimes a little gnawed by mould and rats, sometimes sprinkled with brown specks of blood. They had things that no one else had, at the station and perhaps in the whole metro system: Marquez, Kafka, Borges, Vian, and some Russian classics.

'The guys didn't bring anything this time,' said Zhenya. 'Lekha says that there will be a load of books coming soon from a guy in *Polis*. He promised to bring a couple here.'

'I'm not talking about books!' Artyom waved Zhenya away. 'But what have you heard? What's the situation?'

'The situation? Nothing it seems. There are all sorts of rumours, of course, but that's no different than usual – you know yourself that the traders can't survive without their gossip and stories. They'd wither straight away if you didn't feed them a few rumours. But whether you should believe their rubbish is another question. It looks as though all's quiet. If you compare it with the times when the Hansa was at war with the Reds, that is. But wait!' He remembered something. 'On *Prospect Mir* they have forbidden the sale of weed. Now, if they find any weed on a trader, they will confiscate it all and will chuck him out of the station and put it on his record too. If they find any on you a second time, Lekha says that they won't let you into Hansa for a few years. And that's death to a trader.'

'Come on! What – they've just forbidden it? What are they thinking?'

'They say that they decided that it's a drug since it affects the way you see things. And that your brain starts to corrode if you take it too often. They're, like, doing it for health reasons.'

'They should take care of their own health! Why are they worrying about ours all of a sudden?'

'You know what?' Zhenya said in a low voice. 'Lekha says that they're putting out all sorts of misinfo about things that are bad for your health.'

'What misinfo?' Artyom asked, surprised.

'Misinformation. Here, listen. Lekha once went along the line, past *Prospect Mir*. He made it to *Sukharevskaya*. He was doing some dark business – wouldn't even say what it was. And there he met an interesting old guy. A magician.'

'Who?' Artyom couldn't hold back and burst out laughing. 'A magician? At *Sukharevskaya*? Come on, he's having you on, your Lekha! And what, the magician gave him a magic wand? Or a stick that turns into a flower?'

'You're an idiot.' Zhenya was offended. 'You think you know it all? Just because you haven't met a magician doesn't mean there aren't any. Do you believe in the mutants at *Filevki*?'

'Who needs to believe? They're there, and that's pretty clear. My stepfather told me about them. But I've never heard anything about magicians.'

'Even though I have a lot of respect for Sukhoi, I don't think he knows everything in the whole world either. And maybe he wanted just to scare you. Basically, if you don't want to hear about it then screw you.'

'OK, OK, Zhenya, go ahead. It's interesting anyway. Even if it sounds like . . .'

Artyom grinned.

'OK. They were spending the night by the fire. No one, you know, lives permanently at *Sukharevskaya*. So the traders from other stations stop there because the Hansa authorities see them off from *Prospect Mir* after lights-out. And, well, the whole crowd hangs around there, various charlatans and thieves – they all stick to the traders. And various wanderers rest there too, before heading south. So, in the tunnels beyond *Sukharevskaya*, some kind of ruckus begins. Nobody lives there – not rats, not mutants, and the people that try to pass through those tunnels mostly disappear. Just disappear without a trace. Beyond *Sukharevskaya*, the next station is *Turgenevskaya*. It's next to the Red Line: there was a passage to *Chistye Prudi* there, but the Reds have named it *Kirov* again. Some communist was called that they say . . . People were too afraid to live near that station. They walled up the passage. And now *Turgenevskaya* is there, empty. Abandoned. So the tunnel there – from *Sukharevskaya* to the nearest human settlement is a long way. And it's there that people disappear. If people go one by one, then they almost certainly don't make it through. But if they go in a caravan of more than ten people, then they get through. And it's nothing, they say, just a normal tunnel, clean, quiet, empty, and there aren't any side passages, and there doesn't seem to be anywhere to disappear to . . . Not a soul, not a sound, not a beast to be seen . . . And then, the next day, someone will hear about it, that it's clean and easy, and they'll spit on the superstition and go into the tunnel alone – and then, peek-a-boo. Now you see him, now you don't.'

'You were saying something about a magician,' Artyom quietly reminded him.

'I'm getting to the magician. Wait a minute,' Zhenya said. 'So, here you have it, people are afraid to go alone through this tunnel to the south. And they look for companions at *Sukharevskaya* so they can go through together. And if there's not a market day then there aren't many people and sometimes they have to wait days and weeks until there're enough people to set off. So: the more people, the safer. Lekha says that you sometimes meet really interesting people there. There are plenty of wastrels there too, and you have to know how to differentiate between them. But sometimes you're lucky. So, Lekha meets this magician there. It's not what you think, not some Hottabych that comes out of a lamp . . .'

'Hottabych was a djinn, not a magician.' Artyom carefully corrected him, but Zhenya ignored his comment and continued:

'The guy is an occultist. He'd spent half his life studying all kinds of mystical literature. He told Lekha mostly about this Castaneda chap . . . So the guy, basically, reads a lot, and looks into the future, finds missing things, and knows about future dangers. He says that he sees spirits. Can you imagine, he even . . .' Zhenya paused dramatically. 'He even goes through the metro without a weapon! I mean completely unarmed. He only has a penknife – to cut up food, and he has a plastic staff too. See? So, he says that everyone who takes weed and the people who drink it too – they're all madmen. Because it is not what we think it is at all. It's not any kind of real weed, and those mushrooms, they aren't mushrooms either. Such toadstools have never grown in the central region before. Basically, one day I looked in a mushroom book, and it's true, there's not a word about the kinds of mushroom we have here. And there's nothing even remotely like them . . . Those that eat it thinking that it is just a hallucinogen and they can watch cartoons on it, are totally mistaken, says this magician. And if you cook these toadstools in a slightly different way then you can enter a state where it is possible to regulate events in the real world.'

'That's quite a magician you have there – more like a drug addict!' Artyom declared with conviction. 'A lot of people here play around with weed to relax but, as you know, no one has ever taken it to that degree. The guy is addicted, one hundred percent. And he hasn't got long, I'd say. Listen, Uncle Sasha told me this story . . . There's some station – I don't remember which – where this old man he didn't know came up to him, and starts telling him that he has a powerful extra-sense and that he is waging an ongoing war with similar powerful psychics and aliens, only they are malicious. And they are almost defeating him, and he might not be able to fight them any longer, and all his strength was going into the fight. And the station – it was like *Sukharevskaya*, a kind of half-station where people sit around campfires in the centre of the platform, a ways off from the tunnel mouth, so they can get some sleep before they move on. And there, let's say, there were three guys that walked past my stepfather and the old man, and the old man said to him in horror: "You see, there, that one, in the middle, that is one of the main evil psychics, a disciple of darkness. And on either side of him are aliens. They're

53

helping him. And their leader lives at the deepest point in the metro. And he says, basically, that they don't want to come up to me because you're sitting with me. They don't want regular people to know about our fight. But they're attacking me with their energy right now and I'm putting up a shield. And he says, "I will continue to fight!" You think it's funny, but my stepfather didn't think it was so funny at the time. Imagine: in some godforsaken corner of the metro, who knows what might happen . . . It sounds like rubbish, I know, but all the same. And there's Uncle Sasha telling himself that this old man is crazy, but then the guy who is walking with the two aliens on either side, is looking at him meanly, and there's something flashing in his eyes . . .'

'What crap,' Zhenya said, disbelievingly.

'Crap it may be, but you well know that you should be prepared for anything at the distant stations. And the old man says to him that soon he (the old man, that is) will face the final battle with the evil psychics. And if he loses – and his forces are less than theirs – then it's the end for everyone. Before, he says, there were more positive psychics, and the battleground was even, but now the negatives had started to conquer and this old man was one of the last standing. Maybe even THE last one standing. And if he is killed then the evil ones will win, and that will be it. Checkmate!'

'We're already at checkmate in my opinion,' Zhenya observed.

'Well, let's say not total checkmate. There's still possibilities,' Artyom replied. 'So, in parting, the old man says to him: "My son! Give me something to eat please. I have little strength left. And the final battle is coming nearer . . . And everyone's future depends on its outcome. Yours too!" You get it? The old man was begging for food. That's your magician, I'd say. Also, lost some marbles, I'd say. But for another reason.'

'You're a total fool! You didn't even listen to the ending . . . and anyway, who told you that the old guy was lying? What was his name, by the way? Did your stepfather tell you?'

'He told me, but I don't remember it exactly. Some kind of funny name. Starts with a "Chu." Could it be Chum – or Chump? . . . Bums often have some kind of funny nickname instead of a real name. And what – what was the name of your magician?'

'He told Lekha that they call him Carlos now. Because of the similarity. I don't know what he meant but that's how he explained it. But you should listen to the end of the story. At the end of their conversation, he told Lekha that it's best not to go through the northern tunnel – though Lekha was preparing to go back the next day. Lekha listened to him and didn't go. And he was right. That day some thugs attacked a caravan in the tunnel between *Sukharevskaya* and *Prospect Mir* even though it had been considered safe. Half of the traders were killed. The rest barely managed to fight them off. So there!'

Artyom went quiet and sank into thought.

'Well, generally speaking, it's impossible to know. Anything can happen. Things like that used to happen, that's what my stepfather said. And he also said that at the most distant stations, where people have gone wild and have become primitive, they've forgotten that man is a rational being, and the strangest things happen – things that our logical minds wouldn't be able to explain. He didn't go into it, though. And he wasn't even telling it to me – I just overheard by accident.'

'Ha! I'm telling you: sometimes they describe things that normal people just wouldn't believe. Last time, Lekha shared another story with me . . . Want to hear it? You won't have heard this one from your stepfather, I tell you. A trader from the *Serpukhovskaya* line told it to Lekha . . . So, do you believe in ghosts?'

'Well . . . every time I talk to you I start to wonder if I believe in them or not. But then when I'm on my own or with other people I come back to my senses,' Artyom replied, barely managing to hold back a smile.

'Are you serious?'

'Well, I've read some things, of course. And Uncle Sasha has told me a lot of stories. But, if I'm honest, then I don't really believe in all these stories. In general, Zhenya, I don't really understand you. Here at the station, we're living an unending nightmare with these dark ones – something you don't find in any other part of the metro, I bet. Somewhere in the centre of the metro system there are kids talking about our life here, telling scary stories and asking each other: "Do you believe the tales about the dark ones or not?" And to you that means nothing. You want to scare yourself with yet more things?'

'Yeah but don't tell me that you're only interested in things you can see and feel? You don't really think that the world is organized into things you can see and hear? Take a mole, for example. It doesn't see. It's blind from birth. But that doesn't mean that all the things that the mole doesn't see don't actually exist. That's what you're saying . . .'

'OK, so what's the story you wanted to tell me? About the trader up at the *Serpukhovskaya* line?'

'About the trader? Well . . . Somehow Lekha met this one guy at the market there. He, I guess, was definitely not from *Serpukhovskaya*. He's from the Ring. He's a citizen of the Hansa, but he lives at *Dobryninskaya*. Over there, they have a passage to *Serpukhovskaya*. On the line, I don't know if your stepfather told you, but there's no one living beyond the Ring – that is, until the next station which is *Tulskaya* – where there's a Hansa patrol. They take measures to protect it – they basically think that since the line is uninhabited, you never know what will crawl out of it, and so they made a buffer zone there. And no one goes beyond *Tulskaya*. They say that there's nothing to find there. The stations are all empty, the equipment there is broken – and life is impossible. A dead zone: not an animal, not any kind of vermin, there's not even rats there. Empty. But the trader had one acquaintance, a wanderer type, who once went beyond *Tulskaya*. I don't know what he was looking for there. And he told the trader, that things are not so simple on the *Serphukhvskaya* line. And that it's not empty for no reason. He was saying that you can't even imagine what's going on out there. And there's a reason why the Hansa aren't colonizing the area, even though you might think it would be a fine place for a plantation or a pigsty.'

Zhenya went silent, feeling that Artyom had finally forgotten his robust cynicism and was listening with an open mouth. Then he settled more comfortably on the ground, with an inner feeling of triumph:

'Yeah, well, you're probably not interested in all this crap. Old wives' tales. Want some tea?'

'Wait a second with the tea! Instead tell me why the Hansa didn't colonize the area? You're right, it's strange. My stepfather says that there's a general over-population problem anyway – there isn't room for everyone anymore. So why would they give up the chance of taking a little more space? It's not like them!'

'Ah, so you are interested!? OK, so this stranger went pretty far into it. He was saying that you walk and walk and there isn't a soul. There's nothing and no one, like in that tunnel beyond *Sukharevskaya*. Can you imagine? There's not even a rat! You just hear water dripping. Abandoned stations just sit there in darkness and no one has ever lived there. And you always have a sense of being in danger. And it's oppressive . . . He was walking quickly, and he went through four stations in almost half a day. A desperate person, no doubt. I mean, really, to get into a game like that alone! So, he gets to *Sebastopolskaya*. There's a passage to *Kakhovskaya*. And you know the *Kakhovskaya* line, there's only three stations on it. It's not a line but an unfinished thought. Sort of like an appendix . . . And he decides to spend the night at *Sebastopolskaya*. Having worn out his wits, he's tired . . . He found some wood chips, laid a fire so it wouldn't be all so awful, and crawled into his sleeping bag and went to sleep in the middle of the platform. And during the night . . .'

At this point, Zhenya stood up, stretching, and said with a sadistic smile, 'OK, I don't know about you, but I myself really want some tea!' And, not waiting for an answer, he took the kettle out of the tent, leaving Artyom alone with his impressions from the story.

Artyom, of course, was angry at Zhenya for leaving him there, but he decided to patiently await the end of the story and then he'd give Zhenya a piece of his mind. Suddenly he was reminded of Hunter and his request. It was more like an order, really. But then his thoughts went back to Zhenya's story.

Having returned with tea, he poured some into a tea-glass which had a rare metal outer-casing, the kind they used to have in trains for tea, and he continued, 'So he went to sleep next to the fire and there was silence all around – a heavy silence as though his ears were full of cotton. And in the middle of the night there's a strange sound . . . a totally sanity-challenging and impossible sound. He was immediately covered in cold sweat, and jumped right up. He heard children's laughter. Coming from the tunnel. This is four stations from the nearest people! Rats don't even live there, can you imagine? There was reason to be alarmed . . . So he jumps up and runs under the arches to the tunnel . . . And he sees . . . There's a train coming into the station. A real train. Its headlights are shining, and blinding him – the wanderer could have been blinded by them so it's good he covered his eyes with his hand in time. The windows were lit in yellow and there were people inside and this was all going on in total silence! Not a sound! There wasn't a hum from the engine, not a clatter of wheels. The train glides into the station in total silence . . . You see? The guy sits down, something's wrong with his heart. And there's people in the train windows, like real people who are chatting away inaudibly . . . The train, wagon by wagon, is going past him, and he sees in the last window of the last wagon, there's a seven-year-old child looking at him. Looking at him, pointing at him, and laughing . . . And the laughter was audible. There was such silence

57

that the guy could hear his own heart beating along with this child's laughter . . . The train dives into the tunnel, and the laughter gets quieter and quieter . . . and goes silent in the distance. And again – emptiness. And an absolute and horrifying silence.'

'And then he woke up?' Artyom asked maliciously but with a certain hope in his voice.

'If only! He rushed back, towards the extinguished fire, quickly gathered up his belongings and ran back to *Tulskaya* without stopping. He ran the whole way in one hour. It was so scary. You have to think . . .'

Artyom had gone quiet, frozen by what he'd heard. Silence descended in the tent. Finally, having gathered his wits and coughed, making sure that his voice wouldn't give him away and crack, Artyom asked Zhenya as indifferently as he could:

'And what, you believe all that?'

'Well, it's not the first time I've heard this kind of story about the *Serpukhovskaya* line,' Zhenya replied. 'Only I don't always tell you them. It's not possible to talk about these things with you in a normal way. You start interrupting straight away . . . OK, we've sat here for a while you and me, and it's almost time to go to work. Let's get ready. We can talk more when we get there.'

Artyom got up reluctantly, dragged himself home – he needed to get a snack to take to work. His stepfather was still sleeping, it was totally quiet at the station: most people had probably been let off work and there was a little time left until the night shift began. He should hurry up. Going past the guest tent, in which Hunter was staying, Artyom saw that the tent flaps were pulled aside and the tent was empty. His heart skipped a beat. Finally he understood that everything he'd discussed with Hunter hadn't been a dream, that it had actually taken place, and that the development of events could have a direct impact on him. He knew what fate lay before him.

The tea-factory was located in a dead-end, at a blocked exit from the underground, where there were escalators leading upwards. All the work in the factory was done by hand. It was too extravagant to waste precious electric energy on production.

Behind the iron screens that separated the territory of the factory from the rest of the station, there was a metal wire drawn from wall to wall, on which cleaned mushrooms were drying. When it was particularly humid, they made little fires underneath the mushrooms so that they would dry more quickly and wouldn't get covered in mould. Under the wire there were tables where the workers first cut and then crushed the dried mushrooms. The prepared tea was packed into paper or polyethylene packages – depending on what was available at the station – and they added some extracts and powders to it, the recipe of which was only known to the head of the factory. That was the straightforward process of producing tea. Without the much-needed conversation while you worked your eight-hour shift of cutting and crushing mushroom caps, then it would probably be the most exhausting business.

Artyom worked this shift with Zhenya and a new, shaggy-haired guy called Kirill with whom he'd been on patrol too. Kirill became very animated at the sight of Zhenya – obviously they had met and spoken before – and he quickly took to telling him some story that had apparently been interrupted the last time they spoke. Artyom sat in the middle and wasn't interested enough to listen so he plunged into his thoughts. The story about the *Serpukhovskaya* line, that Zhenya had just told him had started to fade in his memory, and his conversation with Hunter surfaced.

What could be done? The orders given to him by Hunter were too serious not to think them over. What if Hunter would not be able to do whatever it was that he intended? He had committed to a completely senseless act, having dared to venture into the enemy's lair, right into the heat of the fire. The danger he was subjecting himself to was enormous, and he himself didn't even know its true parameters. He could only guess at what awaited him at the five-hundredth metre where the light of the last fire at the border post grows dim – the last man-made flames to the north of *VDNKh*. All he knew about the dark ones was what everyone else knew – but no one else was thinking of going out there. In fact, it wasn't even a known fact that there was a real passageway at the Botanical Gardens where beasts could enter the metro from above.

The likelihood was too great that Hunter wouldn't be able to complete the mission he'd taken upon himself. Obviously, the danger from the north seemed to be so great and was increasing so quickly that any delay was inadmissible. Hunter probably knew something about its nature that he hadn't revealed in his meeting with Sukhoi or his conversation with Artyom.

Therefore he probably was aware of the degree of the risk and understood that he would probably not be up to his task, otherwise why would he prepare Artyom for a turn of events? Hunter didn't resemble an overcautious person, so that meant that the probability that he wouldn't return to *VDNKh* existed and was rather significant.

But how could Artyom give up everything and leave the station without saying anything to anyone? Hunter himself was afraid of warning anyone else, afraid of the 'worm-eaten brains' here . . . How would it be possible to get to *Polis*, to the legendary *Polis*, all alone, through all the evident and mysterious dangers that awaited travellers in the dark and mute tunnels? Artyom suddenly regretted that he had succumbed to Hunter's strong charms and hypnotizing gaze, that he had told him his secret, and agreed to such a dangerous mission.

'Hey Artyom! Artyom! You sleeping there or what? Why aren't you saying anything?' Zhenya shook his shoulder. 'Did you hear what Kirill was saying? Tomorrow night they're organizing a caravan to *Rizhskaya*. They say that our administration has decided to make a pact with them, but meanwhile it looks like we're sending them humanitarian aid, with a view to becoming brothers. Seems they have found some kind of warehouse containing cables. The leaders want to lay them down: they say they're going to make a telephone system between the stations. In any case, a telegraph system. Kirill says that whoever isn't working tomorrow can go. Want to?'

Artyom thought right there and then that fate itself was giving him an opportunity to fulfil his mission – if it came to that. He nodded silently.

'Great!' Zhenya was glad. 'I'll also go. Kirill! Sign us up, OK? What time are they going to set off tomorrow – at nine?'

Until the end of the shift, Artyom didn't say a word, he wasn't in the mood to extract himself from his distracting, gloomy thoughts. Zhenya was left to deal with the dishevelled Kirill by himself and he obviously felt hurt. Artyom continued to chop mushrooms with mechanical movements, and to crumble them into dust, taking the little caps down from the wire, and again chopping them, and so on, indefinitely.

Hunter's face hovered in front of his eyes – frozen at the moment when he was saying that he might not make it back – the calm face of a person who is used to risking his life. And an ink stain marred his heart with the presentiment of trouble.

After work, Artyom went back to his tent. His stepfather wasn't there anymore – he had clearly gone out to take care of business. Artyom fell onto the bed, and buried his face in the pillow, and went to sleep straight away, even though he had planned to think over his situation again in the peace and quiet.

His sleep was delirious after all the conversations, thoughts and worries of the preceding day, and it enveloped him and carried him away into an abyss. Artyom saw himself sitting next to the fire at *Sukharevskaya* station, next to Zhenya and the wandering magician with the unusual Spanish name of Carlos. Carlos is teaching Zhenya how to make weed out of mushrooms and he is explaining that you have to use it just like they use it at *VDNKh* – a clean crime, because these mushrooms aren't mushrooms at all but a new type of rational life on earth, which may with time replace humans. That these mushrooms aren't independent beings, but just elements connected by neurons to the whole unit, spread across a whole metro of a gigantic fungus. And that, in reality, the person who consumes the weed isn't just using a psychotropic material, but is making contact with this new form of rational life. And if you do it right, then you can make friends with it, and then it will help the person that makes contact with it through the weed. But then Sukhoi appears and, threatening Artyom with his forefinger, he says that you absolutely mustn't take weed because if you use it for an extended amount of time then your brain becomes worm-eaten. But Artyom decides to test it and see if it's really true: and he tells everyone that he's going out to get some air but he carefully goes behind the back of the magician with the Spanish name, and he sees that the magician doesn't have a back to his head but his brains are visible, full of wormholes. Long whitish worms curling in circles are chewing into the fabric of his brains and are making new tunnels, and the magician just carries on talking as though nothing is happening . . . Then Artyom gets scared and decides to run away from him, he begins to tug at Zhenya's sleeve, so that he would come with him but Zhenya just waves him away and asks Carlos to go on, and Artyom sees that the worms are crawling down from the magician's head and towards Zhenya, and crawling up Zhenya's back. They are trying to get into his ears . . .

Then Artyom jumps up and takes to his heels and runs from the station with all his might, but then remembers that this was the tunnel you're not supposed to go through alone, and only in groups, so he turns around and runs back to the station but for some reason he can't get to it.

Behind him, suddenly there is a light, and with a clarity and logic that is unusual for dreams, Artyom sees his own shadow on the floor of the tunnel. He turns around and from the bowels of the metro, a train is heading towards him without stopping, gnashing and rattling its wheels with deafening sound and blinding him with its headlights . . .

And his legs refuse to budge, they've lost all power, and they aren't even legs anymore but empty trousers stuffed with rags. And when the train has almost reached Artyom, the visions suddenly lose their colour and disappear.

Instead, something new appears, something totally different: Artyom sees Hunter, dressed in snow-white, in an unfurnished room with blindingly white walls. He stands there, his head hanging down, his gaze drilling into the floor. Then he raises his eyes and looks straight at Artyom. The feeling is very strange, because in this dream Artyom can't feel his own body, but it is as if he is looking at what is going on from all angles at once. When Artyom looks into Hunter's eyes, he is filled with an incomprehensible uneasiness, an expectation of something very significant, something that might happen any second . . .

Hunter starts talking to him, and Artyom has the feeling that what has just happened was real. When he'd had nightmares before, he had told himself simply that he was sleeping, and that everything that was happening was only the fruit of an excited imagination. But in this vision, the knowledge that he could wake up at any moment if he wanted, was totally absent.

Trying to meet Artyom's gaze – even though he had the impression that Hunter couldn't actually see him and was blindly undertaking his task, the hunter slowly and gravely says, 'The time has come. You have to do what you promised me. You have to do it. Remember – this is not a dream! This is not a dream!'

Artyom opened his eyes wide. And again in his head, he heard with horrifying clarity the gruff voice saying, 'This is not a dream!'

'This is not a dream,' Artyom repeated. The details of the nightmare about the worms and the train were quickly wiped from his memory, but Artyom could remember the second vision perfectly in all its detail. Hunter's strange clothes, the mysterious empty white room and the words: 'You have to do what you promised me!' He couldn't get them out of his mind.

His stepfather came in and worriedly asked Artyom, 'Tell me, did you see Hunter after our meeting together? It's becoming evening already and he has gone missing, and his tent is empty. Did he leave? Did he tell you anything yesterday about his plans?'

'No, Uncle Sasha, he was just asking about the conditions at the station and about what was going on,' Artyom lied conscientiously.

'I'm afraid for him. That he's done something silly at his own expense and to our general harm.' Sukhoi was clearly upset. 'He doesn't know who he's been dealing with . . . Eh! What, you're not working today?

'Me and Zhenya signed up to join the caravan to *Rizhskaya* today, to help them get across, and we'll start unwinding the cable from there,' Artyom replied, suddenly realizing that he'd just decided to go. At that thought something broke inside him, he felt a strange lightening and also some kind of inner emptiness, like someone had taken a tumour out of his chest, which had been burdening his heart and interfering with his breathing.

'The caravan? You'd do better to sit at home instead of wading through tunnels. I need to go there anyway, to *Rizhskaya*, but I'm not feeling all that great today. Another time, maybe . . . Are you going out now? At nine? Well, then we'll get to say goodbye then. Get your things together in the meantime!' And he left Artyom alone.

Artyom started to throw things into a rucksack, things which might be useful on the road: a small lamp, batteries, mushrooms, a package of tea, and liver and pork sausage, a full machine-gun clip which he once filched from someone, a map of the metro and more batteries . . . He needed to remember to bring his passport – it would be of no use at *Rizhskaya* of course, but beyond that station he'd be detained or put against a wall by the very first patrol of another sovereign station – depending on their politics. And there was the capsule given to him by Hunter. And that was all he needed.

He threw the rucksack on his back and Artyom looked back for the last time at his home, and walked out of the tent with resolve.

The group that was going with the caravan had gathered on the platform, at the entrance to the southern tunnel. On the rails, there was a cart loaded with boxes of meat, mushrooms and packages of tea. On top of them, there was some kind of clever device, put together by local experts – probably some kind of telegraph apparatus.

In the caravan, apart from Kirill, there was another pair: a volunteer, and a commander from the administration who would establish relations and come to an agreement with the administration at *Rizhskaya*. They had already packed and were playing dominoes while waiting for a departure signal. The machine guns that were assigned to them for the journey were piled beside them. They formed a pyramid with the barrels directed upwards and their spare clips attached to their bases with blue insulation tape.

Finally Zhenya appeared – he'd had to feed his sister and send her to the neighbours before he left since his parents were still at work.

At the very last second, Artyom suddenly remembered that he hadn't said goodbye to his stepfather. Excusing himself and promising that he would be right back, he threw off his rucksack and ran home. There was no one in the tent and Artyom ran to the quarters where service personnel often hung around, but it now belonged to the station's administration. Sukhoi was there, he was sitting opposite the duty officer of the station, the elected head of *VDNKh*, and they were talking about something animatedly. Artyom knocked on the door jamb and quietly coughed.

'Greetings, Alexander Nikolaevich. Could I speak to Uncle Sasha for a minute?'

'Of course, Artyom, come in. Want some tea?' the duty officer said hospitably.

'You off already? When are you coming back?' Sukhoi asked while pushing his chair back from the table.

'I don't know exactly . . .' Artyom mumbled. 'We'll see how it goes . . .'

And he understood that he might never see his stepfather again, and he really didn't want to lie to him, the one man who truly loved Artyom, and say that he would be back tomorrow or the day after and everything would continue as it was.

Artyom suddenly felt a sting in his eyes and to his shame, he found that they were wet. He stepped forward and hugged his stepfather.

'Now, now, Artyom, what's the matter . . . You'll be back tomorrow after all . . . Well?' his surprised stepfather said reassuringly.

'Tomorrow night if everything goes to plan,' Alexander Nikolaevich confirmed.

'Take care of yourself, Uncle Sasha! Good luck!' Artyom uttered hoarsely, shaking his stepfather's hand, and he quickly left.

Sukhoi watched him leave in surprise.

'Why's he come unglued? It's not the first time he's been to *Rizhskaya* . . .'

'Nothing, Sasha, nothing, there will be a time when your boy will grow up. Then you'll be nostalgic for the days when he said goodbye to you with tears in his eyes when he was just going two stations away! So what were you saying about the opinion at *Alexeevskaya* about the patrolling of tunnels? It would be very handy for us . . .'

When Artyom ran back to the group, the commander had given each person a machine gun and said:

'So then, men? Shall we sit down for a moment before we go?' And he sat down on the old wooden bench. The rest of them followed his example silently. 'OK, God be with us!' The commander stood up and jumped down onto the path, taking his place at the front of the group.

Artyom and Zhenya, as the youngest members of the group, climbed up onto the cart and prepared themselves for hard work. Kirill and the second volunteer took their places behind, completing the chain.

'Let's go!' shouted the commander.

Artyom and Zhenya leaned on the levers, and Kirill pushed the cart from behind – and it squeaked, shunting forward and then started gliding ahead. The last two guys walked behind it and the group disappeared into the muzzle of the southern tunnel.

CHAPTER 4

The Voice of the Tunnels

The unreliable light of the lantern in the hands of the commander wandered like a pale yellow stain on the tunnel walls, licking the damp floor and disappearing completely when the lantern was pointed into the distance. There was deep darkness ahead, which was greedily devouring the weak beams of their pocket flashlights from just ten paces away. The wheels of the cart squeaked with a whining and melancholic sound, gliding into nowhere, and the breathing and the rhythmic footfalls of the booted people walking behind it punctuated the silence.

The southern cordons were behind them now, the flickering light of their fires had died away long ago. They were beyond the territory of *VDNKh*. And even though the journey from *VDNKh* to *Rizhskaya* was considered safe, given the good relations between the stations and the fact that there was a sufficient amount of movement between the two, the caravan needed to stay on alert.

Danger was not something that just came from the north or the south – the two directions of the tunnel. It could hide above them, in the airshafts or at the sides in the multiple tunnel branches behind the sealed doors of former utility rooms or secret exits. There were dangers waiting below too in mysterious manholes left behind by the metro-builders, forgotten and neglected by maintenance crews back when the metro was still just a means of transportation, where terrible things now lurked in their depths, things which could squeeze the mind of the most reckless of daredevils in a vice of irrational horror.

That was why the commander's lantern was wandering along the walls, and the fingers of the people at the back of the caravan stroked the safety locks of their machine guns, ready to fix them into firing mode at any moment and to lunge at their triggers. That's why they said little as they walked: chatting weakened and interfered with their capacity to hear in the breathing space of the tunnel.

Artyom was starting to get tired already; he laboured and laboured but the handle, descending and then returning to its former place, gnashed monotonously, turning the wheels again and again. He was looking ahead without success, but his head was spinning to the beat of the wheels, heavily and hysterically, just like the phrases he heard from Hunter before he left – his words about the power of darkness, the most widespread form of government in the territory of the Moscow metro-system.

He tried to think about how he was going to get to *Polis*, he tried to make a plan, but slowly a burning pain and fatigue was spreading in his muscles, rising from his bent legs through the small of his back, into his arms and pushing any complicated thoughts right out of his head.

Hot, salty sweat dripped onto his forehead, at first slowly, in tiny droplets, and then the drops had grown and became heavier, flowing down his face, getting into his eyes, and there was no chance of wiping them away because Zhenya was on the other side of the mechanism, and if Artyom released the handle then it would land all the effort on Zhenya. Blood was pounding louder and louder in his ears, and Artyom remembered that when he was little he liked to adopt an uncomfortable pose in order to hear the blood pounding in his ears because the sound reminded him of the steps of soldiers on parade. And if he closed his eyes, he could imagine he was a marshal leading the parade and faithful divisions were passing him, measuring their paces, and saluting him. That's how it was described in books about the army.

Finally, the commander said, without turning around:

'OK, guys, come down and change places. We've reached half way.'

Artyom exchanged glances with Zhenya and he jumped off the cart, and they both, without speaking, sat on the rails, even though they were supposed to be going to the rear of the cart.

The commander looked at them attentively and said sympathetically:

'Milksops . . .'

'Milksops,' Zhenya admitted readily.

'Get up, get up, there'll be no sitting here. It's time to go. I'll tell you a good little story.'

'We can also tell you a few stories!' Zhenya confidently declared, not wanting to get up.

'Yes, I know all your stories. About the dark ones, about the mutants . . . About your little mushrooms, of course. But there are a few tales you've never heard. Yes, indeed, and they might not even be tales – it's just that no one is able to confirm them . . . That is, there have been people who have tried to confirm the stories, but they couldn't tell us for sure.'

For Artyom, this short speech had been enough to give him a second wind. Now any information about what happened beyond the *Prospect Mir* station had great meaning for him. He hurried to get up from the rails and, transferring his machine gun from his back to his chest, he took up his place behind the cart.

With a little shove, the wheels started singing their plaintive song again. The group moved forward. The commander was looking ahead, peering watchfully into the darkness because not everything was audible.

'I'm interested, what does your generation know about the metro anyway?' the commander was saying. 'You tell each other such tales. Someone went somewhere, someone made it all up. One tells the wrong thing to the next who whispers it to a third, who, in turn, stretches the story over a cup of tea with a fourth person, who pretends that it was his own adventure. That's the main problem with the metro: there aren't any reliable communication lines. It isn't possible to get from one end to the other quickly. You can't get through in some places, it's partitioned in others where some crap is going on, and the conditions change every day. Do you think that this metro system is all that big? Well, you can get from one end to the other in an hour by train. And it takes people weeks to do that now, and that's if they make it. And you never know what is waiting for you at every turn. So, we've set off for *Rizhskaya* with humanitarian aid . . . But the problem is that no one – me and the duty officer included – no one is prepared to guarantee that when we get there, we won't be met with heavy fire. Or that we won't find a burnt-out station without a living soul in it. Or that it won't suddenly become clear that *Rizhskaya* has joined forces with the Hansa and therefore there's no passage to the rest of the metro left to us anymore, ever again. There's no exact information . . . We received some data yesterday – but everything is out of date by evening and you can't rely on it the next day. It's just like going through quicksand using a hundred-year-old map. It takes so long for messengers to get through with the messages they carry that it often happens that the information's not needed anymore or it's already unreliable. The truth is distorted. People have never lived under these conditions . . . And it's scary to think of what will happen when there isn't any fuel for the generators, and there isn't electricity anymore. Have you read Wells' *The Time Machine*? Well, there they had these Morlocks . . .'

This was already the second such conversation in the last two days, and Artyom already knew about the Morlocks and about Herbert Wells, and he didn't want to hear about it all over again. So, disregarding Zhenya's protests, he resolutely turned the conversation back to its original direction.

'So, what does your generation know about the metro?'

'Mm . . . Talking about the devilry in the tunnels is bad luck . . . And about Metro- 2 and the invisible observers? I won't talk about that either. But I can tell you something interesting about who lives where. So, do you know, for example, that at the place that used to be *Pushkinskaya* station – where there's another two pedestrian passages to *Chekhovskaya* and *Tverskaya* – that the fascists have now taken that?'

'What – what fascists?' Zhenya asked, puzzled.

'Real fascists. A while ago, when we still lived there,' the commander pointed upwards, 'there were fascists. There were also skinheads who called themselves the RNE, and others who were against immigration, and there were all kinds of different types, since that was the trend in those days. Only a fool knows what these acronyms mean, now no one remembers, and they themselves probably don't even remember. And then, it seemed, they disappeared. You heard and saw nothing of them. And suddenly, a little while ago, they turned up again. "The metro is for Russians!" Have you heard of that? Or, they say: "'Do a good deed – clean up the metro!" And they threw all the non-Russians out of *Pushkinskaya*, and then from *Chekhovskaya* and *Tverskaya*. In the end they became rabid and started punishing people. They have a Reich there now. The fourth or the fifth . . . Something like that. They haven't crawled any further yet, but our generation still remembers the twentieth century. And what fascists are . . . The mutants from the *Filevskaya* line, basically, exist in actual fact . . . And our dark ones, what are they worth? And there are various sectarians, satanists, communists . . . It's a chamber of curiosities. That's what it is.'

They went past the broken down door to an abandoned administrative room. Maybe it was a lavatory or maybe before it was a refuge . . . Full of furniture: iron bunk-beds and crude plumbing – it was all stolen long ago and nowadays no one tried to get into those dark empty rooms scattered along the length of the tunnels. There's nothing there . . . But truth is, you never know!

There was a weak blinking light ahead. They were approaching *Alekseevskaya*. The station was minimally populated, and the patrol consisted of one person, at the fiftieth-metre – they couldn't allow themselves to go any further. The commander gave the order to stop at forty metres from the fire that had been lit by the patrol at *Alekseevskaya* – and he turned his flashlight on and off several times in a precise sequence, giving the patrol a signal. A black figure was delineated by the light of the flames – a scout was coming towards them. From far off, the scout yelled, 'Halt! Don't approach!'

Artyom asked himself: Could it be possible that one day they wouldn't be recognized at a station with whom they considered themselves to have friendly relations, and they would be met with hostility?

The person was approaching them slowly. He was dressed in torn camouflage trousers and a quilted jacket which displayed the letter 'A' in bold – apparently from the first letter in the station's name. His hollow cheeks were unshaven, and his eyes gleamed suspiciously, and his hands were nervously stroking the body of an automatic machine gun that was hanging from his neck. He looked them right in the face and smiled – he recognized them and, with a little wave showing his trust, he pushed the machine gun onto his back.

'Great, guys! How are you doing? Is it you guys heading to *Rizhskaya*? We know, we know, they warned us. Let's go!'

The commander started to ask the patrolman something but it was inaudible, and Artyom, hoping that he also wouldn't be heard, said quietly to Zhenya:

'He looks overworked and underfed. I don't think they want to join forces with us because they're having the good life.'

'Well, so what?' His friend responded. 'We also have our interests in the matter. If our administration is pursuing it then it means there's something they want from it. It's not out of charity that we are coming to feed them.'

They went past the campfire at the fiftieth-metre where a second patrolman was sitting, dressed just like the one who had met them, and their cart rolled towards the station. *Alekseevskaya* was badly lighted and the people that lived there looked sad and seemed to speak little. At *VDNKh*, they looked on guests with friendliness. The group stopped in the middle of the platform and the commander announced a smoking break. Artyom and Zhenya stayed on the cart to protect it and the others were called to the fireside.

'I've never heard about the fascists and the Reich,' Artyom said.

'I've heard that there were fascists somewhere in the underground,' Zhenya answered, 'but they only said that they were at *Novokuznetskaya.*'

'Who told you?'

'Lekha did,' Zhenya admitted reluctantly.

'He's told you a lot of other interesting things,' Artyom reminded him.

'But there really are fascists there! The guy just got the wrong place. He wasn't lying OK?!' Zhenya said in defence. Artyom became silent and sank into thought. The smoking break at *Alekseevskaya* was supposed to last no less than a half hour. The commander was having some kind of conversation with the local leader – probably about the future cooperation. Afterwards, they were supposed to push on forward, so that they would make it to *Rizhkaya* by day's end. They would spend the night there, decide what needed deciding, and look at the newly discovered cable, and then they would send a messenger back to ask for their next instructions. If the cable could be used for communication between three stations then it made sense to unwind it and to open up a telephone connection. But if it looks unusable then it would be necessary to return to the station at once.

So Artyom had dispensation for no more than two days. During this time, it would be necessary to invent a pretext under which it would be possible to get though the external cordons of *Rizhskaya*, who were even more suspicious and nit-picking than the external patrols at *VDNKh*. Their lack of trust was totally understandable: there, in the south, the wider metro system began, and the southern cordon of *Rizhskaya* was subjected to attacks pretty often. And though the dangers that were threatening the population of *Rizhskaya* were not as mysterious and frightening as those hanging over *VDNKh*, they were different in their amazing variation. The fighters that defended the southern approach to *Rizhskaya* never knew what to expect, and therefore they had to be ready for everything.

Two tunnels go from *Rizhskaya* to *Prospect Mir*. To collapse one of them for some reason didn't seem possible, and the Rizhskys had to put blockades up in both. But this took such a toll on their forces that it became vitally important for them to at least secure the northern tunnel. They joined forces with *Alekseevskaya* and more importantly, with *VDNKh*, and shifted the burden of defence in the northern direction onto them, which provided some peace in the tunnels between stations, so that they could focus on their domestic goals. And at *VDNKh*, they saw this as an opportunity to widen their sphere of influence.

In light of the imminent union, the outposts of *Rizhskaya* were showing increased vigilance: it was necessary to prove to their future allies that they could be counted on to defend the southern borders. That's why it seemed a particularly difficult task to get through the cordons in either direction. And Artyom had a maximum of two days to figure it out.

However, despite the complexities, it didn't seem impossible. The question lay in what he would do after that. Even if he got through the southern outposts, it would be necessary still to find a sufficiently safe route to *Polis*. Since he had had to make an urgent decision, he hadn't had time in *VDNKh* to think about his next moves to make it to *Polis*. At home, he could have asked traders he knew about the dangers out there, without raising suspicions. And he knew that he would raise suspicions immediately if he asked Zhenya or anyone else in the group about the way to *Polis* – and Zhenya would definitely know that Artyom was up to something. He didn't have friends at *Alekseevskaya* or at *Rizhskaya*, and he couldn't trust mere acquaintances with these questions either.

Having taken advantage of the fact that Zhenya walked off to chat with a girl who was sitting nearby on the platform, Artyom furtively got a tiny map of the metro out of his rucksack. It was printed on the back of a card with charred edges that was advertising a market fair (that had been and gone long ago), and he circled *Polis* a few times with a pencil.

The way to *Polis* looked easy and short. In the ancient, mythical times that the commander had been describing when people didn't have to carry weapons, and they went from station to station, even if they had to change trains and take another line – in the times, when the journey from one end to the opposite end, didn't take more than an hour – in the times when the tunnels were only populated by rattling and rushing trains – back then the distance between *VDNKh* and *Polis* would have been quick and clear.

It was directly along the line to *Turgenevskaya* and from there a pedestrian tunnel to *Chistye Prudy*, as it was called on the old map, which Artyom was examining. Or take the *Kirovskaya* line and the

Red Line, the *Sokolnicheskaya* line – straight to *Polis* . . . In the era of trains and fluorescent light, such a trip would take about thirty minutes. But ever since the words 'Red Line' had been written in capital letters, and the red calico banner had hung over the pedestrian tunnel to *Chistye Prudy*, there was no point even thinking of a short-cut to *Polis*.

The leadership of the Red Line had abandoned attempts to force the population of the whole metro to be happy by forcing Soviet power on them, and it had adopted a new doctrine which established communism along a separate line of the metro system. Though it had been unable to dispense with its original dream and continued to call the metro system the 'V. I. Lenin Metropolitan' it had taken no practical steps to pursue the grand plan for a while.

But despite the seemingly peaceful behaviour of the regime, its internal paranoid nature hadn't changed at all. Hundreds of agents of the internal security service, like in the old days, with a certain nostalgia for the KGB, constantly and diligently watched the happy inhabitants of the Red Line, and their interest in guests from other lines was unending. Without the special permission of the management of the 'Reds' no one could get to any other station. And the constant monitoring of passports, the total watching and a general clinical suspicion was imposed on the accidental travellers as well as the spies who were sent there. The former were equated with the latter and the fate of both was rather sad. So there was no point in Artyom thinking about getting to *Polis* through three stations that belonged to the Red Line.

Generally there wasn't an easy route into the very heart of the metro. To *Polis* . . . Just the mere mention of this name in a conversation made Artyom (and most others) fall into a reverential silence. He clearly remembered even now the first time he heard the word in a story told by one of his stepfather's friends. Afterwards when the guest had left, he asked Sukhoi quietly what the word meant. His stepfather then looked at him carefully and, with a vague sadness in his voice, he said, 'That, Artyom, is probably the last place on the earth where people live like people. Where they haven't forgotten what the word "person" means, and, moreover, how the word should sound.' His stepfather smiled sadly and added, 'That is a City.'

Polis was located where four metro lines crossed, and it took up four stations all by itself: *Alexander's Garden, Arbatskaya, Borovitzskaya* and the *Lenin Library*. That enormous territory was the last, genuine seat of civilization, the last place with such a large population that provincial types who happened upon it couldn't help but call it a city. It was given a name – but it meant the same thing anyway: *Polis*. And perhaps it was because this word had a foreign ring to it, an echo of a powerful and marvellous ancient culture which seemed to protect the settlement, that the name stuck.

Polis remained a unique phenomenon in the metro. There, and only there, you could still meet the keepers of old and strange knowledge, which in this severe new world, with its disappearing laws, you just couldn't find anymore. Knowledge for the inhabitants of almost all the other stations, and in essence for the whole metro, was slowly plunging into an abyss of chaos and ignorance, becoming useless along with those who carried it. Driven from everywhere, the only refuge they found was in *Polis*, where they were welcomed with open arms, because their colleagues were in power here. That's why in *Polis*, and only in *Polis*, you could meet decrepit professors, who at some point worked in the departments of famous universities, which were now empty and in ruins, crawling with rats and mould. And the last remaining artists lived there too – the actors, the poets. The last physicists, chemists, biologists . . . Those who stored the best of man's achievements in their skulls, and who knew a thousand years of history. Those whose knowledge would be lost when they died.

Polis was below what used to be the very centre of the city above. Right above *Polis* stood the building of Lenin's Library – the most extensive storehouse of information to come from all ages. There were hundreds of thousands of books in dozens of languages, covering probably all the areas in which human thought was directed. There were hundreds of tonnes of papers marked with all sorts of letters, signs, hieroglyphs, some of which no one could read anymore because the language had died with the last of their speakers. But the whole massive collection of books could still be read and understood, and the people who died a hundred years ago and who wrote them still had a lot to say to the living.

Of all the confederations, empires and powerful stations who had the means to send expeditions to the surface, only *Polis* sent stalkers up to get books. It was the only place where knowledge was valued so much that people were willing to risk the lives of their volunteers for the sake of books, to pay enormous sums to those they hired to do it and forego material assets for the sake of acquiring spiritual assets.

And, despite the seeming impracticality and idealism of the administration, *Polis* stood strong year after year and troubles bypassed

74

it. If any danger threatened it then the whole metro was ready to rally for its protection. The echoes of the last battle that took place there in living memory – between the Red Line and the Hansa – had died down and there was a magic aura of invulnerability and well-being surrounding *Polis* again.

And when Artyom thought about this wonderful city, it didn't seem strange to him at all that the journey to such a place wouldn't be easy. He would have to get lost, go through dangers and tests of strength, otherwise the purpose of the journey would have its charms wasted.

If the way through *Kirovskaya* along the Red Line to the *Lenin Library* seemed impenetrable and too risky, then he'd have to try overcoming the Hansa patrol and go along the Ring. Artyom peered into the charred map even more closely.

Now, if he could be successful in getting through the Hansa territory, by creating some sort of pretext, chatting to the guards at the cordons, breaking through with a fight or by some other means, then the trip to *Polis* would be short enough. Artyom pushed his finger into the map and drew it along the lines. If he went from *Prospect Mir* in the direction of the Ring, through the two stations that belonged to the Hansa, he would come out at *Kurskaya*. Then he could switch over to the *Arbatsko-Pokrovsk* line and from there he could get to *Arbatskaya*, which is to say, to *Polis*. True, *Revolution Square* was on the way, surrendered after the war to the Red Line in exchange for the *Lenin Library*, but the Reds guaranteed free transit to all travellers. This was one of the basic conditions of the peace agreement. And since Artyom was not planning on staying at that station but just going through it, he would ideally be let through freely. Having thought about it, he decided to stick with that plan and to try to iron out the details along the way about the stations he would have to pass through. If something didn't work out, he said to himself, he could always find an alternative route. Looking at the interlacing lines of the numerous passages, Artyom thought that the commander went a bit too far in painting a picture of the difficulties of even the shortest trips through the metro. For example, you could get from *Prospect Mir* not from the right, but from the left – Artyom drew his finger down the map to the Ring – until you got to *Kievskaya*, and there you could go through a pedestrian passage to the *Filevskaya* line or the *Arbatsko-Pokrovskoi* line with just two stops to *Polis*. The task didn't seem so impossible to Artyom anymore. This little exercise with the map had given him confidence in himself.

Now he knew how to act, and no longer doubted that when the caravan got to *Rizhskaya*, he wouldn't be returning with the group back to *VDNKh* but would go on with his journey to *Polis*.

'Studying?' Zhenya asked him having walked right up to Artyom without his noticing.

Artyom jumped up in surprise and tried to hide the map in his confusion.

'Yes, no . . . I was . . . I wanted to find the station on the map where this Reich is, the one that the commander was telling us about before.'

'Well, then, did you find it? No? Oh come on, let me show you,' Zhenya said with a sense of superiority. He oriented himself in the metro much better than Artyom – better than their other contemporaries too, and he was proud of it. He put his finger on the triangle of *Chekhovskaya*, *Pushkinskaya* and *Tverskaya* straight away without mistake. Artyom exhaled with relief but Zhenya thought that it was out of envy.

He decided to console Artyom: 'Don't worry, one day you'll be as good as me in figuring it out.'

Artyom had an expression of gratitude on his face and hurried to change the subject.

'How long are we stopping here?' he asked.

'Young men! Let's be off!' the booming bass of the commander's voice rang out, and Artyom understood that there would be no more resting and he hadn't managed to get anything to eat.

Again it was Artyom and Zhenya's turn to be on the cart. The levers started to grind, boots started to clatter against the concrete, and they were off again into the tunnel.

This time the group moved forward in silence, and only the commander spoke. He had called Kirill to the front and discussed something quietly with him. Artyom had neither the strength nor the desire to hear their conversation. All his energies were taken up by the accursed cart.

The man at the rear, left all alone, felt distinctly uncomfortable, and timidly looked behind himself again and again. Artyom was standing facing him in the cart and could see that there was nothing scary behind him but he was just as reassured when he glanced over his own shoulder to the front. This fear and mistrust followed him always, and it wasn't just him. Any lone traveller was familiar with this feeling. They even had a name for it: 'tunnel fear.' It was when you were going along a tunnel, especially if you had a bad flashlight, and it felt like there was danger right behind your back. Sometimes the feeling was so augmented that you felt someone's gaze at the nape of your neck – or not even a gaze but . . . Who knew who or what was there and how it perceived the world . . . And then, sometimes, it was so intolerably oppressive that you couldn't stand it, and you turned around lightning fast, poking your flashlight into the darkness – and there was no one there . . . Silence . . . Emptiness . . . All was quiet. But while you were looking behind you, and straining your eyes into the darkness until they hurt, and the darkness was condensing behind you again, you wanted to throw yourself in the other direction, to light the tunnel ahead. Was anyone there, had anyone stolen up on you while you were looking the other way? . . . And again . . . The main thing was not to lose control, not to give in to the fear, to convince yourself that it was all crap and that there was nothing to be afraid of, and that you hadn't heard anything anyway . . .

But it was very hard to control yourself – especially when you were walking alone. People had lost their minds. They just couldn't calm themselves down, even when they reached inhabited stations. Then, of course, slowly, they came to themselves again, but they couldn't make themselves go into the tunnel again – or they would immediately be seized by the same feeling of alarm, familiar to every metro-dweller, and it could turn into a pernicious delusion.

'Don't be scared – I'm watching!' Artyom shouted to the man at the back. And the man nodded, but after a couple of minutes he couldn't help it and looked behind himself again. It was hard . . .

'A guy I know at *Seregi* also went a little crazy like that,' Zhenya said quietly, knowing what Artyom had been referring to. 'To be fair, he had a pretty serious reason for it. He decided to go through that tunnel at *Sukharevskaya* – remember I was telling you about it? Where you shouldn't ever go alone and you have to go in a caravan. Well, the guy lived. And, you know why he survived?' Zhenya smirked. 'Because he didn't have enough courage to go beyond the hundredth-metre. When he was heading in he was so brave and resolute. Ha . . . After twenty minutes he came back – his eyes goggling, his hair standing on end, and he couldn't pronounce a single discernible word. So, they didn't get anything out of him – and since then, he speaks incoherently, mostly lowing like a cow. And won't put a foot in the tunnel – just stays at *Sukhareveskaya* begging. He's the local village idiot now. Is the moral of the story clear now?'

'Yeah,' Artyom said uncertainly.

The group moved along for a while in total silence. Artyom sunk into his thoughts again and walked like that for a while, trying to think up something plausible to say at the exit post to get out of *Rizhskaya*.

And so they continued until, after a while, he noticed some kind of strange sound that was getting louder and louder, coming from the tunnel ahead of them. This noise, which had been almost inaudible to begin with, was on the border of audible sound and ultrasound, slowly and imperceptibly gaining strength, so that you couldn't tell when you'd started hearing it. It reminded him of a whistling whisper more than anything – incomprehensible and inhuman.

Artyom quickly looked over at the others. They were all moving rhythmically and silently. The commander had stopped talking to Kirill, Zhenya was thinking about something, and the man at the back was calmly looking forward, having stopped his nervous backward glancing. They didn't hear anything. Nothing! Artyom became scared. The calm and silence of the group became even more noticeable against the background of this whispering, which was getting louder and louder – and it was incomprehensible and frightening. Artyom stopped working the lever and stood up to his full height. Zhenya looked at him in surprise. Zhenya's eyes were clear with no trace of the drugs that Artyom was afraid he might find there.

'What are you doing?' Zhenya asked, annoyed. 'Are you tired or something? You should have said so and not just stopped like that.'

'You don't hear anything?' Artyom asked in bewilderment, and something in his voice made Zhenya's face change expression.

Zhenya listened harder without ceasing to work the lever. The cart, however, was going slower and slower, because Artyom was still standing there with a confused look, catching the echoes of the mysterious noise.

The commander noticed this and turned around.:

'What's wrong with you? Have your batteries run out?'

'You don't hear anything?' Artyom asked him.

And at that moment a foul sensation crept into his soul, that maybe there was no noise and that's why no one heard it. He was just going mad, he was imagining it out of fear . . .

The commander gave the signal to stop so that the squeaking of the cart wouldn't interfere and the grumble of boots would die away. His hands crept up onto his machine gun and he stood motionless and tense, listening, and turning one ear to the tunnel.

The strange noise was right there now, Artyom could hear it

distinctly, and the clearer the sound became the more attentively Artyom peered at the commander's face, trying to make out if he could also hear what was filling Artyom's consciousness with ever-strengthening agitation. But the features of the commander's face gradually smoothed out, and Artyom was overcome with a sense of shame. Moreover, he had stopped the group for nothing and had freaked out and alarmed the others as well.

Zhenya, clearly, couldn't hear anything either even though he was trying. Having given up his work at last, he looked at Artyom with spiteful mockery, looking him in the eye, and asked:

'Hallucinations?'

'Fuck off!' Artyom unexpectedly shouted with irritation. 'What, are you all deaf or something?'

'Hallucinations!' Zhenya concluded.

'Quiet. There's nothing. You just thought you heard it probably. Don't worry, it happens, don't get tense, Artyom. Go ahead and start up again and we'll go on,' the commander said softly, calming the situation, and walking ahead himself.

Artyom had no other option but to return to his work. He earnestly tried to convince himself that the whisper was only in his imagination, that it was just tension. He tried to relax and not to think about anything, hoping he could throw the sound out of his head along with his disturbing and rushing thoughts. He managed to stop the thoughts for a time but, in his empty head, the sound grew more resonant, louder and clearer. He gained strength from the fact that they were all moving further to the south, and when the noise had become so great that it seemed to fill the whole metro, Artyom suddenly noticed that Zhenya was working with just one hand, and that, without noticing it, he was rubbing his ears with the other.

'What are you doing?' Artyom whispered to him.

'I don't know . . . they're blocked . . . they're itching . . .' Zhenya mumbled.

'And you don't hear anything?' Artyom asked.

'No, I don't hear a thing – but I feel pressure,' Zhenya whispered in response, and there wasn't a trace of the former irony in his voice.

The sound had reached an apogee and then Artyom understood where it was coming from. It was emanating from one of the pipes that lay along the tunnel walls. It had been used as a communication line and who knows what else. The pipe was burst and the torn black muzzle was emitting this strange noise. It was coming from the depths of the pipe and. as Artyom tried to figure out why there were no wires, nothing, just complete emptiness and blackness, the commander stopped suddenly and said slowly and laboriously, 'Guys, let's . . . here . . . Let's have a break. I don't feel so well. Something in my head.'

He approached the cart with uncertain steps so he could sit on its edge but he hadn't gone a step before he dropped like a bag to the ground. Zhenya looked at him in confusion, rubbing his ears with both hands and not moving from his place. Kirill for some reason had continued walking alone, as though nothing had happened, not reacting to their shouts. The man at the back sat down on the rails and started to cry helplessly like a baby. The light of the flashlight beamed at the tunnel's ceiling and, lit from below, the scene looked even more sinister.

Artyom panicked. Clearly he was the only one whose mind hadn't been dulled by the sound, but the noise was becoming completely intolerable, preventing any concrete thoughts from developing.

Artyom covered his ears in despair and that helped a little. Then with all his might he slapped Zhenya who was rubbing his ears with a silly expression on his face and yelled at him, trying to overcome the noise, forgetting that he was the only one to hear it: 'Pick up the commander! Put the commander in the cart! We can't stay here, no way! We have to get out of here!' And he picked up the fallen flashlight and went after Kirill who was marching like a sleepwalker into the pitch darkness ahead.

Luckily, Kirill was walking rather slowly. In a few bounds, Artyom managed to chase him down and tap him on the shoulder. But Kirill continued walking and they were getting further and further away from the others. Artyom ran ahead of him and, not knowing what to do, he directed the flashlight into Kirill's eyes. They were closed but Kirill suddenly frowned and broke his stride. Then Artyom, holding him with one hand, used the other to lift Kirill's eyelid and shine the light into his pupil. Kirill screamed, began to blink, shook his head and regained consciousness in a fraction of a second and opened his eyes, looking at Artyom in bewilderment. Blinded by the flashlight, he could almost see nothing, and Artyom had to lead him by the hand back to the cart.

The unconscious body of the commander was lying on the cart, and Zhenya sat next to him, with the same stupid expression on his face. Leaving Kirill at the cart, Artyom went to the man at the back who was still sitting there on the rails, crying. Having looked him in the eye, Artyom met a look of total suffering, and the feeling was so sharp that he stepped backwards in fear that he himself might also start crying in the face of this pain.

'They were all killed. . . . And it was so painful!' Artyom made out the words between sobs.

Artyom tried to get the man to stand up but he pulled away and unexpectedly cried out angrily, 'Pigs! Bad people! I won't go anywhere with you, I want to stay here! They are so lonely, and are in so much pain here – and you want to take me away from here? It's all your fault! I won't go anywhere! Anywhere! Let me go, you hear!'

At first Artyom wanted to slap him thinking that that might bring him back to his senses – but then he was afraid that the guy was so excited that he might just retaliate instead. So, Artyom got down on his knees in front of the man and, even though it was difficult since the noise was so loud, he spoke softly:

'Now, you want to help them though, right? You want to stop their suffering?'

Through his tears, the man looked at Artyom and whispered with a frightened smile: 'Of course . . . Of course, I want to help them.'

'Then you have to help me. They want you to help me. Go to the cart and stand at the lever. You have to help me get to the station.'

'They told you so?' the man looked at Artyom disbelievingly.

'Yes,' Artyom replied confidently.

'And then you'll let me go back to them?'

'I give you my word that if you want to go back to them, then I will send you back,' Artyom confirmed and, without giving the man time to think anymore, he pulled him up into the cart.

He left the man on the cart, mechanically obeying Zhenya, and he and Kirill worked the levers, while the unconscious commander lay there in the middle. Meanwhile, Artyom took the forward position and aimed his machine gun into the darkness, and walked forward with quick steps. He was surprised himself that he could hear the cart following him. Artyom felt that he was doing the unacceptable, having an unprotected rear, but he understood that now the most important thing was to get out of this terrible place as fast as they could.

There were now three of them working the levers and the group was moving faster than before. Artyom felt with some relief that the vicious noise was getting quieter and his sense of being in danger was diminishing. He shouted at the others, telling them to keep up the pace, and suddenly he heard the sober and surprised voice of Zhenya behind him:

81

'What are you, the commander now?'

Artyom signalled to stop, having understood that they had gone past the dangerous zone, and returned to the group and fell to the ground weakly, leaning his back on the cart. The others slowly came to their senses. The man from the back stopped sobbing and was wiping his face with his hands, looking around in perplexity. The commander started to move and rose with a dull groan, complaining of a headache.

Half an hour later, it was possible to go on. Apart from Artyom, no one remembered anything.

'You know, a heaviness pulled me down so quickly and my head was so fogged up – and then suddenly I was out. I've had it happen once before from a gas attack in another tunnel, far from here. But if it had been gas then it would have had a different effect – on everybody at once, without discriminating . . . And you really heard that sound? Yes, this is all strange . . .' The commander was thinking aloud. 'And Nikita was roaring . . . So, Nikita, who were you crying about?' he asked the rearguard.

'The devil knows . . . I don't remember. That is, I did remember about a minute ago but it's flown out of my head . . . It was like a dream: as soon as you wake up, you remember everything and the picture is so clear in your mind. But after a few minutes you regain consciousness a little – and it's all gone, empty. Just fragments remain . . . Well, it's the same now. I remember that I was really, really sorry for someone . . . but who, and why – no clue.'

'And you wanted to stay in the tunnel. Forever. With them. I promised you that if you wanted I would let you go back,' said Artyom, with a sidelong glance at Nikita. 'So, there you go, I'll let you go back,' he added and chuckled.

'No thank you,' Nikita responded gloomily, 'I've reconsidered . . .'

'OK, guys. That's enough hanging about. There's nothing here in this tunnel to stick around for. Let's get there first and then we'll talk about it all. We still have to get back home at some point too . . .' Though why plan ahead on a day like this – God willing they'd just make it to their first destination. 'Let's go!' the commander concluded. 'Listen, Artyom, come and walk with me. You're our hero today,' he added unexpectedly.

Kirill took his place behind the cart, Zhenya despite his protests stayed on the cart with Nikita and they moved forward.

'There was a broken pipe there you say? And your noise was

coming from it? You know, Artyom, maybe we blockheads are all deaf and didn't hear a thing. You probably have a special sense for that crap. You were lucky on this one, boy!' the commander said. 'Very strange, that it came from a pipe. An empty pipe you say? Who the hell knows what goes through them anymore,' he continued, cautiously glancing at the snake-like interlacing pipes along the tunnel walls.

There wasn't much further to go before they'd get to *Rizhskaya*. A quarter of an hour later, they could see the light of the patrol fire, and the commander slowed his pace and gave the correct signal with his flashlight. They let them through the cordon quickly, without delay, and the cart rolled into the station.

Rizhskaya was in better condition than *Alekseevskaya*. Sometime a long time ago, there was a big market above ground at this station. Among those who managed to run to the metro and save themselves were a lot of traders from that market. The people at the station ever since the beginning had been enterprising people and its proximity to *Prospect Mir* and thereby to the Hansa and its main trade routes also gave it a certain prosperity. They had electric light, emergency lights like at *VDNKh*. Their patrols were dressed in old camouflage, which looked more impressive than the decorated quilted jackets at *Alekseevskaya*.

The inhabitants led the guests to their tent. Now a swift return home was not likely, since it was unclear what this new danger was in the tunnel and how to deal with it. The administration of the station and the commander of the small group from *VDNKh* came together for a meeting, and the rest of them were given some time off. Artyom, tired and overwrought, fell face down onto his cot immediately. He didn't want to sleep but he was out of strength. After a couple of hours, the station had promised to have a feast for their guests and, judging from the winking and whispering of their hosts, it seemed there would probably be some meat to eat. But now there was time to lie down and think about nothing.

Noise started up beyond the walls of the tent. The feast was being prepared right in the middle of the platform, where the main camp-fire was. Artyom couldn't resist and looked outside. Several people were cleaning the floor and laying out a tarpaulin, and a little further away they were carving up a pig, cutting it into pieces and sliding them onto steel wire to string them over the fire. The walls of the station were unusual: not marble like at *VDNKh* and *Alekseevskaya* but lined with yellow and red tile. This combination must have looked pretty cheerful at one time. Now, the glazed tile and plastering were covered with a layer of soot and grease – but some of the old feeling of it was preserved. But the most important thing was that at the other end of the station, half buried in the tunnel, was a real train – though its windows were blown in and its doors were open.

You didn't find trains in every passage or station by any means. Over the last two decades many of them, especially the ones that had got stuck in the tunnels and were unsuitable for living inside, were gradually pulled apart by people who used the wheels, the glass and the outer material of the train to make things at their own stations. Artyom's stepfather told him that at Hansa one of the passages was cleared of trains so that passenger trolleys could move between points easily. Also, according to rumour, they were pushed into the Red Line. And in the tunnel that went from *VDNKh* to *Prospect Mir*, there wasn't a wagon left, but that was probably just accidental.

Locals were slowly gathering, and a sleepy-faced Zhenya crawled out of the tent. Half an hour later the local leadership came out with Artyom's commander, and the first pieces of meat were put on the fire. The commander and the station's government were smiling and joking around a lot, seemingly satisfied with the results of their discussions. They brought a bottle of some kind of home-made liquor, there were toasts and everyone was very merry. Artyom gnawed on his meat and licked the dripping hot grease off his hands, looking at the glowing coals, the heat of which brought on an inexplicable feeling of cosiness and peace.

'Was it you that dragged them out of the trap?' said an unfamiliar guy who was sitting nearby and had been looking at Artyom for the last several minutes.

'Who told you that?' Artyom replied to his question with a question, looking at the man. He had a short hair cut, he was unshaven, and under his rough and tough leather coat you could see a soft vest. Artyom could see nothing suspicious about him: his interlocutor looked like a normal trader, the kind that you find at *Rizhskaya*, a dime a dozen.

'Who? Yeah, it was your brigadier said something.' He nodded at someone sitting a little way away and talking animatedly with the commander's new companions.

'Well, yeah it was me,' Artyom reluctantly admitted. And even though he'd been planning to make a couple of useful acquaintances at *Rizhskaya*, now that he was faced with an excellent opportunity, he suddenly didn't feel much like it.

'I'm Bourbon. What's your name?' the guy said.

'Bourbon?' Artyom was surprised. 'Why is that? Wasn't there a king of that name?'

'No, my boy. There was a kind of drink called bourbon. A fiery spirit, you see. It would put you in a good mood, so they say. So what IS your name anyway?' The guy was still interested to know.

'Artyom.'

'Listen, Artyom, and when are you going back?' Bourbon seemed insistent, and it made Artyom suspicious.

'I don't know. Now no one will say when we're going back exactly. If you heard what happened to us, sir, then you should understand why,' Artyom answered coolly.

'Listen, I'm not all that much older than you so you can speak with me without the formality . . . Basically, I'm asking you . . . I have something to propose to you, boy. Not for your whole group but for you personally. Me, well, I need your help. You get it? It won't take long . . .'

Artyom didn't get it at all. The guy was talking haltingly, and something in the way he pronounced his words made Artyom wince inside. He wanted nothing in the world more than to end this incomprehensible conversation.

'Listen, boy, don't you . . . don't get tense.' Bourbon sensed his feelings of mistrust and sought quickly to disperse them. 'Nothing dodgy, it's all above board . . . Well, almost all. Basically, this is it: the day before yesterday some of our guys went along to *Sukharevskaya*, and well, you know, they went straight along the line and they never got there. Only one of them came back. And he doesn't remember anything, came running back covered in snot, howling like your brigadier was telling us. The rest didn't come back. Maybe they got out at *Sukharevskaya*. . . . But maybe they didn't get out at all, because no one has come from *Prospect* for three days now, and no one wants to go to *Prospect* either anymore. And well, basically, I think that there's the same crap there as what you had. As I was listening to your brigadier, I just . . . I got the idea that it might be the same thing. The line is just the same. And the pipes are the same too.' Then Bourbon quickly looked over his shoulder, to check, probably, that no one was listening to him. 'And that crap didn't affect you,' he continued quietly, 'you get it?'

'I'm starting to,' Artyom replied uncertainly.

'Basically, I need to get over there now. I really need to, you see?

85

Really. I don't exactly know what the chances are that I'll lose it, like our boys did, probably like all your guys did. Except you.'

'You . . .' Artyom muttered, 'You want me to take you through the tunnel? To lead you to *Sukharevskaya*?'

'Yeah, something like that.' Bourbon nodded in relief. 'I don't know if you heard about it or not but there's a tunnel beyond *Sukharevskaya*, which, like, is even worse than this one, full of crap, and I need to get through that one too. Bad shit has happened there to the boys. Everything will be fine, don't worry. If you take me, I'll make it worth your while. I'll need to get further, of course, to the south, but I have there, at *Sukharevskaya*, some people, who will dust you off and set you on your road back home and all the rest of it.'

Artyom who had wanted to send Bourbon and his proposals to hell, understood suddenly that this was his chance to get past the southern gates of *Rizhskaya* without a fight and without any other problems. And to go even further . . . Bourbon didn't say much about his next moves, but still he'd said he was going through the accursed tunnel between *Sukharevskaya* and *Turgenevskaya*. And that was exactly where Artyom needed to get. *Turgenevskaya* – *Trubnaya* – *Tsvetnoi Bulvap* – *Chekhovskaya* . . . And then it was only a stone's throw to *Arbatskaya* . . . *Polis* . . . *Polis*.

'What're you paying?' Artyom decided to add for the sake of acting normal.

'Whatever you want. Currency, basically,' Bourbon doubtfully looked at Artyom, trying to make out if the guy understood his meaning. 'I mean, like, Kalashnikov cartridges. But if you want, I can get some food, some spirits or weed.' He winked. 'I can also get you that.'

'No, cartridges are fine. Two magazines. And, well, enough food to get there and back. I won't negotiate.' Artyom named his price as confidently as he could, trying to meet the Bourbon's challenging gaze.

'You drive a hard bargain,' Bourbon responded. 'OK. Two horns for the Kalashnikov. And something to eat. OK, fine,' he mumbled, apparently to himself. 'OK, my boy, so how're you doing there anyway? You should go and sleep, and I'll come and get you soon, when all this ruckus calms down. Pack your stuff, you can leave a note if you can write so that they don't arrange a search. . . . So be ready when I come. Got it?'

CHAPTER 5

In Exchange for Cartridges

He didn't really need to pack his stuff since he hadn't unpacked – there'd been no special reason to do so. The only thing he couldn't work out was how to get his machine gun out of the station so it wouldn't be noticed, so it wouldn't attract attention. They were given bulky military 7.62 calibre machine guns with wooden butts. *VDNKh* always sent their caravans to the nearer stations with these bulky guns.

Artyom lay there, his head buried in the blanket, not answering Zhenya's puzzled questions: why was he snoozing here when everything was so great at the feast, was he sick or something? It was hot and humid in the tent, and it was worse under the covers. Sleep was a long time coming and, when he finally went out, his dreams were unsettling and muddled, as though he was seeing them through clouded glass. He was running somewhere, he was talking to some faceless person, and then he was running again . . .

Zhenya woke him up, shaking him by the shoulder and told him in a whisper: 'Listen, Artyom, there's some guy here for you . . . Are you having some trouble?' he asked carefully. 'Why don't I get all the guys up and we'll . . .'

'No, it's fine, he just needs to talk to me. Go to sleep, Zhen. I'll be back in a sec,' Artyom said quietly, pulling on his boots and waiting for Zhenya to go back to sleep. He was carefully dragging his rucksack out of the tent and gathering up his machine gun, when suddenly Zhenya, having heard a metallic clattering, asked again, 'Now what's happening? Are you sure that everything's OK?'

Artyom had to get him off his back by making up a story that he wanted to show the guy a thing or two because they'd argued, but everything would be fine.

'Liar!' Zhenya said pointedly. 'OK, when should I be worried?'

'In a year,' Artyom mumbled, hoping that this was inaudible enough, and he moved the tent flap aside and went out onto the platform.

'Boy, you're slowing us down,' Bourbon said through his teeth. He was dressed as before, only he had a long rucksack on his back. 'Fuck you! Are you planning to drag that big lump across every cordon with you?' he asked disgustedly, pointing at the machine gun. As far as Artyom could tell, Bourbon didn't have a weapon himself.

The light at the station was fading. There was no one on the platform, everyone had gone to sleep, exhausted from the feast. Artyom tried to walk faster, worried all the time that he would bump into someone from his group, but at the entrance to the tunnel Bourbon trapped him and told him to slow his pace. The patrolmen in the passage noticed them and asked them from afar where they were planning to go in the middle of the night, but Bourbon addressed one of them by name and explained that they had some business to attend to.

'Listen, carefully,' he said to Artyom and turning on his flashlight. 'Now, there'll be guards at the hundredth- and two-hundredth metre lines. So you just keep quiet, above all. I will figure it out with them. Shame that you have a Kalash that's as old as my grandma – you won't hide that thing . . . Where'd you dig up such a piece of crap?'

Everything went smoothly at the hundredth-metre. There was a small fire dying out, and two people were sitting next to it, dressed in camouflage. One of them was snoozing and the second one shook Bourbon's hand like a friend.

'Business? I seeee . . .' he said with a mischievous smile.

Bourbon didn't say a word before the two hundred and fiftieth metre. He just sullenly marched forward. He seemed sort of angry, and unpleasant, and Artyom was starting to regret that he'd come with him. He stepped away from Bourbon and checked to see that his machine gun was in order, and he put his finger on the trigger.

There was some delay at the last guard post. Bourbon either didn't know them well, or they knew him too well. The main guy took him off to the side, putting his rucksack by the fire, and asked him a lot of questions. Artyom, feeling pretty foolish, stayed by the fire and sparingly answered the questions of the duty officer. They were obviously bored and had nothing better to do. Artyom knew for himself that if the duty officer was chatty then everything was fine at the post. If something strange had happened there recently, if something had crawled out of the depths, or someone had tried to break through from the south, or they'd heard a suspicious sound, then they would be crowding around the fire silently, saying nothing, tense, and they wouldn't take their eyes off the tunnel. It looked as though everything had been quiet, and that they could get at least to *Prospect Mir* without worrying.

'You're not from around here I guess. From *Alekseevskaya* or what?' The duty officer was trying to elicit information from Artyom and looking at him right in the face.

Artyom, remembering that Bourbon had ordered him to stay quiet and to talk to no one, muttered something that could have been interpreted in several ways, leaving the guy to his own interpretation. The duty officer, having given up on getting an answer from him, turned to his mate and started discussing a story told by some guy called Mikhail who had been trading at *Prospect Mir* a few days ago and had had some trouble with the station's administration.

Satisfied that they'd given up on him, Artyom sat at the fire and looked at the southern tunnel through the flames. It looked like the same wide and endless tunnel as they had in the northerly direction at *VDNKh* where Artyom had, not so long ago, sat by a fire at the four hundred and fiftieth metre.

By the looks of it, it wasn't different at all. But there was something about it – a particular smell, brought up by the tunnel vents, or was it a particular mood, an aura, that belonged only to this tunnel and gave it an individuality, made it dissimilar to all the rest. Artyom remembered his stepfather saying that there weren't two tunnels alike in the metro. Such supersensitivity had developed over many years of trips and not many had it. His stepfather called it 'listening to the tunnel' and he had such a 'sense of hearing' that he was proud of it and often admitted to Artyom that he had survived many adventures thanks to this sense. Many others, despite their many travels in the metro, had no such thing. Some people developed inexplicable fear, some heard sounds, voices, and slowly lost their minds, but everybody agreed on one thing: even when there wasn't a soul in a tunnel, it was still not empty. Something invisible and almost intangible slowly and viscously dripped onto them, filling them with its being, almost like it was the heavy cold blood in the veins of a stone leviathan.

And now the duty officers' conversation was fading into the background as he tried in vain to see something in the darkness that was swiftly thickening about ten paces from the fire. Artyom started to understand what his stepfather meant when he would tell him

89

about the 'feeling of the tunnel.' Artyom knew that beyond that indistinct boundary, marked by the flames of the fire, where crimson light mixed with shivering shadows, there were more people, other people – but in that moment he couldn't quite believe it. It seemed that life stopped ten paces beyond the firelight, and that there was nothing in front of them, only dead, black emptiness, that answered a shout with the deception of a dull echo.

But if you sit for a while, if you plug your ears, if you don't look into the depths of the tunnel like you're looking for something but instead you try to dissolve your gaze in the darkness, and to merge with the tunnel, to become a part of this leviathan, a cell in the organism, then through your fingers, that are closing off the sounds of the external world, past your auditory organs, a thin melody will flow directly into your brain – an unearthly sound from the depths, indistinct and incomprehensible . . . It's nothing like that disturbing, urging noise, spilling out of the broken pipe in the tunnel between *Alekseevskaya* and *Rizhskaya*. No, it's something different, something clean and deep . . .

It seemed to him that he could dip into the quiet river of this melody for short spells, and suddenly he would understand the essence of this phenomenon – not using reason but using an intuition that was probably awakened by that noise from the broken pipe. The flowing sounds from that pipe seemed to him the same as ether, slowly extending along the tunnel, but they had been rotting inside the pipe, infected by something, seething nervously, and they broke out where tension in the pipe became too much, and the rotting matter pushed itself out into the world, taking its sorrow with it, imparting nausea and madness to all living beings . . .

Suddenly it seemed to Artyom that he was standing on the threshold of an understanding of something important, as though the last hour he had spent wandering in the pitch-black darkness of the tunnels and in the twilight of his own consciousness had pulled the curtain of this great mystery slightly to the side, separating all rational beings from a knowledge of the true nature of this new world which was gnawed into the earth's bowels by previous generations.

But with this realization, Artyom also became scared, as if he had only had a peek through the key hole of the door hoping to find out what was behind it, and seeing only an unbearable light punching through it and singeing the eyes. And if you opened the door then the light would gush out irrepressibly and incinerate the audacious person who decided to open the forbidden door on the spot. However, this light is knowledge.

The whirlwind of all these thoughts, feelings and worries came whipping through Artyom too suddenly and he wasn't at all ready for anything like it and so he recoiled in fright. No, this was all just a fantasy. He hadn't heard anything and hadn't realized anything. It was just a game of his imagination. With mixed feelings of relief and disappointment, he observed how, for an instant, an amazing, indescribable vision was revealed to him. It instantly grew dim, melted, and the mind again was faced with its usual muddy haze. He was afraid of this knowledge and stepped back from it, and now the curtain was lowered again and perhaps forever. The hurricane in his head died down as quickly as it had come and he was left with a devastated and exhausted mind.

Artyom was shaken and sat there trying to understand everything – where his fantasy ended and where reality began – wondering if any of these sensations might be real after all. Slowly, slowly, his soul was filled with bitterness at the fact that he had stood a step away from enlightenment, from the most real enlightenment, but he hadn't been resolute, he hadn't dare give himself to the flow of the tunnel's ether, and now he would be left to wander in the darkness for his whole life because he was once too afraid of the light of authentic knowledge.

'But what is knowledge?' he asked himself again and again, trying to give value to the thing that he had just refused in a hurried and cowardly manner. Sunk in his thoughts, he didn't notice that he had said these words aloud a few times.

'Knowledge, my friend, is light – and non-knowledge is darkness!' one of the duty officers explained to him eagerly. 'Right?' He merrily winked at his friends.

Artyom was dumbstruck and stared at the guy and sat like that for a while until Bourbon returned and got him up and said goodbye to the officers, saying that he had been detained and that they were in a hurry.

'Watch it!' the commander of the post said to him threateningly. 'I'm letting you leave here with a weapon.' He waved a hand at Artyom's machine gun. 'But you won't be coming back through with it. I have clear instructions on that.'

'I told you, you blockhead . . .' Bourbon hissed to Artyom in irritation after they'd hastily walked away from the fire. 'So you can do what you want on the way back. But you'll get a fight. I don't care. I just knew it, I knew that this would happen, fuck you.'

Artyom said nothing, almost not hearing Bourbon chiding him. Instead, he suddenly remembered what his stepfather said that time when he was explaining about the uniqueness of every tunnel – that each one has its own melody and that you can learn to hear it. His stepfather probably wanted simply to express his thought beautifully but, remembering what he felt sitting at the fire moments ago, Artyom thought that he'd heard just such a melody. What he was listening to, really listening to – and hearing! – was the melody of the tunnel. However, the memory of what happened quickly faded and half an hour later Artyom could not be sure that it had all really happened, and that he hadn't imagined it, that it wasn't air blown about by the playing flames.

'OK . . . You probably didn't do it on purpose, you've just got shit for brains.' Bourbon said in conciliation. 'If I'm, like, not very nice to you, I'm sorry. This is stressful work. But, OK, seems we got out so that's good. Now we have to trudge to *Prospect Mir* without being stopped. There we can, like, relax. If everything is quiet then it won't take much time. But beyond that, there's a problem.'

'So it's OK that we're walking along like this? I mean that when we go in a caravan from *VDNKh*, if there's any less than three people then we don't leave, you need a rearguard, and basically . . .' Artyom said, looking behind himself.

'Well, there are plusses of course to going in caravan with a rearguard and all that,' Bourbon started to explain. 'But listen here, there's a concrete minus to that too. I used to be afraid. And forget three people, we used to not go anywhere without at least five people. You think it helped? Doesn't help in the least. Once we were moving a cargo and so we had protection: two in front, three in the middle and a rearguard – everything as it should be. We were going from *Tretyakovskaya* to what's it called . . . used to be called *Marxistskaya*. The tunnel was OK. But something about it I didn't like straight away. A certain decaying . . . And there was a fog. You couldn't see for shit, not five paces ahead – and the flashlights didn't help much. But we decided to tie a rope to the rearguard's belt, drawn from the belt of one of the guys in the middle, and up to the commander at the head of the group. So no one would get lost in the fog. And we're moving at an easy pace, and everything's normal, quiet, there was no need to rush, we hadn't encountered anyone yet (touch wood) and we have about forty minutes to go . . . Though we did it faster than that in the end . . .' His words twisted and he went silent for a little while.

'Somewhere in the middle, this guy Tolyan asks the rearguard something. But the guy doesn't answer. Tolyan waited and asked again. Nothing. Tolyan then pulls on the rope and the end of it appears. It's been bitten right through. Really – bitten through and there's even some wet gunk on the end of it . . . And the guy is no-where to be seen. And they didn't hear a thing. Nothing at all. And I was walking with Tolyan myself. He showed me the end of the rope and my knees quaked. Of course we shouted back at him for the sake of it but didn't hear anything. There wasn't anyone there to answer. So we exchanged glances – and went forward so that we were at *Marxistskaya* in no time.'

'Maybe the guy was playing a joke?' Artyom asked hopefully.

'A joke? Maybe. But he hasn't been seen since. So, there's one thing I've understood: if it's your time, it's your time and no guard's going to help you. Only you go a little slower. And I go everywhere in a twosome, with a partner if you like, except in one tunnel – from *Sukharevskaya* to *Turgenevskaya*, which is a particular situation. If something happens then they'll drag you out. And quickly. Get it?'

'Got it. So, they'll let us into *Prospect Mir*? I still have this thing . . .' Artyom pointed to his machine gun.

'They'll let us onto the radial. But to the Ring – definitely not. They wouldn't let you in anyway, and with that cannon you don't have a hope. But we don't need to get in there. We don't need to hang around there for much time anyway. We'll just make a stop and then go on. You . . . have you ever been to *Prospect Mir*?'

'Only when I was little. But otherwise not,' Artyom admitted.

'Well, why don't I get you up to speed then? Basically, there aren't any guard posts there, they don't need them. There's a market there, and no one lives there so everything is fine. But there's a passage there to the Ring, which means to the Hansa . . . A radial station which doesn't belong to anyone, but the Hansa soldiers patrol it, to keep order. Therefore you have to behave yourself, got it? Or else they'll send you to hell and they'll deny you access to all their stations. So when we get there, you crawl onto the platform and sit quietly. And that samovar of yours,' he nodded at Artyom's machine gun, 'don't go waving it around. I have a . . . I have to sort something out with someone so you'll have to sit and wait. We'll go to *Prospect*, we'll have a talk about how to get through that damn passage to *Sukharevskaya*.'

Bourbon went silent again and Artyom was left to himself. The tunnel wasn't too bad here, the ground was a little damp, and there was a dark, thin stream following the rails, headed in the same direction as they were. But, after a while, there was a quiet rustle and squeaking sound which sounded to Artyom like a nail scratching along glass and it made him wince in aversion. The little beasts weren't visible yet but their presence could already be felt.

'Rats!' Artyom spat out the vile word, feeling a chill pass along his skin. They still visited his nightmares, although his memories of that terrible dark moment when his mother and their entire station were drowned in a flood of rats were almost erased from his memory. Were they actually erased? No, they had just gone deeper, like a needle that wasn't pulled out but gets stuck in the body. It travels around, having been pushed in by an insufficiently trained doctor. At first it will hide and stay still but after a time an unknown force will set it in motion and it will make its pernicious way through the arteries, the nerve ganglions, ripping up vital organs and dooming its carrier to intolerable torment.

The memory of that time, of the blind fury and insatiable cruelty of those beasts, of the experiences of horror that the steel needle left deep in his subconscious only came to disturb Artyom at night. And the mere sight of them, even the vague smell of them, created a sort of electrical discharge in him, forcing his body to shudder in reflex. For Artyom and for his stepfather, and maybe for the other four who escaped with them on the trolley that day, rats were something much more frightening and loathsome than for the other inhabitants of the metro.

There were almost no rats at *VDNKh*: there were traps everywhere and poison had been spread around so Artyom had become unused to them. But they swarmed through the rest of the metro, and he'd forgotten about that or, rather, avoided thinking about it when he had taken the decision to go on this journey.

'What's up boy – you afraid of rats?' Bourbon inquired maliciously. 'Don't like them? You're painfully spoilt . . . but get used to it. They're everywhere . . . But that's OK, it's good even: you won't go hungry,' he added and winked while Artyom was starting to feel nauseous. 'But really,' Bourbon continued seriously, 'you're better to be afraid where there's no rats. If there's no rats then there's been some bad trouble. And if there's no people either then you want to be afraid. But if the rats are running then everything's normal. Business as usual. Get it?'

There're people and there're people and Artyom definitely didn't want to share his suffering with this guy. So he nodded and didn't say anything. There weren't that many rats, and they ran away from the light of the flashlight and you hardly noticed them. But all the same one of them managed to get underfoot and Artyom stepped on something soft and slippery only to hear a shrill squeal. Artyom lost his balance and almost fell face down with all his equipment . . .

'Don't be afraid boy, don't be afraid,' Bourbon cheered him up. 'It gets worse. There's a couple of passages in this shit-hole teeming with them and you have to walk on the rails. And you're walking and crunching them underfoot.' And he snorted meanly for effect.

Artyom frowned. He was silent but he was squeezing his fists. He would have punched Bourbon right in his grinning face with pleasure!

Suddenly an indecipherable din came from far off and Artyom immediately forgot the insult and clasped the handle of his automatic weapon and looked at Bourbon questioningly.

'Don't worry. Everything's fine. We're coming up to *Prospect*,' Bourbon reassured him and patted him patronizingly on the shoulder.

Even though he'd warned Artyom that there were no guard posts at *Prospect Mir*, this was all very unusual for Artyom – to just go straight into another station without first seeing the weak light of a fire designating the border, without any obstacles along the way. When they got to the tunnel's exit, the din got louder and a glow of light became noticeable.

Finally, there were some cast-iron stairs to the left and a little bridge which took you up to the level of the platform. Bourbon's boots rattled up the iron steps and after a few steps the tunnel turned to the left and opened up and they were in the station.

There was a bright white beam of light in their faces: invisible from the tunnel, there was a little table on the side at which sat a man in a strange and unfamiliar old-fashioned, grey uniform, wearing a peak cap.

'Welcome,' he greeted them, averting the flashlight. 'Trading or transit?'

While Bourbon stated the purpose of their visit, Artyom peered at the *Prospect Mir* metro station before him. On the platform, along the pathways, twilight reigned, but there were arches lighted from the inside with a soft yellow light from which Artyom unexpectedly felt a squeeze in his chest. He wanted to be done with all the formalities and to look at what was going on in the station, there, where the arches were, from which this light was coming, so familiar and comforting that it almost hurt. And though it seemed to Artyom that he hadn't seen anything like it before, the sight of this light brought him back to the distant past and suddenly a strange image appeared to him: a small home, flooded with warm yellow light, a woman is half-reclined on a wide ottoman and she is reading a book but you can't see her face amidst the pastel wallpaper and the dark blue square of the window . . . The vision flashed in front of his mind but melted a second later, leaving him puzzled and excited. What had he just seen? Could it be that the weak light coming from the station could project an old slide of his childhood that had been lost in his subconscious onto an invisible screen? Could that young woman who was peacefully reading a book on the spacious and comfortable ottoman be his mother?

Artyom impatiently thrust his passport at the customs officer after agreeing, despite Bourbon's objections, to put his machine gun in their storage room for the duration of his visit. Then Artyom hurried along, attracted to the light behind the columns like a moth, towards the light and the din of a bazaar.

Prospect Mir was different from *VDNKh*, from *Alekseevskaya*, from *Rizhskaya*. The prosperity of the Hansa meant that they had better illumination than the emergency lights that gave light to the stations that Artyom had known during his conscious life. No, these weren't the same lamps that lighted the metro in the old days, they were weak, glowing lights which hung overhead every twenty feet, drawn along a wire that went across the whole station. But for Artyom, who was used to the cloudy-red emergency glow, to the unreliable light of fires, to the weak radiance from tiny pocket flashlights illuminating the inside of tents, the light at this station was totally strange. It was the same light that lit his early childhood, as far back as the time when life was at the surface, and he was charmed to be reminded of something that had long ago ceased to exist for him. So, arriving at the lighted part of the station, Artyom didn't rush into the rows of traders like the others but leant his back against a column and, partly covering his eyes with his hand, he stood and looked at the lamps, again and again, until there was a sharp pain in his eyes.

'You what – gone crazy or something? Why are you staring at them so hard – you want to lose your eyes? You'll be as blind as a puppy, and what'll I do with you?' Bourbon's voice resounded in Artyom's ears. 'You've already gone and given them your balalaika, so you might as well go and have a look around . . . at what the lamps are trying to show you!'

Artyom cast a hostile look over at Bourbon but he obeyed him anyway.

There weren't all that many people at the station but they spoke so loudly, trading, beckoning, demanding, trying to out-yell each other, that it became clear why it was all so audible from afar, from the approach to the tunnel. On both tracks there were scraps of train structures – and some wagons were converted for habitation. Two rows of trays were arranged along the platform that displayed various utensils – some in orderly piles, others in sloppy heaps. On one side of the station there was an iron curtain which stood in the place where there was once an exit to the surface, and on the opposite side there was a line of grey bags which clearly demarcated a line of firing positions. An unnaturally white banner hung from this ceiling on which was painted a brown circle, the symbol of the Ring. Beyond the firing line were four escalators, which led to the Ring circuit, and that's where the territory of the powerful Hansa began (which was closed to foreigners). The frontier guards beyond the fences were dressed in waterproof overalls with the usual camouflage, but for some reason they were grey in colour.

'Why do they have grey camouflage?' Artyom asked Bourbon.

'They're fat animals, that's why,' he answered contemptuously. 'You, now . . . You go ahead and look around while I do a little trading here.'

There was nothing of particular interest to Artyom. There was tea, sticks of sausage, storage batteries for lamps, jackets and raincoats made from pig skin, some tattered books, most of which were pornography, half-litre bottles of a suspicious looking substance with the inscription 'home-brew' written on crooked labels. And there really wasn't one trader selling weed which you used to be able to get hold of anywhere. Even the gaunt little man with the blue nose and watery eyes who was selling the dubious home-brew told Artyom to get lost when he asked if he had a little 'stuff'. There was a trader selling firewood, knotty logs and branches that some stalker had brought down from the surface. It was said to burn for a long time and produce little smoke. Here you paid for things in dimly gleaming Kalashnikov cartridges. A hundred grammes of tea was five cartridges; a stick of sausage was fifteen cartridges; a bottle of home-brew was twenty. They fondly called them 'little bullets': 'Listen, man, look at this, what a cool jacket, it's cheap, just thirty little bullets – and it's yours! OK, twenty-five and you'll take it now?'

Looking at the neatly arranged rows of 'little bullets' on the counters, Artyom recollected the words of his stepfather: 'I once read that Kalashnikov was proud of his invention, that his automatic weapon was the most popular gun in the world. They say that he was particularly happy that thanks to his device the borders of his homeland were kept safe. I don't know, if I had invented that thing I think I would have gone mad. To think that most murders have been committed with the help of your device! That's even scarier then being the inventor of the guillotine.'

One cartridge – one death. Someone's life removed. A hundred grammes of tea cost five human lives. A length of sausage? Very cheap if you please: just fifteen lives. A quality leather jacket, on sale today, is just twenty-five so you're saving five lives. The daily exchange at this market was equal in lives to the entire population of the metro.

'Well, so, did you find anything for yourself?' Bourbon came up and asked.

'Nothing interesting here for me.' Artyom brushed the question away.

'Aha, you're right, it's full of garbage. But, boy, this little station used to be the one place in this stinking metro station where you could find everything you want. You go there and they're all vying with one another: weapons, narcotics, girls, fake documents.' Bourbon sighed dreamily. 'But these cretins,' he nodded at the Hansa flag, 'have made this into a nursery school: you can't do this, you can't do that . . . OK, let's go and get your hoe – we need to keep going.'

After getting Artyom's machine gun, they took a seat on the stone bench before entering the southern tunnel. It was murky there, and Bourbon had picked this spot especially in order to get their eyes used to the weaker light.

'Basically, this is the deal: I can't vouch for myself. I've never done this and so I don't know what I'm doing and if we'll run into trouble. Touch wood, of course, but even so, if we run into something . . . Well, if I start snivelling or go deaf, then that should be OK. As far as I heard, everybody goes crazy in their own way. Our boys didn't make it back to *Prospect*. I think that they didn't get far, and we might bump into them today . . . So you . . . get ready for that, because you're a little soft after all . . . And if I start to see red, I'll shut you up. That's the problem, you see? I don't know what to do . . . Well, OK.' Bourbon finally felt resolved after his hesitations. 'Boy, you're all right I guess, and you won't shoot a guy in the back. I'm going to give you my gun while we go through this passage. Watch it,' he warned, looking Artyom tenaciously in the eyes, 'and don't be funny. I have a limited sense of humour.'

He shook some rags out of his rucksack, and then carefully pulled out a machine gun that was wrapped in plastic packaging. It was also a Kalashnikov but it was cut-off like the ones held by the Hansa border guards, with a hinged butt and a short socket instead of the long one that Artyom had. Bourbon took the magazine out of it and put it back in his rucksack, throwing the rags in after it.

'Hold this!' he gave Artyom the weapon. 'And don't pack it away. It might prove useful. Though the passage looks quiet . . .' And Bourbon didn't finish his sentence but jumped onto the pathway. 'OK, let's go. The sooner you go, the sooner you get there.'

It was frightening. When they went from *VDNKh* to *Rizhskaya*, Artyom knew that anything could happen, but at least people went back and forth along those tunnels every day, and he knew that there was an inhabited station ahead of them where they were expected. It was just as unpleasant as it always was for anyone leaving a lighted and peaceful place. Even when they were headed for *Prospect Mir* from *Rizhskaya*, despite his doubts, he could amuse himself with the thought that ahead of him lay a Hansa station: that there was somewhere to go where he could relax in safety.

But it was terrifying here. The tunnel that lay before them was totally black, and an unusual, total, absolute darkness reigned – it was so thick you could almost touch it. As porous as a sponge, it greedily swallowed the rays of their flashlight, which was hardly sufficient to illuminate even a foot ahead. Straining to the limits of his hearing, Artyom attempted to distinguish the smallest germ of that strange and painful noise but it was in vain. Sounds probably had as hard a time getting through this darkness as light did. Even the bold crashing of Bourbon's boots sounded limp and mute in this tunnel.

On the right wall suddenly there was a gap – the flashlight beam sank into a black spot, and Artyom didn't immediately understand that it was simply a side-passage which exited sideways from the main tunnel. He looked at Bourbon questioningly.

'Don't be scared. There was a transfer passage here,' he explained, 'so that trains could get directly onto the Ring without transferring at other stations. But the Hansa filled it in – they're not fools. They wouldn't leave an open tunnel pointing straight at them . . .'

After that they walked in silence for quite a long time, but the silence was getting more and more oppressive and finally Artyom couldn't bear it.

'Listen, Bourbon,' he said, trying to disperse any hallucinations, 'is it true that some morons attacked a caravan here not long ago?'

Bourbon didn't answer at once and Artyom thought that perhaps he hadn't heard the question and was about to repeat it when Bourbon responded, 'I heard something like that. But I wasn't here then so I can't tell you for sure.'

His words made a dull sound and Artyom barely caught their sense, and had a hard time separating the words he heard from his own grinding thoughts about the fact that everything was so hard to hear in this tunnel.

'What? No one saw it? There're stations at either end – how could that be? Where could they have gone?' he continued, and not because he was especially interested in the answer but simply in order to hear his own voice.

Several minutes went by before Bourbon replied at last, but this time Artyom hadn't wanted to rush him, because there was an echo of the words he had just said resounding in his head and he was too busy listening to them.

'They say that somewhere here there's a . . . kind of hatch. It's covered over. It's not really visible. Well, how likely is it anyway that you'd see something in this darkness?' Bourbon added with a sort of unnatural irritation in his voice.

It took some time for Artyom to remember what they were talking about, and he agonizingly tried to catch hold of the sense of it all and to pose another question simply because he wanted to continue the conversation. Even if it was clumsy and difficult, it was saving them from the silence.

'And is it always so dark in here?' Artyom asked, feeling a bit spooked that his words made such little sound, as though there was something covering his ears.

'Dark? Yes, always. Everywhere is dark. It comes in . . . the great darkness, and . . . it shrouds the world and it will . . . dominate eternally,' Bourbon responded, making strange pauses.

'What's that? A book or something?' Artyom said, noticing that he had to make increasing efforts to catch the sound of his own words, and also paying attention to the fact that Bourbon's language had altered in a frightening way. But Artyom didn't have enough strength to be surprised by this.

'A book . . . Be afraid . . . of truths, concealed in ancient . . . volumes, where . . . words are embossed in gold on paper . . . slate-black . . . they don't decay,' Bourbon said ponderously and Artyom was struck by the thought that the man wasn't turning to speak to him as he had before.

'Beautiful!' Artyom almost yelled. 'Where does it come from?'

'And beauty . . . will be overthrown and crushed, and . . . the prophets will choke, endeavouring to pronounce their pre-monitions . . . for a day . . . the future will be . . . blacker than their most ominous . . . fears and what they see . . . will poison their reason . . .' Bourbon continued quietly.

Suddenly he stopped and he turned his head to the left so sharply that Artyom could hear how his vertebrae cracked and and he looked Artyom straight in the eye.

Artyom started and stepped backwards, groping for his machine gun just in case. Bourbon looked at it with wide-open eyes, but his pupils were contracted into two tiny dots even though in the pitch black darkness of the tunnel they should have been thrown open to their limits in an attempt to capture as much light as possible. His face seemed unnaturally peaceful, not one muscle was tense, and there was even a contemptuous smile which had just disappeared from his lips.

'I've died,' Bourbon said. 'There is no more me.'

And as straight as a cross-tie, he fell face down.

And then that same terrible sound rushed into Artyom's ears but this time it did not expand and amplify gradually as it had the last time. No, it burst suddenly at full volume, deafening him and knocking him from his feet. The sound was more powerful here than it had been when he met it before, and Artyom, laid out on the ground, couldn't muster the will to stand for some time. But once he had covered his ears like before, and yelling as loudly as he could, he rushed and got up from the ground. Then he picked up the flashlight that had fallen from Bourbon's hands, he started feverishly to scan the walls, trying to find the source of the noise – the broken pipe. But the pipes were absolutely intact here, and the sound was coming from somewhere above.

Bourbon was lying there, immobile, still face down, and when Artyom turned him over, he saw that Bourbon's eyes were still open. Artyom tried hard to remember what to do in situations like this, and he put his hand on the man's wrist to look for a pulse. Even if it was as weak as a thread, or inconsistent, he wanted to feel it . . . But it was useless. Then he grabbed Bourbon by the hands and, pouring with sweat, he dragged his ever-heavier body forward, straight out of this place. It was fiendishly hard and made even more so because he had forgotten to remove his companion's rucksack.

After a few dozen steps Artyom suddenly stumbled on something soft and his nose was struck by a sickening and slightly sweet smell. He immediately remembered the words 'we might bump into them' and he redoubled his efforts, trying not to look underfoot, passing bodies stretched out on the rails.

He pulled and pulled Bourbon along. Bourbon's head hung lifelessly and his hands were growing cold and slipping out of Artyom's sweaty hands but he didn't acknowledge it, he didn't want to acknowledge it, he had to get Bourbon out of there and he had promised him, they had an agreement!

The noise gradually began to die down and suddenly disappeared. Again there was a deathly silence and, feeling an enormous relief, Artyom allowed himself to finally sit down on the rails and catch his breath. Bourbon was lying motionless next to him and Artyom was looking with despair at his pale face as he breathed heavily. After about five minutes he made himself get up onto his feet and, taking Bourbon by the wrists, he moved forward stumbling. His head was absolutely empty apart from the vicious determination to drag this person to the next station.

Then his legs buckled and he tumbled onto the cross-ties but after lying there for a few minutes he crawled forward and grabbed Bourbon by the collar. 'I'll get there, I'll get there, I'll get there, I'll get there, I'llgetthereI'llgetthereI'llgetthereI'llgetthere,' he assured himself although he barely believed it. Having lost his strength entirely, he pulled his machine gun down from his shoulder and switched the safety lock to single shots and he directed the barrel to the south, let out a shot and called out: 'People!' But the last sound that he heard was not a human voice but the rustle of rat paws.

He didn't know how long he had lay there like that, gripping Bourbon by the collar, squeezing the handle of his machine gun, when his eyes perceived a ray of light. An unfamiliar old man with a flashlight in one hand and a strange gun in the other was standing above him.

'My young friend,' he was saying in a pleasant and sonorous voice.

'You can forget about your friend. He's as dead as Ramses the Second. Do you want to stay here and reunite with him in the heavens as soon as possible or can he wait for you for a little while?'

'Help me to take him to the station,' Artyom asked the man in a weak voice, covering his eyes from the light.

'I'm afraid that it's necessary for us to reject that idea,' the man said bitterly. 'I am resolutely against turning the metro station of *Sukharevskaya* into a tomb, it's not even that comfortable as it is. And then, if we take this lifeless body there then it's unlikely that anyone in the station will undertake to put him on his final path in a respectable way. What difference does it make whether the body decomposes here or at the station if its immortal soul has already returned to his Creator? Or to be reincarnated, depending on your religious views. Although all religions are mistaken to differing degrees.'

'I promised him . . .' Artyom sighed. 'We had an agreement . . .'

'My friend!' the unfamiliar man said frowning. 'I'm starting to lose my patience. My rules don't tell me to help the dead when there're enough living people that need help. I am returning to *Sukharevskaya*. I'm getting rheumatism from spending a long time in this tunnel. If you want to see your companion as soon as possible I advise you to stay here. The rats and the other lovely creatures will help you with that. And if you are concerned about the legal aspect of the question, then the contract is considered terminated if there is no objection from the other party.'

'But I can't just leave him here!' Artyom quietly tried to convince his rescuer. 'This was a living being. Leave him to the rats?'

'This, by the looks of it, was indeed a living person,' the man responded, inspecting the body sceptically. 'But now it is definitely a dead person and that isn't the same thing. OK, if you want, we can return here and you can make a cremation bonfire or whatever it is that you do in such circumstances. Now, get up!' he ordered and Artyom got to his feet reluctantly.

Despite his protests, the stranger decisively pulled the rucksack off Bourbon's back and threw it over his shoulder and, supporting Artyom, he quickly walked forward. At first Artyom had a hard time walking but it was as if with each step the old man was giving Artyom injections of his ebullient energy. The pain in his feet subsided, and his rational mind returned gradually. He was looking intently into the face of his rescuer. By the looks of him, the man was over fifty, but he looked surprisingly fresh and robust. His arms, which were supporting Artyom, were firm and didn't once tremble with fatigue the whole way back. His short hair was turning grey and his little, sculpted beard surprised Artyom – the man looked too well groomed for the metro, especially given the godforsaken place where it seemed this man lived.

'What happened with you, friend?' the unfamiliar man asked Artyom. 'It doesn't look like an attack, but more like he was poisoned . . . And I really want to hope that it's not what I think it is,' he added, not going into what exactly it was that he feared.

'No . . . He died by himself,' Artyom said, not having the strength to explain the circumstances of Bourbon's death, which he himself was only just starting to get his head around. 'It's a long story. I'll tell you later.'

The tunnel suddenly widened and they appeared to have arrived at the station. Something seemed strange to Artyom here, something unusual and a few seconds later he understood what it was.

'It's what – dark here?' he asked his companion in dismay.

'There's no authorities here,' the man replied. 'So there's no one to provide light for the people. That's why whoever needs light has to get it himself. Some can, some can't. But don't be afraid. Luckily I'm acquainted with the top ranks,' and he quickly climbed onto the platform and held out a hand to Artyom.

They turned into the first archway and went into a hall. There was only one long passage, a colonnade with arches on both sides, and the usual iron walls, the stalled escalators. Barely lighted by weak little fires, and most of it plunged in darkness, *Sukharevskaya* was an oppressive vision and very sad. Crowds of people swarmed around the fires, some were sleeping on the floor, and strange half-bent figures in rags wandered from fire to fire. They were all clustered in the middle of the hall as far from the tunnels as they could be.

The bonfire to which the stranger led Artyom was noticeably brighter than the rest of them and it was located in the centre of the platform.

'One day this station will burn to the ground,' Artyom thought aloud, looking despondently at the hall.

'In four hundred and twenty days,' his companion said calmly. 'So, it's best you leave before then. In any case, that's what I plan to do.'

'How do you know?' Artyom asked and froze, remembering in a flash all that he had heard about magicians and psychics and scrutinizing the face of his companion – looking for the markings of unearthly knowledge.

'The mother heart-python is unsettled,' he answered, smiling. 'OK, that's all, you must have a sleep, and then we'll introduce ourselves and have a talk.'

With these last words, Artyom suddenly was overcome by monstrous fatigue, which had accumulated in the tunnel before *Rizhskaya*, in his nightmares, in the recent tests of his will. Artyom had no more strength to resist and he got down onto a piece of tarpaulin that was spread near the fire and put his rucksack under his head and fell into a long, deep and dreamless sleep.

CHAPTER 6

The Rights of the Strong

The ceiling was so sooty that there wasn't a trace left of the white-wash that had once been applied to it. Artyom looked dully at it, not knowing quite where he was.

'You're awake?' he heard a familiar voice, forcing the scatterings of thoughts to build a picture of yesterday's (was it yesterday?) events. It all seemed unreal to him now. Opaque, like fog, the wall of sleep had separated actuality from recollections.

'Good evening,' Artyom said to the man who had found him. He was sitting on the other side of the fire, and Artyom could see him through the flames. There was a mysterious, even mystical quality to the man's face.

'Now we can introduce ourselves to each other. I have a regular name, similar to all the other people that surround you in your life. It's too long and it says nothing about me. But I am the latest incarnation of Genghis Khan, and so you can call me Khan. It's shorter.'

'Genghis Khan?' Artyom looked at the man disbelievingly. Artyom didn't believe in reincarnation.

'My friend!' Khan objected as though insulted. 'You don't need to look into my eyes and at my behaviour with such obvious suspicion. I have been incarnated in various other and more easily acceptable forms too. But Genghis Khan remains the most significant stage along my path even though I don't remember anything from that life, unfortunately.'

'So why Khan and not Genghis?' Artyom pushed further. 'Khan isn't a surname after all, it's just an professional assignation if I remember correctly.'

'It brings up unnecessary reference, not to mention Genghis Aitmatov,' his companion said reluctantly and incomprehensibly.

'And by the way, I don't consider it my duty to explain the origins of my name to whoever asks. What's your name?'

'I'm Artyom and I don't know who I was in a previous life. Maybe my name was also a little more resounding back then,' said Artyom.

'Nice to meet you,' Khan said, obviously completely satisfied with his answer. 'I hope you will share my modest meal,' he added, lifting and hanging a battered metal kettle over the fire – it was just like the ones they had at the northern patrol of *VDNKh*.

Artyom stood up and put his hand in his rucksack and pulled out a stick of sausage, which he'd acquired on his way from *VDNKh*. He cut off several pieces with his penknife and put them on a clean rag that was also inside his rucksack.

'Here.' He extended it towards his new acquaintance. 'To go with tea.'

Khan's tea was *VDNKh* tea, which Artyom recognized. Sipping the tea from an enamelled metal mug, he silently recalled the events of the day before. His host, obviously, was also thinking his own thoughts, and he didn't bother Artyom.

The madness lashing at the world from the broken pipes seemed to have a different effect on everyone. Artyom was able to hear it simply as a deafening noise that didn't let you concentrate, a noise which killed your thoughts, but spared your mind itself, whereas Bourbon simply couldn't stand the powerful attack and died. Artyom hadn't expected that the noise could actually kill someone, otherwise he would never had agreed to take one step into that black tunnel between *Prospect Mir* and *Sukharevskaya*.

This time the noise had snuck up surreptitiously, at first dulling the senses. Artyom was now sure that all usual sounds had been muted and the noise itself had been inaudible at first, but then it froze the flow of thoughts so they were suddenly covered with the hoarfrost of weakness and, finally, it delivered its crushing blow.

And why hadn't he immediately noticed that Bourbon had suddenly started talking in terms that he couldn't possibly have known, even if he had read lots of apocalyptical prophecies? The noise went deeper into Bourbon, as if bewitching him, and a strange intoxication had taken hold. Artyom himself had been thinking all sorts of rubbish about the fact that he mustn't go silent, that they had to keep talking, but it hadn't occurred to him to try to figure out what was going on. Something had been interfering . . .

He wanted to throw all that had happened out of his consciousness, to forget it all. It was impossible to get his head around it. In all his years at *VDNKh* he had only heard about such things. It had been easier to think that anything he'd heard was just not possible in this world. Artyom shook his head and looked from side to side again.

The same suffocating twilight filled the space. Artyom thought that it had probably never been light here, and that it could only get darker – when the fuel reserves for the fire ended. The clock above the entrance to the tunnel had stopped ticking a long time ago since there was no one who took care of such things. Artyom wondered why Khan had said 'good evening' to him, because according to his calculations it should be morning or midday.

'Is it really evening?' he asked Khan, puzzled.

'It's evening for me,' Khan replied pensively.

'What do you mean?' Artyom didn't understand.

'See, Artyom, you obviously come from a station where the clock works and you all look at it in awe, comparing the time on your wrist watch to the red numbers above the tunnel entrance. For you, time is the same for everyone, just like light. Well, here it's the opposite: nothing is anyone else's business. No one is obliged to make sure there's light for all the people who have made their way here. Go up to anybody here and suggest just that and it will seem absurd to them. Whoever needs light has to bring it here with them. It's the same with time: whoever needs to know the time, whoever is afraid of chaos, needs to bring their own time with them. Everyone keeps some time here. Their own time. And it's different for everybody and it depends on their calculations, but they're all equally right, and each person believes in their own time, and subordinates their life to its rhythms. For me it's evening right now, for you it's morning – and what? People like you are so careful about storing up the hours you spend wandering, just as ancient peoples kept pieces of glowing coal in smouldering crucibles, hoping to resurrect fire from them. But there are others who lost their piece of coal, maybe even threw it away. You know, in the metro, it is basically always night-time and it makes no sense to keep track of time here so painstakingly. Explode your hours and you'll see how time will transform – it's very interesting. It changes – you won't even recognize it. It will cease to be fragmented, broken into the sections of hours, minutes and seconds. Time is like mercury: scatter it and it will grow together again, it will again find its own integrity and indeterminacy. People tamed it, shackled it into pocket-watches and stop-watches – and for those that hold time on a chain, time flows evenly. But try to free it and you will see: it flows differently for different people, for some it is slow and viscous, counted in the inhalations and exhalations of smoked cigarettes, for others it races along, and they can only measure it in past lives. You think it's morning now? There is a great likelihood that you are right: there's a roughly twenty five percent likelihood. Nevertheless, this morning of yours has no sense to it, since it's up there on the surface and there's no life up there anymore. Well, there're no more people, anyway. Does what occurs above have value for those who never go there? No. So when I say "good evening" to you, if you like, you can answer "good morning." There's no time in this station, except perhaps one and it's very strange: now it is the four hundred and nineteenth day and I'm counting backwards.'

He went silent, sipping on his hot tea and Artyom thought it was funny when he remembered that at *VDNKh* the station clock was treated as a holy thing and any failure of it immediately put anyone nearby under the hot hand of blame. The authorities would be astonished to learn that time doesn't exist, that the thought of it had just been lost! What Khan had just described reminded Artyom of a funny thing that he had been surprised by repeatedly as he grew up.

'They say that before, when trains used to run, in the wagons they used to announce "Be careful of the closing doors, the next stop is x,y,z, and the next platform will appear on your left or right," ' he said. 'Is that true?'

'Does it seem strange to you?' Khan raised his eyebrows.

'How could they tell which side the platform would be on? If I'm coming from the south to the north then the platform is on the right. If I'm coming from the north to the south then it's on the left. And the seats on the train were against the walls of the train if I remember right. So for the passengers, the platforms were either in front of them or behind them – half of them on one side and the other half on the other with different perspectives.'

'You're right.' Khan answered respectfully. 'Basically the train drivers were only speaking for themselves because they travelled in a compartment at the front and for them right was absolute right and left was absolute left. So they must have mostly been saying it for their own benefit. So in principle they might as well have said nothing. But I have heard these words since I was a child and I was so used to them that I had never stopped to consider them.'

Some time passed and then he said, 'You promised to tell me what happened to your friend.'

Artyom paused for a moment, wondering if he should tell this man about the mysterious circumstances surrounding the death of Bourbon; about the noise that he had heard twice now in the last twenty-four hours; about its destructive influence on human reason; about his sufferings and thoughts when he could hear the melody of the tunnel . . . And he decided that if there was anyone worth telling it all to, then it would be the person who sincerely considered himself to be the latest incarnation of Genghis Khan and and for whom time doesn't exist. So he started to lay out his misadventure in a muddled, anxious way without observing the sequence of events, attempting to convey the various sensations he felt rather than the facts.

'It's the voices of the dead,' Khan said quietly after Artyom had completed his narrative.

'What?' Artyom asked, surprised.

'You heard the voices of the dead. You were saying that at the beginning it sounded like a whisper or a rustle? Yes, that's them.'

'Which dead?' Artyom didn't quite understand.

'All the people who have been killed in the metro since the beginning. This, basically, explains why I am the last incarnation of Genghis Khan. There won't be any more incarnations. Everyone has come to their end, my friend. I don't know quite how this has happened but this time humanity has overdone it. There's now no more heaven and no more hell. There isn't purgatory either. After the soul flies out from the body – I hope you at least believe in the immortal soul? Well, it has no refuge anymore. How many megatons and bevatons does it take to disperse the noosphere? It was as real as this kettle. And whatever you say, we weren't sparing of ourselves. We destroyed both heaven and hell. We now happen to live in this strange world, in a world where after death the soul must remain right where it is. You understand me? You will die but your tormented soul won't get reincarnated anymore and, seeing as there is no more heaven, your soul won't get any peace and quiet. It is doomed to remain where you lived your entire life, in the metro. Maybe I can't give you the exact theosophic explanation for why this is but I know one thing for sure: in our world the soul stays in the metro after death . . . It will rush around under the arches of these underground tunnels until the end of time because there isn't anywhere for it to go. The metro combines material life with the hypostases of the other world. Now Eden and the Netherworld are here, together. We live amidst the souls of the dead, they surround us in a full circle – all those that were crushed by trains, shot, strangled, burnt, eaten by monsters, those who died strange deaths, about which no living being knows anything and won't ever be able to imagine. Long ago I struggled to figure out where they would go, why their presence isn't felt every day, why you don't feel a light and cold gaze coming from the darkness . . . You are familiar with tunnel horror? I thought before that the dead blindly followed us through tunnels, step by step, hiding in the darkness as soon as we turn to look. Eyes are useless. You won't see the dead with them. But the ants that run along your spine, the hair standing on end, the chill which shakes our bodies – they are all witness to the invisible pursuit. That's what I thought before. But now your story has explained much to me. Somehow they get into the pipes, into the communication lines . . . Sometime a long time ago, before my father and even my grandfather was born, in the city of the dead, which lies above us, there was a little river. People who lived there knew how to lock this river and to direct it into pipes under the earth where it probably flows until today. And it looks like this time someone's buried the River Styx itself in these pipes . . . Your friend was speaking not in his own words – no, it wasn't him. Those were the voices of the dead. He was hearing them in his head and repeating them and then they absorbed him.'

Artyom stared at Khan and could not avert his gaze from the man's face for the duration of his monologue. Indistinct shadows skittered across Khan's face and his eyes were flaring with some internal fire . . . Towards the end of the story, Artyom was almost sure that Khan was mad, that the voices in the pipes had whispered something to him too. And though Khan had saved him from death, and shown him such hospitality, the thought of staying with him for any length of time was uncomfortable and unpleasant. He needed to think about how to move on, through the most evil of all the tunnels in the metro, about which he had heard much – from *Sukhareveskaya* to *Turgenevskaya* and farther.

'So, you'll have to forgive me for my little lie,' Khan added after a short pause. 'Your friend's soul didn't go up to the creator, it won't reincarnate and come back in a new form. It joined the other unhappy ones, in the pipes.'

These words reminded Artyom that he had planned to go back for Bourbon's body, in order to bring it to the station. Bourbon had said that he had friends here, friends who would take Artyom back if they arrived successfully. This reminded him of the rucksack, which Artyom had not yet opened and in which, apart from Artyom's machine gun, there might be something useful.

But to take it over was somehow frightening and superstitions of all kinds climbed into Artyom's head and he decided to open it only slightly and to peek into it without touching or moving anything.

'You don't need to be afraid of it,' Khan said to Artyom unexpectedly as though he could feel his trepidation. 'The thing is now yours.'

'I think what you did is called looting,' Artyom said quietly.

'You don't need to be afraid of retribution, he won't reincarnate,' said Khan, not replying to what Artyom said but to what was flitting about in Artyom's head. 'I think that when they get taken into the pipes, the dead lose themselves and they become part of a whole, their will is dissolved into the will of the rest of them, and reason dries up. There's no more individual. But if you're afraid of the living and not the dead . . . Well, then drag this bag into the middle of the station and empty its contents onto the floor. Then no one will accuse you of thieving, and your conscience can be clean. But you tried to save the guy and he would be grateful to you for that. Consider that this bag is his repayment to you for what you did.'

He was speaking so authoritatively and with such conviction that Artyom gained the courage to put his hand into the pack and he started to take things out of it and lay them on the tarpaulin to see them in the light of the fire. There were four extra cartridges for Bourbon's gun, in addition to the two that he had taken out when he gave the gun to Artyom. It was surprising that the trader had such an impressive arsenal. Artyom carefully wrapped up five of the cartridges he found in their cloth and put them into his rucksack and he put one in the Kalashnikov. The weapon was in excellent condition: thoroughly oiled and looked after. The lock moved smoothly, giving off a dull click when pushed and the safety catch was a bit stiff. All this indicated that the gun was practically new. The handle fitted comfortably into his hand and its shank was well polished. The weapon gave off a feeling of reliability and encouraged calmness and confidence. Artyom immediately decided that if he were to take any one thing from Bourbon it would be this gun.

The 7.62 cartridges that Bourbon had promised him for his 'hoe' weren't there. It wasn't clear how Bourbon had been planning to pay Artyom. Artyom thought about it and came to the conclusion that it may be that Bourbon hadn't been planning to give him a thing but, having passed through the dangerous part, he would sling a shot into the back of Artyom's head and throw him down a shaft and think no more of it. And if anyone had asked him about Artyom's whereabouts then he would have any number of answers: anything can happen in the metro and well, the boy agreed himself to come along.

Apart from various rags, a map of the metro imprinted with notations that only its dead owner would understand, and a hundred grammes of weed, he found a few pieces of smoked meat in plastic bags and a notebook at the bottom of the rucksack. Artyom didn't read the book and he was disappointed in the rest of the stuff. In the depths of his soul, he had hoped to find something mysterious, maybe something precious – the reason that Bourbon was so intent on getting through the tunnel to *Sukharevskaya*. He decided that Bourbon was a messenger or maybe a smuggler or something of the kind. This, at least, explained his determination to get through the damn tunnel at any price and his readiness to be generous. But since there was not much left in the rucksack after he'd pulled out the last pair of linen pieces, Artyom decided that the reason for his insistence had to have been something else. Artyom wracked his brains for a long while about what Bourbon needed at *Sukharevskaya* but he couldn't think of anything plausible.

Then he remembered that he had left the poor man in the middle of the tunnel, left him to the rats, even though he had planned to go back and do something about the body. True, he had only a vague idea of how to give the trader his final honours and what to do with the corpse. Burn it? But you needed strong nerves for that, and the suffocating smoke and the stink of the burning meat and burning hair was sure to filter through to the station, and then he wouldn't be able to avoid unpleasantness. Dragging the body to the station would be heavy and awful. It's one thing to pull a man along by the wrists if you think he's alive and you're pushing away all thoughts of the fact that he is not breathing and has no pulse, but it's another thing to pull along a corpse. So what, then? Just like Bourbon lied to him about his payment, he might have been lying about his friends here at the station. Then Artyom, having dragged the body back here, might just be putting himself in a worse situation.

'So what do you do here with those that die?' Artyom asked Khan after a long bout of thinking.

'What do you mean, my friend?' Khan answered a question with a question. 'Are you talking about the souls of the deceased or about their perished bodies?'

'About the corpses,' Artyom growled. He was becoming fed up with his talk of the netherworld.

'There are two tunnels that go from *Prospect Mir* to *Sukharevskaya*,' Khan said and Artyom thought to himself that trains went in two directions so they always needed two tunnels. So why would Bourbon, knowing about the second tunnel, want to go towards his fate? Was there an even greater danger hiding in the second tunnel? 'But you can only go through it alone,' the man continued, 'because in the second tunnel, near our station, the ground sags, the floor has collapsed and now there's some kind of deep ravine where, according to local legend, a whole train fell through the ground. If you stand on one end of this ravine, it doesn't matter which, then you can't see the other end, and the light of even the strongest flashlight won't illuminate the depths. And so all sorts of blockheads say that it's a bottomless abyss. This ravine is our cemetery. We put all our corpses in there.'

Artyom started to feel ill when he realized that he would have to go back to the place where Khan had picked him up, to drag Bourbon's rat-gnawed body to the station and then to the ravine in the second tunnel. He tried to convince himself that throwing the corpse into the ravine was the same, in essence, as throwing it into a tunnel because you couldn't call either one a burial. But just when he was ready to believe that leaving everything as it was was the best solution to the situation, Bourbon's face appeared in front of his eyes with amazing clarity saying, 'I've died.' Artyom immediately was drenched with sweat. He got up with difficulty, put his new machine gun on his shoulder and said:

'OK, I'm off. I promised him. We had an agreement. I need to.' And with that he started to walk down the hall with stiff legs and onto the iron stairs which led down to the tunnel from the platform.

It was necessary to turn on his flashlight even before he went down the stairs. Thundering down the stairs, Artyom stopped dead for a moment, not wanting to step any further. A heavy air blew a rotting smell in his face, and for an instant his muscles refused to obey him. He tried to force himself to take another step. When he overcame his fear and repulsion and started to walk on, a heavy palm was placed on his shoulder. He cried out in surprise and turned around sharply, his chest tight, understanding that he wouldn't have time to grab the machine gun from his shoulder, he wouldn't have time for anything . . .

It was Khan.

'Don't be scared,' he said to Artyom to calm him. 'I was just testing you. You don't need to go. Your friend's body isn't there anymore.'

Artyom stared at him uncomprehendingly.

'While you were sleeping, I completed the funeral rite. You have no reason to go. The tunnel is empty.' And, turning his back to Artyom, Khan wandered back toward the arches.

Feeling enormous relief, the young man hurried after him. Catching up to Khan in ten paces, Artyom asked him in an emotional voice:

'But why did you do that and why didn't you tell me? You told me yourself that it didn't matter if he stayed in the tunnel or if he was brought to the station.'

'For me it doesn't matter at all.' Khan shrugged his shoulders. 'But to you it was important. I know that your journey has a purpose and that your path is long and difficult. I don't understand what your mission is but its burden will be too heavy for you alone so I decided to help you a bit.' He looked over at Artyom with a smile.

When they had returned to the fire and sat down on the creased tarpaulin, Artyom couldn't help but ask:

'What did you mean when you mentioned my mission? Did I say something in my sleep?'

'No, my friend, you were silent as you slept. But I had a vision and in it I was asked to help by a person who shares part of my name. I was warned of your arrival, and that's why I went out to meet you and picked you up, when you were crawling along with your friend's corpse.'

'That's why?' Artyom looked at him distrustfully. 'I thought it was because you heard shots . . .'

'I heard the shots, there was a loud echo here. But you don't really think that I would go into the tunnel every time I hear a shot? I would have come to the end of my life's path a lot sooner and completely ignominiously if I had done so. But this was an exception.'

'And what about the person who shares part of your name?'

'I can't say who that is, I've never seen him before and have never spoken with him but you know him. You ought to understand this yourself. I've only seen him once and even then not in real life but I immediately felt his colossal strength. He commanded me to help a youth who would come from the northern tunnel and your image stood before me. This was all a dream, but the feeling that it was real

115

was so great that when I woke up I couldn't make out the difference between dream and reality. This powerful man with a bright shaved head, dressed all in white . . . You know him?'

At this point Artyom shook and it was as if everything was swimming before him, and the image that Khan was describing was clear in his mind. The man who shared half a name with his rescuer . . . was Hunter! Khan, Hun . . . Artyom had had a similar vision: when he couldn't decide whether to embark on this journey, he saw Hunter but not in the long black raincoat which he'd worn at *VDNKh* on that memorable day, but in the formless snowy-white garments.

'Yes. I know this man,' Artyom said, looking at Khan in a totally new way.

'He invaded my dreams and I usually never forgive that. But everything was different with him,' Khan said distractedly. 'He needed my help just as you did, and he didn't order me to do it, didn't ask me to submit to his will but it was more like he was asking me persistently. He wasn't able to crawl inside and wander through someone else's thoughts, but he was having a hard time, a very hard time. He was thinking about you in desperation and needed a helping hand, a shoulder to lean on. I extended a hand to him and gave him my shoulder. I went to meet you.'

Artyom was buried in thoughts that were seething and floating up to his consciousness one after the other and dissolving, never making it into words, and then sinking back down to the depths of his mind. His tongue was stiff and the young man took a long time to conjure up even a word. Could this man have really known of his arrival beforehand? Could Hunter have somehow warned him? Was Hunter alive or had he been turned into a bodyless shadow? He was going to have to believe in this nightmarish and delirious story of the nether-world that had been described by Khan – but it was easier and more pleasant to tell himself that the man was just crazy. But the most important thing was that this man knew about the task that faced him – he had called it a 'mission' and though he was probably having a hard time figuring out what it was, he had understood its importance and gravity.

'Where are you going?' Khan asked Artyom quietly, calmly looking him in the eye as though he was reading his thoughts. 'Tell me where your path lies and I will help you make your next step towards your goal if it is within my power. He asked me to do that.'

'*Polis*,' Artyom exhaled. 'I need to get to *Polis*.'

'And how do you intend to get there from this godforsaken station?' Khan inquired. 'My friend, you should have gone up to the Ring from *Prospect Mir* to *Kurskaya* or to *Kievskaya*.'

'The Hansa are there and I don't know anyone there so I wouldn't be able to get through. And anyway, now I can't return to *Prospect Mir*. I'm afraid that I won't be able to stand another journey through that tunnel. I was thinking of getting to *Turgenevskaya*. I looked at an old map and it says that there's a passage there to *Sretensky Bulvar*. There's a half-built tunnel there and you can get to *Trubnaya* through it.' Artyom took the charred map out of his pocket. 'From *Trubnaya* there's a passage to *Tsvetnoi Bulvar*, I saw it on the map and from there, if everything is fine, you can get to *Polis* directly.'

'No,' Khan said sadly, shaking his head. 'You won't get to *Polis* via that route. The map is lying. They printed them way before everything happened. They describe metro lines that were never fully built, they describe stations that have collapsed, burying hundreds of innocents and they don't say anything about the frightening dangers that are hidden along the way and will make most itineraries impossible. Your map is as stupid and naive as a three-year-old child. Give it to me.' He held out his hand.

Artyom obediently gave him the piece of paper. Khan immediately screwed up the map and threw it into the fire. Artyom thought that this was a bit excessive but had decided not to argue about it, when Khan said:

'And now show me the map that you found in your friend's rucksack.'

Rummaging through his things, Artyom found the map but he wasn't in a rush to give it to Khan, thinking about the unfortunate fate that may lie ahead of it. He didn't want to be left without any map. Khan noticed his trepidation and hurried to reassure him:

'I won't do anything to it, don't worry. And trust me, I never do anything without a reason. You might have the impression that some of my actions have no point and are even a little crazy. But there is a point. You just don't get it, because your perception and understanding of the world is limited. You are only at the beginning of your path. You are too young to really know some things.'

Artyom gave Khan Bourbon's map – he didn't have the strength to object. It was a yellowed piece of card the size of a postcard and it had pretty sparkling balls on it and the words 'Happy New Year 2007!'

'It's very heavy,' Khan said hoarsely, and Artyom turned his attention to Khan's palm which held the piece of card. It suddenly fell to the ground as though the card weighed more than a kilo. A second ago, Artyom hadn't noticed anything heavy about it when he held it in his hand. Paper is paper.

'This map is much wiser than yours,' Khan said. 'It contains such knowledge that I don't believe that it belonged to the person who was travelling with you. It's not even that it is marked up with all these notations and signs, although they probably say a lot. No, it has something about it . . .'

His words broke off sharply.

Artyom looked up and peered at Khan. Khan's forehead was carved with deep wrinkles, and the dying fire appeared to flash in his eyes. His face had changed so much that Artyom was frightened and wanted to get out of the station as soon as possible, to go anywhere, even back through the terrible tunnel that he had managed to get through with such difficulty.

'Give it back to me.' Khan wasn't asking but was rather giving an order. 'I will give you another one and you won't know the difference. And I'll throw in anything else you want,' he continued.

'Take it, it's yours.' Artyom easily yielded it, lightly spitting as he uttered the words of agreement.

Khan suddenly moved away from the fire so that his face was in the shadows. Artyom guessed that he was trying to take control of himself and didn't want him to be witness to his inner struggle.

'You see, my friend.' His voice resounded in the darkness, sort of weakly and indecisively, without the power and will it had possessed just a moment before. 'That's not a map. I mean, that's not simply a map. It's a Guide to the metro. Yes, yes, there's no doubt that's what it is. The person who holds it can get across the whole metro in two days because this map is . . . alive or something. It will tell you itself where to go and how to go, it will warn you of dangers . . . That is, it will lead you on your way. That's why it's called a Guide,' Khan moved towards to the fire again, 'with a capital letter. I've heard of them. There are only a few of them in the whole metro and this may be the last one. It's the legacy of one of the most powerful magicians of the last era.'

'The one who sits at the deepest point in the metro?' Artyom decided to flash some knowledge at Khan but immediately stopped short. Khan's face went dark.

'Never speak lightly about things you don't know anything about! You don't know what happens at the deepest point in the metro –

and even I only know a little, and God forbid we ever find out. But I can swear to you that whatever happened there dramatically differs from whatever you heard from your friends. So don't repeat other people's idle imaginings because one day you'll have to pay for it. And it has nothing to do with the Guide.'

'Well, anyway,' Artyom hurried to assure him, not wanting to miss a chance to switch the conversation to a less dangerous tack, 'you can keep the Guide for yourself. After all, I don't know how to use it. And then I'm so grateful to you for rescuing me that even giving you this map doesn't seem to repay the favour.'

'That's true,' the wrinkles on Khan's face smoothed out, and his voice became soft again. 'You won't know how to use it for a long while yet. So if you give it to me, we'll be quits. I have a normal map of the metro lines and if you want I can copy the markings of the Guide onto it and you can have it instead. And then . . .' He fumbled in his bags. 'I can offer you this thing,' and he brought out a strangely shaped flashlight. 'It doesn't need batteries. It's made so that you just charge it like this manually – can you see the two little knobs? You have to press them with your fingers and they manufacture the current themselves and the flashlight shines. It's not too bright of course but there are sometimes situations when this beam seems brighter than the mercury lamps at *Polis* . . . It has saved me many times, and I hope that it will prove useful. Take it, it's yours. Take it, take it, the trade isn't fair anyway – it's me who owes you and not the reverse.'

In Artyom's opinion, the exchange was actually unusually advantageous. What did he need with a map with mystical properties, if he was deaf to its voice? He would have thrown it away anyway, after turning it over again and again and vainly attempting to read the curlicues painted on it.

'So now, the route which you sketched out won't take you anywhere except into an abyss.' Khan continued the interrupted conversation, holding the map with great care in his hands. 'Here you go, take my old one and follow it.' He held out a tiny map, printed on the other side of an old pocket calendar. 'You were talking about the passage from *Turgenevskaya* to *Sretensky Bulvar*? Don't tell me you don't know the evil reputation of this station and the long tunnel that goes from here to *Kitai Gorod*?'

'Well, I have been told that you mustn't go into it alone, that it's only safe to go through in a caravan, and I was thinking to go in a caravan until *Turgenevskaya* and then to run off from them into the transfer passage – they're not going to run after me after all . . .' Artyom answered, feeling vague thoughts swarming in his head.

'There isn't a transfer passage there. The arches are walled up. You didn't know that?'

How could he have forgotten! Of course, he had been told about this before but it had flown out of his head . . . The Reds were frightened of the demons in that tunnel and they walled up the only way to *Turgenevskaya*.

'But is there no other passage there?' he asked carefully.

'No, and the map is silent about it. The passage to lines that are actually constructed doesn't begin at *Turgenevskaya*. But even if the passage did exist I'm not sure that you have enough courage to separate from the group and go into it. Especially if you listen to the latest rumours about that lovely little place while you're waiting to join the caravan.'

'So what should I do?' Artyom asked despondently, scrutinizing the little calendar.

'It's possible to get to *Kitai Gorod*. Oh, now that's a curious station, and the morals there are very amusing – but there, at least, you won't disappear without a trace in such a way that your closest friends wonder to themselves if you ever existed at all. At *Turgenevskaya* that can happen . . . From *Kitai Gorod*, follow me now,' he was tracing a finger on the map, 'it's only two stations to *Pushkinskaya*, and there there's a passage to *Chekhovskaya*, and another one there, and then you're at *Polis*. That would be shorter than the route which you were planning.'

Artyom was moving his lips, counting the stations and transfers on each route. However he counted though, the route that Khan suggested was much shorter and less dangerous and it wasn't clear why Artyom hadn't thought of it himself. So there was no choice left.

'You're right,' he said finally. 'And how often do caravans go there?'

'I'm afraid not often. And there is one small but annoying detail: in order to go into the southern tunnel to *Kitai Gorod*, you have to come to our little half-station from the north,' and he pointed at the damned tunnel which Artyom had only barely made it out of. 'Basically, the last caravan to the south left a while ago now, and we're hoping that there's another group planning on coming through soon. Talk to some people, ask around, but don't talk too much. There're some cutthroats around here and they can't be trusted . . . OK, I'll go with you so you don't get into anything stupid,' he added after thinking it over.

Artyom was going to put on his rucksack when Khan stopped him with a gesture: 'Don't worry about your things. People are so scared of me here that no riff-raff would dare even look at my lair. And while you're here, you're under my protection.'

Artyom left his rucksack by the fire but he took his machine gun with him anyway, not wanting to be separated from his new treasure, and he hurried to follow Khan who was walking in a leisurely fashion towards the fires that were burning on the other side of the hall. He noticed with surprise how under-nourished tramps, wrapped in stinking rags scuttled away from them as they passed and Artyom thought that people really were probably afraid of Khan here. He wondered why . . .

The first fire swam by but Khan didn't slow his pace. It was a very tiny little fire, barely burning, and there were two figures sitting next to it, tightly pressed to each other, a man and a woman. They were whispering quietly in an unknown language, and their whispers dispersed, not quite reaching Artyom's ears. Artyom was so fascinated that he almost turned his head. He could hardly resist looking at this pair.

In front of them was another fire, a big, bright one and a whole camp of people were settled around it. Fierce looking peasant types were sitting there, warming their hands. Loud laughter thundered and the air was so torn with the sound of noisy arguing that Artyom became a bit scared and slowed his pace. But Khan calmly and confidently walked up to the seated men, greeted them and sat down by the fire so that Artyom could do nothing else but follow his example and sit down next to him.

'. . . He's looking at himself and sees that he has the same rash on his hands, and something is swelling and hard and really painful in his armpits. Imagine the horror, fuck's sake . . . Different people behave in different ways. Some shoot themselves straight away, some go crazy and start throwing themselves at other people trying to hug them so they won't die alone. Some run into the tunnel beyond the Ring to the backwaters so they won't infect other people . . . There are all sorts of people. So this guy, as soon as he sees all this, asks his doctor: is there any chance I can get better? The doctor tells him straight: none. After the appearance of this rash you have about two weeks to live. And the battalion commander, I see, is already quietly taking his Makarov out of its holster just in case the guy starts to get violent . . .' The man speaking was a thin old guy with a bristly chin in a quilted jacket with a voice faltering out genuine anxiety as he looked at the grey watery eyes around him.

And though Artyom did not understand what it was all about, the spirit with which the story was told and the pregnant silence among the recently riotous group made him shudder and ask Khan quietly about it in order not to draw any attention to himself.

'What's he talking about?'

'The plague,' Khan answered heavily. 'It's started.'

Those words emitted the stench of decomposed bodies and the greasy smoke of cremation fires and echoes of alarm bells and the howl of manual sirens.

At *VDNKh* and its surroundings there had never been an epidemic; rats as carriers of infection were destroyed, and there were also several good doctors at the station. Artyom had only read in books about fatal infectious diseases. He came across some of them when he was very young and they had left a deep trace in his memory and long inhabited the world of his childhood dreams and fears. Therefore when he heard the word 'plague' he felt a cold sweat on his back and a little faint. He didn't ask Khan anything more, but listened with an unhealthy attention to the story of the thin man in the quilted coat.

'But Ryzhii wasn't that type, he wasn't a psycho. He stood there silently for a minute and says: "Give me some cartridges and I'll go. I can't stay here with you anymore." I heard the battalion commander sigh with relief straight away. It was clear: there's little joy in shooting one of your own even if he's sick. They gave Ryzhii two horns. And he went to the north-east, beyond *Aviamotornaya*. And we didn't see him again. But the battalion commander asks our doctor afterwards about how long it takes the disease to act. The doctor says the incubation period is a week. If nothing appears a week after contact with it then you're not infected. So the battalion commander then decides: we'll leave the station and stay there for a week and then we'll see. We can't be inside the Ring, basically – if the infection penetrates the Ring then the whole metro will die. And so they stayed away for a whole week. They didn't even go up to each other – because how could we know who was infected among us. So there was this other guy, who we called Cup because he really liked to drink. Everyone kept away from him since he'd hung out with Rizhii a lot. When he approached anyone they would run to the other end of the station. Some guy even pointed his barrel at him, telling him

122

to, like, push off. When Cup ran out of water, the guys shared with him of course – but they did it by putting it on the floor and then walking away and no one got near. After a week he went missing. Then people were saying different things, some were even telling lies and saying that some beast had dragged him off but the tunnels there are quiet and clean. I personally think that he noticed a rash on himself and his armpits were hurting so he ran off. And no one else from our forces was infected and we waited a little longer and then the battalion commander checked everyone himself. Everyone was healthy.'

Artyom noticed that despite this assurance, the space around the story-teller was empty even though there wasn't much space at the fire altogether and everyone was sitting close together, shoulder to shoulder.

'Did it take you a while to get here, brother?' A thick-set bearded man in a leather waistcoat asked him quietly but clearly.

'It's about thirty days since we came out from *Aviamotornaya*,' the thin guy replied looking at him uneasily.

'So I have news for you. There's plague at *Aviamotornaya*. There's plague there – do you hear?! The Hansa have closed it as well as *Taganskaya* and *Kurskaya*. They've called a quarantine. I have acquaintances there, Hansa citizens. And there's flame-throwers standing at the passages to *Taganskaya* and *Kurskaya* and everyone who comes within range is blasted. They're calling it disinfection. Apparently, some have an incubation period of a week and for others it takes longer, so you obviously brought the infection back,' he concluded, viciously lowering his voice.

'What, oh come on guys? I'm healthy! See for yourself!' the little guy jumped up from his place and started to convulsively strip off his quilted coat and to show the dirty body underneath it, hurrying, afraid that he wouldn't convince them.

The tension mounted. There was no one left near the thin man, they'd all crowded at the other side of the fire. People were talking nervously and Artyom heard the quiet clanking of gun locks. He looked at Khan questioningly, pulling his gun from his shoulder to firing position, pointed forward. Khan kept his silence but stopped him with a gesture. Then he quickly got up and walked away from the fire without a sound, taking Artyom with him. At about ten paces he froze and continued to look at what was happening.

Quick and busy movements were visible in the light of the fire and they looked like some kind of primitive reckless dance. Talk in the crowd went silent and the action continued in ominous silence. Finally, the man succeeded in pulling off his undershirt and he exclaimed triumphantly:

'See! Look! I am clean! I am healthy! There's nothing there! I'm healthy!'

The bearded guy in the waistcoat pulled a board out of the fire that was burning on one end and carefully approached the thin guy looking at him with disgust. The skin of the overly talkative guy was dark with dirt and glossy with grease, but there was no trace of a rash as far as the bearded guy could see and so after a thorough inspection he commanded him:

'Raise your arms!'

The unfortunate fellow quickly threw his arms up, giving the people crowded on the other side of the fire a view of his armpits which were overgrown with fine hairs. The bearded man made a show of holding his nose as he got closer, meticulously examining and looking for buboes, but he couldn't find any symptoms of plague.

'I am healthy! Healthy! Are you convinced now?' The little man cried out, almost hysterical now.

There was a hostile whisper in the crowd. Taking stock of the overall mood and not wishing to succumb to it, the thickset man declared:

'Well, let's assume that you're healthy. That still means nothing!'

'Why does it mean nothing?' The thin man was taken aback and immediately drooped.

'That's right. You might have not got sick yourself. You might be immune. But you can still carry the infection. You had contact with that Rizhii guy? Were you in the same force? Did you talk with him, share the same water? Did you shake his hand? You shook his hand, don't lie brother.'

'So what, what if I shook his hand? I didn't get sick . . .' The man replied at a loss of what to say. He was frozen powerless, and persecuted by the gaze of the crowd.

'So. It isn't impossible that you're infectious, brother. So, I'm sorry but we can't risk it. It's a prophylactic brother, you see?' The bearded man undid the buttons of his waistcoat, baring a brown leather holster. There were encouraging outbursts and more sounds of snapping gun-locks among the crowd at the fire.

'Guys! But I'm healthy! I didn't get sick! Look, see!' The thin man again raised his arms but now everyone just winced disdainfully and with evident aversion.

The thickset man took his pistol from its holster and pointed it at the guy who it seemed couldn't understand what was going on and he was muttering that he was healthy, squeezing his quilted coat to his chest: it was chilly and he had already started to get cold.

Then Artyom couldn't stand it. Pulling at his gun-lock, he stepped toward the crowd, not exactly knowing what he was about to do. There was a lump in the pit of his stomach and one stuck in his throat too so he wouldn't be able to utter a word. But something in this person, in his empty and desperate eyes, in the senseless, mechanical mutterings, had hooked into Artyom and had pushed him to take a step forward. It wasn't clear what he was going to do next but there was a hand on his shoulder and God what a heavy hand it was!

'Stop,' Khan ordered him quietly, and Artyom was as frozen as a corpse, feeling that his brittle determination had been shattered against the granite of someone else's will. 'You can't help him. You will either be killed or you will bring fury on yourself. Your mission will not be completed in either case and you should remember that.'

At that moment the thin man suddenly twitched, yelled, clinging to his quilted jacket and with a wave he jumped onto the path and dashed into the black trough of the southern tunnel with super-human speed, squealing, as wild as an animal. The bearded man jerked and was after him, trying to take aim at his back but then stopped and waved a hand. This was already going too far, and all of them stood on the platform knew it. It wasn't clear if the chased man remembered what he was running into, perhaps he was hoping for a miracle, or maybe fear had wiped everything out of his head.

After several minutes, there was a howl which tore painfully into the dull silence of the terrible tunnel and the echoes of his footsteps went suddenly silent, as if someone had turned off the sound. Even the echo died immediately, and silence reigned again. This was so strange, so unusual to human hearing and reason, that the imagination tried to fill the gaps and it seemed to them that they could hear a far-off cry. But everyone understood that it was an illusion.

'Jackals always know when one of their pack is sick, my friend.' said Khan and Artyom almost fell backwards as he noticed the predatory fire in Khan's eyes. 'The sick one is a burden to the pack and a threat to its health. So the pack kills the sick one. They tear him to pieces. To pieces,' he repeated, as though he was relishing what he'd said.

'But these aren't jackals,' Artyom finally found the courage to object to Khan, who he was suddenly believing to be the reincarnation of Genghis Khan. 'These are people!'

'And what would you have them do?' Khan parried. 'Degradation. Our medicine is at the level of jackals. And there's as much humanity in us too. So . . .'

Artyom knew how to object to this too but arguing with his only protector at this wild station was not appropriate. But Khan who had been expecting an objection evidently decided that Artyom had given up and he turned the conversation to a different subject.

'So now, while the subject of infectious diseases and the methods to fight them will dominate our friends' discussions, we need to forge some iron. Otherwise they might decide not to move ahead for weeks. Even though weeks around here can fly past unnoticed.'

The people at the fire were excitedly discussing what had happened. They were all tense and upset, the spectral shadow of the terrible danger had covered them, and now they were trying to decide what to do next, but their thoughts, like those of lab mice in a labyrinth, were going in circles as they helplessly poked into blind alleys, senselessly rushing back and forth, unable to find the exit.

'Our friends are very close to panic,' Khan commented smugly, smiling and looking gaily at Artyom. 'Furthermore, they suspect that they just lynched an innocent man and this act does not stimulate rational thinking. Now we are dealing not with a collective but with a pack. A perfect mental state for the manipulation of their psyches! The conditions couldn't be better.'

Artyom felt uneasy again seeing the triumphant look on Khan's face. He tried to smile in response – after all Khan wanted to help him – but the smile came out pitifully and unconvincing.

'The main thing now is authority. Strength. The pack respects strength, and not logical argument,' Khan added, nodding. 'Stand and watch. You'll be able to go on your way in less than a day's time.' And with these words, he took several long strides and wedged himself into the crowd.

'We can't stay here!' His voice thundered and the conversation in the crowd went silent.

People listened to him carefully . . . Khan was using his powerful almost hypnotic gift of persuasion. With his first words, there was an acute feeling of danger hanging above each person, and Artyom doubted that anyone would choose to remain at the station after this.

'He infected the air here! If we breathe this much longer then it's over. Bacilli are everywhere here, and we will definitely get hooked by it if we stay here any longer. We'll die like rats and we'll rot right in the middle of this hall on the floor. No one will choose to come and help us – there isn't a hope! We can only count on ourselves. We need to get out of this demonic station, which is seething with microbes, as soon as we can. If we leave now all together then it won't be hard to get through the tunnel. But we have to do it quickly!'

People made noises of agreement. The majority of them couldn't, like Artyom, protest against the colossal force of Khan's persuasion. In following Khan's words, Artyom obediently worried about all the circumstances and feelings that were proposed in them: the feelings of threat, the fear, the panic, the weak hope which was growing as Khan continued talking about his suggestions for escape.

'How many of you are there?'

Immediately several people started counting the gathered group. There were eight men, not counting Artyom and Khan.

'That's means there's nothing to wait for! We're already ten people so we can get through!' Khan stated and, not allowing the people to come to their senses, he continued, 'Gather your things, we need to leave within the hour! Quick, let's get back to the fire, you also need to get your belongings,' Khan whispered to Artyom, tugging him towards their little camp. 'The most important thing is that they don't realize what's going on. If we delay, they will start to question whether it is worth it for them to leave and go to *Chistye Prudy*. Some of them were headed in the opposite direction, and others just live here, and they have nowhere else to go. It seems that I'll have to take you to *Kitai Gorod*, otherwise, I'm afraid that they'll lose direction or they'll just forget where they're going and why.'

Quickly putting Bourbon's fancy things into his rucksack while Khan rolled up his tarpaulin and put out the fire, Artyom saw what was going on at the other end of the hall. People who were initially animated and quickly gathering up their households were moving less and less certainly. Someone now was squatting by the fire and another was wandering towards the centre of the platform for something, and there were two people discussing something amongst themselves. Having understood what was going on, Artyom pulled on Khan's sleeve.

'They're discussing it,' Artyom warned him.

'Alas, it's an inherent human feature to discuss things,' Khan answered. 'Even if their will is suppressed and even though they are

127

in fact hypnotized, they will still gravitate towards each other and start talking. Man is a social being, and there's nothing you can do about it. In any other situation, I would accept any human activity as a divine concept or as the inevitable result of evolution, depending on who I was talking to. But in this situation, the fact that they're thinking is not good. We need to interfere here, my young friend, and to direct their thoughts along the most useful path,' he concluded, putting his enormous travelling pack on his back.

The fire was put out and the dense, almost tangible darkness squeezed them on all sides. Reaching into his pocket and getting out his flashlight, Artyom pushed on its button. Something buzzed inside the device and the lamp came to life. An uneven, flickering light splashed out from it.

'Go on, go on, press it again, don't be afraid,' Khan encouraged him, 'it can work better than that.'

When they went up to the others, the stale tunnel drafts had had time to blow through their minds so that they were less than convinced in Khan's proposition. The strong man with the beard stepped forward.

'Listen, brother,' he carelessly turned to Artyom's companion.

Without even looking at him, Artyom could feel the air around Khan electrify. It seemed that such familiarity had incensed Khan. Of all the people Artyom knew, it was Khan that he would least like to see furious. There was also the hunter, but he seemed to Artyom to be so much more cold-blooded that it was impossible to imagine him in a rage. He would probably kill people with the same expression on his face that other people have when they were washing mushrooms or making tea.

'We've been discussing it and we think,' the thickset man continued, 'that you're chasing snowstorms here. For me, for example, it's completely inconvenient to go to *Kitai Gorod*. And those guys are against it too. Right Semenych?' He turned for the support of the crowd. Someone in the crowd nodded in agreement, though rather timidly. 'Most of us were going to *Prospect Mir*, to the Hansa, until the business in the tunnel started up. So we're waiting here and then moving on. Nothing is left here anyway. We burned his things. And don't try to get us thinking about the air. This isn't pulmonary plague. And if we're infected, then we're already infected and there's nothing to be done. It's more likely that there wasn't any infection here to start with so you can get lost, brother, with your propositions!' The bearded man's manner was becoming even more familiar.

Artyom was a little taken aback by this onslaught. But, stealing a look at his companion, he felt that the guy was in trouble. There was that blazing orange internal flame in Khan's eyes and there was such savage malice and power coming from him that Artyom felt a chill, and the hair on his head began to rise, and he wanted to bare his teeth and roar.

'Why did you kill him if there was no infection after all?' Khan asked insinuatingly, with a deliberately soft voice.

'It was prophylactic!' the thickset man answered with an insolent look.

'No, my friend, this isn't medicine. This was a crime. What gave you the right to do it?'

'Don't call me friend, I'm not your dog, OK?' the bearded man growled. 'What right did I have? The right of the strong! Haven't you heard of it? And you're not exactly . . . We could get you and your foundling too! As a prophylactic measure! Got it?' With a gesture already familiar to Artyom, the man pulled open his waistcoat and put his hand on his holster.

This time Khan didn't manage to hold Artyom back and the bearded man was in the crosshairs of Artyom's machine gun before he could even unbutton his holster. Artyom was breathing heavily and could hear his heart beating and the blood pounding in his temples, and there wasn't a reasonable thought in his head. He knew only one thing: if the bearded man said one more thing or if his hand continued on its way to his pistol's handle then he would immediately pull the trigger. Artyom didn't want to die like that poor guy had: he wouldn't let the pack tear him to pieces.

The bearded guy froze in place and didn't make a move, with evil flashing in his dark eyes. And then something incomprehensible happened. Khan suddenly took a big step forward, looked the man in the eye and said quietly:

'Stop it. You will obey me. Or you will die.'

The threatening gaze of the bearded man faded, and his hands were powerless, hanging down beside his body. It looked so unnatural that Artyom had no doubt that it was Khan's words and not the machine gun that had had an effect on the man.

'Never discuss the rights of the strong. You are too weak to do that,' said Khan and he returned to Artyom, without even disarming the man.

The thickset man stood still, looking from side to side. People were waiting to hear what Khan was going to say next. His control over the situation had been restored.

'We will consider the matter closed and that consensus has been reached. We leave in fifteen minutes.' And turning to Artyom he said, 'People, you say? No, my friend, they are beasts. They are a pack of jackals. They were preparing to tear us apart. And they would have. But they forgot one thing. They are jackals but I am a wolf. And there are some stations where I am known only by that name.'

Artyom was silent, dumbstruck by what he had seen, finally understanding who Khan reminded him of.

'But you are a wolf cub,' Khan added after a minute, not turning around but Artyom heard the unexpectedly warm notes in his voice.

CHAPTER 7

The Khanate of Darkness

The tunnel was absolutely empty and clean. The ground was dry, there was a pleasant breeze blowing into their faces, there wasn't even one rat, and there were no suspicious looking side passages and gaping patches of blackness to the sides, only a few locked doors, and it seemed that one could live in this tunnel just as well as at any of the stations. But more than that, this totally unnatural calm and cleanliness not only meant they weren't on their guard but it instantly dissipated any fear of death and disappearance. Here the legends about disappeared people started to seem like silly fabrications and Artyom already started to wonder if the wild scene with the unfortunate man who they thought had the plague had actually happened. Maybe it was just a little nightmare that had visited him while he snoozed on the tarpaulin by the wandering philosopher's fire.

He and Khan were bringing up the rear since Khan was concerned that the men might break away from the group one by one – and then, according to him, no one would reach *Kitai Gorod*. Now he was quietly walking next to Artyom, calmly, as though nothing had happened, and the deep wrinkles which had cut through his face during the skirmish at *Sukharevskaya*, were now smooth. The storm had passed, and walking next to Artyom there was now a wise and restrained Khan and not a furious, full-grown wolf. But Artyom was sure the transformation would take only a minute.

Understanding that the next opportunity to draw aside the curtain from the metro's mysteries had arisen, he couldn't hold himself back.

'Do you understand what's happening in this tunnel?'

'No one knows that, including me,' Khan answered reluctantly. 'Yes, there are some things that even I know exactly nothing about. The only thing I can tell you is that it's an abyss. I call this place the black hole . . . You probably have never seen a star? Or did you say you once saw one? And do you know anything about the cosmos? Well, a dying star can look like a hole if, when it goes out, it is affected by its own incredibly powerful energy and it starts to consume itself, taking matter from the outside to the inside, to its centre, which is becoming smaller all the time, but more dense and heavier. And the denser it becomes, the more its force of gravity grows. This process is irreversible and it's like an avalanche: with the ever-increasing gravity, the growing quantity of matter is drawn faster and faster to the heart of the monster. At a certain stage, its power achieves such magnitudes that it sucks in its neighbours, and all the matter that is located within the bounds of its influence, and finally, even light waves. The gigantic force allows it to devour the rays of other suns, and the space around it is dead and black – nothing that falls into its possession has the strength to pull itself away. This is a star of darkness, a black sun, and around it is only cold and darkness.' He went quiet, listening to the conversation of the people ahead of them.

'But what does that have to do with the tunnel?' Artyom couldn't resist asking after a five-minute silence.

'You know, I have the gift of foresight. I sometimes succeed in seeing into the future, into the past, or sometimes I can transport my mind to other places. Sometimes it's unclear, it's hidden from me, like, for example, I don't know how your journey will end – your future is generally a mystery to me. It's kind of like looking through dirty water and you can't make out anything. But when I try to look into what happened here or to understand the nature of this place – there's only blackness in front of me, and the rays of my thoughts don't return from the absolute darkness of this tunnel. That's why I call it the black hole. That's all I can tell you about it.' And he went silent, but after a few moments, he added, 'And that's why I'm here.'

'So you don't know why sometimes this tunnel is completely safe and other times it swallows people? And why it only takes people travelling alone?'

'I know nothing more about it that you do, even though I've been trying for three years to figure out this mystery. So far, in vain.'

Their steps resounded with a distant echo. The air here was transparent, and breathing was surprisingly easy, and the darkness didn't seem frightening. Khan's words didn't put him on his guard or worry him; Artyom thought that his companion was so gloomy not because of the secrets and hazards of the tunnel but because of the futility of his investigations. His preoccupation was self-conscious and even ridiculous in Artyom's opinion. Here was the passage and there were no threats here, it was straight and empty . . . A boisterous melody even started to play in his head, and apparently it then became external without his noticing, because Khan suddenly looked at him mockingly and asked:

'So then, isn't this fun? It's nice here, right? So quiet, so clean, yes?'

'Aha!' Artyom agreed joyfully.

And he felt so light and free in his soul because Khan had understood his mood and was also affected by it . . . He is also walking and smiling and not burdened with heavy thoughts, he also believes that this tunnel is . . .

'So now, cover your eyes, and I'll take you by the hand so you won't stumble . . . Do you see anything?' Khan asked with interest, softly squeezing Artyom's wrist.

'No, I don't see anything, only a little light from the flashlights through my eyelids,' Artyom said a little disappointedly, squeezing his eyes closed obediently – and suddenly he quietly yelped.

'There – you made it!' Khan noted with satisfaction. 'It's beautiful, yes?'

'Amazing . . . It's like when . . . There's no ceiling, and everything is so blue . . . My God, what beauty! And how easy to breathe!'

'That, my friend, is the sky. It's curious, no? If you relax and close your eyes in the right mood here, then lots of people see it. It's strange, of course . . . Even those who have never been to the surface see it. And the feeling is as though you've landed at the surface . . . before it all happened.'

'And you, do you see it?' Artyom asked blissfully, not wanting to open his eyes.

'No,' Khan said darkly. 'Almost everyone sees it but I don't. I only see thick, bright darkness around the tunnel, if you know what I mean. Blackness above, below, and on all sides, and only a small thread of light extends into the tunnel, and we follow it when we're in the labyrinth. Maybe I'm blind. Or maybe everyone else is blind. OK, open your eyes, I'm not a guide dog and I don't intend to take you by the hand to *Kitai Gorod*.' He let go of Artyom's wrist.

Artyom tried to walk on with his eyes squeezed shut but he stumbled on a cross-tie and almost fell to the ground along with his whole load. After that, he reluctantly lifted his eyelids and stayed silent for a long while afterwards, smiling stupidly.

'What was it?' he asked finally.

'Fantasies. Dreams. A mood. Everything together,' Khan replied.

'But it's very changeable. It's not your mood or your dreams. There are a lot of us here and so far nothing has happened, but the mood can change totally, and you will feel it. Look there, we are already coming out at *Turgenevskaya*! We got here fast. But we can't stop here at any cost, not even for a break. People will probably ask to take a break but not everyone feels the tunnel. The majority of them don't even feel what is accessible to you. We need to go on, even though now it will be harder.'

They stepped into the station. The light marble that coated the walls was barely distinguishable from that which covered the walls at *Prospect Mir* and *Sukharevskaya*, but there the walls and ceilings were so smoke-stained and greasy that the stone was almost invisible. Here it was untainted and it was hard not to admire it. People had left this place so long ago that there was no trace of their presence. The station was in surprisingly good condition, as though it had never been flooded, never seen a fire, and if it weren't for the pitch darkness and the layer of dust on the floor, benches and walls, you could have thought that in a minute a stream of passengers would start flowing into it or, after emitting its melodious signal, a train would arrive. It had hardly changed after all these years. His stepfather had described all this with bewilderment and awe.

There weren't any columns in *Turgenevskaya*. Low arches were cut in thick marble at wide intervals. The flashlights of the caravan didn't have enough power to disperse the dusk of the hall and to light the opposite wall so it looked as though there was absolutely nothing beyond the arches, as though there was the end of the universe.

They passed through the station rather quickly and, contrary to Khan's fears, no one expressed the desire to stop for a break. People looked perturbed and they started talking more and more about the fact that they needed to go as fast as they could, and get to an inhabited place.

'Do you feel it, the mood is changing . . .' Khan observed quietly, raising a finger as though trying to feel the direction of the wind. 'We do indeed have to go faster, they'll feel this on their skin no less than I will with my mysticism. But there's something preventing me from continuing on our route. Wait here for a little while . . .'

He took the map that he called the Guide out of his pocket carefully and, having told everyone to stay still, he extinguished his flashlight and took a few long and soft steps and disappeared into the dark.

When he stepped away, one guy came out from among the group

134

and slowly, as though with effort, made his way over to Artyom. He spoke so timidly that at first Artyom didn't recognize the thickset bearded man who had threatened him at *Sukharevskaya*.

'Listen . . . it isn't good that we've stopped here. Tell him, we're afraid. There are a lot of us but anything can happen . . . Damn this tunnel, and damn this station. Tell him we have to go. You hear? Tell him . . . please.' And he looked away and hurried back into the crowd.

This last 'please' made Artyom shudder. He was unpleasantly surprised by it. Taking a few steps forward so that he would be closer to the group and could hear the general conversation, he immediately realized that there was nothing left of his previous good mood.

In his head where a small orchestra had just been playing a bravura march, it was now empty and quiet and he could only hear windy echoes despondently sounding in the tunnels that lay before them. Artyom went quiet. His whole being had frozen, tensely waiting for something, sensing an inevitable change in plans. And he was right. After a fraction of an instant it was as if an invisible shadow swooped in above them and it became cold and very uncomfortable, wiping away all the feelings of peace and confidence which had settled upon them when they were walking through the tunnel. Now Artyom remembered Khan's words about the fact that this wasn't his mood, not his joy, and that a change in circumstances did not depend on him. He nervously turned his flashlight in a circle around him: an oppressive sensation of premonition had piled on top of him. The dusty white marble flared before him dimly, and the dense black curtain under the arches wouldn't be pushed backwards in spite of the panicky flashings of his light. This strengthened the illusion that the world ended beyond the arches. Unable to control himself, Artyom almost ran back to the others.

'Come to us, come, brother,' someone whose face he'd never seen before said to him. They, apparently, were also trying to save the batteries of their flashlights. 'Don't be afraid. You're a person and we're people too. When things like this go on, people have to stick together. Don't you think?'

Artyom willingly acknowledged that there was something in the air. Because he was scared he was unusually chatty, and he started to discuss with the people of the caravan his worries, but his thoughts kept returning to Khan's whereabouts. The man had disappeared over ten minutes before and there was no sign of him. Indeed he knew himself that you shouldn't go into this tunnel alone, you should only go together. How could he have gone off like that, how could he have dared to defy the unwritten law of this place? He couldn't have simply forgotten it, or just decided to trust his wolf's sense of smell. Artyom couldn't believe that. After all Khan had spent three years of his life studying this tunnel. And it didn't take that long to learn the basic rule: never go into the tunnel alone . . .

But Artyom didn't have time to consider what might have happened to his protector up ahead before the man himself appeared noiselessly at his side, and the people were reanimated.

'They don't want to stop here any longer. They're scared. Let's go on, quickly,' Artyom proposed. 'I also feel something's not right here . . .'

'They're not scared yet,' Khan assured him, looking behind him, and Artyom suddenly realized that his hard, husky voice was quivering. Khan continued, 'And you also don't know fear yet so let's not waste breath. I am scared. And remember I don't use words lightly. I am scared because I dipped into the station's gloom. The Guide wouldn't let me take another step, otherwise I would have undoubtedly disappeared. We can't go any further. Something lies ahead . . . But it's dark there and my vision doesn't penetrate and I don't know what exactly is awaiting us there. Look!' He lifted the map up to their eyes with a quick motion. 'Do you see? Shine your flashlight on it! Look at the passage from here to *Kitai Gorod*! Don't tell me you don't notice anything?'

Artyom scrutinized the tiny section of the diagram with such urgency that his eyes hurt. He couldn't make out anything unusual, but he didn't have the courage to admit it to Khan.

'Are you blind? You really don't see anything? It's all black! It's death!' Khan whispered and jerked back the map.

Artyom stared at him cautiously. Khan again seemed like a madman to him. He was remembering the stuff Zhenya had told him about going into the tunnel alone, about the fact that whoever survived the tunnel would go crazy from fright. Could this have happened to Khan?

'And we can't turn back either!' Khan whispered. 'We managed to get through while there was a benevolent mood in there. But now the darkness is unfurling and a storm is brewing. The only thing we can do now is to go forward but not through this tunnel, but through the parallel one. Maybe it's clear right now. Hey!' he shouted at the others. 'You're right! We need to move on. But we can't go along this route. There's destruction and death that way.'

'So how are we going to move on?' asked one of them in puzzlement.

'We'll cross the station and go through the parallel tunnel – that's what we have to do. And as soon as possible!'

'Oh no!' someone in the group burst out. 'Everyone knows that you don't take the reverse direction tunnel if the one you're facing is clear – it's a bad sign, certain death! We won't go in the left-hand tunnel.'

Several voices agreed. The group shuffled their feet.

'What's he talking about?' Artyom asked Khan.

'Apparently it's native folklore,' he said and frowned. 'The devil! There is absolutely no time to convince them and I don't have the strength to either . . . Listen!' he addressed them. 'I'm going into the parallel tunnel. Whoever trusts me can come with me. The rest of you, goodbye. Forever . . . Let's go!' He nodded at Artyom and picked up his rucksack, which was heavy in his hands, and climbed up onto the edge of the platform.

Artyom was frozen with indecision. On the one hand, Khan knew things about these tunnels and the metro in general that far exceeded human understanding, and you could rely on that. On the other, there was the immutable law of these accursed tunnels that you could only go through them with a certain number of people because that was your only hope for success . . .

'What's up there? Too heavy? Give me your hand!' Khan extended his palm down to him and got onto his knees.

Artyom really didn't want to meet his gaze at that moment. He was afraid to see that spark of madness he had been so frightened to see flashing in the man's eyes a few times before. Did Khan understand that he was rejecting the warning calls of not just the people here but of the tunnel itself? Was it enough just to feel the nature of the tunnel? The place on the map, the Guide, at which he'd pointed wasn't black. Artyom was ready to swear that it was a faded orange colour, like all the other lines. So here was the question: which of them was actually blind?

'So? What're you waiting for? You what, don't understand that a delay will kill us? Your hand! For the devil's sake give me your hand!' Khan was yelling but Artyom slowly, with small strides, stepped away from Khan, still staring at the floor, and moved closer to the grumbling group.

'Come on, brother, come with us, no need to hobnob with that jerk, you'll be safer here!' he heard from the crowd.

'Fool! You'll perish with them all! If you don't give a shit about your life then at least think of your mission!'

Artyom summoned the courage to finally lift his head and set his gaze on Khan's dilated pupils, but there wasn't the fire of madness in them, only desperation and fatigue.

He started to doubt himself and he paused – and at that moment someone's hand came lightly down onto his shoulder and it softly pulled him.

'Let's go! Let him die alone, he only wants to drag you along into the grave!' Artyom heard the person say. The meaning of the words made their way to him heavily, he slowly grasped them, and in a moment of resistance he let the man lead him off after the others.

The group set off and moved forward into the darkness of the southern tunnel. They were moving surprisingly slowly, as though affected by the friction of some kind of dense medium – like they were walking in water.

And then Khan, with unexpected lightness, sprang off the platform and onto the path, and in two swift bounds he was at their side. And in one fell swoop he brought down the man who was leading Artyom along, and gripped Artyom and jerked his body backwards. It all seemed to go in slow motion for Artyom. He watched Khan's leap from over his shoulder with mute surprise, Khan's flight seemed to have lasted several seconds. And with the same dull reasoning, he saw how the moustached man in the tarpaulin jacket who was softly gripping him his shoulder, fell hard to the ground.

But from the moment when Khan intercepted him, time started to speed up and the reactions of the others upon hearing the sound of impact, seemed to him to be lightning quick. They were making their first steps toward Khan with their guns fixed on him, and Khan retreated softly to the side, squeezing Artyom to himself with one arm, holding him up, shielding his own body. His other hand was stretched forward and in it he held Artyom's dimly shining new machine gun.

'Go on,' Khan pronounced hoarsely. 'I don't see the point in killing you, you'll die anyway in an hour's time. Leave us. Go on,' he was saying, moving towards the centre of the station, step by step while the frozen figures of the undecided people were starting to turn into vague silhouettes and merged with the darkness.

Some sort of fuss was heard, they were probably helping the moustached man who'd been knocked down by Khan, and the group started to move toward the entrance to the southern tunnel.

They'd decided not to join Khan. Only then did Khan lower the gun and sharply ordered Artyom to get up onto the platform.

'Any more of this and I'll get sick of rescuing you, my young friend,' he said with unconcealed irritation.

Artyom obediently climbed up and Khan followed him. Picking up his stuff, he walked into the black aperture, with Artyom trailing behind.

The hall in *Turgenevskaya* was quite short. On the left, there was a blind alley, a marble wall, and on the other side, there was a piece of corrugated iron over a break in the wall, and that was as far as you could see by the light of a flashlight. Marble, slightly yellowed with age, covered the whole station, which had only three arches. These led to the stairway which connected this station to *Chistyie Prudi* whose name had been changed to *Kirovskaya* by the Reds and which was now walled up with rough grey concrete blocks. The station was completely empty, there wasn't an object on the floor, there were no traces of human activity, not a rat, not a cockroach. While Artyom looked around, he remembered his conversation with Bourbon, which confirmed that rats were afraid of nothing and if there were no rats in a place then there was something wrong there.

Grabbing him by the shoulder, Khan crossed the hall with a quick step, and Artyom could feel, even through his jacket, that Khan was trembling, as though he'd caught a chill. When they put down their bags at the edge of the platform, getting ready to jump onto the path, a weak light suddenly hit them from behind, and Artyom was again surprised by the speed with which his companion reacted to the danger. Within a short moment, Khan was on the ground, spread out and looking at the source of the light.

The light wasn't very strong but it was shining straight into their eyes and it was hard to make out who was in pursuit of them. A moment's delay and Artyom too dropped to the floor. He crawled to his rucksacks and got out the old weapon he was carrying. It was bulky and inconvenient but it made flawless holes of 7.62 calibre and whoever was on the receiving end of it would have a hard time functioning with holes like that in them.

'What's your business?' Khan's voice growled, and Artyom managed to figure out that if the person had wanted to kill them then they would have done so already.

He could see how it probably looked from the outside: helplessly crouched on the floor, in the light of a flashlight and in his crosshairs too. Yes, if he'd wanted to kill them, they would be lying in a pool of blood already.

'Don't shoot!' a voice called out. 'No need . . .'

'Turn off your flashlight!' Khan said, and he moved over to the column to get his own flashlight.

Artyom finally got hold of his weapon and, holding it fast, he rolled over to the side, out of the line of fire and hid in one of the arches. Now he was ready to emerge on the other side and cut off whoever it was, if the person chose to shoot.

But the stranger followed Khan's orders as soon as they were given.

'Good! Now put your weapon on the ground!' Khan said in a less tense voice.

Metal clinked on the granite floor, and Artyom, aiming his weapon forward, crawled sideways and appeared in the hall. He had calculated correctly – fifteen paces in front of him, lit up by the reflections of the flashlight on the arches, with hands up, was that same bearded man who had initiated the skirmish at *Sukharevskaya*.

'Don't shoot,' he said again with a trembling voice. 'I wasn't planning on attacking you. I decided to come with you. You did say that anyone who wanted could come. I . . . I trust you,' he said to Khan. 'I also feel that there's something going on over there, in the right-hand tunnel. They've already left, they all went. But I stayed behind, I want to go with you.'

'Good sense,' Khan said, studiously examining the guy. 'But my friend, you don't inspire trust in me. Who knows why that is,' he added mockingly. 'Basically, we'll examine your proposal. On condition that you hand over your entire arsenal to me. You'll walk in front of us in the tunnel. If you want to play the fool then it won't end well for you.'

The bearded guy pushed his pistol across the floor to Khan with his foot, and carefully put several spare cartridges next to it. Artyom picked them up from the floor and approached him, not lowering his gun.

'I've got him!' he shouted.

'Keep your hands up!' Khan thundered. 'And jump onto the path, quickly. Stand there with your back to us!'

After about two minutes into the tunnel, as they walked in a tight triangle – the bearded guy called Ace, walked five paces ahead of Khan and Artyom – they heard a muted howl. It stopped almost as soon as it had started . . .

Ace looked back at them frightened, forgetting even to shine his flashlight to the side of them. The flashlight was shaking in his hands, and his face, lit from underneath, was forced into a grimace of horror, and that had a greater effect on Artyom than the howl had.

'Yes,' Khan nodded, silently answering the question. 'They made a mistake. But I guess time will still tell whether we have too.'

They hurried on. Casting looks over to his protector from time to time, Artyom noted in him more and more signs of fatigue. His hands were lightly trembling, his stride was uneven, and sweat had gathered in huge droplets on his face. But they hadn't been walking for long at all . . . This path was obviously considerably more tiring for him that it was for Artyom. Thinking about what was draining the strength from his companion, the young man couldn't stop returning to the thought that Khan had seemed to be right in this situation, that he'd saved Artyom again. Had Artyom followed the caravan into the right-hand tunnel, then he would undoubtedly already be dead, he'd have disappeared without a trace.

But there were a lot of them – at least six of them. Had the iron rule not held? Khan had known – he'd known! Whether it really was premonition or if indeed it was thanks to the magic of the Guide . . . It was almost funny that a bit of paper with ink on it could do that. Could that piece of rubbish really help them? Well, the passage between *Turgenevskaya* and *Kitai Gorod* had been orange, definitely orange. Or had it really been black?

'What's this?' Ace asked, suddenly stopping and uneasily looking at Khan.

'Do you feel that? From behind . . .'

Artyom stared in puzzlement at him and wanted to let out a sarcastic comment about jangled nerves because he didn't feel anything in the slightest. The claws of the heavy sensation of depression and danger had even seemed to unclench since they'd left *Turgenevskaya*. But Khan, to his surprise, froze in place, gestured to him to keep quiet, and turned to face the direction from which they'd just come.

'What a keen sense!' he said after a half minute. 'We're in admiration. The queen of admiration,' he added for some reason. 'We must definitely discuss this in more detail if we get out of here. You don't hear anything?' he inquired of Artyom.

'No, everything seems quiet,' Artyom listened and responded. At that moment he was filled with something . . . jealousy? Offence? Vexation, that his protector had said such things about the rough

141

bearded scumbag who had only two hours ago threatened their lives? Please . . .

'That's strange. I think you have the rudiments of the skill to hear tunnels . . . Maybe it hasn't developed itself totally in you yet. Later, later. That will all come later.' Khan shook his head. 'You're right,' he addressed Ace, confirming the man's suspicions. 'Something's coming this way. We have to move and fast.' He listened again and sniffed the air in a very wolf-like manner. 'It's coming from behind like a wave. We have to run! If it covers us, then the game is over,' he concluded, tearing off.

Artyom had to rush after him and break into a run so he wasn't left behind. The bearded guy was now keeping pace with them quickly, moving his short legs and breathing heavily.

They went along like that for ten minutes, and all that time Artyom couldn't understand why they were rushing so much, getting so out of breath, stumbling on the cross-ties if the tunnel behind them was empty and quiet, and there was no evidence that they were being chased. Ten minutes passed before they felt IT. It was definitely rushing after them, hard at their heels, chasing them step after step – something black. It wasn't a wave, but more like a whirlwind, a black whirlwind, cutting through the emptiness . . . And if it overtook them, then the same fate awaited them as had met the other six and all the other daredevils and fools who entered the tunnel alone or at a fatal time, when fiendish hurricanes raged, sweeping up any living thing. Such suppositions and a vague understanding of what was going on, were rushing through Artyom's mind, and he looked at Khan with anxiety. Khan returned his look and everything was clear.

'What, have you got it now?' He exhaled. 'It's a bad business! That means, it's already very close.'

'We have to go faster!' Artyom wheezed as he ran. 'Before it's too late!'

Khan picked up his pace and now he was trotting along with wide paces, saying nothing, not answering Artyom's questions anymore. Even the traces of exhaustion that Artyom had seen in the man seemed to have disappeared and something beast-like had emerged in him again. Artyom had to run to keep up but, when it seemed that they had broken away from the thing that was pursuing them inexorably, Ace tripped on a cross-tie and fell head over heels onto the ground. His face and hands were covered in blood.

Out of inertia, they ran another dozen paces before they took in that Ace had fallen and Artyom thought quickly that he didn't really feel like stopping and going back for the guy – he wanted to leave him to the dogs, the short-arse bootlicker with his amazing intuition. He wanted to keep going before the thing got to them.

It was a disgusting thought but Artyom was seized by such a compulsion to flee and leave the fallen man that his conscience had gone silent. Therefore he felt a certain disappointment when Khan rushed back and, with a powerful jerk, lifted the bearded man to his feet. Artyom had secretly hoped that Khan with his more than disdainful attitude towards others' lives, and indeed their deaths, wouldn't hesitate to forget the guy and leave him in the tunnel like the burden he was, and rush on.

Having ordered Artyom to take one of the injured Ace's arms, he took the other and pulled them along. This made running considerably more difficult. Ace was moaning and grinding his teeth from pain with each step, but Artyom didn't feel anything for him, apart from growing irritation. The long, heavy machine gun was painfully knocking against his legs, and he didn't have a free hand to hold onto it.

But death was very near. If they stopped and waited for half a minute, the ominous vortex would overtake then, whip and tear them into the smallest particles. In the course of a second they would no longer be of this universe and death cries would burst from them with unnatural speed . . . These thoughts didn't paralyse Artyom but, mixed with malice and irritation, they gave him strength and he gained more and more with each step.

And suddenly it disappeared, vanished entirely. The feeling of danger was released so suddenly that one's consciousness was left unusually empty, like the gap after a pulled tooth, and it was as though Artyom was now feeling around with the tip of his tongue for the pit. There was nothing behind them. Just tunnel – clean, dry, clear and completely safe. All that running from fear and paranoid fantasies, the unnecessary belief in some sort of special feelings and intuition, seemed so funny to Artyom now, so silly and absurd, that he burst out laughing. Ace, who had stopped next to him, looked at him with surprise at first and then also started to laugh. Khan looked at them, annoyed and finally spat at them:

'Well, what's so funny? It's nice here right? So quiet, so clean, right?' And he walked on alone. Then Artyom realized that they were altogether only about fifty paces from the station, and that light was clearly visible at the end of the tunnel.

Khan waited at the entrance, standing on the iron stairs. He had

had time to smoke some kind of home-made cigarette, while they, laughing away, completely relaxed, made the fifty paces.

Artyom was penetrated by a feeling of sympathy and compassion for the limping Ace who was moaning through his laughter. He was ashamed at the thoughts that had flashed through his mind back there when Ace had fallen. His mood was dramatically improved, and therefore the sight of Khan, tired, emaciated, scrutinizing them with a strange look of suspicion, seemed a little unpleasant to Artyom.

'Thanks!' Boots rumbled on the stairs and Ace climbed up onto the platform saying to Khan, 'If it weren't for you . . . You . . . Well, it would have all been over. But you . . . didn't leave me there. Thank you! I don't forget things like that.'

'Don't worry,' Khan responded without any enthusiasm.

'Why did you come back for me?'

'You're interesting to me as someone to talk to.' Khan flung his cigarette butt on the ground and shrugged his shoulders. 'That's all.'

After climbing a little higher, Artyom understood why Khan had gone up the stairs to the platform and not continued along the path. In front of the actual entrance to *Kitai Gorod*, the path was heaped with sandbags as high as a man. Behind the sandbags was a group of people sitting on wooden stools with a very serious look about them. Buzz cuts and wide shoulders under beaten-up leather jackets, shabby sports trousers – all this looked rather amusing but, for some reason, it hadn't produced any merriment. Three of them sat there and on a fourth stool there was a deck of cards, which the thugs had strewn carelessly about. There was such abusive language being used that listening to it, Artyom couldn't make out even one normal word in the conversation.

To get through the station you could only pass along a narrow path and up the little stairway, which ended with a gate. But diagonally across from the path, there was an even more imposing pack of four guards. Artyom threw them a look: shaved heads, watery-grey eyes, slightly bent noses, cauliflower ears, wearing training pants with a heavy 'TT' imprinted on the stripe. And there was an unbearable smell of fumes, which was making it hard to think.

'So what do we have here?' the fourth guard said hoarsely, examining Khan and Artyom behind him from head to foot. 'Are you tourists or what? Or traders?'

'No, we're not traders, we're travellers and we have no goods with us,' Khan explained.

'Travellers – grovellers!' the thug rhymed and guffawed loudly. 'Hear that Kolya? Travellers – grovellers!' he repeated, turning to the card players.

They responded enthusiastically. Khan smiled patiently.

The bull of a man leant one hand against the wall blocking their way.

'We have here, a kind of a . . . customs operation, you know what I mean?' he explained. 'Cash is the currency. You want to go through – you pay. You don't want to then you can get lost . . . !'

'Whose prerogative?' Artyom protested indignantly.

That was a mistake.

The bull didn't probably quite get what he'd meant but he'd understood the intonation and he didn't like it. Pushing Khan to the side, he took a heavy step and got right up into Artyom's face. He lowered his chin and gave the young man a severe look. His eyes were completely empty and seemed almost transparent, and they lacked any sign of a reasonable mind. Stupidity and malice, that's what they emitted, and though it was hard to hold his gaze and Artyom was blinking from the tension, he felt how fear and hatred was growing in those eyes as they sat there at the tunnel entrance watching people come past.

'What the fuck?' the guard said threateningly.

He was taller than Artyom by more than a head and three times as wide. Artyom remembered the legend someone had told him about David and the Goliath. Though he was confused which was which, he knew that it ended well for the smaller and weaker of the two, and this gave him a certain optimism.

'Whatever,' he unexpectedly plucked up the courage to say.

This answer upset the man for some reason, and he spread out his short and fat fingers and, with a confident motion, he put all five of them on Artyom's forehead. The skin on his palms was yellow, calloused and it stank of tobacco and car grease, and Artyom didn't have time make out all the many aromas to it because the thug pushed him backwards.

He probably didn't have to apply much force but Artyom flew a metre backwards and knocked Ace, who was standing behind him, over too. They both fell onto the little bridge while the thug returned to his place. But a surprise awaited him there. Khan, who'd thrown his bag on the ground, was standing there gripping Artyom's machine gun in his hands. He demonstratively clicked open the safety catch and with a quiet voice that indicated that nothing good could come of all this – so much so that even Artyom's hair was standing on end upon hearing it – he pronounced:

'Now why so rude?'

He hadn't said anything much but, to Artyom, who was floundering on the floor, trying to get to his feet, burning with shame, these words seemed like a dull precautionary growl which would likely be followed by a quick and hard attack. He stood up, finally, and tore his old machine gun off his shoulder and trained it on the offender, with the safety catch undone. Now he was ready to pull the trigger at any moment. His heart was beating hard and hatred definitely outweighed fear on the scales of his feelings and he said to Khan:

'Let me take care of him.' And he was surprised himself at how unhesitatingly ready he was to kill the man for pushing him over. The sweaty shaved head was clearly visible in the cross-hairs of his scope, and the temptation to pull the trigger was strong. After that, what would be, would be, but most important was to get rid of this piece of filth right now, to wash him in his own blood.

'Alert!' the bull bawled.

Khan pulled the pistol out of his belt with lightning speed, and slid to the side and he took aim at the 'customs officers' who had leapt from their places.

'Don't shoot!' he managed to yell to Artyom, and the animated scene was frozen again: the bull standing there with his hands up on the little bridge and a motionless Khan, aiming at the three thugs who hadn't managed to grab hold of their machine guns from the pile they made nearby.

'There's no need for blood,' Khan said quietly and imposingly, not asking but more like giving an order. 'There's a rule here, Artyom,' he continued, not taking his eyes off the three card-players, who were frozen in absurd poses.

The skinheads probably knew the price of the Kalashnikov and its lethal force at such a distance, and therefore they didn't want to cause any unnecessary suspicion in the man who held them in his sights.

'Their rules force us to pay duty to enter. How much do you take?' Khan asked.

'Three cartridges each,' the guy on the bridge responded.

'Shall we haggle?' Artyom suggested mockingly, pointing the barrel of his machine gun at the guy's belt area.

'Two.' The man offered some flexibility, giving Artyom the evil eye. But he didn't seem sure of what Artyom was going to do.

146

'Give it to him!' Khan ordered Ace. 'Pay for me too and consider it payback.'

Ace readily pushed his hand into the depths of his travelling bag and approaching the guard, he counted out six shining and sharp cartridges. The man quickly squeezed his fist around them and poured them into the protruding pockets of his jacket, and then raised his hands again and looked at Khan, waiting.

'So the duty is paid?' Khan raised his eyebrows questioningly.

The bull nodded sullenly, without taking his eyes off Khan's weapon.

'The incident is settled?' Khan asked.

The thug kept silent. Khan reached into his auxiliary bag and took out another five cartridges and put them in the guard's pocket. They tinkled into the pocket and disappeared together with the tense grimace on the bull's face, which had resumed its usual lazy and suspicious expression.

'Compensation for moral damage,' Khan explained but the words didn't have any effect.

It was likely that the bull hadn't understood them, as he hadn't understood the previous question. He was guessing at the meaning of Khan's wise statements by Khan's preparedness to use money and force. This was the language he understood perfectly, and probably the only one he spoke too.

'You can put your hands down,' Khan said and carefully lifted his gun upwards, taking his aim away from the three gamblers.

Artyom did the same but his hands were shaking – he had been ready to take out the shaved skull of the thug at any moment. He didn't trust these people. However, his agitation was unfounded. The thug, having relaxed and lowered his hands, growled to the rest of his buddies that everything was fine and, leaning with his back to the wall, he assumed an indifferent attitude, letting the travellers go by him into the station. As he passed, Artyom gave him an obnoxious look but the bull didn't take the bait and was looking off to the side.

However, Artyom heard a disgusted 'P-puppydog . . .' and heard spittle hit the floor. He had wanted to turn around but Khan, walking a pace ahead of him, grabbed him by the hand and dragged him along so that Artyom was torn between satisfying his urge to turn back and show the sorry guy a thing or two, and the other cowardly part of him that just wanted to get out of there as soon as possible.

When they had all stepped onto the dark granite floor of the station, they suddenly heard a bellow of stretched vowels behind them: 'He-ey, gimme my piece!'

Khan stopped, took the cartridge clip labelled 'TT' with its rounded bullets and flung it over to the bull. The man rather deftly caught the pistol and put it in his belt, watching annoyed at how Khan had let some extra cartridges fall on the floor.

'Sorry,' Khan opened his palms, 'a prophylactic. Isn't that what it's called?' He winked at Ace.

Kitai Gorod differed from other stations that Artyom had seen: it didn't have three arches like *VDNKh* but was one large hall with a wide platform, with tracks on either side of it, and it gave the alarming impression of an unusual space. The accommodations were lit in the most disorganized way, weak pear-shaped lamps dangling here and there. There weren't any fires here at all, apparently they weren't allowed. In the centre of the hall, generously pouring light around itself, there was a white mercury-vapour lamp – a real miracle for Artyom. But there was bedlam surrounding it so one's attention was distracted and you couldn't keep your eyes on the marvel for more than a second.

'What a big station!' He exhaled in surprise.

'You're only really seeing half of it,' Khan reported. '*Kitai Gorod* is about twice as big as this. Oh, this is one of the strangest places in the world. You have heard, I guess, that all the lines meet here. Look at those rails, to the right of us – that's the *Tagansko-Krasnopresnenskaya* branch. It's hard to describe the craziness and disorder that goes on there, and here at *Kitai Gorod* it meets your orange *Kaluzhasko-Rizhskaya*, and no one from the other lines believes what goes on there. Apart from that, this station doesn't belong to any of the federations, and its inhabitants represent themselves completely. It's a very very curious place. I call it Babylon. With affection,' Khan added, looking around the platform at all the people who were scurrying to and fro.

Life at the station was bubbling. It was vaguely like *Prospect Mir* but the latter was more modest and more organized. Artyom remembered Bourbon's words about the fact that there were better places in the metro than that wretched market which they walked through at *Prospect*.

There were rows of trays along the endless rails and the whole platform was filled with tents. Several of them were made into commercial stalls, others were used as shelter for people. The letters SDAYu were painted on some of them, and that's where travellers could spend the night. They made their way through the crowds and, looking sideways, Artyom noticed on the left-hand track that there was an enormous grey-blue figure of a train. It wasn't complete; there were altogether only three wagons.

There was an indescribable roar at the station. It seemed that the inhabitants never fell silent for a moment and they just constantly talked, screamed, sang, argued desperately, laughed or cried. In several places, overlapping the din, there was a rush of music and this created an unusual holiday mood in underground life there.

At *VDNKh* there were also people who sang enthusiastically, but it was different there. There were only a couple of guitars there, and sometimes people would gather at someone's tent to relax after work. Yes and and there was music sometimes at the three-hundredth metre border where you didn't have to listen hard to hear it coming from the northern tunnel. At the little patrol fire they sang with guitars, but mostly about things that Artyom didn't really understand: about wars that he hadn't taken part in, and which were conducted according to different, strange rules; about life there, above, before.

He especially remembered songs about some Afghanistan place which Andrei really loved to sing – although there wasn't much not to understand in these songs, they were all about sadness for fallen friends and hatred for the enemy. But Andrei could sing so well that everyone who listened was touched so much that their voices quivered and they had goosebumps.

Andrei explained to the younger ones that Afghanistan was quite a country and he described its mountains, the passes, the bubbling brooks, the villages, the helicopters and coffins. Artyom knew what a country was pretty well, since Sukhoi had spent worthwhile time explaining things to him. But while Artyom knew something about governments and their histories, mountains, rivers, and valleys remained as abstract notions to him, and they were mere words which were defined for him by the discoloured pictures his stepfather had shown him in a geography textbook.

Even Andrei hadn't been to any Afghanistan, he was too young for that, but he had just heard the songs from his older army friends.

But did they really play music like this at *VDNKh*? No, the songs were pensive and sad – that's what they sang there and, remembering Andrei and his melancholic ballads, and comparing them to the merry and playful melodies which issued from different corners of the hall, Artyom was surprised again and again how varied, how different music can be and how much it can affect one's mood.

Coming up to the nearest musicians, Artyom stopped without meaning to, and joined the small group of people not just to listen to the words about adventures through the tunnels under the influence of weed but to hear the music itself and to look curiously at the performers. There were two of them: one with long greasy hair, tied down with a leather strap around his forehead, dressed in some kind of strange multi-coloured rags, jingling on the guitar. The other was an elderly man with a significant bald spot from the looks of it, and a pair of glasses that had been repaired many times, in an old faded jacket, and he was charming them with some kind of wind instrument, which Khan called a saxophone.

Artyom hadn't ever seen anything like it. The only wind instrument he knew was the pipe. There were people who knew how to play it well, cutting insulating tubes of different diameters, but they only made them to sell: people didn't like pipes at *VDNKh*. And furthermore the horn looked a little like the saxophone, which sometimes was used to sound the alarm if something was hindering the siren that was usually used.

On the floor next to the musicians lay an open guitar case in which lay a dozen cartridges. When the long-haired one had finished singing his heart out, he said something particularly funny, accompanying it an amusing grimace, the crowd chuckled with joy and applause broke out and another cartridge flew into the case.

The song about the wanderings of the poor devil had ended and the hairy guy leaned on the wall to relax, and the saxophonist in the jacket then took to playing some kind of motif that was unfamiliar to Artyom but evidently popular here because people started applauding and a few cartridges flashed through the air and into the red velvet of the case.

Khan and Ace were discussing something, standing near a tray; they weren't telling Artyom to hurry up, and he could have stayed there another hour probably, listening to the simple songs, if they hadn't suddenly stopped. Two powerful figures approached the musicians with an unsteady gait, and they were very reminiscent of and dressed similarly to the thugs whom they'd met at the entrance to the station. One of the approaching figures crouched and started to unceremoniously remove the cartridges from inside the case, pouring them into the pocket of his leather jacket. The long-haired guitarist rushed at him, trying to stop him, but was quickly knocked

150

over by a fierce blow to his shoulder and had his guitar torn away from him, lifted up in order to smack it down, to shatter the instrument on the side of the column. The second thug pushed the elderly saxophonist against the wall with little effort when the man tried to get away to help his friend.

None of the audience standing around the musicians stepped in. The crowd thinned noticeably, and the ones who were left either covered their eyes or pretended to be looking at the goods for sale lying on a tray nearby. Artyom burned with shame for them and for himself, but he decided not to get involved.

'You've already been here today!' the long-haired musician said, almost weeping, holding his hand to his shoulder.

'Listen you! If you're having a good day that means we're have a good day, got it? And don't you start with me, right? What, you want to go to the wagon do you, you hairy faggot?' the thug screamed at him, throwing down the guitar. It was clear that he had been waving it around more as a warning than anything else.

At the word 'wagon' the long-haired guy immediately stopped short, shook his head quickly and didn't say another word.

'Got it . . . faggot?!' the thug finished, stressing the first syllable, contemptuously spitting at the musician's feet. The musician again said nothing. Convinced that the rebellion was quashed, the two bulls went off slowly, searching for their next victim.

Artyom looked around in dismay and saw Ace nearby who had also been attentively watching the scene.

'Who was that?' Artyom asked, puzzled.

'Well, who did they look like to you?' Ace inquired. 'The usual bandits. There's no governing power at *Kitai Gorod* so there are two groups that control it. This half is under the Brother Slavs. All the riff-raff from the *Kaluzhsko-Rizhskaya* line gather here, all the cutthroats. Mostly they're called the Kaluzhskys, some of them are called the Rizhskys but you won't see the likes of them either at Kaluga or at Riga. But there, you see, where the little bridge is,' he pointed to the stairway that went off to the right and upwards in the middle of the platform. 'There is another hall, and it's identical to this one. There isn't this racket up there, but the Caucasus Muslims are in charge there – basically the Azerbaijanis and the Chechens. It was once a slaughterhouse with each of them trying to take over as much territory as possible. In the end they split the station in half.'

Artyom didn't bother asking what a 'Caucasian' was, having decided that this name, like the incomprehensible and hard to pronounce 'Chechens' and 'Azerbaijanis' were referring to stations he didn't know, where the bandits came from.

'Now both groups behave peacefully,' continued Ace. 'They grab those that decide to stop at *Kitai Gorod* to make some money and charge customs duty. The charge is the same in both halls – three cartridges – so it makes no difference how you enter the station. Of course, there's no order here at all, and they of course don't need it, the only thing is you can't build a fire. If you want to buy some weed? Go for it. Want some spirits? Buy as much as you want. You can load yourself with the kind of weapon that could take down half the metro – no problem. Prostitution flourishes. But I don't advise it,' he added and muttered something about personal opinion with embarrassment.

'And what was that about the wagon?'

'The wagon? It's like their headquarters. And if anyone misbehaves in front of them, you refuse to pay, you owe them money or something like that, then they drag you in there. There's a prison there and a torture chamber – it's like a pit of debt. Better not to land there. Are you hungry?' Ace turned the conversation to a different topic.

Artyom nodded. The devil knew how much time passed since that moment when he and Khan were drinking tea at *Sukharevskaya*. Without clocks he had lost his ability to orientate himself in time. His journeys through the tunnels, full of strange experiences, could have lasted many hours, and also could have flown past in mere minutes. Apart from that, the passage of time inside tunnels was totally different than anywhere else.

In any event, he wanted to eat. He looked around.

'Kebab! Hot kebabs!' a swarthy trader was standing nearby with thick black eyebrows underneath his arched nose.

He had pronounced it a little strangely: he hadn't used a hard 'K' and instead of an 'a' came the sound of 'o.' Artyom had met people before who had spoken with unusual accents but he hadn't ever paid special attention to it.

The word was familiar to Artyom. They made kebabs at *VDNKh* and liked them too. It was pork, obviously. But whatever that trader was waving around seemed a far cry from that. Artyom looked at it tensely and for a long time, and finally recognized the charred carcasses of rats with twisted paws. It made him dizzy.

'You don't eat rats?' Ace asked him sympathetically. 'Here are some.' He nodded at the swarthy trader. 'They won't give you pork.

It's forbidden by the Koran. But rats are OK,' he added, hungrily examining the smoking grill. 'I also used to be disgusted and now I'm used to it. A little cruel, of course, and they're a little bony and apart from that, they smell a little. But these abreks,' again he shot a glance over at him, 'know how to cook a rat and you can't take that away from them. They pickle it in something, and afterwards it becomes as soft as a suckling pig. And with spices! . . . And much cheaper!'

Artyom pushed his palm against his mouth, inhaled deeply and tried to think about something else to distract himself, but the blackened carcasses of rats mounted on spits kept swimming before his eyes: the spits were stuck into the bodies from the back and came out at their opened mouths.

'As you like, but I'm treating! So join us. It's altogether three cartridges for a skewer!' Ace issued his final argument and headed for the grill.

Having warned Khan, Artyom needed to go around the station and find something more normal to eat. Artyom looked through the whole station, he was offered home-brew in all manner of flasks, he greedily but cautiously scrutinized the tempting half-naked girls who stood at lifted tent flaps throwing inviting looks at the passers-by; vulgar though they were, they were so relaxed, so free, and not tense, beaten down by the harsh life women like them were at *VDNKh*. He hung around the booksellers for a bit but there was nothing of interest there. Everything was much cheaper: there were pocket-sized books, that were falling apart, about a great and pure love for women, and books about murder and money for men.

The platform was about two hundred paces long – a little longer than usual. The walls and the amusing columns that were reminiscent of accordions were coated with coloured marble, mostly a grey-yellow, but pinkish in places. The length of the station was decorated with heavy sheets of some kind of yellow metal that had darkened with time, and on them were barely recognizable symbols from a past epoch. The ceilings were darkened from fires, the walls were speckled with a multitude of inscriptions made in paint and soot, and depicting primitive and frequently obscene pictures. On some places there were chunk-sized chips in the marble and the metal sheets were dented and badly scratched.

In the middle of the hall, on the right side, through one of the short flights of stairs, beyond the little bridge, you could see the second hall of the station. Artyom wanted to wander around there too, but he stopped at the iron enclosure, which were made up of two-metre sections like at *Prospect Mir*.

Several people stood by the narrow passage, leaning on the fence. On Artyom's side were the familiar bulldozers in training pants. On the other side, they were swarthy and moustached, of average size, but they didn't look like they could take a joke either. One of them was squeezing a machine gun between his legs, and the other had a pistol poking out of his pocket. The bandits conversed calmly together and you could hardly believe that there had ever been hostility between them. They fairly politely told Artyom that passage to the adjacent station would cost him two cartridges and he'd have to pay the same to get back again. Having learnt his lesson from bitter experience, Artyom didn't dispute the fairness of the tariffs and just walked off.

Having made a circle, carefully studying the stalls and bazaars, he returned to the end of the platform where they'd arrived. The hall didn't end there, there was another staircase leading up. He went up and found a small hall there, split in half in exactly the same way with a cordon. Here, apparently, was another boundary between the two areas. On his right, he saw, to his surprise, a real monument – one of those that you see in pictures of the city. But this wasn't a full figure, just the head of a man.

What a big head! It was no less than two metres high . . . Though it was dirtied on top by something, and its nose was shiny from frequent rubbings by human hands, all the same it demanded respect and was even a little frightening. Fantasies about giants entered his mind. One of the giants lost the battle in his head and now its head was dipped in bronze, to decorate the marbled hall of this small Sodom, buried deeply in the earth's crust, hidden from the all seeing eyes of God . . . The face of the severed head was sad, and Artyom suspected at first that it belonged to John the Baptist of the New Testament, which he had once leafed through. But then he decided that, judging from the scale of it, that it was probably something to do with a big and strong hero who had genuinely been a giant but had lost his head in the end. None of the inhabitants scurrying around could tell him who this severed head belonged to, and he was a bit disappointed.

But near the statue he came across a wonderful place – a real restaurant, set up in a spacious and clean tent of a pleasant, dark-green colour, like at his own station. Inside, plastic vases of flowers with cloth leaves were in the corners, and a pair of tables had oil lamps on them, suffusing the tent with a comfortable, soft light. And the food . . . It was the food of the Gods: the most tender pork with hot mushrooms which melted in your mouth. Restaurants served that at *VDNKh* on holidays, but it had never been so delicious . . .

The people sitting there were solid, respectable types with good and tasteful clothes. Apparently they were important merchants. Carefully cutting pieces of fried crackling, which oozed with hot fat, they unhurriedly placed small pieces of it in their mouths. Meanwhile they sedately conversed with each other, discussing their business, and sometimes threw a politely curious glance over at Artyom.

It was expensive, of course – he had to give over a whole fifteen cartridges from his supply and put them in the wide palm of the fat inn-keeper, and then he regretted that he'd succumbed to temptation, but his stomach was nonetheless happy, calm and warm so the voice of reason was silenced.

And the mug of fermented mixture was sweet, and it pleasantly swirled his head but it wasn't strong, it wasn't that poisonous, turbid home-brew in the dirty bottles and jars that would make you weak at the knees with one sniff. Yes, and it was only for three more cartridges, and what's three cartridges if you exchange them for a phial of a sparkling elixir which helps you to come to terms with the imperfection of this world and restores a certain harmony?

Drinking the fermented mixture in small gulps, sitting alone in silence and peace for the first time in a few days, Artyom tried to resurrect recent events in his memory and to understand where he had got to and where he had yet to go. There was still another section of his designated journey to overcome, and he was again at a crossroads.

He felt like the hero of the almost forgotten fairy tales of his childhood. The memory of them was so distant now that he didn't remember who had told them to him . . . Was it Sukhoi or was it Zhenya's parents, or was it his own mother? More than anything Artyom liked to think that he'd heard them from his mother, and her face even would swim out of the fog for a moment and he could hear her voice reading to him with smooth intonations: 'Once upon a time . . .'

And so, like the fairytale hero, he was standing there and in front of him there were three roads: one to *Kuznetsky Most*, one to *Tretyakovskaya*, and one to *Taganskaya*. He savoured the intoxicating drink, his body seized by a blissful languor. He didn't want to think at all, and all that was circulating in his head was: 'Go straight – you'll lose your life. Go left – you'll lose your horse . . .'

This probably could have gone on forever: he really needed this rest after his recent experiences. It was worth waiting at *Kitai Gorod* – to look around, to ask the locals about the tunnels. He had to meet up with Khan again, to find out if he would be going further with him or if their paths would diverge at this strange station.

It hadn't gone at all according to the lazy plan that Artyom had made. He exhaustedly contemplated the small tongue of flame that was dancing in the lamp on the table.

CHAPTER 8

The Fourth Reich

Pistol shots began to crack, slashing through the merry din of the crowd, and then there was a shrill female scream, and a machine gun rattled. The chubby inn-keeper snatched a small gun from under the counter and ran to the entrance of the tent. Leaving his drink, Artyom leapt up after him, throwing his rucksack on his shoulder, thumbing the safety catch on his gun, regretting as he went that they had made him pay in advance, otherwise he could have slipped away without settling his bill. The eighteen cartridges he had spent could prove very useful one day soon.

At the top, from the stairs, he could see that something terrible was happening. To get down there, he had to push through the crowd of people who had lost their senses out of fear and who were throwing themselves up the stairs. Soon the crush was so bad that Artyom asked himself whether he really needed to get down there, but his curiosity pushed him forward.

On the pathways lay several prostrate bodies, clad in leather jackets, and on the platform, right under his feet, in a puddle of bright red blood, lay a dead woman, face down. He quickly stepped over her, trying not to look down, but he slipped and almost fell. Panic reigned, and half-dressed people were jumping out of their tents, hysterically looking around. One of them was left behind, his foot still stuck in one leg of his trousers, when he suddenly bent over, clutched his stomach and tipped over to the side.

But Artyom couldn't figure out where the shooting was coming from. The firing continued, and heavy-set people in leather were running from the other side of the hall, throwing squealing women and frightened traders out of the way. But these weren't the ones being attacked – it was the bandits themselves, the ones who controlled this side of *Kitai Gorod*. And along the whole platform, it wasn't clear who was creating this slaughterhouse.

And then Artyom understood why he didn't see anyone. The attackers were in the tunnel – and they were opening fire from there, apparently afraid of showing themselves in open space.

This changed things. There was no more time to reflect: they would come out onto the platform when they felt that there was no more resistance – he had to get away from that entrance as soon as possible. Artyom ran forward, tightly gripping his machine gun and looking over his shoulder. The echo of the thundering shots, resounding through the arches, made it difficult to tell from which tunnel the shots were coming – the right or the left.

Finally, he noticed camouflaged figures in the opening of the left-side tunnel. Instead of faces, there was blackness and Artyom felt a chill inside. Only after a few moments did he remember that the dark ones who had encroached on *VDNKh* never carried weapons and weren't dressed in clothes. The attackers were just wearing masks, balaclavas of the kind you could buy at any arms market (they would even give you one for free when you bought an AK-47).

The Kaluga reinforcements had also arrived and were on the ground, hiding behind the corpses, returning fire. You could see how they smashed the plywood boards mounted on the wagon windows, breaking open hidden machine gun positions. Heavy fire thundered.

Looking up, Artyom managed to get a glimpse of the plastic tablet that showed the stations and hung in the middle of the hall. They were attacking from the direction of *Tretyakovskaya* – so this route was cut off. To get to *Taganskaya*, he'd have to go to a part of the station that was now on fire. The only route left to him was to *Kuznetsky Most*.

Jumping onto the path, Artyom headed for the blackened entrance to the one tunnel he could get into. He couldn't see Khan or Ace anywhere. He thought he saw a figure who reminded him of the wandering philosopher but when he stopped for a moment Artyom realized he was mistaken.

He wasn't the only one running into the tunnel – almost half of those escaping were heading that way as well. The passage was ringing with frightened cries – one person was sobbing hysterically. The lights of torches shined here and there, and there was even the uneven flickering of a few fire-torches. Each person was lighting the path for himself.

Artyom took Khan's present out of his pocket and pressed on the handle. After directing the weak light of the torch to the path under his feet, trying not to trip, he rushed forward, catching up to small groups of fugitives – sometimes whole families, sometimes lone women, old men, and young, healthy men, who were dragging parcels that probably didn't belong to them.

He stopped a couple of times to help someone who'd fallen. He lingered with one of them for a moment. Leaning against the ribbed wall of the tunnel, sat an old man, totally grey, with a painful grimace on his face, clutching his heart. Next to him stood an adolescent boy who was looking serenely and dully. From his animal looks and his turbid eyes, you could see that this was an unusual child. Something squeezed Artyom's soul and when he saw this strange pair, even though he was pressing himself forward and cursing himself when he met obstacles, he stopped.

The old man, feeling the attention that was being focused on him and the boy, tried to smile at Artyom and to say something but he didn't have the breath for it. He frowned and closed his eyes, gathering his strength, and Artyom bent over the old man, trying to hear what he was trying to tell him.

But the boy suddenly started to bellow threateningly and Artyom noticed that there was a thread of spit coming from his mouth, and that he was baring his small yellow teeth. Not wanting to deal with any attack, Artyom pushed him aside and the boy moved back and settled clumsily onto the rails, issuing plaintive howls.

'Young . . . man . . .' The old man struggled. 'Don't . . . he . . . That's Vanechka . . . he . . . doesn't understand.'

Artyom just shrugged.

'Please . . . Nitro . . . glycerine . . . in the bag . . . at the bottom . . . One pill . . . Give it to me . . . I can't myself . . .' The old man wheezed horribly and Artyom dug into the bag, quickly finding a new-looking package and he cut through the foil with a fingernail. The pill jumped out and he gave it to the old man who extended his lips into a guilty smile and said:

'I can't . . . my hands . . . don't listen to me . . . Under my tongue . . .' Then his eyelids closed again.

Artyom looked at his black hands in doubt, but he obeyed and put the slippery little ball in the old man's mouth. The stranger nodded weakly and said nothing. More and more fugitives were striding past them hurriedly, but Artyom could only see an endless row of dirty boots and shoes. Sometimes they stumbled on the black wood of the

159

cross-ties and then there was an outburst of swearing. No one paid any attention to the three of them. The teenager was sitting in the same place and was quietly mumbling. Artyom noticed with some indifference and even a little smugness that one of the passers-by kicked him hard and the boy started to howl even more loudly, smearing his tears with his fists and swaying from side to side.

Meanwhile, the old man opened his eyes, sighed heavily and muttered, 'Thank you very much . . . I feel better already . . . Will you help me to get up?'

Artyom supported him by the arm while the man rose with effort, and he picked up the old man's bag, which meant he had to put his machine gun over the other shoulder. The old man began to hobble forward, and went to the boy and started encouraging him to get up. The boy bellowed, offended, but when he saw Artyom come up to them, he started to hiss maliciously and spittle again dripped from his protruding lower lip.

'You see, I just bought the medicine,' the old man said. 'Indeed, I came here especially for it, to this far away place, you know. You can't get it where we live, no one brings it in, and there's no one to ask for it, and I had just finished my supply, I took the last tablet on the way here, and when they didn't want to let us through *Pushkinskaya* . . . There are fascists there now, you know, it's just a disgrace to think that at *Pushkinskaya* there are fascists! I heard that they even want to rename it, either to *Hitlerskaya* or to *Schillerovskaya* . . . Though, of course, they haven't even heard of Schiller. And, imagine, they didn't want to let us through. Those swaggering fellows with their swastikas started to tease Vanechka. And what could he answer, the poor boy, in his condition? I was very worried, my heart went bad, and only then did they let us out. What was I saying? Oh yes! And you see, I especially put them deep into my bag in case anyone searched us, and they would have asked questions, and you know that they could get the wrong idea, not everyone knows what kind of medicine this is . . . And suddenly there's all this firing! I ran off as fast as I could, I even had to drag Vanechka because he had seen some chickens on sticks and he really didn't want to go. And to start off with, you know, it wasn't squeezing so hard, I thought, maybe it will go away, and I don't have to get out the medicine, it's of course worth its weight in gold, but then I understood that I wouldn't manage. And as I reached for a tablet, it got me. And Vanechka, he doesn't understand a thing, I've been trying to teach him for a long time to give me tablets if I don't feel well but he just can't understand it, and he either eats them himself or he gets the wrong thing out of the bag and gives it to me. I tell him thank you, smile and he smiles at me, you know, with such joy, he bellows merrily . . . God forbid something happens to me – there's no one to take care of him at all, and I can't imagine what would become of him!'

The old man talked and talked, ingratiatingly, looking into Artyom's eyes, and Artyom felt very awkward for some reason. Even though the old man was hobbling with all his strength, Artyom thought that they were moving too slowly – everyone was overtaking them. It looked like they would soon be last. Vanechka clumsily walked to the right of the old man, holding his hand. His former serene expression had returned to his face. From time to time he pushed his right hand forward and excitedly gurgled, pointing at some object that had been thrown away or dropped as the fugitives ran from the station, sometimes pointing at the darkness that was thickening in front of them.

'Forgive me, young man, but what's your name? Because we're talking, right, and we haven't even introduced ourselves . . . Artyom? Nice to meet you, and I'm Mikhail Porfirevich. Porfirevich, that's right. They called my father Porfiry, an uncommon, you know, name, and in the Soviet times he was even questioned by various organizations because at that time there were other names in fashion: Vladilen or Stalin . . . And you're from where? *VDNKh*? Well, me and Vanechka, we're from *Barrikadnaya*, I once lived there.' The old man smiled, embarrassed. 'You know, there was a building there, it was such a building, so high, right near the metro . . . But you probably don't remember any buildings do you? How old are you, if you don't mind? Well, of course, that's not important. I had a little flat there, two rooms, on a high floor, and there was such a wonderful view of the city centre. The flat wasn't big but it was very, you know, comfortable, the floors, were of course, oak, and like all flats then there was a gas stove. Lord, I'm thinking right now about just how comfortable. A gas stove! And back then no one cared for them – they all wanted electricity but they just couldn't get it. As you walked in there was a reproduction of a Tintoretto painting, in a pretty gold-plated frame, what beauty! The bed was real, with pillows, with sheets that were always clean and a big desk, with a lamp and it burned brightly. But most importantly, there were bookshelves to the ceiling. My father left me a big library and I collected them too. Ach, why am I telling you all of this? You probably aren't interested in all this old man nonsense . . . And yet still now, you see, I remember, I really miss the things, particularly the desk and the books and recently I really miss the bed. You don't know such luxuries here but we had these wooden beds, handmade, you know, and sometimes we slept right on blankets on the floor. But that's nothing, what's important is what's here.' He pointed to his chest. 'What's important is what goes on inside, and not outside. The important thing is that what's in the head stays the same and who gives a fig about the conditions – 'scuse my French! But you know that bed, it's especially . . .'

He didn't shut up for a minute and Artyom listened the whole time with great interest, even though he couldn't at all imagine what it would be like to live in a tall building, and what the view would be like, and what it would be like to go up in a lift.

When Mikhail Porfirevich paused for a little while, in order to catch his breath, Artyom decided to use the break to turn the conversation in a useful direction. Somehow he had to get through *Pushkinskaya* and to make the transfer to *Chekhovskaya*, and from there get to *Polis.*

'Are there really real fascists at *Pushkinskaya*?' he asked.

'What's that you're saying? Fascists? Ah, yes . . .' The old man sighed confusedly. 'Yes, yes, you know, the skinheads with the armbands, they're just awful. These symbols are hanging at the entrance there and all over the station. You know they used to mean that you couldn't go there – it's a black figure in a red circle with a red diagonal line through it. I thought that they had made some kind of mistake and I asked why they were there . . . It means that the dark ones can't enter. It's some kind of idiocy, basically.'

Artyom turned to him when he heard the words 'dark ones.' He threw a frightened look at Mikhail Porfirovich and asked carefully:

'Are there dark ones there now too? Don't tell me they've reached there too?' A carousel of panic turned feverishly in Artyom's head. How could it be? He'd only been in the tunnel a week and the dark ones were already attacking *Pushkinskaya*. Had his mission already failed? He hadn't succeeded, hadn't come good? It was all for nothing? No, that couldn't be, there would have been rumours, they would have distorted things but there still would have been rumours, right? But it might be the end to everything . . .

Mikhail Porfirevich cautiously looked at him and, stepping a little to the side, carefully asked:

'And you, yourself, what ideology do you adhere to?'

'I? Basically, well, none.' Artyom hesitated. 'And?'

'And how do you feel about other nationalities, about Caucasians, for example?'

'What do Caucasians have to do with anything?' Artyom was puzzled. 'Generally, I don't know much about nationalities. There used to be the French there, or the Germans, the Americans. But I guess none of them are left . . . And as for the Caucasians, if I'm honest, I don't really know any,' he admitted awkwardly.

'It's the Caucasians that they call the "dark ones",' Mikhail Porfirevich explained, still trying to figure out if Artyom was lying, playing the fool.

'But Caucasians, if I remember right, are regular people?' Artyom said. 'I saw a few of them here today . . .'

'Completely normal people!' Mikhail Porfirevich assured him. 'Completely normal people, but those cutthroats have decided that there's something different about them and they persecute them. It's simply inhuman! Can you imagine, they have a ceiling there, right over the pathways, fitted with hooks, and there was a man hanging from one of them, a real man. Vanechka got so excited, that he started to poke it with his finger, to bellow, and then these monsters turned their attention to him.'

At the sound of his name the teenager turned and fixed the old man with a long stare. Artyom had the impression that the boy could hear and could even partly understand what the conversation was about, but when his name wasn't repeated, he quickly lost interest in Mikhail Porfirevich and turned his attention to the cross-ties.

'And once we started talking about nations and, by the looks of it, they really worship Germans. It was the Germans after all who invented their ideology, and you, of course, know, what I'm going to tell you,' Mikhail Porfirovich added quickly and Artyom vaguely nodded even though he didn't actually know, but he didn't want to look like an ignoramus. 'You know, there's German eagles hanging everywhere, swastikas, which are self-explanatory, and there are various German phrases, quotes from Hitler: about valour, about pride and things in that vein. They have parades and marches. While we were there, and I was trying to persuade them to stop antagonizing Vanechka, they were all marching across the platform and singing songs. Something about the greatness of the spirit and contempt for death. But, generally, you know, the German language was perfectly chosen. German was simply created for such things. I can speak a little of it, you see . . . Here, look, I have something written somewhere here . . .' And, breaking step, he extracted a dirty notebook from his inside pocket. 'Wait a second, put your light here, if you don't mind . . . Where was it? Ah, here it is!'

In the yellow circle of light, Artyom saw some jumping Latin letters, carefully drawn on a page of the notebook and even thoughtfully surrounded with a frame of drawn vine-leaves:

Du stirbst. Besitz stirbt.
Die Sippen sterben.
Der einzig lebt – wir wissen es
Der Toten Tatenruhm.

Artyom could also read Latin letters. He had studied them in some textbook for schoolchildren that they dug up at the station library. He looked behind him and he pointed his torch at the notebook again. Of course, he couldn't understand a thing.

'What is it?' he asked, again helping Mikhail Porfirovich along, and quickly pushing the notebook into the man's pocket, and trying to get Vanechka, who was rooted to the spot and growling unhappily, to move forward.

'It's a poem,' the old man replied, and he seemed a bit offended. 'It's in memory of those that perished in war. I, of course, am not planning to translate but broadly speaking, it means this: "You will die. All those close to you will die. Your belongings will disappear. But one thing will cross the centuries – glorious death in combat." But it comes out so pathetically in Russian, doesn't it? While it just thunders in German! Der Toten Tatenruhm! It just sends a chill through you. Hm, yes . . .' He stopped short, apparently ashamed by his outburst.

The walked on quietly for a time. It seemed silly to Artyom and it angered him too that they were probably the last ones walking the tunnel and it wasn't clear what was going on behind their backs – and now the guy was stopping to read poetry. But against his will he was still rolling the last lines of the poem around on his tongue, and for some reason he suddenly recalled Vitalik with whom he went to the Botanical Gardens. Vitalik the Splinter, who the robbers had shot down as they tried to break into the station through the southern tunnel. That tunnel was always considered to be dangerous, and therefore they put Vitalik there. He was eighteen years old, and Artyom was just coming up to his sixteenth year. But that evening they agreed to go to Zhenya's because there was a weed trader who had brought in some new stuff, some special stuff . . . And he got it right in the head, the little black hole was right in the middle of his forehead and the back of his head was blown off. That was it. 'You will die . . .' For some reason the conversation between his stepfather and Hunter came vividly to mind, particularly when Sukhoi said, 'And what if there's suddenly nothing there?' You die and there's nothing beyond that. Nothing. Nothing remains. Someone might remember you for a little while after but not for long. 'People close to you will die too' – or how did it go? Artyom really felt a chill now. When Mikhail Porfirevich finally broke the silence, Artyom was actually glad of it.

'Will you, by any chance, be going the same way as us? Or are you only going to *Pushkinskaya*? Do you intend to get out there? I mean, get off the path. I would really really not recommend that you do that, Artyom. You can't imagine what goes on there. Maybe, you'd like to go with us to *Barrakadnaya*? I would be most happy to talk to you along the way!'

Artyom again nodded indistinctly and mumbled something non-committal: he couldn't just discuss the aims of his journey with the first person he met, even if that person was an inoffensive old man. Mikhail Porfirevich went silent, having heard nothing in answer to what he'd asked.

They walked for quite a long time more in the silence. Everything sounded quiet behind them too and Artyom finally relaxed. In the distance, lights were shining, at first weakly, but then brighter and brighter. They were approaching *Kuznetsky Most* . . .

Artyom knew nothing about the local order of things and so he decided to hide his weapon. After wrapping it up in his vest, he pushed it deep into his rucksack.

Kuznetsky Most was an inhabited station, and about fifty metres before the entrance, in the middle of the path, there stood a sturdy checkpoint. It was only one checkpoint but it had a searchlight, though it was turned off at the moment since it wasn't needed, and it was equipped with a machine-gun position. The machine gun was covered but next to it sat a very fat man in a threadbare green uniform. He was eating some kind of mash from a beaten-up soldier's bowl. There were yet another couple of people in the same outfit with clumsy-looking army machine guns on their shoulders, who nitpickingly checked the documents of those who were coming out of the tunnel. There was a small line in front of them: all the fugitives who had come from *Kitai Gorod*, who had overtaken

Artyom while he had walked slowly with Mikhail Porfirevich and Vanechka.

The people were slowly and reluctantly admitted. One guy had been rejected and he was now sitting in dismay, not knowing what to do and trying from time to time to approach the checkpoint guards who pushed him off each time and called up the next person in line. Each of the arriving people was thoroughly searched and they saw for themselves how a man on whom they'd found an undeclared Makarov pistol was thrown out of the line and, when he tried to argue with them, they tied him up and led him away.

Artyom felt a twirling inside, sensing that trouble was ahead. Mikhail Porfirevich was looking at him in surprise and Artyom quietly whispered that he was armed, but the man just nodded reassuringly and promised him that everything would be all right. It wasn't that Artyom trusted him but thought that it would be very interesting to see how he intended to settle the matter. The old man merely smiled mysteriously.

Slowly, their turn approached. The border guards were now gutting the insides of some fifty-year-old woman's coat, while she took to accusing them of being tyrants, and expressing surprise that people such as them could exist. Artyom agreed with her but he decided not to voice his solidarity audibly. Digging around, the guard, with a satisfied whistle, took several grenades from her dirty brassiere and looked for an explanation.

Artyom was sure that the woman would now tell a touching story about her grandson who needed these things for his work. You see, he works as a welder, and this is part of his welding equipment. Or she'd say that she had found these grenades along the road and she was, as it happens, rushing to give them to the relevant authorities. But, taking a couple of steps backwards, she hissed a curse and rushed back into the tunnel, hurrying to hide in the darkness. The machine gunner set aside his bowl of food and gripped his unit but one of the two border guards, apparently the older one, stopped him with a gesture. The fat one, sighed in disappointment, and turned back to his porridge, and Mikhail Porfirevich took a step forward, holding his passport at the ready.

It was amazing but the senior guard, without the slightest twinge of conscience, having upturned the whole bag belonging to the completely inoffensive-looking woman, quickly leafed through the old man's notebook, and he didn't pay a jot of attention to Vanechka, as though he wasn't there. It was Artyom's turn. He readily gave his documents over to the lean moustached guard and the man started meticulously scrutinizing each page of them, and shined his torch on his stamps for an especially long time. The border guard compared Artyom's physiognomy no less than five times against the photograph, outwardly expressing his doubts, while Artyom gave a friendly smile, trying to portray himself as innocence itself.

'Why is your passport a Soviet model?' the guard finally asked with a stern voice, not knowing what else to pick on.

'I was little, see, when there were still real ones. And then our administration corrected the situation with the first form they could find to fill in.'

'That's out of order.' The man frowned. 'Open your rucksack.'

If he detects the machine gun, Artyom thought, then he could run back. Otherwise they would confiscate it. He wiped perspiration from his forehead.

Mikhail Porfirevich went up to the guard and stood very close to him, and whispered quickly:

'Konstantin Alexeyevich, you understand, this young man is my friend. He's a very very decent youth, I can guarantee it personally.'

The border guard opened Artyom's bag and pushed his hand inside it. Artyom went cold. Then the guard said dryly:

'Five,' and while Artyom figured out what he meant, the old man pulled a fistful of cartridges out of his pocket and, quickly counting out five, he put them into the half-open field bag that was hanging off the guard's belt.

But Konstantin Alexeyevich's hand had continued its rummaging in Artyom's bag and, apparently, the worst had happened, because his face took on a suddenly interested expression.

Artyom felt his heart falling into a precipice and he shut his eyes.

'Fifteen,' the guard said impassively.

After nodding, Artyom counted off ten additional cartridges and poured them into the same bag. Not one muscle flickered on the face of the border guard. He simply took a step to the side and the path to *Kuznetsky Most* was free and clear. With admiration for the man's iron restraint, Artyom went forward.

The next fifteen minutes were spent squabbling with Mikhail Porfirevich who stubbornly refused to accept five cartridges from Artyom, assuring him that his debt to Artyom was much greater.

Kuznetsky Most was no different from most of the other stations that Artyom had managed to see on his journey so far. It had the same marble on the walls and granite on the floors, but the arches here were unusually high and wide, creating an unusual sensation of spaciousness.

But the most surprising thing was that on each of the tracks stood entire trains that were incredibly long and so enormous that they took up almost all the room at the station. The windows were lit up with a warm light that shone through variously coloured curtains, and the doors were welcomingly open . . .

Artyom had not seen anything like it. Yes, he had half-erased memories of swiftly moving and hooting trains with bright squares of windows. The memories were from his early childhood, but they were diffuse, ephemeral, like the other thoughts about what had gone before: as soon as he tried to remember any details, to focus on something small, then the elusive image dissolved right away, and flowed like water through his fingers, and there was nothing left . . . But since he'd grown up he had only seen the train that had got stuck in the tunnel entrance at *Rizhskaya*, and some wagons at *Kitai Gorod* and *Prospect Mir*.

Artyom froze on the spot, captivated, looking at the train, counting the carriages that melted into the haze of the other end of the platform, near the entrance to the Red Line. There, a red calico banner hung down from the ceiling, snatched from the darkness by a distinct circle of electric light, and underneath it stood two machine gunners, in identical green uniforms and peak caps, who seemed small from far away and amusingly reminiscent of toy soldiers.

Artyom had three toy soldiers like them when he lived with his mother: one was the commander with a tiny pistol pulled out of its holster. He was yelling something, looking backwards – he was probably ordering his group to follow him into battle. The other two stood straight, holding their machine guns. The little soldiers were probably from different collections and there was no way to play with them: the commander was throwing himself into battle, and despite his valiant cries, the other two were standing in place, just like the border guards of the Red Line, and they weren't particularly heading for battle. It was strange, he remembered these soldiers so well, and yet he couldn't remember his mother's face . . .

Kuznetsky Most was relatively orderly. The light here, like at *VDNKh*, came from emergency lights that were strung along the length of the ceiling on some kind of mysterious metal construction that had perhaps once illuminated the station itself. Apart from the trains, there was absolutely nothing remarkable about the station.

'I've heard so often that there are so many amazingly beautiful places in the metro but from what I can see they're almost all identical.' Artyom shared his disappointment with Mikhail Porfirevich.

'Come now, young man! There are such beautiful places, you wouldn't believe! There's *Komsomolskaya* on the Ring, a veritable palace!' The old man heatedly took to persuading him. 'There's an enormous panel there, you know, on the ceiling. It has Lenin on it and other rubbish, it's true . . . Oh, what am I saying.' He stopped short and, with a whisper, said to Artyom, 'This station is full of secret agents from the *Sokolnicheskaya* line, that's to say the Red Line, sorry, I call things by their old names . . . So you have to be quiet here. The local leadership looks like it's independent but they don't want to quarrel with the Reds so if they ask them to hand someone over, then they can just hand you over. Not to mention the murders,' he added very quietly, looking timidly from side to side. 'Come on, let's find somewhere to rest. To be honest, I'm terribly tired, and indeed you, in my opinion, are only barely managing to stay on your feet. Let's spend the night here, and then we'll go on.'

Artyom nodded. This day had indeed seemed to be endless and stressful, and rest was absolutely necessary.

Enviously sighing and not taking his eyes off the train, Artyom followed Mikhail Porfirevich. There was joyful laughter and conversation coming from the carriages, and they passed a man standing in the doorway. He looked tired after a day's work and was smoking a cigarette with his neighbour, calmly discussing the events of the day. Gathered around a table, old ladies were drinking tea under a small lamp that was hanging from a wire, and children were running wild. This seemed unusual to Artyom: at *VDNKh*, the conditions were always very tense and people were ready for anything to happen. Yes, people got together in the evenings to sit quietly with friends in someone's tent, but there was nothing like this where doors were open, in full view, and people were visiting each other so easily, children everywhere . . . This station was just too happy.

'And what do they live on here?' Artyom couldn't contain himself as he caught up to the old man.

'What? You don't know?' Mikhail Porfirevich said politely but he was surprised. 'This is *Kuznetsky Most*! You get the best technicians in the metro here, important masters. They bring all sorts of devices to be fixed here from the *Sokolnicheskaya* line, even from the Ring itself. They're flourishing, flourishing. What it would be like to live here!' He sighed dreamily. 'But they're very strict about that . . .'

Artyom hoped in vain that they would also be able to sleep in one of the railroad cars, on a bed. In the middle of the hall stood a row of big tents, the kind that they lived in at *VDNKh*, and the first one they came to had a stencilled inscription on it that said: HOTEL. Next to it was a whole line of fugitives, but Mikhail Porfirevich, calling one of the organizers to the side, tinkled some copper, and whispered something magical starting with 'Konstantin Alexeyevich' and the matter was settled.

'We'll go here,' he said with an inviting gesture, and Vanechka joyfully gurgled.

They even gave them some tea there, and he didn't have to pay anything extra for it, and the mattresses on the floor were so soft that after you'd fallen on them you really didn't want to have to get up. Half-reclining, Artyom carefully blew on the mug of tea and attentively listened to the old man, who was telling him something with a burning look, having forgotten about his cup of tea:

'They have power across the whole branch. And no one will tell you about that, and the Reds will never admit to it, but University is not under their control and everything beyond University too! Yes, yes, The Red Line continues to *Sportivnaya*. There's a passage that starts there, you know, which was once the station *Leninskye Gory*, and then they changed the name but I can only remember the old one . . . But *Leninskye Gory*, was below a bridge actually. And you see, there was an explosion on the bridge and it collapsed into the river and the station was flooded, so there hasn't been any communication with University from the very beginning . . .'

Artyom swallowed a little gulp of tea and felt that everything inside was sweetly freezing in place in anticipation of something mysterious, unusual, that something had started back where the broken rails hovered over a precipice on the Red Line, down in the south-west. Vanechka was gnawing on his nails, only stopping sometimes to look with satisfaction at the fruits of his labour and then starting up again. Artyom looked at him almost with sympathy and felt grateful to the boy that he was being quiet.

'You know, we have a small circle at *Barrikadnaya*,' Mikhail Porfirevich smiled embarrassedly. 'And we get together in the evenings, sometimes people come to us from *Ulitsa 1905*, and now they chased all the differently thinking people, and Anton Petrovich moved to our station too . . . It's nonsense of course, these are

simple literary gatherings, but we sometimes talk about politics . . .
They don't especially like educated people at *Barrikadnaya* – either.
So we just do it on the quiet. But Yakov Yosifovich was saying that,
allegedly, University station didn't perish. That they managed to
block off the tunnel and there're still people there now. Not just
people but . . . You understand, that's where Moscow University
used to be, that's why the station is called University. And so,
allegedly, some of the professoriate were saved at University station,
and some students too. There was some kind of bomb-shelter under
the university, something constructed by Stalin, and I think they
were connected by special tunnels to the metro. And now there's
another kind of intellectual centre there, you know . . . But that's
probably just legend. That there's educated people in power there,
and all the three stations and the shelter are governed by a rector,
and each station is headed by a deacon – all elected for a specified
term. There, studies aren't at a standstill – there are still students, you
know, post-grads, teachers! And culture hasn't died out, not like it
has here, and they write things and they haven't forgotten how to
conduct research . . . And Anton Petrovich even said that one of his
friends, an engineer, told him in secret that they'd even found a way
to go to the surface. They created a protective suit, and sometimes
their scouts are sent into the metro . . . You'll agree that it sounds
improbable!' Mikhail Porfirevich added half-questioningly, looking
Artyom in the eye and Artyom noticed something sad in his eyes, a
timid and tired hope, that made Artyom cough a little and answer as
confidently as possible:

'Why? It sounds completely possible! Take *Polis* for example. I
heard the same about it . . .'

'Yes, it's a wonderful place *Polis* – but how can you get there these
days? They told me that at the council the power has been taken by
the military . . .'

'Which council?' Artyom raised his eyebrows.

'What? *Polis* is governed by a council of the most authoritative
people. And there, you know, authoritative people are either librarians or servicemen. But I don't really know about *Biblioteka Lenina*
exactly, so there's no point in talking about it, but the other entrance
to *Polis* is located right behind the Ministry of Defence, as far as I
remember, or, in any case it was somewhere nearby, and some of the
generals were able to evacuate to it at the time. At the very beginning,
the military men took power, and this junta ruled *Polis* for a sufficiently long time. But the people didn't really like them ruling, there

was disorder – of the blood-spilling kind – but that was a long time ago, a long time before the war with the Reds. Then they came to a compromise and this council was founded. And it happened that within it there were two factions – the librarians and the servicemen. It was a strange combination, of course. You know, the military had probably not met many live librarians in their lives. And here they were, together. And between these factions there was an eternal fight, of course: one would take control, then the other. When the war started with the Reds, defence was more important than culture and the scales tipped to the generals. Then peaceful times began and again the librarians gained influence. And it's like a pendulum, there. Now I hear that the military people have a stronger position, and they're imposing discipline there, you know, curfews and all those other joys of life.' Mikhail Porfirevich quietly smiled. 'Going through there isn't any easier than getting to the Emerald City . . . That's what we call University among ourselves, and the stations surrounding it, for a joke . . . You have to go either through the Red Line or through the Hansa but you can't just go there, as you yourself understand. Before, before the fascists, you could go through *Push-kinskaya* to *Chekhovskaya* and then it's just one transfer to *Borovits-kaya*. It's not a good transfer of course, but when I was younger, I made my way through it.'

Artyom asked what was so bad about the transfer he mentioned, and the old man reluctantly answered:

'You understand, right there in the middle of the tunnel there's a burnt-out train. I haven't been there in ages so I don't know how it is now but before you could see charred human remains sitting in its seats . . . It was just terrible. I don't know how this happened, and I asked some friends but no one has been able to say exactly. And it's very hard to get through this train, because the tunnel has started to collapse and dirt has filled in all the spaces around the train. In the train itself, in the carriages, I mean, various bad things are going on and it would be difficult to explain them. I'm an atheist in general, you know, and I don't believe in all that mystical nonsense . . . and now I don't believe in anything anymore.'

These words led Artyom to the gloomy memories of the noise in the tunnel on his line, and he couldn't restrain himself and he told the old man what had happened to his group, and then what happened with Bourbon and, after hesitating a little, he tried to repeat the explanation that Khan had given him.

'What? What are you talking about? That's utter rubbish!' Mikhail

Porfirevich brushed him off, sternly knitting his brows. 'I've already heard about such things. You remember I was telling you about Yakov Iosefovich? Well, he's a physicist and he explained to me that these disruptions to the psyche occur when people are subjected to the lowest frequencies of sound. They are essentially inaudible. If I'm not mistaken it's around seven hertz, but then my mind is like a sieve . . . And this sound can come about by itself, as a result of natural processes, for example, from tectonic shifts and things like that. I wasn't listening very attentively as he told me about it . . . But that it has something to do with souls of the dead? In the pipes? Please . . .'

This old man was interesting. Artyom heard things from him that he had never heard from anyone else. The man saw the metro from a different angle, an old-fashioned one, an amusing one, and everything, apparently, pulled his soul to the surface of the earth. He was clearly very uncomfortable here, as though these were his first days underground. And Artyom, thinking of the argument between Sukhoi and Hunter, asked him:

'And what do you think . . . ? We . . . people, I mean . . . Will we ever return to the surface? Will we survive and go back?'

And he immediately regretted asking it, because it was as though the question had cut into the old man's very veins, and he became soft straight away, and said, quietly, with a lifeless voice:

'I don't think so. I don't think so.'

'But after all, there were other metro systems, in Petersburg, in Minsk, and in Novgorod.' Artyom listed the names he had learnt by heart. They had always been empty shells of words.

'Ah! What a beautiful city – Petersburg!' Mikhail Porfirevich didn't answer him but sadly sighed. 'You know, Isaak's . . . Or Admiralteistvo, the spire there . . . What grace, what grace! And evenings on Nevsky Prospect – people, noise, crowds, laughter, children with ice cream, pretty girls . . . Music playing . . . In summer especially. It's rarely good weather in the summer there but when it happens . . . the sun, the sky is clear, azure . . . And then, you know, it's just easy to breathe again . . .'

His eyes fixed on Artyom but his gaze was going right through the young man and dissolved in the ethereal distance, where translucent, majestic silhouettes of the dusty buildings rose from the dusky smoke, giving Artyom the impression that he could have turned around and seen it for himself. The old man went quiet, heaved a deep sign, and Artyom decided not to interrupt his reminiscing.

'Yes, there were indeed other metro systems apart from Moscow's. Maybe people took refuge there and saved themselves . . . But think about it, young man!' Mikhail Porfirevich raised a knotty finger in the air. 'How many years have gone by, and nothing . . . Surely they would have found us after all these years if they had been looking for us? No,' he dropped his head. 'I don't think so.'

And then, after five minutes of silence, almost inaudibly, the old man sighed and said, more to himself than to Artyom:

'Lord, what a splendid world we ruined . . .'

A heavy silence hung in the tent. Vanechka, lulled by their quiet conversation, was sleeping, with his mouth slightly open and snuffling quietly, sometimes whining a little, like a dog. Mikhail Porfirevich didn't say another word, and though Artyom was sure that he wasn't yet sleeping, he didn't want to disturb him, so he closed his eyes and tried to fall asleep.

He was thinking that, after everything that had happened to him over the course of that endless day, sleep would come instantly, but time stretched out slowly, slowly. The mattress which had seemed so soft not long ago, now seemed lumpy and he had to turn over many times before he could find a comfortable position. The old man's sad words were knocking and knocking around in his ears. No. I don't think so. There will be no return to the sparkling avenues, the grandiose architectural constructions, the light, refreshing breezes of a warm summer evening, running through your hair and caressing your face. No more sky, it will never be like the old man described again. Now, the sky was receding upwards, enmeshed in the decayed wires of the tunnel ceiling and so it would remain forever. But before it was – what did he say? Azure? Clear? . . . This sky was strange, just like the one that Artyom saw at the Botanical Gardens that time, covered in stars, but instead of being velvet-blue, it was light blue, shimmering, joyful . . . And the buildings were really enormous, but they didn't press down with their mass. No, they were light, easy, as though they were woven out of sweet air. They soared, almost leaving the earth, their contours washed in the endless height of the sky. And how many people there were! Artyom had never seen so many people at once, only perhaps at *Kitai Gorod*, but here there were even more of them; the space in between of these great buildings was full of people. They scurried around and there were a great deal of children among them, and they were eating something, probably real ice cream. Artyom had even wanted to ask one of them if he could try some, he'd never eaten real ice cream. When he was little, he'd really wanted to try some. But there had been nowhere to get any, the confectionery factory had long since produced only mould and rats, rats and mould. But these little children, licking the delicacy, were running away from him and laughing, deftly dodging him, and he didn't even get the chance to look into any of their faces. Artyom didn't know anymore what he was trying to do: take a bite of ice cream or just to look one of the children in the face, to understand if the children did actually have faces . . . and he got scared.

The light outlines of the buildings started to slowly darken and, after some time, they were hanging over him threateningly, and then they started to move closer and closer. Artyom was still chasing the children, and it seemed to him that the children weren't laughing joyfully but evilly, and then he gathered all his strength and grabbed one of the little boys by the sleeve. The boy pulled away and scratched him like a devil, but squeezing the boy's throat with an iron grip, Artyom managed to look him in the face. It was Vanechka. Roaring and baring his teeth, he shook his head and tried to seize Artyom's hand. In panic, Artyom flung him away, and the boy, jumping up from his knees, suddenly lifted his head and let out that same terrible howl which made Artyom run back at *VDNKh* . . . And the children, randomly rushing around, started to slow down, and slowly to look at him from the side, getting closer, and the black bulky buildings towered right over them, drawing closer . . . And the children were filling the decreasing spaces between the buildings, and they took up Vanechka's struggle, full of savage malice and icy sadness, and finally they turned to Artyom. They didn't have faces, only black leather masks with mouths painted on them, and eyes, without whites or pupils.

And suddenly there was a voice that Artyom couldn't place. It was quiet and the vicious battle was drowning it, but the voice repeated itself insistently and, listening closely, trying not to pay attention to the children who were getting closer and closer, Artyom finally figured out what it was saying. 'You have to go.' And it said it again. And again. And Artyom recognized the voice. It was Hunter's.

He opened his eyes and threw off his covers. It was dark in the tent and very muggy, his head was filled with lead weight, his thoughts turned over lazily and heavily. Artyom couldn't seem to come to his senses, to figure out how long he'd slept and whether it was time to get up and get on the road or whether he should just turn over and try to have a better dream.

Then the tent flaps were pulled aside and through it poked the head of the border guard who had let them into *Kuznetsky Most*. Konstantin . . . What was his second name?

'Mikhail Porfirevich! Mikhail Porfirevich! Get up now! Mikhail Porfirevich! Has he died or what?' And not paying any attention to Artyom, who was staring at him in fright, he climbed into the tent and started to shake the sleeping old man.

Vanechka woke up first and started to bellow badly. The guard didn't pay him any attention, and when Vanechka tried to pull on his arm, he boxed him on the ear. And then the old man woke up.

'Mikhail Porfirevich! Get up quickly!' the border guard whispered urgently. 'You have to go! The Reds are asking for you to be handed over as a slanderer and enemy propagandist. I've been telling you and telling you: while you're here, while you're at our lousy station, don't start with your University talk! Did you listen to me?'

'Please, Konstantin Alexeyevich, what is all this?' The old man's head turned in confusion, rising from his cot. 'I didn't say anything, no propaganda. Perish the thought. I was only telling the young man about it, but very quietly, and there were no witnesses . . .'

'Well, take the young man with you! You know what kind of station this is. On Lublyanka they'll gut you and string you up on a stick, and your friend here will be put against the wall straight away so that he doesn't go talking again! Come on, be quick, why are you hanging around? They're coming for you right now! They're just conferring for a moment to decide what to ask the Reds for in exchange – so hurry up!'

Artyom had stood up and had his rucksack on his back. He didn't know whether to get out his weapon or not. The old man was also fussing but a minute later they were already on the road, walking quickly, whereupon Konstantin Alexeyevich himself pressed a hand over Vanechka's mouth with a martyred expression, and the old man looked over at him anxiously, afraid that the frontier guard might twist the boy's neck.

The tunnel leading to *Pushkinskaya* was better defended than the other had been. Here they passed two cordons, at one hundred and at two hundred metres from the entrance. At the first one there was concrete reinforcements, a parapet that cut across the way and forced people along a narrow path by the wall. And to the left of it was a telephone and its wire led right into the centre of the station, probably to the headquarters. At the second cordon there were the usual sandbags, the machine gun and the searchlights, like at the other side. There were duty officers at both posts but Konstantin Alexeyevich led them through both cordons to the border.

'Let's go. I'll walk with you for five minutes. I'm afraid that you can't come here again, Mikhail Porfirevich,' he said as they walked slowly toward *Pushkinskaya*. 'They haven't yet forgiven you for your old sins, and you've done it again. I heard that comrade Moskvin is personally interested, you hear? Well, OK, we'll try to think of something. Be careful as you go through *Pushkinskaya!*' he said as they carried on through the darkness. 'Go through it quickly! We're afraid of them, you see! So, be off and be well!'

Meanwhile, there was nowhere to rush to so the fugitives shortened their stride.

'What made them so bitter about you?' Artyom asked, curiously looking over at the old man.

'Well, you see, I just dislike them very much, and when the war was on . . . Well, basically, you see, my little circle put together some texts . . . And Anton Petrovich – he then lived at *Pushkinskaya* – had access to a typographical press. There was a press at *Pushkinskaya*, where some madmen were printing news . . . And that's where he printed it.'

'But the Reds' border looks harmless: there're two people there, there's a flag hanging, there're no reinforcements. Nothing like the Hansa has,' Artyom suddenly remembered.

'Of course! From this side everything is harmless because their main force is on the inside not the outside.' Mikhail Porfirevich smiled maliciously. 'That's where the reinforcements are. On the borders – it's just decoration.'

They went on in silence, each thinking their private thoughts. Artyom was listening to his sensations about the tunnel. It was a strange business but this tunnel and also the one that led from *Kitai Gorod* to *Kuznetsky Most* were both empty and you didn't feel anything inside them. They weren't filled with anything, they were just soulless constructions.

Then he remembered the nightmare he had just had. The details of it had already been wiped from his memory and all that was left were vague, frightening memories of faceless children and black masses against the sky. But there was the voice . . .

He couldn't follow the thought to its end. In front of him he heard the familiar awful squeaking and the rustle of paws, and then there was the suffocating, sweetish smell of rotting flesh, and when the weak light of their torches reached the place where these sounds were coming from, they saw in front of their eyes such a scene that Artyom thought it might perhaps be preferable to return to the Reds.

At the wall, face down in a row, lay three swollen bodies, their hands tied behind their backs with wire, and they had already been gnawed at by the rats. Pressing his jacket's sleeve to his nose so that he wouldn't smell the heavy sweetish and poisonous air, Artyom bent down over the bodies, and shined his light at them. They were stripped to their underwear, and their bodies showed no evidence of injury. But the hair on each of their heads was stuck together with blood, especially thickly around the black dot of the bullet hole.

'In the back of the head,' Artyom pointed out, trying to make his voice sound calm and feeling that he might suddenly vomit.

Mikhail Porfirevich half opened his mouth and his eyes began to shine.

'What they do, my God, what they do!' he said, sighing. 'Vanechka, don't look, don't look come here!'

But Vanechka, without showing the slightest unease, hunkered down next to the nearest corpse and began to point a finger at it, bellowing animatedly. The torch's beam slipped up the wall and it light up a piece of dirty paper, which was stuck right above the corpses at eye level. Above it, the letters 'Vierter Reich' were painted, accompanied by a depiction of an eagle. It went on in Russian: 'Not one swarthy animal is allowed within three hundred metres of the Great Reich!' And the same 'No through way' sign was also displayed with its circular black outline and little man crossed out.

'Swine,' Artyom said through clenched teeth. 'Because they have different colour hair?'

The old man just shook his head sadly and pulled on Vanechka's collar. He was busy studying the bodies and did not want to be lifted up from his squatting position.

'I see that our typographical machine still works,' Mikhail Porfirevich said sadly, and he moved on.

The travellers went on more slowly. After two minutes they saw the words '300 metres' had been painted on the walls in red paint.

'Three hundred metres to go,' Artyom said, listening uneasily to the echoes of a dog's barking in the distance.

About a hundred metres from the station they were struck by a bright light, and they stopped.

'Hands above your heads! Stand still!' a voice roared through a loudspeaker. Artyom obediently put his hands at the back of his head and Mikhail Porfirevich thrust both his hands into the air.

'I said, everyone, hands up! Walk slowly forward! Don't make any sudden movements,' the strained voice continued, and Artyom couldn't look to see who was speaking because the light was beating right into his eyes and it was too painful to do anything but look down.

Walking with small steps for some distance, they again stood still when they were told and the searchlight was finally turned to the side.

There was a whole barricade erected there, and there were two machine gunners in position and another guy with a holster in his belt, and they were all dressed in camouflage with black berets, aslant on their shaved heads. They had white armbands – with something looking like the German swastika on them but with three points not four. There were some barely visible dark figures in the distance and there was a nervously fidgeting dog by their feet. The surrounding walls were painted with crosses, eagles, slogans and curses aimed at non-Russians. They puzzled Artyom somewhat because they were partly in German. In a visible place, underneath a panel with the silhouette of an eagle on it and a three-pronged swastika, there was that sign again, lit from underneath, the one with the unfortunate little black figure and Artyom thought that it was being displayed like some sort of religious icon for them.

One of the guards made a step forward and lit a long torch, holding it at head level. He slowly walked around the three of them, steadily looking into their faces, apparently trying to find some evidence of non-Slavic features. However, they all looked Russian and he turned his torch away and shrugged his shoulders, disappointed.

'Documents!' he demanded.

Artyom readily extended his passport. Mikhail Porfirevich rummaged in his pocket and finally found his.

'And where are your documents for this one?' the older guard asked, nodding at Vanechka in disgust.

'You see, the thing is, that the boy . . .' the old man started to explain.

'Siiiilence! You will address me as "officer"! Answer the question precisely!' the document checker barked at him and his torch jumped around in his hands.

'Officer, you see, the boy is sick, he doesn't have a passport, he's just little, you see, but, look, he's assigned to me, here, I'll show you . . .' Mikhail Porfirevich began to babble, looking at the officer ingratiatingly, trying to find a spark of sympathy in his eyes.

But the man stood still, straight and stiff, like a rock, and his face was like stone, and Artyom again felt that he wanted to kill someone.

'Where is the photograph?' the officer spat, having flipped through the pages.

Vanechka, who had been standing quietly until that point, tensely watching the dog's silhouette and enthusiastically gurgling from time to time, now turned to the document checker and, to Artyom's horror, he bared his teeth and hooted meanly. Artyom was suddenly so scared for him that he forgot his own hostility toward the man, and his desire to kick him good and properly.

The document checker took an involuntary step backwards, staring at Vanechka unkindly and said, 'Get rid of this. Immediately. Or I'll do it myself.'

'Please forgive him, Officer, he doesn't understand what he's doing,' Artyom was surprised to hear his own voice pronounce.

Mikhail Porfirevich looked at him with gratitude and the document checker quickly rustled through Artyom's passport and returned it to him, saying coldly, 'No questions for you. You can pass.'

Artyom made a few steps forward and froze, feeling that his legs wouldn't obey him. The officer, turned away from him, and repeated his question to the other two about the photograph.

'You see, the thing is,' Mikhail Porfirevich started and, stumbling, he added, 'Officer, the thing is that there's no photographer where we live, and it costs a lot to get them at other stations, and I just don't have the money to get a picture . . .'

'Take off your clothes!' the man interrupted him.

'I'm sorry?' Mikhail Porfirevich's voice quavered, and his legs started to tremble.

Artyom took off his rucksack and put it on the floor, not thinking at all about what he was doing. There are some things that you don't want to do and you pledge to yourself that you won't do, you forbid yourself, and then suddenly they happen all by themselves. You don't even have time to think about them, and they don't make it to the cognitive centres of the brain: they just happen and that's it, and you're left just watching yourself with surprise, and convincing yourself that it wasn't your fault, it just happened all by itself.

If they undressed them and led them like the others to the three-hundredth metre, Artyom would get his machine gun out of his rucksack, would switch it to automatic fire and would take out as many of these camouflaged non-humans as he could, until they shot him down. Nothing else made any sense. It wasn't important that he had only known Mikhail and Vanechka for a day. It wasn't important that they would kill him. What would happen to *VDNKh*? There was no point in thinking what would happen afterwards. There are things that it's just simpler not to think about.

'Undress!' the man articulated carefully, repeating himself. 'A search!'

'But, if you please . . .' Mikhail Porfirevich uttered indistinctly.

'Siiilence!' the man barked. 'Quickly!' and he reinforced his words with a gesture, by taking his gun out of its holster.

The old man started to unbutton his jacket hastily, and the document checker turned his pistol away and silently watched how the old man threw off his jersey, clumsily hopping on one foot to take off his boots, and swaying, trying to undo his belt buckle.

'Faster!' the officer hissed rabidly.

'I'm clumsy . . . you see . . .' Mikhail Porfirevich started, but the document checker had finally had enough and smacked the old man in the teeth.

Artyom rushed forward but two strong arms grabbed him from behind and, as much as he tried to extract himself from them, it was useless.

And then something unforeseeable happened. Vanechka, who was about half the size of the thug in the black beret, suddenly bared his teeth and with an animal roar he rushed at him. The man didn't expect such speed from the wretched boy, and Vanechka managed to grab his left hand and even to hit him in the chest. However, a second later the officer recovered and flung Vanechka off, took a step backwards, held out his hand holding the pistol and pulled the trigger.

The shot, amplified by its echo in the tunnel, resounded in their ears but Artyom thought he could still hear how Vanechka sobbed silently and sat down on the floor. He was leaning over, clutching both hands to his stomach, when the officer kicked him and, with a disgusted expression on his face, pulled the trigger again, aiming at the head.

'I warned you.' He threw a cold look at Mikhail Porfirevich, who was frozen in place, looking at Vanechka with his jaw dropped and rattling sounds coming from his chest.

At that moment, everything went dark in front of Artyom's eyes and he felt such strength inside of him that the soldiers holding him from behind almost fell to the floor when he rushed forward. Time stretched for Artyom and he had enough of it to seize the handle of his machine gun and, clicking the safety lock, he fired a round right through the rucksack into the breast of the officer.

He noticed with satisfaction the black line of dots on the green of the camouflage.

CHAPTER 9

Du Stirbst

'To be hanged,' the commandant concluded. There was a burst of applause which mercilessly tormented his eardrums.

Artyom raised his head with difficulty and looked from side to side. Only one of his eyes could open, the other was totally swollen – the interrogators had tortured him with all their might. He couldn't hear very well either, it was as though sounds were making their way to him through a thick layer of cotton wool. It felt like his teeth were all still in place. But what would he need his teeth for now anyway?

Again the same light-coloured marble, the normal stuff. And this white marble was already setting his teeth on edge. Massive iron chandeliers on the ceiling, once, probably electrical fixtures. Now, there were lard candles in them, and the ceiling above them was completely black. There were only two such chandeliers burning in the whole station, one at the very end where a wide staircase stood, and the other where Artyom was standing in the middle of the hall, on the steps of a little bridge that connected to a side passage that led to another metro line.

Frequent semi-circular arches, almost completely unnoticeable columns, there was a lot of free space. What kind of station is this?

'The execution will take place tomorrow at five o'clock in the morning at *Tverskaya* station,' the fat man who was standing next to the commandant specified.

Like his superior, he was dressed not in green camouflage but in a black uniform with brilliant yellow buttons. There were black berets on both of them, but not as big or as crudely made as those on the soldiers in the tunnel.

There were lots of depictions of eagles and the three-pronged swastika, and slogans and mottos, drawn with great care in Gothic letters. Diligently trying to focus on the blurred words, Artyom read:

'The metro is for Russians!' 'Swarthy people to the surface!' 'Death to the rat-eaters!' There were others too, with more abstract contents: 'March forward to the last battle for the greatness of the Russian spirit!' 'With fire and sword we will establish true Russian order!' Then there was something from Hitler: 'A healthy body means a healthy spirit!' There was one inscription that especially made an impression on him. It was underneath a skilfully drawn portrait of a brave soldier with a powerful jaw and a strong chin, and a rather resolute-looking woman. They were depicted in profile, so that the man was shielding the woman. 'Each man is a soldier and each woman is the mother of a soldier!' the slogan went. All these inscriptions and pictures had somehow absorbed more of Artyom's attention than the words of the commandant.

Right in front of him, behind a cordon, the crowd was restless. There weren't many people here and they were all dressed rather blandly and basically, in quilted jackets and greasy overalls. There were hardly any women to be seen, and if this reflected reality, there wouldn't be many more soldiers in the future. Artyom's head fell to his chest – he hadn't the strength to hold it upright anymore, and if there hadn't been two broad-shouldered escorts in berets supporting him under the arms, he would have fallen already.

He felt faint again, and his head had begun to spin, and he couldn't manage to say anything ironic. Artyom had the impression that they would now turn him inside out in front of all these people.

A stupid indifference about what would happen to him gradually crept up on Artyom. Now he only had an abstract interest in what was surrounding him, as though none of this was happening to him, but he was just reading a book about it. The fate of the main character interested him, of course, but if he was killed then he could just pick another book off the shelf – one with a happy ending.

At first, he had been carefully beaten at length by patient and strong people while others asked him clever and judicious questions. The room had been, predictably, covered with disturbing yellow-coloured tiles, making it easy to wipe away blood. But it was impossible to get rid of its smell.

To start off with they taught him to call the gaunt man with slick, light hair and delicate features who was leading the interrogation 'commandant.' Then they taught him not to ask questions but to answer them. Then they taught him to answer the questions accurately and to the point. Artyom couldn't understand how his teeth were still in his mouth – though a few of them were seriously wobbly and his mouth had a constant taste of blood in it. At first, he tried to justify himself but it was explained to him that that wasn't worth it. Then he tried to stay silent but he was quickly convinced that this too seemed to be the wrong thing to do. It was very painful. It is altogether a strange feeling when a strong man beats you over the head – it's not just pain, but some kind of hurricane, which wipes all the thought from your mind and smashes your feelings to pieces. The real torture happens afterwards.

After a while, Artyom finally understood what he needed to do. It was simple – he needed to manage the expectations of the commandant the best way he could. If the commandant asked whether Artyom was sent by *Kuznetsky Most*, he had to just affirm that with a nod. It took less strength, and the commandant didn't wrinkle his Slavic nose at the response and his assistants didn't hit him. The commandant assumed that Artyom was sent with the aim of collecting military information and performing some kind of sabotage. He agreed again with a nod and then the torturer rubbed his hands together with satisfaction and Artyom had saved his second eye. But it was important not just to nod, he had to listen to exactly what the commandant had asked because if Artyom assented inattentively, the mood would worsen and one if his helpers would try, for example, to break one of Artyom's ribs. After about an hour and a half of this unrushed conversation, Artyom couldn't feel his body anymore, he couldn't see very well, he could scarcely hear and he understood almost nothing. He lost consciousness a few times, but they brought him back to his senses with iced water and ammonia. He must have been a very interesting person to talk to.

In the end, they had an absolutely false idea of who he was. They saw him as an enemy spy and a saboteur, who had appeared in order to stab the Fourth Reich in the back, and having decapitated the leadership, to sow the seeds of chaos and to prepare for an invasion. The ultimate goal was the establishment of an anti-national Caucasian-Zionist regime over the whole of the metro system. Though Artyom generally understood little about politics, such a global aim seemed to him to be worthy and so he told them that was true too. And it was good that he had agreed. Because of this he still had all his teeth. After the final details of the plot were revealed, they allowed Artyom to pass out.

When he could open his eye one last time, the commandant was already reading the sentence. The final formalities had barely been settled when the date of his departure from this world was announced to the public, and they pulled a black hood over his head and face and his vision worsened dramatically. He could see nothing, and he was even more dizzy. He barely managed to stay standing for a minute and stopped struggling when a spasm seized his body and he vomited right onto his boots.

The guard took a cautious step backwards, and the public rustled indignantly. For a moment, Artyom felt ashamed, and then he felt his head swimming and his knees buckling.

A strong arm was holding up his chin, and he heard a familiar voice, which now seemed almost to come from a dream world:

'Let's go. Come with me Artyom! It's all over. Get up!' he said, but Artyom still couldn't find the strength to get up or even to lift his head.

It was very dark, probably because of the hood. But how would he get it off if his hands were tied at the back? Getting it off was essential – to look to see if it was indeed the person he thought it was or if he was imagining it.

'The hood . . .' Artyom managed to say, hoping the person would understand.

The black veil that had been over his eyes then disappeared and Artyom saw Hunter in front of him. He hadn't changed at all since the time Artyom had talked with him, a while back now, a whole eternity ago, at *VDNKh*. How had he got here? Artyom wearily moved his head and looked around. He was on the platform of the exact same station where they had read his sentence. There were dead bodies everywhere; only a few candles in one chandelier continued to smoke. The other chandelier was blown out. Hunter was holding the same pistol in his right hand that had so amazed Artyom the last time, having seemed so huge with its long silencer screwed onto its barrel and its impressive laser sight. A 'Stechkin.' The hunter was looking at Artyom anxiously and attentively.

'Is everything OK with you? Can you walk?'

'Yes. Probably.' Artyom summoned his courage but he was interested in something else at that moment. 'You're alive? Did everything work out for you?'

'As you can see,' Hunter smiled wearily. 'Thanks for your help.'

'But I didn't complete the task.' Artyom shook his head and it was burningly painful, and he was filled with shame.

'You did everything you could.' Hunter patted him soothingly on the shoulder.

'And what's happening at home? At *VDNKh*?'

186

'Everything's fine, Artyom. Everything has already passed. I was able to collapse the entrance and now the dark ones won't be able to get into the metro anymore. We're saved. Let's go.'

'And what happened here?' Artyom looked around, noticing with horror that the whole hall was filled with corpses, and that other than his voice and Hunter's, not another sound could be heard.

'It doesn't matter.' Hunter looked into his eyes firmly. 'You shouldn't worry about it.' He bent over and lifted his sack from the floor. A smoking army hand machine gun was lying in it. His cartridge belt was almost spent.

The hunter moved forward and Artyom tried to keep step. Looking from side to side, he saw something that he hadn't noticed before. Several dark figures were hanging from the little bridge where Artyom had had his sentence read.

Hunter said nothing and was taking long steps, as though he had forgotten that Artyom could barely move. As much as Artyom tried, the distance between then was increasing all the time, and Artyom was afraid that Hunter would just go off, leaving him in this horrible station, which was covered in slippery and still warm blood, and where the only inhabitants were corpses. Do I really deserve this? Artyom thought. Is my life so much more important than the lives of all these people? No, he was glad to have been rescued. But all these people – randomly scattered, like bags and rags, on the granite of the platform, side by side, on the rails, left forever in the poses that Hunter's bullets had found them in – they all died so that he could live? Hunter had made this exchange with such ease, just as though he had sacrificed some minor chess figures to safeguard one of the most important pieces . . . He was just a player, and the metro was a chessboard, and all the figures were his, because he was playing the game with himself. But here was the question: Was Artyom such an important piece to the game that all these people had to perish for his preservation? Henceforth the blood that was flowing along the cold granite would probably pulse in his veins too. It was like he had drunk it, extracted it from others for his existence. Now he would never be warm again . . .

Artyom, with effort, ran forward a bit in order to catch up with Hunter and to ask if he would ever become warm again or would he, even at the hottest firesides, stay this cold and melancholic, like an icy winter's night on a far-flung semi-station.

But Hunter was far in the distance. Maybe it was because Artyom didn't manage to catch him up that Hunter descended onto the tracks and rushed into the tunnel with the agility of an animal. His movements seemed, to Artyom, like the movements of . . . a dog? No, a rat . . . Oh God.

'Are you a rat?' The terrible idea tore from Artyom's mouth, and he was frightened by what he'd said.

'No,' came the answer. 'You're the rat. You're the rat! Cowardly rat! Cowardly rat!' Someone repeated it just above his ear, and spat fruitily.

Artyom shook his head but immediately regretted it. Now, thanks to his sharp movements, the aching blunt pain in his body had exploded. He lost control of his limbs and started to stumble forward, and then he rested his burning forehead on something cool and metallic. The surface was ribbed and it pressed on his skin unpleasantly but it cooled his inflamed flesh, and Artyom froze in that position for a time, not having the strength to make any further decisions. He caught his breath and then carefully tried to open his left eye a little bit.

He sat on the floor, his forehead against a lattice of some sort. It went up to the ceiling and filled the space on both sides of the low and narrow arch. He was facing the hall, and there were paths behind him. All the nearest arches opposite him, as far as he could see, were turned into cages too; there were a few people sitting in each of them. This station was exactly the opposite of the station where he had been sentenced to death. That one was utterly graceful, light, airy, spacious, with transparent columns, wide and high arches, despite the gloomy lighting and the inscriptions and drawings covering the walls. It was like a banquet hall compared with this one. Here everything was oppressive and scary. There was a low, rounded ceiling, like in the tunnels. It was barely twice a man's height. And there were massive, rough columns, each of which was much wider than the arches that cut across between them. The ceiling of the arches were so close to the ground that he could have reached up and touched it were it not for the fact that his hands were tied with wire behind his back. Apart from Artyom there were another two people in the cell. One was lying on the ground with his face buried in a heap of rags, and he was groaning dully. The other had black eyes and brown hair and hadn't shaved for some time, and he was squatting, leaning against the marble wall, watching Artyom with lively curiosity. There were two strong men in camouflage and berets patrolling the length of the cages, one of whom had a big dog on a leash, and he would scold it from time to time. They, it seemed, had woken Artyom.

It had been a dream. It had been a dream. He had dreamt it all.

They were going to hang him.

'What time is it?' he muttered, only slightly moving his inflamed tongue, and looking sideways at the black-eyed man.

'Happast nine,' the man answered willingly, pronouncing his words with the same accent that Artyom had heard at *Kitai Gorod*: instead of 'o' they said 'a' and instead of 'y' they said 'ay'. And then he added, 'In the evening.'

Half past nine. Two and a half hours until twelve – and five hours before . . . before the procedure. Seven and a half hours. And while he was thinking, counting, time was already flying past.

Once Artyom had tried to imagine: what would, what should a person feel and think in the face of death, the night before his execution? Fear? Hatred for his executioners? Regret?

But he was empty inside. His heart was thumping hard in his breast, his temples were throbbing, blood slowly accumulated in his mouth until he swallowed. The blood had the taste of rusty iron. Or was it that wet iron had the taste of fresh blood?

They would hang him. They would kill him.

He would cease to exist.

He couldn't imagine it, couldn't take it on board.

Everyone knows that death is unavoidable. Death was a part of daily life in the metro. But it always seemed that nothing unfortunate would happen to you, that the bullets would fly past you, the disease would skip over you. Death of old age was a slow affair so you needn't think about it. You can't live in constant awareness of your mortality. You had to forget about it, and though these thoughts came to you anyway, you had to drive them away, to smother them, otherwise they could take root in your consciousness and they would make your life a misery. You can't think about the fact that you'll die. Otherwise you might go mad. There's only one thing that can save a man from madness and that's uncertainty. The life of someone who has been sentenced to death is different from the life of a normal person in only one way: the one knows exactly when he will die, and the regular person is in the dark about it, and consequently it seems he can live forever, even though it's entirely possible that he could be killed in a catastrophic event the following day. Death isn't frightening by itself. What's frightening is expecting it.

In seven hours.

How would they do it? Artyom couldn't really imagine how people were hanged. They once had to execute a traitor at their station but Artyom was still little then and didn't understand much, and anyway, they wouldn't perform public executions at *VDNKh*. They would probably throw a rope around his neck . . . either they'd string him up to the ceiling . . . or there would be some sort of stool involved. . . . No, it didn't bear thinking about.

He was thirsty.

With effort he flicked the switch and the train of his thoughts swept onto other rails – to the officer he had shot. The first person he'd ever killed. The scene arose before his eyes again, invisible bullets going into his broad chest, and how they had left burnt black marks in which fresh blood had coagulated. He didn't feel the slightest regret for what he'd done, and this surprised him. Once, he had reckoned that every killed person must be a heavy burden on the conscience of the person who killed them – they would appear in dreams, disturb his old age . . . But no. It seemed it wasn't like that at all. There was no pity. No repentance. Only gloomy satisfaction. And Artyom understood that if the murdered person were to come to him in a nightmare, then he would only turn indifferently away from the phantom and it would then disappear without a trace. But old age . . . There would be no old age anymore.

Time was running out. It would probably involve a stool. When there is so little time, you have to think about something important, about the most important thing, that you never found time to think about before, leaving it all till later . . . About the fact that your life wasn't lived right, and that you'd do it differently if given a second chance . . . No. He couldn't have had any other life in this world, and there was nothing to try to re-do. When the border guard shot Vanechka in the head should he not have rushed for his automatic machine gun but instead have stayed standing at the side? It wouldn't have worked – he would never have managed to chase Vanechka and Mikhail Porfirevich from his dreams. What had happened to the old man? Damn, what would it take to get a mouthful of water!

First they would lead him out of the cell . . . And if he was lucky then they'd lead him through the transfer passage but there'd little time for that now. And if they didn't put that damned cover over his head, he would be able to see something, apart from the rods of the lattice in front of him and the endless rows of cages.

'What station you from?' said Artyom through dry lips, tearing himself away from the lattice and looking up into the eyes of his neighbour.

'*Tverskaya*,' the man responded. Then he asked: 'Listen, brother, what are you in here for?'

'I killed an officer,' Artyom slowly replied. It was hard for him to speak.

'O-oh . . .' the unshaved man offered sympathetically. 'So they're going to hang you?'

Artyom shrugged, and turned again to lean on the lattice.

'Sure they will,' his neighbour assured him.

They will. And soon. Right here at the station, and they won't be transferring him.

If only to get a drink of water . . . To wash this metallic taste from his mouth, to moisten his dry throat, then, maybe, he could speak to this man for a little more than a minute. There was no water in the cage, but on the other side of the space there was a fetid tin bucket. Could he ask his jailers? Maybe they give small indulgences to those who have been sentenced? If he could only have pushed his hand out through the lattice, and wave it a little . . . But his hands were tied behind his back, and the wire was digging into his wrists and he had lost all sensation. He tried to cry out, but only a rattle emerged, which turned into a cough from deep in his lungs.

Both guards approached the cage when they noticed his attempts to get their attention.

'The rat has awoken,' the one with the dog grinned.

Artyom threw his head back to see the man's face and whispered with difficulty, 'Drink. Water.'

'A drink?' The guard with the dog pretended to be surprised. 'What do you need that for? You're just about to be strung up and all you want is to drink! No, we won't be getting you any water. Maybe that way you'll die sooner.'

The matter was settled and Artyom closed his eyes wearily, but the jailers apparently wanted to chat with him some more.

'So, you scum, you've finally understood who you raised your fist to?' the other guard asked. 'And you're even a Russian, you rat! It's because of those morons who will stab you in the back with your own knife, those . . .' He nodded at Artyom's neighbour in the next cage. 'The whole metro will be full of them soon and your simple Russian won't even be able to breathe anymore.'

The unshaved prisoner looked down. Artyom could only find the strength to shrug his shoulders.

'And they smacked that mongrel of yours nicely too,' the first guard added. 'Sidorov said that the tunnel was a bloodbath. And quite right. Subhumans! They need to be destroyed. They are our . . . genofond!' He remembered the difficult word. 'They ruin things. And your old man died too,' he concluded.

'What?' Artyom sobbed. He'd been afraid of that, but he'd hoped that perhaps the old man hadn't died, that maybe he was somewhere here, in the next chamber . . .

'Right. He died. They ironed him a little bit but he up and croaked,' the guard with the dog said happily, satisfied by the fact that Artyom was finally reacting to them.

'You will die. All your relatives will die . . .' He could see Mikhail Porfirevich, without a care in the world, stopping in the middle of the tunnel, leafing through his notepad, and then repeating this last line with emotion. What was it again? 'Der Toten Tatenrum?' No, the poet was mistaken, there aren't any acts of glory anymore. There isn't anything anymore.

Then he remembered how Mikhail Porfirevich had missed his old apartment, and especially his old bed. Then his thoughts started thickening, and were flowing more and more slowly, and then they stopped altogether. He rested his forehead against the lattice again and, with a dulled mind, he started looking at the jailer's sleeve. A three-pronged swastika. Strange symbol. Looks either like a star or like a crippled spider.

'Why only three?' he asked. 'Why three?'

He had to tip his head towards the man's armband so the security guards would understand what he meant.

'Well, how many do you need?' the one with the dog answered indignantly. 'There are three stations, you fool! It's a symbol of unity. And, just you wait, when we get to *Polis*, we'll add a fourth . . .'

'What are you talking about?' the other guard interrupted. 'It's an ancient symbol, a primordial Slavic sign! It's called a solstice. It belonged to the Fritzs and then we took it over. Stations – you pot-head.'

'But there's no more sun anymore . . .' Artyom squeezed out the words, feeling as though there was a muddy veil over his eyes, and his sense of hearing was disappearing into the haze.

'That's it, he's gone mad,' the guard with the dog announced with gratification. 'Let's go, Senya, and find someone else for a chat.'

Artyom didn't know how much time had passed while he sat there deprived of his thoughts and his vision. He occasionally regained consciousness and understood vague images. But everything was saturated with the taste and smell of blood. However, he was glad that his body had taken pity on his mind and killed all thought, and so released his sense of reason was from melancholy.

'Hey, brother!' His neighbour shook his shoulder. 'Don't sleep. You've been sleeping for a long time! It's almost four o'clock!'

Artyom tried to surface from the chasm of his unconsciousness but it was difficult, as though lead weights had been attached to his feet. Reality came to him slowly, like the indistinct outlines on film that has been placed in developing solution.

'What time is it?' he croaked.

'Ten to four,' the black-eyed man said.

Ten to four . . . They'd probably come for him in about forty minutes. And in an hour and ten minutes . . . An hour and nine minutes. An hour and eight minutes. Seven minutes.

'What's your name?' his neighbour asked.

'Artyom.'

'I'm Ruslan. My brother was called Ahmed, and they shoot him straight away. But I don't know what they do with me. My name is Russian – maybe they don't want mistake.' The black-eyed man was happy that he finally managed to start a conversation.

'Where are you from?'

None of this was of interest to Artyom, but the chatting of his unshaven neighbour helped him to fill his head. It didn't matter what it was filling it with. He didn't want to think about *VDNKh*. He didn't want to think about the mission that he had been charged with. He didn't want to think about what was happening in the metro. He didn't want to. He didn't want to!

'I'm from *Kievskaya*. You know it? We call it sunny Kiev . . .' Ruslan smiled, showing a row of white teeth. 'There are lots of my people there . . . I have a wife, children – three children. The oldest one has six fingers on his hands!' he added proudly.

. . . Something to drink. Just a mouthful. Even if it's tepid. he wouldn't mind tepid water. Unfiltered even. Any water. A mouthful. And to be forgotten about again, until the escorts come to get him. He wanted an empty mind again, and not to be bothered. He wanted his head to stop spinning, to stop itching, to stop his thoughts from telling him that he'd made a mistake. He didn't have the right to do what he did. He should have gone off. Turned his back. Covered his ears. Carried on. Made it from *Pushkinskaya* to *Chekhovskaya*. And from there it was just one transfer. So easy. Just one transfer and it would all have been done, his task completed. He would be alive.

Something to drink. His hands had become so numb that he didn't feel them.

It's so much easier for people to die when they believe in something! For those who believe that death isn't the end of everything. For those in whose eyes the world is separated into black and white – who know exactly what they need to do and why, who hold the torch of an idea, of beliefs, in their hands, and everything they see is illuminated by it. Those who have nothing to doubt and nothing to regret. They must have an easy time of dying. They die with a smile on their face.

'We had fruit big like this before! And the beautiful flowers! I give them to the girl for no money and she give me the smile . . .' The words reached Artyom but couldn't distract him anymore.

Steps could be heard from the depths of the hall. Several people were approaching and Artyom's heart tightened and turned into a small nervous lump. Were they coming for him? So soon! He thought forty minutes would have lasted longer . . . Or had his devilish neighbour told him that more time was left because he had wanted to give him some hope? No, it couldn't be . . .

Three pairs of boots stopped at his cage. Two of them were in spotted military trousers, one in black trousers. The lock made a grinding sound and Artyom only just managed not to fall over as the cage door he was leaning on opened.

'Pick him up,' someone said . . .

He was grabbed under the arms and he soared towards the ceiling.

'Break a leg!' Ruslan wished him, as a parting gesture.

There were two machine gunners, but not those that he'd talked to. However, these were just as anonymous looking. A third guy with a bristling moustache and watery blue eyes was wearing a black uniform and a small beret. 'Follow me,' he ordered and they dragged Artyom to the other end of the platform. He tried to walk himself. He didn't want them to drag him like he was a helpless doll . . . If he had to leave this life, he wanted to do it with pride. But his legs wouldn't obey him, they buckled, and he could only clumsily place them on the floor, hampering the forward motion so that the man in the black uniform looked at him severely.

The cages didn't continue to the end of the hall. The row was interrupted in the middle where the escalators to the next level down were situated. There, in the depths, torches were burning and ominous crimson light reflected on the ceilings. There were cries of pain coming from below. Artyom suddenly had a thought about the underworld and he felt a certain relief when they had led him past the escalators. From the last cage, someone yelled to him, 'Farewell my friend!' But Artyom didn't pay him any attention. He could only see a glass of water looming before his eyes.

On the opposite wall there was a guards observation post, a roughly knocked-together table with two chairs and there was a sign with that symbol which said no entry for black people. He couldn't see any gallows anywhere and, for a moment, Artyom had the crazy hope that they had only wanted to scare him and that they weren't really leading him to his hanging but they were taking him to the end of the station so that he could be let go without the others seeing it.

The man with the moustache, who was walking ahead, turned at the last archway, towards the pathways, and Artyom began to believe in his rescue fantasy even more strongly . . .

There was a small platform on wheels standing on the rails, and it was arranged in such a manner that its floor was level with the station floor. There was a thickset man in a spotted uniform, checking a loop of rope that was hanging from a hook screwed into the ceiling. The only difference between him and the others was that his rolled up sleeves showed powerful forearms, and he had a knitted hat pulled over his head with holes cut into it for his eyes.

'Is everything ready?' the man in the black uniform said and the executioner nodded at him.

'I don't like this construction,' he said. 'Why couldn't we use the good old stool? Then it's – pow!' He punched his fist into his other palm. 'Break his neck! But with this thing . . . While he's choking, he'll squirm like a worm on a hook. And when they choke, there's so much to clean up afterwards! There's like guts everywhere . . .'

'Enough!' the man in the black uniform said. Then he took the executioner aside and furiously hissed something at him.

As soon as their superior had stepped away, the soldiers quickly went back to their interrupted conversation.

'So?' the one on the left impatiently asked the one on the right.

'OK, so,' the one on the right whispered loudly, 'I pushed her up against the column and shoved my hand under her skirt and she turned all soft and said to me . . .' But he didn't manage to finish because his superior had returned.

'Never mind the fact that he's Russian – he transgressed! . . . The traitor, the turncoat, degenerate, and traitors should be painfully punished!' He was encouraging the executioner.

They untied his hands, and took off his jacket and jumper so that Artyom stood there only wearing his dirty undershirt. Then they tore the cartridge case that Hunter had given him off the string around his neck. 'A talisman?' the executioner inquired. 'I'll put it in your pocket, it might still come in handy.'

His voice was far from evil, and it was curiously soothing.

Then they pulled his hands together behind his back and pushed Artyom onto the scaffold. The soldiers remained on the platform since they weren't needed. He couldn't escape anyway since it required all the strength Artyom had just to stand there while the executioner fitted the loop over his head. To stand up, not fall and make no noise. Something to drink. That's all that he could think about. Water. Water!

'Water . . .' he croaked.

'Water?' The executioner threw up his hands in disappointment. 'Where am I going to get you any water now? It's not possible, my dear, we're already way behind schedule – now just be patient, not long now . . .'

He jumped off onto the path with a thud and spat on his hands before taking up the rope attached to the scaffold. The soldiers were lined up and their commander had assumed a significant and even solemn look.

'As an enemy spy, who has viciously betrayed his people,' he began.

In Artyom's head there was a dance of thought fragments and images that said wait, it's too early, I haven't yet managed to do what I had to do, and then Hunter's strict face appeared before his eyes and disappeared immediately in the crimson twilight of the station, then Sukhoi's tender gaze appeared and vanished too. Mikhail Porfirevich . . . 'You will die' . . . the dark ones . . . they can't . . . Wait! And over all this, interrupting his memories, the words, his desires, shrouding them in a stuffy dense haze, hung a great thirst. Something to drink . . .

' . . . degenerate, who discredits his own nation . . .' the voice continued to burble.

Suddenly there were shouts in the tunnel and a burst of machine gun fire, and then a loud bang and everything went quiet. The soldiers grabbed their machine guns. Their superior in black turned nervously and quickly said, 'Punishment by death. Go ahead!' And he gave the signal.

The executioner grunted and pulled the rope, planting his feet on the cross-ties. The boards slipped away from Artyom's feet, though he tried to keep touching them, so that he could stay on the scaffold, but they moved further off and it was getting harder and harder to stand. The rope was dragging him back, towards death, and he didn't want it, he didn't want to die . . .

Then the floor slipped out from under him and the loop tightened from the weight of his body. It squeezed his neck, cut into his windpipe, and a rattle issued from his throat. His sight lost its sharpness, and everything was twisted inside him. His body was begging for air, but he couldn't inhale, no matter what he tried, and his body started to coil, convulsively, and there was an awful tickling feeling in his stomach. The station clouded with a poisonous yellow smoke and gunshots roared nearby, and then he lost consciousness.

'Hey, hangman! Come on, come on now. Don't pretend. We've felt your pulse so you can't feign death.' And he was hit across the cheeks, bringing him round.

'I refuse to do mouth-to-mouth on him again!' the other person said.

This time Artyom was absolutely sure that it was a dream, the last seconds of unconsciousness before the end. Death was so close, and the moment her iron fist closed around his neck was as indisputable as the moment the floor fell away from underneath him and he hung over the rails.

'That's enough blinking, you'll be fine!' the first voice insisted. 'We got you out of the loop so you could enjoy life again and you're rolling all over the floor on your face!'

Someone shook him hard. Artyom shyly opened an eye and then closed it, having decided that he was probably in the process of dying prematurely and that the afterlife had already begun. A being was leaning over him and it looked a bit like a person but it was so unusual looking that it reminded Artyom of Khan's calculations about where souls go when they are separated from their transitory bodies. The skin of the being was a matte-yellow, which you could even see in the light of a lantern nearby, and instead of eyes, he had narrow slits, as though a sculptor who was sculpting a person out of a tree had almost finished the face, but had only made an outline of the eyes, and he forgot to chip open the eyes so it could look out onto the world. The face was round with high cheek bones and Artyom had never seen anything like it.

'No, this is not working,' someone declared resolutely from above and they sprayed water in his face.

Artyom swallowed it convulsively and stretched out his hands for the bottle. At first he just held onto the neck of the bottle and only after that did he get up and look around.

He was rushing through a dark tunnel with head-spinning speed, lying on a section car that was no less than two metres long. There was a light smell of burning in the air, and Artyom thought with astonishment that it must be fuelled with petrol. There were four people apart from him sitting on the section car, and there was a big, brown dog with a black undercoat. One of them was the guy who had hit Artyom across the cheeks. There was a bearded guy in a hat with ear-flaps that had a red star sewn onto it and onto his quilted jacket too. He had a long machine gun dangling down his back, one just like the 'hoe' that Artyom had before, but there was a bayonet-knife screwed onto its barrel. The third person was a big fellow whose face Artyom didn't see at once but when he did, he almost jumped off the car: his skin was very dark. Artyom looked at it a bit more and calmed down. He wasn't a dark one, his shade of skin wasn't the same as theirs – and he had a normal, human face with slightly out-turned lips and a flattened nose like a boxer's. The last guy had a relatively regular appearance but he had a beautiful brace face and a strong chin – which reminded him of something on a poster at *Pushkinskaya*. He was dressed in a beautiful leather coat, which was tied with a wide belt with two rows of holes in it and an officer's sword belt, and from the belt hung a holster of impressive size. There was a Degtyaryov machine gun at the back of the section car and a fluttering red flag. When a beam from the lantern accidentally fell on the flag, he could see that it wasn't really a flag but a ragged piece of material with the red and black face of a bearded man on it. All this seemed more like some kind of terrible delirium than the miraculous rescue that Hunter had made for him when he ruthlessly cut his way through *Pushkinskaya*.

'He's regained consciousness!' the narrow-eyed man said joyfully. 'So, hangman, what did they get you for?'

He spoke totally without accent, his pronunciation was no different than Artyom's or Sukhoi's. That was very strange – hearing pure Russian speech from such an unusual being. Artyom couldn't shed the feeling that this was some kind of farce and the narrow-eyed man was only moving his lips while the bearded guy or the man in the leather coat spoke from behind him.

'I shot one of their officers,' he admitted reluctantly.

'Well, good for you! You're just the kind we like! That's what they deserve!' the man with the high cheek bones said enthusiastically, and the big, dark-skinned guy who was sitting at the front turned to Artyom and raised his eyebrows respectfully. Artyom thought that this guy must mispronounce words.

'That means we didn't create such a scene for nothing.' He smiled broadly. He also had a flawless accent, so that Artyom was confused and now didn't know what to think.

'What's your name, hero?' the handsome man in leather asked him and Artyom introduced himself.

'I'm comrade Rusakov. This is comrade Bonsai.' He pointed to the narrow-eyed man. 'This is comrade Maxim.' The dark-skinned one grinned again. 'And this is comrade Fyodor.'

The dog came last. Artyom wouldn't have been surprised if he'd been called 'comrade' too. But the dog was simply called Karatsyupa. Artyom shook their hands one by one, the strong, dry hand of comrade Rusakov, the narrow, firm palm of comrade Bonsai, Maxim's black shovel of a hand and the fleshy hand of comrade Fyodor. He earnestly tried to remember all their names especially the hard to pronounce 'Karatsyupa.' But it seemed that they called each other different names anyway. They addressed the main guy as 'comrade commissar,' and the dark-skinned one they called Maximka or Lumumba, the narrow-eyed one was simply 'Bonsai' and the bearded one with the hat with ear-flaps they called 'Uncle Fyodor.'

'Welcome to the First International Red Fighting Brigade of the Moscow Metropolitan in the name of Ernesto Che Guevara!' comrade Rusakov triumphantly announced.

Artyom thanked him and fell silent, looking around. The name was very long and the ending of it generally blended into something quite unclear – for a while, the red colour had had an effect on Artyom not unlike its effect on a bull and the word 'brigade' was associated for him with Zhenya's stories about the gangster lawlessness somewhere near *Shabolovskaya*. Most of all, he was intrigued by the face trembling on the cloth in the wind and he timidly asked:

'And who have you got there on your flag?' At the last second he decided on the word 'flag' having almost said 'rag.'

'That, my brother, is Che Guevara,' Bonsai explained to him.

'Which chegavara?' Artyom hadn't understood, but seeing rage fill

Rusakov's eyes and the mocking smile on Maximka's face, he figured out that he'd done something foolish.

'Comrade. Ernesto. Che. Guevara.' The commissar rapped the separate syllables. 'The great. Cuban. Revolutionary.'

Now the sounds were all more distinct though it still wasn't intelligible to Artyom, but he decided to widen his eyes enthusiastically and say nothing. After all, these people had saved his life, and angering them right now with his ignorance would be impolite.

The tunnel's soldered ribs flashed past fantastically quickly, and during the length of their conversation they had already managed to fly through one half-empty station and stopped in the twilight of the tunnel beyond it. Here, at the side, there was a little dead-end off-shoot where they could stop.

'Let's see if the fascist reptiles dare to go after us,' said comrade Rusakov.

Now they had to whisper very quietly because comrades Rusakov and Karatsyupa were attentively listening for sounds coming from the darkness.

'Why did you do it? I mean, rescue me?' Artyom asked, trying to choose the right word.

'It was a planned sortie. Some information arrived,' explained Bonsai, smiling mysteriously.

'About me?' Artyom asked in the hope that he could believe Khan's words about his special mission.

'No, just in general.' Bonsai made an indistinct gesture. 'We heard they were planning some kind of atrocity. So comrade commissar decided we had to stop it. Besides, it's our mission – to bother them constantly.'

'They haven't put up road blocks on this side, not even a bright torch, just a few outposts with simple fires,' Maximka added. 'We ran over them straight away. Sadly, we had to use the machine gun. But then, there was the smoke bomb, we had gas masks and we took you, our home-grown SS man, and went back.'

Uncle Fyodor, silent and smoking some kind of weed in a pipe, the smoke from which started to make his eyes tear up, suddenly said, 'Yes, my young friend, it's good that you were appropriated. Do you want a little brew?'

And picking up a half-empty bottle of some kind of murky swill from an iron box, he shook it and offered it to Artyom.

It was going to take a lot of bravery to take a sip. It went down like sandpaper but he felt as though a vice that had been clamped inside him this last twenty-four hours had relaxed.

'So, are you Reds?' he asked cautiously.

'We, my brother, are communists! Revolutionaries!' Bonsai said proudly.

'From the Red Line?' Artyom leaned in.

'No, just simple communists,' the man answered a bit hesitantly and hurried to add, 'Comrade commissar will explain it all to you, he's in charge of the ideology here.'

Comrade Rusakov, having returned after a few minutes, informed them, 'All is quiet.' His handsome masculine face radiated a sense of calm. 'We can take a break.'

There was nothing with which to build a fire. They hung the little kettle over a camping stove and cut up some cold pork. The revolutionaries ate suspiciously well.

'No, comrade Artyom, we aren't from the Red Line,' comrade Rusakov declared firmly when Bonsai related the question to him. 'Comrade Moskvin has taken the position of Stalin, turned his back on a metro-wide revolution, officially denouncing the Interstational and cutting off support for revolutionary activities. He's a renegade and he's a compromiser. Us comrades, we are sticking to Trotsky's line of thinking. You could even draw parallels between Castro and Che Guevara. That's why he's on our fighting banner,' and he pointed to the sad, hanging rag with a broad gesture. 'We have remained true to the revolutionary idea, unlike the collaborationist comrade Moskvin. Us comrades, we condemn them and their line.'

'Aha, and who gives you fuel?' Uncle Fyodor added, puffing on his rolled-up cigarette.

Comrade Rusakov flushed and threw a vicious look at Uncle Fyodor. Fyodor just mockingly tut-tutted and took a deeper pull on his cigarette.

Artyom understood little from the commissar's explanation apart from the main thing: these people had little in common with the Reds who intended to string Mikhail Porfirevich's guts up onto a stick and shoot him at the same time. This calmed him and in an effort to give a good impression, he twinkled. 'Stalin – that's the one in the Mausoleum, right?'

But this time, he'd gone too far. An angry spasm deformed the beautiful and brave face of comrade Rusakov, Bonsai turned away, and even Uncle Fyodor frowned.

'No, no, it's Lenin in the Mausoleum!' Artyom hurried to correct himself.

The stern wrinkles on comrade Rusakov's high forehead smoothed out, and he said severely, 'You still need lots of work, comrade Artyom!'

Artyom really didn't want comrade Rusakov to work on him, but he restrained himself and said nothing in reply. He really understood little about politics, but it had started to interest him, and therefore, he waited until the storm had passed and ventured:

'So why are you against the fascists? I mean, I'm also against them but you guys are revolutionaries after all . . .'

'Those reptiles! Because of Spain, because of Ernst Telmann and the Second World War!' comrade Rusakov spat through his clenched teeth and though Artyom didn't understand a word of it, he didn't want to make a show of his ignorance yet again.

Once they poured boiling water into the mugs, they all became more lively. Bonsai took to exhausting Uncle Fyodor with foolish questions, obviously trying to tease him, and Maximka, having sat down closer to comrade Rusakov, asked quietly, 'So tell me, comrade commissar, what does marxism/leninism say about headless mutants? It has bothered me for a long time. I want to be ideologically strong, and I'm drawing a blank on this one.' His dazzling white teeth sparkled in a guilty smile.

'Well, you see, comrade Maxim,' the commissar replied after a delay, 'this, my brother, is not a simple matter,' and he started thinking hard.

Artyom was also interested in how the mutants were seen from a political point of view and, indeed, he was interested to learn if they existed at all. But comrade Rusakov was silent and Artyom's thoughts slid back down the track that he hadn't managed to get out of in the last few days. He needed to get to *Polis*. He was saved by a miracle, he'd been given one more chance, perhaps his last. His whole body hurt, he had a hard time breathing, deep breaths would set him off coughing, and he couldn't open one eye. He wanted to stay with these people very much! He felt much more calm and confident with them, and the darkness of the unfamiliar tunnel was not condensing around him and oppressing him. The rustlings and scratchings that flew up from the black bowels didn't frighten him, didn't put him on his guard, and he hoped that this respite would last forever. It was sweet to relive his rescue again and again. Even though death had been chomping its iron teeth just above his head,

202

barely brushing against him, the sticky, body-paralysing fear that had seized him before his execution, had already evaporated. The last remnants, hidden under his heart and in his stomach, had been burnt out by the poisonous home-brew of the bearded comrade Fyodor. Fyodor himself, and the friendly Bonsai, and the serious leather-clad commissar, and the enormous Maxim-Lumumba – it was so easy with them, in a way that he had never experienced since he'd left *VDNKh* a hundred years before. None of his belongings were in his possession anymore. The wonderful new machine gun, the five magazines of cartridges, the passport, the food, the tea, two flashlights – they were all lost. Left with the fascists. All he had was a jacket, some trousers, and a twisted cartridge case in his pocket. The executioner had said, 'Maybe it will come in useful.' So what now? To stay here, with the fighters of the Interstational, the brigadiers of . . . of . . . well, it's not important. To live their life and forget his own . . . No. Never. He mustn't stop for a minute, mustn't rest. He had no right. This wasn't his life anymore, his fate belonged to others from the moment he agreed to Hunter's proposition. It was too late now. He had to go. There was no other option.

He sat there quietly for a long time, thinking about nothing in particular. But the gloomy determination was ripening within him with every second, in his emaciated muscles, in his stretched and aching veins. He was like a soft toy from which all the sawdust has been drawn and it has become a shapeless rag that someone has cruelly hung on a metal skeleton. He wasn't himself anymore. He had been scattered together with the sawdust which was picked up by a tunnel draught, broken up into particles, and now, someone new had taken up residence inside his skin, someone who didn't want to hear the desperate entreaties of his bleeding and exhausted body, someone who crushed underfoot the desire to surrender, to stay still, to have a rest, to give up before the endeavour had a chance to assume a complete and realized form. This other person had taken the decision on the level of instinct, and he bypassed consciousness in which there now reigned silence and emptiness. The usual continuous flow of internal dialogue was cut off.

It was like a meandering spring inside Artyom had been made straight. He got up to his feet with wooden and awkward movements and the commissar looked at him in surprise, and Maxim even lowered his hand to his machine gun.

'Comrade commissar, could I . . . speak with you?' Artyom asked in a toneless voice.

Then, Bonsai turned around anxiously, disengaging from the unfortunate Uncle Fyodor.

'Say it straight, comrade Artyom, I don't have any secrets from my fighters,' the commissar cautiously responded.

'You see . . . I am very grateful to you all for saving me. But I have nothing with which to repay you. I would really like to remain with you. But I can't. I have to go on. I . . . have to.'

The commissar said nothing in reply.

'Well, where are you going?' Uncle Fyodor interjected unexpectedly.

Artyom pressed his lips together and looked at the floor. An awkward silence hung in the air. It seemed to him that they were now looking at him tensely and suspiciously, trying to guess at his intentions. Was he a spy? Was he a traitor? Why was he being so secretive?

'Well, if you don't want to say, then don't,' Uncle Fyodor said in a conciliatory tone.

'To *Polis*.' Artyom couldn't resist telling them. He couldn't risk losing the trust for the sake of some silly conspiracy theory.

'You have some kind of business there?' Uncle Fyodor enquired with an innocent look.

Artyom nodded silently.

'Is it urgent?' The man continued to probe.

'Well, look, we're not going to hold you back. If you don't want to talk about your business then fine. But we can't just leave you here in the middle of the tunnel! Right guys?' He turned to the others.

Bonsai resolutely nodded, Maximka took his hands from the barrel of his gun and also confirmed the sentiment. Then comrade Rusakov stepped in.

'Are you prepared, comrade Artyom, in front of the fighters of this brigade, who have saved your life, to swear that you are not planning any harm to the revolutionary cause?' he asked severely.

'I swear it,' Artyom answered readily. He had no intentions of harming the revolution. There were more important things to consider.

Comrade Rusakov looked him in the eye, long and hard, and finally gave his verdict:

'Comrade fighters! Personally I believe comrade Artyom. I ask you to vote for helping him to reach *Polis*.'

Uncle Fyodor was the first to raise his hand, and Artyom thought that it was probably him who had lifted him out of the noose. Then Maxim voted, and Bonsai just nodded.

'You see, comrade Artyom, not far from here, there is a passage that is unknown to the wider masses. It joins the *Zamoskvoretskaya* branch and the Red Line,' said the commander. 'We can set you on your way . . .'

He didn't manage to finish his sentence because Karatsyupa who had been lying quietly by his feet until then jumped up suddenly and started to bark deafeningly. Comrade Rusakov whipped his pistol out of its holster with a lightning fast movement. Artyom didn't have the time to see what everyone else did: Bonsai had already pulled the cord, starting the engine. Maxim took up his position at the rear and Uncle Fyodor took a bottle with a match sticking out of its top from the box that had held his home-brew.

The tunnel at that point dived downwards, so visibility was very bad but the dog continued to strain, and Artyom felt anxious.

'Give me a machine gun too,' he asked in a whisper.

Not far away a powerful flashlight flashed and went out. Then they heard someone barking out orders. Heavy boots trudged along the cross-ties, and someone stumbled quietly and then everything fell silent. Karatsyupa, whose muzzle had been clamped shut by the commissar, struggled free and started to bark again.

'It's not starting,' Bonsai mumbled, slightly defeated. 'We have to push it!'

Artyom was first to climb off the section car and behind him leapt Uncle Fyodor and then Maxim. With effort they wedged the soles of their feet against the cross-ties, and got the large object moving forward. It was shifting too slowly and when they had finally awoken the engine, which started off by making coughing sounds, boots were thundering very near to them.

'Fire!' came the order from the darkness and the narrow space of the tunnel filled with sound. At least four cartridges roared past them, and bullets beat randomly around them, ricocheting, spitting sparks, and hitting pipes and making them ring out.

Artyom thought that they had no way out, but Maxim, straightening out to his full height, held his machine gun in his hands and maintained fire for a long time. The automatic weapons went silent. Then the section car moved a bit more easily and they had to start running after it to jump up onto its platform.

'They're retreating! Push ahead!' was the cry from behind, and the automatic machine guns rattled away behind them with redoubled strength but most of the bullets hit the walls and ceiling of the tunnel.

Swiftly setting the stub of the bottle on fire, Uncle Fyodor wrapped it in some rags and threw it onto the path. A minute later there was a bright flash and the same clap of noise that Artyom heard when he was standing with the noose around his neck rang out.

'And again! More smoke!' Comrade Rusakov ordered.

A motorized section car is simply a miracle, Artyom thought as their persecutors fell far behind, trying to fight their way through the curtain of smoke. The vehicle was moving easily forward and, scaring away the staring bystanders, it swooped through *Novukuznetskay* station where comrade Rusakov flatly refused to stop. They were carried through so quickly that Artyom had barely any time to make out the station at all. There wasn't anything particularly special about it, apart from the meagre lighting. There was a fair number of people there but Bonsai whispered to him that the station was not good at all and its inhabitants were also a bit strange, and the last time that they tried to stop there they had seriously regretted it and only just managed to drag themselves out.

'Sorry, comrade, but we won't be able to help you like we thought,' comrade Rusakov said to Artyom in a more familiar tone than usual. 'Now we won't be able to return here for a while. We're going to our reserve base at *Avtozavodskaya*. If you want you can join the brigade.'

Artyom had to steel himself again and refuse the offer but it was easier this time. He was seized by a cheerful sort of desperation. The whole world was against him, everything was going awry. However, the obstacles that the tunnels put in the way of his mission had awoken in Artyom a rage, and this obstinate rage re-lit his weakening vision with a rebellious fire, devouring in him any fear, sense of danger, reason and force.

'No,' he said firmly and calmly. 'I have to go.'

'In that case, we'll go together until *Paveletskaya* and then we'll part ways,' said the commissar who had remained silent until this point. 'It's a shame, comrade Artyom. We need fighters.'

Near *Novokuznetskaya*, the tunnel forked and the section car took the left-hand path. When Artyom asked what went on down the right-hand path they explained that that way was barred to them: a few hundred metres into it there was an advance post of the Hansa, a veritable fortress. This unremarkable tunnel, it seemed, led directly to the three Ring stations: *Oktyabrskaya, Dobrynskaya* and

Paveletskaya. The Hansa didn't intend to destroy this little inter-tunnel passage and its very important transport link but it was only used by Hansa secret agents. If someone else tried to approach the advance post, they would be destroyed immediately without even being given the chance to explain themselves.

After travelling a while along this passage, they came upon *Paveletskaya*. Artyom thought how right his friend at *VDNKh* had been when he had told him that in the old days you could cross the whole metro system within an hour – and he hadn't believed it at the time. Ah, if only he had a section car like theirs . . .

But anyway, a section car wouldn't really have helped since there were lots of places that you couldn't just pass through like a breeze. No, there was no point in dreaming about it, in this new world there wouldn't be anything like it anymore – in this world each step required an improbable effort and searing pain. The old days were long gone. That magical, wonderful world was long dead. It didn't exist anymore. And there was no point in whining about it for the rest of your life. You had to spit on its grave and never look back.

CHAPTER 10

No Pasarán!

There were no patrols visible in front of *Paveletskaya* station, just a group of dishevelled people sitting thirty metres from the station's exit, moving aside to let the revolutionaries' trolley pass and watching it respectfully.

'What, nobody lives here?' asked Artyom, trying to make his voice sound calm. He certainly did not want to be left alone in this deserted station, without weapons, food, and documents.

'At *Paveletskaya*?' Comrade Rusakov looked at him with surprise. 'Of course they do!'

'So why is there no border guard?' Artyom persisted.

'Because this is *Pa-ve-lets-ka-ya*!' Bonsai interrupted, enunciating the syllables for emphasis. 'Who would bother it?'

Artyom thought to himself how much he agreed with the ancient sage who said, as he was dying, that the only thing he knows, is that he knows nothing. They all talked about the inviolability of *Paveletskaya* station as if it needed no explanation, as though it was something everybody understood.

'What, you mean you don't know?' Bonsai was incredulous. 'Just wait, and see it for yourself!'

Paveletskaya station captured Artyom's imagination at first glance. The ceilings were so high that the flickering flashes of light from the torches that protruded through rings hammered into the walls, did not reach the ceiling, creating a frightening and bewitching sense of the infinite directly overhead. Enormous round arches were supported by slender columns that somehow managed to support the mighty vaults. The space between the arches was filled with bronze castings, tarnished, yet evocative of their past greatness; and although these were only the traditional hammers and sickles, framed as they were by arches, these half-forgotten symbols of a destroyed empire

208

looked as proud and defiant as they did when they were forged. A never-ending row of columns, interspersed with the wavering, blood-coloured torchlight, faded off into the incredibly distant haze, and even there, it seemed never to stop. The flames that licked the graceful marble pillars a hundred or a thousand paces away, seemed simply unable to penetrate the dense, almost palpable, gloom. This station once was, to be sure, the residence of the Cyclops, and therefore everything here was gigantic . . .

Did no one dare to encroach upon it simply because it was so beautiful?

Bonsai shifted the engine to idle, the trolley rolled slower and slower, gradually coming to a halt, while Artyom kept looking intently at the strange station. What was it all about? Why did nobody bother *Paveletskaya*? What was so sacred about it? Certainly not only because it looked more like a fairy-tale underground palace than a building built for the transportation industry?

A whole crowd of ragged and unwashed urchins of all ages gathered around the stopped trolley. They enviously eyed the machine, and one even dared to jump down onto the track and touch the engine, respectfully silent, until Fyodor drove him away.

'That's it, comrade Artyom. Here our paths diverge,' the commander interrupted Artyom's thoughts. 'I talked things over with the other comrades and we decided to give you a little present. Here you go!' And he handed Artyom a submachine gun, probably one of those taken off the killed security guards. 'And here's something more.' He placed in Artyom's hand the lamp that had lit the way of the fascist in the black uniform with the moustache. 'These are all trophies, so take courage from them. They are rightfully yours. We would stay here longer, but we mustn't delay. Who knows how far the fascist bastards will decide to chase us? But they certainly won't dare to stick their noses into the *Paveletskaya*.'

Despite his newly acquired firmness and resolve, Artyom's heart throbbed unpleasantly when Bonsai shook his hand, wishing him success. Maxim slapped him on the shoulder in a friendly way, and bearded Uncle Fyodor thrust him a half-drunk bottle of his potion, not knowing what else to give him:

'There you go, buddy, we'll meet again. And we'll be alive – we won't die!'

Comrade Rusakov shook hands once again, and his handsome, manly face grew serious.

'Comrade Artyom! In parting, I would like to tell you two things.

First, believe in your star. As comrade Ernesto Che Guevara said, Hasta la victoria siempre! And second, and most important, NO PASARÁN!'

All the other soldiers raised their right hand in a fist and repeated the slogan: 'No pasarán!' There was nothing left for Artyom to do but to also raise his fist and shout the refrain, with just as much resolve and revolutionary fervour: 'No pasarán!', although for him personally, the whole ritual was just gobbledygook. But he didn't want to spoil the solemn moment of his departure with stupid questions. Apparently he did everything right, as comrade Rusakov looked at him with pride and satisfaction, and then solemnly saluted him.

The motor revved louder, and, enveloped in a blue-grey cloud of smoke, accompanied by an escort of delighted children, the trolley vanished into the darkness. Artyom was completely alone again, and farther from home than he had ever been before.

The first thing he noticed, as he wandered along the platform, were the clocks. Artyom counted four of them right away. At the *VDNKh*, time was something rather symbolic: like books, like attempts to set up schools for the children – a demonstration that the station residents continued to care, that they did not want to degenerate, that they were still human beings. But here, it seemed, clocks played some other kind of role, a much more important one. Wandering about some more, Artyom noticed other strange things. First, there were no living quarters of any kind at the station, except for some hitched-up subway cars on the second track and on into the tunnel. Only a small part of the train was visible in the hall, which is why Artyom did not notice it right away. Tradesmen of every imaginable kind, and workshops were all over the place, but there wasn't a single tent to live in, not even a simple screen behind which one could spend the night. Some beggars and tramps were lying around on bedding made just of cardboard. People bustling about the station approached the clocks from time to time; some, who had their own watches, would anxiously check them against the red numbers on the display panel, and then go about their business again. If Khan were here, thought Artyom, it would be interesting to hear what he would have to say.

Unlike *Kitai Gorod*, where people showed lively interest in travellers, trying to feed them, to sell them something, to get them to visit somewhere, here everyone seemed preoccupied with their own affairs. They had no business with Artyom, and his sense of loneliness, which at first was displaced by curiosity, grew stronger and stronger.

Trying to ward off a growing depression, he continued observing his surroundings. Artyom expected to see people here who were somehow different, with their own characteristic facial expressions, since life at a station like this could not help but leave its mark. At first glance, people were bustling about, shouting, working, arguing, just like anywhere else. But the more closely he looked, the more the chills went up and down his spine. There was a startling number of young cripples and freaks: one without fingers, one covered with disgusting scabs, with a crude stump in the place of an amputated third hand. The adults were frequently bald and sickly; there were almost no healthy, strong people to be found. Their stunted, deformed look offered a painful contrast to the dark expanse of station in which they lived.

In the middle of the broad platform, there were two rectangular apertures leading into the depths, the passageway crossing over to the Ring, toward the Hansa. But there were neither Hanseatic border guards, nor checkpoints, as there were at *Prospect Mir* – and someone had once told Artyom that the Hansa held all its neighbouring stations in an iron fist. No, there was clearly something strange going on here.

So he did not venture to the opposite edge of the hall. For starters, he had used five cartridges to buy himself a bowl of chopped, grilled mushrooms and a glass of putrid, bitter-tasting water. He swallowed the muck with disgust, sitting on an overturned plastic box that had once held empty bottles. Then he went over to the train, hoping to get a bit of a rest there, since his strength was failing, and he had been feeling more and more sick as he looked around. But the subway train was quite different from the one at *Kitai Gorod*: the cars were all torn up and completely empty, with the seats burnt and fused together; the soft leather sofas had been pulled out and carted off somewhere; there were bloodstains everywhere, and cartridge cases gleamed darkly on the floor. This place was clearly not a proper shelter, but more like a fortress that had withstood more than one siege.

Not much time had passed while Artyom looked over the train, but when he returned to the platform, he hardly recognized the station. The counters were empty, the hubbub had died down and, except for a few tramps clustered on the platform, not far from the transfer passage, there was not a single living soul to be seen on the platform. It had become noticeably darker; the torches were extinguished on the side where he had come into the station, and only a few were burning at the centre of the hall; but in the distance, at the opposite end, a dying fire was still burning. The clock showed it to be a little after eight in the evening. What had happened? Artyom hurried on as quickly as the pain in his body would allow him. The crossing was closed on both sides, not just with the usual metal doors, but with sturdy iron gates. It was exactly the same on the second stairway, but one of the gates was still half-open, and behind it could be seen solid latticework, welded, like the casements at *Tverskaya* station, with heavy reinforcement. Behind that had been placed a table, feebly lit with a small lamp, at which sat the guard, a washed-out grey-blue figure.

'No admission after eight,' he snapped, when asked permission to enter. 'The gate opens at six in the morning,' and turning away, he let it be understood that the conversation was over.

Artyom was taken aback. Why did the life of the station come to an end after eight in the evening? And what was he to do now? The tramps, having crawled into their cardboard boxes, looked positively repulsive, and he didn't want to go near them; so he decided to try his luck at the fire, which glimmered at the opposite end of the hall.

It was clear even from afar that standing at the fire was no group of tramps, but rather border guards or something of the kind: silhouetted against the fire, they seemed to be strong male figures, with the sharp contours of automatic weapons visible. But what was there to guard, sitting there on the platform itself? Guard posts should be set up in the tunnels, the entrances to the station, the farther away the better, but here . . . If some sort of creature crawled out or bandits attacked, the men on duty would not be able to do anything about it.

But drawing closer, Artyom noticed something else: from behind the fire, a clear, white light flashed, seemingly going upwards, but too briefly, as if cut short at the very beginning, not striking the ceiling, but disappearing, contrary to all the laws of physics, after a couple of metres. The searchlight was illuminated infrequently, in distinct intervals, which is probably why Artyom had not noticed it earlier. What in the world could it be?

He walked up to the fire, politely said hello, explained that he was travelling through, didn't know about the closing of the gate, and so missed it; he asked whether he might take a rest here, with the patrol men.

'Take a rest?' sneered the man nearest him. He was a dishevelled, dark-haired man with a large, fleshy nose; he was not tall, but was seemingly very strong. 'This is not a place for resting, kid. If you last till morning, you'll be doing fine.'

To the question of what was so dangerous about sitting by the fire in the middle of the platform, the man said nothing, but only gestured behind him with a nod of the head, to where the searchlight was switched on. The others were busy with their conversation and did not pay Artyom the slightest attention. Then he decided he would finally find out what was going on around here, and went over to the searchlight. What he saw there surprised him, but explained a lot.

At the very end of the hall there was a little booth, such as you sometimes see near escalators, for obtaining transfers to other lines. Bags were piled up around it, reinforced here and there with massive iron plates; one of the patrol men was taking the cover off an extremely formidable-looking type of weapon, and the other was sitting in the booth. On it was mounted the very searchlight that was shining upwards. Upwards! With no damper, no barrier here and not even a trace of one, the steps of the escalator began right behind the booth, leading up to the surface. And that was where the beam of the searchlight struck, anxiously probing from wall to wall, as if trying to find someone in the pitch darkness, but only picking up some kind of some kind of brownish lamp-frame and the damp ceiling from which enormous chunks of plaster were peeling off, and beyond . . . Beyond that, one could see nothing.

Suddenly everything fell into place.

For some reason, here the metal damper that usually separated a station from the surface was missing: it was missing both from the platform and from above. *Paveletskaya* was in direct contact with the outside world, and its residents found themselves under constant threat of attack. They breathed contaminated air, drank contaminated water, which is probably why it tasted so strange . . . That was why there were so many more mutations here among young people than, for example, at the *VDNKh*. That was why the adults looked so sickly: their skulls exposed and polished to a shine, their bodies worn out and subject to decay. They were gradually being devoured by radiation sickness.

But still that was not all, apparently. How could one explain the fact that the whole station 'died' after eight o'clock in the evening, and that the dark-haired duty officer by the fire had said that surviving until morning was a big deal?

Trembling, Artyom approached the man sitting in the booth.

'Good evening,' the man returned his greeting.

He was about fifty, but already quite bald, his remaining grey hairs tangled at the temples and the nape of the neck; his dark eyes looked curiously at Artyom, and his unpretentious, laced-up flak jacket could not conceal his rotund stomach. A pair of binoculars hung on his chest, along with a whistle.

'Have a seat.' He pointed Artyom to the nearest sandbag. 'Those guys over there are having a grand old time, leaving me here alone to bore myself to death. So let's have a chat. Hey, did you hit someone's fist with your eye . . . ?'

And so the conversation began.

'As you see, we haven't been able to do anything halfway decent here,' the duty officer explained sadly, pointing to the aperture leading to the escalator. 'You would need concrete here, not iron; we tried iron, but it was no good. In the autumn, every damn thing is swept away by water. First it builds, then it breaks through . . . It happened several times, and many people perished. Since then, we've been getting by like this. Only life is not tranquil here like it is at other stations; we're always waiting: scum can come crawling in on any given night. During the daytime they don't bother us, because they're either sleeping or roaming around on the surface. But it's after dark that things really get desperate. So, we've adapted here, of course, and after eight o'clock, everyone goes into the passageway, where we live, and those left here are mostly the people who keep things going. But wait . . .' He broke off, flicked a switch on the console, and the searchlight flared up brightly.

The conversation continued only after the white beam had scoured all three escalators, moved along the ceiling and the walls, and finally died out.

'Up there,' pointing toward the ceiling, the duty officer lowered his voice, 'is *Paveletskaya* Railway Station. At any rate, it used to be there. A godforsaken place. I don't even know where its tracks have gone; only that right now something horrible is going on up there. You sometimes hear noises that make your blood run cold. And then when they crawl down . . .' He stopped, and then continued after a minute: 'We call them the newcomers, these creatures that climb down from up there. Out of the train station. So it's not so horrible. Well, a few times some of the stronger of these newcomers wiped out

214

this cordon. Did you see our train there, the one forced off the tracks? That's how far they got. We wouldn't let them go below, where the women and children are; if the newcomers crawled down there, the jig would be up. Our men understood that themselves and so they retreated to the train, dug in there, and finished off a few creatures. But as for themselves . . . just two out of ten remained alive. One of the newcomers left, crawling off to the *Novokuznetskaya* station. Some people wanted to go after him in the morning, since the trail of slime he left behind was so thick; but he turned off at a side tunnel, went down, and we didn't dare follow him. We'd had enough disaster as it was.'

'I heard that nobody ever attacks *Paveletskaya*,' Artyom recalled. 'Is that true?'

'Of course,' the duty officer nodded gravely. 'Who would bother us? If we weren't manning the defences here, they would be crawling from here all the way along the line. No, nobody is going to lift a finger against us. The Hansa have given us almost all of that transfer passage, up to the very end of their blockhouse. They gave us weapons, just so that we would protect them. I tell you, they really love to get others to do their dirty work! By the way, what's your name? I'm Mark.' Artyom told him his name. 'Hold it, Artyom, something is stirring over there,' Mark continued and he quickly switched the searchlight back on. 'No, I'm probably hearing things,' he said uncertainly, after a minute.

Artyom was filled, drop by drop, with an oppressive sense of danger. Like Mark, he looked above attentively, but where Mark saw only the shadow of the broken lamp, Artyom thought he detected sinister, fantastic silhouettes, motionless in the dazzling beam of light.

At first he thought it was his imagination playing tricks on him, but one of the strange contours stirred just a bit, as soon as a bit of light passed over it.

'Wait . . . ,' he whispered. 'Try over in that corner, where there's a big crack, hurry . . .'

And, as if nailed in place by the light beam, somewhere far off, further than the middle of the escalator, something large and bony froze for a moment, and then suddenly swooped down. Mark grabbed the whistle, which almost leapt out of his hand, and blew it with all his might, and in a second all those sitting around the fire rushed from their places and scrambled into position.

It turned out there was another searchlight there. It was weaker,

215

but cleverly combined with an unusual heavy machine gun. Artyom had never seen anything like it: the weapon had a long barrel with a bell muzzle at the end; the trailer was shaped like a web; and the cartridges moved along inside the greased and shining ammunition belt.

'Over there, around the tenth-metre!' The husky, thin fellow who had been sitting near Mark searched about for the newcomer with the beam. 'Give me the binoculars . . . Lekha! At the tenth, on the right side!'

'There it is! We're all here, baby, so sit still,' muttered the gunner, aiming the weapon at the hidden black shadow. 'I've got him!'

A deafening rumble of machine-gun fire burst out; a lamp was blown to smithereens at the tenth-metre; and above, something let out a piercing shriek.

'Looks like we caught him,' declared the husky fellow. 'OK, give me some more light . . . There it is, lying there. Finished, the vermin.'

But from above, for a long time, heavy, almost human, groans could be heard, leaving Artyom on edge. When he proposed finishing off the newcomer to put it out of its misery, they replied:

'If you want, go on, kill it. We aren't a shooting gallery here, kiddo; we keep track of every cartridge.'

Mark was relieved of duty, and went over to the fire with Artyom. Mark lit up a cigarette from the fire, and Artyom began to listen to the general conversation.

'Look, Lekha was telling us yesterday about the Hare Krishnas.' A massive man with a low forehead and a powerful neck was speaking in a low, deep voice. 'They sit at *Oktyabrskoye Pole* and want to get into the Kurchatov Institute to blow up the nuclear reactor and bring enlightenment for everybody, but they have not yet got their act together to do it. Well, that reminded me of what happened to me four years ago, when I was still living at the *Savelovskaya*. One day I was getting ready to go to the *Belorusskaya*. My connection was at the *Novoslobodskaya*, so I went straight through the Hansa. So, I got to *Belorusskaya*, quickly went to the man I needed to meet, we dealt with our affairs, and I figured we ought to celebrate with a drink. So he says to me, you'd better be more careful, drunks often vanish around here. And I say to him: Give me a break, and I won't take no for an answer. So he and I killed a bottle together. The last thing I remember is that he was crawling around on all fours and crying, "I am Lunokhod-1, the lunar rover!" Then I wake up – Mother of God! – tied up, gagged, my noggin shaved, lying in some kind of closet, probably in what used to be a cop shop. What a disaster, say I to myself. After half an hour, some devils come in and drag me to the hall by the scruff of the neck. I had no idea where I was; all the signs carrying place names had been torn down, the walls were smeared with something, the floor bloody, the fires burning, almost the whole station had been dug up, and there was a deep pit below, at least twenty metres, if not thirty. There were stars drawn on the floor and ceiling, all in a single line, you know, the way children draw. Well, I'm wondering, have the Reds got me? Then I turned my head around – not quite. They brought me over to the pit, lowered a rope, and told me to climb down it. And prodded me with an assault rifle. I looked in – there were people piled up at the bottom, digging the pit deeper with pieces of scrap metal and shovels. The earth was being hoisted up with a winch, loaded into wagons, and carted off somewhere. Well, there was nothing I could do, I decided, as long as those fellows were there with their assault rifles – crazy guys, all of them tattooed from head to toe – a criminal enterprise of some kind. Probably I had landed in the Zone. And it's as if these authorities are digging out, they want to escape. And these petty hooligans are their hired hands. But then I realized: that's all nonsense. What kind of metro zone has no cops? I tell them I'm afraid of heights, that I crash down right onto my head, and that they won't get much use out of me. They conferred among themselves and set me to work loading wagons with dirt that had been brought up from below. The scumbags cuffed me, chained me, and now they expect me to load their wagon? Pfft! But still, I couldn't figure out what they were doing. The job, to put it mildly, was not an easy one. I was lucky,' he shrugged his gigantic shoulders, 'but there were some weaker guys there, so whenever someone collapsed into the dirt, the skinheads would pick him up and drag him off to the stairway. Then I went past one time, and I took a look. They had one guy there, a real blockhead, the type who used to stand in Red Square, where the heads rolled, and he had a good-sized axe stuck in him; there was blood everywhere, and heads were impaled on poles. I nearly puked. No, I think to myself, I'd better get out here before they kill me and make me into a stuffed animal.'

'OK, and who was it?' the husky fellow who sat by the searchlight interrupted impatiently.

'I asked the men I was loading with. Do you know who? Satanists! Get it? They decided, you see, that the end of the world has already come, and the metro is the gate to hell. And he said something about a circle or something, I don't remember.'

'Gateway,' the gunner corrected him.

'OK. So the metro is the gateway to hell, and hell itself is a little bit deeper down; and the Devil, you see, is waiting there for them – they just have to reach him. So, they're digging. It's been four years since then. Maybe they've already hit bottom.'

'And where is it?' the gunner asked.

'I don't know! By God, I don't know. Well, I sure got myself out of there: I threw myself into the wagon while the guard wasn't watching, and sprinkled some dirt over me. I rolled along somewhere for a long time; then they dumped out the contents of the wagon, from high up; I passed out, then came to, crept along, crawled out by some sort of tracks, just keeping on, straight ahead; but these tracks kept crossing other tracks, and my sense of direction deserted me. Then somebody picked me up, and when I woke up I was only at *Dubrovka*, get it? And the guy who had picked me up, had gone off already, such a nice guy. So I thought, where am I . . .'

Then they talked about rumours that at Ilich Square and the Rimskaya there was an epidemic of some kind and many people had died, but Artyom paid no attention.

The idea that the metro was the threshold to hell, or maybe even its first circle, mesmerized him, and a bizarre image arose before his eyes: hundreds of people crawling around like ants, endlessly digging a pit with their hands, a shaft leading nowhere, until one day one of their pieces of scrap metal sticks strangely out of the soil, without sinking down below, and then hell and the metro are finally merged into one. Then it occurred to him that at this station, people live almost just like at *VNDKh*: constantly attacking monstrous creatures from the surface, holding off the onslaught alone, and if *Paveletskaya* faltered, these monsters would spread throughout the line. Which meant that the role of *VDNKh* is not so unique as he had previously assumed. Who knew how many such stations there were in the metro, each covering its own turf, doing battle, not for the sake of general tranquillity, but for its own hide. You could go back, retreat to the centre, blow your tunnels up after you – but then you'd be left with less and less residential space, until all those who were still alive would be squeezed into a small patch of land, and would gnaw their way through one another's gullets.

But if *VDNKh* was really nothing special, if there were other exits to the surface that it was impossible to conceal . . . That meant . . .

Artyom decided to discontinue that line of thought. It was just the voice of weakness, of treasonous, sugary, seductive arguments not to continue the journey, to stop striving towards the goal. But he mustn't give up. That was a dead end.

To distract himself, he resumed listening to the others' conversation. At first they were talking about the chances of somebody named Pushka to win some sort of victory. Then the husky fellow started to talk about how some idiots attacked *Kitai Gorod* and shot loads of people, but the timely arrival of the Kaluga brotherhood overpowered them, and the cutthroats went back to *Taganskaya*. Artyom wanted to point out that it was not *Taganskaya* at all, but the *Tretyakovskaya*, but he was prevented from doing so by some scrawny guy whose face was hidden, and who said that the Kalugans had pretty much been kicked out of *Kitai Gorod*, and now a new group controlled it, which nobody had ever heard of before. The husky dude argued heatedly with him, and Artyom started to nod off. This time he dreamed about nothing at all, and slept so soundly that even when the alarm whistle went off and everyone jumped up, he just couldn't wake up.

It was probably a false alarm, because no shots were fired.

When Mark finally woke him up, it was already a quarter to six.

'Get up, time to go on duty!' He cheerily shook Artyom by the shoulder. 'Let's go, I'll show you the passageway that they wouldn't let you into yesterday. Do you have a passport?'

Artyom shook his head.

'Well never mind, we'll smooth it over somehow,' Mark promised, and indeed, after a few minutes, they were already in the passage, and the security officer whistled the go-ahead obligingly, fondling two cartridges.

The passageway was very long, even longer than the station itself. There were canvas tents along one wall, and rather bright little lamps burning ('Hansa takes care of us,' Mark smirked), and along the other was a partition – long, but not high, not more than a metre.

'By the way, this is one of the longest passageways in the whole metro!' Mark said proudly. 'What's behind the partition, you ask? And you don't know? Why it's a marvellous thing! Half of everything we earn goes there! Just wait, it's still early. Things will start up later on. It's almost always the same, in the evening, when the entrance to the station is closed and people don't have anything else to do. Although there can be qualification rounds during the day. No really, you've never heard of it? Why we've got a Totalizator for rat races!

We call it the Hippodrome. I thought everybody knew about it,' he said with surprise, when he finally realized that Artyom was not joking. 'Do you like to gamble much? I'm a gambler myself.'

Artyom was certainly interested in watching races, but had never been fanatical about it. Besides, now, having slept so long, a storm cloud of guilt was growing and darkening over his head. He couldn't wait until evening, couldn't wait at all. He had to get moving; too much time had already been wasted. But the way to *Polis* led through Hansa, and right now there was no way of getting there.

'I probably can't stay here until evening,' said Artyom. 'I have to go . . . to *Polyanka*.'

'But then you'll be going across Hansa,' said Mark with a frown. 'How are you going to get across Hansa if you have no visa, and no passport either? I can't help you there, my friend. But wait, let me throw out an idea. The chief of *Paveletskaya* – not our *Paveletskaya*, but the one on the Ring – is a great fan of these races. His rat, Pirate, is a favourite. He comes here every night, with a security detail and full lighting. How about wagering yourself, personally, against him?'

'But I haven't got anything to wager with,' Artyom objected.

'Wager yourself, as a servant. Or if you want, I'll wager you.' Mark's eyes sparkled with excitement. 'If we win, you get a visa. If we lose – you'll get there just the same, although of course it will be up to you how to get out. Is there an alternative?'

Artyom did not like this plan. It seemed somehow shameful to sell himself into slavery and, what's more, to lose himself to a rat Totalizator. He decided to try to get to Hansa some other way. For a couple of hours, he hung around some stern border guards in dappled grey uniforms – they were dressed exactly like those at *Prospect Mir* – trying to strike up a conversation with them; but they kept mum. After one of them contemptuously called him One-Eye (that was unfair, because his left eye had already begun to open up, although it still hurt like hell) and told him to buzz off, Artyom finally abandoned that fruitless effort and started looking for the most sinister and suspicious people at the station, the weapon and drug traders – anyone who might be a contraband runner.

But no one wanted to convey Artyom to Hansa in exchange for his automatic weapon and his lamp.

Evening came on, and Artyom met it with quiet despair, sitting on the floor of the passageway and wallowing in self-flagellation. Around this time, the passage became more lively; the adults were returning from work, having dinner with their families; the children were making an uproar until time to go to bed; and finally, after the gate was locked, everyone poured out of their stalls and tents, toward the race course. There were lots of people here, at least three hundred, and finding Mark in such a crowd was no easy job. People were betting on how Pirate was running, whether Pushka would beat him just for once, mentioning various nicknames and other runners, but these two evidently had no competition.

The important rat owners approached the starting position, carrying their well-groomed pets in little cages. The chief of *Paveletskaya-Ring* was nowhere to be seen, and Mark also seemed to have disappeared from the face of the Earth. Artyom was even afraid that he was on patrol again today and wouldn't come. What in the world would he do then?

Finally, a small procession appeared at the other end of the passageway. Walking with an escort of two morose bodyguards, an old man with a shaved head, lush, well-groomed moustaches, glasses, and an austere black suit, bore his corpulent body along with no hurry, with dignity. One of the security guards held a cushioned red velvet box with a latticed wall, in which something grey was thrashing about. That, most likely, was the famous Pirate.

The bodyguard carried the box with the rat to the starting line, and the moustached old man walked over to the referee sitting behind a little desk, chucked his aide off a chair, sat down heavily in the empty space, and started up a leisurely conversation. The second security man stood nearby, his back to the wall, legs spread wide, and with his hands on the short black automatic hanging around his chest. Such an imposing fellow was not the sort of person with whom to discuss a wager; even to get close to him was frightening.

Then Artyom saw the sloppily dressed Mark, scratching his long-unwashed head, approaching these venerable people and beginning to explain something to the referee. From that distance, all he could hear was the intonation, but he could certainly see that the moustached old man at first flushed with indignation, then grimaced arrogantly, finally nodded with displeasure, took off his glasses, and started to clean them.

Artyom made his way through the crowd to the starting position, where Mark was standing. 'Everything is hush-hush!' Mark announced, rubbing his hands with glee.

Asked exactly what he had in mind, Mark explained that he had just thrust a personal bet upon the old chief, that his own new rat would outrun the favourite on the first round. He had to put Artyom up for it, Mark reported, but in exchange, he demanded a visa for all of Hansa for Artyom and himself. The chief, to be sure, rejected the proposal, saying that he doesn't engage in the slave trade (Artyom breathed a sigh of relief), but adding that such presumptuous insolence would have to be punished. If their rat lost, Mark and Artyom would have to clean the latrines at *Paveletskaya*-Ring for one year. If the rat won, then, OK, they would get the visa. Of course he was positive that the second option was out of the question, which is why he agreed. He decided to punish the cocky upstarts who had dared to throw down a challenge to his pet.

'And do you have your rat?' Artyom asked cautiously.

'Of course!' Mark reassured him. 'A real brute! She'll tear Pirate to shreds! Do you know how she ran away from me today? I could barely catch her! I chased her nearly to *Novokuznetskaya*.'

'And what's her name?'

'Her name?'

'Sure, what's her name?'

'Well, let's say, Rocket,' Mark proposed.

'Rocket – does that sound menacing?'

Artyom was not sure that the competition was really intended to see whose rat would tear a rival to pieces, but he kept his mouth shut. When Mark explained that he had only caught his rat today, Artyom couldn't stand it.

'And so how do you know she's going to win?'

'I believe in her, Artyom!' Mark proclaimed solemnly. 'And any-how, you see, I've really wanted to have my own rat for a long time. I used to bet on other people's rats; they would lose, and I would think to myself: never mind, the day will come when I will have my own, and she'll bring me luck. But I never decided to do it – after all, it's not that simple. You have to get permission from the referee, and that's such a drag . . . My whole life will go by, some newcomer will gobble me up, or I'll die all on my own, and I'll never have my own rat . . . And then you turned up, and I thought: here we go! It's now or never. If you don't take a risk now, I said to myself, then you'll always be betting on someone else's rat. And I decided: if I'm going to play, then let me play for high stakes. Of course, I want to help you, but excuse me for saying that that's not the main thing. And so I wanted to go right up to that old fart,' – Mark lowered his voice, – 'and say: I'll wager myself against your Pirate! He got so enraged that he forced the referee to certify my rat out of turn. And you know,' he added, barely audible, 'this moment will be followed by a year of cleaning the latrines.'

'Because our rat will surely lose!' Artyom desperately tried to reason with him for the last time.

Mark looked at him attentively, then smiled and said:

'But what if . . . ?'

Having sternly looked over the audience, the referee smoothed his greying hair, cleared his throat with self-importance, and began to read off the nicknames of the rats taking part in the race. Rocket was last, but Mark didn't pay any attention to that. Pirate got more applause than any others, and only Artyom clapped for Rocket, because Mark's hands were occupied, holding the cage. Artyom was still hoping for a miracle that would spare him from an ignominious end in a stinking abyss.

Then the referee fired a blank from his Makarov, and the owners opened the cages. Rocket was the first to break out, and Artyom's heart leapt with joy; but then, while the other rats charged off along the length of the passageway, some slower, some faster, Rocket, not living up to her proud name, got stuck in a corner five metres from the starting line, and there she stayed. It was against the rules to prod the rats. Artyom glanced at Mark apprehensively, expecting that he would either start getting violent, or on the contrary, would languish, overwhelmed with grief. But the stern, proud expression on Mark's face reminded him more of that of the captain of the cruiser who gave the order to sink a warship to prevent the enemy from capturing it, a story about some war between the Russians and somebody else that he'd in a beat-up book lying in the library at the *VDNKh*.

After a couple of minutes, the first rats reached the finish line. Pirate won, second place was some creature with an unintelligible name, Pushka came in third. Artyom cast a glance at the referee table. The old guy with the moustache, wiping the sweat of excitement from his bald pate with the same cloth he had used earlier to clean his glasses, was discussing the results with the referee. Artyom was already expecting that they would forget about them, when the old man suddenly slapped himself on the forehead and, smiling sweetly, beckoned to Mark.

Artyom felt almost like he did at the moment when they took him off for execution, although the sensation was not as strong. Making his way behind Mark to the referee's table, he comforted himself with the fact that, one way or another, the coast was now clear for him to cross Hansa territory; the only trick was to find a way to escape.

But disgrace awaited him.

Shrewdly inviting them to come up to the dais, Moustache turned to the audience and briefly explained the wager, then loudly proclaimed that both rascals were being sent, as agreed, to clean out the sanitary facilities for one year, starting today. Two Hansa border guards appeared from God knows where, took away Artyom's automatic weapon, assuring him that his main opponent in the coming year would not be dangerous, and promising to return the weapon at the end of the sentence. Then, suffering the whistling and hooting of the crowd, they were led off to the Ring.

The passage went under the floor at the centre of the hall, just as at the other station of the same name, but there the similarity between the two *Paveletskayas* ended. The one on the Ring conveyed a very strange impression: on one side, the ceiling was low and there were no real columns at all – arches spanned equal intervals along the wall, with the width of each arch being the same as the width of the gap between them. It seemed as though the first *Paveletskaya* had been easy for the builders, as if the dirt there was softer and all one had to do was push one's way across it; whereas at the other *Paveletskaya*, there was some hard, unyielding rock which was a real pain to chew through.

But for some reason this place did not produce the depressing, melancholy feeling that the *Tverskaya* did. Maybe because here there was so much light, and the walls were decorated with simple designs and imitations of ancient columns, like in the pictures from 'Myths of Ancient Greece.' In short, this was not the worst place for forced labour.

And of course, it was clear right away that this was Hansa territory. First of all, it was unusually clean, comfortable, and large, real lamps cased in glass shone softly from the ceiling. In the hall itself, which, to be sure, was not as spacious as at the twin station, there was not a single kiosk, though there were many work tables piled with mountains of intricate contraptions. Behind them sat people in blue overalls, and a pleasant smell, the light odour of machine oil, hung in the air. Probably the work day ended later than at the *Paveletskaya* radial line. Hansa paraphernalia hung on the walls – an insignia with a brown circle on a white background, posters, appeals to raise labour productivity, and quotes from somebody named A. Smith. Under the largest flag, between the two stiff soldiers in an honour guard, stood a glass table, and Artyom lingered there as he passed, just to satisfy his curiosity about what sacred object might lie beneath the glass.

There, on red velvet, lovingly lit with tiny lamps, lay two books. The first was a magnificently preserved, imposing volume with a black cover and a gold-embossed inscription that read, 'Adam Smith. The Wealth of Nations.' The second was a thoroughly dog-eared copy of a pocket book, a piece of trash with a battered dust jacket that was torn and glued together again, on which thick letters spelled out 'Dale Carnegie. How To Stop Worrying and Start Living.'

Artyom had never heard of either author, so what interested him much more was whether the station chief had used remnants of this very velvet to upholster the cage of his beloved rat.

One line was not blocked, and trolleys travelled by from time to time, most of them hand-powered, loaded with boxes. But once a motorized trolley passed, enveloped in a cloud of smoke, and paused for a minute at the station before continuing further. Artyom was able to get a look at the strong soldiers, with black uniforms and black-and-white-striped vests, who were sitting on it. Each had night vision equipment on his head, a strange, short automatic weapon against his chest, and heavy body armour. The commander, stroking the enormous, dark green, visored helmet that sat on his knees, exchanged a few words with the station security officers, dressed in the usual grey camouflage, and the trolley vanished into the tunnel.

On the second line there was a complete train, in even better condition than the one Artyom had seen at Kuznetsky Bridge. There were probably living quarters behind the curtained windows, but through bare windows one could see desks with printers on them, behind which sat your usual business types; and engraved upon a sign over the door were the words 'CENTRAL OFFICE.'

This station produced an indescribable impression on Artyom. It was not that it amazed him like the first *Paveletskaya*; there were no traces here of that mysterious, sombre splendour that reminded one of the degenerated descendants of bygone superhuman greatness and the power of those who had built the metro. But still, people lived here just as if they were not part of the teeming, decadent, senseless, underground existence outside the Ring line. Life went on in a steady, well-organized way; after the work day there was a well-deserved rest; young people did not go out into a fantasy world of foolish yentas, but to business – the earlier you started your career, the farther up the ladder you could move – and adults were not afraid that as soon as their strength began to ebb, they would be turned out into the tunnel to be eaten by rats. It now became comprehensible why Hansa allowed only a few outsiders into its station, and reluctantly at that. The number of places in paradise is limited; only in hell is entry open to all.

'Why finally I've emigrated!' exclaimed Mark, looking happily about him.

At the end of the platform, another border guard sat in a glass cubicle with the sign 'On Duty,' beside a rather small barrier painted with white and red stripes. When someone drove up to the duty officer, stopping respectfully, the guard came out of the cubicle with an expression of self-importance, inspected documents and sometimes cargo, and finally lifted the barrier. Artyom noted that all the border guards and customs officials were very proud of their posts; it was immediately obvious that they were doing something they enjoyed. On the other hand, he thought, how could one not like such work?

They were taken over to a fence from which the road extended into the tunnel, and turned off to the side, to a corridor for staff quarters. Dreary yellow tile with scooped-out pit holes, proudly crowned with real toilet seats; indescribably filthy overalls; square shovels with some weird stuff growing on them; a wheelbarrow with only one wheel, making wild figure eights; carts that were to be loaded up and carted off to the nearest shaft that led into the depths. And all this was enveloped in a monstrous, unimaginable stench, saturating one's clothes, seeping into each hair from root to tip, penetrating beneath the skin, so that you began to think that it had become part of your very nature and would be with you forever, scaring away your own kind and making them get out of your way before they've even seen you.

The first day of this monotonous work passed so slowly that Artyom decided they had been given an infinite shift: dig, dump, roll, dig again, dump again, roll again, drain, then go back the other way, just so that this thrice-damned cycle could be repeated. There was no end in sight to the work, since new visitors kept coming. Neither they nor the security guards standing at the entrance to the premises and at the endpoint of their route, at the shaft, hid their revulsion for the poor labourers. They stood aside squeamishly, holding their noses, or, the more delicate among them took a deep breath beforehand so as not to have to inhale next to Artyom and Mark. Their faces showed such loathing that Artyom asked himself in surprise, didn't all this crap come from their guts in the first place? At the end of the day, when his hands were worn to a pulp, despite wearing enormous canvas gloves, it seemed to Artyom that he had discovered the true nature of man, as well as the meaning of life.

He now viewed man as a clever machine for the decomposition of food and the production of shit, functioning almost without a hitch throughout a life without meaning, if by the word 'meaning' one has in mind some kind of ultimate goal. The meaning was in the process: to break down the most food possible, convert it even faster, and eliminate the dregs – everything that was left of smoking pork chops, juicy braised mushrooms, fluffy cakes – now rotten and contaminated. Personality traits began to fade, becoming impersonal mechanisms for the destruction of the beautiful and the useful, creating instead something putrid and worthless. Artyom was disgusted with people and felt no less aversion to them, than they to him. Mark was stoically patient, and tried to cheer up Artyom from time to time by saying things like, 'Don't worry about it, they told me beforehand that emigration is always difficult at the beginning.'

And the main thing was that, neither on the first nor the second day did any possibility of escape present itself; the security guards were vigilant, and although the only thing Artyom and Mark would have to do to escape was to enter the tunnel beyond the shaft, heading toward *Dobryninskaya,* that was simply impossible. They spent the night in a nearby closet. The door was locked carefully at night, and whatever the time of day, a guard sat at the glass booth by the entrance to the station.

The third day of their stay at the station arrived. Time here did not pass according to the usual twenty-four-hour day; it crawled along like a slug, in the seconds of an unending nightmare. Artyom had already grown accustomed to the idea that nobody would ever approach him and talk to him again, and that the fate of a pariah was in store for him. It was as though he were no longer human and had turned into an inconceivably monstrous being, whom people saw not just as something ugly and repulsive, but also somehow perceptibly related to themselves – and that scared them and repulsed them even more, as if they might catch this monstrousness from him, as if he were a leper.

First he worked out an escape plan. Then came a resounding void of despair. After that a dull stupor took over, in which his intellect was disconnected from his life; he turned inward, drew in the threads of feeling and sensation, and went into a cocoon somewhere in a remote corner of consciousness. Artyom continued to work mechanically, his motions as precise as those of an automaton – all he had to do was dig, dump, roll, and dig again, roll again, drain, and go back the other way, faster, to start digging again. His dreams lost any meaning, and in them, just as in his waking hours, he endlessly ran, dug, pushed, pushed, dug, and ran.

On the evening of the fifth day, Artyom, pushing the wheelbarrow, tripped over a shovel that had been left on the floor; the wheelbarrow overturned, the contents spilled, and then he fell down into it himself. When he arose slowly from the floor, an idea suddenly popped into his head, and instead of running for a bucket and cloth, he slowly and deliberately headed for the entrance to the tunnel. He himself could feel that he was now so loathsome, so repulsive, that his aura would have to drive anyone away. And just at the moment, due to an improbable confluence of circumstances, the security guard who was invariably hanging around at the end of his route, was, for some reason, not there. Without giving a moment's thought to whether someone might be chasing him, Artyom started off across the ties. Blinded, but hardly stumbling, he walked faster and faster, until breaking into a run; but his reason had not returned to the job of directing his body; it was still holed up, cowering in its corner.

Behind him he heard no shouts, no footsteps of pursuers; only the trolley clattered by, loaded with cargo and lighting its way with a dim lantern. Artyom simply pressed himself against the wall, letting it go past. The people on board either did not notice him or did not consider it necessary to pay him any attention; their gazes passed over him without lingering, and they didn't say a word.

Suddenly he was seized with a feeling of his own invulnerability, conferred on him by his fall. Covered with stinking sludge, it was as if he had become invisible; this gave him strength, and consciousness gradually began to return. He had done it! Who knew how? Against all good sense, despite everything, he had managed to escape from the accursed station, and nobody was even following him! It was strange, it was amazing, but it seemed to him that, if he were only to try right now to comprehend what had happened, to dissect the miracle with the cold scalpel of rationality, then the magic would dissipate immediately, and the beam of the searchlight from a patrol trolley would quickly strike him in the back.

Light shone at the end of the tunnel. He slackened his pace, and after a minute he was at *Dobryninskaya.*

The border guard there satisfied himself with the simple question,

'Did they call for a sanitary technician?' and quickly let him through, waving away the air around himself with one hand while holding the other over his mouth. Artyom had to keep moving, to get out of Hansa territory fast, before the security guards finally gathered their wits, before he could hear behind him the tramp of iron-rimmed jackboots; before warning shots thundered out into the air, and then . . . Faster.

Not looking at anyone, keeping his eyes to the floor, his skin crawling with the disgust those around him felt for him, a vacuum forming around him so that he did not have to elbow his way through the dense crowd, Artyom strode to the border post. And now what was he going to say? More questions, more demands to present his passport. How could he reply?

Artyom's head hung so low that his chin touched his chest, and he saw absolutely nothing around him, so that the only things he remembered about the whole station were the dark, neatly arranged granite slabs of the floor. He kept walking, frozen with anticipation of the moment when he would hear the peremptory order to stand still. Hansa's border was closer and closer. Now . . . Right now . . .

'What kind of rubbish is this?' a gasping voice resounded in his ear. There it was.

'I . . . it . . . I got lost. I'm not from here . . .' muttered Artyom, tongue-tied from nervousness or maybe just getting into his role.

'Well get the hell out of here, do you hear, you ugly mug?!' The voice sounded very persuasive, almost hypnotic, making him want to obey right away.

'Sure I . . . I would . . .' mumbled Artyom, afraid, not knowing how to get out of this one.

'Begging is strictly forbidden on Hansa territory!' the voice said sternly, and this time it was from a greater distance.

'Of course, right away . . . I have little children . . .' Artyom finally realized what button to press, and became more animated.

'What children? Are you nuts?!' The invisible border guard flew into a rage. 'Popov, Lomako, come here! Get this scumbag out of here!'

Neither Popov nor Lomako wanted to soil their hands by touching Artyom, so they just shoved him in the back with the barrels of their automatics. Their superior's angry curses flew after them. To Artyom, this sounded like heavenly music.

Serpukhovskaya station! He had left the Hansa behind!

Finally he looked up, but what he saw in the eyes of the people surrounding him made him look back at the floor. This was not tidy Hansan territory; he was once again in the midst of the dirty, poverty-stricken bedlam that reigned throughout the rest of the metro. But even here, Artyom was too loathsome. The miraculous armour that had saved him along the way, making him invisible, forcing people to turn away from the fugitive and not to notice him, to let him through all the outposts and checkpoints, had now turned back into a stinking, shitty scab.

Evidently it was already past noon.

Now that the initial exultation had worn off, that strange strength, as if borrowed from someone else, which had forced him to keep walking across the stretch from *Paveletskaya* to *Dobryninskaya*, abruptly disappeared and left him alone with himself – hungry, deathly tired, without a penny to his name, giving off an unbearable stench, still showing traces of the blows of the week before.

The paupers next to whom he had sat down along the wall, decided that they could no longer abide such company, crawled away from him, cursing, in various directions, and he was left completely alone. Hugging his shoulders so as not to feel so cold, he closed his eyes and sat there for a long while, thinking about absolutely nothing, until sleep overcame him.

Artyom was walking along an unfinished tunnel. It was longer than all those he had traversed throughout his whole life, rolled into one. The tunnel twisted and turned, sometimes ascending, sometimes descending, but was never straight for more than ten paces. But it just went on and on, and walking became harder and harder; his feet, blistered and bloody, were hurting, his back ached, each new step called forth an echo of pain throughout his body; but as long as hope remained that the exit was not far away, maybe just around that next corner, Artyom found the strength to keep going. But then suddenly the simple, but terrifying thought occurred to him: what if the tunnel had no exit? If both the entrance and exit were closed, if someone invisible and omnipotent had shut him off – left him thrashing around, like a rat unsuccessfully trying to reach the experimenter's finger, in this maze without exit, so that he would keep dragging himself along until he gave out, until he collapsed – and doing this for no reason, just for fun? A rat in a maze. A squirrel in a wheel. But then, he thought, if continuing along the road does not lead to the exit, will refusing any senseless forward motion perhaps bestow liberation? He sat down on a railway tie, not because he was tired, but because he was at the end of his rope. The walls around him disappeared, and he thought: in order to achieve the goal, to complete the journey, all I have to do is to stop walking. Then this thought faded away and disappeared.

When he woke up, he was seized by overwhelming anxiety, and at first could not imagine what had caused it. Only later did he begin to recall bits of the dream, to piece together a mosaic from these fragments, but the fragments just would not hold together; they crumbled; there was not enough glue to hold them together. That glue was some idea that had come to him during his dream; it was pivotal, a vision from the heart, and very important to him. Without it, all that was left was a pile of ragged underwear; but with it – a wonderful picture, full of miraculous import, opening up limitless horizons. But he couldn't remember the idea. Artyom gnawed on his fists, seized his dirty head with his dirty hands, his lips whispered something incomprehensible, and passers-by looked at him with fear and aversion. But the idea just didn't want to return. Then slowly, carefully, as if trying to use a strand of hair to pull out something stuck in a swamp, he started to reconstruct the idea out of the fragments of memory. And – what a miracle! – deftly grabbing hold of one of the images, he suddenly recognized it, in the same primordial form that it had first announced itself in his dream.

To finish the journey, he only needed to stop walking.

But now, in the bright light of waking consciousness, the thought seemed to him banal, pitiful, unworthy of attention. To finish the journey, he needed to stop walking? Well, of course. If you stop walking, then your journey is over. What could be simpler? But is that really the way out? And could that really be the conclusion of the journey?

It often happens that an idea that appears in a dream to be a stroke of genius, turns out to be a meaningless jumble of words when one wakes up . . .

'O, my beloved brother! Filth on your body and in your soul.' The voice was right next to him.

That was as unexpected as the return of the idea, and the bitter taste of that disillusionment instantly vanished. He didn't even think the voice was addressing him, since he had already become so accustomed to the idea that people fled in all directions even before he could utter a word.

'We welcome all the orphaned and wretched,' the voice continued; it sounded so soft, so reassuring, so tender, that Artyom, no longer restraining himself, cast a sideways glance to the left, and then gloomily glanced to the right, afraid to discover that the person speaking was actually addressing somebody else.

But there was nobody else nearby. The person was talking to him. Then he slowly raised his head and met the eyes of a rather short, smiling man wearing a loose-fitting robe, with dark blond hair and rosy cheeks, who was reaching out his hand in friendship. It was vital for Artyom to reciprocate, so, not daring to smile, he too extended his hand.

'Why isn't he recoiling from me like everybody else?' thought Artyom. 'He's even ready to shake my hand. Why did he come up to me on his own, when everyone around was trying to get as far away from me as possible?'

'I will help you, my brother!' the rosy-cheeked fellow continued. 'The brothers and I will give you shelter and restore your spiritual strength.'

Artyom just nodded, but his new companion found that sufficient.

'So allow me to take you to the Watchtower, O my beloved brother,' he intoned and, firmly taking Artyom by the hand, drew him along.

Artyom did not remember much, and certainly didn't remember the road, but only understood that he was being led from the station into a tunnel, but which of the four, he did not know. His new acquaintance introduced himself as Brother Timothy. On the road, and at the grey, mundane *Serpukhovskaya* station, and in the dark tunnel, he never stopped talking:

'Rejoice, O beloved brother of mine, that you met me on your way, for your life is about to undergo a momentous change. The cheerless gloom of your aimless wandering is at an end, because you will attain that which you seek.'

Artyom did not understand very well what the man had in mind, because for him personally, his wanderings were far from over; but the rosy-cheeked and gentle Timothy spoke so smoothly and tenderly that he just wanted to keep on listening, to communicate with him in the same language, grateful for not rejecting him, when the whole world rejected him.

'Do you believe in the one true God, O Brother Artyom?' Timothy inquired, as if by the way, looking Artyom attentively in the eyes. Artyom could only shake his head in an indefinite way and mumble something unintelligible, which could be interpreted as desired: either as agreement or rejection.

'That's good, that's wonderful, Brother Artyom,' Timothy

exclaimed. 'Only belief in the truth will save you from the torments of eternal hell and grant you expiation of your sins. Because,' he assumed a stern and triumphal expression, 'the kingdom of the God of our Jehovah is coming, and the holy biblical prophecies will be fulfilled. Do you study the Bible, O brother?'

Artyom mumbled again, and the rosy-cheeked fellow this time looked at him with some misgivings.

'When we get to the Watchtower, your own eyes will convince you that you must study the Holy Book, given to us from on high, and that great blessings will come to those who have turned to the path of Truth. The Bible, a precious gift of the God of our Jehovah, can only be compared to a letter from a loving father to his young son,' Brother Timothy added, for good measure. 'Do you know who wrote the Bible?' he asked Artyom a bit sternly.

CHAPTER 11

I Don't Believe It

Artyom decided that there was no sense in pretending any more, and honestly shook his head.

'At the Watchtower, they will lead you to this, and to much more, and your eyes will be opened to many things,' proclaimed Brother Timothy. 'Do you know what Jesus Christ, the Son of God, said to his disciples at Laodicea?' Seeing Artyom avert his eyes, he shook his head in mild reproach. 'Jesus said, "I counsel you to buy from me salve to anoint your eyes, that you may see." But Jesus was not talking about physical illness,' stressed Brother Timothy, raising his index finger, and his voice shifted to an exalted, intriguing intonation that promised to the inquiring mind an astonishing sequel.

Artyom was quick to express lively interest.

'Jesus was talking about spiritual blindness which had to be healed,' said Timothy, in explanation of the riddle. 'Like you and thousands of other lost souls who are wandering blindly in the dark. But belief in the true God of our Jehovah is that salve for the eyes which opens your eyelids wide, so that you can see the world as it really is; because you can see physically, but spiritually you are blind.'

Artyom thought that eye ointment would have done him good four days ago. Since he didn't reply, Brother Timothy decided that this complex idea required some further interpretation, and was quiet for a while, to allow what Artyom had heard to sink in.

But after five minutes, a light flickered up ahead, and Brother Timothy interrupted his reflections to report the joyous news:

'Do you see the light in the distance? That is the Watchtower. We're here!' There was no tower at all, and Artyom felt slightly disappointed. It was a regular train standing in a tunnel, whose headlights shone softly in the darkness, illuminating fifteen metres in front of it. When Brother Timothy and Artyom arrived at the train, a chubby man came down from the engineer's cab to meet them, wearing the same type of robe as Brother Timothy; he embraced Rosy-Cheeks and also called him 'my beloved brother,' from which Artyom deduced that this was more a figure of speech than a declaration of love.

'Who is this young fellow?' the chubby guy asked in a low voice, smiling tenderly at Artyom.

'Artyom, our new brother, who wants to walk with us on the path to Truth, to study the Holy Bible, and to renounce the Devil,' explained rosy-cheeked Timothy.

'Then permit the Watchtower to welcome you, O my beloved Brother Artyom!' droned Fatso, and Artyom was again amazed that he too did not seem to notice the unbearable stench that had now permeated his entire being.

'And now,' cooed Brother Timothy, as they were making their leisurely way through the first car, 'before you meet the brothers in the Hall of the Kingdom, you have to clean your body, for Jehovah God is clean and holy, and expects his worshippers to maintain their spiritual, moral, and physical cleanliness, as well as cleanliness of thoughts. We live in an unclean world,' he said, glancing sadly at Artyom's clothes, which were certainly in a deplorable condition, 'and serious efforts are required of us to remain clean in God's eyes, my brother,' he concluded, and hustled Artyom into a nook that was decked out with plastic sheets, set up not far from the entrance to the car. Timothy asked him to undress, and then handed him a bar of grey soap with a nauseating smell, and five minutes later ran water for him from a rubber hose.

Artyom tried not to think about what the soap was made out of. At any event, it not only ate up the dirt on his skin, but also destroyed the disgusting smell emanating from his body. After the procedures were complete, Brother Timothy gave Artyom a relatively fresh robe, like his own, and looked disapprovingly at the cartridge case hanging around his neck, perceiving it to be a pagan talisman, but limited himself to a reproachful sigh.

It was also surprising that on this strange train, stuck, who knows when, in the middle of a tunnel, and now serving as a shelter for the brethren, there was water, and it came out under such strong pressure.

But when Artyom asked about the strange water that was coming from the hose and how it was possible to build such a structure, brother Timothy only mysteriously smiled and declared that the aspiration to please Lord Jehovah really moved people to heroic and glorious acts. The explanation was more than a bit foggy but it would have to suffice.

Then they went into the second wagon where long, empty tables were built between rigid lateral benches. Brother Timothy walked up to a man who was conjuring something over a big cauldron from which a seductive steam was rising, and he returned with a big dish of some kind of thin gruel, which turned out to be quite edible even though Artyom couldn't work out what it was made from.

While he hastily scooped up the hot soup with an old aluminium spoon, Brother Timothy watched affectionately, not missing a chance to proselytize:

'Don't think that I don't trust you, brother, but your answer to my question about belief in our God didn't sound very solid. Can you really imagine a world in which He doesn't exist? Surely our world can't have created itself, not according to His wise will? Could the infinite variety of forms of life, the beauty of the earth,' he gestured around the dining room with his beard, 'could all this be just an accident?'

Artyom looked around the wagon attentively but didn't see any other forms of life in it apart from themselves and the cook. Again, he bent over his bowl and only issued some sceptical rumblings.

Contrary to his expectations, his disagreement didn't embitter Brother Timothy at all. Quite the opposite, in fact. He had visibly enlivened, his pink cheeks were lit with a fervent, fighting flush.

'If this doesn't convince you of His existence,' brother Timothy continued energetically, 'then think about it in a different way. If this world isn't a display of divine will then it means . . .' his voice froze, as if from fright, and only after several long moments, during which Artyom completely lost his appetite, did he finish his thought: 'Then that means that people are left to their own devices, and there's no point to our existence, and there's no point in prolonging it . . . It means that we are completely alone, and no one cares for us. It means that we are plunged into chaos and there isn't the slightest hope of a light at the end of the tunnel . . . And it's frightening to live in such a world. It's impossible to live in such a world.'

Artyom didn't say anything to him in reply, but these words made him think. Until this moment he had in fact viewed his life as total chaos, like a chain of accidents without connection or sense. Though this oppressed him and the temptation to trust any simple truth that might fill his life with meaning was great, he considered it cowardice and through the pain and the doubt, he gained strength in the thought that his life was of no use and that each living thing should resist nonsense and the chaos of life. But he didn't feel at all like arguing with the gentle Timothy right now.

He felt a satisfied and benevolent feeling, and he felt sincere gratitude to the person who had picked him up, tired, hungry and stinking, and who had spoken warmly to him, who now fed him and had given him clean clothes. He wanted to somehow thank him and so when the man beckoned him to join a meeting of brothers, Artyom stood up readily, showing with his every mannerism, that he would go with pleasure to this meeting and wherever he was led.

The meeting was to take place in the next, that is, the third, carriage. It was full of all sorts of people, mostly dressed in the same overalls. In the middle of the carriage there was a small scaffold and the person standing on it towered over everybody at floor level, almost resting his head on the ceiling.

'It's important that you listen to everything,' Brother Timothy told Artyom instructively, clearing their path with gentle nudges and leading Artyom to the very middle of the crowd.

The orator was rather old, and there was a handsome grey beard falling down his chest, and his deep-set eyes of an indeterminate colour looked down wisely and calmly. His face wasn't thin or round, it was furrowed with deep wrinkles but it didn't portray an old man's weakness or helplessness but rather a wisdom. It radiated an inexplicable force.

'That's Elder John,' Brother Timothy whispered to Artyom in a reverential voice. 'You are really lucky, Brother Artyom, as soon as the sermon begins you will receive teachings at once.'

The elder raised his hand; the rustlings and whisperings stopped immediately. Then he began in a deep and sonorous voice:

'My first lesson to you, my beloved brothers, is about how to know what God is asking of you. To do this you must answer three questions. What important information is contained in the Bible? Who is its author? Why should we study it?'

His speech differed from Brother Timothy's meandering manner. He spoke absolutely simply, plainly navigating short propositions. Artyom was at first surprised by this, but then he looked from side to side and saw that the majority of people there were only able to understand words like this, and the pink-cheeked Timothy had no more effect on them than the walls or the table. Meanwhile, the grey-haired preacher informed them that God's truth lay in the Bible: who

He is and which were His laws. After that he turned to the second question and told them that the Bible was written by about forty different people over 1600 years and they were all inspired by God.

'That's why,' the elder concluded, 'the author of the Bible isn't a person but it is God, living in the heavens. And now, answer me this, brothers, why do we need to study the Bible?'

And, not waiting for the brothers to answer, he explained it himself: 'Because to know God and to do His will is a pledge of your eternal future. Not everyone will be pleased that you are studying the Bible,' he warned, 'but don't let anyone prevent you!' He cast a stern look around the congregation.

There was a moment's silence and then the old man, having taken a sip of water, continued: 'My second lesson to you, brothers, is about who God is. So, give me an answer to these three questions: Who is the true God and what is His name? What are His most important qualities? What is the right way to worship Him?'

Someone from the crowd had wanted to answer one of the questions but he was thrown furious looks and John indifferently started to answer the questions himself: 'People worship many things. But in the Bible it says there is only one God. He created everything in heaven and on earth. And since he gave us life, we must worship Him alone. What is the name of the true God?' cried the aged man after a pause.

'Jehovah!' The crowd burst out with one voice.

Artyom looked from side to side warily.

'The true name of God is Jehovah!' the preacher confirmed. 'He has lots of titles but one name. Remember the name of our God and don't call him by his titles like a coward but straight, by name! Who will tell me now, what is the main quality of our God?'

Artyom thought that he would now see that there was someone vaguely educated in the crowd who could answer such a question. And standing nearby, a serious-looking young man put his hand up to answer but the old man beat him to it.

'The nature of Jehovah is revealed in the Bible! And His main qualities are love, justice, wisdom and strength. It is said in the Bible that God is merciful, kind, ready to forgive, magnanimous and patient. We, like obedient children, should be like Him in every way.'

What he said caused no objection amongst the congregation, and the aged man, stroking his magnificent beard, asked, 'So tell me how should we worship our God Jehovah? Jehovah says that we should only worship Him. We must not revere images, pictures, symbols

238

and pray to them! Our God will not share his glory with someone else! Images are powerless to help us!' the voice rumbled threateningly.

The crowd murmured approvingly and Brother Timothy turned his joyful, radiant face to Artyom and said, 'Elder John is a great orator, and thanks to him our brotherhood is growing with every day, and the community of followers of the true faith is spreading!'

Artyom smiled bitterly. The ardent speech of Elder John did not have the same fiery effect on him as it had on the rest of them. But maybe it was worth listening some more?

'For my third lesson I will tell you about Jesus Christ,' said the old man. 'And here are three questions: Why is Jesus Christ called the first-born son of God? Why did He come to the earth as a person? What would Jesus do in the near future?'

Then it became clear that Jesus was called the first-born son of God because he was the first creation of God, an embodiment on earth of the holy spirit and he lived in heaven. Artyom was very surprised by this – he'd only seen the sky once before, on that fateful day at the Botanical Gardens. Someone had once told him that there may be life up there in the stars. Was that what the preacher was talking about?

Then Elder John explained: 'But who among you will tell me why Jesus Christ, the son of God, came to the earth?' And he paused dramatically.

Now Artyom had started to realize what was going on around him, and it became clear that those present belonged to the ranks of the converted and they had been coming to these lectures for some time. Veterans of these lessons never made attempts to answer the elder's questions whereas the new initiates were trying to show their knowledge and eagerness, crying out answers and waving their hands but only until the old man explained it all himself.

'When Adam didn't follow God's command, he became the first person to commit what the Bible calls a sin,' the elder began from afar. 'Therefore God sentenced Adam to death. And gradually Adam grew old and died, but he transferred his sin to his children and therefore we also get older and become ill and die. And then God sent his first-born son, so he could teach man about God's truth, and in his pure example, he showed people an example, and he sacrificed his life to free humankind from sin and death.'

This idea seemed very strange to Artyom. Why was it necessary to punish all men with death in order to later sacrifice your only son so that everything would be returned to its original state? How could that be if He was omnipotent?

'Jesus returned to heaven, resurrected. Later God called him king. Soon Jesus will wipe all evil and suffering from the earth!' the old man promised. 'But we'll speak about this after praying, my brothers!'

Obediently inclined heads gathered and joined in the sacrament of prayer. Artyom bathed in the many-voiced buzz from which separate words could not be distinguished, but the general sense made itself clear. After five minutes of prayer, the brothers began to exchange words briskly, apparently worrying about the arrival of the holy spirit.

Something wasn't sitting right within Artyom. He had a nagging feeling but he decided to stay there for a while because it might be that the most convincing part of the lecture lay ahead.

'And the fourth lesson I will give to you is about the Devil.' And looking around him with a gloomy and damning look, the elder warned, 'Are you all ready for this? Are you brothers strong enough in spirit to know about this?'

Then it was absolutely necessary to answer but Artyom couldn't get a sound out of himself. How could he know if he was sufficiently strong in spirit if he wasn't clear what this was all about anyway?

'And so here are three questions: Where did Satan come from? How does Satan betray people? Why is it necessary for us to resist the Devil?'

Artyom let most of the answer to these questions fly past his ears, distracted by the thought of where he was and how he was going to get out of here. He only heard that the main sin of the Devil was that he wanted people to worship him, which was a privilege for God alone. And he also wondered if it was really true that God was really concerned with each of his followers, and was there one person who is utterly devoted to God?

The language of the aged man now seemed to Artyom frighteningly official and addressed questions that were inappropriate for discussion. From time to time, Brother Timothy looked over at him attentively, searching Artyom's face for the spark of imminent enlightenment but Artyom was just becoming gloomier and gloomier.

'Satan deceives people so they will worship him,' the aged man was saying in the meantime. 'And there are three ways in which he does this: false religion, spiritism and nationalism. If a religion teaches lies

240

about God, it is serving Satan's purposes. Adherents of false religions might easily think that they are worshipping the true God but in reality they are worshipping Satan. Spiritism is when people call upon spirits to protect them, to harm others, to predict the future, and to perform miracles. Behind each of these actions is the evil force of the Devil!' The old man's voice was shaking from hatred and disgust. 'And apart from that, Satan deceives people by inciting nationalistic pride within them and inducing them to worship political organizations,' the elder warned them with an upraised finger. 'People think that their race or nation is superior to others. But it isn't true.'

Artyom rubbed the back of his neck, which was still marred by a red welt, and coughed. He couldn't agree with that last comment.

'Some people are convinced that political organizations will get rid of mankind's problems. People who believe that deny the Kingdom of God. But only the Kingdom of Jehovah will solve the problems of mankind. And now I shall tell you, o my brothers, why you must resist the Devil. In order to make you repudiate Jehovah, Satan may resort to persecutions and actions against you. Some of your near and dear ones may become angry with you for studying the Bible. Others might start mocking you. But to whom do you owe your life?!' asked the elder, and notes of iron rang out in his voice. 'Satan wants to frighten you! So that you'll stop finding out about Jehovah! Don't let him do it! Get! The upper hand! Against Satan!' John's voice crashed like rumbling thunder. 'By resisting the Devil, you will prove to Jehovah that you are in favour of his dominion!'

The crowd roared in ecstasy.

With a wave of his hand, Elder John quelled the general hysteria, in order to end the meeting with a final, fifth lesson.

'What did God intend for the earth?' He turned to the audience, spreading his arms. 'Jehovah created the earth, so that people would live there happily, forever. He wanted a righteous and joyful mankind to inhabit the earth. The earth shall never be destroyed. It shall exist for all eternity!'

Unable to contain himself, Artyom snorted. Angry looks shot in his direction, and Brother Timothy raised a threatening finger.

'The first human beings, Adam and Eve, sinned, deliberately violating God's law,' continued the orator. 'Therefore Jehovah expelled them from paradise, and paradise was lost. But Jehovah did not forget the purpose for which he had created the earth. He promised to transform it into a paradise, in which people would live forever. How did God fulfil his plan?' The elder posed the question to himself.

A lengthy pause indicated that the key moment of the sermon was about to arrive. Artyom was all ears.

'Before the earth could become a paradise, the evil people would have to be eliminated.' John pronounced the words forebodingly. 'It was promised to our forefathers that a cleansing would take place through Armageddon – a divine war for the annihilation of evil. And then Satan would be enfettered for a thousand years. There would be nobody left to harm the earth. Only God's people would remain alive! And King Jesus Christ will rule the earth for a thousand years!' The elder turned his burning gaze to the front ranks of the people who were taking in his words. 'Do you understand what this means? The divine war for the annihilation of evil has already ended! What happened to this sinful earth *was* Armageddon! Evil was incinerated! According to what was prophesied, only God's people would survive. We who live in the metro are the people of God! We survived Armageddon! The Kingdom of God is at hand! Soon there will be neither old age, nor illness, nor death! The sick shall be freed of their ailments, and the old shall become young again! In the thousand-year reign of Jesus, the people who are faithful to God shall turn the earth into a paradise, and God shall resurrect millions of the dead!'

Artyom recalled Sukhoi's conversation with Hunter about how the level of radiation on the surface would not drop for at least fifty years, and that mankind was doomed, and other biological species were on the rise . . . The elder did not explain exactly how the surface of the earth would turn into a flowering paradise.

Artyom wanted to ask him what weird kind of plants were going to bloom in that burned-out paradise, and what kind of people would dare to go up above and settle it, and if his parents had been children of Satan, and if that were why they had perished in the war to annihilate evil. But he didn't say anything. He was filled with such bitterness and such mistrust, that his eyes burned, and he was ashamed to feel a tear run down his cheek. Mustering his strength, he said just one thing:

'Tell me, what does Jehovah, our true God, say about headless mutants?' The question hung in the air. Elder John did not deign even to glance at Artyom, but those standing next to him looked around with fright and repulsion, and they moved away from him, as if he had let out a foul smell. Brother Timothy tried to take him by

242

the hand, but Artyom tore away and, pushing aside the brethren who were crowded around, began to make his way to the exit.

He made it out of the Hall of the Kingdom and went through the dining carriage. There were a lot of people at the tables now, with empty aluminium bowls in front of them. Something interesting was going on in the middle of the room, and all eyes were turned in that direction.

'Before we partake of this repast, my brethren,' a skinny, homely fellow with a crooked nose was saying, 'let us listen to little David and his story. This will fill out the sermon we heard today about violence.'

He moved aside, his place being taken by a chubby, snub-nosed boy with carefully combed, whitish hair.

'He was mad at me and wanted to give me a drubbing,' David began, speaking with the intonation children use when reciting verses they have learned by heart. 'Probably only because I was short. I backed away from him and cried out: "Stop! Wait! Don't beat me! I haven't done anything to you. What did I do to offend you? You'd better tell me what happened!"' A well-rehearsed expression of exaltation came over David's face.

'And what did that awful bully say to you?' the skinny fellow jumped in excitedly.

'It turned out that somebody had stolen his breakfast, and he was only taking out his annoyance on the first person he ran into,' David explained, but something in his voice made it seem doubtful that he himself understood very well what he had just said.

'And what did you do?' asked the thin man, stoking the tension.

'I just said to him, "If you beat me, it won't bring your breakfast back," and I suggested to him instead, to go to Brother Chef and tell him what had happened. We asked for another breakfast for him. After that he shook my hand and was always friendly to me.'

'Is the man who offended little David present in this room?' asked the skinny fellow in the voice of a prosecutor.

A hand shot up, and a strapping twenty-year-old with a doltish and malevolent-looking face began to make his way toward the improvised stage, to tell about the miraculous effect of little David's words upon him. It wasn't easy. The boy was obviously more adept at memorizing words whose meaning he didn't understand. When the presentation was over, and little David and the repentant thug left the stage to the approving sound of applause, the stringy fellow took their place again and addressed the seated audience in an impassioned voice:

'Yes, the words of the meek possess enormous power! As it says in Proverbs, the words of the meek break bones. Softness and meekness are not weakness, o my beloved brethren, for softness conceals an enormous strength of will! And examples from the Holy Bible give us proof . . .' Flipping through the well-thumbed book for the page he wanted, he began to read aloud some story, in tones of rapture.

Artyom moved ahead, followed by surprised looks, and finally made it into the lead car. Nobody stopped him there, and he was about to go out onto the tracks, but Bashni the senior guard, that amiable and unflappable hulk of a man, greeted him cordially at the door, now blocking the way with his torso and, knitting his thick brows, sternly asked if Artyom had permission to exit. There was no way to get around him.

Waiting half a minute for an explanation, the guard kneaded his enormous fists with a dry crackle, and moved towards Artyom. Looking around in all directions, trapped, Artyom remembered little David's story. Maybe, instead of hurling himself against the elephantine guard, it would be worth finding out if maybe somebody stole his breakfast.

Fortunately, just then Brother Timothy caught up with him. Looking at the security man tenderly, he said, 'This young man may pass. We don't hold anybody here against their will.' The guard, looking at him in surprise, obediently stepped aside.

'But allow me to accompany you even just a little way, o my beloved Brother Artyom,' Brother Timothy sang out, and Artyom, unable to resist the magic of his voice, nodded. 'Perhaps the way we live here was something unaccustomed for you, the first time,' Timothy said in soothing tones, 'but now the divine seed has been implanted in you as well, and it is clear to my eyes, that it has fallen into favoured soil. I only want to tell you how you should *not* act, now that the Kingdom of God is near as never before, lest you be turned away. You must learn to hate evil and to avoid the things which God abhors: fornication, which means infidelity, sodomy, incest and homosexuality, gambling, lying, thievery, fits of rage, violence, sorcery, spiritualism, drunkenness.' Brother Timothy reeled them off in a rush of words, nervously looking Artyom in the eye. 'If you love God and wish to please Him, free yourself from those sins! Your more mature friends will be able to help you,' he added, evidently alluding to himself. 'Honour the name of God, preach the

Kingdom of God, take no part in the affairs of this evil world, abjure people who tell you otherwise, for Satan speaks through their mouths,' he muttered, but Artyom didn't hear anything. He was walking faster and faster, and Brother Timothy couldn't keep up. 'Tell me, where shall I be able to find you next time?' he called out from quite a distance, panting, and almost lost in the semi-darkness.

Artyom remained silent, and broke into a run. From behind, out of the darkness, a desperate cry reached him:

'Give the cassock back . . . !'

Artyom ran on ahead, stumbling, unable to see anything in front of him. Several times he fell down, scraping his palms on the concrete floor and skinning his knees, but there was no stopping. He had too clear an image of the black pedestal-mounted machine gun, and now he didn't much believe that the brethren would prefer a meek word to violence, if they could catch up to him.

He was a step nearer to his goal, being not far away at all from *Polis*. It was on the same line, and only two stations away. The main thing was to go forward, not deviating one step from his route, and then . . .

Artyom entered *Serphukhovskaya*. He didn't pause for a second, only checked his direction, and then dived back into the black hole of the tunnel leading ahead.

But, at this point, something unexpected happened to him.

The feeling of terror of the tunnel, which he had already forgotten, came crashing back down upon him, pressing him to the ground, making it difficult for him to walk, or think, or even breathe. It had seemed to him that, by now, he had formed some habits, and that, after all his wanderings, the horror would leave him and would not dare to bother him again. He had felt neither fear nor alarm when moving from *Kitai Gorod* to *Pushkinskaya*, nor when riding from *Tverskaya* to *Paveletskaya*, nor even as he trudged, completely alone, from *Paveletskaya* to *Dobryninskaya*. But now it had returned.

With each step forward, the feeling assailed him more and more. He wanted to turn around immediately and plunge headlong back to the station, where there was at least a little bit of light, and some people, and where his back would not be constantly tickled by the sensation of an intent and malevolent gaze.

He had been interacting with people so much, that he had stopped feeling what had rushed over him when he first left *Alekseevskaya*. But now, once again, he was engulfed by the understanding that the metro was not merely a transportation facility, built at a certain point in time, that it was not merely an atomic bomb shelter, or home to some tens of thousands of people . . . Rather, somebody had breathed into it their own, mysterious, incomparable life, and it possessed a certain extraordinary kind of reason, which a human being could not fathom, and a consciousness that was alien to him.

This sensation was so precise and clear, that it seemed to Artyom as if the terror of the tunnel, which people wrongly took to be their ultimate place of refuge, were simply the hostility of this huge being towards the petty creatures who were burrowing into its body. And now, it did not want Artyom to go forward. Against his drive to reach the end of his path, to reach his goal, it was pitting its ancient, powerful will. And its resistance was growing, with every metre Artyom advanced.

Now he was walking through impenetrable darkness, unable to see his own hands, even if he lifted them right up to his face. It was as if he had fallen out of space and out of the currents of time, and it seemed to him as if his body had ceased to exist. It was as if he were not stepping his way through the tunnel, but soaring as a substance of pure reason in an unknown dimension.

Artyom could not see the walls receding behind him, so it appeared as if he were standing still, not moving forward a single step, and that the goal of his journey were just as unattainable as it had been five or ten minutes earlier. Yes, his feet were picking their way through the cross-ties, which could have told him that he was changing his spatial position. On the other hand, the signal which advised his brain of each new cross-tie, onto which his foot stepped, was absolutely uniform. Recorded once and for all, now it was repeating to infinity. That also made him doubt the reality of his motion. Was he nearing his goal by moving? Suddenly he remembered his vision, which provided an answer to the question tormenting him.

And then, whether from terror of the unknown, evil, hostile thing that was bearing down on him from behind, or in order to prove to himself that he really was still moving, Artyom rushed ahead with triple the force. And he barely managed to stop, guessing by some sixth sense that an obstacle lay ahead, and miraculously he avoided crashing into it.

Carefully probing with his hands along the cold, rusted metal, and then fragments of glass sticking out from rubber gaskets, and steel pancakes which were wheels, he recognized that the mysterious obstacle was a train. This train had been abandoned, apparently. In

246

any case, there was only silence around it. Remembering Mikhail Porfiryevich's horrible story, Artyom made no attempt to climb into it, but rather skirted the chain of subway cars, keeping close to the tunnel wall. Getting past the train at last, he breathed a sigh of relief and hurried onward, again breaking into a run.

In the darkness this was really difficult, but his legs caught on, and he ran, until there appeared ahead, and slightly to one side, the reddish glow of a bonfire.

It brought indescribable relief to know that he was in the real world, and that there were real people nearby. It didn't matter how they would relate to him. They could be murderers or thieves, sectarians or revolutionaries – it didn't matter. The main thing was that they were creatures of flesh and blood, like him. He did not doubt for one second that he would be able to find refuge with these people and to hide from that invisible, huge being which wanted to suffocate him. Or, was he seeking refuge from his own deranged mind?

Such a strange picture came into view that he could not say for certain if he had returned to the real world, or was still roaming the nooks and crannies of his own subconscious.

At *Polyanka* station, only a single small bonfire was burning, but the absence of any other source of light here made it seem brighter than all the electric lights of *Paveletskaya*. Two people were sitting by the bonfire, one with his back turned toward Artyom and one facing him, but neither of them noticed or heard him. It was as if they were separated from him by an invisible wall that cut them off from the outside world.

The entire station, insofar as it could be seen by the light of the bonfire, was piled high with an unimaginable variety of junk. The shapes of broken bicycles, automobile tyres, and pieces of furniture and equipment could be made out. There was a mountain of rubbish, out of which the people seated by the fire from time to time pulled a stack of newspapers or books, and threw them into the flames. There was a plaster bust of somebody or other standing right in front of the fire, on the underflooring, and next to it a cat was curled up most comfortably. Not another soul was present.

One of the people seated by the fire was telling the other something, unhurriedly. Drawing close, Artyom began to pick up what was being said.

'There are rumors going around about the University . . . Absolutely false, by the way. These are just echoes of the ancient myth of an Underground City in the Ramenki District. Which was part of Metro-2. But, of course, you can't refute anything with one hundred percent certainty. Here, in general, you can't say *anything* with one hundred percent certainty. It's an empire of myths and legend. Metro-2 would have been, of course, the chief myth, the golden one, if more people had known about it. Take, for example, even just the belief in the Unseen Watchers!'

Artyom had approached very close, when the person with his back towards him said:

'There's somebody there.'

'Of course there is,' nodded the other.

'You may join us,' said the first, addressing Artyom, but without turning his head towards him. 'In any event, you can't go any farther.'

'Why not?' objected Artyom in some agitation. 'What? Is there somebody there, in that tunnel?'

'No one, of course,' the man patiently explained. 'Who's going to mess around in there? You can't go there now, anyway, I'm telling you. So, sit down.'

'Thank you.' Artyom took a tentative step forward and sank to the floor across from the bust. They were over forty. One was grey-haired, with square glasses, and the other was thin, with fair hair and a small beard. Both of them were wearing old quilted jackets. They were inhaling smoke through a thin tube rigged up to something like a calabash, from which there issued a head-spinning fragrance.

'What's your name?' asked the fair-haired one.

'Artyom,' the young man replied mechanically, busy with studying these strange people.

'His name is Artyom,' the fair-haired man said to the other.

'Well, that's understood,' he replied.

'I am Yevgeny Dmitrievich. And this is Sergei Andreyevich,' said the fair-haired man.

'We don't have to be so formal, do we?' Sergei Andreyevich said

'Sergei, as you and I have reached this age, we might as well take advantage of it. It's a question of status and all that.'

'OK, and what else?' Sergei Andreyevich then asked Artyom.

The question sounded very odd, as if he were insisting that they continue something that had not ever started, and Artyom was quite perplexed.

'So you're Artyom, but so what? Where do you live, where are you going, what do you believe in, what do you not believe in, who is to blame and what is to be done?' Sergei Andreyevich explained.

'Like it used to be, remember?' Sergei Andreyevich said suddenly, for no apparent reason.

'Oh, yes!' laughed Yevgeny Dmitrievich.

'I live at *VDNKh* . . . or at least I did live there,' Artyom began reluctantly.

'Just like . . . Who put their jackboot on the control panel?' the fair-haired man grinned.

'Yes! Nothing left of America!' Sergei Andreyevich smirked, taking off his glasses and examining them in the light.

Artyom looked warily at them again. Maybe he should just get out of here, while the going was good. But what they had been talking about before they noticed him, kept him there by the fire.

'And what's this about Metro-2? If you'll excuse me, I overheard a little,' he admitted.

'So, you want to find out the main legend of the metro?' Sergei Andreyevich smiled patronizingly. 'Just what is it you want to know?'

'You were talking about an underground city and about some kind of observers . . .'

'Well, Metro-2 was generally a refuge for the gods of the Soviet Pantheon during the time of Ragnarök, if the forces of evil were to prevail,' began Yevgeny Dmitrievich, gazing at the ceiling and blowing smoke rings. 'According to the legends, under the city whose dead body lies there, above us, another metro had been built, for the elite. What you see around you is the metro for the common herd. The other one, according to the legends, that's for the shepherds and their dogs. At the very beginning, when the shepherds had not yet lost their power over the herd, they ruled from there; but then their strength gave out, and the sheep ran off. Gates alone were what connected these two worlds, and, if you believe the legends, these were located right where the map is now sliced in two as if by a blood-red scar – on the *Sokolinskaya* branch, somewhere behind the *Sportivnaya*. Later something occurred that closed the entrance to Metro-2 forever. Those who lived here lost any knowledge of what had taken place, and the very existence of Metro-2 became somehow mythical and unreal. But,' he pointed upwards, 'despite the fact that the entrance to Metro-2 no longer exists, that does not at all mean that it has ceased to exist. On the contrary, it is all around us. Its tunnels wind around our stations, and its stations could be just a few steps behind our stations' walls. These two structures are inseparable;

they are like the circulatory system and lymphatic vessels of one organism. And those who believe that the shepherds could not have abandoned their herd to the mercy of fate, say that they are present, imperceptibly, in our lives, direct us, follow our every step, but do not reveal themselves and do not let their existence be known. And that is the belief in Unseen Watchers.'

The cat, curling up next to the soot-covered bust, raised her head and, opening her enormous, lustrous green eyes, looked at Artyom with a startlingly clear and intelligent expression. Her stare was nothing like that of an animal, and Artyom could not immediately be sure that someone else was not studying him carefully him through her eyes. But the cat yawned, stretching out her sharp pink tongue, and, burying her muzzle in her bedding, dropped back to sleep, like an illusion that had vanished.

'But why don't they want people to know about them?' Artyom remembered his question.

'There are two reasons for that. First of all, the sheep are guilty of having rejected their shepherds at their moment of weakness. Second, since the Metro-2 was cut off from our world, the shepherds have developed differently from us, and are no longer human, but beings of a higher order, whose logic is incomprehensible to us and whose thoughts are inaccessible. No one knows what they think of our metro, but they could change everything, even return us to our wonderful, lost world, because they have regained their former power. Because we rebelled against them once and betrayed them, they no longer have anything to do with our fate. However the shepherds are everywhere, and our every breath is known to them, every step, every blow – everything that happens in the metro. They only observe for the present. And only when we atone for our dreadful sin will they turn to us with a gracious gaze and extend a hand to us. And then a renaissance will begin. That is those who believe in the Unseen Watchers say.' He fell silent, inhaling the aromatic smoke.

'But how can people atone for their guilt?' Artyom asked.

'Nobody knows except the Unseen Watchers themselves. Humans don't understand it, because they do not know the dispensation of the Watchers.'

'Then people might never be able to atone for their sin against them?' Artyom was baffled.

'Does that bother you?' Yevgeny Dmitrievich shrugged his

shoulders and blew two more big, beautiful smoke rings, one slipping through the second.

There was silence for a time – at first light and limpid, but gradually getting thicker and louder and more palpable. Artyom felt a growing need to break it any way he could, with any senseless phrase, even a meaningless sound. 'And where are you from?' he asked.

'Before, I lived at Smolenskaya, not far from the metro, about five minutes' walk,' Yevgeny Dmitrievich replied and Artyom stared at him in surprise: how could he have lived not far from the metro? He must have meant that he lived not far from a metro station, in a tunnel – right? 'You had to walk past food stalls, we sometimes bought beer there, and there were always prostitutes standing around near the stalls, and the police had . . . uh . . . a headquarters there,' Yevgeny Dmitrievich continued and Artyom had started to realize that he was talking about the old times, about what had gone on before.

'Yeah . . . Me too, I also lived not far from there, at Kalinsky, in a high-rise,' said Sergei Andreyevich. 'Someone told me about five years ago that he'd heard from a stalker that they had crumbled to dust . . . The House of Books is still there and all the cheap paperbacks were sitting on the tables untouched, can you believe it? And all that was left of the high-rise was a pile of dust and blocks of cement. Strange.'

'So what was life like back then?' Artyom was curious. He loved to ask old men this question and they would stop whatever they were doing and describe the old days with such pleasure. Their eyes would assume a dreamy, distant look; their voices would sound totally different; and their faces looked ten years younger. Images of the past, which were brought to life before their minds' eyes, were nothing like the pictures that Artyom conjured up while they told their stories, but it was nonetheless very enjoyable for all. It was sort of sweet and sort of torturous at the same time and it made the heart ache . . .

'Well, you see, it was a wonderful time. Back then . . . ah . . . we were on fire,' Yevgeny Dmitrievich replied, drawing out his answer.

Here, Artyom definitely did not imagine what the grey-haired man had in mind, and when the other old man realized that, he quickly elucidated.

'We were very lively, we had good times.'

'Yes, that's exactly what I mean. We were on fire,' Yevgeny Dmitrievich confirmed.

'I had a green Moskvich-2141 and I'd spent my whole salary to buy it, to give it a sound system, to change the oil. Once, like a fool, I even had the carburettor replaced with a sports car model and then I used nitrous oxide.' He had clearly transported himself to those good old days, when you could so easily get an old sports car carburettor to put in your car. And his face took on that same dreamy expression that Artyom so loved. It was a shame that Artyom understood little of what he was saying though.

'Artyom probably doesn't even know what a Moskvich is, never mind what a carburettor is.' Sergei Andreyevich interrupted his friend's sweet reminiscences.

'What do you mean he doesn't know?' The thin man threw Artyom an angry look. Artyom took to studying the ceiling, gathering his thoughts.

'So why are you burning books?' He changed the subject as a counteroffensive tactic.

'We've already read 'em,' Yevgeny Dmitrievich responded.

'There's no truth in books!' Sergei Andreyevich added in explanation.

'Anyway, perhaps you should tell us something about how you're dressed – are you a member of a cult or what?' Yevgeny Dmitrievich delivered a decisive blow.

'No, no, of course not,' Artyom hurried to explain. 'But they did pick me up and help me when I was in trouble.' He explained in broad strokes in what poor shape he'd been but didn't go as far as explaining quite how bad it was.

'Yes, yes, that's exactly how they work. I recognize the tactics. Orphaned and wretched . . . ah . . . or something in that vein,' nodded Yevgeny Dmitrievich.

'You know, I was at one of their meetings, and they say very strange things,' said Artyom. 'I stood around for a while and listened, but couldn't stand it very long. For example, that Satan's principal wickedness was that he wanted glory and adoration for himself, too . . . Before, I thought it had been a lot more serious, but it just turned out to be jealousy. Is the world really so simple, and does everything revolve around the fact that someone didn't want to share glory and worshippers?'

'The world is not that simple,' Sergei Andreyevich assured him, taking the hookah from the fair-haired smoker and inhaling.

'And one more thing . . . They say that God's principal qualities are his mercy, kindness, and willingness to forgive, and that he's a God of love, and that he's all-powerful. At the same time, the first time man disobeyed Him, he was kicked out of paradise and made mortal. So then a whole lot of people die – not scary – and in the end, God sends His son to save everyone. And then His son dies a horrible death, and calls out to God before he dies, asking why God had forsaken him. And all this is for what? To purge, with his blood, the sin of the first human, who God had Himself provoked and punished, and so that people could return to paradise and again discover immortality. It's some kind of pointless baloney, because He could have just not punished everyone so severely to begin with for stuff they didn't do. Or he could have discontinued the punishment because the offence had taken place so long ago. But why sacrifice your beloved son, and even betray him? What kind of love is that? What kind of willingness to forgive? Where's the omnipotence?'

'Roughly and bluntly stated, but correct, in general terms,' said Sergei Andreyevich approvingly, passing the hookah to his companion.

'Here's what I can say on the subject,' said Yevgeny Dmitrievich, filling his lungs with smoke and smiling blithely. He paused for a minute, and then continued, 'So, if their God indeed has some qualities or distinguishing aspects, they certainly don't include love, or justice, or forgiveness. Judging from what's happened on earth from the time it was . . . uh . . . created, only one kind of love has been unique to God: He loves interesting stories. First He sets up an interesting situation and then He stands back to see what happens. If the result is a little flat, He adds a little pepper. So old man Shakespeare was right, all the world's a stage. Just not the one he was hinting at,' he concluded.

'This morning alone, you've talked your way into several centuries in hell,' observed Sergei Andreyevich.

'That means you'll have someone to talk with there,' Yevgeniy Dmitrievich told his companion.

'On the other hand, many interesting acquaintances may be made there,' said Sergei Andreyevich.

'For example, among the upper hierarchy of the Catholic Church.'

'Yes, they are surely there. Yet strictly speaking, so are ours . . .'

Both of Artyom's companions clearly didn't much believe that there would someday be a reckoning for everything said now. But

Yevgeniy Dmitrievich's words, about how what has happened to humanity is just an interesting story, led Artyom to a new thought.

'Now, I've read a good many different books,' he said, 'and I'm always amazed that they're nothing like real life. I mean, look, events in books are arranged in a nice straight line, everything is tied to everything else, causes have effects, and nothing doesn't "just happen". But in reality, everything's completely otherwise! I mean, life is just full of senseless events that happen to us randomly, and there's no such thing as everything happening in a logical sequence. What's more, books, for example, come to an end just where the logical chain breaks off; there's a beginning, a development, then a peak, and an end.'

'A climax, not a peak,' Sergei Andreyevich corrected him, listening to Artyom's observations with a bored look.

Yevgeniy Dmitrievich also did not evince any particular interest. He moved the smoking apparatus closer to himself, inhaled some aromatic smoke, and held his breath.

'OK, climax,' continued Artyom, slightly discouraged. 'But in life, everything's different. First, a logical chain might not come to an end, and second, even if it does, nothing comes to a close because of it.'

'You mean to say that life has no plot?' asked Sergei Andreyevich, helping Artyom formulate his words.

Artyom thought for a minute, then nodded.

'But do you believe in fate?' asked Sergei Andreyevich, inclining his head to the side and examining Artyom studiously, while Yevgeniy Dmitrievich turned away from the hookah with interest.

'No,' said Artyom decisively. 'There is no fate, just random events that happen to us, and then we make things up on our own later.'

'Too bad, too bad . . .' sighed Sergei Andreyevich disappointedly, austerely looking at Artyom over his eyeglasses. 'Now, I'm going to present a little theory of mine to you, and you see for yourself if it matches your life or not. It seems to me that life, of course, is an empty joke, and that there's no purpose to it at all, and that there's no fate, which is to say anything explicit and definite, along the lines of you're born and you already know that you're going to be a cosmonaut or a ballerina, or that you'll die in your infancy . . . No, not like that. While you're living your allotted time . . . how do I explain this . . . It may happen that something happens to you that forces you to perform specific actions and make specific decisions, keeping in mind you have free will, and can do this or that. But if you make the right decision, then the things that happen to you subsequently are no longer just random, to use your word, events. They are caused by the choices that you made. I don't intend to say that if you decided to live on the Red Line before it went communist that you'd be stuck there and that corresponding events would happen to you. I'm talking of more subtle matters. But if you again were to find yourself at the crossroads and once more made the needed decision, then later you will be faced with a choice that will no longer seem random to you if, of course, you realize and can understand it. And your life will gradually stop being just a collection of random events; it will turn into . . . a plot, I suppose, where everything is connected by some logical, though not necessarily straight, links. And that will be your fate. At a certain stage, if you have travelled sufficiently far along your way, your life will have turned into a plot to the extent that strange things will occur that are unexplainable from the point of view of naked rationalism or your theory of random events. Yet they will fit very well into the logic of the plot line that your life has by then turned into. I think fate doesn't just happen, you need to arrive at it, and if the events in your life come together and start to arrange themselves into a plot, then it may cast you quite far . . . It is most interesting that a person may not even suspect that this is happening to him, or may conceive what has happened based on a false premise, by attempting to systematize events to match his own world view. But fate has its own logic.'

This strange theory, which at first seemed to Artyom to be complete mumbo-jumbo, suddenly forced him to look at everything that had happened to him from the very beginning, when he had agreed to Hunter's proposal to leave for *Polis*, from a new point of view.

Now all of his adventures, all his travels, which he had previously viewed as unsuccessful and desperate attempts to achieve the goal of his quest, which he pursued wherever it led him, appeared before him in a different light, and it seemed to him to be an elaborately organized system that formed an ornate, yet well-thought-out structure.

Because if one considered Artyom's acceptance of Hunter's proposal as the first step along the way, as Sergei Andreyevich had said, then all subsequent events – including the expedition to *Rizhskaya*, and the fact that Bourbon approached him at *Rizhskaya* and that Artyom didn't recoil from him – constituted the next step, and that Khan came to meet him, although he could have remained at *Sukharevskaya* . . . Yet this could be explained some other way as well; at any rate, Khan himself cited completely different reasons for his actions. Then Artyom was taken prisoner by the fascists, at *Tverskaya,* and should have been hanged, but circumstances so arranged themselves that the International Brigade decided to attack *Tverskaya* precisely on that day. Had the revolutionaries shown up a day earlier or a day later, Artyom's death would have been unavoidable, and then his quest would be ended.

Could it actually be that the persistence with which he pursued his path influenced future events? Could it be that the determination, rage, and desperation that drove him to take every next step created, in some unknown way, a reality that wove a set of chaotic events and someone's thoughts and actions into an ordered system, thereby turning an ordinary life into a plot, as Sergei Andreyevich had said?

At first glance, nothing of the sort could happen. But if you thought about it . . . How else did one explain the meeting with Mark, who offered Artyom the single possible way of getting into the Hansa territory? And the main thing, the very main thing, is that while he was accepting his lot, cleaning out toilets, fate, it would seem, turned away from him, but when he took the bit between his teeth, without even trying to understand his actions, the impossible happened: the guard who was supposed to stay at his post disappeared somewhere, and there wasn't even any pursuit. So when he returned from the diverging crooked path back onto his way, acting in harmony with the narrative pattern of his life, at the stage where he was now, this could already have resulted in a serious warping of reality, repairing it in such a way that the main line of Artyom's fate could develop further without hindrance?

Then this must mean that, should he deviate from his goal or step off his path, fate would immediately abandon him and its invisible shield, which currently safeguarded Artyom from being killed, would directly crumble into pieces, and the thread of Ariadne that he was so carefully following would break, and he would be left face-to-face with a turbulent reality that had been infuriated with his impudent intrusions into the chaotic substance of reality . . . Might it be that whoever once attempted to deceive fate and was flippant enough to continue to persevere even after dire clouds had gathered overhead couldn't just simply step off the path? From then on his life would turn into something completely commonplace and grey, and nothing else would ever happen that was unusual, magical, or unexplainable because the plot had been be interrupted, and he'd put paid to the hero business . . .

Did this mean that Artyom not only hadn't the right, but couldn't deviate from his path? That was his fate? The fate in which he did not believe? And in which he did not believe because he didn't know to interpret what had happened to him, didn't know how to read the signs posted along his road, and continued to naively believe that the road that led to far horizons and which had been constructed just for him was a jumbled tangle of abandoned pathways that led in different directions?

It seemed that he was proceeding along his path, and that the events of his life formed a harmonious plot that held sway over human will and reason, so that his enemies were blinded while his friends saw the light and were able to help him in time. It was a plot that so controlled reality that the immutable laws of probability obediently changed their shape, like putty, in response to the growing power of an invisible hand that moved him over the chessboard of life . . . And if it were actually so, then the question 'What's the point of all this?', which previously could be answered only with sullen silence and gritted teeth, went away. Now, the courage with which he professed to himself (and stubbornly maintained to others) that there was no Providence or any higher plan, that there was no law and no justice in the world, turned out to be unnecessary, because that plan could be divined . . . He did not want to resist this thought. It was too seductive to turn away from it with the same die-hard stubbornness with which he had rejected the explanations offered by religions and ideologies.

As a whole, this meant only one thing.

'I can't stay here any longer,' said Artyom, and got up, feeling as if his muscles were filling with a new, buzzing strength. 'I can't stay here any longer,' he repeated, listening attentively to his own voice. 'I have to go. I must.'

No longer constantly twisting his head around and having forgotten all the fears that drove him to this small fire, he jumped onto the tracks and moved ahead, into the darkness. Artyom's doubts released him, making room for perfect peace and the confidence that he was finally doing everything right. It was as if, having been driven off course, he nevertheless was able to recover his feet on the shining rails of his fate. The ties on which he walked now almost passed under his feet by themselves, requiring no effort on his part. In an instant, he disappeared completely into the darkness.

'It's a beautiful theory, isn't it?' said Sergei Andreyevich, inhaling.

'One would almost think that you believe it,' replied Yevgeny Dmitrievich cantankerously, scratching the cat behind the ear.

CHAPTER 12

Polis

Only one tunnel remained. Only one tunnel, and the goal given to him by Hunter, towards which Artyom stubbornly and recklessly went, would be reached. There were two, maybe three kilometres left to go along a dry and quiet section, and he'd be there. An echoing silence prevailed in Artyom's head, a silence almost like that in the tunnel, but he no longer asked questions of himself. In another forty minutes, he'd be there. Forty minutes, and his trek would be over.

He wasn't even aware that he was walking in impenetrable darkness. His legs continued to steadily mark off the ties. It was as if he had forgotten about all the dangers that threatened him, that he was unarmed, and that he had no identity papers, no flashlight, and no weapons, that he was dressed in an odd-looking set of loose overalls, and that, finally, he knew nothing about either this tunnel or the dangers that lay in wait for travellers through it.

His conviction that nothing posed a threat to him as long as he was following his path filled him. Where had the seemingly inescapable fear of the tunnels gone? What had happened to his fatigue and lack of faith?

The echo spoiled everything.

Because this tunnel was so empty, the sound of his steps carried both ahead and behind. Reflected from the walls, they rumbled and gradually receded and passed into a rustle, and then echoed shortly after, so that it seemed Artyom was not walking in the tunnel alone. After some time, this perception become so acute, that Artyom wanted to stop and listen and find out if the echo of his steps had a life of its own.

He continued to struggle with temptation for several minutes. His pace became slower and quieter, and he listened to hear if this affected the loudness of the echo. Finally, Artyom stopped completely. He stood like that in the impenetrable darkness and waited, afraid to take a deep breath, lest the sound of air entering his lungs interfered with the perception of the slightest murmurs in the distance.

Silence.

Now that he had stopped moving, his perception of the reality of space again vanished. While he was walking, it was as if he was grasping that reality by the soles of his boots. When he stopped in the middle of the ink-black darkness of the tunnel, Artyom suddenly no longer understood where he was.

And it seemed to him, when he again began to move, that the barely perceptible echo of his steps reached his ears before his own foot managed to step down onto the concrete floor.

His heart began to beat more acutely. But, in an instant, he was able to convince himself that paying attention to every rustle in the tunnels was silly and served no purpose. For some time, Artyom tried not to listen to the echo at all. Then, when it seemed to him that the most recent of the fading echoes were drawing closer, he covered his ears and continued to move forward. But even this didn't work for long.

Removing his palms from his ears after a couple of minutes and continuing to walk, he heard – to his horror – the echo of his steps getting louder in front of him, as if they were approaching. But all he had to do was stop and so would the sounds in front of him, after a delay of some fraction of a second.

This tunnel was testing Artyom and his ability to withstand fear. But he didn't give up. He had already been through much too much to be scared by darkness and an echo.

Was it an echo?

It was getting closer. There was no doubt about that. Artyom stopped one last time when the phantom steps could be heard about twenty metres ahead of him. This was so inexplicable and weird that he couldn't stand it. He wiped the cold perspiration from his brow and, with his voice cracking, shouted into the emptiness:

'Is anyone there?'

The echo reverberated frighteningly close, and Artyom didn't recognize his own voice. The rolling echoes chased each other into the depths of the tunnels, shedding syllables: 'anyone there . . . one there . . . there. . . .' And nobody answered. And suddenly, something incredible happened. They started to come back, repeating his question, the dropped syllables recomposing themselves in reverse order and becoming louder, as though someone about thirty paces away had repeated his question in a frightened voice.

Artyom could not endure this. Turning around, he went back, trying not to walk too fast at first, but then he ran, having completely forgotten about not encouraging his fears, and stumbling. But after a minute, he understood that the reverberating footsteps continued to be heard at a distance of twenty metres. His invisible pursuer didn't want to let him go. Gasping, Artyom ran without understanding in what direction, and finally collided with a tunnel cross passage.

The echo immediately abated. Some time passed before he could gather up his will power, get up, and take a step forward. It was the right direction. With each passing metre, the sound of steps shuffling against the concrete became closer, moving towards him. And only the blood pounding in his ears slightly suppressed the ominous rustling. Every time Artyom stopped, his pursuer stopped in the darkness as well, for Artyom was now absolutely sure it was no echo.

This continued until the steps sounded as close as one's outstretched arm. And then Artyom, yelling and blindly swinging his fists, sprang forward to where he reckoned the source of the steps had to be.

His fists made a swishing sound as they cut through the emptiness. Nobody tried to defend themselves against his blows. He flailed the air uselessly, yelling, jumping back, and moving his arms out from his sides in an effort to seize an enemy he could not see in the darkness. Emptiness. There was nobody there. But as soon as he caught his breath and made one more step toward *Polis*, he heard a heavy shuffling sound right in front of him. He again swung his arm, and again there was nothing. Artyom felt he was losing his mind. Straining his eyes until they hurt, he tried to see anything at all, and his ears tried to catch the nearby breathing of some other creature. But there simply wasn't anybody there.

Having stood immobile for several long seconds, Artyom reflected that whatever the explanation might be for this strange phenomenon, it posed no danger to him. Acoustics, more than likely. When I get home, I'll ask my stepfather, he said to himself, but, when he had already brought his foot up to take another step toward his goal, someone quietly whispered, directly in his ear:

'Wait. You can't go there now.'

'Who's that? Who's here?' yelled Artyom, breathing heavily. But nobody answered. He was again surrounded by a deep emptiness. Then, wiping the sweat from his brow with the back of his hand, he hurried off in the direction of *Borovitskaya*. The phantom steps of his pursuer matched his pace as he moved in the opposite direction, gradually fading in the distance until they fell silent. And only then did Artyom stop. He did not and could not know what it had been. He had never heard of anything like it from any of his friends, nor had his stepfather spoken to him of it at night by the fire. But whoever it was who whispered in his ear and ordered him to stop and wait, now – when Artyom no longer feared him, when he had the time to understand what had happened and do some hard thinking about it – it sounded hypothetically convincing.

He spent the next twenty minutes sitting on the rails, swaying from side to side as if drunk, fighting the shakes and recalling the strange voice, which belonged to no human, that ordered him to wait. He moved forward only when the shivering finally began to pass, and the frightful whisper in his head had begun to merge with the quiet rush of the growing air current in the tunnel.

From that point on, he simply walked forward, trying not to think of anything, stumbling at times over cables lying on the floor, but nothing more terrible happened to him. It seemed to him that not much time had passed, although he couldn't say how much, because the minutes all ran together in the darkness. And then he saw a light at the end of the tunnel.

Borovitskaya.

Polis.

Then and there, a rude cry was heard from the station, followed by the sound of shots, and Artyom, springing back, hid in a depression in the wall. From a distance, he heard the lingering cries of the wounded, followed by foul language, and then there was the sound of another burst of automatic fire, amplified by the tunnel.

Wait . . .

Artyom ventured to emerge from his hiding place only a full fifteen minutes after everything had quietened down. Raising his arms, he walked slowly toward the light.

This actually was an entry onto the platform. There was no watch on duty at *Borovitskaya,* apparently relying on the inviolability of *Polis.* An access point made of concrete blocks stood five metres short of the point where the circular arches of the tunnel ended. A prone body lay next to it in a pool of blood.

When Artyom emerged into the field of view of border guards wearing green uniforms and service caps, they ordered him to come closer and stand facing the wall. Seeing the body on the ground, he obeyed immediately.

He was quickly searched, asked for his passport, had his arms twisted behind his back, and finally led to the station. Light. The very same. They told the truth. They always told the truth; legends didn't lie. The light was so bright, Artyom had to squint so as not to be blinded. But the light entered his pupils even through his eyelids, blinding him until it hurt, and only when the border guards blindfolded him did his eyes stop stinging. Returning to the life lived by previous generations of people turned out to be more painful than Artyom could imagine.

The rag was removed from his eyes only at the guard shack, which looked like all others, a small office with walls of cracked tile. It was dark here. Only a candle flickered in an aluminium bowl that lay on an ochre-coloured wooden table. The guard commander was a heavy-set, unshaven man in a green military shirt with rolled-up sleeves. He was wearing a tie on an elastic band. Collecting some of the liquid wax on his finger and observing how it cooled, he watched Artyom for a long time before asking:

'Where are you from? Where's your passport? What's with your eye?'

Artyom decided it didn't make sense to be devious, so he told the truth, that the passport had been left with the fascists, and that his eye had also almost remained there. The commander received this information with unexpected benevolence.

'Yeah, we know. That tunnel opposite comes out precisely at *Checkhovskaya*. We've got a whole fortress built there. There's no fighting for now, but some good folks tell us to keep our ears open. Like they say, si vis pacem, para bellum,' and he gave Artyom a wink.

Artyom didn't understand the last part of what had been said, but preferred not to ask about it. His attention was attracted by the tattoo at the crook of the commander's elbow. It depicted a radiation-deformed bird with two heads, spread wings, and hooked talons. It dimly reminded him of something, but of what, he had no idea. Later, when the commander turned to one of the soldiers, Artyom saw that the same image, smaller, had been tattooed on the commander's left temple.

'And why'd you come here?' continued the commander.

'I'm looking for someone . . . His name is Melnik. It's probably a nickname. I have an important message for him.'

The expression on the face of the commander changed immediately. The idly benevolent smile left his lips, and his eyes sparkled with surprise in the light of the candle.

'You can deliver it to me.'

Artyom shook his head and, apologizing, started to explain that there was no way he could do that, that it was hush-hush, you understand, and that he had been strictly ordered to say nothing to anyone except this very same Melnik.

The commander studied him one more time and signalled one of the soldiers, who handed him a black plastic telephone handset, together with a neatly coiled, rubber-coated telephone cord of the required length. After dialling a number, the border guard spoke into the receiver:

'This is post Bor-South. Ivashov. Get me Colonel Melnik.'

While he waited for an answer, Artyom managed to notice that both of the other soldiers in the room also had the bird tattoo on their temples.

'Who should I say is asking?' asked the commander of Artyom, pressing the side of the handset to his chest.

'Say it's from Hunter. An urgent message.'

The commander nodded and exchanged another couple of phrases with whoever was at the other end of the connection, then concluded the call.

'Be at *Arbatskaya* tomorrow morning at nine, at the station manager's office. You're free until then.' He signalled the soldier standing in the doorway, who immediately moved aside, and then turned to Artyom and added, 'Wait a second . . . It would seem you are an honorary first-time guest of ours. So here, hang on to these, but don't forget to give them back!' He offered Artyom a pair of dark glasses in a shabby metal frame.

Not until tomorrow? Artyom was overcome by burning disappointment and resentment. This was why he came here, risking his own life and that of others? This was why he pressed on, forcing himself to move his feet, even when he had no strength left at all? And wasn't this an urgent business, to report everything he knew to this so-and-so Melnik, who it turned out couldn't even find a spare minute for him?

Or was it that Artyom was simply late, and Melnik already knew everything? Or maybe Melnik already knows something that Artyom himself hasn't a clue about? Maybe he's so late that his entire mission no longer matters?

'Not until tomorrow?' he burst out.

'The Colonel's on a mission today. He'll be back early in the

263

morning,' explained Ivashov. 'Get going, and you'll get some rest besides,' he said, and saw Artyom out of the guard shack.

Having calmed down, but still nursing a grievance, Artyom put on the glasses and thought they looked good. And they hid the shiner under his eye. The lenses were scratched and, moreover, they distorted objects in the distance, but when he went out onto the platform after having thanked the border guards, he understood that he could not manage without them. The light from the mercury lamps was too bright for him. Besides, it wasn't just Artyom who couldn't open his eyes here; many at the station hid their eyes behind dark glasses. They're probably also strangers, he thought.

It was strange for him to see a fully illuminated metro station. There were absolutely no shadows here. At *VDNKh*, as well as at all the other stations and substations where he had been up to now, there were few light sources, and they could not illuminate the entire space of what could be seen and they only shed light on parts of it. There always remained places where not a single beam penetrated. Every person cast several shadows: one from a candle, withered and emaciated; a second, from the emergency light; and a third, black and sharply defined, from an electric lantern. They mixed and covered each other and the shadows of others, sometimes coursing for several metres along the floor, startling you, deceiving you, and forcing you to guess and assume. Yet in *Polis*, every last shadow was eradicated in the ruthless glow of the daylight lamps

Artyom froze in his tracks, looking at *Borovitskaya* with delight. It remained in surprisingly good condition. Not a trace of soot was evident on the marble walls or white ceiling, and the station was tidy. A woman in light-blue overalls laboured over a time-blackened bronze panel at the end of the station, industriously scraping the bas-relief with a sponge and cleaning solution.

The living accommodation here was arranged in the arches. Only two arches were left open at each end to access the tracks; the rest, bricked in from both sides, had been turned into real apartments. There was a doorway in each, and some even had wooden doors and glazed windows. The sound of music carried from one of them. Mats lay in front of several doors, so that those entering could wipe their feet. This was the first time Artyom has seen anything of the kind. These quarters looked so cosy, so calm, that he felt a tightening in his chest, and a picture from his childhood suddenly appeared before his eyes. But what was most surprising was the chain of bookshelves that stretched along both walls the length of the entire station. They occupied the space between 'apartments,' and this gave the entire station a kind of marvellous, strange look, reminding Artyom of descriptions he'd read of medieval libraries in a book by Borges.

The escalators were at the far end of the hall, where the passage to the *Arbatskaya* station was located. The pressure doors remained open, but a small post was located at the passage. Then again, the guards let anyone who wanted to pass unhindered in both directions, without even checking documents.

At the opposite end of the platform, on the other hand, next to the bronze bas-relief, there was a real military camp. Several green military tents were set up there, with markings drawn on them like the ones tattooed on the temples of the border guards. In the same place was a cart with some unknown weapon mounted on it, revealed by the long barrel with flared muzzle sticking out from under a cover. Nearby, two soldiers in dark-green uniforms, helmets, and body armour were on duty. The camp encircled a passage stairway that ascended over the tracks. Flashing arrows indicated this was an 'Exit to the city,' whereupon the established precautions became clear to Artyom. A second stairway led to the same place and was completely blocked off by a wall of huge cement blocks.

People dressed in long, grey robes made of dense cloth sat at stout wooden tables that stood in the middle of the station. Drawing nearer to them, Artyom was surprised to see their temples were tattooed as well, but not with the image of a bird, but with that of an open book on a background of several vertical lines that bore a resemblance to a colonnade. Catching Artyom's intent look, one of the men seated at the table smiled amiably and asked:

'Are you a newcomer? Is this your first time here?'

Artyom flinched at the word 'newcomer,' but pulled himself together and nodded. The man who had spoken was not much older than Artyom and, when he rose to shake Artyom's hand, working the flat of his hand out from the broad sleeve of the robe, it turned out they were of about the same height. Only the man's physique was more delicate.

Artyom's new acquaintance was called Daniel. He was in no hurry to talk about himself, and it was evident that he had decided to talk to Artyom because he was curious about what went on beyond the limits of *Polis*, about what was new on the Ring, and about any news of the fascists and the reds . . .

In half an hour, they were seated in the spindly Daniel's home, in one of the 'apartments' nestled between arches, and were drinking hot tea, certainly brought here by devious routes from *VDNKh*. Of the furniture in the room, there was a table piled with books, tall iron shelves that reached to the ceiling, also crammed to the top with thick volumes, and a bed. A weak electric bulb dangled from the ceiling on a wire, illuminating a skilfully executed drawing of an enormous ancient temple that Artyom did not immediately recognize as the Library erected on the surface somewhere above *Polis*.

After his host had run out of questions, it was Artyom's turn.

'Why do people here have tattoos on their heads?' he asked.

'What, don't you know anything about castes?' said Daniel, surprised. 'And you've never heard of *Polis* Council?'

Artyom suddenly remembered that someone (no, how could he forget? it was that old man, Mikhail Porfirievich, who had been killed by the fascists) had told him that power in *Polis* was divided between the soldiers and the librarians because, formerly, the buildings of the Library and some organization related to the army had stood on the surface.

'I've heard of it!' he nodded. 'The warriors and librarians. So, then, you're a librarian?'

Daniel shot him a frightened glance, paled, and began to cough. After a while, he pulled himself together and calmly said:

'What do you mean "librarian"? Have you so much as seen a living librarian? I wouldn't recommend it! Librarians sit up above . . . You've seen our fortifications down here? Heaven forbid they come down . . . Don't ever confuse these things. I am not a librarian, I am a guardian. We are also called Brahmins.'

'What kind of strange name is that?' asked Artyom, raising his eyebrows.

'You see, we have something of a caste system here. Like in old India. A caste . . . Well, it's like a class . . . Didn't the reds explain that to you? Never mind. There's a caste of priests, or guardians of knowledge, those who collect books and work with them,' he explained, while Artyom continued to marvel at how painstakingly he avoided the word 'librarian'. 'And there's a warrior caste, of those who protect and defend. It's very similar to India, where there was also a caste of merchants and a caste of servants. We have all that, too. And we also use the Hindu names for them among ourselves. The priests are the Brahmins, the soldiers are the kshatriyas, the merchants are the vaishyas, and the servants are the shudras. People become members of a caste once and for the rest of their lives. There are special rites of passage, especially for kshatriyas and Brahmins. In

266

India, it was a tribal matter, ancestral, but with us, it's something you choose yourself when you turn eighteen. Here at *Borovitskaya,* there are more Brahmins; in fact, almost everyone is a Brahmin. Our school is here, our libraries, and cells. There are special conditions at the Library because the Red Line crosses there, and it must be protected, and before the war, there were more of us there. Now they've moved to *Aleksandrovskiy Sad.* Meanwhile, at *Arbatskaya,* it's nearly all kshatriyas, because of the General Staff.'

Hearing yet another hissed ancient Indian word, Artyom sighed heavily. It was unlikely he'd remember all these difficult titles right off. However, Daniel did not pay attention to this and continued his narrative:

'Obviously, only two castes enter into the Council, ours and the kshatriyas, though as a matter of fact, we just call them "war doggies",' he said to Artyom, with a wink.

'So why do they tattoo two-headed birds on themselves?' asked Artyom. 'You, at least, have books. That makes sense. But birds?'

'That's their totem,' said Brahmin Daniel, and shrugged. 'I think that formerly it was a guardian spirit of the radiological defence forces. An eagle, I believe. After all, they believe in some strange thing of their own. Generally speaking, the castes around here don't get along particularly well. There was a time they even feuded.'

Through the blinds, they could see that the station lights had been dimmed. Local night was falling. Artyom started to gather his things.

'Is there a hotel here where I can spend the night? Because I have a meeting tomorrow at nine at *Arbatskaya,* and I've nowhere to stay.'

'If you want, stay here,' said Daniel, shrugging. 'I'll sleep on the floor, I'm used to it. I was just about to prepare dinner. Stay and you'll tell me what else you've seen along the road. Because, you know, I don't ever get away from this place. The guardian vows do not allow us to travel further than one station.'

After thinking about it, Artyom nodded. It was comfortable and warm in the room, and Artyom had taken a liking to his host from the very beginning. They had something in common. In fifteen minutes, he was already cleaning mushrooms, while Daniel was cutting salt pork into small slices.

'Have you ever seen the Library even once with your own eyes?' asked Artyom, his mouth full. They were eating stewed pork with mushrooms from aluminium mess dishes.

'You mean the Great Library?' asked the Brahmin, dourly.

267

'I mean the one up there . . . It's still there, right?' said Artyom, pointing his fork at the ceiling.

'Only our elders go up into to the Great Library. And the stalkers, too, who work for the Brahmins,' answered Daniel.

'So, they're the ones who bring books down from above? From the Library? I mean, from the Great Library,' Artyom said, hurriedly correcting himself as he saw his host scowl once more.

'They do, but only by order of the caste elders. It is not within our power to do so ourselves, so we must use mercenaries,' the Brahmin explained grudgingly. 'According to the Testament, we should have been doing that, preserving knowledge and imparting it to seekers. But in order for knowledge to be imparted, it must first be obtained. Yet who among us will dare to go in there?' he said, lifting his eyes upward with a sigh.

'Because of the radiation?' said Artyom, comprehending.

'That too. But mainly because of the librarians,' said Daniel in a subdued voice.

'But aren't you the librarians? Or, at least, the descendants of the librarians? That's what I've heard.'

'You know? Let's not talk about this at the table. In fact, let someone else explain it to you. I don't like to talk about this subject, really.'

Daniel started to clear the table and then, after thinking for a moment, moved some books from a shelf off to the side, revealing a gap between the volumes standing in the back row, in which a round-bellied bottle of moonshine gleamed. Table glasses were found among the dishware.

After some time, Artyom, who had been examining the shelves with delight, decided to break the silence.

'Wow, you sure do have a lot of books,' he said. 'Over where we are, at *VDNKh*, I don't think you could collect as many in the whole library. I finished reading them all a long time ago. It's rare that something good shows up. Only my stepfather brings anything worth reading, and the itinerant merchants bring nothing but miscellaneous rubbish in their suitcases, all sorts of detective novels. Half the time, you can't tell what's going on in them anyway. That was another reason I dreamed of entering Polis, because of the Great Library. I just can't imagine how many there must be up there if they built such a huge place to keep them,' and he nodded towards the drawing over the table.

The eyes of both of them were shining already. Daniel, flattered by Artyom's words, leaned over the table and said, with great gravity:

'They don't mean a thing, all those books. And the Great Library was not built for them. And it's not books that are stored there.'

Artyom looked at him with surprise. The Brahmin opened his mouth to continue, but suddenly rose from his chair, went to the door, cracked it open and listened. Then he quietly closed the door, sat back down and whispered the rest of what he wanted to say:

'The entire Great Library was built for the one-and-only Book. And it alone is hidden there. The rest are needed to help hide it. In reality, it is this book that is being sought. And it is being guarded,' he added, and squirmed.

'What kind of book is it?' asked Artyom, also lowering his voice.

'An ancient folio. A book of pages, black as anthracite, where all of History is recorded in gold letters. To the end.'

'So why are people searching for it?' whispered Artyom.

'You really don't understand?' said the Brahmin, with a shake of his head. ' "To the end" means to the very end. And there's still some way to go before then . . . So whoever has this knowledge . . .'

A translucent shadow flashed behind the blinds, and Artyom, even though he was looking Daniel in the eye, noticed it and gave him a sign. Interrupting his tale in mid-sentence, Daniel jumped from his seat and darted to the door. Artyom bolted after him.

There was nobody on the platform, but retreating footsteps could be heard from the direction of the passage. The sentries slept peacefully on chairs on both sides of the escalator.

When they returned to the room, Artyom waited for the Brahmin to continue his story, but the latter had sobered up and only glumly shook his head.

'We're forbidden to relate this,' he snapped. 'That part of the Testament is only for the initiated. The alcohol loosened my tongue,' he said, wincing fretfully. 'And don't even think of telling anyone what you heard. If it gets out to anyone that you know about the Book, then there'll be no end of trouble for you. And for me, too.'

And then Artyom suddenly understood why his palms had started sweating when the Brahmin had told him about the Book. He remembered.

'But aren't there several of these books?' he asked, his heart coming to a standstill.

Daniel cautiously looked him in the eyes.

'What do you mean?

'Fear the truths hidden in ancient folios . . . in which the words are lettered in gold and the viper-black paper does not rot,' he recited, while Bourbon's expressionless face loomed in a foggy haze before his eyes, mechanically uttering alien and incomprehensible words.

The Brahmin stared at him fixedly in amazement.

'How do you know that?'

'A revelation. There's not just one Book . . . What's in the others?' asked Artyom, looking at the drawing of the Library as if under a spell.

'Only one is left. There were three folios,' said Daniel, surrendering finally. 'The Past, the Present, and the Future. The Past and the Present disappeared irrevocably centuries ago. Only the last and most important one remains.'

'And where is it?'

'Lost somewhere in the Main Stack Archives. There are more than forty million volumes there. One of them – a completely ordinary book by all appearances, in a standard binding – is It. To recognize It, you have to open the book and skim through it. According to legend, the pages of the folio actually are black. But you'd have to spend seventy years of your life without sleep or rest to skim through all the books in the Main Stack Archive. Yet people can't stay there for more than a day, and second, nobody will let you stand around quietly and look through all the books that are stored there. And that's enough about that.'

He laid some bedding on the floor, lit a candle on the table, and turned off the light. Artyom lay down unwillingly. For some reason, he didn't want to sleep at all, although he could not remember the last time that he managed to get some rest.

'I wonder, can you see the Kremlin when you go up to the Library?' he asked the emptiness, because Daniel had begun to fall asleep.

'Of course you can see it. Only, you can't look at it. It draws you in,' he muttered.

'What do you mean "it draws you in"?'

Daniel lifted himself onto his elbows, and his face, knitted in displeasure, was illuminated by the yellow spot of light.

'The stalkers say that you can't look at the Kremlin when you go out, especially not at the stars on the towers. As soon as you look, you can't tear your eyes away. And if your gaze lingers for a while, the Kremlin starts to draw you inside. There's a reason all the gates stand wide open. That's why stalkers never go up into the Great

Library by themselves. If one happens to glance at the Kremlin, the other will snap him out of it immediately.'

'What's inside the Kremlin?' whispered Artyom, swallowing hard.

'Nobody knows, because nobody who's ever gone in has ever come out again. Up there on the shelf, if you like, there's a book with an interesting history of stars and swastikas, including the ones on the Kremlin towers.' He got up, groped the book from the shelf, opened it to the correct page, and got back under his blanket.

Daniel was asleep within a couple of minutes, but Artyom moved the candle closer and started to read.

'. . . being the smallest and least influential of political groups that fought for influence and power in Russia after the first revolution, the Bolsheviks were not considered serious competitors by any of the opposing sides. They enjoyed no support from the peasantry and relied only on a small number of supporters among the working class and in the navy. V. I. Lenin, who studied alchemy and the invocation of spirits in secret Swiss schools, was able to find his principal allies on the other side of the barrier between worlds. It is precisely in this period that the pentagram emerges for the first time as the symbol of the communist movement within the Red Army.

'As is known, the pentagram is the most widespread and accessible portal between worlds for novices, allowing demons to enter our reality. At the same time, if the creator of a pentagram uses it skilfully, he can control the demons summoned into our world, and they must obey him. Normally, in order to better control a summoned creature, a protective perimeter is drawn around the pentagram, preventing the demon from escaping beyond the ring.

'It is not known how, exactly, the leaders of the communist movement were able to achieve that which the most powerful black magicians of all ages had sought: establishing links to the demon lords who commanded the obedience of hordes of their lesser brethren. Experts are convinced that the lords themselves, sensing the forthcoming war and the most horrible bloodshed ever in the history of mankind, drew nearer to the boundary between worlds and summoned those who could permit them to collect a harvest of human lives. In exchange, they promised support and protection.

'The story of how the Bolshevik leadership was funded by German intelligence is true, to be sure, but it would be foolish and superficial to believe that it was only thanks to his foreign partners that V. I. Lenin and his comrades-in-arms were able to tip the scales in their favour. Even then, the future communist leader had protectors who were immeasurably more powerful and wiser than the military intelligence officials in the Kaiser's Germany.

'Naturally, the details of the secret compact with the powers of darkness are not accessible to modern researchers. However, their result is clear: after a short time, pentagrams appear on banners, on the headgear of Red Army soldiers, and on the armour of its still sparse military equipment. Each of them opened a gate into our world to a demon protector, who guarded the wearer of the pentagram from external violence. The demons received their pay, as usual, in blood. In the twentieth century alone, according to the most conservative estimates, around thirty million inhabitants of the country were sacrificed.

'The Compact with the lords of the summoned powers quickly justified itself: the Bolsheviks seized and consolidated power, and although Lenin himself, who had been the intermediary between the two worlds, could not endure and died only fifty-four years after his birth, eaten from within by the fires of hell, his followers unhesitatingly continued his work. Soon after followed the demonization of the entire country. Schoolchildren pinned their first pentagram to their chests. Few know that, from the outset, the ritual of initiation into the Little Octobrists intended the badge's pin to be used to pierce the child's skin. The demon of the Little Octobrist "star" would thus taste the blood of its future host, entering into a sacral union with its host once and forever. Growing up and becoming a Pioneer, the child would receive a new pentagram, and a part of the essence of the Compact would be revealed to those experiencing insight: a gold-imprinted portrait of the Leader was wrapped in flames, in which he disappeared. Thus, the rising generation was reminded of the heroic deed of self-sacrifice. After that was the Komsomol, and finally, the way was cleared for the chosen to enter into the priestly caste, the Communist Party.

'Myriads of summoned spirits protected everyone and everything in the Soviet state: children and adults, buildings and equipment, while the demon lords themselves took up residence in the giant ruby pentagrams on the Kremlin towers, willingly agreeing to confinement for the sake of their increased power. It was precisely from here that invisible lines of force spread over the entire country, holding it back from chaos and collapse, and subordinating its inhabitants to the will of those who occupied the Kremlin. In some sense, the entire Soviet Union was turned into one giant pentagram whose surrounding protective perimeter became its national boundary.'

Artyom tore himself away from the page and looked around. The candle had burned down and had started to smoke. Daniel was sound asleep, with his face turned to the wall. Artyom stretched, and then returned to the book.

'The supreme test for Soviet power became the clash with National Socialist Germany. Protected by powers no less ancient or powerful than was the Soviet Union, the armour-fettered Teutons were able to penetrate deeply into our country for the second time in a thousand years. This time, their banners were inscribed with a reversed symbol of the sun, light, and prosperity. To this very day, fifty years after the Victory, tanks with pentagrams on their turrets continue in perpetual battle against tanks whose steel bears the swastika, in museum panoramas, on television screens, on sheets of graph paper torn out of school notebooks . . .'

The candle flickered one last time and went out. It was time to go to sleep.

If you turned your back to the monument, you could see a small section of the high wall and the silhouettes of the sharp-pointed towers in the gap between the half-ruined houses. But, as had been explained to Artyom, you couldn't turn around and look at them. And it was also forbidden to leave the doors with the steps unattended because if something were to happen, you'd have to sound the alarm, but if you so much as peeked – that's it, you're done for, and the others suffer, too.

Consequently, Artyom stood still, although the desire to turn around kept eating at him. Meanwhile, he examined the monument, whose bottom had been overgrown with moss. The monument depicted a gloomy old man, sitting in a capacious armchair and leaning on an elbow. Something dripped slowly and thickly from his pitted bronze pupils onto his chest, giving the impression that the monument was crying.

It was unbearable to look at this for very long. So, Artyom went around the statue and attentively looked at the doors. Everything was tranquil, there was complete silence, and there was just the slightest sound of the wind rambling between the picked-over carcasses of buildings. The detachment had departed some time ago, but had not taken Artyom along. They ordered him to stay and stand guard, and if anything happened, to go down into the station and give warning of what happened.

Time passed slowly, and he measured it with steps, which he took around the bottom of the monument: one, two, three . . .

It happened when he got to five hundred: a clatter and growling broke out to his rear, behind his back, where he could not look. Something was nearby, and it could rush at Artyom at any moment. He froze, straining his ears, then dropped to the ground and pressed himself against the base of the statue, holding his weapon ready.

Now it was close at hand, apparently, on the other side of the monument. Artyom distinctly heard its husky animal breathing. Moving around the side of the statue's base, he gradually moved closer to the sound. He tried to stop his hands from shaking and to keep his sight on the place where the creature would appear.

But the breathing and the sound of steps suddenly began to retreat. But when Artyom looked out from behind the statue to take advantage of the opportunity to fire a burst into the back of his unknown enemy, he immediately forgot about both his enemy and everything else.

The star on the Kremlin tower was clearly visible even from here. The tower itself remained only a vague silhouette in the unsteady light of a partially cloud-covered moon, but the star stood out clearly against the sky, riveting the attention of any who looked at it for a completely understandable reason. It glittered. Not believing his eyes, he took out his field binoculars.

The star burned a fierce bright-red colour, illuminating several metres of the space around it, and when Artyom looked closer, he noticed that its fire was irregular. It was as if a tempest was confined inside the giant ruby; it brightened in fits and starts, as if something inside was flowing, seething, flaring . . . The sight was of fantastic beauty not possible in this world, but it was poorly visible from such a distance. He had to get closer.

Shouldering his weapon, Artyom ran down the stairs, jumped over the cracked asphalt in the street, and stopped at the only corner from where he could see the whole Kremlin wall . . . and the towers. A red star beamed from each one of them. Hardly catching his breath, Artyom again looked through the eyepieces. The stars flared with the same seething irregular glow, and he wanted to look at them forever.

Concentrating on the closest of them, Artyom still admired its fantastic flows, until he suddenly seemed to feel as if he could distinguish the shape of whatever was moving inside, under the crystal surface.

To better make out the strange outlines, he had to get a little closer. Having forgotten about all dangers, he stopped in the middle of the open space and now kept his binoculars glued to his eyes, trying to understand what he had managed to see.

The demon lords, he remembered at last. The marshals of an army of unclean spirits that had been summoned to defend the Soviet state. The country, and the whole world as well, had fallen to pieces, but the pentagrams on the Kremlin towers had remained untouched: the governors who had entered into a compact with the demons were long dead, and there was nobody left to free them . . . Nobody? What about him?

I need to find the gates, he thought. I need to find a way in . . .

'Get up! You have to go soon.' Daniel shook him.

Artyom yawned and rubbed his eyes. He had just dreamed something incredibly interesting, but the dream had faded instantly, and he could not recall what he had seen. All of the lights had already been lit in the station, and he could hear the cleaning women sweeping the platform while merrily bantering.

He put on his dark glasses and shuffled off to wash up, having tossed over his shoulder a not-very-clean towel his host had given him. The toilets were located at the same end as the bronze panel, and the line of people waiting to get in was not short. Having got in line, continuing to yawn, Artyom tried to recall at least some of the images from his dream.

The line stopped moving forward, for some reason, and the people in it started to murmur loudly. Attempting to understand what was the matter, Artyom looked around. All eyes were fixed on a bolted iron door. It was now open, and a tall man stood in the frame. Seeing him, Artyom, too, forgot why he was standing there.

It was a stalker.

He had imagined them to look exactly like this, both from his stepfather's stories and the rumours gleaned from itinerant merchants. The stalker wore a stained protective suit, scorched in places, and a long, heavy body armour vest. His shoulders were broad; a light machine gun was casually slung over the right one, while a gleaming, oily belt of ammunition hung like a baldric from the left. He wore rough, laced boots with the pants legs tucked into the top, and there was a large canvas rucksack on his back.

The stalker took off his round special forces helmet, pulled off the rubber face piece of his gas mask, and stood there, flushed and wet, talking to the post commander about something. He was no longer young. Artyom saw grey stubble on his cheeks and chin, and silvery strands in his short black hair. Yet the man radiated power and confidence; he was completely at ease and collected, as if even here, in a quiet and cheerful station, he was ready to meet danger at any moment and not let it catch him unawares.

By now, only Artyom continued to unceremoniously examine the arrival. The people behind him in line first tried to urge him forward, and then simply started to walk around him.

'Artyom! What's the delay? You'll be late if you don't watch out!' Daniel came up to him.

Hearing his name, the stalker turned towards Artyom, looked at him intently, and suddenly took a broad step toward him.

'You from *VDNKh*?' he asked, in a deep resonant voice.

Artyom nodded silently, and felt his knees start to shake.

'You the one looking for Melnik?' the stalker continued.

Artyom nodded once more.

'I'm Melnik. You have something for me?' The stalker looked Artyom in the eye.

Artyom hastily groped around his neck for the cord with the cylindrical case that it now felt odd to part with, as if with a talisman, and extended it to the stalker.

The stalker pulled off his leather gloves, opened the cover and carefully shook something out of the capsule into his palm. It was a small scrap of paper. A note.

'Come with me. I couldn't make it yesterday. Sorry. The call came when we were already on our way to the surface.'

Having said a quick goodbye and thanks to Daniel, Artyom hurried after Melnik, up the escalators that led to the passage to *Arbatskaya*.

'Is there any news from Hunter?' he asked, awkwardly, barely keeping up with the long-striding stalker.

'Haven't heard a thing from him. I fear you'll have to ask your dark ones about him now,' said Melnik, looking back over his shoulder at Artyom. 'On the other hand, you could say there's too much news from *VDNKh*.'

Artyom felt his heart start beating more forcefully.

'What news?' he asked, trying to suppress his worry.

'Not much good,' said the stalker, dryly. 'The dark ones went on the offensive again. There was a heavy battle a week ago. Five people were killed. And it seems there are even more dark ones there now. People are starting to flee that station of yours. They can't stand the horror, they say. So, Hunter was right when he told me something sinister was hidden there. He felt it.'

'Who died, do you know?' asked Artyom, frightened, trying to recollect who was supposed to stand duty that day, a week ago? What day was today? Was it Zhenka? Andrey? Please don't let it be Zhenka . . .

'I wouldn't know. It's not enough the undead are worming their way in there, but some kind of devilment is coming out of the tunnels around *Prospect Mir*, too. People lose their memory, and several people died along the tracks.'

'What's to be done?'

'There's a Council meeting today. The Brahmin elders and generals will have their say, but I doubt they'll be able to help your station with anything. They barely defend *Polis* itself, and then only because nobody dares make a serious attempt on it.'

They came out onto the *Arbatskaya* station. Mercury lamps burned here, too, and just as at Borovitskaya, the living quarters were located in bricked-in arches. Sentries stood next to several of them, and overall, there was an uncommonly large number of soldiers here. The walls, painted white, were hung in places with army parade standards – with embroidered gold eagles – that seemed almost untouched by time. There was activity all around. Long-robed Brahmins walked about, while cleaning women washed the floor and scolded those who tried to pass over the still-wet surface. There were quite a number of people here, too, from other stations. They could be identified by their dark glasses or by the way they folded their hands together to cover their squinting eyes. Only living and administrative quarters were located on the platform; the shopping arcades and food vendors were removed to the passages.

Melnik led Artyom to the end of the platform where the office premises began, seated him on a marble bench lined with wood that had been burnished by contact with thousands of passengers, asked him to wait, and departed.

Looking at the intricate stucco work under the ceiling, Artyom thought about how *Polis* had lived up to his expectations. Life here really was arranged in a completely different way; people weren't as cutthroat, exasperated, or browbeaten as at other stations. Knowledge, books, and culture seemed to play a thoroughly fundamental role. They had passed by at least five book stalls in the passage between *Borovitskaya* and *Arbatskaya*. There were even playbills posted announcing the performance of a play by Shakespeare tomorrow night and, just as at *Borovitskaya*, he could hear music playing somewhere.

The passage and both stations had been maintained in excellent condition. Although blotches and seepage were evident on the walls, all damage was immediately patched by repair teams, who scurried about everywhere. Out of curiosity, Artyom glanced down the tunnel, where he saw everything was in perfect order; it was dry, clean, and an electric light burned at intervals of one hundred metres as far as the eye could see. From time to time, handcars loaded with crates passed by, stopping to discharge the occasional passenger or take on a box of books that *Polis* sent out through the entire metro.

'All of this might soon come to an end,' thought Artyom, suddenly. '*VDNKh* can no longer withstand the pressure from these monsters . . . No wonder,' he said to himself, recalling one night on watch, when he had to repel an attack by the dark ones, and all of the nightmares that tormented him after that fight.

Was it true that *VDNKh* was falling? That meant that he would no longer have a home He wondered if his friends and stepfather had managed to flee; if so, there was a chance of meeting them one day in the metro. If Melnik told him that he had completed his mission and could do nothing more, then he promised himself he'd head back home. If his station was destined to act as a lone covering force in the path of the dark ones, and if his friends and relatives were slated to die defending the station, then he'd rather be with them instead of taking refuge in this paradise. He suddenly had the urge to return home, catch sight of the row of army tents, the tea-factory . . . And chew the fat with Zhenka, and tell him of his adventures. It was a sure thing he wouldn't believe half of it . . . If he were still alive.

'C'mon, Artyom,' Melnik called. 'They want to talk to you.'

He had managed to rid himself of his protective suit and was wearing a turtleneck, a black navy fore-and-aft cap with no insignia, and pants with pockets, the same as Hunter's. The stalker somehow reminded him of the Hunter, not by his appearance, of course, but by his behaviour. He was just as collected and resilient, and spoke in the same way, using short, telegraphic sentences.

The walls in the offices were lined with stained oak, and two large oil paintings hung there, opposite each other. Artyom easily recognized the Library on one of them, while the other depicted a tall building covered in white stone. The label under the picture read: 'General Staff, Russian Federation Ministry of Defence.'

A large wooden table stood in the middle of the spacious room. About ten men sat in chairs around the table, studying Artyom. Half of them wore grey Brahmin robes; the other half, military officer uniforms. As it turned out, the officers sat under the painting of the General Staff, while the Brahmins sat under the Library painting.

A person of short stature but of commanding bearing sat solemnly at the head of the table. He wore austere glasses and had a large bald spot. He was dressed in a suit and tie, but had no tattoo to designate membership in any caste.

'To business,' he began, without introducing himself. 'Tell us everything you know, including the situation with the tunnels from your station to *Prospect Mit.*'

Artyom proceeded to describe in detail the history of the *VDNKh* battle against the dark ones, then about Hunter's mission, and finally, about his trek to *Polis.* When he related the events in the tunnels between *Alekseevskaya, Rizhskaya,* and *Prospect Mir,* the soldiers and Brahmins started to whisper among themselves, some incredulous, others animated, while an officer who sat in the corner diligently recording the narrative occasionally asked him to repeat what he had said.

When the discussions finally stopped, Artyom was allowed to continue his story, but his recital elicited little interest in his listeners until he got to *Polyanka* and its inhabitants.

'If you will!' interrupted one of the officers, indignantly. He was about fifty years old, of compact build, with slicked-back hair, and he wore steel-framed glasses that cut into the meaty bridge of his nose. 'It is known without a doubt that *Polyanka* is uninhabited. The station was deserted a long time ago. It's true that dozens of people pass through the station every day, but nobody can live there. Gas erupts there from time to time, and there are signs everywhere warning of the danger. And well, of course, cats and paper waste are long since gone, too. The platform is completely empty. Completely. Cease your insinuations.'

The other officers nodded in agreement, and Artyom fell silent, perplexed. When he stopped at *Polyanka,* the thought entered his mind, for an instant, that the tranquil conditions that prevailed at the station were unreal for the metro. But he was immediately distracted from such thinking by the inhabitants, who were more than real.

The Brahmins, however, did not support the angry outburst. The oldest of them, a bald man with a long, grey beard, regarded Artyom with interest and exchanged some words with those sitting nearby in an unintelligible language.

'This gas, as you know, has hallucinogenic properties when mixed in certain proportions with air,' said the Brahmin sitting at the old man's right hand, in a conciliatory manner.

'The point is, can we now believe any of the rest of his story?' retorted the officer, frowning at Artyom.

'Thank you for your report,' said the man in the suit, interrupting the discussion. 'The Council will discuss it and inform you of the result. You may go.'

Artyom started to make his way to the exit. Was his entire conversation with the two hookah-smoking inhabitants of *Polyanka* really just a hallucination? But that would then mean the idea of his having been selected – of his being able to bend reality while fulfilling his destiny – was just a product of his imagination, an attempt at self-consolation . . . Now even the mysterious encounter in the tunnel between *Borovitskaya* and *Polyanka* no longer seemed a miracle to him. Gas? Gas.

He sat on the bench next to the door and didn't even pay attention to the distant voices of the arguing Council members. People went by, handcars and railmotor cars drove through the station, and the minutes passed, while he sat and thought. Did he actually have a mission, or did he make the whole thing up? What'll he do now? Where'll he go?

Someone tapped him on the shoulder. It was the officer who made notes during his narrative.

'The members of the Council state that *Polis* cannot assist your station in any way. They are grateful for your detailed report on the situation in the subway system. You are free to go.'

That was it. *Polis* can't help with anything. It was all for nothing. He had done everything he could, but it changed nothing. All that remained was to return to *VDNKh* and stand shoulder-to-shoulder with the remaining defenders. Artyom heaved himself up from the bench and went off slowly, with no particular destination in mind.

When he had almost reached the passage to *Borovitskaya*, he heard a quiet cough behind him. Artyom turned and saw the Brahmin from the Council, the same one who had sat at the old man's right hand.

'Wait a moment, young man. I believe you and I need to discuss something . . . privately,' added the Brahmin, smiling politely. 'If the

Council is not in a position to do anything for you, then perhaps your obedient servant can be of more help.'

He took Artyom by the elbow and led him away to one of the brick residences in the arches. There were no windows here, and no electric lights. Only the flame of a small candle lit the faces of several people who had gathered in the room. Artyom was not able to get a good look at them, because the Brahmin who brought him quickly blew out the flame, and the room was plunged into darkness.

'Is it true about *Polyanka*?' asked a woolly voice.

'Yes,' answered Artyom, unwaveringly.

'Do you know what we Brahmins call *Polyanka*? The station of destiny. Let the kshatriyas think it's the gas that brings about the gloomy enchantment, we won't protest. We would not restore the sight of our most recent enemy. We believe that people encounter messengers of Providence at this station. Providence has nothing to say to most of them, so they simply pass through an empty, abandoned station. But those who have met someone at *Polyanka* should have a most attentive attitude towards such an encounter and remember what was said to them there for the rest of their lives. Do you remember?'

'I've forgotten,' lied Artyom, not particularly trusting these people, who reminded him of the members of a sect.

'Our elders are convinced that you have not come here by chance. You are not an ordinary person, and your special abilities, which have saved you several times along the way, can help us, too. In exchange, we will extend a helping hand to you and your station. We are the guardians of knowledge, and that includes information that can save *VDNKh*.'

'What's *VDNKh* got to do with anything?' burst Artyom. 'You all talk only about *VDNKh*! It's as if you don't understand that I came here not just for the sake of my station, and not because of my own misfortune! All, all of you, are in danger! First *VDNKh* will fall, then the whole line will follow, and then the entire metro will come to an end . . .'

There was no response. The silence deepened. Only the cadenced breathing of those present could be heard. Artyom waited a bit longer and then, unable to stay silent, asked:

'What must I do?'

'Go up, into the great stack archives. Find that which is ours by right, and return it to us here. If you can find what we seek, we will give you the knowledge that will help destroy the threat. And may the Great Library burn if I lie.'

CHAPTER 13

The Great Library

Artyom went out into the station, looking from side to side with a mad look in his eye. He had just entered into one of the strangest agreements of his life. His employers refused to even explain what, exactly, he was supposed to find in the stack archives, promising to provide him with details later, after he had already gone up to the surface. And though it had occurred to him, for a moment, that they were talking about the Book Daniel had told him about the night before, he didn't dare ask the Brahmins about it. Then, too, both of them had been pretty drunk yesterday, when his hospitable host had told him this secret, so there was reason to doubt its truth.

He would not be going to the surface alone. The Brahmins intended to outfit an entire detachment. Artyom was to go up with at least two stalkers and one person from the caste, to whom he was to immediately give what had been found, should the expedition meet with success. That same person would show Artyom something that would help eliminate the threat hanging over *VDNKh.*

Now, having emerged from the impenetrable gloom of the room onto the platform, the terms of the agreement seemed absurd to Artyom. As in the old fairy tale, he was required to go he knew not where, to fetch he knew not what, and in exchange, he was promised he knew not what kind of miraculous salvation. But what else could he do? Return with empty hands? Is that what the hunter expected of him?

When Artyom had asked his mysterious employers how he would find what they were looking for in the giant stacks of the Library, he was told that he would understand everything in due course. He would hear. He didn't ask any more questions, fearful that the Brahmins would lose their confidence in his extraordinary abilities, in which he himself did not believe. Finally, he was strictly warned that the soldiers must not learn anything, else the agreement would no longer be in force.

Artyom sat down on a bench in the centre of the hall and started to think. This was an incredible chance to go out onto the surface, do what he had only done once before, and do it without fear of punishment or consequences. To go up on the surface – and not alone, but with real stalkers – to carry out a secret mission for the guardian caste . . . He hadn't even asked them why they so detested the word 'librarian.'

Melnik slumped down on the bench next to him. Now he looked tired and overwrought.

'Why'd you say yes?' he asked, without expression and looking in front of him.

'How'd you find out?' asked Artyom, surprised. Less than a quarter hour had passed since his conversation with the Brahmins.

'I'll have to go with you,' continued Melnik in a dull voice, ignoring the question. 'I answer to Hunter for you now, whatever's happened to him. And there's no backing out on an agreement with the Brahmins. Nobody's done it yet. And above all, don't think about blabbing to the military.' He got up, shook his head, and added: 'If you only knew what you're getting into . . . I'm going to sleep. We'll be getting up tonight.'

'But aren't you in the military?' asked Artyom, catching up to him. 'I heard them call you "Colonel".'

'Yeah, I'm a colonel, just not in their chain of command,' answered Melnik grudgingly, and left.

Artyom spent the rest of the day learning about *Polis*, walking about aimlessly through the limitless space of stairs and passages, examining the majestic colonnades and marvelling at how many people this underground city could accommodate. He studied the whole of the 'Metro News' penny sheet, which was printed on brown wrapping paper, listened to vagrant musicians, leafed through books at stalls, played with puppies that were being offered for sale, listened to the latest gossip, and could not shake the feeling that he was being followed all this time and was under constant observation. Several times, he even wheeled around suddenly, hoping to catch someone's attentive look, but it was no use. He was surrounded by a swarming crowd, and nobody paid any attention to him.

Finding a hotel in one of the passages, he slept for several hours before appearing at ten in the evening, as had been agreed, at the gate of the exit into the city at *Borovitskaya*. Melnik was running late, but the sentries had been informed and offered Artyom a cup of tea while he waited.

Interrupting himself for a minute to pour boiling water into an enamelled cup, the elderly sentry continued his story:

'So . . . I was assigned to listen to the radio. Everyone hoped to catch a transmission from government bunkers beyond the Urals. But it was no use, because the first thing they hit was the strategic targets. That's how Ramenki got smeared, and all of the out-of-town summer residences, with their basements thirty metres deep, how they got smeared, too . . . They might have even spared Ramenki . . . They didn't try too hard to hit the peaceful population . . . Nobody knew then that this war was to the very end. So, maybe they might have spared Ramenki, but there was a command point right next to it, so they slammed it . . . And as far as civilian casualties were concerned, it was all, as they say, collateral damage, you should pardon the expression. But at that time nobody believed that yet, so the brass had me sit and listen to the airwaves over next to *Arbatskaya*, in a bunker. And initially, I heard a lot of strange stuff . . . Siberia was quiet, though other parts of the country were broadcasting. Submarines – strategic, nuclear – went on the air. They'd ask whether to strike or not . . . People didn't believe that Moscow no longer existed. Full captains were sobbing like kids over the radio. It's strange, you know, when salty naval officers, who hadn't uttered a swear word in their entire lives, are crying and asking for someone to check and see if their wives or daughters are among the survivors . . . "Go, look for them here," they'd say . . . And later, they'd all react differently. There were those who said, "That's it! The hell with it, it's an eye for an eye!" and they'd get in close to their shores and launch everything against the cities. Others, on the contrary, decided that since everything was already going to hell in a hand basket, there wasn't any sense in continuing to fight. Why kill more people? But that didn't have any effect. There were enough out there who wanted to avenge their families. And the boats answered for a long time. They could run under water for half a year while on station. They found some of them, of course, but they couldn't find all of them. Well, that's an earful of history. To this day, when I think about it, I get the shakes. But that wasn't the point. I once picked up a tank crew that miraculously survived a strike; they were ferrying their tank from their unit, or something . . . It was a new generation of armour technology that protected them from the radiation. So, here were these three guys in this tank, and they light out at full speed from Moscow, headed east. They drove through some burning villages, picked up some broads, and went on, stopping to top off with some straw distillate and then getting back on the road. When the fuel finally ran out, they were in some backwater, where there wasn't anything left to bomb. The background radiation there, too, remained pretty high, of course, but still it was nothing like it was next to the cities. They laid out a camp, dug their tank in hull-down, and ended up with a sort of fortification. They pitched tents nearby, eventually built mud huts, set up a manual generator for electricity, and lived for a fairly long time around that tank. For two years, I spoke to them almost every night and knew all of what was going on in their personal lives. Everything was quiet at first, they set up a farmstead, and two of them had kids that were . . . almost normal. They had enough ammo. They saw some weird stuff there, and creatures were coming out of the forest the likes of which the lieutenant we were talking to couldn't even describe properly. Then they went off the air. I spent another half year trying to raise them, but something happened out there. Maybe their generator or transmitter broke down, or maybe they ran out of ammo . . .'

'You were talking about Ramenki,' recalled his partner, 'about how it got bombed, and I thought, for as long as I've been serving here, nobody can tell me anything about the Kremlin. How is it that it remained whole? Why didn't it get hit? I mean, that's where'd you expect to find right proper bunkers . . .'

'Who told you it didn't get hit? Man, did it get hit!' the sentry assured him. 'They just didn't want to demolish it, because it's an architectural monument, and also because they were testing new weapons against it. So that's what we got . . . It would've been better if they'd wiped it off the earth from the beginning.' He spat and fell silent.

Artyom sat quietly, trying not to distract the veteran from his reminiscences. It was rare that he was able to hear so many details of how everything had come about. But the elderly sentry remained quiet, lost in some private thought, and eventually Artyom seized the moment and decided to ask a question that had preoccupied him earlier, too:

'But there's subway systems in other cities, aren't there? At least, I heard there were. Is it true there's no people left anywhere? When you were a radio operator, didn't you hear any signals?'

'No, I didn't hear anything. But you're right. People in Petersburg, for example, should have been able to save themselves. Their subway stations are deeply embedded, some even deeper than what we've got here, and the setup was the same. I travelled there when I was young, I remember. On one line, they had no exits onto the tracks. Instead, they had these hefty iron portals. When the train arrived, the portal doors would open together with the doors of the train. I remember this quite me surprised at the time. I asked everyone, but nobody could properly explain why things were set up that way. One told me it was to prevent flooding, another told me it saved a heap of money on finishing work. Later, I became friends with this one subway worker, and he told me that something had devoured half of one construction team, and that the same was going on with other teams. They were finding only the gnawed bones and the tools. Of course, the public was never told anything, but those iron doors were installed all along the line, just to be on the safe side. And that was, let me think, back when . . . Anyway, what the radiation may have spawned there is hard to imagine.'

The conversation broke off as Melnik and one other person, short and thickset, with deeply set eyes and a massive jaw overgrown by a short beard, came up to the gate. Both were already wearing their protective suits and had large haversacks slung on their backs. Melnik silently inspected Artyom, placed a large black bag next to Artyom's feet, and motioned towards the army tent.

Artyom slipped inside and, opening the zipper on the bag, took out a black set of overalls like the ones Melnik and his partner wore, an unusual gas mask, with a full-face window and two filters on the sides, high laced boots, and most important, a new Kalashnikov assault rifle with a laser sight and folding metal stock. It was an exceptional weapon. The only thing Artyom had seen like it had been carried by the elite Hansa units who patrolled the line in railmotor cars. A long flashlight and round helmet with a fabric cover lay at the bottom of the bag.

He hadn't had the time to finish dressing when the tent flap lifted and the Brahmin Daniel entered. In his hands, he held an identical zippered stretch bag. They stared at each other in amazement. Artyom was the first to realize what was what.

'You're going up? You're our chaperone? You're going to help us go look for I don't know what?' he asked, jeeringly.

'*I* know what it is,' snarled Daniel, 'but I have *no* idea how you intend to look for it.'

'Neither do I,' admitted Artyom. 'I was told it'd be explained later . . . So here I am, waiting.'

'And I was told that a clairvoyant is being sent up to the surface, and that he's supposed to feel where to go.'

'*I'm* the clairvoyant?' snorted Artyom.

'The elders believe that you have a gift and that your destiny is special. Somewhere in the Testament is a prophecy foretelling the appearance of a youth, led by fate, who will find the hidden secrets of the Great Library. He will find that which our caste has attempted to find for this past decade without success. The elders are convinced that this person is you.'

'Is it that book you told me about?' asked Artyom.

For a long time, Daniel didn't answer, then he nodded his head.

'You're supposed to feel it. It's not hidden from everyone. If you're really that same "youth, led by fate", then you won't even have to run around the stack archives. The book will find you,' he said, running his eyes over Artyom searchingly, and then added, 'What did you ask from them in exchange?'

There was no use keeping back the truth. Artyom was only unpleasantly surprised that Daniel, who was supposed to give him information capable of saving *VDNKh* from the ghoul invasion, knew nothing of this danger or of the conditions of his agreement with the Council members. He briefly summarized the agreement for Daniel and explained the catastrophe he was trying to prevent. Daniel attentively heard him out, and was still standing motionless and thinking about something when Artyom left the tent.

Melnik and the bearded stalker were already waiting in full combat dress, holding their gas masks and helmets in their hands. His partner now carried the light machine gun, while Melnik clasped a copy of the assault rifle that Artyom had been given. A night vision device was hanging around his neck.

When Daniel stepped out of the tent, he and Artyom looked at each other with a swagger, then Daniel gave a wink and both started to laugh. They both now looked like real stalkers.

'We lucked out . . . Before rookies go on important missions, they spend two years training under stalkers, fetching firewood from the surface. But you and I, we're sitting pretty!' said Daniel, whispering, to Artyom.

Melnik looked at them disapprovingly, but said nothing. He motioned for them to follow. They came up to the passage arch and, after going up the stairs, stopped at the next cement block wall, where there was an armoured door guarded by a reinforced sentry detail. The stalker greeted the sentries and gave the sign to open the door. One of the soldiers got up from his seat, went to the door and pulled at the bolt heavily. The thick steel door moved smoothly to the side. Melnik let the other three pass, saluted the sentries, and went out last.

A short buffer zone about three metres in length began beyond the door, between the wall and the pressure doors. Another two heavily armed soldiers and an officer stood watch there. Before giving the order to raise the iron barrier, Melnik decided to brief the rookies.

'Listen up. No talking en route. Either of you ever been on the surface? Never mind . . . Give me the map,' he said to the officer. 'Until we get to the vestibule, walk in my footsteps and don't wander. Don't look around, don't talk. When we leave the vestibule, don't even think about going through the turnstiles, or you'll lose your legs. Keep following me. I don't want to see any independent activity. Then I'll go outside. Ten over there,' he pointed at the bearded stalker, 'will stay behind and cover the station vestibule. If everything is clear, then as soon as we're on the street, we'll immediately turn left. It's not too dark right now, so don't use your flashlights out there. We don't want to attract attention. Did you get the word about the Kremlin? It'll be on the right, but one tower can be seen above the buildings as soon as you come out of the metro. Don't look at the Kremlin, no matter what! I'll personally smack anyone who does upside the head.'

So it's true, about the Kremlin and about the stalker's rule not to look at it, no matter what, thought Artyom in amazement. Suddenly, something stirred within him, some fragmented thoughts and images . . . Stirred, and then calmed down.

'We're going up to the Library. We'll go as far as the doors and steps. I'll go in first. If the stairs are clear, Ten'll keep his sights on 'em and we'll go up; then we'll cover Ten and he'll come up. No talking on the stairs. If you spot danger, signal with your flashlight. Don't shoot unless it's absolutely necessary. Shots can attract them.'

'Who?' Artyom could not stay quiet.

'What do you mean, "who"?' repeated Melnik. 'Who would you expect to meet in the Library? Librarians, of course.'

Daniel swallowed hard and paled. Artyom looked at him, then at Melnik and decided this was no time to pretend he was a know-it-all.

'And who's that?'

Melnik raised his eyebrows in surprise. His bearded partner put a hand over his eyes. Daniel looked at the floor. For a long time, the stalker looked at Artyom with eyebrows raised and when he finally understood that Artyom wasn't joking, he coolly answered, 'You'll see for yourself. The main thing to remember is this: you can keep them from attacking if you look them straight in the eyes. Straight in the eyes, got it? Don't let them get behind you . . . That's all. Move out!' He put on his gas mask, then his helmet, and gave the sentries the thumbs-up.

The officer took a step to the master switch and opened the pressure doors. The steel barrier crawled upward, slowly. The show had begun.

Melnik waved his hand, indicating it was OK to come out. Artyom pushed the transparent door, raised his rifle, and jumped out into the street. And although the stalker had demanded that he follow in his footsteps and not wander, it wasn't possible to obey . . .

The sky had changed completely since that time when Artyom had seen it as a boy. Instead of a limitless, transparent sky-blue space, dense grey clouds now hung low overhead, and the first drops of an autumn rain had begun to ooze from this cotton-like sky. A cold wind blew in gusts, and Artyom felt it even through the cloth of his protective suit.

There was a mind-boggling, inconceivable amount of space here, to the right and to the left and in front. This boundless space was both spellbinding and strangely depressing at the same time. For a fraction of a second, Artyom wanted to return to the *Borovitskaya* vestibule, underground, and feel protected by the nearby walls and immerse himself in the comfort of an enclosed, limited space. He was able to deal with this oppressive feeling only by forcibly distracting himself to study the nearest buildings.

The sun had already set, and the city was gradually descending into a dingy twilight. The skeletons of low apartment houses, dilapidated and pitted by decades of acid rainstorms, stared at the travellers with empty orbits of broken windows.

The city . . . It was a dismal, yet magnificent sight. Hearing no calls, Artyom stood still, looking about as if mesmerized; he could finally compare reality with his dreams and with nearly equally blurry childhood memories.

Daniel, who likely also had never been on the surface, froze next to him too. The last to emerge from the station vestibule was Ten. The stalker slapped Artyom on the shoulder to get his attention and pointed to the right to where, in the distance, the silhouette of the cathedral's dome stood out against the sky.

'Look at the cross,' droned the Ten's voice through the gas mask's filters.

At first, Artyom noticed nothing in particular, and didn't actually see the cross. Only when a giant winged shadow took flight from the crossbar with a lingering, bloodcurdling wail did he understand what Ten had meant. After a few flaps of its wings, the monster had gained altitude and began to glide downward in wide circles, searching for prey.

'That's where they nest,' said Ten with a wave of the hand.

Staying close to the wall, they moved to the entrance of the Library. Melnik led the group, staying several steps ahead while Ten was stepping backward, half-turned, covering the rear. It was precisely because both stalkers were distracted that Artyom was able, even before they had drawn even with the statue of the old man sitting in the armchair, to cast a glance at the Kremlin.

Artyom had not intended to do it, but when he saw the monument, it was as if he had been jolted, and something cleared up in his mind. A whole piece of yesterday's dream suddenly popped to the surface. But now it didn't seem to be only a dream, because the panorama and Library colonnade that he had seen exactly resembled the view that was before him now. Did that mean that the Kremlin looked the same as he had imagined in his visions?

Nobody was looking at Artyom, even Daniel wasn't nearby, as he tarried behind with Ten. It was now or never, said Artyom to himself.

His mouth became dry and blood began to pound in his temples.

The star on the tower really did glitter.

'Hey, Artyom! Artyom!' Someone shook his shoulder.

A numb awareness came alive with difficulty. A bright flashlight beam assaulted his eyes. Artyom started to blink his eyes and shaded them with his hand. He was sitting on the ground with his back against the granite base of the monument. Daniel and Melnik were bending over him. Both were looking into his eyes with worry.

'His pupils are constricted,' stated Melnik. 'How'd you manage to lose him?' he asked Ten, with annoyance. The latter stood at some distance and kept his eyes on the street.

'Something made a noise back there, and I couldn't turn my back to it,' explained the stalker. 'Who could guess he was so quick . . . Look, he almost made it to the Manezh within a minute . . . And he would have kept going. It's a good thing our Brahmin has a head on his shoulders,' he said and slapped Daniel on the back.

'It shines,' said Artyom to Melnik in a weak voice. 'It shines,' he said, looking at Daniel.

'It shines, OK, it shines,' repeated Daniel, reassuringly.

'Weren't you told not to look over there, dumbass?' said Melnik to Artyom, angrily, now convinced the danger had passed. 'You going to obey your superiors?' he asked, and cuffed him on the back of his head.

The helmet reduced the educational value of the blow, and Artyom continued to sit on the ground, batting his eyes. Having finally run out of obscenities, the stalker grabbed him by the shoulders, shook him hard, and put him on his feet.

Artyom gradually recovered himself. He grew ashamed that he was not able to resist temptation. He stood, looking down at the toes of his boots, hesitating to look at Melnik. Luckily, Melnik didn't have time to read any sermons, as he had been distracted by Ten, who was standing in the intersection. He had signalled his partner to join him and was pressing his finger to a filter on his gas mask, indicating a need for silence. Artyom decided to stay out of trouble by now following Melnik everywhere and never to turn in the direction of the enigmatic towers.

Approaching Ten, Melnik also froze in his tracks. The bearded man was pointing into the distance, away from the Kremlin, to where the long-crumbling high-rises along Kalinin Prospekt gave the appearance of grinning, rotten teeth. Carefully drawing near to them, Artyom looked out from behind the stalker's broad shoulders and immediately understood the situation.

Right in the middle of the Prospekt, about sixty metres from them, he saw three human silhouettes standing motionless in the gathering dusk. Human? At such a distance, Artyom wouldn't have bet they were, indeed, people, but they were of medium height and stood on two legs. This was encouraging.

'Who's that?' Artyom asked hoarsely, whispering, while trying to identify the distant figures through the fogged window of his gas mask. Were they people or some spawn that he had heard spoken of?

Melnik silently shook his head, making it known that he didn't know any more than Artyom. He shone the beam of his flashlight at the motionless beings and made three circular motions. Then he switched his flashlight off. In answer, a bright spot of light came on in the distance, moved in a circle three times, and went out.

Tension eased immediately and the electrified atmosphere

returned to normal. Artyom sensed this even before Melnik gave the all clear.

'Stalkers,' explained the guide. 'Remember, for next time: three circles with a flashlight is our recognition signal. If you get the same response, you can go forward without fear. You won't come to harm. If you get no response, or some other response, then run. Don't wait.'

'But if they have a flashlight, it means they're human and not some kind of monsters from the surface,' objected Artyom.

'I don't know what's worse,' said Melnik, cutting off Artyom. Without further explanation, he moved up the stairs to the Library entrance.

The heavy oak door, almost as tall as two people, gave slowly, almost unwillingly. The door's rusted hinges shrieked hysterically. Melnik slipped inside, put his night-vision unit to his eyes while holding his rifle level with one arm. After a second, he signalled the others to follow.

They could see a long corridor before them, with the twisted framework of iron coat racks along the sides. This was once a cloakroom. In the distance, in the fading day's light coming weakly in from the street, were the white marble steps of a wide, rising staircase. The ceiling was about fifteen metres high, and the wrought railing of the second floor gallery could be distinguished about halfway up the wall. There was a brittle silence in the hall, responding to their every step.

The walls of the vestibule were covered by moss that stirred slightly, as if it were breathing, and strange, vine-like plants as thick as one's arm hung from the ceiling almost to the floor. Their stalks shimmered with a greasy lustre in the flashlight beams and were covered with large, malformed flowers that exuded a suffocating odour that made one's head spin. They also swayed ever so slightly, and Artyom didn't feel like venturing to find out if the wind blowing through the broken second-floor windows caused them to move, or whether they moved on their own.

'What's this?' asked Artyom, addressing Ten and touching the vine with his hand.

'Greenery,' came the filtered reply. 'House plants after being irradiated, that's what. Morning glories. Did a proper job of growing 'em, those botanists . . .'

Following Melnik, they reached the stairs and started to ascend, keeping to the left wall while Ten covered them. The lead stalker did not take his eyes off the black square of the entrance to other rooms that could be seen ahead of them. The others ran their flashlight beams over the marble walls and the rusty moss-pitted ceiling.

The wide marble stairs on which they stood led to the second floor of the vestibule. There was no ceiling above it, and thus both vestibule floors combined into a single huge space. The vestibule's second level formed three sides of a rectangle. In the centre, there was a space through which the stairs ascended, and there were areas along the edges with wooden cabinets. Most of them had either burned or rotted, but some looked as if people had used them just the day before. There were hundreds of small drawers in each section.

'The card catalogue,' said Daniel quietly, looking around with reverence. 'The future can be foretold using these drawers. The initiated know how. After a ritual, you blindly pick one of the cabinets, then randomly pull out a drawer and take any card. If the ritual is properly performed, then the name of the book will foretell your future, provide a warning, or predict success.'

For a second, Artyom wanted to go up to the nearest cabinet and find out what section of the card catalogue the fates had brought him to. But his attention was distracted by a giant cobweb which stretched several metres across a broken window in a far corner. A bird of considerable size was caught in thin filaments of apparently extraordinary strength. It was still alive, twitching weakly. To his relief, Artyom did not see whatever it was that had managed to spin this unnatural web. Besides them, there wasn't a soul in the vast vestibule.

Melnik signalled them all to stop.

'Now listen,' he said to Artyom. 'Don't listen to what's outside . . . Try to hear the sounds from inside you, in your head. The book is supposed to call you. The Brahmin elders think that it is most likely on one of the levels of the Main Stack Archives. But the folio can be any place at all, in one of the reading rooms, in a forgotten library cart, in a hall, in one of the matron's tables . . . So before we try to find a way into the archives, try to sense its voice here. Close your eyes. Relax.'

Artyom squeezed his eyes shut and started to listen intently. In the complete darkness, the silence fell apart into dozens of tiny noises: the creaking of wooden shelves, the noise of draughts passing down corridors, vague murmurs, howls that carried from the street, and a noise like a geriatric cough that carried from the reading rooms . . . But Artyom was unable to hear anything that resembled a call or a voice. He stood like that, motionless, for five minutes, and then five more, ineffectively holding his breath, which might have obstructed his efforts to differentiate the voice of the living book from the farrago of dead book sounds.

'No,' he said, guiltily shaking his head and finally opening his eyes. 'There's nothing.'

Melnik said nothing, nor did Daniel, but Artyom caught his disappointed look, which was self-explanatory.

'Maybe it's really not here. So, we'll go to the stack archives. Or more precisely, we'll try to get there.' After a minute, the stalker made up his mind and signalled the others to follow him.

He stepped forward through the wide doorway where only one of the two original door panels remained on its hinges. It was charred along its edges and covered with strange characters. There was a small, round room on the other side, with a six-metre-high ceiling and four entrances. Ten followed Melnik and Daniel, taking advantage of the fact that they could not see him, took a step to the nearest surviving cabinet, pulled out one of the drawers, and took a card out of it. Running his eyes over the card, his face took on a puzzled look, and he shoved the card into his breast pocket. Understanding that Artyom had seen everything, he pressed a finger to his lips in a conspiratorial manner and hurried after the stalkers.

The walls of the round room were also covered with drawings and signs, and a sofa, with broken springs and upholstered in cut-up imitation leather, stood in a corner. In one of the four passages, an overturned book stand lay near some spilled pamphlets.

'Don't touch anything!' warned Melnik.

Ten sat down on the sofa, causing the springs to squeak. Daniel followed his example. Artyom, as if under a spell, stared hard at the scattered books on the floor.

'They're untouched . . .' he mumbled. 'We have to put out rat poison at our station's library, or the rats would eat everything . . . So, what? There're no rats here?' he asked, again recalling what Bourbon had said, about how the time to worry wasn't when a place was crawling with rats, but when there weren't any rats around at all.

'What rats? Are you kidding?' Melnik made a discontented face. 'Where are you going to find rats around here? They ate them all a long time ago . . .'

'Who?' asked a puzzled Artyom.

'What do you mean "who"? The librarians, of course,' explained Ten.

'So are they animals or people?' asked Artyom.

'Not animals, that's for sure,' said the stalker, shaking his head pensively, and said nothing else.

A massive wooden door located far down one of the passages gave a long creak. Both stalkers immediately darted in different directions, taking cover behind the embedded columns at both ends of the arch. Daniel slipped from the sofa to the floor and rolled to the side. Artyom followed his example.

'Up further is the Main Reading Room,' whispered the Brahmin to Artyom. 'They show up there once in a while . . .'

'Cut the chatter!' interrupted Melnik, fiercely. 'Don't you know librarians can't stand noise? For them, noise is like waving a red rag in front of a bull?' He swore and indicated the door to the reading room to Ten.

Ten nodded. Staying close to the walls, they began to slowly move towards the huge oak door panels. Neither Artyom nor Daniel was less than a step behind. Melnik was the first to go in. Leaning with his back against one of the door panels and raising his rifle so that the barrel pointed up, he took a deep breath, let it out, and then sharply pushed the panel open with his shoulder, simultaneously pointing the barrel at the opened black mouth of the Main Hall.

They were all there in an instant. The hall was a room of incredible size, with a ceiling that disappeared twenty metres above the floor. Just as in the vestibule, heavy, thick vines with flowers hung from the ceiling. The walls of the hall were covered in the same unnatural morning glories. On each side of them there were six giant windows, where a part of the glazing remained unbroken. However, the illumination was very weak: light from the moon barely penetrated a dense tangle of fat, gleaming stalks.

Earlier, rows of tables had been arranged to the left and right, to accommodate readers. Much of that furniture had been hauled off, and some had been burned or broken, but about a dozen tables remained untouched. These stood closer to a decorated, cracked panel at the opposite wall, in whose exact centre rose a sculpture that was indistinct in the semi-darkness. Plastic signs reading 'Observe silence!' were screwed onto surfaces everywhere.

The silence here was completely different from that of the vestibule. Here it was so thick, you could almost touch it. It seemed to entirely fill this ancient, rough hall, and you felt afraid to disturb it.

They stood there, searching the space in front of them with their flashlights, until Melnik concluded, 'Probably the wind . . .'

But at that very instant, Artyom noticed a grey shadow that crossed in front of them, between two broken tables, which disappeared into a black gap in the bookshelves. Melnik saw it, too. Placing his night-vision device to his eyes, he jerked his rifle up and, stepping carefully over the moss-overgrown floor, started to approach the mysterious access.

Ten moved after him. Even though Artyom and Daniel had been motioned to remain where they were, they couldn't stand it and also followed the stalkers. Remaining at the entrance alone was too spooky. At the same time, Artyom could not resist looking around with delight at the hall, which retained vestiges of its former grandeur. This not only saved his own life, but everyone else's, too.

Galleries encircled the entire perimeter of the room at a height of several metres; these were rather narrow walkways enclosed by wooden railings. You could look through the windows from the galleries, and furthermore, there were doors leading to office spaces both in the wall they were standing next to and in the walls on both sides of the ancient panel. The gallery was accessible via twin stairs that were located on both sides of the reading sculpture or via an identical set of stairs that ascended from the entrance.

And it was down those stairs that humped, grey figures now descended, deliberately and silently. There were more than a dozen of them, creatures that did not quite melt into the gloom. They would have been about Artyom's height if they hadn't been bent over double so that their long forelegs, which amazingly resembled arms, all but touched the floor. The creatures moved on their hind legs, taking waddling steps, yet with surprising nimbleness and silence. From a distance, they most closely resembled gorillas, pictures of which Artyom had seen in his childhood in a biology book his stepfather had tried to teach from.

Artyom had no more than a second for all these observations because, as soon as his flashlight beam fell on one of the humped figures, casting a sharp, black shadow on the wall behind it, a diabolical chirring sound rang out all around them, and the creatures, no longer attempting stealth, rushed down.

'Librarians!' yelled Daniel, with all his strength.

'Down!' ordered Melnik.

Artyom and Daniel threw themselves to the floor. They chose not to fire, recalling the stalker's warning that shots, or any loud noises, would attract and aggravate librarians. Their hesitation was dispelled by Melnik, who threw himself to the floor next to them and was the first to open fire. Several creatures fell down with a roar; others threw themselves headlong into the darkness, but only in order to steal closer. After several instants, one of the monsters suddenly appeared two metres from them and made a long jump, attempting to seize Ten by the throat. Falling onto the floor, Ten managed to cut the creature down with a short burst.

'Run! Get back to the round room and try to get to the archives! The Brahmin should know how to get there; they teach them that! We'll stay here, cover you, and try to fight them off,' said Melnik to Artyom, and without a further word crawled off to join his partner.

Artyom motioned to Daniel and both bolted for the exit, staying low to the ground. One of the librarians sprang from the darkness to meet them, but it was swept away in a hail of lead. The stalkers were keeping an eye on the pair.

Exiting the Main Reading Room, Daniel darted back to the vestibule from where they had come. For an instant, Artyom thought that his partner had been frightened by the librarians so much that he was trying to run away. But Daniel wasn't running for the stairs that led to the exit. Going around them, he ran past the surviving card catalogue cabinets to the opposite end of the vestibule. There, the room narrowed and ended in three pairs of doors, in front and on both sides. The right-hand doors led to a staircase where absolute darkness prevailed. Here the Brahmin finally stopped to catch his breath. It took Artyom a few seconds to catch up, as he had never expected such agility from his companion. Standing still, they listened. They heard gunfire and cries from the Main Hall, so the fight was continuing. It wasn't clear who would get the upper hand in the battle, and they couldn't waste time waiting to see who won.

'Why are we going back? Why did we start out going the other way?' asked Artyom, catching his breath.

'I don't know where they were taking us.' Daniel shrugged. 'Maybe they intended to take us some other way. The elders taught us only one way, and it leads to the archives exactly from this side of the vestibule. Now we go up the stairs one floor, then along the corridor to another set of stairs, then through the duplicate card catalogue, and then we'll be in the archives.'

He pointed his rifle into the darkness and stepped into the stairwell. Artyom followed, lighting the way with his beam.

There was an elevator shaft in the middle of the stairs; it went down about three floors and went up about the same distance. Apparently, the shaft had once been glassed-in, as in places, sharp glass shards, now frosted with decades of dust, could still be seen poking out of the cast-iron structure. The square well of the shaft was girdled by rotted wooden stairsteps that were strewn with broken glass, spent brass cartridges, and dried piles of excrement. There was no trace of railings, and Artyom had to press himself against the wall and carefully watch where he stepped so as not to slip and fall into the opening.

They went up one floor and found themselves in a small square room. There were three outlets from here, too, and Artyom realized that, without his guide, it was unlikely he'd find his way out of this labyrinth. The left-hand door led to a wide, dark corridor whose end he could not see by the light of his flashlight. The right-hand door was closed and had been boarded up in criss-cross fashion for some reason. On the adjacent wall was written, in soot: 'Do not open! Deadly danger!'

Daniel led Artyom straight ahead, down a passage that ran at an angle to another corridor that was narrower and full of new doors. The Brahmin did not move so quickly down this corridor, and stopped often to listen. The floor here was of inlaid parquet, and forbidding signs reading 'Observe silence!' hung on the walls, which were painted yellow as were the walls throughout the Library. Rooms and trashed offices could be seen behind doors that were wide open. Rustling could sometimes be heard from behind closed doors, and once, Artyom thought he heard steps. Judging from his partner's face, this spoke of nothing good, and both hurried to get out of there as quickly as possible.

Then, as Daniel had expected, a doorway to another stairwell appeared on their right. It was lighter here compared to the murk of the halls, as there were windows at each flight of stairs. From the fifth floor, you could see the courtyard, some outbuildings, and the burned-out skeletons of some technical equipment. But Artyom was not able to examine the courtyard for long, as two grey humped figures emerged from behind the corner of the building he and Daniel were in. They made their way slowly across the courtyard, as if they were searching for something. Suddenly, one of the creatures stopped and raised its head, and Artyom felt as if it was looking directly at the window at which he was standing. Recoiling, Artyom squatted on his heels. He didn't have to explain what had happened to his partner, who grasped everything.

'Librarians?' he whispered with alarm, also squatting so as not to be visible from the street.

Artyom nodded silently. Daniel then wiped the plexiglass of his gas mask, as if this would help him dry his forehead, which was perspiring from worry. He then collected his thoughts and hurried up the stairs, dragging Artyom behind him. One flight up, and then another set of winding corridors . . . Finally, the Brahmin stopped uncertainly in front of several doors.

'I don't remember anything about this place,' he said, perplexed. 'There's supposed to be an entrance to the duplicate card catalogue. But nobody told us there'd be several doorways.'

He pondered, then half-heartedly jerked the handle of one of the doors. It was locked. The other doors were locked, too. Uncomprehendingly, as if he refused to believe it, Daniel shook his head and pulled the handles once more. Then Artyom tried as well, also without result.

'They're locked,' he said. There was despair in his voice.

Suddenly Daniel gave a little shudder, and Artyom, looking at him in alarm, took a step away from his partner, just in case. But Daniel only laughed.

'Why don't you knock?' he suggested to Artyom and added, with a sobbing laugh: 'Sorry, it's probably a fit of hysterics.'

Artyom felt the incongruous laughter filling him, too. The tension that had been building over the past hour was starting to show and, try as they might to control themselves, their silly giggling broke through to the outside. For a minute, both stood with their backs to the wall and laughed.

'Knock!' repeated Artyom, holding his belly and regretting not being able to take off his gas mask to wipe away his tears.

He stepped up to the closest door and knocked on it three times with his knuckles. After a second, three resounding knocks came in response from the other side of the door. Artyom's throat dried immediately and his heart started pounding frantically in his chest. Someone was standing behind the door, listening to their laughter and biding their time. What the . . . ? Daniel threw him a look that was mad with fear and backed away from the door. And from the other side, someone knocked again, louder and more demandingly.

And then Artyom did what Sukhoi had once taught him. Pushing off from the wall he kicked the lock of the next door over. He hadn't counted on it working, but the door opened with a crash. The lock's steel mechanism had torn out of the rotten door, together with some wood.

The room behind this door was unlike any of the other rooms or corridors of the Library through which they had passed. For some reason it was very humid and oppressive here, and by the light from their flashlights, they could see a small hall that was densely over-grown with strange plants. Thick stalks, heavy oily leaves, a mixture of scents so intense it even penetrated their gas mask filters, a floor covered with tangled roots and trunks, thorns, flowers . . . The roots of some of them disappeared into preserved or shattered flowerpots or tubs. The now-familiar vines entwined and supported rows of wooden cabinets that were identical in appearance to those in the big vestibule, but rotted through entirely owing to the high humidity. This became clear as soon as Daniel tried to open one of the drawers.

'It's the duplicate card catalogue,' he told Artyom, with a sigh of relief. 'We're not far, now.'

They heard another knock on the door behind them, and then someone carefully tried the doorknob, as if testing it. Moving the vines aside with their rifles and trying not to trip over the roots that ran along the floor, they hurried to pass through the ominous secret garden hidden in the depths of the Library. There was another door at the other end of the hall, and this one was not locked. They passed down the last corridor and finally stopped.

They were in the stack archive. They felt it immediately. There was book dust in the air. The library was breathing calmly, and the murmur of billions of pages could be heard ever so slightly. Artyom looked around, and it seemed to him he could smell the odour of old books, a favourite of his childhood. He looked at Daniel inquiringly.

'That's it, we're here,' confirmed Daniel then added, in a hopeful tone: 'Well?'

'Well . . . it's spooky,' admitted Artyom, not understanding immediately what his partner was expecting.

'Do you hear the book?' clarified the Brahmin. 'From here, its voice should be more distinct.'

Artyom closed his eyes and tried to concentrate. The inside of his head was empty and reverberated, as if inside an abandoned tunnel. Standing like that for a while, he again began to hear the little noises that filled the Library building, but he wasn't able to hear anything resembling a voice or a call. Worse, he felt nothing, and even if one assumed that the voice Daniel and the other Brahmins spoke of was some completely different type of sensation, that changed nothing.

'No, I don't hear anything.' He spread his hands.

'Never mind,' sighed Daniel after a silence. 'Let's go to another level. There're nineteen of them here. We'll keep looking until we find it. We better not go back with empty hands.'

Going out onto the service staircase, they went up several floors of concrete steps before stopping to again try their luck. At this level, everything looked like the place they came to initially: a medium-sized room with glazed windows, several office tables, the now-familiar growth on the ceiling and in the corners, and two corridors, going off in different directions, filled with endless rows of book-shelves along both sides of a narrow passageway. The ceiling in both the room and the corridors was low, just over two metres in height, and after the incredible vastness of the vestibule and the Main Reading Room, it seemed that not only would it be difficult to squeeze between the floor and ceiling here, but to breathe as well. The stacks were densely packed with thousands of various books, and many of them appeared to be completely untouched and marvel-lously preserved, evidence that the Library was built so that even when people abandoned it, a special microclimate was preserved inside. Seeing such fabulous wealth even made Artyom forget, for a minute, why he was there, and he dived into one of the rows, looking at the spines and running his hand over them reverently. Concluding that his partner had heard what he had been sent here for, Daniel initially didn't interfere, but then finally realized what was going on. He grabbed Artyom rather roughly and pulled him further on.

There were three, four, six corridors; a hundred, two, of stacks; thousands and even more thousands of books, revealed in the impenetrable darkness of the stack archive by a yellow spot of light. The next level, and the next . . . All for nothing. Artyom felt nothing that could be said to be a voice or a call. Absolutely nothing unusual. He recalled that if the Brahmins at the meeting of *Polis* Council considered him to be the chosen one, endowed with a special gift and led by fate, then the military had its own explanation for his visions: hallucinations.

He had begun to feel something on the last few floors, but it wasn't what he had expected or wanted. It was the vague feeling of some-one's presence that reminded him of the notorious fear of the tunnels. Although all of the levels they had visited seemed completely abandoned, and there were no signs here of librarians or other creatures, he nevertheless kept wanting to turn around and he had this crazy feeling that someone was attentively observing them through the bookshelves.

Daniel tapped him on the shoulder and directed the flashlight at his boot. A long lace, which the Brahmin wasn't too good at tying, dragged behind him on the floor.

'While I tie this, you go on ahead and take a look. Maybe you'll hear something, after all,' he whispered and squatted down.

Artyom nodded and proceeded to move ahead slowly, step by step, looking back at Daniel every second. Daniel was having a difficult time; it wasn't easy to tie a slippery lace while wearing thick gloves. Moving forward, Artyom first shone a light down the endless row of shelves to his right, then sharply threw his beam to the left, trying to catch sight of crooked grey shadows of librarians in the rows of dusty and age-warped books. Having moved about thirty metres ahead of his partner, Artyom suddenly distinctly heard a rustling two rows ahead of him. His rifle was already at hand, so he pressed his flashlight against the barrel and with one bound was at the corridor where he reckoned someone was hiding.

He saw two rows of shelves, crammed to the top with volumes, receding into the distance. Emptiness. The beam darted to the left; maybe the enemy was hiding there, in the opposite direction. Emptiness.

Artyom held his breath, attempting to attentively distinguish the slightest noise. There was nothing; only the illusory murmuring of pages. He returned to the passageway and threw his beam to where Daniel was struggling with his bootlace. It was empty. Empty?

Not looking where he was going, Artyom rushed back. The spot of light from his flashlight jumped frantically from side to side, illuminating row after row of identical shelves in the darkness. Where had he stopped? Thirty metres . . . About thirty metres, he should be here . . . But there's nobody. Where could he have gone without first telling Artyom? If he had been attacked, why hadn't he resisted? What happened? What could have happened to him?

No, he had already gone back too far. Daniel should have been a lot closer . . . But he wasn't anywhere! Artyom felt he was losing control of his actions, and that he was starting to panic. Stopping at the same place where he had left Daniel to tie his bootlace, Artyom leaned his back limply against the end of a shelf. Suddenly, from the depths of the bookshelf row he heard a quiet inhuman voice that broke off into a eerie squawk:

'Artyom . . .'

Suffocating from fear and almost unable to see anything through his fogged gas mask, Artyom turned abruptly towards the voice, and, attempting to keep the corridor in his rifle's unsteady sights, he moved forward.

'Artyom . . .'

The voice was just around the corner! Suddenly, a thin fan of light cut through a shelf, leaking between some loosely shelved books at floor level. The beams moved back and forth, as if someone was repeatedly waving a flashlight left and right . . . Artyom heard the jangling of metal.

'Artyom . . .' It was barely discernible, but this time it was a familiar whisper, and there was no doubt the voice belonged to Daniel.

Artyom cheerfully took a broad step forward, hoping to see his partner, whereupon the same eerie guttural squawk he had heard initially split the air not more than two paces away. The flashlight beam continued to pointlessly rove over the floor, back and forth.

'Artyom . . .' The strange voice repeated the call.

Artyom took another step, glanced to the right and felt the hair on his head stand on end.

The row of shelves ended here, forming a niche, and Daniel sat on its floor in a pool of blood. His helmet and gas mask had been torn off and were lying on the floor some distance away. Though his face was as pale as that of a corpse, his open eyes were conscious and his lips attempted to form words. Behind him, half merged into the gloom, there hid a humped, grey figure. A long, bony hand, covered with bristly silver fur – and not a paw, but a real hand with powerful, incurved claws – was pensively rolling the flashlight that had dropped to the floor and now lay a half metre from Daniel. The other hand was buried in the ripped-open belly of the Brahmin.

'You're here,' whispered Daniel.

'You're here . . . ,' rasped the voice behind Daniel's back, with exactly the same intonation.

'A librarian . . . Behind me. I'm dead anyway. Shoot. Kill him,' Daniel said in a weakening voice.

'Shoot. Kill him,' repeated the shadow.

The flashlight once again deliberately rolled on the floor to the left, only to return to its starting point to repeat the cycle yet again. Artyom felt he was losing his mind. Melnik's words, about how the sound of gunshots could attract the nightmarish monsters, churned in his head.

'Go away,' he said to the librarian, not expecting, however, that he would be understood.

'Go away,' came the almost-affectionate reply, but the clawed hand continued to search for something in Daniel's stomach, causing Daniel to groan quietly, while a drop of blood drew a thick line from the corner of his mouth to his chin.

'Shoot!' said Daniel, louder, having gathered some strength.

'Shoot!' demanded the librarian from behind his back.

Should he shoot his new friend himself and, in doing so, attract other creatures, or should he leave Daniel to die here and run, while there was still time? By now, it was doubtful Daniel could be saved; with his ripped-open belly and eviscerated entrails, the Brahmin had less than an hour left.

A pointed grey ear appeared from behind Daniel's tipped-back head, followed by a huge green eye that sparkled in the flashlight's bean. The librarian slowly looked out from behind his dying partner, almost shyly, and his eyes sought Artyom's. Don't turn away. Look right there, right at him, right in his pupils . . . The pupils were vertical; those of an animal. And how strange it was to see vestiges of intelligence in these sinister, impossible eyes!

Now, up close, the librarian in no way resembled a gorilla, or even a monkey. His predatory face was overgrown with fur. The mouth was full of long fangs and reached almost from ear to ear, while the eyes were of such a size that they made the monster unlike any animal Artyom had ever seen, either in real life or in pictures.

It seemed to him that this went on for a very long time. Having plunged into the creature's gaze, he could no longer tear himself away from those pupils. Only when Daniel emitted a deep, lingering groan did Artyom snap out of it. He placed the tiny red dot of his sight directly on the unkempt grey fur of the librarian's low forehead and thumbed the selector of his rifle to semi-automatic fire. Upon hearing the soft metallic click, the monster spluttered angrily and again hid behind Daniel's back.

'Go away . . . ,' it said suddenly from behind Artyom's back, mimicking Artyom's intonation perfectly.

Artyom woozily stopped in his tracks. This time, the librarian hadn't just echoed his words, it was as if he had remembered them and understood their meaning. Could this be?

'Artyom . . . While I can still speak . . .' Daniel started to speak, having gathered his strength and attempting to focus his gaze, which grew cloudier with every minute. 'In my breast pocket . . . an envelope . . . I was told to give it to you if you found the Book . . .'

'But I didn't find anything,' Artyom shook his head.

'Didn't find anything,' echoed the eerie voice behind Daniel's back.

'It doesn't matter . . . I know why you agreed to do this. It wasn't for you . . . Maybe it'll help you. It doesn't matter to me if I obeyed the order or not . . . Just remember this, you can't go back to Polis . . . If they find out you came up empty-handed . . . And if the military finds out . . . Go through other stations. Now shoot, because it really hurts . . . I don't want . . .'

'Don't want . . . hurts . . .' mixing the words, the librarian repeated, hissing, and his arm made a sudden movement in Daniel's ripped stomach, which caused the latter to jerk convulsively and cry out with all his might.

Artyom could not take any more. Throwing caution to the wind, he thumbed his rifle back to automatic and, pursing his lips, pulled the trigger, stitching bullets into his partner and the beast that hid behind his body. The unexpectedly loud noise tore the silence of the Library into ribbons. Shrill chirring sounds followed, stopping suddenly, all at the same time. The dusty books absorbed their echo like a sponge. When Artyom next opened his eyes, it was finished.

Approaching the librarian, which had dropped its bullet-riddled head onto the shoulder of its victim and even in death still hid shyly behind him, Artyom lit up the eerie picture and felt his blood cooling in his veins, while his palms perspired from tension. Then he fastidiously poked the librarian with the toe of his boot and its body fell back, heavily. It was dead, there could be no doubt.

Trying not to look at the bloody mess that had been Daniel's face, Artyom started to slowly undo the zipper of the dead man's protective suit. The clothing had quickly become soaked in thick, black blood, and a transparent vapour rose from it into the cool air of the stack archive. Artyom started to feel nauseated. The breast pocket . . . The fingers inside his protective gloves awkwardly tried to undo the button, and it occurred to him that such gloves might have delayed Daniel for the minute that cost him his life.

A rustling could distinctly be heard in the distance, followed by the patter of barefoot steps along the corridor. Artyom twisted around nervously, and ran the flashlight beam over the passageways. Having assured himself that he was alone for the moment, he continued to struggle with the button. The button finally yielded and his stiff fingers managed to remove a thin grey envelope from deep inside the pocket. The envelope was inside a polyethylene bag that had a bullet hole in it.

In addition, Artyom found a bloodstained pasteboard rectangle in the pocket, undoubtedly the card Daniel had taken out of the card catalogue drawer in the vestibule. The card read: 'Shnurkov, N. E., Irrigation and the prospects for agriculture in the Tadzhik SSR. Dushanbe, 1965.'

Pattering and indistinct muttering could now be heard a very short distance away. There was no time left. Collecting Daniel's rifle and flashlight, which had fallen out of the librarian's claws, Artyom took off and ran back the way he came as fast as he could, almost not seeing where he was going, past the endless rows of bookshelves. He didn't know for sure if he was being followed, as the noise of his boots and the pounding of blood in his ears prevented him from hearing any sounds behind him.

As soon as he jumped into the stairwell and began to tumble down the concrete steps, he realized that he didn't even know on what floor the entrance they had used to enter the archives was located. He could, of course, go down to the first floor, knock out the stairwell glass, and jump out into the courtyard . . . He stopped for a second and looked outside.

Exactly in the centre of the courtyard, with their faces pointed up, several grey creatures stood motionless, looking at the windows, and – it seemed – directly at him. Petrified, Artyom pressed himself against a side wall and resumed his descent, treading softly. Now that he had stopped tramping his boots down the stairs, he could hear the patter of bare feet, which got louder and louder. Then, having completely lost control of himself, he resumed a headlong rush down the stairs.

Jumping out at the next level so as to fitfully look around in search of a familiar door, not finding it and then flinging himself onward, stopping and squeezing into dark corners when it seemed he could hear steps nearby, desperately looking around in dead-end passages and crawlways and again entering the stairs to go down one more floor or go up two more levels – perhaps he overlooked something? – understanding that the infernal noise with which he was desperately trying to find an exit from this labyrinth would attract every monstrous inhabitant of the Library but unable to calm himself down, Artyom pointlessly and unsuccessfully tried to find the exit. That is, until he made out a familiar, half-bent silhouette against the background of a knocked-out window as he was about to enter the stairwell again. Artyom moved back, dived into the first passage that presented itself, pressed his back to the wall, pointed his rifle at the opening from where he reckoned the librarian had to appear, and held his breath . . .

Silence.

The brute either decided not to pursue Artyom alone, or was waiting for Artyom to blunder and come out of hiding. He didn't have to go back the same way, though. The passage led onward. Thinking hard for a second, Artyom began to step backward from the opening, keeping his sight trained on it.

The corridor turned to the side, but at that very place the turn began, there was a black hole in the wall. The area was strewn with shards of brick and sprinkled with lime. Obeying an impulse, Artyom stepped through the hole, into a room full of broken furniture. Pieces of photographic and movie film were scattered over the floor. A slightly open door could be seen ahead, from behind which a narrow wedge of pale moonlight fell onto the floor. Stepping carefully on the treacherously creaky parquet, Artyom reached the door and looked out.

He recognized the room, although now he was at its opposite end. The imposing statue of the person reading, the incredible height of the ceiling and the gigantic windows, the path which led to the grotesque wooden portal of the exit, as well as the disturbed rows of reading tables along the sides: without a doubt, he was in the Main Reading Room. He stood on the enclosed wooden balustrade of the narrow gallery that girdled the hall at a height of four metres. It was from this gallery that the librarians came down at them. He had no idea how he had managed to get here from the stack archives, not to mention from the other side, bypassing the route he and Daniel had travelled to get there. But there was no time to reflect. The librarians could be hard on his heels.

Artyom ran down one of the two symmetrical stairs that led to the pedestal of the monument, and sprang to the doors. Not far from the carved wooden arch of the exit, several deformed bodies of librarians lay spread-eagled on the floor, and as he passed by where the battle had taken place, Artyom almost fell after losing his footing in a pool of thickening blood.

The heavy door was opened unwillingly, and a bright white light blinded him at once. Recalling Melnik's instructions, Artyom gripped his flashlight in his right hand and hastily described a triple circle, giving the sign that he was approaching with peaceful intentions. The dazzling beam immediately went to the side and Artyom, having thrown his machine gun behind his back, slowly moved forward into a round room with columns and a couch, still not knowing who was coming to meet him.

A light machine gun stood on its tripod on the floor, and Melnik was leaning over his partner. Ten was reclining with his eyes closed on the couch, making short moaning sounds from time to time. His right leg was twisted unnaturally, and, having seen him, Artyom understood that it was broken at the knee and bent, not forward, but backward. He could not imagine how such a thing might occur and what strength the one who had been able to so mutilate the stalwart tracker must have possessed.

'Where's your comrade?' Melnik tossed the question at Artyom, turning away from Ten for a second.

'The librarians . . . in the depository. They attacked,' Artyom tried to explain. For some reason he didn't want to say that he had killed Daniel himself, out of mercy.

'Did you find the Book?' the tracker asked just as abruptly.

'No,' Artyom shook his head, 'I didn't hear anything there and I didn't feel anything.'

'Give me a hand lifting him up . . . No, better take his rucksack, and mine, too. See what his leg looks like . . .' They nearly tore it off. 'Now he can only be carried piggy-back,' Melnik nodded at Ten.

Artyom gathered all the equipment, three rucksacks, two machine guns and the light machine gun, about thirty kilos of weight in all, and it wasn't easy lifting it. It was even more difficult for Melnik, shouldering the limp body of his partner with some difficulty, and even the short trip down the staircase – toward the exit – took them several long minutes.

They could no longer see any librarians all the way to the doors, but when Artyom flung open the heavy wooden doors, letting through the groaning tracker, a squawking howl was heard from the darkest bowels of the building, full of hatred and anguish. Artyom felt shivers running through him again and he hurried to shut the door. Now the main thing was to reach the metro as soon as possible.

'Lower your eyes!' Melnik ordered when they were on the street.

'The star will be right in front of you now. Don't even think of looking over the roofs . . .'

Barely moving his stiffening legs, Artyom obediently stared at the ground, dreaming only of overcoming those inconceivably sprawling two hundred metres from the library to the descent to *Borovitskaya*. However, the tracker wouldn't allow Artyom to enter the metro.

'It's impossible to go to the police now. You don't have the Book, and you lost their guide,' Melnik pronounced, gently lowering his wounded comrade to the ground and breathing heavily. 'The Brahmins would hardly like it. And, mainly, this means that you are not the chosen one and they have entrusted their secrets to you. You'd disappear without a trace if you returned to the police. They have specialists there, regardless whether they are intelligent or not. And even I won't be able to protect you. Now you have to leave. It's best you go to *Smolenskaya*. Go straight through, there are few houses, and there's no need to go deep into any alleys. Maybe you'll get there. If you hurry, before sunrise.'

'What sunrise?' Artyom asked, puzzled. The news that he would have to reach the other metro station on the surface alone, to which, judging by the map, was about two kilometres away, was for him like a kick in the head.

'The sun. People are night animals, and it's better for them if they don't show themselves on the surface by day. But there are those who crawl out of the ruins to warm themselves in the sun and you'll regret it a hundred times over if you interrupt them. And I'm not just talking about the light: you'll go blind in two seconds flat, and the dark glasses won't save you.'

'But why am I going alone?' Artyom asked, still not believing his ears.

'Never fear. You'll be walking straight ahead the whole way. You'll exit onto Kalininskiy and continue along it, there aren't any turns. Don't show yourself on the way, but stay really close to the houses, they live everywhere there. Go on, until you reach the intersection with a second broad avenue, this will be Sadovoye Koltso. There you turn left and straight ahead to a white stone apartment building. It was once the House of Fashion . . . You'll find it right away, right opposite, across Sadovoye, stands a half-ruined very tall building, the trade centre. There will be sort of a yellow arch behind the House of fashion on which "Metro Station *Smolenskaya*" is written. Turn into it, you'll come to a small square, a sort of inside courtyard, and you'll see the station itself there. If everything is quiet, try to get below. One entrance is closed there and guarded, they keep it for their own trackers. Knock on the gate like this: three fast raps, two slow, then three fast. They should open it. Tell them that Melnik sent you and wait for me there. I'm taking Ten to the infirmary and will leave right away. I'll be there before noon. I'll find you myself. Take the machine guns with your, we don't know how it all will turn out.'

'But there's another station, closer, on the map, you know . . . *Arbatskaya*,' Artyom had recalled the name.

'There is such a station. But you don't have to go near it. And you don't even want to. You'll pass right by it, stay on the other side of the street and move quickly, but don't run. That's it. Don't waste any time!' he concluded, and he nudged Artyom towards the exit from the vestibule. Artyom didn't want to argue anymore. Having thrown one of the machine guns over his shoulder, he held the second at the ready, went into the street and hurried back toward the monument, covering his eyes with his right hand so as not to see the beckoning radiance of the Kremlin's stars by accident.

CHAPTER 14

There Up Above

Before reaching the old stone man in the easy chair, Artyom turned left in order to cut across the corner of the street along the Library steps. Passing it, he glanced at the majestic building and a shiver went down his spine: Artyom remembered the terrible inhabitants of the place. Now the Library once more was immersed in dreary silence. The custodians of the predominant silence in it most likely had dispersed among the dark corners, licking their wounds after their impudent incursions and preparing to pay the next adventurers back for it.

The pallid, drained face of Daniel appeared before his eyes. It occurred to Artyom that the Brahmin, not without reason, had been frightened of these creatures, refusing even to speak of them. Had he seen his own death in his nightmares? His body would remain forever lying in the stacks, embracing the librarian who had killed him. Of course, if these creatures disdain carrion . . . Artyom winced. Would he ever be able to forget how his partner, who had become almost a friend to him in only two days, had died? It seemed to him that Daniel would trouble his dreams for a while longer, trying again and again to speak with him in the night, putting together indistinct words with his bloodstained lips.

Exiting onto the broad avenue, Artyom hastily turned over in his mind the instructions given him by Melnik. Go straight to the Kalininskiy intersection with Sadovoye Koltso, do not turn off any-where . . . Try to guess again which of the streets is Koltso itself. Don't go into the middle of the road, but also don't press up to the walls of the houses, and mainly, get to *Smolenskaya* before the sun comes up.

The famous Kalininskiy high-rises, which Artyom knew from the yellowed postcards with views of Moscow, began half a kilometre from the very place where he was standing. Now, low, detached houses stood along the sides of the street, which curved left into New Arbat. The outlines of buildings, clear close-up, blurred when he moved away and they blended into the twilight. The moon was hidden behind low clouds. The meagre milky light barely filtered through them and only when the misty curtain had dissipated, did the ghostly silhouettes of the homes again take shape for a short while. But even in such lighting, in the alleys that dissected the street every hundred metres, the powerful contour of an ancient cathedral could be seen on the left. A huge winged shadow once more circled over the cross-capped dome.

Perhaps it was for that reason Artyom stopped, in order to look at the soaring beast in the air, that he noticed it. It was hard to determine in the twilight whether his imagination was drawing the strange figure that had stopped dead in the depths of the alley and had fused with the partly destroyed walls of the houses. And only when he examined it further, did it appear to him that this blob of darkness moved a little and possessed its own free will. It wasn't easy to determine precisely the form and dimensions of the creature at such a distance, but it clearly stood on two legs and Artyom decided to act as the stalker had told him. Switching on his flashlight, he aimed the beam into the alley and made a circular movement with it three times.

There was no response. Artyom waited for it in vain for a minute until he realized that staying in that same place could be very dangerous. But before he could go on, he illuminated the motionless figure in the alley again. What he saw forced him to turn off his flashlight immediately and try to pass the alley as soon as he could.

It clearly had not been a man. Its silhouette had become more distinct in the spot of light, and it was no less than two and a half metres, its shoulders and neck were missing and the large round head emerged directly from a powerful body. The creature had hidden, biding its time. Despite this apparent indecisiveness, Artyom felt in his bones a threat from it.

He did the hundred and fifty metres to the last alley in less than a minute. Taking a hard look, he understood that it wasn't even an alley, but an opening burnt into a residential neighbourhood by some kind of weapon: they had either bombed here or simply demolished a whole row of buildings with heavy military equipment. Artyom looked with curiosity at the half-ruined homes fading into the distance but then his attention was fixed on the unclear, motionless shadow. It was enough to put the beam of the flashlight on it for a second to dispel all doubt: it was that very same creature or its mate. Standing right in the middle of the alley in the same block, it wasn't even trying to hide.

If the creature was the same one he had observed in the block behind him earlier, that meant it had snuck along the street parallel to the one he was walking along, Artyom thought. It turned out that it had covered this distance twice as fast as he: for at the very moment he reached the next crossing, it was already waiting for him there. But something else was even worse: this time he also saw a similar figure in the alley to the right of the avenue. As the first one, it was standing there, frozen in place, like a statue. For a moment Artyom thought that perhaps they weren't living beings, but signs placed here by someone for intimidation or as a warning . . .

He was already running to the third intersection, stopping only at the last detached house to look carefully around the corner into the alley and make certain that the mysterious pursuers had outpaced him once more. There already were several of the huge figures, and now they were a little easier to see: the layer of clouds that had been covering the moon had thinned out a little.

And as before, the creatures stood there, not stirring, as if waiting until he appeared in the opening between the houses. And for all that, had he not deceived himself, taking stone or concrete stubs of collapsed structures for living beings? His acute senses were able to stand him in good stead down below, in the metro. On the surface lay a deceptive world, unknown to him, and here everything was different and life went on with different rules. He was no longer justified in relying on his impressions and intuition.

Having tried to dart past a new alley as quickly and inconspicuously as possible, Artyom pressed himself against the wall of a house, waited a second and again looked around the corner. He gasped: the figures were moving, and in a surprising manner. Stretching still higher and raising its head as if sniffing the air, one of them unexpectedly dropped onto all fours and disappeared around the corner in one long bound. The rest followed it several seconds later. Artyom moved back, hid and, sitting onto the ground, caught his breath.

There were no more doubts – they were pursuing him. It was as if the creatures were leading him, moving along parallel streets. They were biding their time until he passed a new opening. They would appear in an alley to make certain that he had not deviated from his route and they continued their silent shadowing of him. Why? Choosing a suitable moment for an attack? Simply out of curiosity? Why hadn't they made up their minds to come out to the avenue, preferring to hide in the gloomy shadows? He again recalled Melnik's words which forbade him to turn away from the straight road. Was it because they were laying in wait for him there and Melnik knew about this danger?

In order to calm down, Artyom replaced the clip in his machine gun, pulled back the bolt, and turned the laser gunsight on and off. He was well armed and, in contrast to the library, was able to shoot here without any dangers; it would be easier to defend himself. Taking a deep breath, he got to his feet. The stalker had forbidden him to stop and waste time. He had to hurry. It seemed that here, on the surface, one always had to hurry.

Passing another block, Artyom slowed his pace in order to look around. The street here had got wider, forming something like a square, part of which, cut off from the road by a fence, had been converted into a park. In any case, it looked as if there had been a park there at some time: trees still stood in places, but they were not at all the trees Artyom had happened to see in postcards and photographs. Thick, gnarled trunks carried spreading crowns to a height of a five-storey building which stood to the rear of the park. Most likely, the stalkers went to such parks for the firewood that heated and lit the whole metro. Strange shadows flickered in the spaces between the trunks and, somewhere in the distance, a faint fire flickered. Artyom would have taken it for the flame of a bonfire if it were not for its yellowish color. The building itself also looked sinister: it created the impression that it had been the arena of brutal and bloody clashes more than once. Its upper floors had collapsed and in many places bullet holes showed black. In places only two walls remained intact, and the dim night sky was visible through empty windows.

The buildings parted beyond the square and a broad boulevard intersected the street. Above him, appearing out of the darkness, like watch towers, rose the first high-rise buildings of New Arbat. Judging by the map, entry to *Arbatskaya* should have been located nearby, to his left. Artyom again looked at the gloomy park. Melnik had been right: one didn't want to delve deeply into this labyrinth while trying to find a descent into the metro within it. The longer he stared at the black bushes scattered next to the base of the ruined structure, the greater it seemed to him that he saw those most mysterious figures that had been following him earlier moving among the roots of the giant trees.

A swooping puff of wind shook the heavy branches, and the crowns creaked under the strain. The wind carried some drawn-out wail from afar. The thicket itself was quiet, but not because it was dead. Its silence was akin to the hush of Artyom's mysterious pursuers and it seemed it too was waiting for something.

Artyom was overtaken by the feeling that if he stopped here, examining the park's innermost depths, he could not escape retribution. He better gripped his machine gun, looked around to see if the creatures had approached, and moved forward.

But only several seconds later he stopped again, when he was crossing the boulevards in front of the start of Kalininskiy Prospekt. Such a view was revealed here that Artyom simply was unable to force himself to go further.

He was standing at an X-shaped intersection of wide roads, along which vehicles must have driven at one time. The junction had been constructed in an unusual way. Part of the asphalt road went into a tunnel and then emerged at the surface again. On the right, boulevards went into the distance. It was possible to recognize them by a black line of trees, just as huge as those past which he had just made his way. A large, square, covered with asphalt was seen on the left – a complex tangle of numerous paths, beyond which the brush began again. Now it was possible to see further, and Artyom asked himself whether the rising of the frightful sun was already nearing.

The roads were strewn with deformed and burnt carcasses of automobiles. Nothing else was left here: in two decades of trips to the surface, stalkers had succeeded in getting hold of everything they possibly could. Gasoline from fuel tanks, batteries and generators, headlights and traffic signals, seats torn out with flesh still on them – it had even been possible to find all this at *VDNKh*, and at any huge market in the metro. The asphalt had been dug out, and craters and wide cracks could be seen everywhere. Grass and soft stems poked through, bending beneath the weight of their crowning balls filled, apparently, with seeds. The murky gorge of New Arbat came into view directly ahead of Artyom. On one side, formed, for some unknown reason, of undamaged houses, resembling open books in layout, and on the other of partly collapsed high-rise buildings, about twenty storeys high. The road to the Library and the Kremlin remained behind Artyom.

He was standing in the middle of this majestic cemetery of

civilization and felt like an archaeologist, uncovering an ancient city, the remnants of a bygone power and beauties of which even many centuries later forced those seeing it to experience the chill of awe. He tried to imagine how the people who populated these gigantic buildings, who moved in these vehicles, then still sparkling with fresh paint and rustling softly along the smooth road surface warmed with the rubber of wheels and who descended into the metro only to get from one point of this boundless city to another more quickly had lived. It was impossible. What had they thought about every day? What had bothered them? Just what can bother people if they don't have to be concerned about their lives every second and constantly fight for it, trying to extend it at least for a day?

At this moment the clouds finally dissipated and a piece of the yellowish disc of the moon was seen, striated with strange drawings. The bright light that fell through the hole in the clouds inundated the dead city, intensifying its gloomy magnificence a hundredfold. The houses and trees, until now looking like only flat and disembodied silhouettes, had returned to life and acquired dimension.

Unable to move from the place, Artyom looked, spellbound, from side to side, trying to suppress the chill that had overtaken him. Only now did he begin to understand the anguish which he had heard in the voices of the old men recalling the past, who had returned in their imagination to the city in which they previously had lived. Only now did he start to sense how far man now was from his former achievements and conquests. Like a proudly soaring bird, mortally wounded and dropping to the ground in order to hide in a crevice and, having concealed itself there, dies quietly. He recalled an argument of his stepfather and Hunter he had overheard. Will man be able to survive, and even if he can, will he be that same man who had conquered the world and confidently ruled it? Now, when Artyom himself was able to evaluate from what heights mankind had fallen into the precipice, his faith in a beautiful future evaporated once and for all.

The straight and broad Kalininskiy Prospekt moved away from him, gradually tapering, until it dissolved in the dark distance. Now Artyom was standing on the road completely alone, surrounded only by the ghosts and shadows of the past, trying to imagine just how many people once had filled the pavements day and night, how many cars had swept past at fantastic speed in that same place where he was standing, how comfortably and warmly the now empty and black windows of the homes had glowed. Where had it all vanished? The world seemed more deserted and abandoned, but Artyom understood that it was an illusion: the earth had not been abandoned and lifeless, it had simply changed owners. Having thought about it, he turned back, toward the Library.

They were standing motionlessly only a hundred or so metres from it, as was he, in the middle of the road. There were no fewer than five of the creatures, and they no longer intended to hide in the alleys, although they also had not tried to attract his attention. Artyom couldn't understand how they had managed to steal up on him so quickly and silently. These figures were especially distinct in the moonlight: powerful, with developed rear extremities and, perhaps, even taller than they had seemed to him at first. Though Artyom was unable to see their eyes at such a distance, he knew nonetheless that now they, biding their time, were examining him and sniffing the damp air, getting to know his scent. It must have been that the smell of gunpowder was known to them and had affixed itself to him and so the beasts still had not decided to attack, observing Artyom from a distance and searching for a sign of uncertainty or weakness in his behaviour. Perhaps they were just accompanying Artyom to the boundary of their domain and did not intend to inflict any harm on him? How could he know how creatures that appeared on the earth contrary to the laws of evolution would act?

Trying to maintain his self-control, Artyom swung round and with feigned nonchalance continued on, looking over his shoulder every ten paces. At first the creatures stayed put, but then his worst fears began to be realized. Getting down on all fours, they slowly plodded after him. But as soon as they were only a hundred metres from him, they again stopped fast. Although he'd become accustomed to his strange escort, Artyom was afraid to let it out of his sight and held his machine gun at the ready. They walked like this together, along the empty avenue, flooded with moonlight: a man, alert, wound up like a spring, stopping and looking back every half minute and, behind him, five or six strange creatures, leisurely keeping pace with him.

However, it soon seemed to him that the distance they had been maintaining was becoming shorter. Moreover, remaining in a group before this, now the beasts started to fan out, as if trying to outflank him. Artyom never had to deal with a pack of hunting predators before, but for some reason he had no doubts that the creatures were preparing to attack. It was time to act. Turning sharply around, he

317

shouldered his machine gun and caught one of the dark figures in its sight.

Their behaviour really had changed. This time they didn't stop to wait until he moved further away. They continued to approach him almost imperceptibly, gradually creating a semi-circle. He had to try to frighten them away before they succeeded in shortening the distance to the range at which an attack would follow.

Artyom lifted the barrel a little and fired into the air. The clatter reverberated from the walls of the high-rises and echoed to the other end of the avenue. The empty clip fell to the asphalt with a clanking sound. And then a deafening roar full of fury was heard and the beasts dashed forward. They were able to cover the dozens of metres separating them from Artyom in several seconds, but he too was ready. As soon as the beast closest to him was in his sight, he gave it a short burst and started running toward the houses.

Judging by the fit of screaming the creature emitted, he had managed to hit it. It was impossible to guess whether it delayed the remaining beasts or, conversely, it had infuriated them.

And then a new cry was heard, not the threatening roar of the beasts hunting him, but a long, piercing squawk, which made his blood curdle. It reached him from above and Artyom understood that a new participant had joined the game. Obviously, the noise of the shots had attracted the attention of a flying monster similar to the one that had spun its nest on the cathedral's dome.

A huge shadow swept over his head like a shot. Turning back for a moment, Artyom saw that the beasts had scattered, and only one of them, apparently the one he had wounded, was left in the middle of the street. Continuing to scream, it clumsily lurched towards the building, also hoping to conceal itself there. But it had no chance of being saved: describing another circle several dozen metres high, the monster folded its enormous leathery wings and fell upon the victim. It dived down so swiftly that Artyom wasn't even able to see what happened next. Having gripped the beast screeching its final agony, the gigantic hulk lifted its quarry aloft without any visible effort and leisurely carried it to the roof of one of the high-rises.

His pursuers didn't immediately break cover, concerned that the monster may return, and Artyom had no time to lose. Pressing himself to the walls of the houses, he ran forward, where, according to his calculations, Sadovoye Koltso should be located. He was able to cover about half a kilometre before he was out of breath and he looked back to check whether the beasts hunting him had gathered their wits. The avenue was empty. But going several more dozen metres and looking into one of the alleys leading away from New Arbat, Artyom, to his horror, noticed familiar still shadows in it. Now he was beginning to understand why these creatures were in no hurry to come out into the open and preferred to track their victims from the narrow side streets. While hunting for him, they feared attracting the attention of the larger monsters and becoming their prey.

Now Artyom had to turn around to look every minute: he remembered that the beasts were able to move extremely quickly, and at the same time practically silently, and he feared that they could catch him unawares. The end of the avenue was already visible when they again raced from the alleys and began to surround him. Taught by experience, Artyom at once shot into the air, hoping that that would attract the winged monster as before and frighten off the beasts. They actually froze for a while, standing up on their hind legs and craning their necks. But the sky remained empty – the monster, apparently, still had not been able to deal with its first victim. Artyom understood sooner than his pursuers and rushed to the right, skirted one of the houses and dived into the nearest entrance. Though Melnik also had warned him against it, saying that the houses were inhabited, running into such a powerful and mobile enemy as the beasts chasing him in the open would have been insane. They would have torn Artyom to pieces before he was able to pull back the bolt of his machine gun.

It was dark in the entrance, and he had to turn on his flashlight. In the round spot of light rose shabby walls covered with obscenities scrawled several decades before, a foul staircase, and the broken doors of ruined and burnt out apartments. Bold rats scampering around like they owned the place, adding to the picture of desolation.

He had chosen the entry wisely, the staircase windows looked out onto the avenue, and, climbing to the next floor, he was able to ascertain that the beasts had not decided to follow him. They were stealing up to the front doors but, instead of going into one, surrounded it, squatting on their haunches and again turning into stone statues. Artyom didn't believe that they would back off and allow their prey to elude them. Sooner or later they would try to reach him from outside, if, of course, nothing was hiding in the entrance which Artyom himself would be forced to flee.

He climbed a storey higher, illuminated the doors and discovered that one of them was closed. He put his shoulder to it and was convinced that it was locked. Without thinking twice, he put the muzzle of the machine gun up to the keyhole, fired and flung the door open with a kick. When it came down to it, it was all the same to him in which of the apartments he put up a defence, but he was unable to miss his chance to look at an untouched dwelling of the people of a bygone era.

First he slammed shut the door and blocked it with a cabinet standing in the hallway. This barricade would not sustain a serious attack, but at least they couldn't get past it unnoticed. After that, Artyom approached the window and carefully looked outside. It was practically an ideal firing position – from the height of the fourth floor he was able to see perfectly the approaches to the entrance. There were about ten beasts sitting in a semi-circle around it. Now the advantage was his and he wasted no time in using it. Switching on the laser gunsight, he put the red dot on the head of the largest of the beasts and, taking a breath, pulled the trigger. A short burst sounded and the creature soundlessly fell onto its side. The others dashed off in different directions at lightning speed, and a moment later the street was empty. But there was no doubt they didn't intend to go far. Artyom decided to wait it out and be certain that the death of their colleague really had frightened off the remaining beasts.

In the meantime, he had a little time in which to study the apartment.

Though the glass here, as in the whole house, had been broken long ago, the furniture and all the fittings had been preserved surprisingly well. Small pads had been spread around the floor resembling the rat poison they used at *VDNKh*. Perhaps that was why Artyom had not noticed one rat in the rooms. The longer he walked around the apartment, the more he was convinced that the residents had not abandoned it in a hurry, but had preserved it, hoping sometime to return. No food had been left in the kitchen to attract rodents or insects, and much of the furniture was carefully wrapped in cellophane.

Moving from room to room, Artyom tried to imagine what the everyday life of the people who had lived here had been. How many of them lived here? What time did they get up, arrive home from work, have dinner? Who sat at the head of the table? He knew about many of the jobs, rituals and things only through books, and now, seeing a real dwelling, was convinced that much of what he had imagined earlier was totally wrong.

Artyom carefully lifted the semi-transparent polyethylene film and examined the book shelves. Several colourful children's books stood among the detective stories he knew from the bookstalls in the metro. He grasped one of them at the spine and gently pulled it out. While he paged through the decorative depictions of happy animals, a sheet of cardboard fell from the book. Bending over, Artyom lifted it off the floor: it turned out to be a fading photograph of a smiling woman with a small child in her arms.

He was petrified.

His heart went into palpitations. Having just been dispersing the blood through his body in measured beats, it suddenly had sped up, beating inappropriately. Artyom terribly wanted to remove his tight gas mask to get a jolt of fresh air, if it had not been poisonous. Carefully, as if concerned that the picture turn to dust from his touch, he took it from the shelf and lifted it to his eyes.

The woman in the picture was about thirty years old, and the little one in her arms not more than two, and it was difficult to determine if it was a boy or girl from the funny cap on its head. The child was looking straight at the camera, and its expression was surprisingly grown up and serious. Artyom turned over the photograph and the glass of his gas mask became clouded. On the other side was written in a blue ballpoint pen: 'Little Artyom is 2 years and 5 months old.'

It was as if they had pulled a rod out of him. His legs went weak and he slid down to the floor, placing the picture in the moonlight falling from the window. Why did the smile of the woman in the photograph seem so familiar to him, so like his own? Why had he begun to feel suffocated as soon as he saw her?

More than ten million people had been living in it before this city perished. Artyom is not the most widely used name, but there had to have been several tens of thousands of children with such a name in a megapolis of many millions. It was as if they called all the present inhabitants of the metro the same. The chance was so small that it simply made no sense to consider it. But why then did the smile of the woman in the photograph seem so familiar to him?

He tried to recall scraps of memories about his childhood that sometimes flashed before his mind's eye. A comfortable small room, soft lighting, a woman reading a book . . . A wide ottoman. He leapt up, passing through the rooms like a whirlwind, trying to find in one of them furniture similar to that of which he had dreamed. It seemed to him in an instant that the furniture in one of the rooms was arranged the same as in his memories. The couch looked a bit different, and a window was not there, but this picture may have left something of a distorted imprint on the consciousness of a three-year-old child . . .

Three years old? The age on the photograph was different, but this too meant nothing. There was no date with the inscription. It could have been taken at any time, it didn't have to be several days before the residents of the apartment had to leave it forever. The photo may have been taken half a year, even a year before this, he convinced himself. Then the age of the boy in the hat in the picture would coincide with his own . . . Then the probability that he himself was portrayed in the picture. . . . and his mother . . . would be much greater. 'But the photograph could have been taken three or five years before this,' an alien voice coldly stated inside him. Could have.

Suddenly another thought entered his head. Flinging open the door to the bathroom, he glanced around and almost missed what he was looking for: the mirror was covered with such a layer of dust that it didn't even reflect the light from his flashlight. Artyom removed a towel left by the apartment's owners from its hook and wiped off the mirror. The area he cleared revealed his reflection in gas mask and helmet. He illuminated himself with the flashlight and looked into the mirror.

His drawn, emaciated face was not entirely visible beneath the plastic visor of the gas mask, but the look of the deeply sunken dark eyes barely making its way back from the mirror suddenly seemed to him similar to the look of the boy in the photograph. Artyom brought the photograph to his face, looked intently at the boy's tiny face, and then looked at the mirror. Again he held the light on the picture and again he looked at his own face beneath the gas mask, trying to recall how it looked the last time he saw his reflection. When was that? Not long before he had left *VDNKh*, but it was impossible to say how much time had passed since then. Judging by the man he saw in the mirror now, several years . . . If only he could pull off this damned mask and compare himself with the child in the photo! Of course, people now and then become unrecognizable while growing up, but something remains in the face of everyone that reminds one of their distant childhood.

There was one possibility: when he returned to *VDNKh*, he could ask Sukhoi if the woman smiling at him now from the piece of paper looked like the woman, condemned to be devoured by the rats, who had handed the child's life over to him at the station. Looked like his mother. Though her face was then distorted in a grimace of despair and supplication, Sukhoi would recognize her. He had a fine memory, he would be able to say precisely who was in the photo. Was it her or not?

Artyom examined the picture again, then with an unaccustomed tenderness, he stroked the woman's image, carefully put the photograph into the little book out of which it had fallen and put it away into his rucksack. It was strange, he thought, only several hours ago he was in the largest storehouse of knowledge on the continent, where he could take for himself any of the millions of very different volumes, many of which were simply invaluable. But he had left them gathering dust on the shelves, and the thought never even crossed him mind to profit from the riches of the Library. Instead, he was taking a cheap children's book with unpretentious drawings and yet he felt as if he had gained the greatest of the world's treasures.

Artyom returned to the hall, intending to leaf through the remaining books from the shelf, and perhaps even look into the cupboards in search of photograph albums. But, lifting his eyes towards the window, he felt the almost imperceptible changes there. An uneasiness seized him: something wasn't right. Approaching nearer, he understood what was wrong: the night's colour was changing, and yellowish-rose tints had appeared in it. It was getting light.

The beasts were sitting next to the entrance, hesitating to go inside. The dead body of their companion was nowhere to be seen, but whether the winged giant had carried it away or they had torn it to pieces themselves was unclear. Artyom didn't understand what kept them from taking the apartment by storm, but for the time being it suited him.

Would he manage to reach *Smolenskaya* before sunrise? More importantly, would he be able to get away from his pursuers? It was possible to remain in the barricaded apartment, hide from the rays of the sun in the bathroom, wait until they chased away these predatory creatures, and set out when darkness fell. But how long would the protective suit last? How long was his gas-mask filter estimated to last? What would Melnik undertake, not finding him in the agreed place at the agreed time?

Artyom approached the door leading to the stairwell and listened. Silence. He carefully moved the cabinet away and slowly opened the door a little. There was no one there, but, having illuminated the staircase with his flashlight, Artyom noticed something he had not seen earlier.

A thick, transparent slime coated the steps. It looked as if someing had just crawled down them, leaving a trail behind. The trail had not approached the apartment door where he had spent all this time, but this didn't console Artyom. Did it mean the abandoned houses were not as empty as they had seemed?

Now he no longer wanted to stay in the apartment, let alone sleep here. There was only one possibility: to drive away the beasts and to try to run to *Smolenskaya*. And to do it before the sun burnt his eyes and the unseen monsters awoke.

This time he aimed not as carefully, but tried to damage the predatory beasts as much as possible. Two of them roared and tumbled to the ground and the others disappeared into the alleys. It seemed the road was clear.

Artyom ran down, carefully, concerned about an ambush, looked out of the entrance and rushed with all his strength toward Sadovoye Koltso. What a nightmarish thicket must be there, in the gardens on this ring, he thought, if even the thin strips of trees on the boulevards had, after all these years, been converted to dark labyrinths . . . Not to mention the Botanical Gardens and what must be growing there.

His pursuers had given him a head start while gathering into a pack and he was able to reach almost the very end of the avenue. It was becoming ever more light, but the sun's rays, apparently, did not daunt these beasts at all: breaking into two groups, they rushed along, shortening with every passing second the distance separating them from Artyom. Here, in the open space, the advantage was with them: Artyom was unable to stop to fire. At the same time, they were shifting to all fours, and their silhouettes did not rise more than a metre above the ground. They almost merged with the road. No matter how fast Artyom tried to run, the protective suit, rucksack, two machine guns and fatigue, accumulated during the seemingly endless night, were making themselves felt.

Soon these hellhounds would overtake him and take their toll, he thought with despair. He recalled the deformed but powerful bodies of the monsters lying in pools of blood at the entrance where his burst of machine-gun fire had toppled them. Artyom had no time to examine them, but even one look was enough to engrave them on his memory for a long time: glossy brown hair, huge round heads, and mouths studded with dozens of small sharp teeth that, it seemed, grew in several rows. Going over in his mind all the animals known to him, Artyom was unable to recall one that would have been able to produce such beasts even after the effects of radiation.

Fortunately, there were no trees growing at Sadovoye Koltso. It was simply one more broad street, extending right and left from the intersection as far as the eye could see. Before breaking into a run again, Artyom let off a short burst at the beasts without looking. They were already less than fifty metres from him and again had broken up into a semi-circle so that some were moving almost level with him.

At Sadovoye he had to look for the road among several huge craters five to six metres deep, and make a detour in one place in order to skirt a deep crevice that split the road surface in two. The structures standing close by looked strange: rather than being burnt, they appeared more to have been melted. It created the impression that something peculiar had happened here, that this region had endured much more than Kalininskiy Prospekt. And something like several hundred metres in the distance arose a building of inconceivable size. It looked like a medieval castle, and was a majestic and sombre background to this troubled landscape, untouched by time or fire. Artyom glanced up for a split second, and he let go a sigh of relief: a scary winged shadow soared over the castle and that could become his salvation. He only had to attract its attention so that it busied itself with his pursuers. Lifting the machine gun in one hand and aiming the barrel at the flying monster, he squeezed the trigger.

Nothing happened.

He had run out of ammunition.

It was difficult to drag the reserve machine gun hanging on his back forward while running. Diving into one of the nearest alleys, Artyom leaned against the wall and changed weapons. Now he didn't have to let the beasts come close while he emptied the magazine in the second machine gun.

The first of them already had appeared from around the corner and sat on its hindquarters with the customary movement, extending itself to all its huge height. It had grown bolder and had approached so close that now Artyom was able to see its eyes for the first time: small, concealed beneath massive brows, burning with an evil green fire similar to the gleam of that mysterious flame in the park.

There was no laser sight on Daniel's Kalashnikov, but one normally couldn't miss from such a distance. He framed the figure of the beast standing stock in his sight. Artyom squeezed the machine gun more tightly to his shoulder and pulled the trigger.

Moving slowly to the centre, the bolt stopped. What had happened? Could he really have confused the machine guns in his haste?

Absolutely not, for his weapon had a laser sight . . . Artyom tried to wrench the bolt. It was stuck.

A whirlwind of thoughts swirled in his head. Daniel, the librarians . . . That was why his comrade had not resisted when that grey monster attacked him in the labyrinth of books! His machine gun simply had not worked. He, most likely, had pulled the bolt just as spasmodically while the librarian dragged him into the depths of the corridors . . .

There was silence as two more beasts appeared, like spectres. They were studying Artyom intently. He was looking in despair at Daniel's machine gun. It seemed that they were drawing their own conclusions. The closest of the creatures, most likely the leader, jumped and now was only five metres from Artyom.

At this moment a gigantic shadow swept over their heads. The beasts pressed themselves to the ground and lifted their heads. Taking advantage of their confusion, Artyom dashed to one of the arches, no longer hoping to come out of this mess alive, but just trying instinctively to postpone the moment of his death. He had not the slightest chance against them in the alleys, but the way back, to Sadovoye Koltso, already had been cut off.

He ended up in the middle of an empty square, bounded along the edges by the walls of houses, in which arches and passages could be seen. That same gloomy castle that had impressed him at Sadovoye Koltso rose into the sky behind the building he was facing. Finally tearing his gaze away from it, Artyom saw writing on the building opposite: 'The Moscow V.I. Lenin Underground Railroad' and a bit lower, '*Smolenskaya* Station.' The high oak doors were ajar.

It was hard to say how he managed to evade them. He felt a premonition of danger and the sensation of a light air current, was aware of a predator dashing towards its prey. The beast landed only a half metre from him. Easing sideways, he broke into a run and dashed with all his might towards the entrance to the metro. His home was there, his world, there beneath the ground he again would become master of the situation.

The *Smolenskaya* vestibule looked exactly as Artyom had expected: dark, grey, empty. It at once became clear that the people at this station often came to the surface: the ticket booths and office facilities were open and ransacked and everything of use had been moved underground many years ago. Neither the turnstiles nor the booths for the staff remained – their concrete foundations a mere reflection of what once had been. The arch of the tunnel was visible, and several escalators reached down to incredible depths. The flashlight's beam was lost somewhere in the middle of the descent and Artyom was unable to ascertain that there really was an entrance there. But it was impossible to stay where he was: the beasts had already penetrated into the vestibule. He knew because he heard the creaking of the door. In a few seconds they would reach the escalators, and that tiny head start he still had would disappear.

Awkwardly stepping along the shaking grooved steps, Artyom began his descent. He tried to hop across several steps, but his foot slipped on the damp covering and he crashed downward, striking the back of his head on a corner. He managed to stop only when he had hit about ten steps with his helmet and the small of his back. Searching the section of the way behind him with his light, Artyom discovered exactly what he was looking for and was afraid to find: the stationary dark figures. As was their custom, before they attacked, they stood stock still, studying the situation or conferring inaudibly. Artyom turned round and again tried to jump over two steps. This time it turned out better for him, and, sliding his right hand along the rubber of the handrail, while grasping his flashlight in his left, he ran for about another twenty seconds before he fell again.

He heard heavy stomping from behind. The creatures were determined. Artyom hoped with his whole being that the old stairs woefully creaking beneath his lighter weight would just collapse, not sustaining the weight of his pursuers. But the clatter approaching from the shadows was evidence that the escalator was handling the load well. A brick wall with a large door in the middle appeared in the beam of his flashlight. Only about twenty metres remained to it, no more. Rising to his feet with difficulty, Artyom covered the final stretch in fifteen seconds. It seemed like an eternity.

The door was made of steel plates and echoed resonantly, like a bell, at the blows of his fists. Artyom pounded at it with all his might. The approaching shadows, which he saw dimly in the semi-darkness, were spurring him on. Only after several seconds did he understand, a sudden chill overcoming him, what a terrible mistake he had just made: instead of knocking at the door with the prearranged code, he had only alarmed the guards. Now it was most probable that there was no way it would be unlocked under any circumstances. It didn't matter who was trying to enter. And the fact that the sun was rising already made it even less likely that the door would be opened.

Just how did the prearranged signal sound? Three quick, three slow, three quick? Absolutely not, that's an SOS. It was exactly three at the beginning and three at the end, but he was no longer able to recall quick or slow. And if he were to begin to experiment now, he could forget about any hope of getting inside. Better the SOS . . . At least then the guards would understand that a man was on the other side of the door.

Having banged on the steel once more, Artyom pulled the sub-machine gun from his shoulder and, with hands shaking, replaced the clip in it. Then he pressed the light to the weapon's barrel and nervously outlined the upward stretching arches with it. Long shadows from the surviving lamps covered each other in the wandering beam of his light, and it was impossible to guarantee that a dark silhouette didn't lurk in one of them . . .

As before, it remained completely quiet on the other side of the iron door. Lord, it's really not *Smolenskaya*, Artyom thought. Maybe this entrance was blocked up decades ago and no one has used it since then? He had got here completely by accident, not following the instructions of the stalker at all. And he may have been wrong!

The stairs creaked very near to him, about fifteen metres away. Not able to bear it, Artyom let loose a burst of machine-gun fire in the direction from which the sound had been heard. The echo pained Artyom's ears.

But nothing like the howl of a wounded beast was heard. The shots were wasted. Not having the courage to look away, Artyom pressed his back against the door and again began to pound with his fist on the iron: three quick, three slow, three quick. He thought he heard a heavy metallic grinding sound from the door. But just at that moment the figure of a predator flew from the shadows with a startling speed.

Artyom held the submachine gun suspended in his right hand, and pressed the trigger almost by accident when he instinctively recoiled backwards. The bullets swept the body of the creature in the air, and instead of seizing Artyom by the throat, it collapsed on the last steps of the escalator, having flown not two metres. But only a moment later it raised itself and, ignoring the blood gushing from its wound, moved forward.

Then, staggering, it leapt again and pressed Artyom to the cold steel of the door. It was no longer able to attack: the last bullets had struck its head, and the beast was dead already by the end of its lunge. But the inertia of its body would have been enough to crack Artyom's skull, had he not been wearing a helmet.

The door opened, and a bright, white light burst out. A frightened roar was heard from the escalators: judging by the sound, there were no fewer than five of these beasts there now. Someone's strong hands grasped him by the collar and pulled him inside and the metal clanged once more. They shut the door and bolted it.

'Are you injured?' someone's voice next to him asked.

'Damned if he knows,' another answered. 'Did you see who he brought with him? We barely scared them away the last time, and even then only by using gas.'

'Leave him. He's with me. Artyom! Hey, Artyom! Come to your senses!' someone familiar called, and Artyom opened his eyes with difficulty.

Three men were leaning over him. Two of them, most likely the gate guards, were dressed in dark grey jackets and knitted caps and both wore bullet-proof vests. With a sigh of relief, Artyom recognized Melnik as the third.

'So is this him or what?' one of the guards asked with some disappointment.

'Then take him, only don't forget about the quarantine and the decontamination.'

'Any more lectures?' the stalker grinned. 'Stand up, Artyom. It's been a long time,' he said, extending his hand to him.

Artyom tried to stand up, but his legs refused to work. He swayed and began to feel sick, and he was groggy.

'We have to get him to the infirmary. You help me, and you close the pressure doors,' Melnik commanded.

While the doctor examined him, Artyom studied the white tiles of the operating room. It was sparkling clean, there was the sharp smell of bleach in the air, and several fluorescent lamps were fastened just beneath the ceiling. There were also a few operating tables there, and a box with instruments ready for use hung next to each one.

The condition of the little hospital here was impressive, but why peaceful *Smolenskaya* needed it was unclear to Artyom.

'No fractures, only bruises. Several scratches. We have disinfected them,' the doctor said, wiping his hands with a clean towel.

'Can you leave us for a bit?' Melnik asked the doctor. 'I would like to discuss something in private.'

Nodding knowingly, the medic left.

The stalker, having sat down on the edge of the couch on which Artyom was lying, demanded the details of what had happened.

By his estimate, Artyom was supposed to show up at *Smolenskaya* two hours earlier, and Melnik had already started planning to go up to the surface to try to find him. He listened to the end to the story about the pursuit, but with no special interest, and he called the flying monsters by a dictionary word, 'pterodactyl,' but only the story about how Artyom had concealed himself at the front door really impressed him. Learning that while he was sitting snugly in his apartment someone was creeping along the staircase, the stalker frowned.

'Are you certain that you didn't step in the slime on the stairs?' He shook his head. 'God forbid you bring that crap into the station. I've been telling you not to go near the houses! Consider yourself really lucky that it didn't decide to drop in on you when you were making your visit . . .'

Melnik stood up, went to the entrance where Artyom's boots had been left and meticulously examined the soles of each of them. Not having found anything suspicious, he put them back.

'As I've also said, the road to *Polis* is prohibited to you for the time being. I have not been able to tell the Brahmins the truth; therefore, they think that you both disappeared during the trip to the Library, and I was sent out to search for you. So what happened there to your partner?'

Artyom told him the whole story once more from beginning to end, this time honestly explaining just exactly how Daniel had died. The stalker winced.

'It's better you keep this to yourself. To be honest, I liked the first version a lot more. The second will cause too many questions from the Brahmins. Their man was killed by you, you didn't find the books, so the reward remained yours. And, by the way,' he added, looking sullenly at Artyom, 'what was in that envelope?'

Raising himself on his elbow, Artyom took from his pocket a bag covered with dried blood, looked at Melnik attentively and opened it.

CHAPTER 15

The Map

There was a sheet of paper, taken from a school notebook and folded four times, and a leaf of thick drafting paper with rough pencilled drawings of the tunnels. This was exactly what Artyom had expected to see inside the envelope – a map and the keys to it. While he was running toward *Smolenskaya* across Kalininskiy Prospect, he hadn't had time to think about what may have been inside the bag that Daniel had passed to him. The miraculous resolution of a seemingly insoluble problem, something capable of taking from the *VDNKh* and the whole of the metro an incomprehensible and inexorable threat.

A reddish-brown spot had spread in the middle of the sheet of explanations. The paper, glued fast with the Brahmin's blood, would have to be dampened a bit to reveal its message and great care would have to be taken not to damage the finely written instructions on it.

'Part Number . . . tunnel . . . D6 . . . intact installations . . . up to 400,000 square metres . . . a water fountain . . . not in good working order . . . unforeseen . . .' The words sprang at Artyom. Trying to jump from the horizontal lines, they merged into one whole, and their sense remained absolutely incomprehensible to him. Having despaired of shaping them into something sensible, he handed the message to Melnik. The latter took the sheet into his hand with care and fastened his covetous eyes onto the letters. For some time he didn't say anything, and then Artyom saw how his eyebrows crept upwards with suspicion.

'This can't be,' the stalker whispered. 'It's just all nonsense! They couldn't have overlooked something like this . . .'

He turned the sheet over, looked at it from the other side, and then began to read it again from the very beginning.

'They kept it for themselves . . . They didn't tell the military. Not a surprise, really . . . Show them something like this and they'll immediately take it as something old,' Melnik mumbled indistinctly while Artyom patiently awaited some explanations. 'But did they really overlook it? It's faulty . . . Well, let's assume it is OK . . . That means they must have checked it!'

'Can it really help?': Artyom finally couldn't stand it.

'If everything written here is true, then there's hope,' the stalker nodded.

'What's it about? I didn't understand a thing.'

Melnik didn't answer right away. Once more he read the message to the end, then thought for several seconds and only after that did he begin his tale:

'I had heard about such a thing before. Legends were always flying about, but there are thousands of them in the metro, you see. And we live by legends, and not by bread alone. About University, about the Kremlin and about *Polis* you can't make out what is the truth and what was contrived around a bonfire at Ploshchad Ilicha. And so you see . . . Generally, there were rumours that somewhere in Moscow or outside of Moscow a missile unit had survived. Of course, there is no way that could have happened. Military facilities are always the number one target. But the rumours said they were unsuccessful, or they didn't see it through, or they forgot it – and one missile unit wasn't damaged at all. They said that someone had even walked there, had seen something there, and, allegedly, the installations were beneath a tarpaulin, brand new in the hangars . . . True, there's no need for them in the metro – you can't reach your enemies at such a depth. They stand – well, let them remain standing.'

'What have missile installations got to do with it?' Artyom looked at the stalker in amazement and lowered his feet from the couch.

'The dark ones come to *VDNKh* from the Botanical Garden. Hunter suspected that they come down into the metro from the surface right in that area. It's logical to assume that they live right up there. As a matter of fact, there are two versions. The first says that they come from a place that is like a beehive, figuratively speaking, not far from the metro entrance. The second says that in truth, there is no beehive, and the dark ones come from outside the city. Then there's the question: why haven't we noticed more of them anywhere else? It is illogical.

'Although, perhaps, it's a matter of time. Generally, this is the situation: if they arrive from somewhere far away, we won't be able to do anything with them anyhow. We blow up the tunnels beyond

332

the *VDNKh* or even beyond *Prospect Mir* – sooner or later they'll find new entrances.

'Barricading ourselves in the metro will be our only option, closing ourselves in tight, and forgetting about returning to the surface and forever subsisting on pigs and mushrooms. As a stalker, I can say with certainty that we won't last so long. But! If they have a beehive, and it is somewhere close by as Hunter thought . . .'

'Missiles?' Artyom said at last.

'A salvo of twelve rockets with high explosive fragmentation warheads covers an area of 400,000 square metres,' Melnik read, finding the necessary place in the message. 'Several such salvos from the Botanical Garden will turn them to dust.'

'But you just said that these are legends,' Artyom objected.

'Well, the Brahmins say they aren't.' The stalker waved the sheet. 'It even explains here how to find our way to the location of this military unit. True, it also says that the installations are partially inoperable.'

'Well, just how then do we get there?'

'D-6. It mentions D-6 here. Metro-2. The location of one of the entrances is indicated. They maintain that the tunnel leads from there towards this unit. But they stipulate themselves that unforeseen obstacles may arise on trying to get through to Metro-2.'

'Unseen observers?' Artyom recalled a conversation he had heard once.

'Observers? That's rubbish and nonsense.' Melnik wrinkled his face.

'The missile unit was also just a legend,' Artyom added.

'And it remains a legend as long as I haven't seen it myself,' the stalker cut him short.

'And where is the exit to Metro-2?'

'It's written here: *Mayakovskaya* station. That's strange . . . As many times as I've been to *Mayakovskaya*, I never heard anything like that.'

'So what will we do now?' Artyom was curious.

'Come with me,' the stalker answered. 'You have a bite, relax, and I'll think about it for a while. We'll discuss it tomorrow.'

Only when Melnik began to talk about food did Artyom suddenly become aware of how hungry he was. He sprang to the cold, tiled floor and was at the point of hobbling toward his boots when the stalker stopped him with a gesture.

'Leave your shoes and all your clothes, put them there in that box.

They will clean and disinfect them. They will also check your rucksack. Over there on the table are trousers and a jacket, put those on.'

Smolenskaya looked gloomy: a low semi-circular ceiling and narrow arches in massive walls lined with marble that was once white. Although decorative false columns overhung from the arches and well-preserved plasterwork adorned the walls at the top, all of it only accentuated his first impression.

The station gave the impression of a citadel besieged for a long time that its defenders had adorned in their own manner, giving the place an even more stern appearance. The double cement wall with the massive steel doors along both sides of the pressurized gate, the concrete firing points at the entrances to the tunnels, all said that the inhabitants here had grounds to fear for their safety. Women were hardly seen at *Smolenskaya*, but all the men were carrying weapons. When Artyom asked Melnik directly what happened at this station, the latter only vaguely shook his head and said that he could not see anything unusual here.

However, a strange sensation of tension hanging in the air did not leave Artyom. It was as if everyone here was waiting for something. The stalls were arranged in a line in the centre of the hall, and all the arches were left free, as though they were afraid to obstruct them so as not to hinder an emergency evacuation. At the same time, all the housing was situated exclusively in the spaces between the arches.

Halfway along each train platform, where it went down to the rails, sat duty personnel, who constantly kept the tunnels under observation from both sides. The almost total silence at the station added to the picture. The people here spoke in low voices among themselves, sometimes going into a whisper altogether, as if they were afraid that their voices may drown out some kind of troubling sounds coming from the tunnels.

Artyom tried to recall what he knew about *Smolenskaya*. Did it perhaps have dangerous neighbours? No, on one side the rails led to the bright and safe *Polis*, the heart of the metro, and the other tunnel led to *Kievskaya*, about which Artyom remembered only that it was populated mainly by those very same 'Caucasians' he had seen at *Kitai Gorod* and in the cells of the fascists, at *Pushinskaya*. But these were normal people, and they were hardly worth being so concerned about . . .

A dining room was located in the central tent. Dinner-time,

judging by everything, had already passed, because only a few people remained at the crude, homemade tables. Sitting Artyom at one of the tables, Melnik returned a few minutes later with a bowl in which an unappetizing grey, thin gruel smoked. Under the reassuring glance of the stalker, Artyom dared to try it and didn't stop until the bowl had been emptied. The local dish turned out to be simply remarkable in taste, although it was difficult to define from what specifically it had been prepared. One could say for certain that the cook hadn't spared the meat.

Having finished eating and putting the earthen bowl aside, Artyom calmly looked around. Two men still sat at the neighbouring table, speaking quietly. While they were dressed in conventional quilted jackets, there was something in their appearance that caused him to imagine them in full protective suits and with automatic rifles at the ready.

Artyom caught the look one of them exchanged with Melnik. Not a word was spoken aloud. The man in the quilted jacket examined Artyom casually and returned to his leisurely conversation.

Several more minutes slipped by in silence. Artyom attempted to speak once more with him about the station, but Melnik answered reluctantly and curtly.

Then the man in the quilted jacket stood up from his seat, walked to their table and, leaning towards Melnik, said, 'What will we do with *Kievskaya*? It's coming to a head . . .'

'OK, Artyom, go have a rest,' the stalker said. 'The third tent from here is for guests. The bed has already been made up. I made the arrangements. I'm going to stay here for a while, I have to talk to these guys.'

With a familiar unpleasant feeling as if they had sent him away so that he couldn't overhear adult conversations, Artyom obediently stood up and pushed off towards the exit. At least he'd be able to study the station alone, he consoled himself.

Now, when he was able to take a closer more attentive look, Artyom discovered several more small peculiarities. The hall had been perfectly cleared, and the assorted junk with which the majority of the inhabited stations in the metro were unavoidably filled was completely missing here. And *Smolenskaya* was larger and did not give the appearance of an inhabited station. It suddenly reminded him of a picture from a history book in which a military encampment of Roman legionnaires was depicted. Correctly and symmetrically organized space, which faced in all directions, nothing of excess, sentries placed everywhere and reinforced entrances and exits . . .

He didn't manage to walk around the station for very long. Having been confronted by the frankly suspicious glances of its inhabitants, Artyom understood after only several minutes that they were watching him, and so he preferred to retreat to the guest tent.

A made-up cot really did await him there, and in a corner stood a plastic bag with his name on it.

Artyom sunk into the springs of the squeaking cot and opened the bag. Inside were the things that he had left in the rucksack. Digging in it for a second, he drew from the bag the children's book he had brought from the surface. He wondered if they had checked his little treasure with a Geiger counter. Certainly the dosimeter would have begun to click nervously near the book, but Artyom preferred not to think about it. He leafed through a few pages, making out the slightly faded pictures on the yellowed paper, delaying the moment when he would find his own photograph between the next pages.

Would it be his?

Whatever happened to him now, to the *VDNKh*, and to the whole metro, first he must return to his own station in order to ask Sukhoi, 'Who's in this photo? Is it my mother or not?' Artyom pressed his lips to the picture, then again laid it between the pages and concealed the book back into the rucksack. For a second it had shown to him that something in his life was gradually falling into place. And a moment later, he was asleep.

When Artyom opened his eyes and left the tent, he didn't even consider how much the station had changed. Fewer than ten complete housing units remained there. The rest had been broken or burned. The walls were covered with soot and pocked by bullets, the plaster was crumbling from the ceiling and lay on the floor in large pieces. Around the edges of the platform flowed ominous black rivulets, the precursors of a coming flood. There was hardly anyone in the hall, only a small girl playing with toys alongside one of the tents. From the other platform, where the staircase of a new exit from the station went, muffled screams were heard. Only two surviving emergency lighting lamps dispelled the darkness in the hall.

The submachine gun that Artyom had left at the head of the cot, had disappeared somewhere. Searching the whole stall in vain, he resigned himself to the fact that he had to go unarmed.

Just what had happened here? Artyom would have liked to

question the little girl who was playing, but she, having just seen him, desperately broke into tears so that to get anything from her proved to be impossible.

Leaving the little girl choking in her tears, Artyom carefully passed through the arch and glanced at the path. The first thing that caught his glance was the three bronze letters screwed to the marble facing: 'V. .NKh.' Where the 'D' should have been only a dark trace was visible. A deep crack went across the whole inscription along the marble.

He had to check what was happening in the tunnels. If someone had captured the stations, then, before going back for assistance, he had to explore the situation in order to explain exactly to his allies from the south what danger threatened them.

Immediately after the entrance to the line, there was such an impenetrable darkness that Artyom could see no further than the elbow of his own arm. Something was uttering strange, chomping sounds in the depth of the tunnel, and it was insane to go there unarmed. When the sounds stopped for a short while, he began to hear the water babbling along the floor, flowing round his boots and rushing back, towards *VDNKh*.

His legs shook and refused to step forward. The voice in his head warned over and over again that it was dangerous to go on, that the risk was too great and he would not be able to discern anything in such darkness anyhow. But another part of him, not paying any attention to all those sensible arguments, was pulling him deeper, into the darkness. And, having surrendered himself, he, like a wind-up toy, made one more step ahead.

The darkness surrounding him became total and nothing was visible. A strange sensation arose in Artyom, as if his body had disappeared. Only the rumour of his former self remained and he depended wholly on his mind.

Artyom moved forward for some time more, but the sounds from the direction he was heading did not get nearer. Then others were heard. The rustle of steps, the exact duplicate of those he had been hearing earlier, in the same darkness, but he was unable to recall where exactly and under what circumstances. And with every new step reaching him from the unseen depth of the tunnel, Artyom felt as if a black, cold horror was seeping, drop by drop, into his heart.

In several moments he, not being able to endure it, turned and broke headlong for the station, but, not seeing the cross-ties in the darkness, tripped over one of them and fell, knowing that now the inevitable end had come.

He broke out in a sweat and didn't even consider immediately that he had fallen out the cot during a dream. His head was unusually heavy, a dull pain pulsed in his temples, and Artyom spent another few minutes on the floor, until he finally came to, but even then he was unable to lift himself to his feet.

But at that moment, when his head had cleared a little, the remnants of the nightmare completely vanished, and he was no longer able even to recall approximately just what he had dreamed. Lifting the curtain, he glanced outside. Besides some sentries, there was no one – evidently, it was now night. Deeply inhaling and exhaling the customary damp air several times, Artyom returned to the tent, stretched out on the cot and slept like a log without any dreams.

Melnik woke him. Dressed in a dark insulated jacket with turned-up collar and military trousers with pockets, he looked as if he intended to leave the station any minute now. He had on his head that very same old black field cap, and two large bags, which seemed familiar to Artyom, stood at his feet.

Melnik moved one of them toward Artyom with his boot and said:

'Here. Shoes, a suit, a backpack and weapons. Change your shoes and get ready. You don't have to put on any armour, we don't intend to go to the surface, just bring it along. We leave in half an hour.'

'Where are we going?' Artyom asked, half awake, eyes fluttering and trying to restrain a yawn.

'*Kievskaya*. If you are OK, then along the Ring to *Byelorusskaya* and to *Mayakovskaya*. And there we'll see. Get ready.'

The stalker took a seat on a stool standing in the corner and, pulling a scrap of newspaper from his pocket, began to roll himself a cigarette, looking at Artyom from time to time. Under this watchful eye Artyom was nervous and fumbled everything.

However, after about twenty minutes, he was ready. Not saying a word, Melnik rose from the stool, grabbed his bag and walked to the platform. Artyom looked round the room and followed him.

They passed through an arch and exited toward the paths. Climbing along the wooden staircase added to the path, Melnik nodded to the sentry and began to walk towards the tunnel. Only now did Artyom notice how strangely the entrances to the lines were arranged. On the side of the platform that led to *Kievskaya*, half the path was blocked by a concrete weapon emplacement with narrow gun slots. A metal grate obstructed the passage as well. And there were two sentries on duty. Melnik gabbed with them in short, unintelligible phrases, after which one of the guards opened the hinged lock and pushed the grate.

Along one side of the tunnel stretched spooled black insulation wire, from which weak lamps hung every ten or fifteen metres. But even such poor lighting seemed a real luxury to Artyom. However, after three hundred steps, the wire had become detached, and in this place one more sentry awaited them. There were no uniforms on the patrol members, but they looked much more serious than the military at *Polis*. Knowing Melnik by sight, one of them nodded at him, letting him pass ahead. Stopping at the edge of the lighted space, the stalker took a flashlight from his bag and switched it on.

After another several hundred metres voices were heard ahead and the glows of flashlights appeared. Melnik's submachine gun slid down from his shoulder and ended up in his hands in an imperceptible movement. Artyom followed his example.

Most likely it was another, long-range patrol from *Smolenskaya*. Two strong, armed men in warm jackets with fake fur collars were arguing with three peddlers. The patrol had round knitted caps on their heads, and on the chest of each hung night-vision instruments on leather straps. The two peddlers had weapons with them, but Artyom was ready to bet anything that they were just traders. Huge bales of rags, a map of the tunnels in their hands, the special roguish look, the animatedly shining eyes in the beams of the flashlights, he had seen all of this repeatedly. They let peddlers into all the stations usually without any problems. But, it seemed, no one expected them at *Smolenskaya*.

'Well it's OK, pal, we are going by,' one of the traders was trying to convince a patrol member, a lanky moustached man in a quilted jacket that fit too tightly.

'We have our belongings here, take a look for yourself, we will be trading at *Polis*,' echoed the other peddler, a chunky guy with hair down his eyes.

'What harm is there from us for you? There's only good; here, take a look, jeans just like new, your size for certain, brand name, I'll give them to you for free.' The third had taken the initiative.

The sentry shook his head in silence, blocking their passage. He answered next to nothing, but as soon as one of the peddlers, taking his silence for agreement, tried to step ahead, both sentries nearly simultaneously clacked the bolts of their submachine guns. Melnik and Artyom stood five paces behind them, and though the stalker lowered his weapon, the tension was felt in his attitude.

'Stop! I am giving you five seconds to turn around and leave. It's a secure station, they don't allow anyone here. Five . . . four . . .' One of the sentries began to count.

'Well, how are we supposed to get there, through the Ring again?' One of the peddlers was about to get perturbed, but another, shaking his head resignedly, tugged him by the sleeve and the traders picked up their bales from the ground and dragged themselves back.

Waiting for a minute, the stalker gave Artyom a sign, and they began to walk to *Kievskaya* right behind the peddlers. When they were passing the sentries, one of them silently nodded to Melnik and put two fingers to his head, as if giving a salute.

'A security station?' Artyom was curious, when they themselves had passed the cordon. 'What's that mean?'

'Go back and ask,' the latter snapped, stopping Artyom from asking any more questions.

Although Artyom and Melnik were trying to hold a bit further back from the peddlers walking ahead, the sound of their voices came ever closer, and then suddenly stopped short. But they hadn't passed even twenty paces, when the beam of a light struck them in the face.

'Hey! Who's there? What do you need?' someone cried nervously, and Artyom recognized the voice of one of the traders.

'Calm down. Let us pass, we won't bother you. We're going to *Kievskaya*,' the stalker answered quietly, but clearly.

'Pass, we'll let you go ahead. No use breathing down our necks,' they declared from the darkness after conferring briefly.

Melnik shrugged his shoulders with displeasure and leisurely moved ahead. After about thirty metres that very same trio of peddlers was waiting for them. Upon Artyom and Melnik's approach, the traders politely lowered their wares to the floor, parted and allowed them to pass. The stalker, as if nothing had happened, began walking further on, but Artyom noted that his pace had changed. Now he walked silently, as if hoping to muffle the sounds. Although the peddlers immediately followed them, Melnik didn't look at them once. Artyom himself had been trying to overcome the desire to turn round for a rather long time, about three minutes, but then he looked back anyhow. 'Hey!' a tense voice was heard from behind. 'Wait up there!' The stalker stopped. Artyom began to feel perplexed. Why was Melnik so obediently responding to some petty traders?

'Are they so bitter because of *Kievskaya* or because they are

340

protecting *Polis*?' one of the peddlers asked on catching up with them.

'Naturally because of *Kievskaya*,' Melnik replied, and Artyom felt a pang of jealousy: the stalker hadn't wanted to tell him anything.

'Yeah, I can understand that. It's getting scary at *Kievskaya* now. Well, it's all right. Soon these neatniks from your guard will have to be hot. Everyone will be running to you from *Kievskaya*. Do you understand just who will remain living at the station? It'd be better to be shot,' the lanky peddler mumbled.

'Have you rushed the guns yourself?' the other spitefully har-rumphed. 'Pshaw! Don't pretend you're a hero!'

'Well, you haven't been too hot yourself, either,' the lanky one responded.

'And just what's going on?' Artyom couldn't contain himself.

The two peddlers immediately looked at him as if he had asked a question so stupid that even a child knows the answer. The stalker kept quiet. And the peddlers grew silent and they walked for some time in complete silence. Whether because of this or, perhaps, because the prolonged silence was growing spooky, Artyom suddenly no longer wanted to hear any explanation. And when he had decided he was about to give up on them, the lanky one finally and reluctantly pronounced:

'The tunnels to Park Pobedy are there, right ahead . . .'

Hearing the name of the station, his two fellow travellers pressed closer to each other and Artyom imagined for a second there was the rush of dank tunnel air and the tunnel walls were collapsing. Even Melnik shrugged, as if trying to warm himself. Artyom had never heard anything bad about Park Pobedy and was not able to recall one tale associated with this station. So just why, suddenly, had he become so uneasy at the sound of its name?

'What? Is it getting worse?' the stalker asked gravely.

'What do we know? We are just ordinary folks. We pass it some-times. Stay there, you'll understand,' the bearded one mumbled vaguely.

'People disappear,' the thickset peddler stated under his breath. 'Many are frightened, so they run. One can never make out who has disappeared or who ran away on their own, and it's even more awful for the rest.'

'All these tunnels are damned,' said the lanky one, and he spat at the ground.

'But the tunnels are blocked.' Melnik was stating a fact.

'They've been blocked for a hundred years, but what about since then? Well, if you're a stranger, then it's better you should understand us! Everyone knows there that there is a fear of the tunnels, even though they have been blown up and blocked three times. And anyone can feel it in their skin as soon as they show up here, even Sergeich over there.' The lanky one pointed at his bearded companion.

'Exactly,' the shaggy Sergeich confirmed and he crossed himself for some reason or other.

'But they're guarding the tunnels, aren't they?' Melnik asked.

'The patrols are here every day,' the bearded one nodded.

'And have they ever caught anyone? Or seen someone?' the stalker prodded.

'How would we know?' the peddler gestured helplessly. 'I haven't heard. But they try to catch someone.'

'And what do the locals say about it?' Melnik wasn't backing off.

The lanky one said nothing, he only gestured sombrely but Sergeich glanced back and said in a loud whisper:

'It's the city of the dead,' and thereupon he crossed himself again.

Artyom wanted to burst out laughing: he had already heard too many stories, fables, legends and theories about just where in the dead are found in the metro. And of souls in the pipes along the tunnel walls and the gates to hell, which they are digging at one of the stations . . . now there's a city of the dead at Park Pobedy. But the ghostly draught had caused him to suppress his laughter, and, despite the warm clothing, it had chilled him. Worst of all was the fact that Melnik fell silent and ceased all inquiries. Artyom hoped that his companion was just scornfully waving aside such an absurd idea.

They passed the rest of the way in silence, each of them immersed in his own thoughts. The way proved to be completely quiet, empty, dry and clear but, despite everything, the heavy sensation that something bad awaited them intensified with every step.

As soon as they stepped into the station, this feeling rushed over them, like subterranean waters, just as uncontrollable and just as turbid and chilling.

Fear ruled completely here, and this was apparent at first glance. Was this that 'sunny *Kievskaya*,' about which the man from the Caucasus who was staying with him in a cell in fascist captivity had spoken? Or did he have in mind a station with the same name located at *Filevskaya* branch?

You couldn't say say that the station was neglected and that all its inhabitants had fled. It turned out there were many people here, but *Kievskaya* gave the impression that it did not belong to its residents. They all were trying to stay close together. Tents were stuck to the walls and to each other in the centre of the hall. The distance between them required by the fire safety regulations was not observed anywhere: clearly, these people were frightened of something more dangerous than fire. Those passing by, immediately and wearily looked away when Artyom looked them in the eyes, and, avoiding the strangers, tore from their path, as beetles scurrying along cracks.

The platform, squeezed between two rows of low, round arches, went downward at one side with several of the escalators and, at the other, was raised at the short staircase where the side passage to the other station had been opened. Coals smouldered in several places, and there was a tantalizing aroma of roast meat. Somewhere a child was crying. Though *Kievskaya* was located on the edge of the city of the dead that the frightened peddlers had spoken of, it was fully alive.

Quickly saying goodbye, the peddlers disappeared into the passage to the other line. Melnik, prudently having looked along the sides, resolutely began to walk to the side of one of the passages. It was immediately apparent he had been here regularly. Artyom was unable to fathom why the stalker had questioned the peddlers in such detail about the station.

Had he been hoping that a hint of the true state of affairs be revealed accidentally? Was he trying to flush out possible spies?

They stopped after a second at an entrance to some office facilities. The door here had been knocked off, but a guard stood on the outside. The authorities, Artyom guessed.

A smoothly shaven elderly man with well combed hair came out to meet the stalker. He wore the old, blue uniform of a subway worker, aged and faded by washing, but surprisingly clean. It was clear how he managed to look after himself at this station. The man saluted Melnik, for some reason placing only two fingers to his forehead, and not sincerely, as the patrols had done in the tunnel, but ludicrously. He squinted derisively.

'Good day,' he said in a pleasant deep voice.

'Good day, sir,' the stalker replied and he smiled.

In ten minutes they were seated in a warm room and drinking the best of mushroom tea. This time they didn't leave Artyom out as he had expected, but they allowed him to take part in a discussion of serious matters. Unfortunately, he didn't understand anything of the conversation between the stalker and the station chief, who Melnik called

Arkadiy Semyonovich. At first Melnik asked about a certain Tretyak, then he set about inquiring whether there were any changes in the tunnels. The chief reported that Tretyak had left on personal business, but was supposed to return quite soon, and he proposed they wait for him. Then they both got deeper into the details of some kind of agreements, in such a way that Artyom soon completely lost the thread of the conversation. He just sat there, sipped the hot tea, the mushroom smell of which reminded him of his home station, and looked around. *Kievskaya* clearly had known better times: the walls of the room were hung with moth-eaten carpets with the design preserved. In several places, immediately above the carpets, were fastened pencil sketches of tunnel junctions in wide gilded frames, and the table at which they sat looked like an antique, and Artyom couldn't imagine how many stalkers had been needed to drag it down from someone's empty apartment and how much the station proprietor had agreed to pay for it. On one of the walls hung a sabre that had grown dark with age, and alongside was a pistol of a prehistoric type, clearly unsuitable for firing. At the far end of the room, on a wardrobe, lay a huge white skull that had belonged to an unknown being.

'There is absolutely nothing in these tunnels.' Arkadiy Semyonovich shook his head. 'We keep watch so the people remain calm. You have been there yourself and you know well that both lines have been blocked about three hundred metres from the station. There is no chance that anyone could show up. It's superstition.'

'But people are disappearing?' Melnik frowned.

'They are disappearing,' the chief agreed, 'but it's unknown to where. I think they run off. We don't have any cordons at the passages, and there,' he waved his hand towards the stairs, 'is a whole city. They can go where they like. Both to the Ring and to *Filevskaya*. Hansa, they say, is letting people out of our station now.'

'But what are they afraid of?' asked the stalker.

'Of what? Of the fact that people are disappearing. You go around in circles.' Arkadiy Semyonovich gestured helplessly.

'It's strange,' Melnik said suspiciously. 'You know, while we are waiting for Tretyak, let's go down to the guard again. Just to get acquainted. Or they will worry the Smolenskie.'

'I understand,' the chief nodded. 'Well, you go to the third tent now, Anton lives there. He is commander of the next shift. Tell him you were sent by me.'

It was noisy in the tent with the painted number '3.' Two little lads about ten years of age, played on the floor with the cartridge cases of automatic weapons. Alongside them sat a young girl, who was looking at her brothers with eyes wide with curiosity, but who had not decided to participate in the game. A neat middle-aged, woman in an apron was slicing some kind of food for dinner. It was comfortable here, a delicious domestic smell hung in the air.

'Anton has gone out, have a seat and wait,' the woman offered, smiling cordially.

The boys had begun to gaze at them watchfully, then one of them approached Artyom.

'Do you have any cartridge cases?' he asked, looking at him sullenly.

'Oleg, stop your begging at once!' the woman said sternly, not stopping what she was preparing.

To Artyom's surprise, Melnik put his hand into the pocket of his trousers, fumbled about and withdrew several unusual oblong cartridge cases, clearly not from a Kalashnikov. Jamming them into his fist and jingling them like a rattle, the stalker extended the treasure to the child. His eyes immediately lit up, but he didn't have the courage to take the gift.

'Take them, take them!' The stalker winked at him and dumped the cartridge cases into the child's outstretched palm.

'Now I'll win! Look, how big! It'll be Spetsnaz!' the boy yelled happily.

Watching, Artyom had seen that the cartridge cases with which they played had been laid out in equal rows and, apparently, represented tin soldiers. Even he himself had played like that once, only he had been lucky: he still had real little tin soldiers, though from various collections.

As a battle unfolded on the floor, the father of the children entered the tent. He was a short, thin man with wet dark-blond hair. Seeing the strangers, he nodded at them in silence and, not uttering a word, stared intently at Melnik.

'Papa, Papa, did you bring us some more cartridge cases? Oleg now has more, they gave him some long ones!' the second boy nagged, plucking at the father's trouser leg.

'From the authorities,' the stalker explained. 'We are going on duty with you into the tunnels. Like reinforcements.'

'More reinforcements are out of the question,' muttered the boss of the tent, but the lines of his face had become smooth. 'My name is Anton. We'll just have a bite to eat and go. Have a seat.' He pointed at the stuffed sacks that served as chairs in this home.

Despite the guests' resistance, both partook of a smoking bowl with tubers unfamiliar to Artyom. He looked at the stalker questioningly, but the stalker confidently stabbed a piece on his fork, put it into his mouth and began to chew. Something resembling satisfaction was reflected in his poker face, and this imparted bravery to Artyom. The tubers were totally unlike mushrooms to the taste, they were sweet and a little fatty, and he ate his fill of them in only a few minutes. At first Artyom wanted to ask what they were eating, but then he thought that it would be better for him not to know. They were tasty and OK. Some places they consider rats' brains a delicacy . . .

'Pop, can I go with you, on duty?' having eaten half his portion and spreading the rest along the edges of his plate, the child to whom the stalker had given the cartridge case asked.

'No, Oleg,' the host answered, frowning.

'Olezhenka! What's this about duty? Just what are you thinking? They don't take little boys there!' wailed the woman, taking her son by the hand.

'Mom, what do you mean, little boy?' Oleg said, examining the guests uncomfortably and trying to speak with a deep voice.

'Don't even think about it! Do you want to drive me to hysterics?' The mother had raised her voice.

'Well, fine, fine,' the child mumbled.

But as soon as the woman had gone to the other end of the tent to fetch something else for the table, he tugged his father by the sleeve and loudly whispered:

'But you took me the last time . . .'

'The conversation is finished!' the host said sternly.

'It doesn't matter . . .' Oleg muttered his final words to himself under his breath so that they couldn't be heard clearly.

Having finished eating, Anton stood up from the table, unlocked a metal box standing on the floor, and took an old army AK-47 out of it and said:

'Shall we go? It's a short shift today, I'll be back in six hours,' he reported to his wife.

Both Melnik and Artyom stood immediately. Little Oleg looked in desperation at his father and fidgeted uneasily in his seat, but decided to say nothing.

At the dark tunnel orifice sat a pair of guards on the edge of the platform, legs hanging downward and a third blocked the passages and peered into the darkness. There was stencilling on the wall. 'The *Arbatskaya* Confederation. Welcome!' The letters were half-erased, and it was immediately clear that it hadn't been repainted for a very long time. The guards conversed in a whisper and even hushed one another if one of them suddenly raised his voice.

Besides the stalker and Artyom, two more local men accompanied Anton. Both of them were sombre and not talkative, they looked at the guests malevolently, and Artyom never caught what their names were.

Having exchanged some short phrases with the people protecting the entrance to the tunnel, they stepped down to the paths and slowly moved forward. The tunnel's round arches were perfectly conventional here, the floor and walls appeared untouched by time.

And yet the unpleasant feeling about which the peddlers had spoken had begun to envelop Artyom as soon as he took his first steps.

A dark, inexplicable fear crept out from the depths to greet him. It was quiet on the line. Some human voices were heard in the distance: mostly likely there was a patrol located there, too.

It was one of the strangest posts that Artyom had seen.

Several men sat around on bags filled with sand. In the middle stood a cast-iron stove and, some distance further away, a pail of fuel oil. Only the tongues of flame penetrating the slits in the stove and the light of the flickering wick of an oil lamp suspended from the ceiling illuminated the faces of the patrol members. The lamp swung a little from the stale tunnel air, and therefore, it seemed that the shadows of the people sitting motionless were living their own private lives. The lookout members were sitting with their backs to the tunnel. The air was irritating their eyes.

Protecting their eyes from the blinding rays of the flashlights of the replacements with their hands, the lookouts gathered themselves up to go home.

'Well, how was it?' Anton asked of them, ladling out a scoop of fuel oil.

'How can it be here?' the senior shift member grinned gloomily. 'Like always. Empty. Quiet. Quiet . . .' He snuffed and, having hunched up, began walking towards the station.

While those remaining moved their bags closer to the stove and planted themselves, Melnik turned to Anton: 'Well, shall we continue on and take a look at what's there?'

'There's nothing to see there, it's just blocked, I've already seen it a hundred times. Look, if you want, it's about fifteen metres from here.' Anton pointed over his shoulder in the direction of Park Pobedy.

The tunnel was half destroyed before the blockage. The floor was covered with rock and dirt fragments, the ceiling had sagged in some places and the walls were crumbling and had converged. The warped opening of an entrance to unknown office facilities at the side had grown black, and at the very end of this appendix the rusty rails had been thrust into a pile covered with concrete blocks, mixed with cobblestones and soil. The metal utility line pipes that also stretched along the walls were immersed in this earthen layer.

Lighting the collapsed tunnel with the flashlight and not finding any secret trap doors, Melnik shrugged his shoulders and turned toward the lopsided door. He aimed the beam inside and glanced there, but didn't cross the threshold.

'Are there no changes on the second line either?' he asked of Anton, turning towards the stove.

'It was all like that both ten years ago and now,' the latter replied.

They were silent for some time. With flashlights extinguished, the light once more came only from the loosely covered stove and from the tiny flame behind the sooty glass of the oil lamp, and the darkness around became dense. All the lookouts had bunched around the stove as close as was possible: the yellow beams blocked out the darkness and cold, and one could breathe more freely here. Artyom had endured as much as he could, but the need to hear at least some kind of a sound forced him to overcome his shyness: 'I have never been to your station before,' coughing, he told Anton, 'I don't understand, just why do you have duty here if there's nothing there? You don't even watch in that direction!'

'That's the order of things,' Anton explained. 'They say that is why there's nothing here, since we are on duty.'

'And what's up there further, beyond the blockage?'

'One has to think it's the tunnel All the way to,' he stopped for a second, turning back and looking at the impasse, 'all the way to Park Pobedy.'

'Does anyone live there?'

Anton gave no reply, only vaguely shaking his head. He was silent for a while, but then asked with interest:

'Well, generally speaking, don't you know anything about Park Pobedy?' and, not even waiting for an answer from Artyom, continued, 'Lord knows what is still there now, but previously it was a huge twin station, one of those that was built last of all. Those who are older and visited there back then . . . well . . . until . . . Anyhow, they say that it was made very luxuriously, and the station lay very deep, not like the other new construction. And the people there, one has to think, lived in clover. But not for long. Until the tunnel caved in.'

'But how did it happen?' Artyom asked.

'They say,' Anton glanced at the others, 'that it collapsed by itself. They designed it poorly, or construction materials were stolen, or something else. But it's already so long ago that no one remembers for certain.'

'Well, I heard,' one of the lookouts said, 'that the local authorities blasted both lines to hell. Either they were in competition with Park Pobedy or something else . . . Maybe they were afraid that Park would subjugate them with time. But here at *Kievskaya*, you yourself know at that time who was in command . . . Who was trading fruit at the market earlier. The hot people, who are accustomed to dismantling things. A box of dynamite in this tunnel, a box in that, a bit further from their station, and it's done. Like it's bloodless and the problem is solved.'

'But what happened with them later?' Artyom was curious.

'Well, we just don't know, by then we had already arrived here . . .' Anton was on the verge of beginning, but the talking look-out interrupted him:

'And what could happen? Everyone died. You have to understand, when a station is cut off from the metro, you can't survive there for long. The filters pack up, or the generators, or it begins to flood. And you can't afford to be on the surface even now. I heard, at first they supposedly tried to dig, but later they gave up. Those who served here in the beginning say they heard screams through the pipes . . . But soon even that stopped.'

He gave a cough and stretched out his hands toward the stove. Having warmed his hands, the lookout looked at Artyom and added, 'It wasn't even the war. Just who fights like that? They had women with them, you know, and there were children. Old folks . . . A whole city. And for what? Simple, they didn't divide up any money. It seems they didn't kill anyone themselves, but oh well. So you were asking, "What's there, on that side of the blockage?" Death is there.'

Anton shook his head, but didn't say anything. Melnik looked at Artyom with attention, and nearly opened his mouth, as if intending to add something to the story he had heard, but had second thoughts. Artyom had got really cold, and he also stretched toward the stove. He tried to imagine what it meant to live at this station, the inhabitants of which believe that the rails leaving their home lead directly to a kingdom of death.

Artyom gradually began to understand that the strange duty in this broken-up tunnel was not so much necessary, but more of a ritual. Who were they trying to scare away while sitting here? Who were they able to stop coming to the station, and into the rest of the metro? It became even colder, and neither the cast-iron stove nor the warm jacket given him by Melnik spared him any longer from the chill.

Unexpectedly the stalker turned towards the tunnel leading to *Kievskaya* and got up from his seat, listening and watching. Even Artyom understood the reason for his concern in several seconds. Quick, soft steps were heard from there, and in the distance the glow of a weak flashlight was being thrown about, as if someone was hurrying, jumping over the ties, hurrying with all his might to get to them.

The stalker jumped from his seat, pressed against the wall and aimed his submachine gun at the spot of light.

Anton calmly stood up, peering into the darkness, and by his easy posture it was clear that he couldn't imagine any serious danger which would come from that side of the tunnel.

Melnik clicked the switch of his flashlight, and the dark crawled away unwillingly. At about thirty feet from them, in the middle of the track bed, a fragile little figure stood still with his arms lifted.

'Pop, Pop, it's me, don't shoot!' The voice was a child's.

The stalker brought his beam to bear in that direction and, shaking himself, lifted himself from the ground. The child was standing by the stove in only a minute, examining his boots with embarrassment. It was Anton's son, the one who had asked to go on duty with him.

'Has something happened?' his father asked worriedly.

'No . . . I just wanted to be with you very much. I'm no longer a little boy to be sitting in the tent with Mom.'

'How did you get here? There's a guard there!'

'I lied. I said that Mom sent me to see you. It was Uncle Petya, he knows me. He only said that I mustn't look into any of the side paths and get here quickly, and he allowed me to pass.'

'We'll be talking to Uncle Petya again,' Anton promised solemnly. 'And you think for a while how you will explain this to your mother. I won't let you go back alone.'

'Can I stay with you?' The child wasn't able to contain his delight and began to hop about.

Anton moved to the side, sitting his son on the warm bags. He took off his jacket and was on the verge of wrapping him up, but the child immediately scrambled down to the floor and, taking the stuff brought with him from his pocket, spread it out on a cloth: a handful of cartridge casings and several more objects. He sat beside Artyom, and the latter had time to study all these things.

A small metal box with a handle that turned was the most interesting. When Oleg held it in one hand and turned the handle with the fingers of the other, the little box, emitting ringing metallic sounds, began to play a simple mechanical melody. And it was amusing that it was worth leaning it against another object, because that one began to resonate, amplifying the sound by many times. It came from the iron stove best of all, but it wasn't possible to leave the device there long, because it got hot too quickly. It had become so interesting to Artyom that he decided to try it himself.

'What on earth!' the boy said, giving him the hot box and blowing on his burnt fingers. 'I'll show you such a trick later!' he promised conspiratorially.

The next half hour slipped by slowly. Artyom, not noticing the angry glances of the lookouts, endlessly turned the handle and listened to the music, Melnik whispered something to Anton, and the child played on the floor with his cartridge cases. The melody from the tiny music box was rather dreary, but charming in its own way. It was just impossible to stop.

'No, I don't understand,' the stalker said and stood up from his seat. 'If both tunnels have been brought down and are being protected, just where, in your opinion, do the people disappear to?'

'And who said that it's all in these tunnels?' Anton looked him up and down. 'And there are passages to other lines, two altogether, and lines to *Smolenskaya* . . . I think someone simply is making use of our superstitious beliefs.'

'Just what superstitions!' interrupted the lookout who had told them about the blowing up of the tunnel and the people who were left on the other side. 'The curse of our station is that it stopped with Park Pobedy. And we all are damned that we live at it . . .'

'And you, Sanych, are muddying the waters,' Anton cut him short with displeasure. 'Here the people are asking about serious things and you are spreading your tales about!'

'Let's take a walk. I saw some doors along the way and a side exit. I want to take a look,' Melnik said to him. 'The people are frightened at *Smolenskaya*, too. Kolpakov was personally interested.'

'Well, now he has got interested, right?' Anton smiled sadly.

'They are even throwing questions at *Polis* already.' The stalker pulled a folded sheet of newspaper from his pocket.

Artyom had seen such papers at *Polis*. At one of the passages stood a tray where it was possible to buy them, but they cost ten cartridges and paying so much for a sheet of wrapping paper with poorly printed gossip on it was not worth it. Melnik, it seemed, didn't regret the cartridges.

Several short articles huddled under the proud name 'Metro News' on the roughly cut yellowish sheet. One of the pieces was even accompanied by a black and white photograph. The banner ran: 'Mysterious Disappearances at *Kievskaya* Continue.'

'The smokers are still alive, they say.' Anton carefully took the newspaper in his hands and smoothed it out. 'OK, let's go, I'll show you your side branches. Will you stop reading?'

The stalker nodded. Anton stood, looked at his son and said to him:

'I'll be right back. Look, don't be naughty here without me,' and, turning toward Artyom, asked, 'Look after him, be a pal.'

There was nothing left for Artyom to do but nod.

As soon as his father and the stalker had gone a bit further away, Oleg jumped up, took the box away from Artyom with a naughty look, yelled at him, 'Catch me!' and broke into a run towards the dead end. Recalling that the boy was now his responsibility, Artyom guiltily looked at the rest of the lookouts, lit his flashlight and went after Oleg.

He didn't investigate the half-destroyed office facility, as Artyom feared he might. He was waiting right next to the blockage.

'See what happens now!' the lad said.

Oleg scrambled onto the stones, reached the level of the pipes and disappeared into the blockage. Then he took out his box, placed it against the pipe and turned the handle. 'Listen!' he said.

The pipe began to hum, resonating, and it was as if it all had been filled from within by the simple, doleful melody the music box was playing. The boy pressed his ear to the pipe and, as if bewitched, continued to turn the handle, drawing the sounds from the metallic box.

He stopped for a second, listening, smiled happily and then jumped down from the pile of stones and extended the music box to Artyom:

'Here, try it yourself!'

Artyom was able to imagine how the sound of the melody would change as it passed through the hollow metal pipe. But the child's eyes were so bright, that he decided not to behave like the ultimate pain in the neck. Leaning the box against the pipe, he pressed his ear to the cold metal and began to turn the handle. The music began to resound so loudly that he nearly jerked his head away. The laws of acoustics were not familiar to Artyom, and he was unable to understand by what miracle this piece of metal could so amplify the melody inside such a feebly tinkling box.

Turning the handle for several more seconds and playing the short tune a good three times, he nodded to Oleg:

'It's splendid.'

'Listen again!' he began to laugh. 'Don't play, just listen!'

Artyom shrugged and looked at the post to see if Melnik and Anton had returned, and once more placed his ear to the pipe. What could one possibly hear now? The wind? The echo of a scary noise that flooded the tunnels between *Alekseeva* and *Prospect Mir*?

From an unimaginable distance, making their way through the earth's stratum with difficulty, came muffled sounds. They came from the direction of the dead Park Pobedy. There could be no doubt about it. Artyom stood stock still, listening, and, gradually becoming chilled, understood: he was listening to something impossible – music.

Someone or something several kilometres away from him was duplicating that melancholy melody from the music box one note after another. But this was not an echo: the unknown performer had erred in several places, shortened a note somewhere, but the motif remained completely recognizable. And, mainly, it was not at all a ringing chime, the sound resembled more of a hum . . . Or singing? The indistinct chorus of a multitude of voices? No, a hum all the same . . .

'What, is it playing?' Oleg asked of him with a smile.

'Hush! I'm still listening! What is it?' Barely parting his lips, Artyom mumbled hoarsely.

'Music! The pipe is playing!' the boy explained simply.

The melancholy, oppressive impression that this eerie singing produced in Artyom, it seemed, was not passed on to the lad. For him, it was simply a happy game, and he could never ask how he could hear a melody from a station cut off from the whole world, where all the living had vanished into thin air more than a decade ago.

Oleg again climbed up onto the stones, on the verge of preparing to start his little machine again, but Artyom suddenly felt inexplicably fearful for him and for himself. He grabbed the lad by the hand and, not paying any attention to his protests, dragged him back to the stove.

'Coward! Coward!' Oleg screamed. 'Only children believe in these tales!'

'What tales?' Artyom stopped and looked him in the eyes.

'That they take the children who go into the tunnels to listen to the pipes!'

'Who takes them?' Artyom dragged him closer to the stove.

'The dead!'

The conversation stopped: a lookout speaking about damnation roused himself and gave them such a once over that the words stuck in their throats.

Their adventure had ended right on time: Anton and the stalker were returning to the post, and someone else was walking with them. Artyom quickly planted the boy in his seat. The child's father had asked him to look after Oleg, and not to indulge in his whims . . . And who knew what superstitions Anton himself believed?

'Excuse me, we've been delayed.' Anton sank onto the sacks beside Artyom. 'He wasn't naughty, was he?'

Artyom shook his head, hoping that the lad had enough sense not to brag about their adventure. But he, it seemed, understood everything himself just fine. Oleg again laid out his cartridge cases with an enthralled look.

The third man who had arrived with Anton and the stalker, a balding, skinny man with sunken cheeks and bags under his eyes, was unfamiliar to Artyom.

He approached the stove only for a minute and nodded at the lookouts, and Artyom examined him closely, but he didn't say anything to him. Melnik introduced him.

'This is Tretyak,' he told Artyom. 'He'll be going on ahead with us. He's a specialist. A missile man.'

CHAPTER 16

The Songs of the Dead

'There are no secret entrances there, and there never were. Really, don't you know that yourself?' Tretyak had raised his voice with displeasure, and his words flew at Artyom.

They were returning from duty – back to *Kievskaya*. The stalker and Tretyak walked a little behind the others and animatedly discussed something. When Artyom also fell back to take part in their conversation, they began to whisper, and he was left to join the main group again. The young Oleg, who was skipping along, trying not to drop behind the adults, and refusing to climb onto his father's shoulders, immediately and happily grabbed him by the hand.

'I'm a missile man, too!' he announced.

Artyom looked at the boy with surprise. He had been alongside when Melnik introduced Tretyak to him and most likely had heard this word by chance. Did he understand what it meant?

'Only don't tell anybody!' added Oleg hurriedly. 'The others aren't allowed to know it. It's a secret.'

'OK, I won't tell anyone.' Artyom played up to him.

'It's no shame, quite the opposite. You should be proud of it, but others might say bad things about you out of envy,' the boy explained, although Artyom hadn't even intended to ask anything.

Anton was walking about ten paces ahead, lighting the path. Nodding at his frail figure, the child loudly whispered:

'Papa said not to show anyone, but you know how to keep secrets. Here!' He took a small fragment of cloth from an inside pocket.

Artyom shined his flashlight on it. It was a torn tab – a circle of a thick, rubberized substance, about seven centimetres in diameter.

On one side it was completely black, on the other was portrayed the intersection of three incomprehensible oblong objects on a dark background, not unlike one of the six-pointed paper snowflakes with which they decorated *VDNKh* for the New Year.

One of the objects was standing upright and Artyom recognized it as a cartridge from a machine gun or a sniper's rifle, but with wings attached to the bottom. But he did not recognize the other two identical, yellow ones, with rings on both sides. The mysterious snowflake was enclosed in a stylized wreath, such as on old cockades, and there were letters around the circle of the tab. But the colour on them was faded so that Artyom was able to read only, '. . . troops and ar . . .', and also the word '. . ussia', which was written below, beneath the figure. If he had had a little more time, he might have been able to understand what the boy showed him, but he didn't.

'Hey, Olezhek! Come here, there's something for you!' Anton called to his son.

'What is it?' Artyom asked the boy, before he grabbed the tab from him and concealed it in his pocket.

'RVA!' Oleg carefully articulated, beaming with pride, then he winked at him and ran to his father.

Having climbed to the platform by stepladder, the outlook members began to disperse and go home. Anton's wife was waiting for him right at the exit. With tears in her eyes, she flung herself to meet young Oleg, caught him by his arm, and then bawled at her husband:

'Are you trying to upset me? What am I supposed to think? The child left home several hours ago! Why am I supposed to think about everyone? You're like a child yourself, you couldn't bring him home!' she cried.

'Len, please, not in front of people,' Anton muttered, looking round in embarrassment. 'I just couldn't leave the watch. Think about what you are saying, an outpost commander and suddenly he leaves his post . . .'

'A commander! Go ahead and command! As if you don't know what is going on here! Over there, a neighbour's youngster disappeared a week ago . . .'

Melnik and Tretyak quickened the pace and didn't even stop to say goodbye to Anton, leaving him and his wife in private. Artyom hurried after them. For a long time after, although one could no longer make out the words, the weeping and reproaches of Anton's wife reached them.

All three were heading to the office facilities, where the station's chief of staff was located. After several minutes they already were seated in the room with the hanging threadbare carpets. The chief himself, having nodded knowingly, left when the stalker asked to leave them alone.

'It seems you don't have a passport?' Melnik remarked, turning towards Artyom.

He shook his head. The document had been confiscated by the fascists and, without it, he had been turned into a social outcast.

Hansa, the Red Line and *Polis* would not accept him. While the stalker was beside him, no one asked personal questions of Artyom, but, having found himself alone, he would have to wander between the cast-off flag stations and the uncivilized stations, such as *Kievskaya*. And he couldn't even dream of returning to *VDNKh*.

'I won't be able to take you to Hansa without a passport. I'll have to find the necessary people for it first,' Melnik said, as if confirming his thoughts. 'It may be possible to obtain a new one, but of course this will take time. The shortest route to *Mayakovskaya* is along the Ring, like it or not. What do we do?'

Artyom shrugged his shoulders. He was inclined to agree with the stalker. It was impossible to wait, and he also wasn't able to get around Hansa to *Mayakovskaya* himself. The tunnel that adjoined it from the other side came straight from *Tverskaya*. To return to the lair of the fascists, let alone to the station that had been transformed into a dungeon, would be folly. A dead end.

'It will be better if Tretyak and I go together now to *Mayakovskaya*,' Melnik said. 'We'll look for an entrance to D-6. We will find it, return for you, and perhaps something will come up about a passport. If we don't find an entrance, we'll come back anyway. You won't have to wait for us long. We can get there quickly. We'll get it done in a day. Will you wait?' He looked at Artyom quizzically.

Artyom shrugged his shoulders again. He felt that they were treating him like a child. He'd served his purpose and told them about the danger and now they didn't want him under their feet.

'Excellent,' the stalker said. 'Expect us us towards morning. And we'll travel straight here so as not to lose any time. As regards food and lodging, we will discuss it all with Arkadiy Semyonovich. He won't hurt you. It seems that's it . . . No, it's not all.' He felt in a pocket and withdrew from there that same bloodstained sheet of paper on which was the layout and keys. 'Take it, I copied it for myself. Who knows how things will turn out. Only don't show it to anyone . . .'

Melnik and Tretyak left in less than an hour later, having spoken beforehand with the station chief. The punctual Arkadiy Semyonovich immediately took Artyom to his tent and, inviting him to have dinner with him in the evening, left to rest.

The tent for guests stood a little out of the way and although it also was maintained in fine condition, Artyom felt very uncomfortable in it from the very outset. He glanced outside and again was convinced that the rest of the quarters were crowded together, and all of them were located as far as possible from the entrances to the tunnels. Now that the stalker had gone and Artyom was alone in the unfamiliar station, the sensation of unease that he had experienced earlier returned. It had been scary at *Kievskaya* in just the same way, simply frightening, without any obvious cause. It was already getting late. The voices of the children were dying away, and the adults only rarely left their tents. Artyom did not want to stroll around the platform at all. Having read through the letter from the dying Daniel a third time, Artyom couldn't stand it and left for dinner with Arkadiy Semyonovich half an hour earlier than the agreed time.

The office facility's anteroom now had been converted into a kitchen, and an attractive girl, a little older than Artyom, was working there. Meat and some kind of root vegetables were stewing in a large frying pan, and boiling next to them were some of the white tubers which he'd eaten at Anton's. The station chief himself sat next to a stool and paged through a tattered booklet, on the cover of which was painted a picture of a revolver and women's legs in black stockings. Seeing Artyom, Arkadiy Semyonovich laid the book aside with embarrassment.

'It's boring for us here, of course.' He smiled knowingly at the youth. 'Come with me into the office. Katerina will lay the table for us there. And we'll drink for a while.' He winked. Now the room with the carpets and skull looked completely different: lit by a table lamp with a green cloth lampshade, it had become a little more comfortable. The tension which had haunted Artyom on the platform, dissipated without a trace in the rays of this lamp. Arkadiy Semyonovich drew a small bottle from the cupboard and poured a brown liquid with a head-reeling aroma into an unusual round-bellied glass. Only a little came out, a finger's worth, and Artyom thought that this bottle must have cost more than a whole box of the home-brew he had tried at *Kitai Gorod*.

'A little cognac.' Arkadiy Semyonovich responded to his curious look. 'Armenian, of course, but it's almost thirty years old. Bottoms up.' The chief dreamily looked up at the ceiling. 'Don't be afraid, it's not contaminated, I checked it myself with the dosimeter.'

The unfamiliar drink was very strong, but the pleasant flavour and sharp aroma made it palatable. Artyom didn't swallow it all at once, but tried to savour it, following the example of his host. A fire was slowly breaking out inside him, it seemed, but it gradually cooled and turned into an acceptably comforting heat. The room had become even more agreeable, and Arkadiy Semyonovich even more likeable.

'A surprising thing,' screwing up his eyes in satisfaction, Artyom commented.

'It's good, right? About a year and a half ago the stalkers found completely untouched groceries at *Krasnopresenskaya*,' the station chief explained, 'in a cellar, as they often had done previously. The sign had fallen off and no one had noticed it. But one of us recalled that earlier, before it had crashed, sometimes he had looked in there, so he decided to check it. It had been there so many years it had became better. Because we knew each other, he gave me two bottles for a hundred bullets. They ask two hundred for one at *Kitai Gorod*.'

He took one more small swallow, then thoughtfully looked at the lamp's light through the cognac.

'They called him Vasya, this stalker,' the chief informed him. 'He was a good man. Not some kind of kid who runs after nothing, but a serious young man. He fetched all the good things. As soon as he returned from above, he came to me first. Well, he says, Semyonych, some new supplies.' Arkadiy Semyonovich smiled weakly.

'Did something happen to him?' Artyom asked.

'He loved *Krasnopresenskaya* very much He repeated all the time that it was a real El Dorado there,' Arkadiy Semyonovich said sadly. 'Nothing touched in one Stalinist high-rise . . . It's understandable why it was there all safe and sound . . . The zoo was right across the road. Just who would poke their head in there, at *Krasnopresenskaya*? Such fear . . . He was desperate, Vasyatka, he was always taking risks. And he got into a mess at the end. They dragged him into the zoo, and his partner barely managed to bolt. So, let's drink to him.' The chief breathed heavily and poured one more for each of them.

Recalling the unusually high price of the cognac, Artyom was on the verge of protesting, but Arkadiy Semyonovich decisively placed the round-bellied glass into his hand, explaining that a refusal would insult the memory of the reckless stalker who had obtained this divine drink.

By that time, the girl had set the table and Artyom and Arkadiy

Semyonovich moved on to ordinary, but decent, moonshine. The meat had been prepared delightfully.

'It's unpleasant for you at the station.' After an hour and a half Artyom was frank. 'It's scary here, something is oppressive . . .'

'We're used to it.' Arkadiy Semyonovich vaguely shook his head. 'And people live here. It's no worse than at some . . .'

'No, don't think that I don't understand.' Having decided that the *Kievskaya* chief had taken offence, Artyom hastened to calm him. 'You, certainly, are doing all that is possible . . . But there is something going on here. Everyone talks about just one thing: that people are disappearing.'

'They lie!' Arkadiy Semyonovich cut him off. But then he added, 'Not all are disappearing. Only the children.'

'Are the dead taking them?'

'Who knows who is taking them? I myself don't believe in the dead. I have seen dead in my lifetime, make no mistake. They don't take anyone anywhere. They themselves lie quietly. But there, beyond the blockage,' Arkadiy Semyonovich waved a hand in the direction of Park Pobedy and nearly lost his balance, 'is someone. That's definite. And it is impossible for us to go there.'

'Why?' Artyom tried to focus on his glass, but it had been growing fuzzier the whole time and seemed to creep away somewhere.

'Wait a little, I'll show you . . .'

The station chief moved away from the table with a crash, got up with difficulty and, rocking, went to the cupboard. Digging around on one of the shelves, he carefully lifted into the light a long metal needle with a barb by the thick end.

'What's that?' Artyom frowned.

'That's what I would like to know . . .'

'Where did you get it?'

'From the neck of a lookout who was guarding the right tunnel. Hardly any blood came out, but he lay there all blue, and foaming at the mouth.'

'Did they come from Park Pobedy?' Artyom was guessing.

'Damned if anyone knows,' mumbled Arkadiy Semyonovich and at the same time he upset their glasses. 'Only,' he added, putting the needle back into the cupboard, 'don't tell anyone.'

'But why haven't you told anyone yourself? They'll help you and people will settle down.'

'Well, no one would settle down, everyone would run away, like rats! They're already running now . . . Not to defend themselves from anyone here, there is no enemy. He isn't visible, and that's why it's frightening. So, I show them this needle, and what? Do you think everything will settle? That's ridiculous! Everyone will disappear, the bastards, and leave me here alone! And what kind of a station chief will I be without people? A captain without a ship!' He had raised his voice, but he let out a squeak and was silent.

'Arkasha, Arkasha, you don't have to be like that, everything's OK . . .' The girl sat down, startled, beside him, and stroked his head. Artyom sadly understood through the alcoholic fog that she wasn't the chief's daughter.

'All of them, the sons of bitches, will run! Like rats from a ship! I'll be alone! But we won't give in!' He hadn't calmed down.

Artyom stood up with difficulty and unsteadily walked toward the exit. The guard at the door quizzically snapped his fingers in his face, nodding at Arkadiy Semyonovich's office.

'Dead drunk,' Artyom muttered. 'It's better not to touch him until tomorrow.' And, rocking slightly, he plodded towards his tent.

He had to find the way. He tried a few times to get into someone else's quarters, but crude male curses and piercing female squeals told him that he had gone into the wrong tent. The moonshine had turned out to be more potent than cheap home-brew, and he had started to feel its full strength only now. The arches and columns floated before his eyes and, to top it off, he was beginning to feel sick.

At a normal hour, perhaps, someone would have helped Artyom reach the guest tent, but now the station seemed completely empty. Even the posts at the exits from the tunnels were likely to have been abandoned.

Three or four dim lamps remained lit in the whole station, and, apart from those, the whole platform had been plunged into darkness. When Artyom stopped and looked around more attentively, it began to appear to him that the gloom had been filled by something and it was stirring quietly. Not believing his eyes, he plodded in the direction of one especially suspicious place with the curiosity and bravery of a drunk. Not far from the transfer to the *Filevskaya* line, at one of the arches, the movements of blobs of darkness were not gradual, as in other corners, but sharp and almost deliberate.

'Hey! Who's there?' Having approached to a distance of about fifteen steps, he cried out.

No one answered, but it seemed to him that an elongated shadow was oozing out of a particularly dark spot. It almost merged with the gloom. However, Artyom was certain that someone was looking at him from the darkness. He was shaking but kept his balance and took another step.

The shadow abruptly decreased in size, as if it had shrunk, and slipped away. A sudden, sickening smell struck his nostrils and Artyom recoiled. What did it smell like? A picture of something he had seen in the tunnel on the approaches to the Fourth Reich arose in front of his eyes: bodies heaped on each other with hands tied behind their backs. The smell of decomposition?

At that very moment with a hellish speed, like an arrow flying from a crossbow, the shadow dashed towards him. A pallid face covered with strange spots, with deeply sunken eyes, appeared in front of his eyes for a second.

'The dead!' wheezed Artyom.

Then his head split into thousands of parts, the ceiling began to dance and turn over, and everything was fading away. Emerging and submerging into a feeble quiet, some kind of voices could be heard, some kind of visions flashed up then disappeared.

'Mama won't let me, she'll be upset,' the child said from not far away. 'It was really impossible today, she cried all evening. No, I am not afraid, you are not frightful, and you sing beautifully. I just don't want Mama to cry again. Don't feel hurt! Well, for a short while maybe . . . Will we return before morning?'

'. . . Time's a-wasting. Time's a-wasting,' a low male voice repeated.

'We don't have all day. They're close enough already. Get up. Don't lie there. Get up! If you lose hope, if you flinch or give up, others will quickly take your place. I'm continuing the struggle. You should, too. Get up! You don't understand . . .'

'Who is it again? To the chief? As a guest? Well, of course, I'll bring one! Go ahead, you help too . . . Shake a leg, at least. Severe . . . Don't you care what he has there jingling in his pockets. Well, OK, I'm joking. That's all. We've gone as far as we can. And I won't, I won't. I'm leaving . . .'

The tent's flap was dramatically moved aside, and the beam of a flashlight struck him in the face.

'Are you Artyom?' He could barely make out the face, but the voice sounded young. Artyom jumped up from the cot, but his head suddenly began to spin, and he felt ill. A dull pain throbbed in the back of his head and each time he touched it, it felt like fire. His hair was matted there, most likely from dried blood. What had happened to him?

'May I come in?' the arrival asked and, not waiting for permission, stepped into the tent, closing the flap behind him. He shoved a tiny metallic object into Artyom's hand. Having finally turned on his own flashlight, Artyom looked at it. It was a cartridge converted to a screw-on capsule, exactly the same as the one Hunter had presented to him. Not believing his own eyes, Artyom tried to open the top, but it slipped. His hands were sweating from the excitement. Finally a tiny piece of paper fell into the light. Was it really a missive from Hunter? 'Unforeseen complications. The exit to D-6 has been blocked. Tretyak has been killed. Wait for me, don't go anywhere. We need time to get organized. I will try to return as soon as possible. Melnik.' Artyom re-read the note yet again, to analyse its contents. Tretyak has been killed? The exit to Metro-2 is blocked? But then this meant that all their plans and all their hopes had turned to dust and ashes! He looked at the envoy in a befuddled manner.

'Melnik has ordered you to stay here and wait for him,' the visitor confirmed.

'Tretyak is dead. They killed him. With a poisoned needle, Melnik said. We don't know who did it. Now he'll be leading a mobilization effort. That's it, I have to run. Will there be an answer?' Artyom thought a little about what he could write to the stalker. What can I do? What is there to hope for now? Maybe drop everything and return to *VDNKh* to be with those near and dear in the last minutes? He shook his head. The envoy turned around in silence and exited. Artyom dropped to the cot and began to meditate. There was simply nowhere for him to go right now. He was neither able to go to the Ring nor return to *Smolenskaya* without a passport and without an escort. His only hope was that Arkadiy Semyonovich would be just as hospitable in the coming days as he had been the day before.

It was 'day' at *Kievskaya*. The lamp burnt twice as brightly, and alongside the office facilities, where the station chief's apartment was located, another mercury lamp gave off the light of day. Wincing from the pain in his head, Artyom plodded to the chief's office. A guard stopped him at the entrance with a gesture. Noise came from within. Several men were conversing in raised voices. 'He's busy,' the guard explained. 'Wait if you'd like.'

Several minutes later Anton flew from the room like a shot. The office boss ran out right on his heels. Although his hair was perfectly combed once more, he had bags beneath his eyes, and his face was noticeably swollen and covered with silver stubble.

'But what can I do? What?' the chief cried, chasing after Anton, and then, spitting, smacked himself with his hand on the forehead. 'Are you up?' Having noticed Artyom, he smiled wryly.

'I have to stay here with you until Melnik returns,' Artyom declared apologetically.

'I know, I know. They reported it. Let's go inside, they gave me an order concerning you.' Arkadiy Semyonovich invited him into the room with a gesture.

'So, I've been told to photograph you for a passport while you wait for Melnik. I still have the equipment here from when *Kievskaya* was a normal station . . . Then maybe he'll acquire a blank passport and we'll make the document for you.'

Sitting Artyom onto a stool, he pointed the lens of a small plastic camera at him. There was a blinding flash, and Artyom spent the next five minutes completely blinded, looking around helplessly.

'Excuse me, I forgot to warn you . . . You're starving. Come in, Katya will feed you, but I won't have any time for you today. It's getting worse for us here. Anton's oldest son disappeared during the night. He's giving the whole station a hard time now . . . And for what? And those here told me they found you this morning between the platforms? With a bloody head? What happened?'

'I don't remember . . . Most likely I fell down when I was drunk.' Artyom hadn't answered immediately.

'Yes . . . It's good that we had a sit-down yesterday,' the chief grinned. 'OK, Artyom, it's time for me to get to work. Drop by a little later.'

Artyom slid down from the stool. The young Oleg's face was in front of him. Anton's oldest son . . . Was it really him? He recalled how the night before the boy had turned the handle of his music box, placed it on the iron of the pipe and then said that only small children are afraid that the dead would take them away if they walked into the tunnels and listened to the pipes. A chill swept over Artyom. Was it true? Did it happen because of him? Once more he glanced helplessly at Arkadiy Semyonovich, began to open his mouth, but he went outside without speaking.

Returning to his tent, Artyom took a seat on the floor and sat in silence for some time, looking into the void. Now it was beginning to seem to him that, having chosen him for this mission, someone unknown had damned him at the same time: almost everyone who had decided to share at least part of the way with him had died. Bourbon, Mikhail Porfirievich and his grandson, Daniel . . . Khan had disappeared without a trace, and even the fighters of the revolutionary brigade who had rescued Artyom may have been killed at the very next crossing. Now Tretyak. But the young Oleg? Had Artyom brought death to his companions?

Not understanding what was going on, he jumped up, threw his rucksack and machine gun onto his back, grabbed a flashlight and went out to the platform. He walked mechanically to the place where they had assaulted him during the night.

Approaching closer, he froze. The dead man looked at him through the dim haze of a drunken memory. He remembered it all. It was not a dream. He had to find Oleg or at least help Anton search for his son. It was his fault. He hadn't looked after the lad. He had allowed Oleg to play his strange games with the pipes, and now he was here, safe and sound, but the boy had disappeared. And Artyom was convinced that he had not run away. Something bad and inexplicable had happened here during the night, and Artyom was doubly guilty, because he may have been able to prevent it, but he had been incapable.

He looked at the spot where the terrifying stranger had hidden in the shadows. A heap of garbage had been dumped there, but, sifting through it, Artyom only frightened a stray cat. Having searched the platform without result, he approached the tracks and jumped down to the rails. The guards at the entrance to the tunnel lazily looked him over and warned that he went into the crossings at his own risk and that no one there would take any responsibility for him.

This time Artyom didn't go through the same tunnel as the day before, but took the second, the parallel one. As the lookout commander had said, this crossing was also blocked. The guard post was located at the blockage: an iron barrel served as a stove, and there were bags piled around. Alongside them there was a handcar, loaded with buckets of coal.

The lookouts sitting on the bags were whispering about something and, on his approach, jumped up from their seats, intently eying Artyom. But then one of them gave the OK and the others calmed down and settled in as before. Taking a closer look, Artyom recognized Anton as the commander, and hurriedly mumbling something awkward, turned and began to walk back. His face was on fire; he was unable to look into the eyes of the man whose son had disappeared because of him.

Artyom plodded on, lowering his head, repeating under his breath: 'It wasn't my fault . . . I wasn't able . . . What could I have done?' The splash of light from his flashlight skipped ahead of him.

Suddenly he noticed a small object lying desolately in the shadow between two ties. Even from the distance it seemed familiar to him, and his heart beat faster. Bending over, Artyom picked the small box off the ground. He turned the handle and the box answered with that tinkling dreary melody. Oleg's music box. Thrown or accidentally dropped by him here.

Artyom threw down his rucksack and began studying the tunnel walls twice as hard. Not far away was a door leading to office facilities, but Artyom discovered behind it only a ruined public loo. Twenty more minutes of tunnel inspection didn't get him anywhere.

Returning to his rucksack, the young man sank to the ground and leaned back against the wall. Throwing back his head, stared at the ceiling, exhausted. After a second he once more was on his feet and the beam of the flashlight, fluttering, revealed a black gap, hardly noticeable in the darkened concrete of the ceilings. There was a loosely closed hatch just above the very place where Artyom had picked up Oleg's music box. However, there was no way to reach the hatch. The ceiling was more than three metres high.

A solution presented itself to him in a flash. Grasping the box he had found and throwing his rucksack onto the rails, Artyom raced back to the lookouts. He was no longer afraid to look Anton in the eyes. Slowing his pace at the approach to the post so the lookouts wouldn't panic, Artyom approached Anton and in a whisper told him about his discovery. Two minutes later they left the post, to the questioning looks of the rest, alternately operating the handles of the handcar.

They stopped the handcar directly beneath the hatch. The handcar was just high enough that Artyom, climbing onto Anton's shoulders, could reach and move the cover, haul himself inside and then pull up his partner. Although the tight corridor went off in both directions, Anton decisively moved in the direction of Park Pobedy.

Several seconds later it became clear that he had been right. An oblong cartridge case shone in the dim light. It was one of those that Melnik had given the lad the day before. Inspired by the discovery, Anton broke into a trot. He went about another twenty metres, to the place where the access corridor ran into the wall, and another hatch, also half open, blackened an opening in the floor. Anton confidently began to lower himself down. Before Artyom could manage to object, he had already disappeared. There was a crash from the opening, swearing, and then a choked voice said, 'Be careful when you jump, it's about a three-metre drop. Come on. I'll shine the light for you.' Placing his hands on the edge, Artyom hung down and, rocking several times, unclenched his fingers, trying to get both legs between the ties.

'How will we get ourselves back out of here?' he asked, straightening up.

'We'll figure something out.' Anton dismissed the problem with a wave of his hand.

'Are you certain that they didn't think you were dead?'

Artyom shrugged his shoulders. Despite the pain in the back of the head, the thought that some being had attacked him last night at *Kievskaya* seemed absurd now that he was sober.

'We'll go to Park Pobedy,' Anton decided. 'If there's trouble about, the threat can only come from there. You should feel it, too, you were with us at the station yourself.'

'But why didn't you say anything to us yesterday?' Artyom asked, catching up to Anton and trying to keep pace with him.

'The boss didn't allow it,' he answered sullenly. 'Semyonovich is really afraid of panic, and he has said not to spread rumours. He fusses over his position. But everyone has his limits. I told him ages ago that they couldn't keep it a secret forever . . . Three children have disappeared in the last two months and four families have fled the station. And there was our guard with that needle in his neck. No, he says panic will ensue and we'll lose control. He's a coward.' Anton spat out in sudden anger.

'But who made that needle . . . ?'

Artyom stopped in the middle of his sentence, and Anton stopped dead in his tracks.

'What's that again? Did you see it?' the lookout asked, taken aback.

Artyom did not reply. And so he stopped, staring at the floor and only moving the flashlight from side to side in order to see better what the lookout was pointing at. A gigantic figure had been crudely drawn in white on the floor. It was a twisting outline about forty centimetres wide and about two metres long, resembling a crawling snake or worm. From one side a bulge resembling a head was visible, and that gave it even greater similarity to a huge reptile.

'A snake,' Artyom offered.

'Maybe they just spilled some paint?' Anton tried to joke.

'No, they didn't just spill something. Here's the head . . . It's looking in that direction. It's crawling to Park Pobedy . . .'

'So, we'll follow it . . .'

Several hundred metres further on, they found three cartridge cases in the middle of the path. They both started walking more briskly.

'Good lad!' Anton said with pride. 'Wouldn't you just know he would think of leaving a trail!'

Artyom nodded. He was becoming ever more certain that, while the unknown creature had been able to get to him without a sound, the boy was still alive. But would Oleg have agreed to go with his mysterious kidnapper willingly? Then why would he have marked his trail? Artyom grew quiet for several minutes, and so did Anton. The pungent darkness dissipated the recent joy and hope, and he once more became just a little frightened.

In hoping to make amends to the father, he had forgotten all the warnings and terrible tales retold in whispers. He had forgotten the stalker's order not to leave *Kievskaya*. Anton was tearing ahead to find his son, but why was Artyom going to the ominous Park Pobedy? Why was he neglecting himself and his primary mission? For a second he recalled the strange people from *Polyanka* and the discussion about fate and he felt relieved. But the relief only lasted about ten minutes. Just up to the next symbol portraying a snake.

This figure was twice as large as the earlier one and it looked as if it was supposed to convince travellers they were going in the right direction. However, Artyom was not entirely happy about it.

The tunnel seemed endless. They walked and walked forever, and more than than two hours already had passed by Artyom's calculations.

The third painted giant snake was more than ten metres long, and they heard something there. Anton froze, turning his ear towards the tunnel, and Artyom listened too. Strange sounds were coming from the depths of the crossings in fits and starts; at first he couldn't make them out, but later he understood: a chant similar to the one the pipes had played to the music box at *Kievskaya* was being accompanied by the pounding of drums.

'Not far now,' Anton nodded.

Time, which had already been slipping by slowly, nearly stood still. Looking at his partner, Artyom realized with startling clarity that he was nodding too dramatically, as if his head were twitching in convulsions. When Anton began to glide down onto his side, looking comically like a toy animal stuffed with rags, Artyom thought that he might catch him, because there was plenty of time for it. Then a light prick in his shoulder stopped him from doing so. Taking a puzzled look at where it smarted, Artyom discovered a feathered steel needle stuck in his jacket. Nothing came of his intention to pull it out. His whole body was petrified, and then suddenly it was as if it had disappeared. His feeble legs gave way to the forces of gravity and Artyom ended up on the ground. At the same time, he remained almost totally conscious but it became increasingly difficult to breathe. He was unable to move his extremities. He heard footsteps near him, swift and weightless. The approaching being could not be human. Artyom had learned to recognize human footsteps long ago, on the patrols at *VDNKh*. A sudden, unpleasant smell reached his nose.

'One, two. Strangers, laid out,' someone overhead said.

'I'm a good shot, it was far away.'

'The neck, shoulder,' another responded.

The voices were strange: devoid of any intonation, flat, they reminded one mostly of the monotone drone of the wind in the tunnels. However, they were definitely human voices.

'To eat, well-aimed. That's what the Great Worm wants,' the first voice had continued.

'To eat. One – you, two – me, we carry the strangers home,' the second added.

The picture before him gave Artyom a start: they tore him from the ground jarringly. For a fraction of a moment a face flashed in front of his eyes: narrow, with dark, deep-set eyes. Then they put out the flashlights and it became pitch black. And only with the flood of blood to his head did Artyom understand that they were dragging him somewhere roughly, like a sack. The strange conversation continued for a time, although the phrases were intermixed now with an intense groaning.

'A paralysing needle, not poison. Why?'

'That's what the commander ordered. That's what the priest ordered. The Great Worm wanted it that way. It's OK to save the meat.'

'You're smart. You and the priest are friends. The priest is teaching you.'

'To eat.'

'One, two, the enemies are coming. There's a smell of gunpowder in the air, fire. A bad enemy. How do they get here?'

'I don't know. The commander and Vartan are doing the interrogation. You and I are the hunters. It is good that the Great Worm is happy. You and I will get a reward.'

'A lot to eat? Boots? A jacket?'

'A lot to eat. No jacket. No boots.'

'I'm young. I hunt the enemies. It is good. There's a lot? A Re-Ward . . . I'm happy.'

'This day is OK. Vartan brings a new young one. You, I, we hunt the enemies. The Great Worm is happy, the people sing. A holiday.'

'A holiday! I'm happy. Dances? Vodka? I dance with Natasha.'

'Natasha and the commander, they dance. Not you.'

'I am young, strong, the commander is very old. Natasha is young. I hunt enemies, brave, it is good. Natasha and I, we dance.'

Not too far away new voices could be heard and an argument had broken out. Artyom guessed that they had brought them to the station. Here it was almost as dark as in the tunnels, only one small campfire was burning in the whole place. They threw them nonchalantly onto the floor next to it. Someone's steel fingers gripped him by the beard and turned him face up. Several people of an unimaginably strange appearance were standing around. They were almost stark naked, and their heads were shaved bare, but it seemed they were not at all cold. On the forehead of each could be seen a wavy line, similar to the pictures at the crossing. Their small stature caused them to appear unhealthy: sunken cheeks, pale skin, but they radiated some kind of superhuman strength. Artyom recalled with what difficulty Melnik had borne the wounded Ten from the Library, and he compared this with how quickly these strange creations had brought them to the station. A long, arrow was in nearly each one's hand. Artyom recognized with surprise that they were made from the plastic sheathings that are used for spacing and insulating bundles of electrical wires. Huge steel bayonets hung on their belts, as from old Kalashnikov machine guns. All these strange people were approximately of the same age. There was no one here older than thirty. They scrutinized them in silence for some time, then the only one of the men wearing a beard and with a red line on his forehead said, 'OK. I am happy. These are the enemies of he Great Worm, the people of the machines. Evil people, tender meat. The Great Worm is satisfied. Sharap, Vovan are brave. I will take the people of the machines to the prison and interrogate them. Holiday tomorrow, all good people will eat the enemies. Vovan! Which needle? The paralyser?'

'Yes, the paralyser,' a thickset man with a blue line on his forehead said.

'A paralyser is good. The meat won't be spoiled,' the bearded one said.

'Vovan, Sharap! Get the enemies and come with me to the prison.'

The light began to recede. New voices were calling nearby, someone inarticulately expressed his delight, someone wailed mournfully. Then singing could be heard, low, barely audible, and not good. It seemed as if the dead really were singing, and Artyom recalled the tales that made their way around Park Pobedy. Then they put him on the ground again, flung Anton alongside and before long he lost consciousness.

It was as if someone had shoved him, suggested that he had to get up right away. Stretching, he lit a lantern, covering it with his hand so as not to hurt the sensitive, half-asleep eyes, and inspected the tent (where was the machine gun?!) and he went to the station. He was so homesick, but now, when he again had turned up at *VDNKh*, he was not at all happy about it. The smoky ceiling, emptied tents filled with bullet holes and the heavy ash in the air . . . Here, it seemed, something awful had happened, and the station was strikingly different from how he remembered it. In the distance, most likely from the passage at the other end of the platform, wild howls were heard, as if they were slicing up someone there. Two emergency lamps sparsely lit the station, their weak beams penetrating the lazy tufts of smoke with difficulty. There was no one on the whole platform, except for a small girl playing on the floor next to one of the neighbouring tents. Artyom was on the verge of asking her what had happened here and where the rest had disappeared to, but, catching sight of him, the girl began to cry loudly, and he thought better of it.

The tunnels. The tunnels from *VDNKh* to the Botanical Garden. If the inhabitants of his station had gone anywhere, then it would be there. If they had run to the centre, to Hansa, they wouldn't have left him and the child alone.

Jumping onto the track, Artyom moved toward the dark void of the entrance. It's dangerous without weapons, he thought. But there was nothing to lose, and he had to reconnoitre the situation. Had the dark ones suddenly been able to penetrate the defences? Then any hope lay with him. He had to find out the truth and report it to the southern allies.

The darkness enveloped him just beyond the entrance and fear came with the darkness. He could see absolutely nothing visible ahead, but he could hear disgusting chomping sounds. He regretted once more his lack of a machine gun, but it was too late to retreat. Steps began to sound in the distance, and then came ever closer. It was as if they approached when Artyom was moving forward and stopped when he stopped. Something similar had happened to him, but when and how, he couldn't recall. It was very frightening, approaching the unseen and unknown . . . An adversary? His trembling knees did not allow him to move quickly, and time was on the side of the terror. A cold sweat ran down his temples. He felt more ill at ease with every passing second. Finally, when the steps were only about three metres from him, Artyom could not hold back, and, stumbling, falling and lifting himself up, he raced back to the station. Falling a third time, his weakened legs refused to sustain him, and he understood that death was imminent.

'. . . Everything on this earth is a consequence of the Great Worm. Once the whole world consisted of stone and there was nothing on it except stone. There was no air, and there was no water, there was no light and there was no fire. There was no man and there was no beast. There was only dead stone. And then the Great Worm made it his home.'

'But how did the Great Worm get here? From where does he come? Who bore him?'

'The Great Worm has always been. Don't interrupt. He made a home for himself in the very centre of the world and said, "This world will be mine. It is made from hard stone, but I will gnaw my own passages in it. It is cold, but I will warm it with the heat of my body. It is dark, but I will light it with the light of my eyes. It is dead, but I will inhabit it with my creations." '

'Who are the creations?'

'The creations are the creatures the Great Worm issued from his womb. Both you and I, all of us, are his creations. There you have it. And then the Great Worm said, "Everything will be as I said, because this world henceforward is mine." And he began to gnaw passages through the hard stone, and the stone softened in his belly, saliva and juice moistened it, and the stone became alive and began to bear the fungi. And the Great Worm having gnawed the stone, let it pass through himself, and he did it thus for thousands of years, until his passages went through all the earth.'

'A thousand? What? One, two, three? How many? A thousand?'

'You have ten fingers on your hands. And Sharap has ten fingers . . . No, Sharap has twelve . . . That won't do. Let's say Grom has ten fingers. If you take you, Grom and other people so that all together there were as many as you have fingers, they each of them all would have ten times ten each. This is a hundred. And a thousand, this is when it is ten times each 100.'

'That's a lot of fingers. I can't count them.'

'It's not important. When the Great Worm's paths appeared on the earth, his first work was finished. And then he said, "So, I have gnawed thousands and thousand of paths through the hard stone and the stone has been scattered into crumbs. And the grit has passed through my womb, and has become soaked with the juice of my life, and it has become alive. And earlier the stone had occupied all the space in the world, but now an empty place has appeared. Now there is a place for the children I shall bear." And his first creations came forth from his womb, the names of whom they no longer remember. And they were big and strong, like the Great Worm himself. And the Great Worm loved them. But there was naught for them to drink, for in the world there was no water and they died of thirst. And then the Great Worm grieved. Grief was unknown to him before then, for there had been no one to love him, and he had not known solitude. But, having created new life, he had loved it, and it was difficult to part with it. And then the Great Worm began to cry, and his tears filled up the world. Thus water appeared. And he said, "See, now there is also a place so that one may live in it and water, so that one may drink it. And the earth, sated by the juice of my womb, is alive, and it bears fungi. Now I shall make some creatures, I shall bear my children. They will live in the paths that I have gnawed and drink of my tears and eat the fungi grown in the juice of my womb." And he feared giving birth once more to huge creations like himself, for you see there was not enough space or water or fungi. At first he created the fleas, and then the rats, then the cats, and then the chickens, and then the dogs, and then hogs and then man. But it did not turn out as he had thought: the fleas began to drink blood, and the cats to eat rats, and the dogs to oppress cats, and man to kill them all and eat them. And when man for the first time killed and ate another man, the Great Worm understood that his children had become unworthy of him and he cried. And each time that man eats man, the Great Worm cries, and his tears flow through the passages and flood them. Man is good. The meat is tasty. Sweet. But one can eat only his enemies. I know.'

Artyom clenched and unclenched the fingers on his hands. His hands were tied behind his back with a piece of wire and they had become numb, but at least they were responding again. Even the fact that his whole body ached was now a good sign. The paralysis from the poisoned needle had turned out to be temporary. The idiotic idea spun in his head that he, in contrast to the unknown storyteller, had no memory of how chickens had got into the metro. No doubt, some merchants had succeeded in bringing them from some market somewhere. They had brought swine from one of the *VDNKh* pavilions, he knew, but chickens . . . He tried to see what was next to him, but around him was absolute, inky darkness. However, someone was not too far away. It had already been half an hour since Artyom had come to. Gradually he was becoming aware of where he was.

'He is stirring, I can hear it,' a hoarse voice said. 'I'll call the commander. The commander will do the interrogation.' Something had moved, then stopped. Artyom tried to stretch his legs. They too turned out to be bound with wire. He tried to roll over onto his other side and hit something soft. A long, drawn-out moan, full of pain, was heard.

'Anton! Is that you?' Artyom whispered. There was no answer.

'Aha . . . The Great Worm's enemies have come to . . .' someone said derisively in the darkness.

'It would have been better had you not come to.' It was that same broken, sage voice that had been relating the story about the Great Worm and the creation of life for the past half hour. It immediately became clear that his keeper differed from the other inhabitants of the station: instead of primitive, chopped phrases, he had been speaking properly, somewhat pompously, and even the timbre of his voice was completely human, unlike that of the others.

'Who are you? Release us!' Artyom wheezed, moving his tongue with difficulty.

'Yes, yes. That's just what they all say. No, unfortunately, wherever you were headed, your travels are over. They are going to torture and grill you. And what will you do?' the voice answered from the darkness with indifference.

'Are you . . . also imprisoned?' Artyom asked.

'We all are in prison. They are releasing you this very day.' His unseen companion giggled.

Anton groaned again and began to stir. He mumbled something unintelligible, but had not yet regained consciousness.

'Why are we are sitting together in the darkness like cave-dwellers?'

A lighter was struck and the spot of flame lit the face of the speaker: he had a long grey beard, dirty, matted hair and dull, mocking eyes lost in a network of wrinkles. He could be no less than sixty. He was sitting on a chair along the other side of the iron bars that broke the room in two. There was something like it at *VDNKh*, too. It had a strange name: the 'monkey house'. Artyom had seen monkeys only in biology textbooks and children's books. In any event, the facility was used as a prison.

'There's no way I can get used to the damned darkness, I have to use this trash,' the old man lamented, covering his eyes. 'Well, why have you come here? Aren't there enough places on that side or something?'

'Listen,' Artyom didn't allow him to finish speaking. 'You are free . . . You can let us out! Before these cannibals return! You're a normal man . . .'

'Of course I can,' he answered, 'but of course, I will not. We make no deals with the enemies of the Great Worm.'

'What the hell is the Great Worm? And what are you talking about? I've never even heard of it, so I can't be its enemy . . .'

'It's not important whether you have heard of him or not. You came from that side, from where his enemies live, and that means you must be spies.' The derisive rasping in the old man's voice had changed to a steely clacking. 'You have firearms and flashlights! Damned mechanical toys! Machines for killing! What more evidence do you need to understand that you, the infidels, that you are the enemies of life, the enemies of the Great Worm?' He jumped up from his chair and approached the bars. 'It is you and those, who like you, are guilty of everything!' The old man put out the overheated lighter, and in the encroaching darkness he was heard blowing on his burning fingers. Then a new voice called out. This one hissed and chilled the blood. Artyom grew frightened. He remembered Tretyak, killed by a poisoned needle.

'Please!' he began to whisper fervently. 'Before it's not too late! Why are you doing this?'

The old man said nothing and a minute later the place was filled with sounds: slaps of unshod feet on concrete, hoarse breathing, the whistling of air drawn through nostrils. Although Artyom didn't see any of those entering, he felt that all of them were studying him closely, looking, sniffing, listening to how loudly Artyom's heart beat in his chest.

'The fire people. He smells like smoke, he smells like fear. One is the smell of the station from that side. The other is foreign. One, the other, they are enemies,' someone hissed at last.

'Let Vartan do it,' another voice ordered.

'Light the fire,' someone commanded.

The lighter was struck once more. In the room, besides the old man in whose hand the flame fluttered, stood three shaved savages, shading their eyes with their hands. Artyom already had seen one of them, the thickset and bearded one. The other also seemed strangely familiar to him. Looking Artyom directly in the eyes, he took a step forward and stopped at the bars. The smell from him wasn't like from the rest: Artyom detected a faint stench of decomposed flesh emanating from this man. They couldn't stop staring at him. Artyom winced: he understood where he had seen this face earlier. It was the creature who had attacked him in the night at *Kievskaya*. A strange feeling seized Artyom. It was similar to the paralysis, only this time his mind was affected. His thoughts stood still, and he obediently opened his consciousness to the silent probing.

'Through a hatch . . . The hatch had remained open . . . They had come for the boy. For Anton's son. They stole him in the night. I am guilty of it all, I allowed him to listen to your music, through the pipe . . . I climbed into the handcar. We didn't tell anyone else. We arrived together. We didn't close it . . .' Artyom answered the questions that arose in his head. It was impossible to resist or conceal anything from the soundless voice demanding the answers from him. Artyom's interrogator knew in a minute everything that was of interest. He nodded and stepped back. The fire was extinguished. Slowly, like feeling returning to a numbed hand, Artyom regained control.

'Vovan, Kulak! Return to the tunnel, to the passage. Close the door,' one of the voices ordered. Most likely it belonged to the bearded commander. 'The enemies are to remain here. Dron will guard the enemies. There is a holiday tomorrow, the people will eat the enemies, they will honour the Great Worm.'

'What have you done with Oleg? What have you done with the child?' Artyom began wheezing after them.

The door thudded hollowly.

CHAPTER 17

The Children of the Worm

Several minutes passed in total darkness, and Artyom, having deciding that they had left them alone, began to pull himself up, trying at least to sit. His tightly tied legs and hands were numb and sore. Artyom recalled the words of his stepfather explaining to him once that even leaving a bandage or tourniquet on too long, could kill the skin. Although, it seemed to him that it didn't matter now.

'Enemy, lay quietly!' A voice rang out. 'Dron will spit a paralysing needle!'

'It's not necessary.' Artyom froze obediently. 'You don't have to shoot.' He had a glimmer of hope. Perhaps he could convince his jailer to help him get out. But how can you talk to a savage who barely understands you?

'And who is this Great Worm?' He asked the first thing that came to his head.

'The Great Worm makes the earth. He makes the world, he makes man. The Great Worm is everything. The Great Worm is life. The enemies of the Great Worm, the people of the machines are death.'

'I have never heard of him,' Artyom said, choosing his words carefully. 'Where does he live?'

'The Great Worm lives here. Next to us. Around us. The Great Worm digs all the passages. Then man said he does it. No. The Great Worm. He gives life, he takes life. He digs new passages, the people live in them. Good people honour the Great Worm. Enemies of the Great Worm want to kill him. That is what say the priests.'

'Who are those priests?'

'Old people, with hair on their head. Only they can. They know, they listen to the desires of the Great Worm and they tell the people. Good people do it thus. Bad people do not obey. Bad people are enemies, the good eat them.'

Recalling the overheard conversation, Artyom began gradually to comprehend what was what. The old man relating the legend of the Worm was, probably, one of those priests.

'The priest says: it is forbidden to eat people. He says the Great Worm will cry when one man eats another,' Artyom reminded him, trying to express his thoughts exactly as the savage would.

'It is against the will of the Great Worm to eat people. If we stay here, they will eat us. The Great Worm will be sad, he will cry,' he added carefully.

'Of course the Great Worm will cry,' a derisive voice was heard from the darkness. 'But emotions are emotions, and you will not replace a protein food in a ration with anything.'

It was that same old man speaking. Artyom recognized his timbre and intonation. Only he didn't know if he had been in the room all the time or had just stolen in unnoticed. I didn't matter. He wasn't going to get out of the cell now. Then another thought entered Artyom's head, and it chilled him. How lucky that Anton had not come round yet and wasn't hearing this.

'And the child? The children that you steal? Do you eat them, too? The boy? Oleg?' he asked almost soundlessly, staring into the darkness with eyes open wide from fear.

'We do not eat little ones,' the savage replied, although Artyom thought the old man was answering. 'Little ones cannot be evil. They cannot be enemies. We take little ones in order to explain how to live. We talk about the Great Worm. We teach them to honour him.'

'Good boy, Dron,' the priest said. 'Favourite student,' he explained.

'What happened to the boy you stole last night? Where is he? It was your monster who dragged him away, I know,' Artyom said.

'Monster? And just who brought forth these monsters?!' the old man exploded. 'Who brought forth these mute, three-eyed, armless, six-fingered things who die during birth and are unable to reproduce? Who deprived them of human appearance, promised them paradise and flung them to die in the blind gut of this cursed city? Who is to blame for this and who is the real monster?'

Artyom was silent. The old man said no more and only breathed heavily, trying to calm down. And Anton finally came to.

'Where is he?' he said in a hoarse voice. 'Where is my son? Where is my son? Give me my son!' He began to scream and, trying to get free, began to roll about the floor, hitting the bars of the cage, then the wall.

'Violent,' the old man remarked in his former derisive tone. 'Dron, calm him.'

A strange sound was heard, as if someone had coughed. Something whistled through the air, and Anton was calm again after several seconds.

'Very instructive,' the priest said. 'I will go and bring the boy, let him see his papa and say goodbye. A good laddie, by the way, his pop can be proud of him, he resists hypnosis so well . . .'

He began to shuffle along the floor, and then the door creaked.

'No need to fear,' the jailer softly said unexpectedly. 'Good people do not kill, they do not eat the children of enemies. Little ones do not sin. It is possible to learn to live well. The Great Worm forgives young enemies.'

'My God, just what is this Great Worm? This is completely absurd! Worse than non-believers and Satanists! How can you believe in him? Has anyone ever seen him, your Worm? Have you seen him or something?' Artyom tried for sarcasm, but lying on the floor with his arms and legs tied didn't make it easy. Just as when he had been waiting in prison to be hanged, he became indifferent to his own fate. He put his head on the cold floor and closed his eyes, expecting an answer.

'It is forbidden to look at the Great Worm. Banned!' the savage snapped.

'And such a thing cannot be,' Artyom replied reluctantly. 'There is no Worm . . . And people made the tunnels. They all are shown on maps . . . There is even a round one, where Hansa is, and only people can build round ones. I don't suppose you even know what a map is . . .'

'I know,' Dron said quietly. 'I study with the priest, he shows us. There are not many passages on the map. The Great Worm has been making new passages, and they aren't on the map. Even here, our home, there are new passages – sacred ones, and they are not on the map. The people of the machines make the maps, they think they dig the passages. Stupid, proud. They don't know anything. The Great Worm punishes them for this.'

'Why does he punish them?' Artyom didn't understand.

'For arr . . . arr-o-gance,' the savage articulated carefully.

'For arrogance,' confirmed the voice of the priest. 'The Great Worm made man last, and man was his favourite offspring. For he did not give intellect to the others, but gave it to man. He knew that intellect is a dangerous toy, and therefore he ordered, "Live in the world with yourself, in the world with the earth, in the world with life and all creatures, and honour me." After this, the Great Worm went to the very bowels of the earth, but said beforehand, "The day will come and I shall return. Behave as if I were with you." And the people obeyed their creator and lived in the world with the earth he had created and in the world with each other and in the world with the other creatures and they honoured the Great Worm. And they bore children, and their children bore children, and from father to son, from mother to daughter they handed down the words of the Great Worm. But those who had heard his order with their own ears died, and their children died, and many generations were replaced, and the Great Worm has not yet returned. And then, one after the other, people stopped observing his covenants and did as they wanted. And there appeared those who said, "There never was a Great Worm and there is not now." And others expected that the Great Worm would return and punish them. He would burn them with the light of his eyes, devour their bodies and cause the passages where they live to crumble. But the Great Worm has not returned and has only cried for the people. And his tears have risen up from the depths and flooded the lower passages. But those who have turned from their creator have said, "No one created us, we always have been. Man is beautiful and mighty, he cannot have been created by an earthworm!" And they said, "All the earth is ours, and was ours, and will be, and the Great Worm did not make the passages in it, but we and our ancestors." And they lit the fire and began to kill the creations which the Great Worm had created, saying:, "Here, all the life that is around is ours and everything here is only to satisfy our hunger." And they created machines in order to kill more quickly, in order to sow death, in order to destroy the life created by the Great Worm and to subdue his world. But even then he did not rise up from the extreme depths to which he had gone. And they laughed and began to do more against that of which he had spoken. And they decided in order to degrade him, to build such machines that would replicate his likeness. And they created such machines and they went inward in them and they laughed:, "Here," they said, "now we ourselves can rule as the Great Worm, and not as one, but as dozens. And the light strikes from our eyes, and the thunder rolls when we are creeping, and people leave their womb. We created the Worm, and not the Worm us." But even this was not enough for them. The hatred grew in their heart. And they decided to destroy the very earth where they lived. And they created thousands of different machines: that belched flame, and spat iron, and rendered the earth into parts. And they began to destroy the earth and every living thing that was in it. And then the Great Worm could not bear it and he condemned them: he took from them their most valuable gift, intellect. Insanity overtook them, they turned their machines against each other and began to kill each other. And they no longer remembered why they did it and what they were doing, but they were unable to stop. Thus did the Great Worm punish man for his arrogance.'

'But not everyone?' a child's voice asked.

'No. There were those who always remembered the Great Worm and honoured him. They renounced the machines and light and lived in the world with the earth. They were saved, and the Great Worm did not forget their loyalty, and he preserved their intellect, and he promised to give them the whole world when his enemies have fallen. And so shall it be.'

'And it will be so,' the savage and child repeated together.

'Oleg?' Artyom called out, hearing something familiar in the child's voice. The child did not reply.

'And to this day the enemies of the Great Worm live in the passages burrowed by them, because there is nowhere else for them to take shelter, but they continue to worship, not him, but their machines. The patience of the Great Worm is enormous, and it has been sufficient for long centuries of human outrages. But even it is not eternal. It has been foretold that when he makes the last strike at the dark heart of the country of his enemies, their will shall be crushed, and the world will fall to the good people. It has been foretold that the hour shall come and the Great Worm will summon the rivers and the earth and the air for aid. And the earthly layer will sink, and the seething currents will rush, and the dark heart of the enemy will rush to oblivion. And then finally the just will triumph and there will be happiness for the good, and life without diseases and fungi for one's heart's content, and every kind of beast in abundance.'

A flame was lit. Artyom had succeeded in leaning his back against the wall, and now he no longer had to bend agonizingly in order to keep the people on the other side of the bars in his field of view. A small boy sat cross-legged on the floor in the middle of the room with his back to him. Over him loomed the withered figure of the priest, lit by the flame of the burning lighter in his hand. The savage with the blowpipe in his hands stood alongside, leaning against the door jamb. All eyes were fixed on the old man who had just finished

381

his narrative. Artyom turned his head with difficulty and looked at Anton, who was fixed in that convulsive pose in which the paralysing needle had caught him. He stared at the ceiling and was not able to see his son, but he certainly heard everything.

'Stand up, sonny, and look at these people,' said the priest. The boy immediately got to his feet and turned toward Artyom. It was Oleg.

'Go closer to him. Do you recognize any of them?' the old man asked.

'Yes.' The boy nodded affirmatively, looking sullenly at Artyom.

'It is my pop and I was listening to your songs with this one. Through the pipe.'

'Your pop and his friend are bad people. They have been using machines and have been disparaging the Great Worm. Do you remember, you told me and Uncle Vartan what your papa did when the bad people decided to destroy the world?'

'Yes.' Again Oleg nodded.

'So tell us again,' the old man placed the lighter into his other hand.

'My pop worked in the RVA. The rocket forces. He was a missile man. I wanted to be just like him, too, when I grow up.'

Artyom's throat dried up. How had he not been able to work out this riddle earlier? So that's where the lad had got that strange tab and so had declared that he was a missile man, just like the slain Tretyak! The coincidence was almost incredible. There remained in the whole metro people who had served in the rocket forces . . . And two of them had ended up in *Kievskaya*. Could this have been by chance?

'As a missile man . . . These people created greater evil for the world than all the rest put together. They sent machines and equipment that burnt and destroyed the earth and almost all life on it. The Great Worm forgives many who stray, but not those who gave the orders to destroy the world and sow death in it, and not those who carried it out. Your father has caused intolerable pain to the Great Worm. Your father destroyed our world with his own hands. Do you know what he deserves?' The old man's voice had become stern.

'Death?' the boy asked uncertainly, while glancing first at the priest and then at his father, doubled up on the floor of the monkey cage.

'Death,' the priest confirmed. 'He must die. The sooner the evil people who have imparted pain to the Great Worm die, the sooner his promise will be fulfilled, and the world will be reborn and delivered to the good people.'

'Then papa must die,' concurred Oleg.

'That's the boy!' the old man tenderly patted the boy on the head.

'And now run, play with Uncle Vartan and the kiddies again! Only, look out, be careful in the darkness, don't fall! Dron, lead him and I'll sit some more for a while with them. Return in half an hour with the others and grab the sacks, we'll be ready.'

The light was extinguished. The swift, rustling steps of the savage and the light tread of the child faded into the distance. The priest gave a cough and said to Artyom, 'I'll have a little chat here with you if you aren't opposed to it. We usually don't take captives unless they are children, and then they are all puny and born sickly . . . But we are seeing more and more adults who are deaf. I would be glad to talk with them and maybe they would not mind, only, well, they eat them too quickly . . .'

'Why then do you teach them that it is bad to eat people?' Artyom asked.

'The Worm will cry there and so on? Well, how can I put it? It is for them in the future. For you, of course, you will miss this moment, and even me, too, but now the basis of a future civilization is being laid down: of a culture which will live with nature in the world. Cannibalism is a necessary evil for them. There is nothing without animal protein, you see. But the legends will remain, and when the direct need to kill and stuff your face with those like you fades away, they will stop doing it. Only then will the Great Worm remember. It is unfortunate only to be living in this dandy time . . .' The old man again began to laugh unpleasantly.

'You know, I've already seen so many things in the metro,' Artyom said. 'At one station they believe that if you dig deeply enough, you can dig all the way to hell. At another, that we already are living on the threshold of paradise, because the final battle of good and evil is over and those who survived were chosen for entry into the Heavenly Kingdom. After that, the story about your Worm doesn't sound all that convincing somehow. Do you at least believe in it yourself?'

'What's the difference what I or the other priests believe in?' The old man grinned. 'You won't be alive much longer, just a few hours, so I'll just tell you something. One cannot be so frank with someone as with he who will carry all his revelations to the grave. So, what I myself believe in is not important. The main thing is that the people believe. It is difficult to come to believe in a god whom I have created

383

myself.' The priest stopped for a short while, thinking, and then continued. 'How could I explain it to you? When I was a student, I studied philosophy and psychology at the university, although I doubt that's anything to you. And I had a professor: an instructor of cognitive psychology, a most knowledgeable man, who laid out the intellectual process systematically – he was a real pleasure to listen to. And then I put to him a question as all others do at that age: Does God exist? I had read various books, had conversations, as is customary, and I was inclined to the view that most likely He did not. And somehow I decided that this professor in particular, a great expert on the human soul, could answer for me precisely this question that so pained me. I went to see him in his office, on the pretext of discussing a paper, and then I asked, "In your opinion, Ivan Mikhalych, does God actually exist?" Then he really surprised me. For me, he said, this question isn't worth asking. I myself was from a family of believers, used to the idea that He exists. From the psychological point of view, I did not try to analyze the truth because I did not want to. And generally, he said, for me it was not so much a question of knowledge based on principle, as everyday behaviour. My faith was not that I was sincerely convinced of the existence of a higher power, but that I was fulfilling the prescribed commandments, praying at night and going to church. I would be better for it, more at peace. And that's it.' The old man went silent.

'And what?' Artyom couldn't contain himself.

'Whether I believe in the Great Worm or not isn't so very important. But commandments from divine lips live for centuries. Just one more thing: create a god and teach his word. And believe me, the Great Worm is no worse than other gods and has survived many of them.'

Artyom closed his eyes. Neither Dron nor the chief of this surprising tribe, nor even such strange creations as Vartan, had the slightest doubt that the Great Worm exists. For them it was a given, the only explanation of what they could see around them, the only authority for action and a measure of good and evil. What else could a man who had never seen anything except the metro believe in? But there was in the legends of the Worm something that Artyom was still unable to understand.

'But why do you incite them so against machines? What's so bad about these mechanisms? Electricity, lighting, firearms, and so on. Your teachings mean that your people live without them,' he said.

'What's bad about machines?!' the old man's tone changed

dramatically: the good nature and patience with which he had just set forth his thoughts evaporated. 'You intend an hour before your death to preach to me the benefits of machines! Well, look around! Only a blind man won't notice that if mankind owed some kind of a debt, then he wouldn't rely so much on machines! How dare you snicker about the important role of equipment here, at my station? You nobody!'

Artyom hadn't expected his question, way less seditious than the previous, about his belief in the Great Worm, to provoke such a reaction from the old man. Not knowing how to respond, he remained silent. The priest's heavy breathing could be heard in the darkness, as he whispered some kind of curses and tried to calm himself. He resumed speaking only after several minutes.

'I am out of the habit of speaking with non-believers.' Judging by the voice, the old man had regained control of himself. 'I got carried away in speaking with you. Something is keeping the young ones, they aren't bringing the sacks.' He paused meaningfully.

'What sacks?' Artyom responded to the ploy.

'They will prepare you. When I spoke of torture, I wasn't being strictly accurate. Pointless cruelty goes against the grain of the Great Worm. My colleagues and I, when we understood that cannibalism had taken root here, and we could no longer do anything about it, decided to look after the culinary side of the problem. And so someone recalled that the Koreans, when they eat dogs, catch them alive, put them in sacks and beat them to death with sticks. The meat benefits a lot from it. It becomes soft, tender. One man's multiple haematomas, as it were, are another man's cutlet. So don't judge us too severely. I myself would perhaps be happier to die first and then suffer the sticks. Inevitably, there will be internal bleeding. A recipe is a recipe.' The old man even clicked the lighter in order to get a look at the effect he had produced. 'However, something is keeping them, it shouldn't have happened . . .'he added.

A whistle interrupted him. Artyom heard cries, running, children's crying and that ominous whistle again. Something had happened at the station. The priest listened to the noise uneasily, then extinguished the fire and grew silent.

Several minutes later heavy boots began to rumble on the threshold, and a low voice murmured, 'Is anyone alive?'

'Yes! We're here! Artyom and Anton!' Artyom yelled at the top of his lungs, hoping that the old man had no pipes with poisoned needles hanging around his neck.

'Here they are! Cover me and the lad!' someone screamed. There was a dazzling, bright flash of light. The old man dashed towards the exit, but a man barring the way hit him in the neck. The priest began to wheeze and fell.

'The door, hold the door!' Something had come crashing down, plaster began to fall from the ceiling and Artyom blinked. When he opened his eyes, two men were now standing in the room. They were not run-of-the-mill soldiers and Artyom hadn't seen anyone like them before. Dressed in heavy long bullet-proof vests over tailored black uniforms, both were armed with unusual short machine guns with laser gun sights and silencers. In addition, massive titanium helmets with face guards, like the Hansa Spetsnaz, and large titanium shields with eye slits added to the impressive sight. A flame-thrower was visible on the back of one. They quickly inspected the room, illuminating it with a long and inconceivably strong flashlights, that were shaped like cudgels.

'These?' one of them asked.

'Them,' the other confirmed. Efficiently examining the lock on the door of the monkey cage, the first moved back, took several steps and leapt, striking the cage with his boots. The rusty hinges broke and the door collapsed half a foot from Artyom. The man lowered himself onto one knee in front of Artyom and lifted his face guard. Everything now fell into place: Melnik was looking at Artyom through squinted eyes. His wide serrated knife slipped along the wires entangling Artyom's legs and hands. Then the stalker cut the wire that had been binding Anton.

'Alive,' Melnik remarked with satisfaction. 'Can you walk?'

Artyom began to nod, but was unable to lift himself to his feet. His numbed body was still not totally under his command. Several more men ran into the room. Two of them immediately took up a defensive position at the doors. There were eight fighters in all in the party. They were dressed and equipped just like those who had stormed into the room, but several of them wore long leather cloaks, as Hunter had. One of them lowered a child to the ground, covering him with the shield he wore on his arm. The child immediately raced into the cell and bent over Anton.

'Papa! Papa! I lied to them so they'd think I was on their side! I showed them where you are! Forgive me, Papa! Papa, don't be silent!' The boy could hardly contain his tears. Anton looked at the ceiling with glassy eyes. Artyom was frightened that two paralysing needles in a day could turn out to be too much for the watch commander.

Melnik placed his index finger on Anton's neck. 'He's OK,' he concluded after several seconds. 'He's alive. Bring a stretcher!'

While Artyom talked about the impact of the poisoned needles, two fighters unrolled a cloth stretcher on the floor and loaded Anton onto it. On the floor, the old man began to stir and mumble something.

'And who's this?' Melnik asked, and, having heard from Artyom the explanation, said, 'We'll take him with us and use him as cover. How's the situation?'

'All quiet,' reported a fighter guarding the entrance door.

'Let's get back to the tunnel,' the stalker said

'We have to return to base with the wounded and the hostage for interrogation. Here you go.' He threw Artyom a machine gun. 'If all goes as planned, you won't have to use it. You don't have any armour, so you'd better stay under our cover. Watch the youngster.'

Artyom nodded and took Oleg by the hand, nearly tearing the boy away from the stretcher on which his father lay.

'Let's build the "turtle",' Melnik ordered. The fighters formed an oval in a moment, sticking out their linked shields, above which only helmets were seen. Four carried the stretcher with their free hands. The boy and Artyom were inside the formation, fully covered by shields. They gagged the old man, tied his hands behind his back, and placed him at the head of the formation. After several strong jabs, he stopped trying to break loose and calmed down, staring sullenly at the floor. The first two fighters, who had special night vision instruments, served as the eyes of the 'turtle'. The instruments were fastened directly to the helmets, so that their hands remained free. The party bent down on command, covering their legs with the shields and moved ahead swiftly. Squeezed between the fighters, Artyom held Oleg's hand tightly and pulled him along. He couldn't see anything, and could work out what was happening only by the curt discussions.

'Three on the right . . . Women, a child.'

'On the left! In the arch, in the arch! They're shooting!' Needles began to clang on the metal of the shield.

'Take them out!' Machine gun pops were heard in response.

'There's one . . . Two . . . Keep moving, keep moving!'

'From behind! Lomov!'

'Some more shots.'

'Where, where? Don't go there!'

'Ahead, I said! Hold the hostage!'

'Damn, it flew right in front of my eyes . . .'

'Stop! Stop! Halt!'

'What's there?'

'It's all blocked! There are about forty people there! Barricades!'

'Is it far?'

'Twenty metres. They are not firing.'

'They are approaching from the sides!'

'When did they manage to build barricades?'

A rain of needles fell on the shields. On signal, they all got down onto one knee so that now the armour covered them completely. Artyom bent down, covering the boy. They placed the stretcher with Anton on the floor. The rain of needles intensified.

'Do not respond! Do not respond! We'll wait . . .'

'It hit my boot . . .'

'Ready the light . . . On the count of three, flashlights and fire. Whoever has the night vision equipment, choose the targets now . . . One . . .'

'How they shoot . . .'

'Two! Three!' Several powerful flashlights lit up simultaneously and the machine guns opened up. Somewhere ahead Artyom could hear the cries and moans of the dying. Then the firing unexpectedly ceased. Artyom listened.

'Over there, there, with the white flag . . . Are they giving up or what?'

'Cease fire! We'll talk. Put the hostage in front!'

'Stop, you bastard, there! I've got him, I've got him! Smart old man . . .'

'We have your priest! Let us leave!' Melnik called out. 'Let us return to the tunnel! I repeat, let us leave!'

'Well, what's there? What's there?'

'Zero reaction. They're silent.'

'Maybe they don't understand us?'

'So, hold the light on him for me a little better . . .'

'Take a look.' Then the negotiations suddenly stopped. It was as though the fighters were absorbed in thought. At first it was just those who were at the front, then the one's covering the rear quieted down. The silence was tense, not good.

'What's there?' Artyom asked uneasily. No one answered him. The people even stopped moving about. Artyom felt the palm of the hand he was holding the boy with start to sweat. It shook him.

'I feel . . . He is looking at us . . .' he said quietly.

'Release the hostage,' Melnik suddenly pronounced.

'Release the hostage,' repeated another fighter. Then Artyom, could bear it no longer and he straightened up and looked over the shields and helmets. Ahead, ten steps from them, in the intersection of three blinding beams of light stood, not squinting and not shielding his eyes with his hands, a tall stooped man with a white rag in his extended gnarled hand. The man's face could be seen clearly. He was similar to Vartan, the one who had interrogated him several hours ago. Artyom ducked behind the shields and released the safety on his machine gun and chambered a round. The scene he had just observed remained before him. Simultaneously eerie and bewitching, it suddenly reminded him for a moment of an old book, *Tales and Myths of Ancient Greece* which he had loved to look at when he was a child. One of the legends told about a monstrous creation in semi-human form, whose look turned many brave warriors to stone. He drew a breath, mustered all his willpower, having forbidden himself to look the hypnotist in the face, jumped over the shields like an imp on a spring and pulled the trigger. After the strange, noiseless battle between machine guns with silencers and blow pipes, the Kalashnikov's salvo seemed to jar the station's domes. Although Artyom was convinced it was not possible to miss from such a distance, what he feared most, happened: the creature had guessed his intentions and, as soon as Artyom's head appeared above the shields, his gaze fell into the trap of those dead eyes. He succeeded in squeezing the trigger, but an unseen hand deftly pushed the barrel aside. Almost the whole salvo missed, and only one round struck the creature in the shoulder. It issued a guttural sound that pierced the ears, and then, with one elusive movement, disappeared into the darkness. We have several seconds, Artyom thought. Only several seconds. When Melnik's party had broken through to Park Pobedy, there had been the element of surprise on his side. But now, when the savages had organized a defence, there was no chance, it seemed, to overcome the barrier created by them. Running the other way remained the only way out. The words of his jailer flashed in his head: tunnels that are not on the metro map leave the station.

'Are there other tunnels here?' he asked Oleg.

'There is one more station, beyond the passage, just like this one, like a reflection in a mirror,' the boy waved a hand. 'We played there. There are still tunnels like here, but they told us it was forbidden to go there.'

'We are falling back! Towards the crossing!' Artyom bellowed, trying to lower his voice and imitate Melnik's commanding bass.

'What the devil?' the stalker snarled with displeasure. It seemed he had come to his senses. Artyom grabbed him by the shoulder.

'Quickly, they have a hypnotist there,' he began to jabber. 'We can't penetrate this barrier! There's another exit there, beyond the crossing!'

'True, it's a double, this station . . . Let's go!' the stalker accepted the decision. 'Hold the barricade! Back! Slowly, slowly!'

The others slowly, as if unwillingly, began to move. Urging them with new orders, Melnik was able to compel the party to reform and begin the retreat before new needles flew at them from the darkness. When they began to stand up along the steps of the passage, the fighter who was bringing up the rear let out a scream and grabbed at his shin. He continued to climb with his stiffening legs for several seconds but then a monstrous cramp brought him down, twisted him, as if he were wrung out laundry and he collapsed onto the ground. The party stopped. Beneath the cover of the shields, two free fighters rushed to lift their comrade from the ground, but it was all over. His body was turning blue before their eyes, and foam was appearing on his gums. Artyom already knew what it meant, and so did Melnik.

'Take his shield, helmet and machine gun! Quickly,' he ordered Artyom. 'Let's go, let's go!' he screamed to the rest.

The titanium helmet was soiled with the awful foam, and he would have to take it from the dead man's head. Artyom was unable to force himself to do it. Limiting himself to the machine gun and shield, he took his place at the rear of the formation, covered himself with the shield, and moved behind the others. Now they were nearly running. Then someone threw a smoke bomb far ahead and, availing themselves of the confusion, the party began to climb down to the tracks. Another fighter cried out in surprise and fell to the ground. Now only three were able to carry the stretcher with the wounded Anton. Artyom was reluctant to show himself from behind the shield and fired back several times without looking. Then things grew strangely quiet: the needles were no longer flying at them, although, judging by the rustle of the steps and voices all around, the pursuit had not ceased. Summoning his courage, Artyom looked out from behind his shield. The party was ten metres from the entrance to the tunnel. The first fighters had already stepped inside. Two, turning, swept the approaches with their lights and covered the rest. But there was no need for it: the savages, it seemed, did not intend to follow them into the tunnels. Crowding around in a semi-circle, lowering their pipes and shading their eyes with their hands from the blinding light of the flashlights, they awaited something in silence.

'Enemies of the Great Worm, listen!' The bearded leader appeared from the crowd. 'The enemies are going into the holy passages of the Great Worm. Good people do not go after them. It is forbidden to go there today. Great danger. Death, and damnation. Let the enemies give back the old priest and leave.'

'Don't let him go, don't listen to them,' Melnik commanded slowly. 'Let's go.'

They continued moving cautiously. Artyom and several other fighters were moving backwards and not taking their eyes off the station they were leaving behind. At first no one actually came after them. A voice was heard from the station: someone was arguing, at first not loudly, but then beginning to scream.

'Dron cannot! Dron must go! For the teacher!'

'Forbidden to go! Halt! Halt!' A dark figure dashed from the darkness into the beams of the flashlights with such speed that it was impossible to hit it. Immediately behind it others too appeared in the distance. Not able to target the first savage, one of the fighters tossed something forward.

'Get down! Grenade!' Artyom flung himself onto the ties with his face down, covering his head with his hands, and opened his mouth as his stepfather had taught him. The incredible sound and deafening force of the shock wave hit his ears and pressed him to the ground. He lay there for several minutes, opening and closing his eyes, trying to come to his senses. His head pounded, coloured spots circled before his eyes. Clumsy, endlessly repeated words were the first sound he heard after coming to his senses. 'No, no, don't shoot, don't shoot, don't shoot, Dron doesn't have a weapon, don't shoot!' He turned his head and looked around. In the intersection of the beams, with hands lifted high, the savage who had been guarding them while they were imprisoned in the monkey cage stood. Two fighters kept him in their sights, awaiting orders, and the rest got up from the ground and shook themselves. A heavy dust from the rock hung in the air while a pungent smoke crept from the side of the station.

'What? Did it collapse?' asked someone.

'From one grenade . . . The whole metro holds on by a hair . . .'

'Well, they won't try to get in here any more. Until they get rid of the blockage . . .'

'That should tie them up. Let's go, there's no time, we don't know when they'll come to their senses,' the approaching Melnik ordered.

They halted only an hour later. During this time, the tunnel split in two directions, and the stalker, who was walking ahead, chose which way to go. Huge, cast-iron loops were seen in one place. Most likely at some time they had strong shutters hanging from them. Next to them was scattered the debris of a pressurized gate. Except for that, nothing of interest was found: the tunnel was completely empty, pitch-black and lifeless.

They walked slowly. The old man stumbled at every step, and several times he fell to the ground. Dron walked unwillingly and mumbled to himself about a prohibition and damnation, until they stuffed a gag into his mouth. When the stalker finally allowed them to stop and he had dispatched sentries with night vision instruments fifty metres on both sides, the exhausted priest collapsed to the floor. The savage continued pleading inarticulately through the gag, until the escorts brought him closer to the old man and he dropped to his knees in front of him and stroked the old man's head with his bound hands. The young Oleg rushed to the stretcher on which his father lay and began to cry. Anton's paralysis had passed, but he was unconscious, just as after the first needle had struck him. The stalker, meanwhile, beckoned Artyom to his side. Artyom was no longer able to contain his curiosity.

'How did you find us? I was already thinking, you know, they were going to eat us,' he admitted to Melnik.

'You think it was difficult? You left the handcar right under the hatch. The lookouts noticed it when Anton didn't show up for tea. They just didn't try to poke around in there themselves. They placed a guard and reported it to the chief. You actually didn't wait for me even for a little while. Then I left for *Smolenskaya* again, to the base, for corroboration. We assembled at the alarm, but we needed time. While we got equipped, I began to remember what's what at *Mayakovskaya*. It was a similar situation: there was a crumbling side tunnel there as well where Tretyak and I had separated. We had been looking for the entrance to D-6 on the map. We were about fifty metres apart. He, most likely, had got closer to it. I'd been gone for only three minutes. I shouted to him, but he didn't respond. I ran to him. He was lying there all blue, swollen, his lips cracked by this crap. I grabbed him by the legs and dragged him to the station. While I was dragging him, I recalled Semyonych and his story about the poisoned watchman. I shined my light at Tretyak and there was a needle in his leg. Then everything began to fall into place. I sent the messenger to you as soon as possible so that you would remain at the station, arrange your affairs, and return. But I was unsuccessful.'

'Are they really at *Mayakivskaya*, too?' Artyom was surprised. 'But just how did they get there from Park Pobedy?'

'This is how they get there.' The stalker removed his heavy helmet and placed it onto the floor. 'You will, of course, forgive me, but we didn't just come for you, but for intelligence as well. I think there must be one more exit to Metro-2 from here. These cannibals of yours also made it through to *Mayakovskaya*. There, by the way, it's the same story as here: children disappear from the station at night. And only the devil knows where they get to, and we see neither hide nor hair of them.'

'That is . . . you want to say . . .' The thought itself had seemed so unbelievable to Artyom that he didn't dare utter it aloud. 'In your opinion, is the entrance to Metro-2 somewhere around here?' Was the gate to D-6, that mysterious metro phantom, really located in the immediate vicinity? Rumours, stories, legends and theories of Metro-2 that he had heard throughout his life swirled in Artyom's head.

'Let me tell you something else,' the stalker winked at him. 'I think we're already in it. It has just been impossible to verify it.'

Requesting a flashlight from one of the fighters, Artyom began to study the tunnel's walls. He caught the surprised looks of the others, knowing that must look really stupid, but he couldn't help himself. And he only partly understood what had he expected to see on reaching Metro-2. Golden rails? People living as they once had, not knowing about the horrors of present-day existence, in fairy-tale abundance? Gods? He passed from one lookout to the other, but, as he didn't find anything, turned towards Melnik. He was speaking with the fighter who was guarding the savages.

'What about the hostages? Finish them off?' the escort asked casually.

'First we'll have a little talk,' the stalker answered. Bending down, he pulled the gag from the old man's mouth. Then he did the same with the second prisoner.

'Teacher! Teacher! Dron is coming with you. I am coming with you, Teacher!' the savage immediately began to lament, swaying from side to side above the groaning priest. 'Dron is violating the prohibition of the holy passages, Dron is ready to die at the hand of the enemies of the Great Worm, but Dron is coming with you, to the end!'

'What else is there? What's this about a worm? What about the holy passages?' Melnik asked.

The old man was silent.

Looking at the escorts in fright, Dron hurriedly said, 'The holy passages of the Great Worm are forbidden for good people. The Great Worm may appear there. Man can see. It is forbidden to look! Only the priests can. Dron is afraid, but is coming. Dron is coming with the teacher.'

'What worm?' The stalker wrinkled his nose.

'The Great Worm . . . The creator of life,' explained Dron. 'The holy passages are further. One cannot go every day. There are forbidden days. Today is a forbidden day. If you see the Great Worm, you will turn to ashes. If you hear him, you will be cursed, you will die quickly. Everyone knows. The elders say so.'

'What? Are all the morons like this there?' The stalker looked at Artyom.

'No,' he shook his head, 'talk to the priest.'

'Your Eminence,' Melnik addressed the priest tongue in cheek. 'You will excuse me, I am just an old soldier . . . How best to express it . . . I don't know haughty language. But here there is one place in your possession that we are searching for. Supposedly accessible . . . Things are kept there . . . Flaming arrows? Grapes of wrath?' He gazed into the old man's face, hoping that he would respond to one of his metaphors, but the priest stubbornly remained silent, sullenly staring at him from beneath his brows. 'The hot tears of the gods?' The stalker was continuing, to the surprised looks of Artyom and the others, to try get answers. 'Zeus' lightning bolts?'

'Stop playing the fool,' the old man finally interrupted him with contempt. 'There is nothing transcendental to trample with your dirty soldier boots.'

'Missiles,' Melnik at once became business-like. 'The missile unit just outside Moscow. An exit from the tunnel by *Mayakovskaya*. You must remember what I'm talking about. We have to get there right away, and it would be better for you to help.'

'Missiles . . .' the old man repeated slowly, as if testing the flavour the word.

'Missiles . . . You, probably, are about fifty years old, right? You still remember. They named the SS-18 "Satan" in the West. It was the only insight of a blind-from-birth human civilization.'

'Are you really so great?! You have destroyed the whole world. Are you really so great?'

'Listen, Your Eminence, we don't have time for this.' Melnik cut him off. 'I am giving you five minutes.' His fingers cracked as he stretched out his hands.

The old man made a face. It was as if neither the combat dress of the stalker and his fighters, nor the poorly concealed threat in Melnik's voice had the slightest impact on him.

'And what, what can you do to me?' he smiled. 'Torture me? Kill me? Go ahead, I'm already old, and in our faith there are not enough martyrs. So just kill me, like you killed hundreds of millions of other people! As you killed my whole world! Our whole world! Go ahead, squeeze the trigger of your damned machine, as you pressed the triggers and buttons of dozens of thousands of different lethal devices!' The old man's voice, at first weak and hoarse, quickly turned steely. Despite his matted grey hair, tied hands and short stature, he no longer looked pathetic: a strange force emanated from him, his every new word sounded more convincing and menacing than the last. 'You don't have to smother me with your hands, you don't even have to see my agony . . . You and all your machines will be damned! You have devalued both life and death . . . Do you consider me a madman? But the true madmen are you, your fathers and your children! Wasn't it really a perilous madness to try to subjugate the whole earth to yourselves, throw a bridle on nature and cause it to cramp and convulse? Where were you when the world was destroyed? Did you see how it was? Did you see what I saw? The sky, at first melting, and then engulfed with lifeless clouds? Boiling rivers and seas, expelling onto the shores creatures boiled alive, and then converted into frozen custard? The sun, disappearing from the sky, not to reappear for years? Homes turned to dust in a split second, and the people living in them turned to ashes? Did you hear their cries for help?! And those who died from epidemics and maimed by radiation? Did you hear their curses?! Look at him!' He pointed at Dron. 'Look at all those without arms, without eyes, with six fingers! Even those who have obtained new capabilities!'

The savage fell to his knees and seized on every word of his priest with awe. And Artyom himself felt something similar. Even the other soldiers unwillingly took a step back. Only Melnik continued, screwing up his eyes, to look the old man in the eyes.

'Have you seen the death of this world?' the priest continued. 'Do you understand who is to blame for it? Who converted boundless green forests into scorched deserts? What did you do with this world? With my world? Earth has not known a greater evil than your damned mechanized civilization. Your civilization is a cancerous tumour, it is a huge amoeba, greedily soaking up everything is useful and nourishing and belching out only fetid, poison wastes. And now you once more need missiles! You need the most frightful weapons created by a civilization of criminals! Why? In order to complete what you started? Murderers! I hate you, hate you all!' he yelled in a rage, then had a coughing fit and fell silent. No one breathed a word until he stopped coughing and continued, 'But your time is coming to an end . . . And even if I do not survive until then, others will come to replace me, those will come who understand the perniciousness of technology, those who will be able to manage without it! Your numbers are dwindling and you will not be here much longer. It's sad that I will not see your agony! But we are nurturing sons who will! Man will repent that he destroyed everything of value to him in his arrogance! After centuries of deception and illusions, he finally will learn to distinguish between evil and good, between the truth and a lie! We are cultivating those who will populate the earth after you. And so that your agony is not dragged out, we soon will drive the dagger of mercy into your very heart! Into the flabby heart of your rotted civilization . . . That day is near!'

He spat at Melnik's feet.

The stalker didn't respond right away. He gave the old man, trembling in his rage, the once over. Then, folding his arms across his chest, asked with interest, 'And what? You conceived some kind of worm and made up a tale just to inspire your cannibals to hate technology and progress?'

'Shut up! What do you know of my hatred of your damned, of your diabolical technology! What do you understand about people, and of their hopes and goals and needs? If the old gods allowed man to go to hell and died themselves along with their world, it makes no sense to revive them . . . In your words I hear the bloody arrogance, the contempt, the pride, that brought mankind to the brink of disaster. So, though there be no Great Worm, though we dreamed him up, you will very soon be convinced that this fabricated underground god is mightier than your celestial beings, those idols that tumbled from their thrones and were broken asunder! You laugh at the Great Worm! Go ahead and laugh! But you will not have the last laugh!'

'That's enough. The gag!' the stalker ordered. 'Don't touch him for now, he may come in handy for us again.'

They once more stuffed a rag into the mouth of the resisting old man as he cried out obscenities. The savage stood quietly, his shoulders drooped helplessly, but he did not take his lacklustre eyes off the priest.

'Teacher! What's it mean – there is no Great Worm?' he uttered gravely at last. The old man didn't even look at him. 'What's it mean? The teacher dreamt up the Great Worm?' Dron spoke dully, shaking his head from side to side.

The priest did not answer. It seemed to Artyom that the old man had used up all his vital energy and will in his speech and was exhausted now.

'Teacher! Teacher . . . There is a Great Worm . . . Are you misleading them! Why? You are speaking an untruth – to confuse the enemies! He exists . . . Exists!' Unexpectedly, Dron began to howl. Such despair was heard in his half wailing, half crying, that Artyom wanted to approach him to comfort him. The old man, it seemed, already had said adieu to life and had lost any interest in his pupil, for now other questions troubled him.

'He exists! He exists! He exists! We are his children! We all are his children! He is and always was and always will be! He exists! If there is no Great Worm . . . That means . . . We are completely alone. . . .'

Something terrifying was happening to the savage who had been left bereft. Dron went into a trance, shaking his head, as if hoping to forget what he had heard, emitting the same note, and the tears dropping from his eyes mixed with the drool from his mouth. He didn't even make an attempt to dry himself, snatching with his hands at his shaved skull. The soldiers released him, and he fell to the ground, covering his ears with his hands, striking himself on the head. He began to roll around wildly and uncontrollably, and his screams filled the whole tunnel. The fighters tried to quiet him, but even kicks and blows couldn't stop the howls bursting forth from his breast.

Melnik looked with disapproval at the cannibal, then he unbuttoned the holster at his hip, pulled his Stechkin with the silencer from it, aimed at Dron and pulled the trigger. The silencer gave a quiet bang, and the savage went instantly limp. The inarticulate screaming he had been making stopped suddenly, but the echo repeated his last sounds for several more seconds, as if extending Dron's life for a moment: 'ooooooooooonnn. . . .' And only now did it begin to occur to Artyom what the savage had screamed before his death. 'Alone!'

The stalker slid the pistol back into the holster. Artyom was unable to lift his eyes towards him, looking instead at the silenced Dron and the priest sitting not far away. He did not react in any way to the death of his pupil. When the clap of the pistol had sounded, the old man hardly twitched, then looked in passing at the savage's body and turned away with indifference again.

'Let's go on,' Melnik ordered. 'Half the metro will come running here with all this noise.'

The party formed up instantly. They put Artyom at the rear, equipped with the powerful flashlight and bullet-proof vest of one of the fighters who was carrying Anton. A minute later they had moved deep inside the tunnel. Artyom was not fit for the role of last man. He moved his legs with difficulty, stumbling on the ties, looking helplessly at the fighter walking ahead. Dron's dying bawling rang in his ears. His despair, disillusionment and unwillingness to believe that man had been left completely alone in this horrifying, gloomy world, had been transferred to Artyom. Strange, but only having heard the savage's howl, the full hopeless nostalgia for an absurd, fabricated divine being, he began to understand the universal feeling of solitude that fed mankind's faith.

If the stalker turned out to be right and they had been descending into the bowels of Metro-2 for more than an hour already, then the mysterious structure would turn out to be just an engineering design, cast off long ago by its proprietors and captured by semi-rational cannibals and their fanatical priests. The fighters began to speak in whispers. The party entered an empty station of an extremely unusual design. A short platform, low ceiling, enormously thick columns of ferroconcrete and tiled walls instead of the customary marble indicated that no one had asked that this station be easy on the eyes, and its singular mission consisted of protecting as effectively as possible those who used it. Bronze letters on the wall grown dim from time were formed into the incomprehensible word 'Sovmin.' In another place appeared 'Dom Pravitelstva RF.' Artyom knew that there were no stations under those names in the usual metro.

Melnik, it seemed, did not intend to hang about here. Quickly looking around, he spoke softly to his fighters about something and the party moved on. Artyom was overcome with a strange feeling that he was unable to express in words. Unseen Observers changed from menacing, wise and incomprehensible powers into phantasmagorical ancient sculptures illustrating ancient myths and crumbling from the dampness and draft of the tunnels. At the same time, the other beliefs that he had bumped into during this journey were lost in the gibberish of his consciousness. One of the greatest secrets of the metro was opening before him. He was walking through D-6, called by one of his companions the Golden Myth of the Underground. However, instead of a wave of happiness, Artyom was experiencing an incomprehensible bitterness. He was beginning to understand that some secrets should remain as secrets because they do not have any answers, and there are questions the answers to which it is better no one knows. Artyom was aware of the cold breath of the tunnels on his cheek, following the trail of his falling tears. He shook his head, just as Dron had done a little while ago. He began to shiver from the dank draft carrying the smell of dampness and desolation, as well as from his feelings of loneliness and emptiness. For a split second it seemed that nothing in the world made sense. His mission and man's attempts to survive in a changed world were worthless. There was nothing: just an empty, dark tunnel he was supposed to plod his way through, from 'Birth' station to 'Death' station. Those looking for faith had simply been trying to find the side branches in this line. But there were only two stations, and only tunnel connecting them.

When Artyom gathered his wits, it turned out that he had fallen several dozen paces behind the others. He didn't immediately understand what had forced him to come to his senses. Then, looking along the walls and listening closely, he realized: on one of the walls hung a loosely closed door, through which a strange, increasingly loud sound reached him. It was some kind of a dull murmur or dissatisfied rumbling. It probably hadn't been audible when the others were passing the door. But now it was becoming difficult not to notice the noise.

The others had already moved a hundred metres beyond it. Overcoming the desire to dash after them, Artyom held his breath, approached the door and shoved it. A long, wide corridor revealed itself. It ended in the black square of an exit. The murmur was coming from there. Increasingly, it sounded like the roar of a huge animal. Artyom did not dare step inside. He stood, as if bewitched, staring into the dark emptiness and listened until the roar had intensified many times and he saw in the beam of his flashlight something incredibly huge hurtling towards him. He recoiled, slammed the door, and hurried to catch up with the others.

CHAPTER 18

The Authority

They had already noticed his absence and had stopped. A white beam darted about the tunnel. When it fell on him, Artyom raised his hands just in case and screamed:

'It's me! Don't shoot!' The flashlight went out. Artyom hurried forward, expecting a dressing-down now. But, when he reached the others, Melnik only asked quietly, 'Didn't you hear anything just now?'

Artyom nodded. He didn't want to talk about what he had just seen. He thought it might just have been his imagination. He knew that he had to treat his impressions carefully in the metro. What was it? It had looked like a train racing by, but it couldn't have been. There hadn't been enough electricity in the metro to move the trains for dozens of years. The second possibility was even more improbable. Artyom recalled the warnings of the savages regarding the holy passages of the Great Worm.

'So, the trains don't run any more, right?' he asked the stalker.

Melnik looked at him with displeasure.

'What trains? Once they stopped running, they never moved again until they were ransacked for parts. Do you know something about these sounds? I think it's subterranean water. There's a river quite near here. We passed beneath it. Screw it! There are more important problems. We still don't know how to get out of here.'

Artyom didn't want to let the stalker think that he was dealing with a madman so he remained silent and let the subject drop. It was probably the river. The unpleasant sounds of flowing water and the babble of thin black tiny brooks along the edges of the rails had disturbed the sombre hush of the tunnel here. The walls and arches gleamed with moisture, a whitish film of mould covered them, and here and there were puddles. Artyom had become used to fearing water in the tunnels and this line made him particularly uncomfortable. His stepfather had told him about flooded tunnels and stations. Luckily, they lay deep or were located far away, so that a disaster was unlikely to spread to a whole branch. The further they moved, the dryer it became around them. The tiny brooks gradually disappeared, the mould on the walls was found more rarely, and the air became lighter. The tunnel went down, leaving everything empty. For the umpteenth time, Artyom recalled Bourbon saying that an empty line was most terrifying of all.

The others, it seemed, also understood this and often looked back at Artyom stumbling along last, but, having looked him in the eyes, they hastily turned back around. They walked straight ahead the whole time, not lingering at the grates cut away from the side branches and the thick cast-iron doors with locks that could be seen in the walls. Only now was it becoming clear to Artyom just how great were the dimensions of the labyrinth that had been dug into the earth beneath the city by dozens of generations of its inhabitants. The metro consisted of numerous passages and corridors, spreading into the depths of a gigantic cobweb. Some of the doors the party passed were open. The beam of a flashlight peeping into them for some seconds showed abandoned rooms and rusty bunk beds. Desolation reigned everywhere, and Artyom searched for even the slightest trace of human presence in vain. Even the metro had abandoned this grandiose structure very long ago.

The march seemed to go on forever. The old man was walking ever more slowly, he was all in, and neither jabs to his back nor the foul language of the fighters could force him to pick up the pace any longer. The party had not halted for longer than the half a minute the fighters carrying the stretcher with Anton needed to change hands.

Surprisingly, Oleg held on tenaciously. Although he was obviously tired, he didn't complain once. He only sniffled stubbornly, trying to keep pace with everyone. Up ahead, a lively discussion broke out.

Peeping from behind the broad backs of the fighters, Artyom understood what was going on. They had entered a new station. It looked almost the same as the previous one: low arches, columns thick as elephant legs, concrete walls coloured with oil paint. The platform was so wide that one was unable to see clearly what was on its other side. A cursory glance suggested that two thousand people could have waited here for a train. But there wasn't a soul here, and the last train had been sent to an unknown destination so long ago that the rails were covered with a black rust and the rotted ties were overgrown with moss. The station's name, made up of cast bronze letters, caused Artyom to shudder. It was that same mysterious word, 'Genshtab'. He immediately recalled the military personnel at *Polis*, and the poor lights wandering in the god-forsaken square near the demolished walls of the Defence Ministry building. Melnik lifted a gloved hand. The party froze at the same instant.

'Ulman, behind me,' the stalker spat out, and he nimbly climbed up to the platform. The robust fighter who was walking next to him followed the commander. The soft sounds of their stealthy steps dissolved at once in the quiet of the station. The other members of the party, as if on command, took up defensive positions, keeping the tunnel in their sights in both directions. Finding himself in the middle of them, Artyom decided that he might be able to examine the strange station under the cover of his comrades.

'Will Papa die?' He felt the boy pulling on his sleeve. Artyom lowered his eyes. Oleg was standing, staring at him pleadingly, and Artyom understood that the child was ready to cry. He shook his head in a calming manner and patted the boy on the head.

'Is it because I told where Papa worked? Did they hurt him for that?' Oleg asked. 'Papa always told me never to talk to anyone,' he sobbed. 'He said that people don't like missile men. Papa said that it wasn't shameful and bad and that the missile men had been protecting the country. That others just envy them.'

Artyom glanced at the priest apprehensively, but the old man, fatigued by the journey, had sat down on the floor and was staring blankly into the emptiness, paying no attention to their conversation.

Melnik and Ulman returned several minutes later. The party crowded around the stalker, and he put the others in the picture:

'The station is empty. But it has not been abandoned. In several places there are images of their worm. And something else . . . We found a diagram on the wall that was hand drawn. If one is to believe it, this branch leads to the Kremlin. The central station and transfer to the other lines is there. One of them goes off in the direction of *Mayakovskaya*. We have to move off in that direction. The track should be free. We won't poke our noses into the side passages. Questions?'

The fighters glanced at each other, but no one said anything. Then the old man, who had been sitting indifferently on the ground until now, became upset at the word 'Kremlin,' and began shaking his head and mumbling something. Melnik bent down and tore the gag from his mouth.

'You can't go there! You can't! I won't go to the Kremlin! Leave me here!' the priest began to babble.

'What's wrong?' the stalker asked with displeasure.

'We can't go to the Kremlin! We can't go there! I won't go!' the old man kept repeating like a wind-up toy, fidgeting.

'Well, it's fine that you won't go there,' the stalker answered him. 'At least, your fellows won't be there. The tunnel is empty, clean. I don't intend to go into the branch lines. It's best that I go straight through, via the Kremlin.'

People started whispering. Recalling the sinister glow on the Kremlin towers, Artyom understood why it wasn't only the priest who was afraid to show himself there.

'Everyone!' Melnik said. 'We are moving forward. There's no time to waste. They have a taboo day today and there is no one in the tunnels. We don't know when it will end, so we have to press on. Get him up!'

'No! Don't go there! You can't! I won't go!' The old man, it seemed, had gone totally out his mind. When a fighter approached him, the priest slipped out of his hands with an imperceptible serpentine movement, then with feigned obedience froze at the sight of the machine gun muzzles aimed at him.

'Well, get lost!' His triumphant laughter turned into a choking wheeze after several seconds, a spasm twisted his body and he foamed profusely at the mouth. His face became a hideous mask, with his mouth sharply angled upwards. It was the most terrifying smile Artyom had seen in his whole life.

'Ready,' Melnik reported. He approached the old man who had fallen to the ground and, hooking him with the tip of his boot, turned him over. The stiffened body moved heavily and rolled over face downwards. At first Artyom thought that the stalker had done it so as not to see the dead man's face, but then he understood the real reason. Melnik illuminated the tightly drawn wires around the old man's wrists with his flashlight. The priest was squeezing the needle he had driven into his left forearm in his right fist. Artyom could not understand how he had contrived to do it, where he had hidden the poisoned dart and why he had not used it earlier. He turned away from the body and covered young Oleg's eyes with the palm of his hand. The party had stopped dead still. Although the order to move had been issued, not one of the fighters had stirred. The stalker looked them over. One could imagine what was going on in the fighters' heads: just what awaited them at the Kremlin if the prisoner preferred suicide to avoid going there? Not losing any time on opinions, Melnik stepped towards the stretcher with the groaning Anton, bent down and took one of the handles.

'Ulman!' he called. After a second of wobbling, the broad-shouldered scout took up position at the second handle of the stretcher. Submitting to an unexpected impulse, Artyom approached them and grabbed a rear handle. Someone else stood beside him. Saying not a word, the stalker straightened up and they moved forward. The others followed them, and the party once more assumed combat formation.

'It's not too far now,' Melnik said quietly. 'About two hundred metres. The main thing is to find the crossing to the other line. Then, on to *Mayakovskaya*. I don't know what's further ahead. There's no Tretyak . . . We'll think of something. Now we have one road. It's impossible to turn off it.'

His words about the road woke something in Artyom and he again recalled his own trip. Having thought about it, he didn't immediately recognize what Melnik was talking about but as soon as he heard the stalker's reference to the dead Tretyak, he started and loudly whispered to him:

'Anton . . . The wounded man . . . it seems he served in the RVA . . . So he's a missile man! That means we still will be able to do it! Won't we?'

Melnik looked over his shoulder at the watch commander on the stretcher.

He, it seemed, was really ill. The paralysis in Anton had passed long ago, but now delirium tormented him. His groans were replaced by unclear but furious commands, desperate entreaties, sobbing and muttering. And the closer they approached the Kremlin, the louder the wounded man's cries became and the more intently he bucked on the stretcher. 'I said! Don't argue! They're coming . . . Hit the ground! Cowards . . . But just how . . . just how are the others?! No one will be able there, no one!'

Anton argued with comrades only he could see. His forehead was covered with perspiration, and Oleg, running alongside the stretcher, took advantage of a short respite while the fighters changed hands to dab at his father's forehead with a rag. Melnik shined his light at the watch commander, as if trying to understand whether he would come to his senses. His eyeballs flashed back and forth beneath their lids and Anton clenched his teeth and his fists were clenched. He threw his body one way and then the other. Only the canvas straps stopped him from falling from the stretcher, but it was becoming increaingly difficult to carry him.

After another fifty metres, Melnik lifted his hand and the party again came to a halt. A crudely painted symbol was shown in white on the floor: the now customary twisting line thrust its thickened head at a fat, red mark that cut across the line lying ahead. Ulman gave a whistle.

'The red light's lit, it says there's no road,' someone laughed nervously from the rear.

'It's for the worms, it doesn't concern us,' the stalker cut him short. 'Forward!'

However, now they were moving ahead more slowly. Melnik, having put on the night vision device, took up the position at the head of the party. But it was not only out of caution they had stopped hurrying. At the 'Genshtab' station, the tunnel began to angle more sharply downward, and an invisible, but tangible haze of some presence was creeping from the Kremlin. Shrouding the people, it convinced them that something inexplicable, huge and evil was hidden there, in the pitch dark depths. It was not the same feeling as Artyom had experienced before. It wasn't like the dark vortex that had pursued him in the lines at *Sukharevskaya*, nor like the voices in the pipes, or the superstitious fear generated and fed by the people in the tunnels leading to Park Pobedy. He felt more strongly that this time something inanimate, but alive nonetheless, was concealed. Artyom looked at the stalwart Ulman walking on the other side of the stretcher. He suddenly really wanted to talk with him. It wasn't important what they talked about. He just wanted to hear a human voice.

'And why do the stars at the Kremlin glow on the towers?' The question had been tormenting him.

'Who told you that they glow?' the fighter asked with surprise. 'There's no such thing there. It's like this with the Kremlin: each person sees what he wants to see. Some say that it hasn't been there for ages. It's just everyone hopes to see the Kremlin. They just want to believe that this holy of holies was left intact.'

'And what happened to it?' Artyom asked.

'No one knows,' Ulman replied, 'except your cannibals. I was still young, about ten years old then. And those who did the fighting say that they didn't want to destroy the Kremlin so dropped some kind of a secret development on it . . . Biological weapons. Right at the beginning. They didn't notice it right away and didn't sound the alarm, but when they understood what was what, it was already too late, because it had consumed everyone there, it even swallowed up the people from the neighbourhoods. They had been living outside the wall up to then and felt wonderful.'

'But how does it . . . swallow?' Artyom was not able to shake off a vision: of the stars shimmering with the unearthly light on the tops of the Kremlin towers.

'Did you know there was such an insect as the doodlebug? It would dig a funnel in the sand, and climb down to the bottom and open its mouth. If an ant ran past and accidentally touched the edge of the hole, that was it. End of its career. The doodlebug would move, the sand would pour to the bottom and the ant went straight down, falling into its mouth. Well, it's the same thing with the Kremlin. It stands on the edge of a funnel it can fall into and will suck you down,' the fighter smirked.

'But why do people go inside?' persisted Artyom.

'How would I know? Hypnosis, most likely . . . So take for example these cannibalistic illusionists of yours. They almost forced us to stay there . . .'

'So just why then are we making our retreat towards it?' Artyom asked with a puzzled look.

'Those aren't questions for me, but for the boss. But I understand that you have to be outside and look at the walls and towers for it to grab you. But it seems we're already inside . . . What is there to see here?'

Melnik turned round and angrily hissed at them. Ulman immediately stopped short and shut up. And a sound his voice had been covering up could be heard. Was it a soft gurgling coming from the deep? A rumbling? It didn't seem to presage anything terrible, but it was persistent and unpleasant, and there was no way of ignoring it. They passed by a trio of powerful pressurized doors arranged one behind the other. All the doors were opened wide, invitingly, and a heavy iron curtain was raised to the ceiling. 'Doors,' Artyom thought. 'We are on a doorstep.'

The walls suddenly parted, and they ended up in a marble hall, so spacious that the beam of the powerful flashlights hardly reached the opposite wall. The ceiling, in contrast to other secret stations, was high here and thick, richly adorned columns supported it. Massive gilded chandeliers, turned black by time, still flashed brilliantly in the beam of a flashlight. The walls were covered with huge mosaic panels. They depicted an old man with a beard with people in work clothes smiling at him, and young girls in modest garments and light white headscarves, and soldiers in out-dated service caps, a squadron of fighters being carried along the sky, a rumbling tank column and finally the Kremlin itself. There was no name at this surprising station, but its absence was just enough to understand where they were. The columns and walls were covered with a thick layer of grey dust. It was obvious that no feet had encroached here for decades; and it was strange to think that even the intrepid savages had fled this place Further on there was an unusual train on the track. Its only two carriages were heavily armoured and painted in a protective dark green colour. The windows had been replaced with narrow slits resembling gun slots. The doors, one on each carriage, were locked. It occurred to Artyom that perhaps the inhabitants of the Kremlin had not been able to use their own secret track for escape. They got to the platform and stopped.

'So this is what it's like here . . .' The stalker lifted his head toward the ceiling, as far as his helmet allowed him. 'How many tales I've heard . . . But it's not like that at all . . .'

'Where to now?' Ulman asked.

'No idea,' Melnik confessed. 'We have to investigate.'

This time he didn't abandon them and the people slowly moved around all together. The station resembled a conventional one in some respects: along the edges of the platform two tracks had been built and an elongated hall ended in two escalators, forever stopped, that exited to magnificent rounded arches. The one closest to them went up and the other plunged to a quite unimaginable depth. Somewhere here, there had to be an elevator. The former residents of the Kremlin would hardly have had, as mortal beings have, two minutes to creep down an escalator.

Melnik was spellbound and so were the others. Trying to reach the high arches with their beams, scrutinizing the bronze sculptures installed inside the hall, admiring the magnificent panels and astonished by the grandeur of this station, a true underground palace, they even began to whisper so as not to violate its peace. Looking along the walls with admiration, Artyom completely forgot about the dangers and about the priest who had finished himself off, and about the intoxicating radiance of the Kremlin stars. Only one thought remained in his head: he was trying so hard to imagine how unspeakably beautiful this station must have been in the bright light of those magnificent chandeliers.

They were approaching the opposite end of the hall where the steps of the down escalator began. Artyom wondered what was concealed down there. Another station perhaps, from which trains were sent directly to secret bunkers in the Urals? Or tracks leading to countless corridors of dungeons? A deep fortress? Strategic reserves of weapons, medicines and foodstuffs? Or simply an endless dual ribbon of steps leading downward, as far as the eye could see? Wouldn't that deepest point of the metro of which Khan had spoken be located here? Artyom imagined the most improbable pictures, deferring that moment when, reaching the edge of the escalator, he would finally see just what really was located below. That's why he was not first at the handrail. The fighter who had just been telling him about the doodlebug had reached the arch earlier. Uttering a shriek, he shrunk back in fright. And a moment later it was Artyom's turn. Slowly, like certain magical creatures, which had been sleeping for hundreds of years, but were suddenly were awake and flexing muscles that had become numb from ages of sleep, both escalators began to move. The steps crawled downward with a strained creak. It was inexpressibly eerie . . . Something here did not add up, did not correspond to what Artyom knew and understood about escalators. He felt it, but was unable to grasp the slippery shadow of understanding by the tail.

'Do you hear how quiet it is? It's not the motor moving it, you know. The machine room is not working. Ulman facilitated it.'

But of course, that was it. The creak of the stairs and the grinding of the ungreased gears, and all the sounds that the revived mechanism emitted. Was that all? Artyom again heard the disgusting gurgling and slurp that had reached him in the tunnel. The sounds were coming from the depths where the escalators led. He gathered his courage and, approaching the edge, illuminated the inclined tunnel along which the blackish brown ribbon of steps crawled ever faster. For something like a moment it seemed that the Kremlin's secret had been opened up before him. He saw something dirty, brown, oily, overflowing and unambiguously alive oozing through the slits between the steps. It emerged from these slits in short spurts, rising and falling in step along the whole length of the escalator as far as Artyom could see. But it was not a meaningless fluctuation. All these spurts of a living substance were part of one gigantic whole, which was straining to move the steps. And somewhere far below, at a depth of several dozen metres, this very dirty and oily stuff spread freely about the floor, swelling and clearing away, overflowing and quivering, emitting those same strange and revolting sounds. The arch was like a monstrous jaw to Artyom, the domes of the escalator tunnel a throat, and the steps themselves, the greedy tongue of a terrible ancient god awakened by strangers. And then it was as if a hand touched his consciousness, stroking it. And his head emptied, as in the tunnel. And he wanted only one thing – to step onto the escalator and ride below, where the answer to all his questions waited. The Kremlin's stars once more flashed before his imagination's gaze . . .

'Artyom! Run!' A glove slapped him on the cheeks, burning his skin. He roused himself and was stupefied: the brown slush was creeping up through the tunnel, swelling visibly, expanding, frothing like steaming pig's milk. His legs would not obey, and his flash of consciousness was extremely short. Whatever controlled him set him free for only a flash in order to grasp him firmly and draw him back into the haze once more.

'Pull him!'

'The lad first! And don't cry . . .'

'Heavy . . . And the wounded guy is still here . . .'

'Drop it, drop the stretcher! Where are you going with the stretcher!'

'Wait a moment, I'll climb it too, it's easier with two . . .'

'Your hand, give me your hand! Quickly!'

'Mother of God. It's already come out . . .'

'Tighten it up . . . Don't look! Don't look there! Do you hear me?'

'On his cheeks! That's it!'

'To me! That's an order! I'll shoot!'

Strange pictures were flickering: green, the side of a railcar sown with rivets, an inverted ceiling for some reason, then a soiled floor . . . darkness . . . green armour again . . . then the world stopped swaying, grew calm and froze.

Artyom raised himself up and looked around. They were sitting around him on the roof of the armoured train. All the flashlights had been turned off, only one was lit, a small pocket light, which lay in the centre. Its light was not enough to see what was happening in the hall, but something could be heard bubbling, seething and overflowing from all sides. Someone again was carefully, as if trying by touch, to reach into his mind, but he shook his head and some of his fog dissipated. He looked and mechanically recounted the members of the party huddled on the roof. Now there were five of them, not counting Anton, who still had not come to, and his son. Artyom dully noted that one fighter had disappeared somewhere, but then

410

his thoughts again faded away. As soon as his head emptied, reason once more began to slide into a turbid abyss. It was difficult to fight it alone. Melnik recognized what was happening, and Artyom tried to grasp this thought; he had to think about whatever he liked, if only to keep his mind occupied. It was apparent the same thing was happening to the others.

'This is what happened to this trash when it was exposed to the radiation . . . They were exactly right, biological weapons! But they didn't think what the cumulative effect would be. It's also good that it stays behind the wall and doesn't get out into the city . . .' Melnik was saying.

No one answered him. The fighters had calmed down and listened absent-mindedly.

'Speak, speak! Don't be quiet! This crap will stay in your sub-conscious. Hey, Oganesian! Oganesian! What are you thinking about?' The stalker shook one of his subordinates. 'Ulman, dammit! Where are you looking? Look at me! Don't be quiet!'

'Sweet . . . It's calling . . .' the strong Ulman said, fluttering his eyelashes.

'Just how sweet! Didn't you see what happened to Delyagin?' The stalker slapped the fighter on the cheek with all his might, and Ulman's lethargic look brightened.

'Hold hands! Everyone is to take each other's hand!' Melnik cried at the top of his lungs.

'Don't be quiet! Artyom! Sergey! At me, look at me!' And a metre below bubbled and seethed that terrible mass that, it seemed, already had covered the whole of the platform. It was becoming ever more persistent, and they were no longer able to withstand its pressure.

'Guys! Fellows! Don't give in! But press on . . . altogether! Let's sing!' The stalker was not giving up, calling his soldiers to order, handing out slaps in the face or bringing them to their senses with light touches. 'Rise up, huge country . . . Rise up for a mortal fight!' he dragged it out, wheezing and out of tune. 'With the dark fascist force . . . Against their curs-ed hordes . . .'

'Let noble fu-ry. . . . Boil up like a wave,' Ulman carried on. It seethed around the train with double the strength. Artyom hadn't begun to sing along: he didn't know the words to this song, and anyhow it occurred to him that the fighters had begun to sing, for some hidden reason, about the power of darkness and a boiling wave. No one knew any more words than the first verse and the refrain, except Melnik, and he sang the next quatrain alone, his eyes flashing menacingly and not allowing anyone to be distracted: 'As two-oo different poles, We are hostile to all! For Wo-rl-d and peace, we battle, They for a reign of darkness . . .' Almost everyone sang the refrain this time, even little Oleg tried to echo the adults. The discordant choir of coarse, male voices, cracked and hoarse from smoking, resounded, returning in an echo, in the boundless dark hall. The sound of the singing soared to the high arches painted with the mosaic, bounced off them, fell and sank into the teeming, living mass below. And although this picture of seven healthy men, perched on the roof of a train and, while holding hands, singing these senseless songs would have appeared absurd and funny to Artyom in any other situation, now it resembled more a chilling scene from a nightmare. He really, truly wanted to wake up. 'Let no-o-o-ble fu-ry bo-il up like a wa-a-a-ve. . . . A people's war is going on, a sa-a-a-cred wa-a-a-r!' Artyom himself, although he was not singing, diligently opened his mouth and rocked in time to the music. Not having caught the words in the first verse, he even decided that it was about either the people living in the metro, or about the opposition to the dark ones, under whose onslaught his home station was soon supposed to fall. Then in one verse he heard fascists, and Artyom understood it was about the battle of the Red Brigade fighters with the inhabitants of *Pushkinskaya* . . . When he tore himself away from his reflections, he discovered that the choir had fallen silent. Perhaps even Melnik himself didn't now the next verses.

'Guys! Let's do "Combat", hey?' The stalker was trying to persuade his fighters. 'A combat, my father, my father-combat, You didn't hide your heart behind the guys' back . . .' He had only just started, but then he too fell silent. A stupor enveloped the party. The fighters began to unclench their hands and the circle disintegrated. Everyone was quiet, even Anton who had been raving and muttering the whole time. Feeling a warm and turbid slush of indifference and fatigue filling the emptiness that had occurred in his head, Artyom tried to push it out, thinking about his mission, then telling himself nursery rhymes as he remembered them, then simply repeating: 'I think, think, think you will not worm yourself into me . . .' The fighter whom the stalker had called Oganesian suddenly stood up and brought himself to his full height. Artyom lifted his eyes to him with indifference.

'Well, it's time for me. Take care,' he said taking his leave. The rest dully looked at their comrade, not answering, only the stalker nodded at him. Oganesian approached the edge and unhesitatingly

412

stepped forward. He didn't even scream, but from below was heard an unpleasant sound, a combination of a splash and a hungry rumbling.

'It calls . . . It . . . calls,' Ulman said in a sing-song voice and also began to get up. Artyom was spellbound.

'I think you won't worm yourself into me!' He got stuck on the word 'I,' and now he simply repeated it, not even noticing that he was speaking aloud: 'I, I, I, I, I.' Then he strongly, irresistibly wanted to look down in order to understand whether the heaving mass there was as deformed as it had appeared to him at first. But had he suddenly been wrong about it? Recalling again the stars on the Kremlin towers, distant and beckoning . . . And here the small Oleg sprang lightly to his feet and, taking a short run, threw himself down with a happy laugh. The living quagmire below chomped quietly, receiving the boy's body. Artyom understood that he envied him and also intended to follow.

But several seconds later, as the mass closed over Oleg's head, perhaps at that very moment when it had taken his life from him, his father screamed and regained consciousness. Breathing heavily and exhaustedly looking from side to side, Anton lifted himself and set about shaking the others, demanding an answer from them: 'Where is he? What's happened to him? Where is my son? Where is Oleg? Oleg! Olezhek!' Little by little the faces of the fighters began to regain intelligence. Even Artyom began to become conscious. He was no longer certain what he really had seen as Oleg jumped into the seething mass. Therefore, he didn't answer, just tried to calm Anton, who, it seemed, felt in a mysterious way that what had happened was irrevocable. And then his hysterics broke into the numbness felt by Artyom and in Melnik, and the others. His agitation and his baleful despair were transferred to them, and the unseen hand firmly grasping their consciousness, was yanked away.

The stalker made several test shots at the bubbling mass, but with no success. Then he told the fighter armed with the flame-thrower to remove the backpack with the fuel from his shoulders and, when told to, toss it as far as possible from the train. Having ordered two others to direct their flashlights on the spot where the backpack would fall, he prepared to fire and gave the go-ahead. Spinning in place, the fighter hurled the backpack and almost flew right after it himself, barely managing to hold on to the edge of the roof. The backpack flew into the air and began to fall about fifteen metres from the train.

'Get down!' Melnik waited until it touched the pulsing, oily surface, and squeezed the trigger.

Artyom watched the backpack's flight while stretched out on the roof. As soon as the shot rang out, he hid his face in the fold of his elbow and grasped the cold armour with all his might. The explosion was powerful: Artyom nearly flew off the roof as the train rocked. A dirty, orange glow of blazing fuel splashing along the platform reached his blinking eyes. Nothing happened for a minute. The squelching and chomping of the quagmire did not weaken, and Artyom was already preparing for it to recover from the annoying unpleasantness and begin to envelop his mind again. But instead, the noise began gradually to move further away.

'It's leaving! It's leaving!' Ulman bellowed right beside his ear. Artyom lifted his head. In the light of the flashlights he could clearly see that the mass, which recently had occupied nearly the whole huge hall, was shrinking and retreating, returning to the escalator.

'Hurry!' Melnik jumped to his feet. 'As soon as it slides down, everyone behind me, right to that tunnel!'

Artyom was surprised how Melnik could be so certain, but he wasn't about to ask, having put the stalker's previous indecisiveness down to whatever had been controlling his mind. Now the stalker was transformed. He was again the sober, decisive commander who did not put up with any arguments. Not only was there no time to think about it, but he didn't even want to. The only thing that now occupied Artyom was how to get out of this damned station as soon as possible before the strange being that dwelled in the Kremlin's basements recovered its wits and returned in order to consume them. The station no longer seemed marvellous and beautiful to him. Now everything here was hostile and repulsive. Even the workers and peasants looked down in outrage from its wall panels. They still smiled, but it was strained and sickly sweet.

Having jumped pell-mell to the platform, they tore to the opposite end of the station. Anton had come to completely and ran as fast as the others, so that now nothing was delaying the party. After twenty minutes of mad racing through the black tunnel, Artyom began to gasp, and even the others had begun to tire. The stalker allowed them to slow to a quick march.

'Where are we going?' Artyom asked, overtaking Melnik.

'I think right now we are beneath *Tverskaya* . . . We should exit soon toward *Mayakovskaya*. We'll sort it out there.'

'But how did you know which tunnel to enter?' Artyom was curious.

'It was shown on the map we found at Genshtab. But I only recalled that at the last moment.'

As they arrived at the station, everything flew from their heads. Artyom pondered. Had his delight with the Kremlin station, with the pictures and the sculptures, and its space and magnitude come to nothing? Or was it some trickery, evoked by the terrible entity lurking in the Kremlin? Then he remembered the disgust and fear that the station had inspired in him when the drug had dissipated. And he began to doubt that these were his real feelings. Maybe the 'doodlebug' forced them to feel an irresistible desire to run from there at breakneck speed when they caused it pain? Artyom was no longer sure of his true feelings. Did a monstrous creation of his mind release him or did it continue to dictate thoughts to him and inspire his emotional experiences? At what moment did Artyom fall under its hypnotic influence? And was he sometimes free to make his own choices? And could his choice ever be free? Artyom again recalled the meeting with the two strange residents of *Polyanka*.

He glanced back: Anton was walking two paces behind him. He no longer badgered anyone about what happened to his son. Someone had already told him. His face had hardened and gone dead, his gaze was turned inward. Did Anton understand that they were only a step away from rescuing the boy? That his death had become a ridiculous accident? But it had brought the others through. Accident or victim?

'You know, we all most likely were saved only thanks to Oleg. It is because of him that you . . . regained consciousness,' he said to Anton, not specifying how this had come about.

'Yes,' Anton agreed indifferently.

'He told us that you served in the rocket forces. Strategic.'

'Tactical,' Anton replied.

'The "Tochka" and the "Iskander".'

'And multiple fire systems? "Smerch", "Uragan"?' having held back a little, the stalker, who had been listening to their conversation, asked.

'I can operate those, too. I was a career soldier, and they taught it to us. And everyone was interested in it. Everyone wanted to try it. Until I saw what it led to.'

There was not the smallest sign of interest in his voice, and there was no uneasiness regarding the fact that his secret was known to strangers. His answers were short, mechanical. Melnik, nodding, again moved away from them, going on ahead.

'We need your help very much,' Artyom said, carefully testing the waters. 'Understand, we have terrible things happening at *VDNKh*,' he began. And he immediately stopped short: after what he had seen in the last twenty-four hours, what happened at *VDNKh*, however awful, didn't seem like anything exceptional, capable of overwhelming the metro and finally destroying man as a biological species. Artyom considered this thought, and reminded himself that it could be coming from the strange entity. 'We have some creatures getting through from the surface,' he continued, having collected his thoughts. But Anton stopped him with a gesture.

'Just say what has to be done, and I will do it,' he uttered colourlessly. 'I have the time now . . . How can I return home without my son?'

Artyom nodded nervously and walked away from the man leaving him along with his thoughts. Now he felt unclean, seeking help from a man who had just lost a child . . . He had been deprived of him through his, Artyom's, fault . . .

He caught up with the stalker again. Melnik was clearly in a good mood. Having left the party stretched out behind him, he was humming something to himself and, seeing Artyom, smiled at him. Listening to the melody Melnik was trying to reproduce, Artyom recognized that very song about the sacred war they had been singing on the roof of the train.

'You know, at first I decided this is the song for our war with the dark ones,' he said, 'and then I understood that it is about fascists. Who composed it? The communists from the Red Line?'

'This song is already about a hundred years old, if not a hundred and fifty.' Melnik shook his head.

'They composed it first for one war, then adapted it for another. It's good that it is suitable for any war. As long as man is alive, he will always deem himself to be the light of the world, and consider his enemies as the darkness. And they will be thinking like that on both sides of the front,' Artyom added to himself. 'Whatever it means.' His mind again flashed to the dark ones. 'Maybe it means that people, let's say the *VDNKh* inhabitants, are the evil and darkness for them?' Artyom thought better of it and forbade himself to think of the dark ones as ordinary enemies. If one open the door for them only half way, nothing would hold them back . . .

'So you were saying about this song that it is eternal,' Melnik unexpectedly spoke. 'That dawned on me, too. In our country all eras are much the same. Take people . . . You won't change them in any way. They're as stubborn as mules. So, it would seem the end of the world is already at hand and you cannot go outside without an anti-radiation suit, and every kind of trash that earlier you only saw at the cinema has multiplied . . . No! You don't impress them! They're the same. Sometimes it seems to me that nothing has ever changed. Well, I visited the Kremlin today,' he smiled wryly, 'and I was thinking: there's not even anything new there. I'm not even certain when they hit us with this crap: thirty years ago or three hundred.'

'Were there really such weapons three hundred years ago?' Artyom was doubtful, but the stalker didn't reply. They'd seen two or three depictions of the Great Worm on the floor, but there had been no sign of the savages themselves. The first drawing had put the fighters on their guard, and they'd regrouped in such a way that it was easier to defend themselves, but the tension had dissipated after they'd encountered the third drawing.

'They weren't jabbering nonsense. Today was a holy day and they stay at the stations and don't go into the tunnels,' Ulman noted with relief.

Something else occupied the stalker. By his calculations, the missile unit was very close by. Checking the hand-drawn map every minute, he absently repeated:

'Somewhere here . . . Isn't this it? No, not that corner, but where is the pressurized gate? We ought to be approaching it already . . .'

Finally, they stopped at a fork: to the left was a dead end with a grille, at the end of which they could see the remains of a pressurized gate, and to the right, as far as the light of the flashlight could reach, there was a straight tunnel.

'That's it!' Melnik determined. 'We're there. Everything tallies with the map. There, behind the grille, the tunnel has collapsed like at Park Pobedy. And that must be the passage into which they took Tretyak. So . . .' Illuminating the map with his pocket flashlight, he thought aloud, 'The line goes directly from this fork to the division, and this one, to the Kremlin, we came from there, right.' Then he climbed behind the grille with Ulman and they wandered around the dead end for about ten minutes, inspecting the walls and ceiling with the flashlight.

'OK! There's a passage in the floor this time, a round sort of top, similar to a sewer manhole,' the returning stalker reported. 'Every-one, we are there. Take a break.'

As soon as everyone had removed their rucksacks and had sprawled out on the ground, something strange happened to Artyom: despite the awkward position, he fell asleep instantly. Either the fatigue accumulated in the last twenty-four hours had taken its toll or the poison from the paralysing needle was producing some side effects.

Artyom again saw himself, asleep, in the tent at *VNDKh*. As in his earlier dream, it was gloomy and abandoned at the station. Artyom knew beforehand what would happen to him now. Already accus-tomed to saying hello to the little girl who was playing, he didn't ask her about anything, heading instead directly toward the tracks. The distant cries and entreaties for mercy didn't frighten him. He knew that he was seeing the unwelcome dream again for another reason, one that concealed in the tunnels. He was supposed to uncover the nature of the threat, reconnoitre the situation and report about it to his allies from the south. But as soon as he was shrouded in the darkness of the tunnel, his confidence in himself and in the fact that he knew why he was here and how he had to go on vaporized. He was as frightened as when he went beyond the limits of the station alone for the first time. And exactly as then, it wasn't the darkness itself nor the rustle of the tunnels that scared him, but the unknown, the inability to foretell what danger the next hundred metres of the line concealed.

Vaguely recalling how he had behaved in previous dreams, he decided not to give in to fear this time, but to go forward, until he met the one who was concealed in the dark, waiting for him.

Someone was coming towards him. Not hurrying, as he was, not walking with his cowardly, slinking short steps, but with a confident heavy tread. Artyom stopped in his tracks, catching his breath. The other one also stopped.

Artyom promised himself that he wouldn't run this time regard-less of what happened. When, judging by the sound, only about three metres of darkness separated them, Artyom's knees shook, but somehow he found the strength to make one more step. But, feeling a light flutter of the air on his face as someone approached, Artyom couldn't bear it. Flinging out a hand, he pushed the unseen being away and fled. This time he didn't stumble and he ran for an intolerably long time, an hour or two, but there was no trace of his home station, there were no stations at all, nothing at all, only an endless, dark tunnel. And this proved to be even more terrible.

'Hey, that's enough of a nap, you'll sleep through the meeting.' Ulman pushed him on the shoulder.

Artyom roused himself and looked guiltily at the others. It appeared that he had dropped off for only for a few minutes. They were all sitting in a circle. In the centre was Melnik with the map, pointing and explaining.

'Well,' he said,' it's about twenty kilometres to our destination. If we keep up a good pace and nothing gets in our way, it's possible to make it in half a day. The military unit is located on the surface, but there is a bunker under it and the tunnel leads to it. However, there's no time to think about that. We have to split up.' He looked at Artyom. 'Are you up? You are returning to the metro, I will appoint Ulman to look after you,' he said. 'The others and I are going to the missile division.'

Artyom was on the verge of opening his mouth, intending to protest, but the stalker stopped him with an impatient gesture. Leaning towards the heap of rucksacks, Melnik started to distribute the supplies.

'You take two protective suits, we have four left, and we don't know what it will be like there. There's one radio for you and one for us. Now the instructions. Go to *Prospect Mir*. They are waiting for you there. I have sent some messengers.' He looked at his wristwatch. 'In exactly twelve hours go up to the surface and look for our signal. If everything is OK and we are on the air, we'll move to the next stage of the operation. Your mission is to find the best way to the Botanical Gardens and then to get up high in order to help us direct and correct the fire. The "Smerch" has a limited destruction area and we don't know how many missiles are still there. And the gardens aren't small. Don't worry,' he said to Artyom, 'Ulman will be doing it all, you are there as company. We have use for you too, of course. You know what these dark ones look like.

'The Ostankino tower is very suitable for guidance. It's wider in the middle: there was a restaurant there. They served tiny sandwiches with caviar there at prices that were out of sight. But people didn't go there because of them, but for the view of Moscow. The Botanical Gardens can be seen clearly from there. Try to get to the tower. If you can't get to the tower, there is a multi-storey building alongside, sort of white, shaped like the letter P, and almost uninhabited. So . . .

This is a map of Moscow for you, and this one is for us. It's a shambles there around the squares. You simply look and communicate. The rest, follow us. It's nothing too complex,' he assured them. 'Questions?'

'And if they don't have a nest there?' Artyom asked.

'Well, we can't do the impossible,' the stalker slapped his palm on the map. 'And I have a surprise here for you,' he added, winking at Artyom.

Reaching into his backpack, Melnik took out a white polyethylene bag with a worn coloured picture on the side. Artyom looked inside and took out the worn passport and the children's book with the cherished photograph that he had found in the neglected apartment at Kalinskiy inside. Having raced after Oleg, he had left his treasures at *Kievskaya*, and Melnik had gone to the trouble to collect them and carry them with him all this time. Ulman sitting alongside looked at Artyom with a puzzled look, then at the stalker.

'Personal things,' Melnik said, smiling. Artyom wanted to thank him but the stalker had already got up from his seat and was giving orders to the fighters going with him.

Artyom went up to Anton who was absorbed in his own thoughts.

'Good luck!' Artyom extended his hand to the lookout. Anton silently nodded, putting his rucksack onto his back. His eyes were totally empty.

'Well, that's all! We won't say goodbye. Note the time!' Melnik said. He turned and, without saying another word, was off.

CHAPTER 19

The Final Battle

Having moved the heavy cast-iron lid of the closed manhole aside, they began their descent. The narrow, vertical shaft was composed of concrete rings, from each of which jutted a metal bracket. As soon as they were left alone, Ulman changed. He spoke to Artyom in short, monosyllabic phrases, mainly giving orders or admonishing him. As soon as the lid of the hatch had been removed, he ordered Artyom to put out the flashlight and, putting on the night vision instrument, dived inside first. Artyom had to crawl down, holding on to the brackets. He didn't really understand what all these precautions were for, as, after the Kremlin, they hadn't encountered any danger along their way. Finally, Artyom decided that the stalker had given Ulman special instructions and, having been left without a commander, he was enthusiastically filling the role himself. Ulman smacked Artyom on the foot, giving the sign to stop. Artyom obediently froze, waiting until the other man explained to him what was happening. But, instead of explanations, a soft thump was heard from below. It was Ulman jumping to the floor. A few seconds later, Artyom heard muffled gunshots.

'You can come down,' his partner said to Artyom in a loud whisper, and a light came on.

When the brackets ended, he released his hands, and dropped about two metres, landing on a cement floor. Lifting himself up, he dusted off his hands and looked around. They were in a short corridor, about fifteen paces long. The opening of the manhole yawned above them in the ceiling. There was another hatch just like it in the floor, with the very same cast-iron grooved cover. Beside it, in a pool of blood, lay a dead savage face downwards, squeezing his blow pipe tight in his hand even after death.

'He was guarding the passage,' Ulman replied quietly at Artyom's questioning glance, 'but he had fallen asleep. Most likely he didn't expect anyone to crawl in from this side. He had put his ear to the hatch and dropped off.'

'You killed him . . . what, while he was sleeping?' Artyom asked.

'So what? It wasn't a fair fight.' Ulman sniffed. 'If nothing else, now he'll know not to sleep on duty. Anyway, he was a bad person: he wasn't observing their holy day. He was told not to go into the tunnels.'

Dragging the body to the side, Ulman opened the hatch and again put out his flashlight. This time the shaft was extremely short and led to an office filled with trash. A mountain of metal plates, gears, springs and nickel-plated handrails, enough parts for a whole coach, completely hid the manhole from prying eyes. They were heaped on top of each other in disarray right up to the ceiling and stayed there only by some kind of miracle. There was a narrow passage between this pile and the wall, but getting through it without touching and bringing a whole mountain of metal down was almost impossible.

A door buried in dirt up to its middle led from the office to an unusual square tunnel. A line from the left there: either there was an obstruction or they had stopped laying the track for some reason. To the right there was a standard tunnel, round and wide. It seemed as if there was a border between two intertwined subterranean worlds here. Even breathing was different: the air was damp but not so ghastly and stagnant as in the secret D-6 passages. They weren't sure where to go. They decided not to move out at random, as there was a frontier post of the Fourth Reich located on this line. Judging by the map, it was only about twenty minutes from *Mayakovskaya* to *Chekhovskaya*. Digging into the bag with his things, Artyom found the bloodied map he had got from Daniel, and worked out the true direction from it. Less than five minutes later they reached *Mayakovskaya*.

Sitting down on a bench, Ulman took the heavy helmet off his head with a sigh of relief, wiped his red, damp face with a sleeve and ran his fingers through his dark-blond crew cut. Despite his powerful frame and having the habits of an old tunnel wolf, Ulman, it seemed, was only slightly older than Artyom.

While they were looking for somewhere to buy food, Artyom was able to inspect the station. He no longer knew how much time had passed since his last meal, but his aching stomach was no laughing matter. Ulman had no supplies on him: they had left in a hurry and brought only what was necessary.

Mayakovskaya resembled *Kievskaya*. It was just a shadow of the once elegant and airy station. In this half of the ruined station people huddled in ragged tents or out on the platform. The walls and ceiling were covered with damp patches and trickling water. There was one small campfire for the whole station but no fuel.

The inhabitants talked among themselves quietly, as if at the bedside of a dying man. However, there was a shop even here: a patched up three-man tent with a folding table displayed at the entrance. The selection was modest: skinned rat carcasses, dried up and shrunken mushrooms, procured here God knows when, and even uncut squares of moss. A price tag lay proudly next to each item – a piece of news print with carefully handwritten numbers. There were almost no shoppers except them, only an undernourished stooped woman holding a small boy by the hand. The child was pulling towards a rat lying on the counter, but his mother admonished him:

'Don't touch! We've already eaten meat this week!' The boy obeyed, but he didn't forget about the carcass for long. As soon as the mother turned away, he once more tried to reach for the dead animal.

'Kolka! What did I tell you? If you are bad, the demons will come out of the tunnels to get you! Sashka didn't obey his mommy and they took him!' the woman scolded him, succeeding at the last moment to pull him away from the counter.

Artyom and Ulman couldn't make up their minds. Artyom began to think that he could survive until they got to *Prospect Mir* where the mushrooms would at least be fresher.

'Some rat, perhaps? We fry them in front of the customer,' the shop's bald owner said with some dignity. 'Certificate of quality!' he added enigmatically.

'Thanks, I've already eaten,' Ulman hastened to turn him down. 'Artyom, what do you want? I wouldn't take the moss. World War Four will start in your gut from it.'

The woman looked at him with disapproval. In her hand were only two cartridges which, judging by the prices, was just enough for the moss. Noting that Artyom was looking at her modest capital, the woman hid her fist behind her back.

'Nothing here,' she snarled spitefully.

'If you don't intend to buy anything, get lost!'

'We're not all millionaires! What are you staring at?'

Artyom wanted to answer, but he was carried away by the sight of her son. The boy was very similar to Oleg. He had the same

423

colourless, fragile hair, reddish eyes and turned-up nose. The boy put his thumb in his mouth and smiled shyly at Artyom, looking at him a bit sullenly. Artyom felt as if his lips were spreading into a smile in spite of himself, and his eyes were swelling with tears. The woman intercepted his glance and flew into a rage.

'Damned perverts!' she screeched, her eyes glaring. 'Let's go home, Kolienka!' She pulled the boy by the hand.

'Wait! Stop for a minute!' Artyom pressed several shells out of the reserve clip of his machine gun and, catching up to the woman, gave them to her. 'Here . . . These are for you. For your Kolia.'

She looked at him with distrust, then her mouth twisted scornfully.

'Just what do you think you can get for five cartridges? That he'll be your child?'

Artyom didn't immediately understand what she had in mind. Finally, it came to him and he was on the verge of opening his mouth to start making excuses, but he wasn't able to utter a thing, and he just stood there, staring blankly. The woman, satisfied with the effect she had produced, replaced her rage with mercy.

'Agreed certainly! Twenty cartridges for half an hour.'

Stunned, Artyom shook his head, turned and nearly took off running.

'Jerk! OK give me fifteen!' the woman cried after him.

Ulman was still standing there, discussing something with the seller.

'Well, what about the rats? Haven't you made up your mind?' the owner of the tent inquired courteously, having seen the returning Artyom. 'A little bit more and she'll start bargaining with me.'

Artyom understood. Pulling Ulman behind him, he hurried from this Godforsaken station.

'Where are we going in such a hurry?' the fighter asked when they were walking through the tunnel in the direction of *Byelorusskaya*. While trying to cope with the lump rising in his throat, Artyom told him what had happened. His story did not especially impress Ulman.

'So what? She has to live somehow,' he responded.

'Why is such a life necessary at all?' Artyom's face convulsed. 'Do you have any ideas?'

Ulman shrugged his broad shoulders.

'What's the sense of such a life? You cling to it, you endure all this filth, humiliation, you trade your children, stuff your face with moss, for what?' Artyom stopped short, recalling Hunter, who had been talking about the survival instinct, about the fact that one would fight like a wild animal for his life and the survival of others with all his might. Then, at the very beginning, his words had inflamed a hope and desire in Artyom to fight like that frog who had whipped the cream in the jar with its feet, turning it into butter. But now the words uttered by his stepfather for some reason seemed more reliable.

'For what?' Ulman teased him.

'Well, all right young man, "for what" are you living?' Artyom regretted that he had got involved in this conversation. As a fighter, he had to give Ulman his due, he was superb, but as a companion he wasn't especially interesting. And Artyom could see it was useless to argue with him regarding the sense of life.

'Well, personally I am "for what",' he answered sullenly, not able to bear it.

'Well, for what?' Ulman began to laugh. 'For the rescue of mankind? Leave it. It's all nonsense. You aren't saving it, so it's someone else. Me, for example.' He shined the flashlight on his face so that Artyom could see him and made a heroic face. Artyom looked at him jealously, but said nothing. 'And then,' the fighter continued, 'they all just cannot live for it.'

'And what about you, is life without meaning?' Artyom tried to ask the question ironically.

'How is it without meaning? It makes sense for me, the same way as for everyone. And generally, searches for the meaning of life usually happen during puberty. But for you, it seems, it's taken longer.' His tone was not offensive, but mischievous, so that Artyom wouldn't sulk. Inspired by his success, Ulman continued, 'I remember when I was seventeen. I was trying to understand it all, too. It passes. There is only one meaning in life, brother: to make and bring up children. But let them be tormented by the question. And answer it how they can. Well, that's the theory,' he smiled again.

'And then just why are you coming with me? Are you risking your life? If you don't believe in rescuing mankind, then what?' Artyom asked after some time.

'First, I was ordered to,' Ulman said severely. 'Orders are not questioned. Second, it's not enough to make children, you have to raise them. And how will I grow them if your riffraff from *VDNKh* eat them up?' Such self-confidence exuded from him, his strength and his words, that the picture of the world was so seductively simple and organized, that Artyom no longer wanted to argue with him. On

425

the other hand, he felt that the fighter was inspiring a confidence in him too.

As Melnik had said, the tunnel between *Mayakovskaya* and *Byelorusskaya* turned out to be peaceful. True, something was banging in the ventilation shafts but they slipped past normal sized rats a few times, and that reassured Artyom. The section was surprisingly short – they had not even been able to complete the argument when the lights of the station appeared ahead.

Being close to Hansa had a profound influence on *Byelorusskaya*. It was immediately apparent that it was rather well protected. A blockhouse had been constructed ten metres before the entrance: a light machine gun stood on sacks filled with dirt, and the guard detail consisted of five men. Checking their documents (and here the new passport came in handy), they asked them politely whether they were from the Reich. No, no, they assured Artyom, no one here has anything against the Reich, it was a trading station, observed full neutrality, and did not interfere in the conflicts between the powers, as the chief of the guard called Hansa, the Reich and the Red Line.

Before continuing their trip along the Ring, Artyom and Ulman decided they could take a break and have a bite. Sitting in an affluent, even chic, snack bar, Artyom obtained information about *Byelorusskaya* as well as eating an excellent and inexpensive cutlet.

A round-faced, fair-haired man sitting at the table opposite, who introduced himself as Leonid Petrovich, was tucking away an epic portion of bacon and eggs, and when his mouth was empty, he told them with pleasure about his station. *Byelorusskaya* survived because of the transit of pork and chicken. Huge and very successful enterprises were located beyond the Ring – closer to *Sokol* and even to *Voykovskaya*, though the latter was dangerously close to the surface. Kilometres of tunnels and engineering lines had been converted to a huge livestock farm that fed all of Hansa, and delivered goods both to the Fourth Reich and to the eternally half-starved Red Line. Moreover, the residents of *Dynamo* had inherited from their enterprising predecessors an aptitude for the tailor's trade. They sewed the pigskin jackets that Artyom had seen at *Prospect Mir*. No external danger from this end of the *Zamoskvoretskaya* line existed, and in all the years of living in the metro, no one even once had put either *Sokol*, *Airport*, or *Dynam* out of business. Hansa laid no claims to them, being satisfied by the ability to collect a duty from the transportation of the goods, and at the same time they rendered them protection from the fascists and the Reds. Nearly all of the

426

residents of *Byelorusskaya* were involved in business. Farmers from Sokol and tailors from *Dynamo* had the sense to make a profit from the wholesale deliveries. Bringing a batch of hogs or live chickens on handcars and trams pulled by men, the people from that side, as they called them here, unloaded their belongings – for these purposes special cranes even had been installed on the platforms – settled up their accounts and left for home. Life bustled at the station. The resolute traders (at *Byelorusskaya* they were called 'managers' for some reason) drifted from the 'terminal' – the unloading locations – to warehouses, jingling bags with cartridges and dispensing instructions to sinewy loaders. Small carts on well lubricated wheels, laden with boxes and bundles, rolled noiselessly towards rows of counters, or to the Ring boundary line, from where Hansa buyers took the merchandise, or to the opposite edge of the platform, where Reich emissaries awaited the unloading of their orders. There were quite a few fascists here, but not the ordinary ones, mainly officers. However, they behaved themselves. They were a little arrogant, but within the bounds of decency. They looked with hostility at the swarthy dark-haired men, of whom there were enough among the local tradesmen and loaders, but they didn't try to impose their beliefs and laws.

'And we have banks here, too, you know . . . Many of them, from the Reich, come to us supposedly for goods, but really they come to invest their savings,' his companion shared with Artyom.

'I doubt that they will touch us. We are like Switzerland for them,' he added incomprehensibly.

'You have it good here,' Artyom noted politely.

'It's not just us, it's all about *Byelorusskaya* . . . So where are you from?' Leonid Petrovich finally asked out of respect. Ulman pretended that all his attention was on his cutlet and he had not heard the question.

'I'm from *VDNKh*,' Artyom replied, glancing at him.

'What do you say! How terrible!' Leonid Petrovich even put down his knife and fork. 'They say things are really bad there? I heard they are hanging on by a thread. Half the people have died . . . Is it true?'

A lump stuck in Artyom's throat. For better or for worse, he had to reach *VDNKh*, see his own kind, perhaps, for the last time. How had he been able to waste valuable time eating? Moving the plate away, he asked for the bill and, despite Ulman's protests, pulled him along with him, past the counters with meat and clothing in the openings of the arches, past the piles of merchandise, past the bartering peddlers, bustling loaders, the sedately strolling fascist officers, towards the crossing to the Ring line. Over the entrance hung a white cloth with a brown circle in the middle. Two machine gunners in the familiar grey camouflage checked their documents and inspected their things. Artyom had not succeeded in getting through to the Hansa territory with such ease before. Ulman, still chewing a piece of cutlet, dug into his pocket and presented an unknown type of ID to the border guards. They silently moved away a section of the barrier, allowing them in.

'What kind of a pass is that?' Artyom was curious.

'So . . . The award booklet for the medal, "For Service to the Fatherland'," Ulman laughed it off. 'Everyone is indebted to our colonel.'

The crossing to the Ring was a strange mixture of fortress and warehouses. The second Hansa border began beyond the footbridges over the tracks: real redoubts had been erected there with machine guns and even a flame-thrower. And further away, next to a memorial – a bronze, bearded guy with a machine gun, a frail girl and a pensive lad with weapons (most likely, the founders of *Byelorusskaya* or heroes of a battle with mutants, Artyom thought) – a whole garrison of not less than twenty soldiers was deployed.

'This is because of the Reich,' Ulman explained to Artyom. 'It's like this with the fascists: trust but verify. They didn't touch Switzerland, of course, but they subjugated France.'

'I have gaps in my knowledge of history,' Artyom acknowledged with embarrassment. 'My stepfather couldn't find a tenth grade textbook. Though I have read a little about ancient Greece.'

An endless chain of loaders with bundles on their shoulders trailed past the soldiers like ants. The movement was well organized: the bearers descended on one escalator, and they came up, unladen, on the other. A third was intended for the remaining passers-by. Below sat a machine gunner in a glass booth, watching the escalator. He checked Artyom and Ulman's documents again and issued them papers with the stamp, 'Temporary Registration – in Transit' and the date.

This station also was named *Byelorusskaya*, but the difference from its radial twin was striking: they were like twins separated at birth, one of whom ended up in a royal family and the other who was adopted and grew up poor. All the prosperity of that first *Byelorusskaya* faded in comparison with the Ring station. It gleamed with shining white walls, fascinated with intricate stucco work on the ceiling and dazzled with neon lamps, of which only three were burning in all the station, but even their light was more than enough. The loaders on the platform were divided into two parts. One group walked to the tracks through arches on the left, the other to the right, casting off their bundles into piles and returning at a run for new ones. Two stops had been made at the tracks: for merchandise, where a small crane had been installed, and for passengers, where a ticket office stood. Once every fifteen or twenty minutes a cargo handcar went past the station. They were outfitted with a peculiar body – board planking on which they had loaded boxes and bundles. Besides the three or four men who stood at the handles of the handcar, there also was a guard on each.

The passenger handcars arrived more rarely – Artyom and Ulman had to wait more than forty minutes. As the ticket collector explained to them, the passenger handcars waited until enough people had gathered so as not to send the workers on errands for no reason. The fact that somewhere in the metro it was still possible to buy a ticket – a cartridge for each stage – and pass from station to station, as before, completely fascinated Artyom. He even forgot about all his problems for a while and simply stood and observed the loading of the merchandise. It showed him how fine life in the metro must have been earlier when huge sparkling trains, not manual handcars, moved along the tracks.

'That's your carrier coming!' the ticket collector announced and he began to ring a small bell. A large handcar, to which was attached a tram with wooden benches, rolled to a stop. Having presented their tickets, they sat down on unoccupied seats. After waiting another few minutes for tardy passengers, the trolley moved on. Half the benches were situated so that the passengers were sitting facing forward and half facing to the rear. Artyom had got a seat facing backwards and Ulman was sitting in the remaining seat, with his back to him.

'Why are the seats arranged so strangely, in different directions'? Artyom asked of his neighbour, a hale old woman of about sixty years old who was wearing a woollen shawl riddled with holes. 'It's uncomfortable you know.'

She threw up her hands.

'And what? Would you leave the tunnel running wild? You young people are thoughtless! Didn't you hear what happened over there the other day? Well, such a rat,' the old woman gestured in dismay, 'jumped out of an interline, and dragged away a passenger!'

'It wasn't a rat!' a man in a quilted jacket interrupted, turning round. 'It was a mutant! They have a lot of mutants running about at *Kurskaya* . . .'

'And I say, a rat! Nina Prokoievna, my neighbour, told me. Do you think I don't know?' The old woman was indignant.

They argued for a long time, but Artyom was no longer listening to their conversation. His thoughts once again had turned to *VDNKh*. He had already decided that, before he went up to the surface to set out for the Ostankino tower with Ulman, he would definitely try to get through to his home station. He still didn't know how he would convince his partner but he had a bad feeling that this might be his last chance to see his home and friends. And he couldn't ignore it. Who knew what would happen later? Though the stalker had said that there was nothing complicated about their task, Artyom didn't really believe that he would be meeting him any time again. However, before starting his own, perhaps, final climb up, he had to at least return to *VDNKh* for a little while. How it sounded . . . *VDNKh* . . . Melodic, endearing. 'I could listen and listen to it,' Artyom thought. Had his casual acquaintance at *Bye-lorusskaya* really been speaking the truth? Was the station really on the point of falling to the onslaught of the dark ones? Were half its defenders already dead? How long had he been absent? Two weeks? Three? He closed his eyes, trying to imagine his beloved arches, the elegant, but reserved lines of the domes, the delicate forging of the copper ventilation grids between them and rows of tents in the hall. The handcar gently swayed in time to the lulling chatter of the wheels, and Artyom didn't notice that it was putting him to sleep. He was dreaming about *VDNKh* again . . .

Nothing surprised him any more, he wasn't listening and not trying to understand. The goal of his dream was not at the station, but in the tunnel. Leaving the tent, Artyom went right to the tracks, jumped down and headed south, towards the Botanical Gardens. The darkness no longer frightened him, but something else did: the forthcoming meeting in the tunnel. Who awaited him there? What was the point of it? Why did his courage always fail him in the end?

His twin finally appeared in the depths of the tunnel. Soft confident steps gradually approached, as before, and Artyom felt his nerve failing. However, this time he comported himself better. His knees shook but he was able to control himself and wait until he came right up to the unseen creature. He was covered in a cold, sticky sweat, but did not break into a run when the light ripple of the air told him that the mysterious being was just a few centimetres from his face.

'Don't run . . . Look into the eyes of your fate . . .' a dry, rustling voice whispered into his ear. And here Artyom recalled – and just how had he been able to forget about it in his past nightmares? – that he had a lighter in his pocket. Groping for it, he struck the flint, preparing to see who was speaking to him. And he immediately went numb, feeling only that his feet were taking root in the ground. A dark one stood next to him, not moving. Its dark eyes were without pupils and wide open, searching for his glance. Artyom cried as loudly as he could.

'Damnation!' the old woman was holding her hand to her heart, breathing heavily. 'How you frightened me, you tyrant!'

'Please forgive him. He's with me and . . . He's nervous,' Ulman said turning around.

'Just what did you see there, that you shouted out?' The old woman shot him a curious glance from beneath half closed, swollen eyelids.

'It was a dream . . . I had a nightmare,' Artyom answered. 'Excuse me.'

'A dream?! Well you young people are impressionable.' She again started moaning and bickering.

Actually, Artyom had slept for a rather long time – he even had slept through the stop at *Novoslobodskaya*. But he didn't have time to remember what he had understood at the end of his nightmare as the passenger handcar arrived at *Prospect Mir*.

The situation here was strikingly different from the satisfying prosperity of *Byelorusskaya*. There was no business recovery at *Prospect Mir*, not even a sign of it, but on the other hand one immediately noticed a large number of military personnel: Spetsnaz and officers with the chevrons of the engineering troops. From the other edge of the platform, on the tracks, stood several guarded cargo motorized trolleys with mysterious boxes covered with tarpaulins. In the hall, nearly fifty poorly dressed people with huge trunks were sitting right on the floor, looking round hopelessly.

'What's going on here?' Artyom asked Ulman.

'It's not what's happening here, it's what you have going on at *VDNKh*,' the fighter replied. 'It's obvious they intend to blow up the tunnels . . . If the dark ones crawl through from Prospect Mir, Hansa will have to answer for it. Most likely, they are getting ready for a pre-emptive strike.'

While they were crossing to the *Kaluzhka-Rizhskaya* line, Artyom grew convinced that Ulman's guess was most likely correct. The Hansa Spetsnaz was also active at a radial station where it wasn't supposed to be. Both entrances to the tunnels leading to the north, towards *VDNKh* and the Botanical Gardens, were fenced off. Someone had constructed some makeshift blockhouses here, where the Hansa border guards were on duty. There were no visitors in the marketplace, almost half the stands were empty, and people whispered nervously, as if inevitable misfortune was looming over the station. Several dozen people were crowded into one corner, whole families with bundles and bags. A chain had been strung around a table with the sign, 'Refugee Registration.'

'Wait for me here, I'll go find our man.' Ulman left him at the shopping area and disappeared.

But Artyom had a few things he wanted to do himself. Climbing down onto the rails, he went up to a blockhouse and started talking with a sullen border guard.

'Can one still get to *VDNKh*?'

'We are still letting them through, but I don't advise going there,' the guard answered. 'Haven't you heard what's happening there? Some kind of vampires are getting in, so many that they can't be stopped. They've taken over nearly the whole station. Obviously it's really hot there. If our miserly leadership had decided to let them have some free ammo, if only to hold them off till tomorrow.'

'What's happening tomorrow?'

'Tomorrow we're going to blow everything to hell. We are placing dynamite three hundred metres from *Prospect* in both tunnels and everything will be just a fond memory.'

'But why don't you just help them? Certainly Hansa has the power?'

'I told you. There're vampires there. It's swarming with them, there's not enough backup.'

'But what about the people from *Rizhskaya*? And from *VDNKh* itself?'

Artyom couldn't believe his ears.

'We alerted them several days ago. They're trickling in. Hansa is taking them. We aren't animals. But they had better hurry. When the time runs out, it's so long. So you should try to get there and back as soon as possible. What do you have there? Business? Family?'

'All of it,' Artyom replied, and the border guard nodded knowingly. Ulman was standing in the arch, quietly speaking with a tall young man and a stern man in a machinist's coat and with the full regalia of the station chief.

'The vehicle is up above and the tank is full. In any event, I still have a radio and protective suits, and another Pecheneg and a Dragunov sniper rifle.' The youth pointed at two large black bags. 'We can go up at any time. When do you need us up there?'

'We'll be monitoring the signal every eight hours. We should already be in position by then,'

Ulman answered. 'Is the pressurized gate working?' he addressed the chief.

'It's OK,' the chief confirmed.

'When you give the word. Only we'll have to drive off the people so they aren't frightened. That's all I have. So, we'll rest for about five hours or so and then full speed ahead,' Ulman summed up. 'So, Artyom? Lights out?'

'I can't,' Artyom told him, pulling his partner aside. 'I have to get back to *VDNKh*. To say goodbye and just to look around. You were right, they will be blowing up all the tunnels from *Prospect Mir*. Even if we come back alive from there, I won't see my station any more. I have to! Honestly.'

'Listen, if you are just afraid of going up, to your dark ones, just say so,' Ulman nearly started, but on seeing Artyom's look, he stopped short. 'It was a joke. Excuse me.'

'Honest, I have to,' Artyom repeated. He couldn't explain his feeling, but he knew that he had to get to *VDNKh* at any cost.

'Well, if you have to, then you have to,' the fighter replied, embarrassed. 'You won't have time to get back, especially if you intend to say goodbye to someone there. Here's what we'll do: we'll ride from here along *Prospect Mir* in the vehicle with Pashka – that's him with the cases. We had intended to go directly to the tower earlier, but we can take a detour and run by the old entrance to the *VDNKh* metro. Everything new has been turned upside-down, your people have to know that. We'll wait for you there. In five hours and fifty minutes. Whoever doesn't make it is late. Did you get a suit? Do you have a watch? Here, take mine, I'll get one from Pashka.' He unfastened the metal bracelet.

'In five hours, fifty minutes.' Artyom nodded, shook Ulman's hand and raced towards the blockhouse. Seeing him again, the border guard shook his head.

'And nothing else strange is happening in this crossing?' Artyom asked. 'Are you here about the pipes or what?'

'It's nothing. They patched them up. They say your head will spin when you are going by,' the border guard answered.

Artyom thanked him with a nod, turned on his flashlight and walked into the tunnel. Different thoughts raced through his head for the first ten minutes: about the danger of the crossing laying ahead, about the considered and reasonable way of life at *Byelorusskay*, then about the 'carriers' and real trains. But gradually the tunnel's darkness sucked these trivial thoughts, this confusion of flashing pictures and snatches of phrases, from him.

At first he grew calm, empty, then he began to think about something else. His journey was coming to an end. Even Artyom could not say how long he had been away. Maybe two weeks had passed, perhaps more than a month. How simple, how short the trip had seemed to him when, sitting on the handcar at *Alekseevskaya*, he had been looking at his old map in the light of the flashlight, trying to plan a route to *Polis* . . . An unknown world lay before him then, about which he knew nothing for certain. It had been possible to develop a route by considering only the length of the journey and not how it would change the traveller walking it. Life had turned out to be very different, confused and complex, mortally dangerous. Even casual companions, sharing small segments of his trip with him, had paid for it with their lives. Artyom remembered Oleg. Everyone has his own predestination, Sergei Andreyevich had told him at *Polyanka*. Could it have been that the terrible, nonsensical death spared other people and allowed them to continue their affairs? Artyom grew cold and uncomfortable. To accept such a proposition, to accept this sacrifice, meant that he had to believe that his journey could only be at the cost of somebody's life . . . Could it be that in order to fulfil his predestined fate others had to be trampled, destroyed, crippled? Oleg, of course, had been too young to ask why he had been born. But if he had thought about it, he would hardly have agreed to a fate. The faces of Mikhail Porfirievich, Daniel and Tretyak passed before his eyes. Why did they die? Why did Artyom himself survive? What gave him this capacity, this right? Artyom was sorry that Ulman, who with one mocking remark could dispel his doubts, was not with him now. The difference between them was that the trip through the metro had forced Artyom to see the world as if through a multi-faceted prism, but Ulman's Spartan life had taught him to view things simply: through the sight of a sniper's rifle. He didn't know which of the two of them was right, but Artyom no longer was able to believe that there can be only one, single true answer to every question. Generally in life, and especially in the metro, everything was unclear, changing and relative. Khan had explained this to him at first using the example of the station clock. If such a basis for perceiving the world, as time, turned out to be farfetched and relative, then just what could be said about other indisputable views of life? All of it: from the voice of the pipe in the tunnel through which he was walking, and the shining of the Kremlin stars to the eternal secrets of the human soul, had several explanations. And there were many answers to the question, 'why?' The people Artyom had encountered, from the cannibals at Park Pobedy to the fighters of the Che Guevara brigade, knew how to answer it. All of them had their own answers: the sectarians and the Satanists, the fascists and the philosophers with the machine guns, like Khan. It was for this reason that it was difficult for Artyom to choose and accept only one of them. Getting a new version of the answer every day, Artyom was unable to compel himself to believe what was true, because the next day another, no less precise and comprehensive one, might arise. Whom should he believe? And in what? In the Great Worm – the cannibalistic god, shaped like an electrified train and populating the barren, scorched earth with living beings; in the wrathful and jealous Jehovah; in his vainglorious reflection – Satan; in the victory of communism in the whole metro; in the supremacy of the fair-haired men with turned-up noses over curly haired, swarthy races Something suggested to Artyom that there were no differences in any of it. Any faith served man only as a crutch supporting him. When Artyom was young, his stepfather's story about how a monkey took up a cane and became a man made him laugh. After that, apparently, the clever macaque no longer let the cane out of his hand because he couldn't straighten up. He understood why man needs this support. Without it, life would have become empty, like an abandoned tunnel. The desperate cry of the savage from Park Pobedy when he realized that the Great Worm was only a contrivance of his people's priests still resonated in Artyom's ears. Artyom felt something similar, finding out that the Unseen Observers did not exist. But for him, repudiation of the Observers, the Snake and other metro gods made life easier. Did that mean that he was stronger than the others? Artyom understood that was not true. The cane was in his hands, and he was supposed to become brave enough to recognize it. His awareness that he was carrying out an assignment of huge importance, that the survival of the whole metro was in his hands and that this mission hadn't been entrusted to him by chance, served as his support. Consciously or not, Artyom looked for proof in everything that he had chosen for carrying out this mission, but not like Hunter, but someone or something greater. To destroy the dark ones, to save his home station and those near and dear from them and to stop the destruction of the metro – that was his task. And everything that had happened to Artyom during his travels proved only one thing: he was not the same as everyone. Something special had been intended for him. He was supposed to make mincemeat of and destroy the vermin which otherwise would make short work of the remnants of mankind. While he was walking along this path, faithfully interpreting the signs being sent his way, his will for success was overcoming reality, playing with statistical probability, warding off bullets, blinding monsters and enemies, and compelling allies to be at the right location at the right time. How else could he understand why Daniel had turned over to him the plan of the missile unit's location, and this unit by some miracle had not been destroyed decades ago? How else to explain that, against all common sense, he had met one of the few, maybe only living missile men in the whole metro? Had Providence had placed powerful weapons into Artyom's hands personally and sent him a man to help deliver a death blow to the inexplicable and merciless force, crushing it? How else could all the miraculous rescues of Artyom from the most desperate situations be explained? While he believed in his own predestination, he was invulnerable, although people who accompanied him perished one after the other. Artyom's thoughts turned to what had been said by Sergei Andreyevich at *Polyanka* about fate. At that time those words had driven him forward, like a new, lubricated spring installed in the worn-out, corroded mechanism of a wind-up toy. But at the same time, they were unpleasant for him. Maybe it was because this theory deprived Artyom of his own free will and forced him to submit to the story line of his own fate. But, on the other hand, how was it possible for him to refute the existence of this line of thinking after everything that had happened to him? He could no longer believe that his whole life was only a succession of random events.

Too much already had happened, and it was impossible to get out of this rut just like that. If he had gone so far, then he had to go even further – such was the inexorable logic of the path chosen. Now it was already too late to hold any doubts. He must go forward, even if this meant bearing the responsibility not only for his own life, but also for the lives of others. All the sacrifices had not been in vain. He had to accept them, he was obligated to take his path to the end. That was his fate. Just how had he lacked this clarity earlier? He had doubted his own election, distracted by stupidity and hesitating all this time, but the answer always was right there. Ulman had been right: there's no need to complicate life.

Artyom was walking now, briskly beating out the pace. And he hadn't heard any noise from the pipes; nothing dangerous had been encountered at all in the tunnels all the way to *VDNKh*. However, Artyom had come across people who were going to *Prospect Mir*: he was moving against the flow of those unfortunates, who were exhausted, had cast off everything and were running from the danger. They viewed him as a madman: he alone was walking into the lair of terror itself at the same time the others were trying to abandon the cursed place.

There were no patrols at *Rizhskaya* or at *Alekseevskaya*. Immersing himself in his thoughts, Artyom didn't notice when he had approached *VDNKh*, though not less than an hour and a half had passed. Climbing into the station and looking around, he unwillingly shuddered – how much it reminded him of that *VDNKh* he saw in his nightmares.

Half the lighting was not working, there was the odour of burning gunpowder in the air, and somewhere in the distance were heard the moans and the anguished crying of women. Artyom held the machine gun at the ready and moved ahead, carefully skirting the arches and examining the shadows closely. It was as if the dark ones had been able, at least once, to penetrate the fences and reach the station itself. Some of the tents had been cleared away, and in several places there were dried traces of blood on the floor. People were still living here and there, and a flashlight sometimes even shone through the canvas. Distant gunfire could be heard from the northern tunnel. The exit to it was covered with bags of dirt piled as high as a man. Three men were pressed against this breastwork, observing the tunnel through gun slots and keeping the approaches in their sights.

'Artyom? Artyom! Where did you come from?' a familiar voice hailed him. Turning around, he noticed Kirill – one of the men he had left *VDNKh* with at the very beginning of his journey. Kirill's arm was in a sling, and the hair on his head seemed even more unkempt than usual.

'Well, I've come back,' Artyom answered vaguely. 'How are you holding out here? Where's Uncle Sasha, where's Zhenka?

'Zhenka? He was caught . . . They killed him, a week ago,' Kirill said gloomily.

Artyom's heart fell.

'And my stepfather?'

'Sukhoi is alive and well, he's in charge. He's in the infirmary right now.' Kirill waved a hand in the direction of the staircase leading to a new exit from the station.

'Thanks!'

Artyom raced away.

'And just where have you been?' Kirill cried after him.

The 'infirmary' was sinister. There weren't many real wounded here, only five men. Other patients occupied the majority of the space. Diapered like infants and confined in sleeping bags, they were laid out in a row. All of them had their eyes wide open and they mumbled incoherently through their half-open mouths. It wasn't a nurse watching over them, but a rifleman holding a phial with chloroform in his hands. From time to time one of those in diapers began to fidget along the floor, howling and transferring his agitation to the rest, and then the guard would place a rag soaked with chloroform to the man's face. The man didn't fall asleep, nor did he close his eyes, but he went quiet for some time and calmed down.

Artyom didn't see Sukhoi right away: he was sitting in the office, discussing something with the station doctor. Leaving, he ran into Artyom and was stupefied.

'You're alive . . . Artyomka! Alive . . . Thank God . . . Artyom!' he had begun to mutter, touching Artyom on the shoulder, as if wishing to convince himself that Artyom was indeed standing in front of him. Artyom embraced him. And he, like a child, was afraid in the depths of his soul that he would return to the station and his stepfather would begin to scold him: he would say, where did you disappear to, how irresponsible, how long were you going to behave like a little boy . . . But instead, Sukhoi just held him close and didn't let go for a long time. When the fatherly embrace finally ended, Artyom saw that Sukhoi's eyes were filled with tears and he blushed. Briefly, he told his stepfather where he had disappeared to and what he had managed to do during that time, and he explained why he had returned. Sukhoi only shook his head and criticized Hunter. Then he came to his senses, saying that he would not speak ill of the dead. Though, he didn't know what had happened to Hunter.

'Do you see what's going on here?' Sukhoi's voice again hardened.

438

'Every night they pour in and there aren't enough bullets. A handcar arrived from *Prospect Mir* with supplies, but it's peanuts.'

'They want to blow up the tunnel at *Prospect Mir* to cut off both *VDNKh* and the other stations completely,' Artyom reported.

'Yes . . . They are afraid of the ground water. They aren't venturing close to *VDNKh*. But this won't help for long. The dark ones will find other entrances.'

'When will you be leaving here? There's only a little time left. Less than a day. You have to get everything ready.'

His stepfather took a long look at him, as if checking him over.

'No, Artyom, I only have one way out of here, and it's not to *Prospect Mir*. We have thirty wounded men here. What are we to do with them? Throw them away? And who will maintain the defences while I am saving my hide? How can I go up to a man and say to him: "Well, you are staying here so that you can hold them off and die, but I'm going"? No . . .' He took a breath. 'Let them blow it up. We'll hold out as long as we can. I have to die like a man.'

'Then I'll stay with you,' Artyom said. 'They have the missiles and they will manage without me. What's my purpose anyway? At least I'll help you . . .'

'No, no. You must go,' Sukhoi interrupted him. 'We have a fully operational pressurized gate and the escalator is working again. You can make your way to the exit quickly. You must go with the others. They don't even know what they're dealing with!'

Artyom suspected that his stepfather was sending him away from the station just to save his life. He tried to object, but Sukhoi didn't want to hear anything.

'Only you alone in your group know how the dark ones are able to drive people mad.' He pointed at the diapered wounded.

'What's wrong with them?'

'They were in the tunnels, they couldn't hold out. We managed to drag these out, and that's good. But the dark ones tore so many apart while they were alive! Incredible strength. The main thing is, when they approach and begin to howl, there are few who can stand it. You understand that. Our volunteers handcuffed themselves together so they wouldn't run away. But those who managed to get loose are lying here. There are only a few wounded because if the dark ones reach you, it's hard to get away.'

'Zhenka? . . . did they get him?' Artyom asked, swallowing. Sukhoi nodded. Artyom decided not to get the details.

'Let's go while there's a lull.' Taking advantage of his silence,

Sukhoi added, 'We'll have a chat and drink some tea. We still have some left. Are you hungry?' His stepfather embraced him and moved into the command room.

Artyom looked around in amazement: he could not believe that in the weeks since he had left that *VDNKh* had managed to change so much. The once comfortable, homelike station had now been cast into anguish and despair. He wanted to flee from here as soon as possible. A machine gun clattered behind them. Artyom gripped his weapon.

'That's a warning,' Sukhoi said. 'The most terrible time will start in a few hours. I feel it already. The dark ones come in waves, and we have killed only one recently. Never fear, if something serious begins, our guys will use the siren – they sound a general alarm.'

Artyom pondered. His dream of walking into the tunnel . . . Now it was impossible, and a real meeting with a dark one would hardly end just as harmlessly. There was no point in mentioning it when Sukhoi would never allow him to go into the tunnel alone. He had to reject such a mad idea. He had more important things to do.

'I knew that you and I would see each other again, that you would come,' Sukhoi said, pouring the tea once they were in the command room. 'A man arrived here a week ago looking for you.'

'What man?' Artyom was put on his guard.

'He said you and he are acquainted. Tall, skinny, with a small beard. He had a strange name, similar to Hunter's.'

'Khan?' Artyom was surprised.

'That's it. He told me that you would come back here again, and was so certain that I was put at ease at once. And he also gave me something for you.' Sukhoi reached for the wallet in which he kept notes and objects known only to him and pulled out a sheet of paper folded a couple of times. Unfolding the paper, Artyom lifted it to his eyes. It was a short note. The words written in a sloppy fleeting hand baffled him. 'He who is brave and patient enough to peer into the darkness his whole life will be first to see a flicker of light in it.'

'And didn't he give you anything else?' Artyom asked with a puzzled look.

'No,' replied Sukhoi. 'I thought it was a coded message.'

But the man had come here especially for this. Artyom shrugged his shoulders. Half of everything Khan had said and done seemed complete nonsense to him but, on the other hand, the other half had compelled him to look at the world otherwise. How was he to know to which part this note pertained?

They drank tea and chatted for quite a while. Artyom was unable to throw off the feeling that he was seeing his stepfather for the last time, and it was as if he was trying to talk long enough with him to last him for the rest of his life. Then the time to leave arrived.

Sukhoi tugged the handle and, with a grinding sound, the heavy cover lifted a metre. Stagnant rainwater poured down from outside. Standing in slime up to his ankles, Artyom smiled at Sukhoi, though the tears were welling up in his eyes. He was on the point of saying goodbye when, at the last moment, he remembered the most important thing. Withdrawing the children's book from his rucksack, he opened it to the page with the photograph inside and handed it to his stepfather. His heart began to beat anxiously.

'What is it?' Sukhoi was surprised.

'Do you recognize her?' Artyom asked hopefully. 'Look closer. Isn't this my mother? You would have seen her when she gave me away to you.'

'Artyom,' Sukhoi smiled sadly, 'I hardly saw her face. It was very dark there and I was looking at a rat. I don't remember her at all. I remember how you then grabbed my hand and didn't cry at all, and then she was gone. I'm sorry.'

'Thank you. Bye.' Artyom was on the verge of saying, 'Daddy,' but a lump got caught in his throat. 'Maybe we'll meet again . . .' He tightened his gas mask, bent over, slipped beneath the curtain and ran up along the rickety steps of the escalator, carefully pressing the crumpled photograph to his breast.

The escalator seemed simply endless. One had to climb it slowly and very carefully. The steps creaked and chattered beneath his feet, and in one place they unexpectedly moved downwards, and Artyom barely managed to yank away his foot. Moss-covered remnants of huge branches and small saplings were scattered everywhere, carried here by the explosion, perhaps. The walls were overgrown with bindweed and moss and, through holes in the plastic covering of the side barriers, the rusty parts of the mechanism could be seen. He didn't once glance back. Everything was black up above. That was a bad sign. Suddenly he thought, what if the station pavilion crumbled and he couldn't overcome the obstacle? If it were just a moonless night, it wouldn't be too bad: but it wouldn't be easy guiding the fire of the missile battery in poor visibility. The closer to the end of the escalator, the brighter the glares on the walls and the thin beams penetrating the slits became. The exit to the exterior pavilion was blocked, not by stones but by fallen trees. After several minutes of searching, Artyom discovered a narrow trapdoor through which he could just about squeeze. A huge gap, almost the length of the whole ceiling, yawned in the roof of the vestibule through which the pale lunar light fell. The floor was covered with broken branches and even with whole trees. Artyom noted several strange objects next to one of the walls: large, dark-grey leather spheres, as tall as a man, rolling in the brush. They looked repulsive and Artyom was afraid to go any closer to them. Switching off his flashlight, he exited onto the street. The upper station vestibule stood among an accumulation of the expanded frames of once graceful merchants' pavilions and kiosks. Ahead he could see an enormous building. It was strangely bent and one of the wings was half demolished. Artyom looked around: Ulman and his comrade were not around. They must have been delayed along the way. He had a little time left to study the surroundings.

CHAPTER 20

Born to Creep

After catching his breath for a minute, he listened, trying to detect the heartrending howl of the dark ones. The Botanical Gardens were not far from here, and Artyom couldn't understand why these beasts had not reached their station along the surface before now. Everything was quiet, but somewhere in the distance wild dogs howled sadly. Artyom didn't want to run into them. If they had managed to survive on the surface all these years, something must have distinguished them from the dogs the metro residents kept.

Moving a little further away from the entrance to the station, he discovered something strange: a shallow, crudely dug trench encircled the pavilion. A stagnant dark liquid filled it as if it were a tiny moat. Jumping the trench, Artyom approached one of the kiosks and looked inside. It was completely empty. On the floor was broken glass. Everything else had been taken. He investigated several other kiosks, until he stumbled onto one which promised to be more interesting than the others. Outwardly, it resembled a tiny fortress: it was a cube welded from thick sheets of iron with a tiny window made of plate glass. A sign over the window read 'Currency Exchange'. The door was secured with an unusual lock. It wasn't opened with a key, but with the correct digital combination. Approaching the little window, Artyom tried to open it, but he couldn't. He noticed some faded handwriting on the windowsill. Forgetting the danger, Artyom turned on his flashlight. It looked as if whoever had written it had been left handed but he was able to read the uneven letters. It said, 'Bury me the human way. Code 767.' And as soon as he understood what it might mean, an angry chirr was heard overhead. Artyom recognized the sound right away. The flying monsters above Kalinskiy had cried exactly like that. He hastily put out the flashlight, but was too late: he heard the call again, directly above him.

Artyom desperately looked around, searching for somewhere to hide. He decided to try the numbers written on the windowsill. Pressing the buttons with the digits in the necessary sequence, he pulled the handle toward him. He'd been right. A dull click was heard inside the lock, and the door gave with difficulty, creaking on its rusty hinges. Artyom wriggled inside, locked himself in and again turned on his light. In a corner, resting with its back to the wall, sat the shrivelled mummy of a woman. It was squeezing a thick felt-tip pen in one hand, and in the other a plastic bottle. The walls were covered with neat female handwriting from top to bottom. An empty tin of pills, bright chocolate wrappers and soda cans lay on the floor, and in a corner stood a half-opened safe. Artyom wasn't afraid of the corpse. He felt only pity for the unknown girl. For some reason he was sure that it was a girl. The cry of the flying beast was heard once more, and then a powerful blow on the roof shook the kiosk. Artyom fell to the floor, waiting.

The attack was not repeated, and the squeals of the creature began to grow more distant, so he decided to stand up. When it came down to it, he was able to hide as long as he liked in his shelter: the girl's corpse had not been disturbed all this time, though certainly enough hunters had feasted on those around it. Of course, he might have been able to kill the monster, but he would have had to go outside. And if he missed or the beast turned out to be armoured, a second chance wouldn't present itself. It was more reasonable to wait for Ulman. If he was still alive.

Artyom began to read the handwriting on the walls to pass the time. 'I write because I am bored and so I don't go insane. I've been sitting in this stall for three days already and I am afraid to go outside. I have seen ten people who were not able to run into the metro, they suffocated and are lying right in the middle of the street even now. It's good that I managed to read in the paper how to glue adhesive tape to the seams. I will wait until the wind carries the cloud away. They wrote that there won't be any more danger after a day. 9 July. I tried reaching the metro. Some kind of iron wall starts beyond the escalator. I wasn't able to lift it and no matter how much I beat on it, no one opened it. I started feeling really bad after ten minutes, so I came back here. There are many dead around. Everything is horrible, they are all swollen up and they smell. I broke the glass in a grocery stall and took the chocolate and mineral water.

Now I won't starve to death. I have felt terribly weak. I have a safe full of dollars and roubles and nothing to do with them. That's strange. It turns out they are only bits of paper. 10 July. They have continued bombing. An awful roar was heard all day to the right, from *Prospect Mir*. I thought no one was left, but yesterday a tank passed at a high speed. I wanted to run out and attract their attention, but I couldn't. I really miss Mom and Leva. I've been throwing up all day. Later I fell asleep. 11 July. A horribly burnt man has passed by. I don't know where he has been hiding all this time. He was forever crying and wheezing. It was really awful. He went toward the metro, then I heard a loud bang. Most likely he was knocking on that wall, too. Then everything went quiet. Tomorrow I'll go take a look and see whether they opened it for him or nor.'

A new blow shook the booth – the monster wasn't giving up on its catch. Artyom staggered and nearly fell on the dead body, barely able to hold himself up by grabbing onto the counter. Bending down, he waited another minute, then continued reading.

'12 July. I'm not able to leave. I'm shivering, I don't understand whether I am sleeping or not. I was talking to Leva for an hour today and he said he will marry me soon. Then Mom arrived and her eyes were flowing. Then I was left alone again. I'm so lonely. When it all ends, when will they rescue us? Some dogs are here and are eating the corpses. Finally, thank you. I have been throwing up. 13 July. There's still some canned food, chocolate and mineral water, but I don't want it any more. It'll be another year before life returns to normal. The Great Patriotic War went on for 5 years. Nothing can be longer. Everything will be OK. They will find me. 14 July. I don't want it any more. I don't want it any more. Bury me the human way, I don't want to be in this damned iron box . . . It's cramped. Thanks for the Phenazepam. Good night.'

Alongside was some more handwriting, but ever more incoherent and ragged, and drawings: imps, young girls in large hats or bows, human faces. 'Obviously she was hoping that the nightmare that she survived would soon be over,' Artyom thought. 'A year or two, and everything would come full circle, everything would be as it was before. Life would go on and everyone would forget about what had happened. How many years have passed since then? Mankind has only further distanced itself from returning to the surface during this time. Did she dream that only those who managed to get down into the metro would survive?'

Artyom thought about himself. He had always wanted to believe that once people were able to get out of the metro in order to live again as they had before, they would be able to restore the majestic buildings erected by their ancestors, and settle down in them so as not to squint at the rising sun and to breathe not the tasteless mixture of oxygen and nitrogen filtered by gas masks, but to swallow with delight the air suffused with the fragrances of plants . . . He didn't know how they smelled before, but it was supposed to be wonderful. His mother had reminisced about flowers. But, looking at the shrivelled body of the unknown girl who didn't live to see the cherished day when her nightmare ended, he began to doubt that he would. How did his hope to see the return of a previous life differ from hers? During the years of existence in the metro, man had not amassed the strength to climb the steps of the shining escalator leading to his past glory and splendour in triumph. On the contrary, he was reduced, becoming used to the darkness. Most people had already forgotten the absolute authority mankind had once had over the world, others pined for it, and a third group cursed it.

A horn sounded from outside and Artyom threw himself to the window. A very unusual vehicle stood on a patch of ground in front of the kiosks. He had seen automobiles before: in his distant child-hood, then in pictures and photographs in books and, finally, during his previous climb to the surface. But not one of them looked like this. The huge six-wheeled truck was painted red. Behind its cab, which had two rows of seats, the metal body of the truck had a white line along the side, and some pipes piled on the roof. Two rotating blue lights blinked. Instead of struggling out of the booth, he shone his flashlight through the glass, waiting for an answering signal. The truck's headlights flashed on and off several times, but Artyom was unable to leave the kiosk: two huge shadows were diving headlong one after the other. The first grabbed the roof of the truck with its talons and was trying to lift the vehicle up, but it was too heavy. Lifting the vehicle's body a half metre from the ground, the monster tore off both pipes, squealed with displeasure and dropped them. The second creature struck the automobile in the side with a screech, counting on turning it over. A door swung open, and a man in a protective suit jumped to the asphalt with a bulky machine gun in his hands. Lifting the barrel, he waited several seconds, evidently allow-ing the monster to come closer, and then let loose a spray of bullets. Offended chirring was heard from overhead. Artyom hastily opened the lock and ran outside. One of the winged monsters was describing a wide circle about thirty metres above their heads, preparing to strike again but the other couldn't be seen anywhere.

'Get in the vehicle!' yelled the man with the machine gun. Artyom raced towards it, scrambled into the cab and sat on the long seat. The machine gunner let off a burst of shots several more times, then jumped onto the footboard, slid into the cab and slammed the door behind him. The vehicle roared off.

'You feeding the pigeons?' Ulman hooted, looking at Artyom through his gas mask. Artyom thought that the flying beasts would pursue them, but instead, having flown past about another hundred metres behind the vehicle, the creatures turned back towards *VDNKh*.

'They are defending a nest,' the fighter said. 'We've heard about that. They would not just have attacked the vehicle like that. They aren't big enough. Where is it, I wonder?'

Artyom suddenly understood where the monsters had their nest, and why not one living thing, including the dark ones, dared be seen next to the exit from *VDNKh*.

'Right in our station's hall, above the escalators,' he said.

'It that so? Strange, usually they are higher, they nest on buildings,' the fighter replied. 'Most likely, it's another type. Right . . . Sorry we were late.'

It turned out to be rather cramped in the suits and with the bulky weapons in the vehicle's cab. The rear seats were occupied by some of rucksacks and cases. Ulman had taken the outside seat, Artyom had ended up in the centre, and left of him, behind the wheel, sat Pavel, Ulman's friend from *Prospect Mir*.

'What's there to excuse? It wasn't on purpose,' the driver said. 'Something the colonel didn't warn us about. We had the impression a steamroller had passed over the street that runs from *Prospect Mir* to *Rizhskaya*. Why that bridge hasn't collapsed I don't know. There wasn't anywhere to hide. We barely got away from some dogs.'

'Haven't you seen any dogs yet?' Ulman asked.

'I only heard them,' Artyom responded.

'Well, we had a good look at them,' Pavel said, turning the wheel.

'What about them?' Artyom was interested in learning from him.

'It wasn't anything good. They tore off the bumper and nearly gnawed through the wheel, even though we were moving. They only stopped when Petro took out the leader with the sniper rifle,' he nodded at Ulman.

It wasn't easy going: the ground was covered with trenches and holes. The asphalt was cracked and they had to make their way carefully. In one place they got stuck and it took about five minutes to cross a mountain of concrete rubble left from a collapsed bridge. Artyom looked out the window, squeezing the machine gun in his hands.

'It's going OK.' Pavel was talking about the vehicle.

'Where did you find it?' Artyom asked.

'At the depot. In pieces. They weren't able to fix it, so it couldn't go to fires while Moscow was burning down. Now we use it from time to time. Not for what it was built for, of course.'

'Got you.' Artyom again turned towards the window.

'We've been lucky with the weather.' Pavel, it seemed, wanted to talk. 'There's not a cloud in the sky. That's good. We'll be able to see a long way from the tower. If it turns out we reach it.'

'I'd rather be up there than walking from house to house,' nodded Ulman.

'True, the colonel was saying that almost no one lives in them, but I don't like the word "almost".'

The vehicle turned left and rolled along a straight, broad street, divided in two by a plot of grass. On the left was a row of almost undamaged brick homes, on the right stretched a gloomy, black forest. Powerful roots covered the roadway in several places and they had to go round them. But Artyom managed to see all this only in passing.

'Look at it. What a beauty!' Pavel said with admiration. Straight ahead of them the Ostankino tower supported the sky, rising like a gigantic club threatening enemies brought down long ago. It was a perfectly fantastic structure. Artyom had never seen anything like it even in the pictures in books and magazines. His stepfather, of course, had told him about some Cyclopean structure located only two kilometres from their station, but Artyom hadn't been able to imagine how it would astound him. For the rest of the way, his mouth was open his mouth in surprise and stared at the grandiose silhouette of the tower, devouring it with his eyes. His delight at seeing this creation of human hands was mixed with the bitterness of finally understanding that nothing like it ever would be created again.

'It has been so close all this time, and I didn't even know.' He tried to express his feelings.

'If you don't come to the surface, there's much you will not understand in this life,' Pavel responded. 'Do you at least know why

448

your station is named what it is – *VDNKh*? It means Great Achievements of Our Economy, that's what. There was a huge park there with all kinds of animals and plants. And this is what I am telling you: you are really lucky that the "birdies" spun their nest right at the entrance to your station. Because, some of these structures have been softened so much by the X-rays now they can't even sustain a direct hit from a grenade launcher.'

'But they respect your feathered friends,' Ulman added.

'It is, so to say, your roof.' Both men began to laugh, and Artyom, who couldn't be bothered to set Pavel straight regarding the name of his station, stared once more at the tower. He noticed that the enormous structure had leaned a little, but it seemed to have attained a delicate balance and hadn't fallen. How in hell could something put here decades ago remain standing? Neighbouring houses had been swept away, but the tower proudly rose among this devastation, as if it had been magically preserved from the enemy's bombs and missiles.

'It's interesting how it has survived,' Artyom muttered.

'They didn't want to demolish it, most likely,' Pavel said. 'Anyhow, it's a valuable infrastructure. It was twenty-five per cent higher you know, and there was a pointed spire on top. But now, you see, it's broken off almost right at the observation deck.'

'But why spare it? Didn't they really care anymore? Well, I suppose that it might not have gone well with the Kremlin.' Ulman was doubtful.

Sweeping through the gate behind the steel rods of the fence, the vehicle approached the very foundation of the television tower and stopped. Ulman took the night vision instrument and the machine gun and jumped to the ground. A minute later he gave the go-ahead: everything was quiet. Pavel also crawled out of the cab and, having opened the rear door, undertook dragging out the rucksacks with the equipment.

'There should be a signal in twenty minutes,' he said. 'We'll try to catch it from here.'

Ulman found the rucksack with the radio transmitter and began to assemble a long field antenna from the multiple sections. Soon the radio antenna reached six metres in height and lazily swung too and fro in the slight breeze. Sitting at the transmitter, the fighter put the headset with the microphone to his head and began to listen for a transmission. Long minutes of waiting wore on. The shadow of a 'pterodactyl' covered them for an instant, but after describing a few circles over their heads, the monster disappeared behind the houses; apparently one encounter with armed people had been enough for it to remember a dangerous enemy.

'And what do they look like anyhow, these dark ones? You're our specialist on that,' Pavel asked Artyom.

'They look very scary. Like . . . people inside out,' Ulman was trying to describe them. 'The complete opposite of a human. And it's clear from the name itself: the dark ones – they are black.'

'You don't say . . . and where did they come from? No one even heard of them before, you know. What do they say about that?'

'It doesn't matter what you never heard of in the metro.' Artyom hastened to change the subject. 'Who from Park Pobedy knew anything about the cannibals?'

'That's true,' the driver brightened up. 'They found people with needles in their neck, but no one was able to say who had done it. What nonsense the Great Worm is! But this is where these dark ones of yours are from . . .'

'I have seen him,' Artyom interrupted him.

'The worm?' Pavel asked, not believing him.

'Well, something like it. A train, maybe. Huge, it bellows so that you block your ears. I didn't manage to see what happened – it tore right past me.'

'No, it couldn't be a train . . . What would power it? Mushrooms? Trains are driven by electricity. You know what it reminds me of? A drilling rig.'

'Why?' Artyom was taken aback. He had heard about drilling rigs, but the idea that the Great Worm who had gnawed the new passages about which Dron had spoken may turn out to be such a machine hadn't occurred to him. And wasn't all belief in the worm built on denying machines?

'Don't say anything to Ulman about the drilling rig, and the colonel, too: they'll all think I'm nuts.' Pavel said. 'The thing is, I had been gathering information at *Polis* earlier. I tracked down every plainclothes detective, and in short, I was involved with subversives and the internal threat. And one day an old guy ran into me and he was convinced that in one recess in a tunnel next to *Borovitskaya*, a noise was constantly heard, as if a drilling machine was operating behind the wall. Of course, I would have immediately determined he was insane, but previously he had been a builder and knew a lot about such things.'

'But who would need to dig there?'

'No idea. The old man raved on that some miscreants wanted to dig a tunnel through to the river so that all *Polis* could bathe, and he had somehow overheard their plans. I immediately gave a warning only no one believed me. I rushed to look for this old man in order to present him as a witness, but he, as luck would have it, had got lost somewhere. An agent provocateur, maybe. And maybe,' Pavel looked carefully at Ulman and lowered his voice, 'he really heard how the military are digging something secret. And they buried my old man at the same time. Since then I have had ideas about a drilling rig and they are putting me down as a nutcase. It's hardly worth saying that they begin to taunt me straight off about the rig.' He went quiet, looking searchingly at Artyom: what was his attitude to his story?

Artyom vaguely shrugged his shoulders.

'Not a damned thing heard, empty air!' the approaching Ulman spat angrily. 'We can't get it from here, son of a bitch! We have to get higher: Melnik most likely is too far away.'

Artyom and Pavel immediately started picking up. No one wanted to think about other explanations for why the stalker's team hadn't made contact. Ulman folded the antenna into sections, put the radio into the rucksack, lifted his machine gun onto his shoulder and walked off first toward the glass vestibule that was concealed behind the television tower's mighty pillars. Pavel handed one case to Artyom, took the knapsack and rifle himself, cracked the vehicle's doors and they followed Ulman.

Inside it was quiet, dirty and empty: people, apparently, once ran from here in a hurry and never returned again. The moon surprisingly shone through the broken, dusty glass onto overturned benches and the broken counter of the ticket office, onto the security post, with the remnants of a service cap forgotten in haste, and onto the broken turnstiles at the entrance, and illuminated stencilled instructions and cautions for visitors to the television tower. They turned off their flashlights and, looking around a little, found the exit to the staircase. The useless elevators that had been able to take people up in less than a minute stood on the first floor with their doors flung feebly open. Now the team was approaching the most difficult area. Ulman explained that they had to get to a height of more than three hundred metres. Artyom did the first two hundred steps with ease. Weeks of travelling around the metro had toughened his legs. He began to flag at three hundred and fifty. The winding staircase stretched upwards, and there was no perceptible difference between the floors. It was damp and cold inside the tower, and, apart from naked concrete walls, all that could be seen was abandoned equipment rooms, through the occasional open door.

Ulman decided to take the first break after five hundred steps but he took only five minutes to rest. He was afraid of missing the moment when the stalker tried to communicate with them.

Artyom lost count after the eight hundredth step. His legs were filled with lead, and each one now weighed three times as much as at the beginning of the climb. Lifting his foot off the floor became very difficult. The floor pulled it back, like a magnet. Perspiration flooded his eyes, and the grey walls floated, as if in a fog, and the insidious steps began to clutch at his boots. He was not able to stop and rest: behind him, panting, was Pavel who was carrying twice as much as Artyom. After about fifteen more minutes, Ulman again allowed them to take a break. Even he looked tired. His chest heaved heavily under the shapeless protective suit, and his hand rummaged along the wall in search of a support. Pulling a canteen with water from the knapsack, the fighter first extended it to Artyom. A special valve was provided in the gas mask through which a catheter passed: one was able to suck water through it. Artyom understood that the others wanted a drink, but he was unable to tear himself away from the rubber tube until the canteen was half empty. Afterwards, he settled to the floor and closed his eyes.

'Come on, it's not much further!' Ulman shouted. He jerked Artyom to his feet, took the case from him, loaded it onto his own shoulders and moved forward.

Artyom didn't remember how long the final part of the climb took. The steps and walls merged into one dull whole. Beams and spots of light from behind dull stains on the viewing glass looked like radiant clouds and for some time he was distracted by the fact that he was admiring their iridescent tints. The blood pounded in his head, the cold air tore his lungs and the staircase went on forever. Artyom sat down on the floor several times, but they picked him up and forced him to walk. Why was he doing this? So that life could continue in the metro? Right. So that they could grow mushrooms and pigs at *VDNKh* in the future, and so that his stepfather and Zhenkina's family lived there in peace, so that people unknown to him could settle at *Alekseevskaya* and at *Rizhskaya*, and so that the uneasy bustle of trade at *Byelorusskaya* didn't die away. So that the Brahmins could stroll about *Polis* in their robes and rustle the pages of books, grasping the ancient knowledge and passing it on to subsequent generations. So that the fascists could build their Reich,

452

capturing racial enemies and torturing them to death, and so that the Worm people could spirit away strangers' children and eat adults, and so that the woman at *Mayakovskaya* could bargain with her young son in the future, earning herself and him some bread. So that the rat races at *Paveletskaya* didn't end, and the fighters of the revolutionary brigade could continue their assaults on fascists and their funny dialectical arguments. And so that thousands of people throughout the whole metro could breathe, eat, love one another, give life to their children, defecate and sleep, dream, fight, kill, be ravished and betrayed, philosophize and hate, and so that each could believe in his own paradise and his own hell . . . So that life in the metro, senseless and useless, exalted and filled with light, dirty and seething, endlessly diverse, so miraculous and fine could continue. He thought about this, and it was as if a huge crank turned in his back and nudged him to take one more step and another and still another. Thanks to that, he continued to move his feet. And suddenly it all ended. They tumbled into a spacious area – a broad, circular corridor, a closed ring. Its inner wall was faced with marble, and Artyom at once felt as if he were at home. And there was an outer wall . . . The sky began at immediately behind the completely transparent outer wall, and somewhere far, far below were strewn tiny little homes, split into neighbourhoods by roads and patches of parks, and there were huge black craters and the rectangles of surviving tall buildings. . . . The whole, boundless city, like a grey mass moving toward the dark horizon, could be seen from here. Artyom got down onto the floor, leaning against the wall, and he looked for a very long time at Moscow and the sky slowly turning pink.

'Artyom! Get up, that's enough sitting! Come, give us a hand.' Ulman shook him by the shoulder. The fighter handed him a large bundle of wire, and Artyom stared at it blankly. 'This damned antenna won't pick up anything,' Ulman pointed at the twisted six-metre probe scattered on the floor. 'We'll try the loop. Over there's a door to the engineering balcony, a floor below us. The exit is right there on the Botanical Garden side. I'll stay here with the radio, you go outside with Pashka, he'll uncoil the antenna, you secure it. Be lively 'cause it will start to get light soon.'

Artyom nodded. He remembered why he was here and he got a second wind. Someone had tightened that invisible crank in his back and that inner spring began once more to unwind. Only a short while remained to the goal. He took the spool and moved towards the balcony door. The door didn't give, and Ulman had to fire a whole salvo into it before the glass, riddled by his bullets, cracked and spilled out. A powerful gust of wind almost knocked them off their feet. Artyom stepped onto a balcony enclosed by a grate the height of a man.

'Wow, look at them.'

Pavel extended the field binoculars to him and waved his hand in the appropriate direction. Artyom pressed the binoculars to his eyes and looked over the city until Pavel pointed him in the right direction. The Botanical Gardens and *VDNKh* coalesced into one, dark impassable thicket, among which rose the peeling white cupolas and roofs of the Exhibition's pavilions. Only two gaps were left in this dense forest, a narrow path between the main pavilions ('Glavnaya Alleya' Pavel whispered timidly) and this. A huge patch had formed right in the middle of the Gardens, as if even the trees had drawn back in disgust from an unseen evil. It was a strange and repulsive sight: a large city like a gigantic life-giving organ, pulsing and quivering, that stretched out for several square kilometres. The sky gradually was being painted with morning colours, and this terrible tumour was becoming ever more visible: a living membrane entangled with veins, tiny black figures crawling out of cesspool exits, running about in a businesslike way, like ants . . . Ants especially, and their mother city reminded Artyom of an enormous anthill. And one was walking away from the paths – he saw it well now – towards a white round structure standing on its own, an exact copy of the entrance to the *VDNKh* station. The black figures reached the doors and disappeared. Artyom knew the route all too well. They really were right next door, and hadn't come from some remote place. And it would be possible to really destroy them, simply destroy them. Now the main thing was that Melnik didn't fail. Artyom heaved a sigh of relief. For some reason he was reminded of the black tunnel from his dreams, but he shook his head and set about unwinding the cable. The balcony encircled the tower, but the forty-metre wire wasn't enough to go right round. Tying off the end to the grate, they went back in.

'I have it! There's a signal!' Ulman began to yell cheerfully on seeing them. 'We have comms! The colonel is turning the air blue, he's asking where we were earlier.' He was pressing the headphones to his head, listened some more and added, 'He says everything is even better than we had thought. They found four installations, all in excellent condition. They had been preserved . . . In oil, beneath a

454

tarpaulin . . . He says Anton is a hero. He's familiar with it all. They'll be ready soon. We have to report the coordinates. He sends you greetings, Artyom!'

Pavel unfolded the large map of the area that had been divided into quarters and, looking through the binoculars, began to dictate the coordinates. Ulman repeated them into the microphone of his radio.

'We'll seal up the station itself too in any case.' The fighter consulted the map and called out several more digits. 'That's all, they've got the coordinates, now they'll do the aiming.' Ulman removed the earphones and rubbed his forehead. 'It'll still take some time, your missile man there is the only one who knows how. But that's nothing, we'll wait.'

Artyom took the binoculars and again went out onto the balcony. Something had dragged him to this disgusting anthill, some oppressive feeling, an intangible and inexpressible anguish, like something heavy pressing on his chest, not allowing him to breathe deeply. The black tunnel once more rose up before his eyes and suddenly it was clear, distinct, as Artyom had not seen it even in the nightmares that had pursued him relentlessly. But now it was possible not to be afraid: these vampires didn't have long to lord it in his dreams.

'That's all! It's taken off! The colonel says wait for the greeting! Now we're going to fry these black bitches of yours!' Ulman yelled.

And at that moment the city beneath their feet vanished, the sky disappeared into a dark abyss, the happy cries behind his back abated – and there remained only one empty black tunnel, along which Artyom had strolled so many times . . . for what? The time thickened and congealed. He pulled a plastic lighter from his pocket and struck the flint. A small happy flame jumped out and began to dance on the wick, illuminating the space around it. Artyom knew what he would see and understood that now he must not fear it, and, therefore, he simply lifted his head and looked at the huge black eyes without whites and pupils. And he heard it.

'You are the chosen one!' The world had been turned upside-down. In those unfathomable eyes he suddenly saw in a fraction of a second the answer to everything that had, for him, been left incomprehensible and inexplicable. The answer to all his doubts, hesitations and searches. And the answer turned out not to be what Artyom had been expecting.

Having disappeared into the gaze of the dark one, he suddenly saw the universe with its eyes. New life was being reborn and hundreds and thousands of individual minds were being joined together into a single whole . . . The resilient black skin allowed the dark one to endure both the scorching sun and the January frosts, the soft telepathic tentacles enabled it to caress any creation and to painfully sting an enemy, and it was totally immune to pain . . . . . . The dark ones were the true inheritors of the ruined universe, a phoenix that had risen from ashes of mankind. And they possessed a mind – inquisitive, living, but completely unlike the human mind.

But, somehow, it connected with him, with Artyom. He saw people with the eyes of the dark ones: embittered, living beneath the earth, talking back with fire and lead, destroying the bearers of the flag of truce who had been sent to them with a song of peace. And they had wrested the white flag from them and stabbed them in the throat with the shaft. Artyom understood the growing despair at the inability to establish contact and to reach a mutual understanding, because, in the depths, in the lower passages, sat unreasonable, infuriated creatures who had destroyed their own world, who continued to bicker among themselves and who would die out soon if no one could re-educate them. The dark ones were extending a helping hand to people. And again the people seized it with hatred. He saw the desire to rid themselves of these embittered but very clever creations. But he also saw the desperate searches to find one of the unfortunates – one who could become a bridge between the two worlds, who could explain to the people that there was nothing to fear, and who could help the dark ones communicate with them.

He understood that there was nothing dividing people and the dark ones. He understood they were not competing for survival but were two organisms intended by nature to work together. And together – with man's technical knowledge and with the ability of the dark ones to overcame perils – they could take mankind to a new level, and the world, having ground to a halt, could continue to rotate about its axis. Because the dark ones were also part of mankind, a new branch of it, born here, in the ruins of a megalopolis swept away by war. The dark ones were the consequence of the final war, they were the children of this world, better adapted for the new terms of the game. And they sensed man not only with their customary organs, but also with tentacles of consciousness. Artyom recalled the mysterious noise in the pipes, he recalled the savages who could cast a spell with only a glance, and the revolting mass in the heart of the Kremlin that could assault one's reason . . . Man had not been able to cope with their influence on the mind, but it was as if the dark ones were created for it. Only they needed a partner, an ally . . . A friend. Someone who could help establish communications with their deaf and blind elder brothers – with people. And so began the long, patient search for an intermediary, a search crowned with luck and delight, because such an interpreter, the chosen one, had been found. But, before contact had been established with him, he disappeared. The tentacles of the Commoner looked for him everywhere, sometimes grabbing him in order to begin discourse, but he, afraid, tore away and ran. But he had to be supported and rescued, stopped, warned of the danger, urged on and again taken home where communication with him would be especially strong and clear. Finally, contact could become established and then the chosen one could another timid step towards understanding his mission. His fate. He had been intended for this because he had opened the door to the metro, to the people and to the dark ones.

Artyom briefly thought about asking what had happened to Hunter. But this thought began to whirl in the vortex of new improbable sensations and it vanished into the seething whirlpool of experiences and disappeared without a trace. Now nothing distracted him from his primary goal, and he once again opened his mind to their mind. He now stood on the threshold of something incredibly important. He had experienced this feeling at the very beginning of his Odyssey, when he was sitting next to the bonfire at *Alekseevskaya*. And it was this clear understanding that kilometres of tunnels and weeks of wandering had led him to a secret door, and knowing that opening it would give him access to all the secrets of the universe and allow him to tower over the wretched people gouging out their world in the unyielding frozen earth. His long trip was forcing Artyom to throw the door open and bathe in the light of absolute knowledge that would gush out. And let the light blind him: eyes were a clumsy and purposeless instrument, suitable only for those who have not seen anything in their life except the sooty arches of the tunnels and the filthy granite of the stations. Artyom now had to extend his hand towards the one offered to him. Though it was frightening it was, undoubtedly, friendly. And then the door would be opened. And everything would be different. Unseen new horizons spread before him, beautiful and majestic. Joy and determination filled his heart, and there was only a drop of remorse that he had not understood all this earlier, that he had driven away his friends and brothers.

He grabbed the door's handle and pulled it down. The hearts of thousands of dark ones far below were ignited with joy and hope. The darkness before his eyes dissipated and, putting the binoculars to his eyes, he saw that hundreds of black figures on the distant ground had stopped still. It seemed to him that all of them now were looking at him, not believing that so long awaited a miracle had occurred and the senseless fratricidal hostility had come to an end.

At this second, the first missile drew a fiery smoky trail in the sky with lightning speed and struck the very centre of the city. And immediately three more of the very same meteors streaked across the reddening sky. Artyom jerked back, hoping that the salvo could still be stopped. But he suddenly understandood that everything was already over. An orange flame swept over the 'ant hill', a pitch-black cloud shot upwards, new explosions circled him from all sides and the city crashed down, emitting a tired, dying moan. It was clouded by the thick smoke of the burning forest. From the sky more missiles fell, and each death reverberated with a melancholy pain in Artyom's soul.

He tried desperately to discover in his consciousness at least a trace of that presence which just had filled and warmed him, and which had promised salvation for him and all mankind, which had given meaning to his existence. But nothing was left of it. His consciousness was like a deserted metro tunnel. Artyom keenly felt that the light by which he would be able to illuminate his life and find his way would never appear again.

'We really gave it to them, hey? They'll know not to bother us!' Ulman was rubbing his hands. 'Ah, Artyom? Artyom!'

The whole Botanical Gardens and *VDNKh* were turning into one fiery mass. Huge puffs of fatty black smoke lazily lifted into the autumn sky, and the crimson glow of the monstrous fire blended with the delicate rays of the rising sun. It had become unbearably stuffy and close. Artyom grabbed his gas mask, tore it off and, greedily, took a full breath of the bitter, cold air. Then he wiped his falling tears and, not paying any attention to the cries, began to descend the staircase. He was returning to the metro. He was going home.